FOR THEY SHALL INHERIT

Also by Malcolm Macdonald

WORLD FROM ROUGH STONES
THE RICH ARE WITH YOU ALWAYS
SONS OF FORTUNE
ABIGAIL
GOLDENEYE

FOR THEY SHALL INHERIT

a novel

MALCOLM MACDONALD

St. Martin's Press
New York

Library of Congress Catalog Number 84-52352

ISBN 0-312-29818-8

First published in Great Britain under the title of *In Love and War* by Hodder & Stoughton Ltd.

First U.S. Edition

10 9 8 7 6 5 4 3 2 1

For the one
who started it
and in a way
(his own)
finished it, too.
With baffled affection

The writer would like to thank Ida Whitehill of Cheadle Hulme, Cheshire, England, for sending him photocopies of the diary of Thomas Walsh of Manchester (her aunt's father-in-law), who was a boiler engineer on the Venezuelan railway in the 1880s.

CONTENTS

CONTENTS

PART ONE

THE FLIGHT
OF THE GRAND SOARER

CHAPTER ONE

"**T**HIS'LL MAKE THEM JUMP,**"** Clive said as he rammed the gunpowder even harder into the copper pipe. "Let them dare call it 'childish amusement' after *this*!"

Freddy looked on and smiled. He tried to lick his lips, to wet them, but the tip of his tongue was dry with excitement. A small, sensible voice within told him this latest "experiment" was folly; but too many forces were pulling him onward.

Above all he wanted to see how mighty an explosion they could make if they really tried. For the past month or so, ever since that wonderful day when he had spotted *The Pyromaniac's Delight* among a grubby heap of secondhand books on a stall in Aston market, life had been all bangers and rockets and smoke bombs. From feeble little squibs that hardly woke the cat, from puny indoor mortars whose crimson flares could barely reach the low rafters of the potting shed roof, they had progressed – alarmingly as grown-ups saw it, stupendously in their own estimation. Now, as easy as pie, they could make a soaring skyrocket whose charred remains fell so far off they were never found. And the terrible cannonades of one of their thunderpots had ruined at least one shooting party.

That was the day on which the grown-ups had forbidden them all further pyromania; the day on which Clive had said, "Let's go out in a real fire of glory!" and Freddy had answered – shyly, slyly – "Yes! Let's make a Sebastopol special!" And they had looked at each other in a trembling kind of excitement, daring themselves to go back on this resolve, which neither boy had meant to be taken quite so literally.

Too late now, for here they were, actually making the bomb.

In Freddy's case a more subtle force urged him onward: the force of class – for this was England and the year was 1863.

Freddy was socially the inferior of the two boys; indeed the gap between them was so great that they ought not to have been companions at all. For Clive was Clive Mortimer, the squire's son, while Freddy was only Freddy Oxley, son of a local tool and diemaker who worked in one of the Mortimer factories. So whatever Clive did was right. Freddy was relieved of the ultimate decision. He might share the blame but Clive alone had the responsibility.

True, it was Freddy who had found the book in the first place – Freddy who had suggested they should put its experiments into practice – Freddy who had bought the sulphur and carbon black and Chile saltpetre that made the bangs – and Freddy who had later extended their chemistry into the glorious and multicoloured realms of cadmium and cobalt and strontium. But Clive was a Mortimer and there was an end of it. The Mortimers ruled everything hereabouts. This was Sir Toby Mortimer's garden, all twenty acres of it. The casing of their bomb was of copper pipe from a Mortimer rolling mill. And it was Sir Toby's marble steps, all the way from Carrara in Italy, under which they were going to place and explode the charge.

The choice of this site had been practical enough. A badger had recently begun to dig out an earth under one of the steps; it made a convenient place to kindle a fire and, when the ashes glowed red, throw in the tight-packed, tight-sealed copper tube and run. At least, that was how they justified it later. Truly, though, both knew in their hearts that if the badger had not been so obliging, they would themselves have dug the hole. That great sweep of marble, from the fountains on the terrace above to the carefully manicured formal gardens below, was the only conceivable setting for this last, spectacular experiment.

"It can't possibly ram any tighter than that," Clive said. He turned to his young companion and added generously, "Give it one for luck?"

The copper tube, pinched and folded at the bottom, was clamped tight in the vice by that fold. Freddy took the wooden tamper, placed it firmly in the open mouth of the tube and gave it a ritual but expert blow with the mallet. The gunpowder, already tamped as hard as oak, yielded not at all. Freddy nodded his approval.

As if he had waited for that signal, Clive said, "We'd better close it off then."

Working together, with few words, they gingerly flattened the open end against the workbench, folded it, pinched it in the vice, folded it again ... and so on until Freddy feared that one more tightening of the handle would burst the copper seam. "That should do it," he said.

"Enough!" Clive confirmed. "You slip ahead and see how the fire's going."

Freddy ran out of the shed and down one of the paths toward the formal garden, slowing to a walk only when he spotted Hawkins, one of the senior undergardeners. The man saw him and changed direction. "If you was going to feed that fire under the steps," he said crossly, "you may turn about now. You must be mad."

"You didn't put it out?" Freddy asked anxiously.

"No point. It's nearly out anyway. What was you thinking of? Did you suppose there was a badger there?"

"Isn't there?"

The man spat disgustedly. "You could have cracked the marble."

Clive came sauntering up, his arm stiff from the concealment of the copper bomb. "Race you to the lakes!" he said, to rescue Freddy.

They broke back into a walk as soon as they were beyond Hawkins' sight. Clive took out the bomb, big as a policeman's truncheon and twice as fat. He hefted it contentedly, whacking the palm of his hand – living dangerously, as he supposed.

"I've just thought of something," Freddy said, looking at it. "It's a pity we couldn't have got some sort of round container. I mean spherical-round."

"Why?"

"I don't know. I just have a feeling it'd be more compact and would give a bigger e x p l o s i o n." He loved the word *explosion* and always lingered over it.

"The Fenian bombs in *Punch* are always round," Clive agreed dubiously.

"Too late now," Freddy said. "But it's something to think about."

The fire was not "almost out," it was glowing a fierce

orange, dulled only by the strong sunlight, and perfect for their purpose.

Now that the moment had come they were both too scared to consummate it. There was at least ten times as much powder in this charge as in the biggest of their previous bangs – and all those earlier charges had been tamped in cardboard tubes, not in stout copper. The suppressed voices of good sense clamoured louder than ever to stop, to turn back – even now.

"I'll just peep over the top of the steps," Freddy said. "Make sure there's no one around."

"Good egg."

Freddy had intended this move as an honourable postponement, a sop to reason – and even a hint that, in the few moments his scrutiny would occupy, the wiser counsels of conscience might indeed prevail. Yet in some curious way the effect was opposite. His words, his creeping up the broad expanse of marble steps, his peeping out over the acre of empty terrace, all somehow committed them to the action.

The house, a stately and much altered Elizabethan manor, shimmered in the August afternoon sun. The quiet of centuries seemed to hang about its ivied walls. The ballroom windows stared out over the terrace, somnolent and blank. The water, playing listlessly in the fountains, laid a drowsy, splashing hiss upon the air. Not for the first time Freddy imagined the comforts and luxuries of such a home, and he envied his friend.

His lips pressed tight together. He turned and rose to his feet. "Safe enough," he said. "Chuck it on." He began to saunter down the steps.

"Don't be a fool. You come back down here first."

"No! You chuck it on."

Clive half-obeyed but just prevented himself at the last moment. He held the bomb like a pointer, its tip toward the glowing recess.

"Go on!" Freddy gave a wild, challenging laugh that – Clive was never able to explain it properly – commanded obedience. Like a felon destroying some incriminating evidence he threw the tube beneath the steps and ran.

He ran like a demon.

Nothing happened.

Freddy, moving through the unreal air of a dream, continued his slow progress down the steps. The Lord of Creation, unable to fear.

Still nothing happened.

Clive watched, half-aghast at the certainty of Freddy's death, and half in awe at his coolness.

For Freddy the universe had become a kind of dream. There was no sensation beneath his feet; the steps were made of whipped cream. His body had no substance; the breezes chased one another through his frame. No birds sang. The flowers trembled in their efforts not to vanish. All at once he saw the world as a kind of painted backdrop, of which he and Clive – and everyone – were mere mechanical elements. At any moment now the *real* actors would come on and the real drama begin.

If he was smart, he thought, he could slip out of this half-world and join them, and they might not notice.

He reached the bottom of the steps, ten feet below and thirty away from the glowing badger hole and the reluctant bomb. He turned to look – perhaps to find a long pole and poke the bomb to life? "For Christ's sake!" he heard Clive shout from another time and space.

The great marble steps lifted. He heard the explosion not so much in his ears as in the pit of his lungs. The marble lifted, cracked asunder, shattered, rose, and spun.

The shimmering arcs of splintered, sunstruck marble held him entranced. He knew what danger he was in, yet the knowledge was somehow arcane, like the knowledge of Latin grammar. It seemed to have no practical bearing on the here-and-now. Its remoteness liberated him from all fear. He stood and watched the explosion unfold before him as if it, and he, and all the world were immersed in clear golden treacle.

Small chunks of stone whizzed lazily by his charmed head. Larger fragments rose, spinning and wheeling, suddenly black against the brilliant afternoon as they soared over the terrace. There was an almighty shattering of glass, which frittered itself away into a gentle pitter-patter of descending stone. The envoi was sung by a chorus of protesting jackdaws, specks of fright upon a newly livid sky.

Eternity passed in approving silence. Freddy knew true ecstasy at last.

"What a stunner!" Clive said, breathless from his return sprint up the formal garden.

Freddy still forgot to breathe.

"You're not hurt are you?" Anxiety edged Clive's tone. "You were mad to stand there like that."

Still awestruck, Freddy shook his head.

"What a stunner!" Clive rekindled his joy. "Let's go and see the damage."

Freddy did not move. He wanted the pleasure to last forever. Clive's rough push broke the spell. "Come on!"

Together they clambered up the tangle of marble steps and gazed in awe at the gaping hole, large enough now for a whole colony of badgers.

What had that simple mixture of sulphur and carbon and saltpetre done! That splendid geometry of the steps – surely it was gone now – gone beyond recovery. And all in a fraction of a second!

They leapt the gap and hastened upward to the terrace.

At first it seemed nothing had changed. The fountains still splashed; the ivy still hung upon the walls; the old leaded windows still gleamed blankly in their shrouded quietude.

Then the two pyromaniacs saw the gashes in the red tiles of the roof, and the gaping hole, black on black, in one of the ballroom windows.

"Oh Christopher!" Clive said, all joy gone. The damaged roof might not have been so bad but the new ballroom windows were his father's pride and delight – his great legacy in the evolution of the stately old home.

There were twenty of them – massive affairs of teak and polished plate glass almost half an inch thick; designed to last for ever, one of them had not even reached its first anniversary.

"Cut along home, Freddy," Clive said in sepulchral gloom. "I'm bound to get it in the neck, now. No need for two of us to face the cannon. I'll say I did it all by myself."

Disconsolately he walked across the terrace toward the shattered window. Freddy was at his side.

They entered the ballroom to find it full of housemaids and footmen, standing aghast, waiting for the housekeeper or butler – or anyone with majesty enough to cope with this enormity.

The flying marble slab that had shattered the plate glass had gone on to plough a huge furrow clear across the gleaming parquet floor; the ballroom was a ruin.

Clive was marvellous, Freddy thought. The sight of the servants reminded the young master who he was. His head came up. His back stiffened. His eyelids drooped. "Don't just stand there," he said with languid majesty as he sauntered toward them. "Get buckets and things and start cleaning up this dreadful mess."

It was sheer bravado, of course; everyone knew that. But they admired him for the way he carried it off – none more than Freddy. One day, he thought, I shall behave like that.

The young master swept out past them and went upstairs to soak the cheeks of his backside in spirit, a vain bid to harden them against the wrath to come. Freddy just hung around, knowing he was bound to be flogged as well, and wanting to avoid the ignominy of being dragged by the ear from his parents' home by one of Sir Toby's undergardeners.

And so it proved. The pain of the flogging was excruciating, of course, Sir Toby being both angry and powerful. It was the most dreadful torment either boy had ever had to endure. But the blood that was drawn by that pliant and screaming horsewhip forged between them a brother-bond that was to endure all their lives – through hurt and betrayal, both real and imagined.

CHAPTER TWO

THE HORSEWHIPPING, for all its terror, was soon forgotten. The sting went in minutes; the last dull ache in days; the final blue-brown marbling of the bruise in weeks. What then remained, for both boys, was the memory of an awesome power, a power they had for a moment controlled, a power they had unleashed – but a power which from that moment on had become unstoppable.

There were other, similar moments in their lives, of course. Once they dammed the Blythe, the stream that flowed through the garden. It was no ordinary boys' dam, either; as Sir Toby later said to Lady Mortimer, "When that pair go at it, they *go* at it, by Hades!" No, this dam was large enough to drive a small mill. The boys had not intended anything so utilitarian; they merely wished to create a Little Venice beside the Elysian Grove. To get the dam built had cost them the sovereign that Clive's Great Aunt Maud had given him for Christmas, and, a greater sacrifice, Freddy's birthday shilling from his grandad; for that guinea a gang of diddicoys with donkeys and scoops had agreed to build their dam. In a single morning they had scraped up enough sand and gravel to pen back many thousand gallons. By late afternoon the stream had obligingly delivered that quota of water. By evening an angry band of flooded cottagers, living upstream at Sandal's Cottages, had waited in deputation upon Sir Toby. The boys had tried to abate the flood by cutting an overflow channel to one side of the dam wall. The spirit of the waters, keen to show off his new might, had gone rushing out, scouring away the dam, and bringing a second, even angrier deputation of wet cottagers to Sir Toby's back door, this time from downstream.

Those moments while the little rivulet of clear stream had gouged and swelled to a massive, unstoppable flood of churned-up headwater had been like a slowed-down re-enactment of the Great Explosion. A pale echo, to be sure, and yet an equal reminder of those unseen and wilful forces in the world around us, forces that skilled men may tap and turn into wealth but that quickly slip beyond the grasp of the unskilled and then are free to whistle up the spirits of havoc.

Not all their ventures ended in disaster. They made a Robinson Crusoe raft that lasted several weeks, and though both of them nearly drowned several times, that was more to do with the places and distances to which the vessel carried them than with any essential defect in the craft itself.

With two diaphragms of tinplate and a length of taut copper wire they made a talking machine that enabled one of

them in the potting shed to talk to the other in the hothouse.
True, they ought not to have stretched the wire at the height of
the average human neck – but then Hawkins ought also to have
looked where he was going. And the talking machine *was* an
undoubted success. Anyway, the wound soon healed.

Their only absolute, total failure was the experimental
recreation of A Day in the Life of Ug the Prehistoric Ironsmith.
But, as Clive often remarked in later years, the events of that
afternoon did point up several deficiencies in the organization
and equipment of the local volunteer fire brigade, the remedying
of which had undoubtably saved a great deal of property – and,
of course, lives – in subsequent years. What was one small
plantation of balsam poplars, however beautiful, to set beside
that?

For each of these disasters and near-tragedies they received
the usual stigmata of boyhood. Time and again they were
forbidden to have anything to do with each other – a prohibition
that their differences in class and prospects ought to have made
unnecessary in any case. But neither rewards nor punishments
– nor even simple reasoning – could prevail against the delight
of their mutual company. Clive had only to see the sprightly,
cocky shape of Freddy, leading with his left shoulder as he
walked, bursting with some grand new scheme and grinning as
if it were already achieved ... and all his promises and fear of
retribution flew to the winds. Freddy had only to think of the
tall, languid outline of his partner in so many past adventures,
had only to remember how his easygoing calm had made many
an awkward moment negotiable ... and he could more readily
have "given up" gravity than he could Clive.

"It'll be different when he goes to Eton," Sir Toby told
Lady Mortimer. "He'll mix with his own sort and develop
some judgement."

Clive did in time go to Eton. His recounting there of his
adventures ensured that at least a dozen O.E.s regretted all
their lives they had never known Freddy Oxley in their youth.
And Clive's attempt to introduce the Wall Game to the village
– or, more specifically, to the wall at the end of the Rose
Garden – was just one more of what his mother came to call
"those sal-volatile moments of life." Eton proved no cure for
boys suffering from boyhood.

"That awful little Freddy Oxley will be apprenticed soon," Sir Toby next assured his lady. "I'll put him to Dixon – the hardest, surliest man I know. That'll curb him."

Freddy was in time apprenticed, and to Dixon. But in the remainder of his forecast Sir Toby was wrong. Dixon was not so much a hard and surly man as an average socialist. The angry political animal was all Sir Toby had ever seen. The man himself was something more complex. He was hard, all right. The smallest unevenness in a bit of filing, the slightest weep in a hand-forged weld, the faintest trace of bloom on a piece of supposedly annealed copper – and the curses and blows would rain down. But he appreciated good work, too; for him good craftsmanship and honest socialism were the two great moral forces in the world.

Once, when Freddy's ears were still red-raw from Dixon's corrective hand, a philosophic mood came over the man. "I know what you're thinking, lad. You're thinking it'd've done the job, that weld of yourn. And so it would!"

Freddy looked up in surprise.

"Aye," Dixon confirmed. "It'd've stood till the Last Trump. But that's not the point. It'd've been wrong until the Last Trump, too – *that's* the point! There's enough folk in the world think like that as it is, wi'out me fashioning one more out o' you." He looked around and lowered his voice, drawing Freddy closer to him in conspiracy. "You get them here. 'Can't you make it quicker?' they ask. 'Aye,' I tell them. 'If you're willing to make it wrong.' Or 'make it thinner,' they say. 'Use less metal – it'll still be strong enough to get by. Don't use six studs, use four ...' All that caper. Cutting corners all the time. 'It won't last even one man's lifetime,' I answer. 'Bugger that!' they say." He imitated "their" wink. "'*Half* a lifetime'll do us. Then they'll have to throw it out and come back to us and buy another. More profit for us. More work for you.'"

Beginner though he was, Freddy realized that these conversations had never actually taken place; they were part of some token moral dialogue that went on endlessly in the fellow's mind. As if to confirm it, Dixon went on: "That's capitalism for you, lad. They're just the same with folk. They want to get the most out of you for the least they can put into you – the least into your pocket, the least into your belly. They don't mind if they make you thinner and you last only half a lifetime. They'll just throw you out and buy another of you. That's what we've got to fight against. And making things properly is one of the champion ways of doing it."

Another time he said, "There's justice for things as there's justice for people, see? You forge a hinge badly, you make it so the rain can enter or all the wear goes on one of the knuckles – and you've not done right by that hinge. You've not done it justice."

Hinges were on Dixon's mind that week because the firm had taken delivery of a new machine that could stamp out cheap iron hinges from plate only half as thick as a man would need if he was to forge it "justly."

Freddy took in all these arguments, saw the points the man was making, conceded their probable rightness, and yet felt he himself was somehow always going to live in a world where they didn't quite apply – a parallel world where they would *nearly* apply but where there would always be some extenuating or exceptional circumstance to bend them aside. He never said so, of course; he simply nodded sagely and got on with the immediate practical business of avoiding Dixon's verbal and physical scoldings. Once the skills began to grow in his fingers, which is the only proper place for skills to grow, it became easy enough, and the work, though long and hard, enriched him with its own rewards.

Clive Mortimer was a "capitalist," of course. Freddy had discovered as much the first (and, after seeing Dixon's response, the only) time he introduced that name into their conversation. The thought of dear old Clive "grinding down the poor" – or, rather, the impossibility of such a thought – merely strengthened Freddy's conviction that he was going to live in that parallel world, more complex, less navigable, than Dixon's simple universe, where it was always dawn and unknown flowers were always just in bud.

These experiments in human apprenticeship – Clive at Eton, Freddy at the mill – had precisely the opposite effect to that for which Sir Toby, his wife, the servants, Hawkins and the other gardeners, the cottagers (both upstream and downstream), and every other victim of their development had prayed. Clive had always been coolest under fire. Eton confirmed him in that and now, when his vacations and Freddy's days off coincided, it began to rub off on Freddy, too.

For his part Freddy had always been a most ingenious young man. Whenever they came to some practical impasse, he was the one who said, "We could get over it like this." And when Clive said, "Come on then. Let's do that," Freddy would say, "Or, another way ..." until there were so many solutions to their problem, all of them sound and sensible, that Clive would resign the confusion to him and his decision. Now that native resourcefulness began to be backed by adult skills – craft skills handed down over centuries – some of it could not help but rub off on Clive, too.

The Mortimers were in despair.

"It's your own fault," Sir Toby's younger brother unfeelingly pointed out. "Should have given young Clive a full complement of brothers and sisters."

Sir Toby could hardly go into the gynaecological origins of this deficiency, but he did provide Lady Mortimer with an alternative paraphrase of his brother's rebuke. "Perhaps it's a bit unfair to blame the lad entirely," he said. "Every growing boy needs the companionship of his fellows. Only natural for him to turn to scruffs like young Oxley. Let's invite two of his schoolfellows down for Easter, eh? They'll soon elbow the little tyke aside."

And so it was ordered.

The two thus favoured were Tony Knox-Riddell (who was rumoured to be sired, on the wrong side of the sheets, by a now elderly royal duke) and the Hon. Howard Gray (whose father governed places here and there about the empire).

Alas for Sir Toby, he was as dazzled by what his capitalist friends said about Eton as was Dixon by what his socialist friends said about the upper classes; neither could see the truth for the Truth.

Tony Knox-Riddell and the Hon. Howard Gray were far keener to meet the famous Freddy Oxley than merely to stay at the fabled Mortimer Hall, for all its pleasures and treasures. The three young men, as they now were, came up to Birmingham by train, where the family coach met them and brought them out through Solihull to the Hall. They made all the right sounds of appreciation, of course. They admired the Rubenses and the Hogarths and the great ceiling by Sir James Thornhill, Hogarth's father-in-law; but what they really wanted to see was the repaired cracks in the grand marble staircase out in the garden ... the tidemark of the Great Diluvium on the cottages, both upstream and downstream ... the charred memorials to Ug the Prehistoric Ironsmith ... and all the other fabulous sites associated with the legendary Freddy Oxley.

That evening they met the legend himself. It had to be arranged with care for the entire staff were on pain of dismissal for any failure to prevent such a meeting. The Elysian Grove was the most easily defensible location. Every avenue to it led straight to its heart, where stood a marble reproduction of Pallas Athene, her arms, conjecturally restored by the copyist, welcoming the unwary from all points of the compass. To one side of the grove, invisible from anywhere beyond its confines, was a small folly of a temple, built with its domed roof frozen in the very act of collapsing; the tumbling stones were cunningly held in space by a concealed binding of iron straps and pegs, converting them into a makeshift staircase to the stars – or, at least, to the uncollapsed portion of the dome above. There the meeting had been arranged.

"Capital place to bring a wench!" Gray said, looking around knowingly. "Those Georgian squires knew how to do things."

"I say!" Knox-Riddell exclaimed, pointing into the great, sunken basin of water that occupied most of the floor of the folly. Three huge goldfish were swimming lazily around in it. All were deformed.

"The defect is inherited," Clive said. "My uncle brought them from China."

"How do they feed? How did they get so big?"

"They swim in here from the lake. There's a concealed pipe. Hush a moment!" He looked up at the evening sky, through the artificial gape in the dome. "Foxy?" he called.

"Gone to earth!" came back the challenge.

Clive smiled. "Code," he explained. The others were thrilled. One by one they climbed the precarious stairway and emerged into the chill light of the fading evening sun.

As so often happens when anticipation magnifies an event out of all proportion, the moment of meeting was an anticlimax.

Freddy Oxley did not bristle with bombs – or secrets; he carried no astounding scars; short said, he entirely lacked the air of a fellow to whom other boys would gladly sacrifice an entire holiday. Indeed, with his handed-down artisan clothing, his hobnail boots, his cropped hair, his work-blackened hands, and his common accent, he was a distinct let-down.

Freddy could feel it. He understood exactly what had happened – how Clive had built him up into some sort of hero, how they had been lured here by the promise of an adventure sandwiched somewhere between the lethal and the downright criminal ... How dreadfully ordinary he must seem after all that. He was ashamed of himself.

Even Clive could feel it, though loyalty was his other name. "Well," he said with a light laugh, after all other conversational resources had been exhausted, "what have you planned for us this hols, young 'un?"

More than all the world Freddy wanted not to let his friend down. Desperately he racked his brains for some scheme of ultimate devilment. He remembered how calm Clive had been after the explosion. It helped him now to keep a cool outward face to the world, and even to put a light smile on its lips. How the idea finally came to him he could never say. True, while he was waiting for them he had fashioned an aerial dart out of a piece of paper in his pockets – some announcement of a trade union meeting. True, he launched it on the air at that moment. But as they watched it spiral gracefully down and park itself in the shrubbery, he was almost as astonished as they to hear himself saying, in laconic tones that only Clive could have taught him: "I thought we might have a go at building a Grand Soaring Machine. Big enough to carry one or two of us, you know."

The last of the sun was golden on his polished cheeks as he looked from one to the other and smiled. They digested his words, took in the enormity of the proposal – and spontaneously they all began to laugh and cheer.

CHAPTER THREE

FREDDY'S SUGGESTION that they build and fly a soaring machine did not come entirely out of the blue. Only the previous week he had been down at the Mechanics Institute, leafing through some old bound volumes of *The Mechanics Magazine*, and there he had seen the drawings of Sir George Cayley's original soarer. This contrivance of cloth and springy timber – really a giant kite, some five hundred square feet in area, with a little canoe on wheels slung beneath it – had actually flown across a small valley at Brompton Hall in Yorkshire in 1853 with a rebellious coachman at the controls. *And I was only three ...* Freddy had thought. What had happened in the intervening fourteen years? Had Sir George given up all interest in flying? Perhaps his coachman had been killed in some further experiment?

No one at the Institute seemed to know. Anyway, who wanted to fly? It could never be more than the hobby of a rich man, and an eccentric rich man at that. So when Freddy found himself among the sons of three very rich men and under some pressure to produce an idea of daring and originality, it was hard for him not to remember Sir George Cayley's wonderful soaring machine.

He produced a piece of charcoal from his pocket and sketched its outlines on the curve of the dome. The other three risked their footholds, and the secrecy of their hiding place, to crowd the parapet and watch.

The overall shape was something like a fanciful skate (the fish not the ice shoe), "a chineesey sort of skate," as Knox-Riddell put it.

"We could make these of willow," Freddy said, as he drew the last of the struts, "and bind them with jute."

"And we can steal some bedlinen for the sails," Gray said.

"And there's that explorers' wagon we made a couple of years ago," Clive remembered. "We could take the wheels off that."

"We'd have to soak the bedsheets in linseed oil or something," Freddy said. "Just like a kite. Or they'll spill too much wind. It's going to need weeks to harden."

The longer they thought about it, the more obvious it became that one brief vacation would never suffice for the building of the Grand Soarer, as their imaginations now pictured it; and yet the idea was so marvellous that none of them would even dream of abandoning it.

"We can come back in the summer," Knox-Riddell said. "We'll all have left Eton by then. And you" – he nodded at Clive – "won't be going up to Balliol for a couple of months."

Grinning at this salvation they considered it from every angle and found it flawless. "And the intrepid Oxley can be building the thing meanwhile," Gray pointed out.

"Why intrepid?" Clive asked.

"Well, I'm bloody sure *I'm* not going to sit in the helmsman's seat! Aren't you?"

Freddy felt a subtle kind of disappointment. By their conversation they were demoting him to a mere mechanic; they had taken over his idea. "At least the frame could be built before you all vanish," he said.

Accidentally he had hit on the right words to restore his position as the founder of this feast. His suggestion – that they, three young lords of creation, by returning to Eton, the country's foremost seat of learning, would be "vanishing" – struck them all as quaint and even laughable. Yet they felt the truth at the heart of it; for the first time in their lives they envied someone like Freddy.

And indeed, when the time came, when they took their last look for several months at the sturdy willow framework whose manufacture had cost them the entire holiday, it did seem that they were the ones who were vanishing and that the centre of the world remained here with Freddy.

The seeming completeness of the framework was, however, an illusion. Freddy still had to bind every joint in several layers of raffia, each one held in a skin of boiled linseed oil that would take weeks to harden properly. The wheels, which had belonged to a child's toy cart before they were purloined for the "explorer's wagon," were merely pushed onto wooden axles. They probably wouldn't survive a single outing. Freddy would have to make proper bearings and sweat them onto heart-of-oak or lignum vitae, if he could steal some from the mill. And several forays around Mortimer Hall in search of bedsheets had proved abortive. Clive had thought all he needed to do was accidentally rip a pair and they would become available; but not a bit of it. The ruined sheets were turned sides-to-middle and handed up to the menservants' quarters. And what happened when they became threadbare, he asked? Why then they were sent out to The Poor or sold to the rag-and-bone man. Clive and his friends began dimly to grasp that there was an economy at work which they, up near its fountainhead, had never even glimpsed.

In the end they had to wait until they returned to Eton, where theft, or "poaching," came more easily. Whether or not the sheets actually belonged to Queen Victoria herself the boys never knew; certainly they bore no royal monogram. But equally certainly they came from the drying yards at Windsor Castle; Gray had once been a pageboy to the Order of the Garter and knew his way around the royal household. They were still barely dry when a mystified Mrs. Oxley untied the parcel and put them out to air.

"The sheets are of excellent quality," Freddy wrote back in unwitting endorsement of the royal taste. "They should oil up well and carry us to the clouds this summer."

His letters to Eton were more eagerly awaited than any the three boys had received there before. Not even when Knox-Riddell had suspected he would get his Honourable had he run with such anticipation to the windowledge where letters from home were laid out. But then, early in June, Freddy's literary efforts became vague, scrappy, and – worst of all – infrequent. It was some weeks before the explanation for this change was forthcoming.

It all happened after he was sent one evening to fetch some papers for Mr. Wilde, the factory overseer. Now Mr. Wilde was not just the overseer of the one small mill where Freddy was apprenticed, he was the general overseer of all the Mortimer factories in the Midlands. He was also a justice of the peace. So it was no surprise to Freddy to learn that Mr. Wilde lived in a grand new house in the grand new crescent terrace overlooking Heronfield Park – at number twelve, to be precise.

Night had fallen by the time Freddy reached the terrace. It was early summer and the cloudless sky had drawn a thin mist from the still-cool earth; the gaslamps stretched around the curve of the terrace, laying a crescent of lighted islands strewn like an opulent necklace along the broad pavement. The park itself lay beyond the feeble reach of the yellow gas fishtails, but its presence could be felt whenever the night breeze stirred in the shrubs and still-young trees. He could just make out the high palisade of green-painted iron spears that railed it off from dogs, courting couples, and other threats to good order. He knew those spears; the final batch of them had been forged at the mill in the very week he had begun his apprenticeship there. He remembered how they had looked, black from the forge, lying in counted piles on the mill floor. It was hard to believe they were the same objects that now ranged with such mathematical precision all around the park.

There was a kind of wonder about the transformation. It was the same with the Grand Soarer, he realized – everything these days came back to the flying machine. Take the willow switches he and the others had spent days selecting and cutting and unbarking and shaving ... looking at them now, bent out of their natural form, disciplined to the outline of the machine and bound with all the precision and strength he could muster, it was almost impossible to remember that these had once been free-growing branches, dipping with haphazard charm beside the river.

These amazements occupied him until he found number twelve – its "gothick" letters lifted straight from the hymnbook and magnified upon the fanlight over the door; the spiky outlines were softened only slightly by the gentle glow of gaslight from within. Distractedly, lost for the ten-thousandth time in pleasurable anticipation of his first flight, he wandered up the front steps and rang the doorbell.

The front steps! Whatever was he thinking of? The jangle of bells from the area below reminded him with a jolt who he was. Working so much on the Soarer he had begun to think of himself as one of the local Eton set. He thought of fleeing but already he could hear a footman coming into the lobby.

Tell the fellow that the gate on the steps leading down to the area was stuck! No – the house was too new for that. Tell him Mr. Wilde ordered him to use the front door. Impossible.

The door opened inward. A young footman of around seventeen, Freddy's own age but taller, looked him up and down suspiciously. Freddy put the best face possible on it. "Mr. Wilde has sent me for the papers he left upon his desk," he said. He tried to sound as much like Tony Knox-Riddell as possible. His success was only partial but it was enough to throw the footman into a quandary.

"Be so good as to wait," he said, only just managing not to add *sir*. In his confusion he left the door slightly ajar as he turned for advice from the butler.

But for that carelessness the whole of Freddy's life might have taken an entirely different course. For through the crack of the door, and on through the crack of the inner door as the footman opened it, he saw such a vision of loveliness that his heart stood still and his mouth fell open and all thought of his errand, and even of the Grand Soarer, deserted him.

She was about his own age, an upstairs maid, just bringing down a warming pan from the sheets of some early-to-bed. She had fine, fair hair, and though it was neatly combed up inside her cap the bulge of it showed its length. She was no slim and slank little sapling, either; her figure was generously feminine and yet her face had an elfin delicacy that won his heart at this very first glance. She turned her eyes upon him, great searching pools of an almost violet blue, and from that instant he was in thrall to her. The soft, tender lamplight made even the air about her seem desirable. She swept out of sight, though he craned to follow her. A door swished on two-way hinges.

She had seen him, hadn't she? She had paused? For the merest fraction of a second something had passed between them – surely?

There was a sudden darkness before him. He looked up into the eyes of a minor god, a towering cliff of disapproval, the butler. But the god's voice came straight off some barrack square: "If you don't get off my front steps toot sweet, laddie, I'll have your last drop of blood."

Alone on the pavement, suddenly chill, he felt as Lucifer cast down from heaven. Disconsolately he set his feet to the steps that his class and errand should have dictated in the first place, down to the servants' hall. A scullery maid answered his knock. Committed now to the voice of Knox-Riddell, he repeated his message. It impressed her into a suspicion of a curtsey as she let him into the boot lobby. Then, seeing how dank and cheerless it was there, she added, "Come in where it's more comfortable, I'm sure."

The servants' hall was brighter and better furnished than many an artisan's home. The equivalent at Mortimer Hall, being of a much earlier age, was ruder by far – and in any case it was years since Freddy had been welcome there. The room into which the little skivvy had shown him was unoccupied except for a coachman, fast asleep by the boiler; the gentle mewing of hot water wove in and out of his snores. Freddy's observant eye was busy taking in every detail, trying to imagine *her* living and moving among it all, when the door opened. He expected the footman with the box of papers but his stomach turned a new somersault when he saw it was herself, the fair vision from above.

"Hello," he said, knowing that if he had left it a second later, his voice would have shattered under the hammer of his heart. She paid him no heed. What an awesome power she had – to stand over there, at the very far side of the room, ignoring him, ignoring his greeting, and yet to stoke his blood to such a fever, to pull a trapdoor beneath his innards, to dry his throat, to set his every muscle ashiver, to rivet his eyes to her. She made him aware of himself as never before. His hands were twice their usual size, and hot, and clammy. How long since he had cleaned his boots, for heaven's sake? His clothes felt shabby and threadbare.

She rescued him, again without being aware of it. She could fill the most trivial, everyday acts with magical appeal. Surely he had never seen a drawer opened with such grace. Never had anyone taken out a teaspoon with such delicacy, nor examined it with such style, nor polished it with such tenderness, nor replaced it with such an elegant kind of hesitancy – nor stood just so, in such heartrending uncertainty.

A monstrous thought then struck him – a thought so

wonderful, so terrifying, he could hardly bear to repeat it even to himself. Her only purpose in coming down here was *to see him*. No! To see him *again*! Was it possible? Was it even thinkable? She an upstairs maid and he a mere apprentice?

True, his time was all but out, yet – even so ... was it possible? "Mere" apprentice was not his own self-portrait, mind; rather it was the conventional description in all the penny dreadfuls. He had never actually felt terribly "mere" – until now. After all, how many apprentices could boast three close friends at Eton – not alone that, but three friends who really rather looked up to him and took something of a lead from him? No, he could think of a lot of people who were "merer" by far.

He cleared his throat, testing, really, to see whether or not his voice had deserted him. She turned sharply and stared at him. He gulped, and melted all over again. Those eyes! That perfect little face! Those tiny, adorable ears!

"Did you speak?" she asked.

He knew it was a command, not a question. "Yes. When's your day off?" he asked.

She tossed her head and swept from the room. "You've got a nerve!" she said.

But he had seen the smile she tried so hard to suppress, the glance she had been powerless to prevent. Their eyes had met and some brief, urgent plea had passed from her to him. *Persist!* it begged. *Only persist!* He knew some of the ways of girls by now. He had horsed around with the ones down at the mill for years – not, of course that he would compare ... no, even to think the comparison was ... no!

Still, he knew the glance that meant *persist*.

The footman came at last with the wanted papers, securely held in a legal briefcase. "It's locked," he warned pointedly, risking as much rudeness as he dared, for he was still a little uncertain of Freddy's class.

His bluntness angered Freddy, but he contained it, thinking he might gain the greater advantage if he increased the fellow's uncertainty rather than by a straight challenge. Besides, he wanted to learn at least the name of his angel. Inspiration suddenly gripped him – he could do both in one and the same stroke.

He remembered the tones in which Clive and his friends had discussed women – not women of their own class, to be sure, but those of the humbler sort. "That little filly who was down here just now ..." he began, still in his borrowed Eton tones.

"Ann?" the other was startled into saying.

Ann! Ann-gelic ... Ann. What an unimaginably beautiful name! It soared far above all other women's names. Why had he never seen it before when it was so obvious now? Ann, Ann ... he could repeat it for ever and never grow tired of it.

"Ann," he said with a dismissive insouciance, the pretence at which cost all his powers. "Pretty little thing."

"She'd match you," the fellow sneered. "You've both got guinea ideas on a farthing's income, I'd say. Aye, you and that Ann Howard – two out the same mould."

Almost too angry to speak Freddy made for the door. As a parting shot he looked around and said, "Interesting. I've never actually been in a servants' hall before."

But he no longer deceived, or even half-deceived, the footman. "I could tell that," the fellow said. "Mebbe you'll remember to wipe your boots next time."

As he ascended once more to the street Freddy had ruefully to admit he had come off second best. But what did it matter? What did anything matter beside the single, great, wonderful, amazing discovery that such a beautiful young woman existed outside the imagination of poets, that she had been interested enough at the mere sight of him to come down for a second look, and that, despite all her flouncing away, she wanted to see him again.

Ann ... Ann ... he murmured the name all the way back to the works. And when the great Mr. Wilde cursed him for a loafer he hardly even heard.

CHAPTER FOUR

THE IDLE APPRENTICE was a figure of Hogarth's time. A century later, in Freddy's time, an idle hour was a rare luxury. What few he had he should have been spending in the abandoned barn behind the derelict gamekeeper's cottage in the neglected corner of the Mortimer estate. Instead he polished his boots, scoured his hands red raw, slicked his hair down with water, and went scurrying off to Ferndown Crescent by Heronfield Park. There he would stroll up and down, and count the railings, and kick small stones, and watch the courting couples making the best of the unlocked hours, and sigh his heart toward the attic windows of number 12.

From time to time he tried to resume his work with the Grand Soarer but it was no use. Darkness would fall upon the old barn before he realized he must have been standing there, heavens knew how long, remembering her voice, the shade of her cheek, the sweep of her hair, those astonishing eyes ... while the linseed oil dried upon his hands. And his next free moment would bring him once more back on watch at the park palisades.

Every servant in the house knew he was there, of course. Now and then he would see one of them, drawing a curtain, raising a blind, adjusting a sash. Usually it was the young footman, who would glance cautiously about him and then make a rude gesture. Sometimes it was the other upstairs maid; she would notice him, turn from the window, and beckon at someone deeper in the room. But only twice did that someone draw close enough to the daylight for him to see; and both times it was, of course, herself, the sweet tormentor of his days and dreams. Oh they all knew he was there, well enough.

Did she never take an hour off? Probably it was in the afternoons.

One evening the pattern was different. In addition to the usual comings and goings at the windows, there was a face – or, rather, a brow and a glimpse of an eye – that kept peeping up over the kerb around the basement area. It was the face of a woman, but its exposures were too brief for him to identify her. He was fairly certain it was the scullery maid, the one who had first let him in. He racked his brains for some errand that might gain him admittance for the second time. Just when he had screwed up his courage to the point where he was ready to march across the street, down the steps, and boldly announce that he desired a word with Miss Ann Howard, who should come leisurely up those same steps but Miss Ann Howard in person; and at her side was the other above-stairs maid. Both were gorgeously dressed in summer finery, for the evening was warm and the sun was still an hour short of setting.

He expected, or hoped – that is to say, he fervently desired – they would cross the street and enter the park by the gate to his left. But they hesitated; and he realized he'd stationed himself a little too close to it. If they were to go to it straightway now, it would betray a shocking want of deviousness, which is the very etiquette of courtship. Their hesitation was brief. Impelled by that unwritten code they strolled off in the other direction, arm in arm, chatting amiably, as if he were invisible – had always been invisible.

Freddy took off his hat and wiped his brow as he began, awkwardly and unhappily, to follow them, matching his pace to theirs but keeping to his side of the road. The welcoming coolness of the damp hatband as he replaced it was like a douche of common sense.

Why? he asked himself. Why am I doing this? What sort of figure am I cutting in their eyes – in *her* eyes?

He saw that his obsessive behaviour marked no real change of character, however drastically it had altered his habits. He wanted to know Miss Ann Howard, and when he wanted a thing he always pursued it singlemindedly, either until he got it or until he drew close enough to see it was not worth the wanting. But he realized, too, that outwardly he must seem a very different sort of person, especially to her. An outcast dog hoping for one kind glance.

He turned on his heel and began a purposeful walk toward the first gate – the one they had spurned; he suspected that they were making for the other entrance, farther up the crescent. As soon as he was inside the park he chose the path that linked the two entrances. It meandered somewhat, and the shrubs were at the peak of their summer luxuriance, so there was no place in all its length where he could gain a view of the farther gate, watch them enter, and thus pick his moment.

In any case such fine calculation would have run quite against his present mood, which was brash and full of purpose, kill or cure. As he strode along he hammered out his thoughts between the fist of one hand and the palm of the other. Yet to call them "thoughts" is to exaggerate; they were more like exhortations. He did not plan a single word of what he would say when they met – only that he would be plain, blunt, courteous, and manly.

He was walking rather fast, he realized. There is a nice gradation between a stride that is hasty and one that is resolute. He slowed himself down and took off his hat to mop his brow yet again. *And don't frown so*, he commanded himself when he felt the ridges beneath his damp kerchief.

"I don't know why you even notice him," Sally, the companion, was saying to Ann.

"How many other apprentices did you ever hear old Wilde mention by name?" Ann challenged. "Go on – tell me one."

Sally was still scornful. "But I *mean* – an apprentice! Oil under their fingernails. Iron filings in everything."

"Well, it's happened anyway."

"What's happened? What are you talking about? Nothing's happened."

"He noticed me. I noticed him. That happened."

Sally looked about her in bewilderment. "Well, all I can say is that some people are very easily satisfied."

"No!" For a fleeting moment Ann felt it important to get her meaning across. "Don't you see? If something happens, it's more important than something that didn't happen. Like dreams. I mean – this really happened." She saw that Sally was not grasping the point and gave up. What did it matter? She herself knew perfectly well what she meant.

And anyway, at that moment they almost ran into the young apprentice himself; their mutual approach had been masked by a sharp bend and a huge clump of bamboo and deutzia.

Freddy smiled and raised his cap. She could see he was all nerves. She wanted to say something to help him, though she was overwrought herself.

Freddy knew that if he delayed a fraction of a second longer his voice would desert him, and anyway, the momentum of their walking would carry them past each other. "What a pleasant evening," he said. And then he added, "Miss Howard."

"Oh," she said, and smiled at him in what she hoped looked like encouragement.

He was transfigured. He wanted to touch her face, her lips, her hair ... to stare into her eyes while she stared into his and let no words pass between them because none would be necessary. He wanted to leap forward to that moment now.

"Why, 'pon my soul, he's dressed little better than a beggar," Sally said, looking him up and down as if he were a waxwork. "But what did you expect – he's nought but an apprentice!"

His impulse was to insult her back but he checked it and smiled instead. His eyes danced as he replied, "Set beside two such beauties, the Prince of Wales himself wouldn't look up to much."

Sally pressed her lips tightly together but he could tell by her eyes that she was pleased. Emboldened he went on, "In fact, I can't understand why the whole park hasn't come to a standstill, just to look and wonder."

Ann turned triumphantly to Sally and, referring to some previous conversation about Freddy's character, said, "Bashful, eh! My eye!" She laughed.

Freddy laughed.

People nearby stopped momentarily and turned to look. They smiled: knowing smiles, melancholy smiles, happy smiles, pitying smiles – at those siren trills of youth and innocence.

"Won't you present me to your friend, Miss Howard?" Freddy asked.

Ann drew breath but Sally cut in quickly, "Perhaps if she knew your name she might consider it."

Freddy saw the nudge she gave Ann as she spoke and understood that Ann did, indeed, know his name. He grinned to show he was not being serious; he allowed his voice to stray toward the tones of his friends from Eton; and he said, "Do forgive me. I thought everyone knew. I'm Frederick Mortimer. I'm sure you've heard of my older brother Clive?"

Sally was scandalized. "The cheek!" She turned to continue their walk.

Ann lingered, in half a mind to go. He could see he had disappointed her. He had broken one more of those unwritten conventions. "Only joking," he said. "I'm Freddy Oxley – as I'm sure you know."

"Oh hark!" Sally said. "You're sure of yourself."

"Miss Pickering," Ann said, "let me present Mr. Frederick Oxley."

Freddy bowed his head at Sally, who gave him a brief, cool smile in return.

"Miss Pickering's right," Ann reproved him mildly. "You shouldn't ought to assume we knew your name."

He hung his head and glanced mischievously at Sally, determined to win her over. "Even in these matters," he said, "I'm nought but an apprentice. Still" – regaining his usual cheerful composure – "it would be odd if a beautiful and charming young lady, seeing some idiot making a fool of himself outside her house evening after evening, didn't make *some* inquiry."

"You're forgiven," Ann said brightly. "Shall we walk about a bit?"

He looked at Sally, as if seeking her permission. "Perhaps Miss Pickering would find that too uncongenial?"

The direct approach took Sally by surprise. She just stared back blankly.

"And much as I would hate to be deprived of her company ..." he went on.

But Ann was swift to head him off. "Oh, don't mind Sal. Her bark's always worse than her bite."

So he stepped nimbly between them, spun himself about, and took each by the arm, propelling them gently forward.

Ann was softly pliable, Sally, a stick insect of unwillingness. "You'll get into trouble," she told him, "going about saying you're a Mortimer."

He laughed. "Old Clive wouldn't mind. Anyway, we are brothers of a kind." He remembered the hesitant razor nicks in their forearms, how little pain there had been, the raspberry jam of their mingled blood, the sense of growing three years older in half a second.

Sally's arm was as tense as steel. "There you go again!"

But Ann said, "Wait a minute! Are you *that* one?"

"What one?"

"The floods up at Sandal's Cottages? And that fire in the ... and the bomb? Did you blow up ..."

He wanted to let her know they had moved on from such childish pranks, and yet she was so excited by the possibility that *he* was the perpetrator of all those outrages that he didn't want to belittle them, either. So all he said was, "We've set out upon something really big now. Important, I mean."

But Ann leaned forward and said to Sally, "You weren't around here in those days, Sal. It was the talk of the district for weeks." To Freddy she said, "What's he like? I've seen him, of course. He looks ... well, very nice."

"We're building a soaring machine now."

"For sawing wood?" Sally asked.

"No – *soar*ing." He withdrew his arms and imitated a gull. "Like a kite, you know, only without a kitestring."

Sally understood. "A big paper dart."

"Very big." He took their arms again. Ann was now the more tense of the two. He went on: "Big enough to take a man. And it's not made of paper. Come and see it if you like. How much time have you got?"

"Is Clive Mortimer going to fly in it?" Ann asked. "I'll bet he's brave enough."

Freddy sniffed. "I'm going to be the first. After all, I'm the one who's building it for them." Then, realizing he had made himself sound like a mere mechanic, he added, "Well – *with* them, actually. They spent all their Easter hols helping me."

"Who's *they*? He hasn't got any brothers, has he?"

"Oh, just a couple of other friends of ours. The Flying

Four we call ourselves. The Honourable Howard Gray, the Honourable Tony Knox-Riddell, Clive, and yours truly." He smiled at Sally. "Three schoolboys and a mere apprentice."

He added the self-deprecation to avoid being bowled over by Ann's enthusiasm. "You really really know these people?" she was asking. "What are they like?"

Sally was distressed at her. "They're like the simpering idiots who come to us At Home and make the dullest, emptiest conversation in the world. That's what."

Freddy remembered the yarns the four of them had spun while making the framework of the Grand Soarer. Knox-Riddell was going to cross Africa, from Cape to Cairo and open up the Lost Civilizations of the interior; he told them the tale of it as if it had already happened. Clive, inspired by this, described the buried city he had discovered after a sandstorm in the Great Arabian Desert. Gray, for variation, had described *Une Grande Horizontale* Tour of Europe – a different fabulous woman each night. Freddy had learned much, without being as stimulated by it as the others. And then, to bring them back to the work in hand – though not back to earth – he had given them a birdseye tour of Birmingham and the Midlands as seen from the cradle of the Grand Soarer.

Simpering idiots with dull, empty conversation, indeed! What a stupid woman this Sally Pickering was; eaten alive with sourness and criticism. He forced himself to swallow his impatience with her; indeed, it became something of a challenge to win her over.

"They're all first-class fellows," he said, in exactly their tones.

Ann giggled. "Ooh I love it when you talk like that. Doesn't he do it well, Sal?"

"Yes, like Ma Wilde's pug dog walking on his back legs for a nibble of fancy cake."

"Oh Sal!" Ann was getting cross.

"No," Freddy said tolerantly. "Miss Pickering's right. We shouldn't try to be what we aren't – except as a joke, of course." He leaned forward and looked up into her eyes. "You do know I was joking."

She tried not to smile. He saw that winning her over was quite possible. Perhaps he shouldn't overdo it? He realized how much a little mild opposition from her had helped him with Ann – who felt obliged to compensate for her friend's coolness.

"But," he went on, "if the unusual thing happens, if we find ourselves close friends with people who would not normally give us the time of day – well, we should be grateful. That's all."

"You mean you and these fellows?" Ann said.

With his smile he tried to say that he thought her by far the most wonderful person in the world. "I also mean a mere apprentice and two of the most scorching beauties ever, Miss Howard."

Sally laughed at last. She gave him a daring little push with her hip, adding, "No one's going to keep you down for long, are they!"

He gave her arm a squeeze but it was to Ann that he said, "One unkind word could do it. Or even a glance."

At that moment her interest in him turned from flirtatious curiosity into something much deeper. Their eyes dwelled in each other's until neither could bear the wonder of the possibilities that were just beginning to occur to them both.

CHAPTER FIVE

IT WAS A FURTHER WEEK before the two upper maids could get away again. The arrangement was that they would come straight to the old barn, thus leaving Freddy free to get on with his construction. The sheer size of the machine brought about an immediate change in Ann. While Freddy was opening the barn door, hoisting its half-collapsed structure and walking it carefully through its arc, he kept his eyes on her face, smiling, encouraging her to smile. The wonder of her beauty and the fact that she was there, she was really there, with him, renewed itself from moment to moment. So he saw the transformation happen.

Until that evening she must have thought of the Grand Soarer as some kind of glorified kite. But now, seeing it hang from the old rafters, with a span that would easily cover two large carriages, she began to grasp the true scope of the venture. She gazed from it to him and back again. "Will it really fly?" she asked.

"Come back in July and I'll tell you."

"Oh, I'd love to see it happen. I'd adore to see you go right up in the air in it."

"Well, I'd have to ask the others. They'll probably say it's only for people who helped build it."

"Just say the word! You said yourself it wasn't finished. We'll help, won't we, Sal?" She walked into the barn and looked up at it. "Yes. That sail, or wing, or whatever you call that oilcloth – that's only tacked in. Sal and I can finish that."

"It's work for cobblers," he warned. "Not little button-holes for milady."

"Give us a bodkin and I'll show you! Buttonholes indeed!" In a wheedling tone she added, "Oh please – dear Frederick?"

He was about to correct her, for he hated to be called Frederick – or had done until that moment. Then he decided that if anyone in all the world should be allowed to use the name it was Ann. He held out his hand. "Welcome to the Flying Four, Miss Howard. I supose we'd better call ourselves the Flying Five now. Or" – turning to Sally – "the Flying Six?"

Sally shrugged. "I don't mind."

He laughed at her. "Careful with the enthusiasm or you'll bust a vessel."

Ann, not yet understanding that they both enjoyed this kind of sparring, stepped in and said, "You'd better call me Ann, then." As an afterthought she added, "And Sally."

"On alternate days?"

It was Sally who laughed.

"You know what I mean," Ann said crossly, taking off her gloves.

Freddy's original idea had been to stretch the sheeting directly over the frame. That appeared to be the system in

Cayley's original machine. But, thinking about it – and thinking about it, and thinking about it – he had realized that thick sisal twine, sewn through ordinary bedsheets, even those of regal quality, would create a weakness that could easily propagate right across the sail. The willow frame was too flexible in itself to support the fabric – indeed, the boot was on the other foot, for only the tensioning of the fabric would finally make the framework rigid.

At first he thought of buttonholing each hole but saw it would take until doomsday. Someone at the Institute told him of a firm in Handsworth who made brass eyelets for sails; but even at friendly rates they were a farthing each. In the end he cut and stripped another set of willow sticks, much thinner than the first lot, about finger thickness, and made a second frame that would fit within the outline of the first, leaving an inch or so to spare all round. The idea was to fix the sheeting to this much lighter frame and then secure it to the main frame by a simple running lockstitch; this would spread the pull of the twine, and all the strains of flight, evenly throughout the fabric.

He explained these ideas to the girls as he unhitched the pulley rope and carefully lowered the machine onto the upright logs and applecrates that served as his manufacturing jig.

"When it flies," Ann asked, "where are you going to sit? Or stand – or lie?"

He pointed toward a corner of the barn where stood the only finished portion of the machine – a kind of low, elongated bassinet or wickerwork canoe on four light but sturdy wheels. "I'll be in that thing. It'll be slung beneath the sail. Well, not slung but connected by struts – rigidly, you know. And there'll be two smaller sails sticking out at the back, one fixed and one that you can move like a rudder, to steer it. We're following Sir George Cayley's original design as closely as possible, except where we can see obvious improvements."

"Kites don't need rudders," Sally commented.

"Yes but kites are tethered. You can steer them from the ground. This will be completely free once it's in the air."

He saw that neither of them fully grasped the idea, even now.

"Free?" Ann echoed.

"As the lark at sunrise."

This light of admiration in her eyes was nectar to him. "I think you're mad," she said.

"I always told you," Sally agreed complacently.

After that they came and helped him regularly every Saturday night and whatever evening they could manage in the week, for their evenings off moved at the Wildes' convenience. With their help and advice on the finer points of stitchery the work went better and the machine was stronger than it ever would have been without them.

And because they had something to do, a dream to realize together, it made Freddy's and Ann's relationship quite different from the commonplace of walking around the park, kicking stones, chatting brightly, sparring in the age-old ways of lovers and lasses, watching couples more advanced in their courtship as they slipped away among the bushes, and wondering how many more snatched kisses and squeezings of hands were needed as a pre-investment in those more robust and private favours.

His fellow apprentices measured romantic progress on the traditional how-far-did-she-let-you-go scale. It was something Freddy had never understood and now it bewildered him more than ever. When he admired the swell of Ann's bosom it was not in that sniggering, lecherous spirit but with something closer to wonder, to adoration. Exclude the human and emotional side of it and he could get the same feeling out of looking at a good piece of engineering – one of the latest locomotives, say. He admired anything that was perfection of its kind, admired it to that point of wonder which we call worship. And Ann was as close to his idea of feminine perfection as it was possible to get. He could admire her form, quite frankly, and still feel a million miles away from his giggling fellows down at the factory.

It was as if he and Ann, by working together and by living for the climactic day of the flight, now soon upon them, had gained a uniquely different scale of judgement. And a better one, too, he thought. For where else could a kiss and a caress in the park lead *except* to some public-secret bower among the shrubbery, if not today then tomorrow, if not tomorrow then next week? But now, when they were coating the fabric, say, and their hands brushed together, or when, later and more daring, they would pause to admire their handiwork and he would put his arms around both their waists (but less lightly around Ann's), then the very existence of the machine, both as an achievement and a goal, gave these growing intimacies a context that mere elemental courtship could never provide.

Sometimes, when night had consumed the evening and it was time to go, Sally, the perfect chaperone, would give them a few moments alone, and he would put his arms about her and whisper I love you in her ear, and she would put her darling lips up to his and fill him with such sweet minglings of love and yearning. He wanted almost to become her, to be inside her mind, to share her understanding of the world and of him – never to be separated from that perfect union of their thoughts. Sometimes he wondered how she felt. She was more passionate than him. People said only degraded women had passions like that. But Ann ... well, there were times when the fury of her love overwhelmed him. Her body writhed against him, little moans escaped her lips, she would lead his hands to ever-greater licence with her; his mind and will were prisoners of her compulsion. Yet when finally, and after many a cautious reconnaissance, the tips of his fingers strayed as far as halfway down one breast, she moaned *no* with a pleading note of desperation, and curtseyed her body out of his embrace.

He wanted to tell her that even – no! – he wanted her to understand without his having to tell her that even if she were naked, even if he ran his hands all over her, it would be an act of worship not of lechery. But he could be patient now. He knew that when the right moment came she would understand it – and without a word spoken.

Meanwhile, stitch by stitch, coat by coat, the Grand Soarer took shape.

Eton went down early in July but the young men had metropolitan and social obligations, so it was close to the end of the month before Clive and Gray and Knox-Riddell appeared once more at Mortimer Hall. By then the machine was as ready to fly as she ever would be.

Freddy didn't finish until seven of an evening, and it was more like eight by the time he'd changed and had his supper. The fellows couldn't wait that long, of course. They had already lowered the craft to the floor and wheeled it out into the old threshing yard. There they took turns to indulge each other's fantasies with mock flights, imitating the rush of the wind and the cawing of jackdaws, whose musclebound style of soaring seemed closest to the way they imagined their own rigid craft would perform.

When Freddy came, alone, for it was Friday, which was never one of the nights off in the Wilde household, they fell upon him in an orgy of delight and congratulation. He had not intended to take all the praise upon himself but suddenly he found he was too shy to mention the girls. Only when the fellows suggested he should immediately take it up on its maiden flight did he at last, and awkwardly, confess their help.

"What! What? Fillies eh! What's all this?" They nudged and cajoled. "Sly little bugger! Look at him – face like a beetroot!"

Clive, more accustomed than the others to sensing Freddy's mood, asked, "Serious, young'un?"

Freddy nodded. "Pretty much so." It was easier for him now to fall into their vernacular.

"Tell us about it. Stow it, you two!"

"They're two very charming young women," Freddy began. He almost said ladies, but to call women who were not ladies, "ladies" would have implied something quite different. "They're upper maids at Mr. Wilde's house in the Ferndown Crescent."

"Our general manager," Clive explained.

The term "upper maids" triggered some tribal response in the others. Gray leered and dug Freddy in the ribs. "So while we've been down and out at Eton, you've been up and in here! You're a true dark horse, Foxy me old swell."

There was a lot of new wealth entering Eton at that time so it was naturally the fashion to pretend to be desperately poor.

"We've been hard up," Knox-Riddell laughed. "He's been hard *and* up!"

Freddy, torn between the flattery of their envy and the purity of his love, said gruffly but with a grin, "There was nothing like that." He felt a traitor both to the brotherhood of young men and to the chivalry he owed Ann.

Gray peered into the barn, at the piled hay and the dark corners, and said simply, "More fool you! It's a fellow's duty, don't you know. Get it where you can, and how you can, and whenever you can."

He always spoke like a man of large experience. Freddy wondered if he had, in fact, ever done It. If so, naturally, it would only have been with a housemaid or a whore – and people of Gray's class, it seemed, were able to make very little distinction between the two. He began to sense that it might have been a mistake to invite the girls to the grand maiden flight. An easy charmer like Gray or a genuinely charming but thoughtless young fellow like Knox-Riddell could turn their heads without even trying. Clive alone he would trust, without any reservation.

"So what's your idea?" Clive asked. "When's the flight to be?"

"It'll have to be tomorrow evening, after work. Miss Pickering and Miss Howard finish at four on Saturdays but we go on till six. I can't get here until seven."

"We'll keep 'em warm for you," Gray promised. He began to dance around, singing, "I'll be Getting Gertie's Garters in the Garden."

"Cut that!" Clive warned him, eyeing Freddy.

"Let's hope this wind will have blown itself out by then," Freddy said. "It's working up to quite a gale."

They horsed around for a while longer, taking it in turns to pretend to fly. Then, when the buffeting of the wind threatened to upend the machine, they pushed it back into the relative safety of the barn. Before they closed the door, they ran their eyes and fingers one last time over the shining monster.

"She looks so *right*," Knox-Riddell said.

"Yes!" Freddy answered excitedly, glad of at least one point where their minds could meet without qualification. "That's just it. In *all* engineering, if a thing *is* right then it also looks right. Have you seen these new Thornton Class locos? On the Great Western? You don't need to see 'em working – they don't even need to be fired up – even in a picture you can *see* they're about a hundred times better than anything we ever had before."

They made their various ways home. Gray and Knox-Riddell went directly to the Hall; Clive walked home via Freddy's.

On their way Freddy outlined his misgivings about the other two and the girls.

"You're serious, aren't you," Clive said.

"Yes. The point is – they're not a pair of fillies. They're not just bits of fluff."

"Of course not. Don't worry. I'll make sure the others behave themselves. We're all a bit excited tonight. Understandably. But they know what's what once the flag of possession is flying."

A short while later he said, "Gosh but I envy you, young Fredders. The freedom you have to meet girls. I took a fall for a young charmer in London last week – couldn't exchange more than half a dozen words with her. They keep them as tight as new pine cones." He grinned. "What's it like, eh?"

"It's always very proper. I mean, Miss Pickering is always there to play gooseberry on us."

"Still, you can talk, can't you? Talk about anything you want? Laugh ... joke ... be serious? Just talk? That would be wonderful I think." He punched Freddy playfully. "Don't ever envy me, young'un."

Freddy laughed. "As if I would." Then he returned to his chief worry. "As long as you make Gray and Knox-Riddell understand ..."

Clive had a sudden inspiration. "I know! I'll tell them to think of your girls as if they were someone's sisters."

"They *are*, actually. Both of them."

"Yes but I mean" – he tried to find a different way of putting it and couldn't – "you know, somebody's *sisters!*"

CHAPTER SIX

THE WIND ROARED. Sleep, which had been shallow at best, deserted Freddy shortly after two that night – the birth hour of novel ideas, when the censors of reason are the last to awaken. The novel idea that now crept into Freddy's mind was that the wind offered him a safe chance to see how the Grand Soarer would respond to the stresses of flight. He might also, in passing, pick up some hints on handling her. Was that sane or lunatic, he wondered? At that hour who could tell?

For weeks he had tried to imagine these things. He remembered how quickly the purling little stream by the Elysian Grove had become an unstoppable flood, how the inert-looking powder packed in the copper pipe had, in a fraction of a second, done the work of twenty horses, and how speedily the gentle flame kindled by Ug the Prehistoric Iron-smith had grown to a roaring wall of hell. These dabblings with the powers of water, earth, and fire had left him in no doubt of the challenge of this last, unconquered element. The paper darts he flew and watched, the gliding of doves and jackdaws, were like the purling streams of Elysium and the gentle flames of the forge when compared with the forces he must now master if he was to hold aloft one fifth of a *ton* of man and machine.

The wind that now howled through the hip of his bedroom roof was surely of that order? It occurred to him, in that mad hour when genius and delusion merge, that if he could somehow manoeuvre the Grand Soarer outside and tether her to weights upon the ground, he might be able to make her rise and soar up and down a yard or two, to the limit of those tethers; in that way he might acquire some experience in "flying." Certainly the only other way was to actually fly the thing. And what speeds would be needed to raise the machine and almost 150lb

48

of man into the air? Forty miles an hour? Sixty? Enough to kill, anyway; he felt sure of that. He tried to imagine his own death but found it impossible. Nevertheless, thrice bitten was quadruple shy. He rose and dressed.

It was one of those strange summery gales – a steady wind that filled a cloudless sky. The moon and stars shone with an almost painful brilliance through a solid belt of air that moved over the flat Midlands at the speed of an express train, without an eddy, with never a slack or a squall. If he closed his eyes, he could imagine he stood already at the prow of some giant aerial craft nosing its way through the air. Would men ever do such a thing? And would the Grand Soarer play any part in that progress? His hair stood on end at the thought.

The wind hurried him across Lovelace Common, by Halfmoon Coppice, to the great Blythe Hundredacre, where he reached the barn at last. The first problem was that the door was downwind. It would be madness to bring the Soarer out on that side and then try to manoeuvre her edgewise into the teeth of the gale. He went around to the windward side of the building. How the ancient structure groaned and rattled!

On the far side he saw, what he had forgotten, that the barn had another door, larger than the first. They had never used it because it was visible from the attics of Mortimer Hall; to have done so would have tempted fate. Would it even open? Well, it would simply have to. There was no other possible way to get the Soarer out.

Fortunately, opposite the door and thus directly upwind from the barn, about thirty paces away, stood a lone Scots pine. If he could just get a block and tackle about that ...

Block and tackle! Exactly what he had used for hoisting the Soarer before it had been joined to its carriage. It was still in the barn. He fetched it and tied it to the pine tree. Then he carried its hook back to the door they had never opened. The doorbolt would not slide so he hit it with the hook. The housing, eaten with rust, fell apart at the third blow. He slipped the hook over the bolt and took up the loose end of the rope.

At his very first pull the door toppled over and splintered to a thousand shards on the ground. The hinges, too, had rusted away. Only gravity, or a century of custom, had held it in place. Or, on this night, the wind.

Now the wind had a new playground, the interior of the barn; and a new plaything, too – the Grand Soarer. The ancient structure began to shake. The Soarer rocked and shivered on its unsprung carriage. Desperately Freddy seized up the hook and strained against the gearing of the tackle to carry it to the ring on the prow. It was like running through industrial soap. He trapped the loose end of the rope beneath one of his feet just as it was about to go snaking out of reach.

He also trapped himself. For here he was with the hook in his left hand, the ring just beyond his most heroic stretch, and the last inch of free rope beneath his foot. If he let go, he might lose it for good.

Could he drop everything and try instead to push the Soarer forward? The shattering groans from all the timbers around howled *no!* As his mind bounced back and forth between the one impossibility and the other he heard a cry of "Frederick!"

Ann!

"Here!" he called, unable to turn and therefore to see that she was already around his side of the barn and watching him in horror.

"Come away!" she cried. "It's not safe."

"You come here."

After several more vain entreaties she saw that nothing would move him. Fearfully she let the wind nudge her to his side – or, rather, to just behind him. "What are you doing? You're mad!"

"We've got to save her. Pick up …"

"It's only a load of old willow and bedsheets, Frederick."

"Hell, woman," he roared. "Will you just do as I ask!"

Angry, but also fearful for his life, she said, "All right. What must I do?"

"That's better. Pick up the rope I'm standing on and walk with it towards the tree. Don't for Christ's sake let go."

She obeyed.

"Quicker!" he shouted.

But however fast she went it would not be quick enough.

The barn was shrieking like the damned at crack of doom. The Soarer was shuddering up and down.

He stretched his free right hand forth to the limit of his reach. As soon as he could touch the ring on the Soarer's nose he grasped it firmly and shouted to her, "Come back now!"

"What?"

"Pull! Come toward me. Pull as you come."

She understood quickly and began the easier task of walking downwind to him – easier, that is, until the slack was taken up and all the strain came upon him. He stood like one of those ancient martyrs about to be torn apart by teams of horses. The invincible force of the tackle, with all of Ann's buxom weight magnified eightfold behind it, tugged at his left arm and shoulder. The immovable object of the Soarer shuddered and bounced at his right. Racked between them he thought the pain would surely kill him.

But it did not. He survived that first rending onslaught and then, miraculously, the Soarer began to move. And it kept on moving. The physical relief to his tortured muscles was huge but the mental relief – the knowledge that the immovable object was, after all, movable – was even greater.

The machine stopped. One of the wheels had lodged against a shard of the fallen door. This time he accepted the pain in the certainty of its worth. And again the Soarer moved. Thus they progressed, inch by tortured inch, until more than half the machine was out in the open. The leading set of wheels reached the heavier timber that had formed the midrail of the door. Looking at its thickness he knew his arms would be pulled out of their sockets before the Soarer would surmount that obstacle. "Stop!" he called.

"You needn't shout." Her heaving on the rope had brought her to his side, and there was a loose coil of slack at their feet. She saw the problem at once. "Hold this," she said and then, without waiting for him to obey, she bent and, lifting his foot like a blacksmith with a carthorse, thumped it down on the loose end of the rope. "I'll deal with it," she added.

She ran to the machine, ducked beneath the leading edge of the sail, and stooped to tug at the timber that was blocking the progress of the wheels. It would not budge.

"Try pushing it with your feet," he called to her. "Sit beyond it and push it toward me with your feet."

If she could wedge it behind the wheel, he could let go his hold and pay out the hook until it engaged with the ring.

She understood. She crawled into the shadow of the sail and sat with her knees half-raised and her heels against the wood. It shifted too easily now, hurling her flat on her back. The wind, howling off the vast Hundredacre, raced in beneath her skirts and threw them roughly up over her body and face. She shrieked and rolled away quickly, but not quickly enough to prevent Freddy from seeing she wore nothing beneath her petticoat – not even stockings.

He froze with the shock. He wanted time to stop, to go back, to undo that moment, to erase even the memory of it.

A dark shape blew past him toward the machine. In his surprise he took it for a sack, carried on the wind. Then a large black dog. Then, most improbable of all, an ape. The shape resolved itself.

"Clive!" he shouted in relief. "Thank God!"

Clive dragged the heavy timber from the Soarer's path. It broke in two. He worked the shorter length of it in behind the wheels, to provide at least a temporary stop. Freddy relaxed his arms a little.

Stooping low again Clive scuttled toward Ann, who had just succeeded in rolling herself around, head-to-the-wind, so that she could rise without risking a further exhibition. Gallantly he helped her to her feet and then cradled her across the wind, still ducking low beneath the sails. When they reached the very outward tip of it, where Freddy had left a nib of willow sticking out, like a bat's thumb, as a handling and towing point, he stopped. The gale tore his words away but it was obvious to Freddy that he was telling her to hold it there and push. Clive himself then ran swiftly to the other extremity, where he grasped a similar nib. They both took up the strain, heaving with every last ounce of their strength.

In no time the gap between the hook and the ring was closed. Freddy snapped them together and all-but collapsed with relief. Clive ran to him and grabbed the rope. "Stout fellow!" he called. "We're not out of danger yet, though."

Ann was there, too.

He watched them pulling in unison, like everyone's picture of mariners, while the balm of warm blood and relaxation surged through his shoulders. His fingers still seemed cemented together. One by one he peeled them apart and flexed them.

The image of Ann's nakedness recurred again and again in his mind. What made it so compulsive was not so much the fact that she had been reduced – simplified – to that one elemental glimpse, but that she had been moving, wriggling, writhing. His image of sacred nudity was not like that. The thought struck him then that Clive must have seen her, too. Memory and imagination mingled. Clive became the black dog, became the ape, became a ravening beast. Freddy was ashamed at the accusations his mind felt but could not frame.

At that moment the barn collapsed. With a last rising groan of its tortured wood and a roar of crumbling brick its centuries came down in rubble. A great cloud of dust, like a coven of pale, hastening ghosts, fell downwind. Clive danced for joy. "You saved her! You saved her!" He showered congratulations upon Freddy.

When he grew calmer he again took up the strain on the rope; but this time Freddy stopped him. "Something else I want to do," he shouted. "Tie her off at that."

He went to the heap of bricks and shattered timber, all that remained of the barn, and searched for the coils of rope that used to hang inside the door. He found them without much difficulty, and brought them back to the Soarer.

"What now?" Clive asked.

Talking was difficult. Freddy held up a finger, much as to say, "All will soon be clear."

On his second return from the rubble he dragged one of the ancient rafters, a rough-hewn treetrunk, felled perhaps before the Black Death had ravaged Europe. He dropped it beneath one of the sail tips, tying it to the nib with the rope he had brought earlier. He left about two yards slack. He took another heavy timber and tied the other tip in the same way.

Then he went to Clive, who once again had a protective arm around Ann's shoulder. "Want to get the feel of her," he shouted.

Clive let go of Ann with some haste. "Eh?"

"Give us a hand to get the feel of her."

"What?"

"I'll sit in the cradle. You move the tail. Up, down, side-to-side. I want to see ... feel ... the wind in her sails. See?"

Clive laughed uproariously. "You're a card all right!" He made for the tail but stopped. "No, look, I won't be able to see you."

He was right. The sail would be in the way. Freddy turned to Ann. "You stand here." He pointed to a spot directly in front of the machine. "Watch me and relay my signals."

They quickly agreed a set of signals and for the next ten minutes Freddy sat, or lay, at the helm while Clive raised, lowered, and swung the tail to his directions, as relayed by Ann. The storm, though past its peak, still had plenty of puff. At first he could find no combination of sail angle and rudder that would cause the Soarer to soar. Several times he came tantalizingly close as the willow spars creaked under the strain. Then quite suddenly she lifted several inches. In his excitement he jerked the rudder too violently and the lifting effect was lost.

But he soon achieved it again. And then again. And then he could achieve it at will. When the Soarer lifted a couple of feet he understood why it had been so difficult to get off the ground at all. Every time the prow rose Clive lifted the tail to keep the angle level. Inevitably he was a second or so late each time. But in those brief moments when the prow was up and the tail down Freddy felt a surge of lifting power that made his blood race. On the ground the sail was at such a shallow angle that it gave no lift; but in the air, where the tail could drop, the wind got under the sail like a giant's fist.

Now he was sure she would fly, and would need nothing like a sixty-mile-an-hour pull to get her going – if only he could lower the angle of the sail.

"Next time let the tail go," he shouted to Clive.

He had to say it several times before Clive believed he was serious, but when the tail was free, Freddy gave a great shout of joy as she whanged herself up to the full reach of her tethered wings and threatened to split the willow framework. He swung the rudder around until he found a point where the strain was eased and the stay ropes slackened. Then, by hunting up and down around that point, he was able to make the machine rise and fall at his command.

His laughter went up to heaven. Clive and Ann pranced around like leaping children; they caught hands and danced a wild, wind-pummelled ringaroses – all-fall-down and rolling in the grass in their excitement.

"Look!" Freddy shrieked.

He could steer it from side to side now, to the limit of its tether.

The revelling pair rose on hands and knees and crawled toward the craft, ducking under the great projecting sail.

"Stupendous!" Clive shouted.

"Stupendous," Ann mimicked.

How swiftly the control of the Soarer became almost second nature. He could lower her to an inch off the ground and then raise her, as slow or as fast as he wished, to the limit of her tether. So skilled did he become he could even make the tip of her prow, where the pulley hook went through the ring, define a perfect circle.

Ann was quick to make a game of it. She would put her hand somewhere within reach and Freddy had to steer the point of the prow to try and touch her open palm. Her mouth was open in a smile; her tongue lay invitingly on her lip. The game became a ritual of their courtship, for every time he reached her open palm she would dart it to some other place and he would have to follow. She never let him catch her. They both laughed, he at his skill, she at hers.

And out of Freddy's sight Clive lay at ease in the wind-swept grass, almost at Ann's feet. He was trying not to be jealous of Freddy. Above him, inches away, the gale still played the wanton with Ann's skirts, often lifting them above her knees. That first time she had split the skies with her shriek, but now, though she knew he was there, she seemed not to mind at all.

CHAPTER SEVEN

CLIVE FELT AWFUL – also stupendous.

He lay in the grass, with the frills of Miss Howard's petticoats flapping around his face, with flashes of Miss Howard's ankles and calves before his eyes, and he could not think of her as someone's sister. He remembered her shriek when the wind had thrown up her skirts ... her pale, generous, moonlit thighs ... the dark delta of her hair ... the hot-cross-bun of her ample derrière as she rolled into the come-hither dark. The memories besieged his mind's eye, shutting out all warnings. There were other thoughts, too – satanic whispers about her vulnerability.

Until now he had unthinkingly expected that the parts of a woman beneath her clothing would be like the drawings in those magazines from Paris – you'd see the shading, the crayon outlines, the marks of the water-colour brush. The utter reality of it had shocked him, the natural colour, the full, everyday solidity.

He shook his head violently as if that might dislodge something inside and so block this flow of disloyal, shocking, unstoppable images.

At last Freddy was confident he could steer the machine. The wind had dropped further, making the degree of lift less reliable. He lowered her to the ground and climbed stiffly out. "Oh, my muscles will take a year to recover," he complained happily. Then, in a more businesslike tone, "We'd better tie her down securely. This gale could just as easily get up again."

Clive crawled to one tip and tightened up the slack; Ann managed the other. Freddy, for good measure, piled several rafters beneath the tail, raising it until the main part of the sail was horizontal. "Let's get out of this wretched wind," he said.

Ann skipped between them, linked arms with both, and urged them toward the derelict cottage, which still stood unharmed, four-square to the elements. "Can we break in there?" she suggested. "Will the owners mind?" She giggled and secretly tickled the inside of Clive's arm.

He broke from her guiltily, looking for an escape. But his cunning body was already stooping among the rubble, selecting a good soft bale of hay. It chuckled and said, "We'll bring our armchairs with us."

He took two bales. Ann picked up one. Freddy took two. They broke in via a kitchen window. But they discovered that the flagstones had been salvaged and the earth floor was too uneven for comfort. "Upstairs," Freddy suggested. "The floors are wooden there. Leave your bale, Ann. I'll come back for it."

He led, Ann followed, Clive brought up the rear. Miss Howard smelled of sweet musk. The rustle of her clothing was silken to his ears. She was well aware of his eyes upon her; he could tell, just from the sway of her hips, careful inches from his eyes.

"We can do it! We can fly!" Freddy cried out suddenly, as if he had only just realized it was now quiet enough for conversation.

"You can, old boy," Clive told him. "Yours shall be the glory."

"Rats!" Freddy said.

"Where?" Ann asked nervously.

"No, I mean nonsense. We all share the glory. Share everything."

He left them alone while he returned briefly below for her haybale.

Clive, nervous at being near her, went over to the window. With his sleeve he wiped away the dust and cobwebs. He was as careless with his clothes as young Billy Wilde, she thought – Mr. Wilde's son. But why should they bother? Hadn't they an army of servants to follow behind them? Oh if she had servants, she'd never stoop to pick up a stitch!

Clive could see the Grand Soarer, safely tethered in the wind at the edge of the big, open field. The moon, now descending in the sky, gleamed on its oilcloth sail. Everything was black and silver.

"I'm Ann Howard, by the way," she said.

"Forgive me. How rude of me. Freddy told me how beautiful you are so naturally I didn't imagine you could be anyone else. I'm Clive Mortimer."

She was so thrilled that she laughed. She had a lovely laugh, rich and musical. "No need to tell me that, sir. When Frederick first ..."

"Look here. I say, you can't go calling me sir. At least, not when we're on Grand Soarer business."

"Oh?" She waited.

"Yes. At least call me Mr. Mortimer, Miss Howard."

She smiled archly. "If you say so, Mr. Mortimer."

"I do."

"Oh good," Freddy said from the doorway. "I forgot you hadn't formally met. Sorry."

They spread the hay from two bales on the floor and arranged the other three in an oblique horseshoe, so that they could lounge, feet to the middle. We're like the spokes of a wheel, Freddy thought. Ann thought: I'm like a flower between two green leaves.

Clive, trying to avoid his thoughts, said, "The same guardian angel must have awakened all three of us."

"I don't think I truly got off to sleep." Freddy turned to Ann. "What brought you, dearest?"

"I just woke up with a feeling of danger."

"Did you climb out?"

"No. Sal let me out. We crept down and she locked the door again after me. We had an argument about whether I should come at all."

"How will you get back in?"

"Bessie gets up at half five to do the boiler and the grates. She'll let me in. I'll slip her a penny and she'll hold her tongue." Then, realizing it was beginning to sound as if she often spent the night out, she added, "I hope."

"You're at Mr. Wilde's I understand," Clive said.

"Yes."

"Well, you know he's our general manager. Why don't I just have a word in his ear?"

The other two laughed. Clive felt isolated.

"We've got to find some way to get her tail a bit lower,"

Freddy said. And for the next ten minutes he tried to convey to them the sensation of flying, but the excitement dwindled away into a catalogue of improvements he thought the craft might need. As with a lot of technical people, his enthusiasms could vanish in a thicket of joyful jargon without his even realizing it.

The other two listened for the most part in admiring silence. Every now and then Clive stole a glance at Miss Howard, who seemed more lovely than ever as the moonlight strengthened. He understood how Freddy had fallen under her spell.

Ann, who felt the heat of his admiration like a brazier at her side, was cast into confusion, though she had a young woman's instinctive knack of hiding it behind a calm face and a still body. She loved Freddy. She thought he was the cleverest and decentest young man she'd ever met. She knew he was going to do something extraordinary with his life; even Mr. Wilde had said as much once at the luncheon table when she had been serving. Of course he knew nothing about her and Freddy.

But oh, if only he wasn't still so young! It was going to take him years, starting as he did from nothing. And years were what she had not got, or so she felt. At the end of every day, after she had raked out the fires and carried the coals and dusted the rooms and fetched hot water and toiled through all the other tasks of an upstairs maid, she would ease her aching body and look at her work-grimed hands, and she'd feel time racing by and all the precious energy of youth vanishing down the cracks of drudgery. She didn't want to be old and careworn by the time life started doling out the rewards.

Once, when young Billy Wilde had trapped her on the upstairs landing and kissed her without any warning, she'd been so flattered it cost all her strength to say no to the other things he'd suggested. And his admiration had made her so happy all day, and all that week; if he'd asked her again at the end of it, she might have agreed. Admiration was like a change of blood to her, taking away the coarse, tired, everyday stuff and replacing it with something hotter, finer, and more lively.

So she sat there, loving Freddy, and already feeling sorry for a betrayal that had not yet happened.

When Freddy had run out of improvements he reached forward and tapped one of the moonshadows with a slow forefinger. "They're racing," he said. "If I'm to be fit to guide that thing tomorrow – or later today – I'd better get some sleep."

Clive moved his feet, creating space.

"No," Freddy responded. "I meant at home. I couldn't possibly sleep here. My muscles are …"

"Well I can't go back to the Crescent for hours yet," Ann objected.

"Oh. Of course." Freddy fell silent.

That silence, to him, became pregnant with unspoken reproaches. To remain in the cottage now, to settle to a sleep he had already declared impossible, would be like saying to Clive, "I don't trust you." Yet he did trust him. With his life. He'd certainly trust him with Ann's honour.

"You'll be warm and dry here," he told her.

She stared at him, open-mouthed. Couldn't he see the risk?

"I say," Clive cried. "You can't expose Miss Howard's reputation to …" An awkward grunt supplied the missing sentiments.

"Expose it?" Freddy asked. "Who to? Would you go cantering on about it?"

Clive gulped. Ann said, "But Frederick …" and subsided. They glanced at each other and hastily averted their eyes.

"Mr. Mortimer is a gentleman," Freddy pointed out to her. "Nowhere in the world is a woman's reputation and honour safer than in the trust of an English gentleman." He smiled and his tone changed. "Besides, he's my friend. I want you two to get to know each other. And" – his tone became pleading now – "I must get some sleep or I may make a mistake tomorrow and, well, get hurt."

He rose stiffly and went out to the stairhead. Clive followed him. "Look, young'un," he said, "it's all very well but I really had better leave, too."

"I'd rather you stayed," Freddy assured him. "That broken window's an invitation to any passing tramp or blackguard. She doesn't bite, you know."

Clive sighed; then he raised his voice and asked, "What does Miss Howard herself say? I'll be ruled by her."

Ann, still seated among the hay, cleared her throat and said carefully, "If Frederick says it's all right, then I'm sure it is."

Freddy felt marvellous as he skipped away downwind on his homeward run. Could there be any stronger token of friendship than what had just passed between himself and Clive!

The lane was called the Old Way, though where it was the old way from, or to, no one could now say. Probably from some long-dissolved monastery to some equally forgotten convent. A very old way indeed.

Clive picked up one of the unbroken bales and said to Ann, "I'll sleep in the front room." But he lingered in lifting it.

"You don't trust honour and friendship all that much then?" Ann teased. They both heard the brittle edge to her voice.

"I was thinking of you, actually." He took strength from her nervousness.

"I don't feel in the least bit tired." As he grew in confidence, she became calmer, too.

"Nor me." He sat contentedly on the bale.

"Let's talk a bit," she suggested, managing to imply that talk, at least, would create no obligations between them.

"What about?"

"Anything you like. Tell me about your friends from school, these fellows who are going to help Frederick and you fly the Grand Soarer tomorrow."

"You must be very proud of Freddy," Clive said. There was no hint of Judas in his tone.

"Why?" She seemed genuinely surprised.

"Well" – he gave an awkward laugh – "aren't you and he, you know ..?"

She stretched her left hand into the moonlight, showing off no ring.

"Isn't he your young man?" Clive persisted.

"One of them," she conceded. Everything was temporary, she assured herself – even, at times like this, the truth.

"He's an amazing young fellow, you know. We've been friends since we were very young."

"He told me." She smiled at him and nodded. "He told me everything." She wanted him to know he could decently drop the subject.

"He really is remarkable, too."

"Mmmm." She gazed across at the descending moon as an actress to her key light.

"Of course, he's lucky to have found you," Clive added gallantly. From the shadows where he sat he watched her intently. He no longer thought about what he was doing, or why. Thoughts get in the way.

"I wish I could see your face," she told him.

"Do you?"

"I think you're poking fun at me."

"Oh I assure you, Miss Howard, I most certainly am not."

She peered toward him, miming annoyance at his concealment.

Awkwardly then, walking on his kneecaps, he came into the spill of the moonlight. "Better?" He wished he could have moved more elegantly but to have stood and then walked a mere two paces would have given the action a deliberateness – a menace even – that he wanted to avoid. And then to have fallen to his knees at her side would have seemed far too explicit.

"You don't look very comfortable," she told him.

He stretched himself out, half lying in the hay, keeping his body raised on one elbow.

"That's better," she told him. "Now why d'you say Frederick's so lucky?"

From her earlier response he was surprised she now chose to mention Freddy at all. But then he saw her purpose and grinned. "Anyone would be lucky to make a friend who is so charming." Suddenly he remembered how slender was their acquaintance. He flinched from her eyes, which seemed to gaze directly into the murk of his soul. "And so beautiful," he added, to fill the silence.

She smiled happily. She had never imagined that a young man with so soft a voice and so perfect an accent would tell her these things. She lay back against the haybale. The movement had the effect of thrusting out her ample bosoms. He remembered the milkwhite thighs, the neat delta of hair ... the vulnerability.

"Yes," he sighed. "Very lucky indeed."

Until now, thighs like that had been mere tokens of the imagination, drawings or photographs, studio products pasted to a slip of board and passed with a snigger and a leer in dorm or chapel ...

His disloyalty suddenly shamed him. He cleared his throat and said in an altogether stiffer tone, "Good old Fredders will do something remarkable in life, I'm sure."

She seemed so unaware of him that he wondered if he had even spoken aloud.

His thoughts ran unchecked in their riot: These thighs were *here*, in this very room, only inches away from him, nestling warmly under a few thin layers of skirt ...

"Yes – remarkable." He definitely said that aloud.

... skirts that could so easily ...

"It's all a matter of time, isn't it, though," she said suddenly.

"What is?"

"Frederick making something of himself. He starts with less than nothing. It'll take years and years and years."

Clive took his mental hands off her skirts. "You can't be sure of that," he said encouragingly.

"I know it for a fact."

He thought of one poor fellow, Robinson, who'd been withdrawn from school because his father, once a prosperous City merchant, had failed. There had been others, too, less spectacular. He tried to think of ways to tell her that right across the spectrum of human enterprise there were new lights kindling and old ones dowsing, all the time.

"Impatience!" he chided. "Things seem so permanent, I know. Yet you need look no further than my own family. My great-grandfather was only a small farmer, you know. You'd be amazed at ..."

"What would you have told your great-granma, then?" Ann asked.

"In what way?"

"Would you have talked to her about impatience? You

paid me a nice compliment just now, and don't think I'm not grateful. But every evening, pretty near every evening, I look at my face as I wash out the day's grime and I see there's another little wrinkle growing, or a new blotch, or, I don't know, a sort of *greyness* you can't never wash out. And I could tell you a thing or two about impatience." She slumped, deliberately causing her bosoms to vanish into the general softness of her. She wanted him to see how swiftly charms could disappear. She wanted him to understand the mild but endless panic that was consuming her life away.

He was still young enough to feel immortal – with all the callow powers of observation that entails. Yet her words and her gesture somehow penetrated the protective delusion and he saw, with a clarity that seared him, an intimation of the woman toward whom she was growing: A grey servant, not yet thirty, but with her skin already foxed by the grime of a thousand coal scuttles and ten thousand slop pails. There were half a dozen such young-old maids in every house he knew.

By her action she had transformed the atmosphere between them. The tension vanished, even his lust was muted. He wanted to help, and the urge was altruistic.

"My mum," Ann was saying, "I mean she's seen it all before. She always says to me she says, 'If you see a bit of open country, my gel, you go! Don't you wait for all the howsomevers and on-the-other-hands. Fortune's got no double knock.'"

"Oh Miss Howard," he sighed. "I do so wish life could be different for you."

"All of us you mean? All the servants?"

"No – you. Just you." This brusque reminder of her status startled him. For a moment he did not know what else to add. "Good Lord," he said awkwardly, to mask the deficiency, "I've never talked to anyone like this before!"

"You mean to a servant girl. I don't suppose you think we don't have ..."

"No I mean to anyone." The profound truth of his own words seized him. He saw it as a means to regain that intimacy of their minds whose loss he now felt keenly. "I've never talked like this to any other young woman. I have no sisters, as I suppose you know. Nor brothers either. I may as well tell you,

I feel very uncomfortable, talking with you here like this. And I suppose you must think me a perfect fool." He stopped himself at that point and sat in dumb misery. The words had just gushed out of him; he hadn't intended saying anything like that. The verbal pathway vanished in a disorderly undergrowth of immature feelings and shrivelled lust.

She gasped. "But of course I don't! My – the very idea! I should just think you're the very opposite of a fool, Mr. Mortimer."

"Oh for God's sake call me Clive. Please? When we're alone."

"Only if you'll call me Ann."

He sat up, cheerful again, and faced her. "Ann!" It was as easy as that! He grinned and held out a hand, formally.

She took it. "Clive!" Their clasp lingered, pleasing to both of them. "Do I really make you feel uncomfortable?" she asked.

"Not you, but our situation. We get no practice at it, do we? We're so hedged around with ..."

"There's no need, you know."

"It's easy to say." After a pause he added, "Aren't you uncomfortable?"

"Not any more." She smiled and let go his hand at last. "You're easy to talk to, really. I could stay here and talk and talk and talk."

He laughed. "That's true. You're quite right." He relaxed still further. "What shall we talk about?"

"Anything. Let's make a rule: We can talk about anything."

"Fine. I was going to say about rules ..."

"Oh why do we have rules anyway?" she broke in. "Strikes me it's a disease with some people."

"Like who?"

"Like Mrs. Holroyd for one. You know – the Wildes' housekeeper. She's got rules for every minute of the day."

"For the household? It must make for smooth ..."

"Yes but listen! Don't twice-cross your apron strings or it means you'll have two men falling out over you. Don't ladder-lace your boots or it's a signal to the men – ladders, you see? Girls should only lace them criss-cross. And don't eat sweetmeats without plain brown bread or biscuits – bad thoughts feed on sugar in the blood. Don't warm both feet at the fire at the same time – blood from the feet goes straight to the head and hot blood can turn your brain."

"Are you sure she's not pulling your leg? She must have her tongue in ..."

"No! Not her – it's a disease like I said. All her pleasure comes from *not* doing things. I don't mean doing nothing. She's never idle, not Mrs. Holroyd. But from deliberately not doing this, deliberately not doing that. If ... if ..." She caught her breath several times, trying to find some way of making it compellingly obvious to him. At last she said, "If all of life was like one big garden, like your garden over at Mortimer Hall, she'd be saying, 'I'm not going down there. And I'm not going down there. And I'm not going down there. I'm going to spend my days walking round and round this one fountain – 'cos it's safe!' I mean she looks straightaway for things not to do. There!"

"But you! You want to see all the garden. Is that it, Ann?"

"I think it's silly putting up trespass notices all over the place before you've even been down half the paths. I mean if you wander off down one of them and you find a quicksand at the end of it or a mad bull or something, well and good. That's when to put up the signs."

"Good Lord, Ann, you're absolutely right. I've never thought of it like that but you're ..."

"It's the same all over. You've got to know, haven't you? I have, anyway. Never mind your Doubting Thomas. It's no good telling me this is wrong, that's right, don't do this, do that. I mean I've got to *know*."

He laughed uncomfortably. "Here am I, Ann, about to go to Oxford, and here's you, what, left school at twelve? And I suppose there's more wisdom in your little toe than in the whole of me."

The compliment pleased her. "It's my mum, really. She always tells me, 'Keep your fancy free, gel,' she says. 'Don't let the first likely lad turn your head. See what's in the market. Make sure.'"

There was a Latin name for her philosophy. Not stoicism. Epicureanism? Oh, it was on the tip of his tongue.

"Like, I love Frederick, all right? So suppose I say I'm never going to kiss and cuddle with any other fellow? Isn't that as good as saying my love or whatever it is is too feeble to stand it?"

"Yes but there's also the matter of ..."

"But suppose I did kiss and cuddle with another fellow, and then I still said I love Frederick, well now – isn't that like saying it's strong!"

"But what if you couldn't say it?"

She appeared nonplussed for the moment but then she brightened. "Well, better to find out sooner rather than later."

"And is Freddy to be allowed this same latitude? To sample the entire ..."

"I thought you said you knew him."

"I do."

"Well, he never would, would he! Not 'Good old Fredders!' " She giggled to soften her cheek at daring to mimic him. "I mean he'll fiddle around till the cows come home with *things*, like that machine out there, trying to get it right. But not people. Not with people."

Cynicism? Or was that in Ancient Rome? Pragmatism? No, that didn't sound very classical.

He suddenly realized that her silence was thrusting some initiative upon him.

"D'you really think I'm beautiful?" she asked.

"You're so beautiful, Ann, it makes me ache inside."

"Ache?"

"With longing, I mean."

"Oh?"

"It makes me long to kiss you." He could say it now because she had made it sound like some novel and powerful way of strengthening her love for Freddy.

She lay back upon the straw and reached forth one arm to him. He slithered and wriggled across to her, stretched himself full length at her side, and lowered his lips to hers. She was soft and sweet and yielding. Her mouth was a marshmallow cauldron of strange elixirs that fired him and stupefied him and drained his will. She murmured approvingly and moved her head this way and that, perpetually renewing the contact of their lips from every angle.

"Oh Ann!" he gasped as they broke.

"Oh Clive!" She gripped his hair with tender firmness and pulled his lips back on hers.

Long minutes they kissed, and long minutes more. They changed positions, restlessly. They crushed their lips together. They lay inches apart and brushed them light as down. She leaned over him and pecked him like a bird. Her tongue rasped the unshaven stubble at the corner of his mouth. She had always thought a gentleman's skin would be especially smooth, so now she felt as if she had caught Clive out, discovered one of his most intimate secrets. She giggled again. They laughed. They whispered each other's names like open-sesames on caverns of vast wealth. They lay still, shivering at the mere pleasure of feeling the other's breath on skin, in ear, in hair, down neck. They murmured *mmmm?* and answered *mmmm!*

His fingers played with the easy buttons of her blouse; easily they popped into freedom; easily his fingertips roved, this way and that, over all her young and soft, young and easy flesh. But as they grew more bold and began to sweep down, she became tense again. And when they closed over one ample melon of a breast she moaned, "No!" and shrank herself away, leaving his hand poised above him, printed on the early morning sky.

"Oh," she cried as though she feared the move might have wounded him. And she fell upon him and kissed him a score of times, as if each kiss were a nursing touch, ice bags to a fever, balm to an ache.

"No?" he asked. "A quicksand? A mad bull? You're fast enough with the no-trespassing sign. Where's your philosophy now?"

She made one grim chuckle. "It was easy enough to talk about it."

"It still is. Are you afraid?"

"Of what?"

"That I won't behave ... like a gentleman."

"Oh no!" She kissed him again, fervently. "I'll never be afraid of you in that way, Clive darling. You'd never think of me as some servant girl you've surprised on an upstairs landing and pushed into some dark corner."

"Well of course not. How could you ..."

"I mean we've met *socially*, haven't we."

"It's deeper than that, I'm afraid." He sighed. "What a web!"

"But just give me a day or two," she begged.

"Oh what a tangled web!"

CHAPTER EIGHT

FOR THE SECOND TIME in twenty-four hours Freddy thought the pain in his arms would kill him. It was two in the afternoon. He and another apprentice were passing a large zinc sheet back and forth between a set of giant nip rollers to impart to it a double curve, like a dished mudguard or a banana skin halved along its length. Backed with oak, these curved sheets would form the striker surfaces of a vast impulse turbine intended for a sawmill in Canada.

The work entailed holding the sheet above their heads, one at each end, the nip roller in between, and walking back and forth while the rollers imparted the double curves, never letting it sag too much, nor lifting it with too much force. At the end of each back-and-forth walk Freddy had to reach out one hand (still supporting the sheet with the other) and deftly give the screw of the anvil roller one measured twist, to increase the curvature another fraction. And every so often they had to pass the sheet out of the rollers altogether and check both curvatures against a template.

When he had first seen it done, Freddy thought it must surely be the most skilled work on earth; and it had, indeed, taken him ages to master. But now that it posed no further challenge he thought it the hardest, most odious work in the whole shop. They had made only four since dinner. There were twelve more to go. It would take all afternoon and it was going to kill him.

So any apprehension he might have felt at the sight of Mr. Wilde hastening into the workshop and talking earnestly with the foreman, Mr. Brewster, was overwhelmed by the relief of his tortured muscles when Brewster shouted "Oxley!" and beckoned him over.

"Nothing amiss, I hope, sir," he said ritually as he approached.

"You're to go home and get changed and wait," Brewster said.

"Wait for what, sir?" He was more worried now.

"For me to collect you," Mr. Wilde said. "Half an hour?"

"Yessir."

Mr. Wilde consulted his watch. "Quarter to three, we'll say."

At twenty minutes short of the hour Freddy was in his Sunday – indeed his only – best, hopping up and down in Copt Lane, wondering what it all might mean. He was not one to go inventing dramas. Nor did he live in that haphazard Old Testament landscape where a capricious Jehovah might at any moment heap him with boils, pestilence, or demands for supreme sacrifice. In any case, what was the very worst that might have happened? Ann's nocturnal absence had been noted perhaps. And the sequel? Not his dismissal, or that would have taken place back at the workshop. An instant visit to the vicar? Put up the banns at once? He almost wished it true.

When he saw Mr. Wilde's open landau he almost *believed* it true. For there beside him, one each side, sat Ann and Sally, also in their summer finery. They were laughing. But why had they come the long way round? He had expected to see them coming down Copt Lane, not up it.

"Jump up, young man!" Mr. Wilde called out. "We've tormented you long enough."

Freddy was to sit in solitary state, it seemed, in the body of the carriage. As he obeyed he questioned Ann with his eyebrows. She grimaced and shrugged, as much in the dark as him. Her manner was nervy, on edge.

"And how is our young Icarus?" Mr. Wilde asked jovially.

Freddy knew the name. Sir George Cayley had referred to

it – some Ancient Greek who had tried to fly. "May I ask who told you, sir?" he answered.

"I could say 'a little bird'." Mr. Wilde laughed. Ann looked at him again, and again an exchange of gestures told him it was not her. "In fact, it was Daedalus himself – Icare! clamabat. Icare! Quove sub axe volas? Let's hope you do better, young fellow."

It was all beyond Freddy.

"You may wonder why we are proceeding so slowly," Mr. Wilde continued. "I'm saving these fine, mettlesome bays, you see. D'you think they'll bear you up into the empyrean, eh? Pegasus One and Pegasus Two, what!"

"You mean you don't mind, sir?" Freddy asked, incredulous.

"I'll be in a better position to answer that this evening."

Freddy gave up. He was sure that, whatever the secret, Ann was in on it – despite her gestured denials. Then, as they approached the Blythe Hundredacre, he understood why they had come this way. His heart almost stopped. There was the wreckage of the derelict barn ... there was the machine, sparkling in the afternoon sun ... there were Clive and Knox-Riddell and Gray – all these were expected. He gave them no more than a glance because there, too, in a canvas-covered stand that had seen service at many a local pageant and cricket match, were Sir Toby Mortimer and his lady and a dozen or more of their friends. A great cheer went up as they saw the landau approaching.

Freddy's stomach caved in. His heart began to race. His throat went dry. "But it may not work," he croaked.

"You'll be a laughing stock if it doesn't," Mr. Wilde warned – naught to Freddy's comfort.

Yet this dour comment had the right effect. Freddy, with his back to the wall, and the last ditch beyond it, decided he might as well put a brave face on the business. As the landau drew near the Grand Soarer he leaped over the door and landed springily on the turf. The other three lads ran laughing up to him, asking if he'd made his will – said his prayers – eaten a hearty breakfast ... and so on.

He took it all in good part while he gave the machine a quick but careful scrutiny. Sir Toby came over and said, awkwardly, "Well young Oxley, I know we haven't often seen eye to eye but I wish you luck all the same. Don't know what the four of you are trying to prove but I wish you well of it."

Freddy thanked him. Sir Toby turned to the landau. "Are those the two, Wilde?" he asked.

"The very two, Sir Toby."

"Well, young ladies, if these sails split asunder today, we'll know who to blame, eh?"

Sally laughed nervously. Ann assured him they wouldn't break.

"Well, anyway," he said, "you made a splendid job of it. Come in out of this dreadful sun. It'll give you freckles." He wafted the landau over to the stand. Knox-Riddell and Clive ran beside it, returning with the horses, which they unhitched like a pair of professionals. For the first time Freddy noticed that haymakers had been busy here since last night, cutting a broad fairway, north to south, through the grass.

"How are the old arms?" Clive asked solicitously.

"I'll live!" Freddy laughed. "Thank you for looking after Ann last night."

Clive smiled wanly. "You're a lucky man."

"Did she ... er ... did you and she ..."

"What?" Clive gulped.

"... talk about me at all?"

Clive laughed most heartily. "Did we! I may tell you I nearly died of boredom."

They arranged matters so that the towline was held by a simple round turn through the ring on the prow of the helmsman's cradle. Freddy, holding the loose end, could let it go whenever he chose and so assume total control of the craft. The shafts of the landau had been replaced by a single pole of larch slung between the horses; the landward end of the towline was secured to an iron ring at its end. All this Freddy had prepared weeks ago. Clive, sitting astride one of the horses, would be their driver. Gray and Knox-Riddell were to hold a sail-tip each so as to align the machine properly, for her wheels were not steerable; they would also steady her against any sudden squall.

The gale had blown out but the wind was still brisk. It had veered northwesterly, too, and now blew diagonally across the fairway. Freddy wondered if it would make any difference. He had long planned to launch directly into the wind, the way birds do; but now he felt that the horses would get up more speed on the stubble. He'd have to see. He wished these first attempts at launching could have been made without an audience.

He climbed into the cradle. A great cheer went up, but it dissolved into laughter. He realized they were all preparing to take this event either way – as the act of a hero or the folly of a clown. The structure crackled alarmingly under his weight. He gave each strut an experimental shake, producing yet more crackles. Clive passed the end of the towline through the ring, round to the left, through the ring again, round to the right, and handed Freddy the loose end. Freddy turned it twice around his left hand. With his right he grasped the rudder, levering its business end clear of the ground. The air and light around him seemed suddenly unreal; he became a spectator of himself; all his movements turned into alien rituals.

"Ready?" Clive asked.

"I suppose I must be. I can't think of anything we forgot."

Clive clasped his shoulder. "Happy landfall – as we bird-men say!"

Freddy watched him walking away across the stubble; what a good man Clive was! At that moment their friendship was even stronger than his love for Ann. *This might be the last minute of my life,* he thought. He glanced across at the spectators, seeking Ann. The two servant girls had been placed a little apart from the others, not quite in and not quite out of the party. Perhaps the danger of it all had just occurred to Ann, too, for she was standing rigid, with both gloved hands up to her mouth. He let go the rudder and gave her an encouraging wave.

She appeared not to see him. He waved again. Now she waved back.

So did Sir Toby. Clive, mounted by now and taking it for a signal, lashed the horses to a sudden frenzy. The towline grew taut at once and jerked the machine out of the grasp of Gray and Knox-Riddell. Freddy, squatting in the cradle, was bowled over backwards. He fought a hopeless battle to regain his grasp of the rudder and he almost let go of the towline.

"Stop!" he called, several times, but Clive could not hear him above the thunder of the hooves.

At last Freddy had no choice but to let go of the rope.

From the spectators' point of view that first run was an anticlimax. Freddy did not hear their cries of "oh!" and "is that to be all?" but even at this distance he could sense their impatience. Nevertheless, from his point of view the run had unlocked one of the secrets of launching into flight. The moment he had let go of the towline the craft had briefly raised itself into the air. The maiden flight of the Grand Soarer had been six-foot long and had reached all of three inches in altitude! To the onlookers it must have seemed like one more unevenness in the ground, but to the helmsman it had been true flight. What it meant, as Freddy was quick to see, was that the rope was hitched too high; the towing ring should have been lower. In its present position the towing force was acting to keep the craft pressed to the ground. Also, having his weight nearer the back must have helped.

"Sorry!" Clive shouted breathlessly as he rehitched the team for a more leisurely return to the starting line.

"Don't be," Freddy answered happily. "I just discovered something vital. I could skin myself for not having thought of it before."

Derisory but still good-natured cheers greeted their return; they modulated into surprise when Freddy leaped out and stood in front of the machine, where he proceeded to kick a hole in the prow of the cradle, about a foot below the towing ring. Then, with the buzz of excited voices in his ears, he ran over to the wreckage of the barn and poked around until he found what he was looking for – a short, smooth stub of wood (it was actually the handle of an old hammer), which he brought back to the Grand Soarer. He placed it inside the cradle, spanning the hole he had kicked in the prow. "Now, pass the towline through the hole and round that," he told Clive.

"Why all this?" Gray asked.

Freddy tapped the original towing ring. "That's too high. The tow is pulling her down, not up. She'll launch easily now, you'll see."

This time he tied only half the round turn, for fear that the ragged edges of the hole might trap the line, even after he let it go. "*I'll* give the start signal this time," he warned. "Keep your eyes on me."

"Yes milord!" Clive laughed.

They all took up their positions again. This time there was no waving to the gallery.

"Go!" Freddy yelled.

The sudden strain twisted the hammer handle in its make-shift housing, nearly wrenching Freddy's hand off at the wrist. Gristle groaned, tendons creaked, but excitement masked all pain.

In ten paces the horses were at a gallop. Before they had covered twenty the Grand Soarer was living up to its name.

It almost didn't, though. Freddy had forgotten that cross-wind. A fraction of a second after the wheels ceased their soft thunder on the grass he remembered it – just in time. The wind was from a quarter-left. The right sail dipped. His helmsman's instinct, though not yet a full day old, made him swing the rudder and shift his weight in the cradle to steady her. He kept a hold of the towline still.

The sails shivered. The spars creaked. And a fifth of a ton of dead weight came surging alive to rise with ponderous grace upon nothing but air.

Immediately, of course, it swung away downwind, pulling diagonally at the horses and slewing them around. They stopped.

"Go on! Go on!" Freddy yelled. He still held the towline, though it was now quite slack.

But it was too late. The craft, barely six feet off the ground, was losing way. He shifted his weight to put down the nose, fighting the wind along his brief glideway to the ground. He reached it with so little momentum that she stopped almost at once. Still clutching the rope he leaped out and turned her back to face the start line.

Gray and Knox-Riddell came running up to assist. "You did it! You did it!" they cried excitedly.

"We all did it," Freddy said.

"Everyone's gone mad. Didn't you hear the shouting?"

"Not a thing."

"The women were screaming."

The spectators had left the stand and were crowding around the start line. They had all touched the machine before, when they had first arrived; but now it was as if that brief moment of flight had transformed it and imbued it with some potent magic. They all touched it again and ran their elegantly gloved hands over the oilcloth and frame, still unable to *quite* believe what their eyes had just seen.

"You're not going again?" Ann asked.

"Oh yes. That didn't count. I didn't even let go of the towline. That was just a bit of kite flying."

"Why didn't you let go?" Sir Toby asked.

"Because I didn't get enough height, sir. Nor enough speed."

"I think we should leave well alone," Sir Toby said. "You've proved your point. Why take more risks?"

"Toby my dear," Lady Mortimer interjected. "If this young man wishes to endeavour to the limit, we ought not to stand in his way."

She had not consciously set eyes on Freddy since the sal-volatile days of his early teens; she hardly recognised the dashing young man who had commandeered her afternoon. When she saw him at the helm of this remarkable machine ... saw him lift it like magic into the empty air ... his daring had stirred her. She did not want these faint hearts to rob her of her second vicarious flight.

Looking at her eyes, Freddy saw only what he expected to see: a steely hardness that was quite lacking in either of her menfolk. *She wouldn't much mourn my death*, he thought.

He accepted her support with a grateful smile. "Please don't worry," he announced generally. "She does steer properly. She responds very well. There'll be no danger."

This time he arranged with Clive that the team would gallop up the eastern edge, the downwind edge, of the launching fairway; but as soon as she soared up and the wind carried her off at a diagonal, Clive would turn the team and drive them directly upwind as fast as they'd go. Freddy would let go the rope when they reached the long grass on the opposite edge of the fairway.

This new arrangement worked perfectly. By the time he let go of the line he was more than twenty feet off the ground.

By now his steersmanship was almost automatic, though he still had to concentrate.

But that very act of concentration, by some strange paradox of the mind, had the effect of liberating him, the real Freddy, and placing him in some godlike seat, remote from humankind.

Looking down at the broad, sunlit Hundredacre, the meandering Blythe, the Warwick road, the Old Way, as they twisted below him, then at the polkadot faces and the exclamation marks of sober male dress, he recaptured that feeling he first experienced on the day of the Great Explosion. He had never quite forgotten it though its precise quality had since eluded him. Now he felt it again in all its primitive force. The world was a sham. Its façade was about to be torn apart to reveal a more real world that had always lurked behind it. And he, forewarned by this strange premonition of collapse, would be able to leap nimbly from the one to the other, and leave behind all the constraints of his present existence.

Curiously, on both occasions he had been close to death. Deliberately close – almost flirting with it, like a child saying, "Can't catch me!" Was this the intimation of an afterlife – or just a dangerous delusion?

He circled the launching ground. It occurred to him that he was now steering her more by shifting his weight than by moving the paddle of the rudder. The wind soughed through the spars. This time he heard the cries of wonder and acclaim.

He made one mistake: He left too little height to level off and face into the wind for his landfall. In fact, he was still on that curve, and still tilted over, when the lower pair of wheels touched the grass. Their sudden deceleration caused the sail to dip even more. The nib of willow at its tip, the "bat's thumb," dug into a tussock of grass to one side of the fairway and the inaugural flight of the Grand Soarer came to an inglorious end, with Freddy spinning like a dervish. But she held together.

Freddy, though hurled from the cradle, was more dazed than hurt. Even so, that low-speed encounter with what Sir Toby later called "terror firmer" left him with no illusions about the prospects of surviving a crash from twenty feet at forty miles an hour.

The other fellows rushed to help him, shouting, "Are you all right?" and "Don't move if you're hurt!"

"What we really need," he said as he rose and dusted the hayseed from him, "is a steam winch here at this end of the fairway, a pulley down the far end, and an endless rope between them. Also I think the sails should be remade to slope upward a bit, like wings, so we can land at an angle without hitting the grass."

They all laughed uproariously and told him what a card he was.

Ann, whose heart had been in her mouth every second that Frederick was airborne, saw how alive – how more-than-alive – the achievement had made him. He was flushed with something almost godlike. She felt less worthy of him than ever. Last night her life had arrived at a great divide. Today it yawned before her, wider still, making all choice equally impossible.

What a mess she had made of things!

CHAPTER NINE

"I FEEL SUCH A SHAM," Clive said.

"Don't!" Ann touched his arm unhappily. "You're not to blame. You didn't want it to happen."

"To us, you see, this Grand Soarer business was never anything more than a bit of a lark, a kind of ultimate dare. Poor old Fredders was the only one who took it seriously. He thinks it can be George Stephenson and the Stockton and Darlington all over again." He stamped his foot with annoyance. "But why should he! What good will it ever be? It'll never be a way of getting about the country – anyone can see that. And even as a rich man's sport – well, its pleasures would be exhausted within two days – as we've proved."

"You're talking as if *you* sent him away. It wasn't you. It was Mr. Wilde."

Clive sighed. "But haven't I just taken the advantage of it!"

"Why did Mr. Wilde send him over to the Soho works, anyway?" Ann asked.

"I don't know. It's some engineering thing. I don't even pretend to understand it. Something to do with difficulties they've been having with some moulds. Wilde thinks Freddy will find the answer. He will too, probably."

Their casual stroll had brought them to a ferny little grove in the Informal Garden. Hardly anyone came here, certainly not so late in the evening. He took her arm. "I love every minute with you, Ann darling – and hate myself for it. But I can't help it."

She sniffed. "Don't worry. I know very well I'm 'just a bit of a lark,' too."

He leaped in front of her and forced her to look at him. "Don't you dare even think that again, Ann. I love you. For the ten-thousandth time, I love you. I'm beset, besieged, and besotted by you, by thoughts of you. I can't get you out of my mind for one instant, day or night."

She gazed up into his eyes and saw there an admiration that was new to her. At least, she had never seen it in Frederick's eyes. It was an adoration tinged with violence. Suddenly she knew the name for it: hunger. Frederick loved her truly, she never doubted it; but that raw kind of hunger was not in him.

It both frightened and flattered her. She wanted to run from Clive. She wanted to stay and see where it might lead them.

She lowered her gaze but she felt his eyes still upon her, like a burn. He was waiting for her response – and so, in a way, was she. When it came, its mildness surprised her. She nuzzled his cheek with the tip of her nose, a sad, cool touch. "You know it can never be."

"If you really think you're only a bit of amusement for me," he began. Then he changed tack to something more accusing: "I notice you never refuse a chance to meet me."

"I can't seem to help myself either," she answered. "I'm in such a turmoil."

"I mean to marry you," he added, like a warning.

"You know it's impossible, Clive."

"How can you say that so calmly?" He turned away from her and added bitterly, "You accept everything so easily. 'It can never be ... it's impossible.' How d'you know?"

"Your parents would cut you off without a penny. You know it. You may be the only son, but still they'd do it."

This was her body preparing her to marry Frederick yet scheming to keep its dreams afloat.

He protested. "You speak as if that would be the end of the world. We'd be alive, wouldn't we? We'd still have each other. We'd have all our lives before us."

"But ... there's Frederick."

Angrily he kicked a stone into the undergrowth; a blackbird fled among the saplings with an ear-shattering alarm. "Yes," he said. "There's Frederick! Pay no attention to me. I couldn't do it to him. When the moment came, I couldn't do it. But by God, Ann, I want you! I'll never stop wanting you."

Despite the fervour of his words she sensed a collapse inside him. Something within her was angered at it. She drifted close to him again and, putting up her hands, slowly pulled at the ribbons of her bodice until it was undone. The white fingers of her gloves had a conjuror's eloquence in that tree-dark twilight, giving a deftness and a finality to everything they did. "There!" they said for her, and invited him to do the rest.

"No," he murmured. But the shiver behind the word was more honest. "We'd regret it so."

"I regret it now," she said simply. "I love Frederick and none of this can change that. But when I'm with you I'm just so sorry this has all happened, and it's my fault because I wanted to flirt and play with you that night, and I led you on, and now I owe it to you." The pitter-patter of half truths eased the air between them.

He shook his head and, taking up the ribbons, tied them neatly together again.

At once she tugged them apart and stared at him in defiant expectation – also with a trace of annoyance that he had driven her to such directness. "Also I want to," she added flatly.

He raised his hand, intending to caress her half-naked breast but, funking it at the last moment, let the movement carry it onward until he touched her face.

It was an unconsciously astute move for it enabled her to retreat again into the mists of ambiguous promise. Fervently she clasped his hand to her cheek. Softly she leaned against it. Ardently she kissed his open palm. Adrift once more on that warm ocean of tenderness, she closed her eyes and said, "I think about it all the time, too. Beset ... besotted ... just the way you said it. I can't seem to stop wanting it with you." She pushed his hand back where he had intended placing it. At his touch there she shivered and clung to him.

When he took no bolder liberty she opened her great searching eyes and asked him what was the matter.

"I love you too much," he explained.

She smiled and, bending earthward, tugged him to fall with her.

"Not here." The words squeezed out of him like a shameful admission.

"Where then?" For one wild moment she had visions of a huge romantic boudoir somewhere in Mortimer Hall.

"You know that widow woman who takes in washing, down the little backwater by Hen Wood mill? Has two daughters."

"The lacemakers?"

"Yes."

"What about her?"

He could barely get out the words. "She, er, lets out her parlour."

The blankness of her gaze forced him to add, "To oblige needy ladies and gentleman."

She was numb with disappointment. He saw it and blurted out, "Not me! It was Gray. When he was here last month – he discovered it. Gray will discover anything like that. It didn't take him two hours. He also discovered she lets out her daughters, too. But it's the room I'm thinking of."

Ann was silent, torn between the promptings of common sense and a poetic urge to believe him.

"You're so good and fine," he told her. "Where else could we go? Here? With stinging nettles and everything – and we'd

be afraid all the time of being found out. Or the old gamekeeper's cottage? In all that filthy hay? I want to lie beside you,
Ann, and be at perfect peace. I want time to stop. I want the
world to go away – to stay beyond the door. I want to hold
you for ever in a cool, soft bed, between cool, fresh sheets,
with candlelight, and warm water, and a flask of cool wine
there."

The fact that he had already planned it in such detail
seemed fitting to her. Now he would lead all the way. She
could resign everything to him.

She retied her ribbon. They went back to retrieve her
cloak, which she had left over the bole of a tree. "Wear it inside
out," he said. "She won't recognise you again. Keep your head
down. I'll pretend you're a lady of fashion. I'll do all the
talking."

She put a finger to his lips. "You do too much already,"
she told him. "You talk as if I'd be ashamed to be seen with
you."

The widow's parlour was like no cottage parlour Ann had
ever seen. It was more like a grand bedroom at the Royal in
Birmingham, which she had seen once when she had had to
take Mrs. Wilde's gown for the Trade Society Ball – copper
pans, polished oak furniture, chintz curtains, brass candlesticks,
and imitation Turkey rugs. And, dominating the room, of
course, the one item of equipment that had paid for all the rest –
a vast feather bed.

The hire was a half-crown for the hour or six shillings a
night. They took it for four hours but Clive had to pay the full
night rate; a week's wages squandered on a few hours with her!
And all because he thought she was beautiful, because of that
hunger in him. As she watched the silver coins counted out, her
own power gave her a visceral thrill.

As a concession the widow woman agreed to waive the
sixpenny charge for the wine, a bottle of light hock. She sent
her daughter in to kindle the fire, "in case it might turn a bit
chill," she said with a wink. Clive watched the girl at her work.
Not a bad looker, but nothing like the Venus whom Gray had
described. He tried not to imagine Gray and her together, in
this room, on this bed.

Watching him keenly Ann saw an echo of that same

hunger in his eyes as they followed the girl's movements. Anger flared inside her. How *could* he!

When the girl had gone, Clive turned to see Ann looking at him steadily; it filled him with guilt at the depth of his need for her and for the coming betrayal of Freddy.

"You're a man, I suppose," she said, as if he just about deserved forgiveness for it.

"Meaning?"

She forgot that sudden, sharp bite of her anger and gave her words a more general drift: "You handled the old lady pretty well. You had her eating out of your hand."

"I'm sorry?" He did not follow her.

"Gray discovered this place, did he!" she taunted. "In your own backyard? I'll bet the Mortimers are her landlords."

"I expect we are. But I honestly didn't know this sort of thing was going on here."

"You've never been here before?" she asked with a cajoling laugh.

"Oh Ann – d'you think I could possibly bring you here if I had. It's bad enough knowing about Gray and that girl ..."

"How d'you know it wasn't her sister?"

"It was both of them."

She turned her back on him. "God! You men!" She wondered why she was so angry all of a sudden. Because it was the least expected response – and thus restored an illusion of freedom to her? Because she had been so mistrustful of him – and her suspicions had proved so unworthy? Because his goodness only heaped her guilty feelings about Frederick? Because the judas goat of her body had led her into this trap? She shivered at the number of reasons she could find.

His fingers lightly stroked her neck. "If you prefer," he said, "we can just lie down on the bed and sip our wine and talk."

A fat tear brimmed suddenly in each eye. She did not want his goodness. The nicer he was, the worse it made her seem. She remembered how Gray had behaved toward her – at odd moments, whenever he'd had the chance. Arrogant, contemptuous, absolutely sure of himself, never doubting that he was driving her wild with desire – when all the time, if her bosom had heaved and fluttered with any emotion, it had been with laughter, and with the joy of feeling several lifetimes older than such a puppy. Nevertheless, she wanted Clive to be like that, so she could feel contempt for him, even as she seemed to yield. In that way she would keep herself, her real self, inviolate. She yearned for this experience; her body craved it, even now. Yet she also wanted to remain a partial spectator to it. She wanted to keep back something of her virginity, her true virginity, which was in her mind, and give it intact and pure to Frederick when their time came; but Clive's decency was not going to let her. It was a refiner's fire that would transform every particle of her.

"Would you prefer that?" he pressed.

How could she tell him? The room shuddered and dissolved in the brimming salt before her eyes. "Oh just do whatever you want," she said wearily.

"Then we'll lie down side by side and talk," he said.

Gently he pulled her until the nudge of the mattress behind her knees collapsed her upon it. He stooped to unlace her boots. Suddenly he looked up and smiled. "They're ladder-laced!"

She gave a little laugh, against her will, and, reaching forward, pinched his nose fondly. Somehow the gesture liberated them. She watched him unlacing and tugging at her boots, saw the trembling of his fingers, heard the shiver of his breath, and suddenly she knew he was as virgin as herself. In that instant everything changed.

Until then, because he had conducted all the arrangements, she had assumed he knew it all and would induce her step by step into *his* familiar wonderland. But now she saw he had no more ownership there than her; they were both at the equal mercy of their imaginations.

Secure yet still experimental in her new status, she stretched forth her one liberated foot and stroked him where she had never before stroked any man. He looked suddenly up at her, pursed his lips, and whistled.

Her other free boot came away too easily, causing him to lurch back. She gazed at the swelling she had caused and smiled. He was on his knees before her now. She gave her skirts an inch or two of a hitch. His hands reached forward and took over from hers. Their eyes dwelled in each other's as he continued with the slow revelation of her charms. They were both too beset by happiness even to smile; each saw there only a wonder that this was possible, that it was happening.

When her knees were bared she pushed down his head. His lips, kissing now one thigh, now the other, followed the hem up, up ... Thus she had often imagined it. The tightening gather of the cloth upon her lap began to hinder him. She slipped her fingers around it and lay back with an expansive sigh. But she kept her thighs together.

It was going to be all right. Because she was no longer the follow-me creature of his experience, because she could say – not in so many words, but by subtle movements of her body – do this, do that, here! there! ... she could remain, in part, spectator to their pleasure – and comptroller of his.

His kiss foundered in the delta of her hair. She resisted the finger pressure on her thighs. Harder he pressed, and tighter she clenched until he raised his head and said, "Oh please!" Even then she did not help. A delicious dead languor filled her limbs as she lay there, utterly passive, and let him push apart and open her. His gasp filtered to her from a distant world. "T h a t   i s   s o   b e a u t i f u l ..." Each word a century long. Lips closed on lips and kissed lingering.

It was not going to be all right. She – that cool observer within – was shrivelling away, dissolving in strange juices that now began to eddy through her. Parts of her that once had no sensation – bones and dumb organs – now swelled and tingled. She lost control of her breathing. Something inside her ribcage – or no, it was in her stomach – or in both places and in neither – something began to rise like dough gone mad. It crowded her out.

She was naked. He was wearing his strange, wonderful, bony, lean, muscular, softskinned, mansbody. She was over him, melons in his mouth. Darts of consuming thrills stretched veins of blood turned to lemonade, to firewater, to sheer spirit, from her nipples to the soles of all her feet. She could never have dreamed of this; all those knocks and disappointments she had requited on her patient flesh could not have prepared her for anything like this.

For Clive it was the totality of her that came as such a thrill. In waking dreams he had enjoyed, yesterday, the vicarious idea of a pair of bosoms, today the secondhand vision of a thigh, tomorrow the enforced imagining of a furrowed groin; but to unify them required a vision far superior to his. Now she achieved it for him; the conjunction was immaculate. From the top of his head, nestling in the dear warmth of her, to the tip of his toes, knuckling into her curling soles, the touch of joy was seamless.

His flesh melted into hers, feminine, masculine, two parts of one perfected sex. When he moved, she gave their one moan of pleasure. When she breathed, his blood renewed itself. Her divine body kindled his love for his, such ordinary clay.

"You are my wife," he whispered as he began the long, unstoppable rise to a climax deep within her.

She ought to have listened more acutely, for the words were not idly chosen; but she was hardly there any more.

CHAPTER TEN

WHEN ANN TOLD FREDDY she was pregnant, it was as the end of the world for him. He went to work as usual but hung over his bench like the living dead. If for a few short moments he could forget Ann's perfidy, his mind immediately leaped to that of Clive. Which was worse? He shuttled between the one and the other in a downward spiral of despair. Where in all the world was sanctuary for comradeship?

Dixon, Freddy's first master in the early days of his apprenticeship, was intrigued enough to fall in beside Freddy on their homeward way that evening. "What's up, lad?" he asked – never being one for a devious approach. "Let's drop in for a quick one."

"Nothing's up," Freddy told him. But several unaccustomed pints of beer later, "nothing" had turned into the story of Clive's betrayal – edited to make it romantic rather than physical.

Dixon was surprised to hear that the close friendship between the two lads had persisted beyond their childhood. He thought it was dead these many years. Now he did his best to make it so.

"This is *it*," he said. "This is your class struggle as it really is. You can read about it in books and you'd think it was something old Karl dreamed up specially for other writers to do other books about, and for trade union men to frighten their comrades with. But this is it, lad."

Freddy was unable to focus either on the man or his thoughts.

Dixon went on, "You had something you wanted, right? Something you valued. Well that's not allowed, son. He *had to* take it off you – whether he wanted it or not, he had to take it. They're as trapped by the class system as what we are."

Freddy was puzzled. Had Ann been *his* in that way? Like *his* job or *his* earnings? He shook his head. "It wasn't like that," he tried to explain. "The young lady wasn't *mine* like that."

"Not the point, son. The point is – did the high and mighty Clive Mortimer see it like that? 'Course he didn't! According to his lights, she was yours. So he had to take her off of you. Pleasure is their birthright, they think. It's a disease with them, see. Just as our disease is saying yes-sir, no-sir, thank-you-very-much-sir, where'd-you-like-to-kick-me-next-sir?"

"I wanted to kill him, Mr. Dixon."

Several responses occurred to the older man. In the end he said, "I think you might do better than that, Mr. Oxley. Killing's too quick, too kind. And too stupid. They've got the law all rigged up against you if you do that."

"Better?" Freddy seized upon the word and all it seemed to promise.

Dixon looked at him in silence, a long moment. "Have another," he said jovially at last.

"No – honest ..."

But the next pint was already being ordered. "I've been

waiting two years for the right moment to tell you this," Dixon said. "You've got brains, lad. You're one of the brightest I've ever known. You could be a real leader. The sort of man the working classes are dying for want of. You could change the course of history if you set your mind to it. I'd swear it."

"How?" Despite his mood Freddy was enthralled. Dixon was so intense, so possessed, so convincing.

Dixon told him.

As Freddy listened, he found himself agreeing with almost everything old Dixon said. And yet in some peculiar way none of it quite applied to him, to this case, to Clive – especially to Clive.

Still, he didn't reject the man out of hand. For the first time in his life he realized that other people's ideas are like spare parts in the factory store; you could take the bits you wanted and use them to make something of your own. As soon as he expressed it like that, to himself, the notion was so simple that he marvelled he had not seen it before. It appeared to mark an important stage in his life, as if the lack of it had made every previous thought and action seem childish.

On that same day Lady Mortimer was having her own argument with Clive. "You could postpone Oxford, dear, and go to Melbourne. Help Uncle Wystan with his woolgathering or woolbroking or whatever he calls it. This whole idea of marrying the Howard woman is quite absurd, and out of the question. I'm sure once you've gone, she will see sense and marry this young creature from her own class."

" 'Young creature from her own class'!" Clive echoed scornfully. "We're discussing Freddy Oxley! As you very well know."

"To my cost! It was an evil day that he was born! But what a fine chance this would be for him to make amends – for all the harm he's done us."

"You pretend to dislike him so much but you're quite happy, apparently, for him to raise one of *your* grandchildren! There'll be a quarter of your blood in Ann's baby."

"Happy is hardly the word! I dislike him heartily. I detest him. I detest the thought of his having anything to do with my grandchild. But, 'if thine eye offend thee ...' is a good principle.

I detest everything to do with this whole squalid affair. I most especially loathe the way we are forced to beget our offspring. I wish with all my heart we could manage it after the manner of the trees. Or seaweed. But as we can't, and as we are 'stuck,' as your father puts it, with the consequences, we must make the best of it all. And that means, in my case, cutting off a tainted quarter of myself rather than letting it infect the legitimate line."

"You can't stop me marrying her."

She smiled thinly. "I don't think that necessity will arise. Thank heavens the Howard woman seems to have *some* sense – though where it was on that particular night, I ..."

"It wasn't just one night."

She shuddered fastidiously, as if he had confessed to coprophilia, but she stuck relentlessly to her line. "I'm quite sure she won't have anything to do with you – once she hears you'll be cut off without a farthing – which is what I shall insist upon with your father. This idea of your living quietly in France is absurd."

Clive ought to have left it at that, but he could not resist adding, "She will marry me. She's not at all the sort of person you imagine. Surely no woman would deliberately choose to deny her own child a name."

His mother pursed her lips thoughtfully, conceding the point. "We must take care of that, then," she said. "If Howard now supposes that marrying Oxley is beneath her, we must sweeten the pill. Mmmm?"

The opportunity arrived soon enough – the following day, in fact. Freddy came to see her at Mortimer Hall. He chose to speak to her rather than to Sir Toby because he remembered her ruthlessness on the day of the flight.

It was the first time he had been to the Hall, openly and in broad daylight, since the evening of the Great Explosion. There were strange echoes of that occasion, even today, as he slowly mounted the grand staircase leading up to the front door. Then, as now, he was hollow with fear. Then, as now, the outcome was wholly in the lap of the gods – or at least it depended entirely on how well he acquitted himself.

But there were differences. This time, for instance, he had a card or two of his own to play.

"Old Soakum," the butler, took one look at him, glanced about himself, and hissed, "Piss off round the back, you! The very idea!"

It was important to Freddy's self-esteem to be admitted at the front door. He said, in a voice whose calm surprised him, "What I have to say is entirely to her ladyship's advantage. If you send me away, I'll write to her – then you'll know all about the back door!"

With a scowl Old Soakum left him standing there. But in less than a minute he was back, saying, "You'd better come in, Oxley. And make sure you wipe those clodhoppers. Her ladyship will see you in the gun room."

Freddy smiled and followed the rotund figure into the gloom of the ancient building. Their footsteps rang out on the polished flagstones. The oak-panelled walls were rich in armorial achievements. Pennants that were a mere forty years old – though they looked as if they had been flaunted at Agincourt – hung from gilded poles. Modern portraits in the stiff style of Kneller, purporting to recapture semi-researched Jacobean ancestors, stared down contemptuously upon Freddy, piqued, perhaps, that their promotion from swineherd to courtier had come a century and a half too late for them to enjoy the fruits of it. Freddy knew none of this, of course. To him the house and family had all the magnificence it so plainly wore upon its sleeve.

Lady Mortimer had chosen the gunroom because it was a "nothing" room. She was obviously going to have to buy off little Oxley and little Howard; there was nothing like a purseful of small change for keeping people in their places. Yet the bailiff's office would have lent their transaction the solid colours of the Hall's daily commerce; she was too squeamish for that. And any other room would have accorded Oxley some degree of social status – which was quite out of the question, of course. Anyway, she felt secure here. She gazed around the glass cases, filled with everything from ancient flintlocks to the most gorgeous modern fowling pieces, all gleaming and polished (and securely chained, too, since the Chartist riots of twenty years ago) and she took heart.

"Young Oxley, milady," the butler spat out the words. His venom surprised her. Indeed, it seemed almost like an affront, as if he had borrowed her attitudes from her without a by-your-leave.

It vexed her, too. If she now behaved as coldly as she had intended, it would seem as if she were taking her cue from her own butler. So she smiled in welcome – which she had certainly not intended doing.

Again the boy's clean-cut young-manliness surprised her. It tricked her into saying, "Do please be seated, Mr. Oxley." She had intended calling him only by his surname, and making him stand, a petitioner at the court of his betters, throughout. "You have something you wish to communicate to me?"

Freddy remained standing. "I think we have a joint interest in this business, Lady Mortimer," he said.

His use of the socially equal "Lady Mortimer" instead of the servile "milady" made one of her eyebrows twitch, but she held her tongue. At first she could not imagine why, for to remain silent after such an insult was most unlike her. But some instinct warned her that a larger game was now afoot. Precisely what, she could not say, but she never mistrusted her instinct. She watched the young man closely.

He began belligerently, "Your son, having betrayed his friendship with me, now wishes to lower – as you must see it – the name of Mortimer by a marriage none of you would call suitable."

She hid her amusement. The boy's insolence was too absurd. "You imply that you would? Call it suitable, I mean?"

"I had not intended to offer an opinion as to that, Lady Mortimer, but since you are kind enough to ask it, I may say that I believe the honour would be done *to* your family, not *by* it."

This time there was no smile to suppress; there ought to have been, but there was not. Indeed, she ought to have laughed in his face. The words had the ring of Eton but they were delivered in the flat accent of the Midlands. They ought to have been ludicrous. Yet in some extraordinary fashion this young fellow managed to deliver them with every air of authority. He was altogether too sure of himself. Beyond murmuring, "How interesting," Lady Mortimer held her tongue.

"Let me tell you something even more interesting, then,"

Freddy went on. "I daresay the two things you most want at this minute are, one: You want an end to my association with Clive. And two ..."

"You mean it hasn't yet ended!"

"An apology from him could do wonders." Freddy hoped he looked and sounded convincing. He'd thought this out very carefully – once Dixon had pointed him in the right direction.

"An apology? That's all it would need?" she asked in disbelief. "A sorry and a handshake? Do you really *feel* so little? Lord – I'd want him to die a thousand different ways." In the normal course of events the last thing she'd have concerned herself with would be the attitudes of a lad of Oxley's class to matters of honour. But she was still following that instinct of hers, which was amazed at the young man's air of command – and intrigued at his apparent lack of jealousy.

He shrugged helplessly. This was not the hoped-for response. How little he understood people like her, he thought.

Her eyes narrowed. "Tell me," she said. "I have no right to ask this but I'd be grateful if you'd answer me honestly – which has wounded you the most, my son's betrayal or that of Miss Howard?"

"They're one and the same thing, surely," he answered at once.

"Do you really think so!" She saw his bewilderment was quite genuine and became even more intrigued. All sense of the vast social gulf between them was, for the moment, suspended. "Go on," she prompted. "What's the second thing I want most in all the world?"

He heard the gentle mockery but could not explain it.

"You want Miss Howard off your hands. Am I right?" At the sudden bark of the question his confidence began to recover.

"Go on." Her face was a mask.

"I need to hear you say it." He began to feel himself in command again – or at least back on the firm ground of his prepared script.

"You're a very self-assured young man. How old are you, may I ask?"

"Soon eighteen – but I came of age last week. Prematurely, you might say. Am I right in what I believe? Do you ..."

"Yes yes yes! Of course you're right. Go on." Not yet eighteen! It made his air of authority, his self-possession even more interesting.

"I" – he spoke the word with generous grandeur – "would be willing to take Miss Howard off your hands."

For a moment his attempt at *noblesse oblige* goaded Lady Mortimer back into her intended posture. She exploded: "Considering that it was you who introduced her to my son in the first place, I should think ..." But again her instinct restrained her. She bit back the rest of the sentence. "What's past is past. Do go on. Take her off our hands, you say. You mean marry her?"

"I mean marry her and accept the paternity of the child."

"The one implies the other."

"It's necessary to be explicit. For instance, it's also necessary to point out that, in the normal course, I'd not be ready to marry – that is, I'd not be capable of supporting a wife – for at least two years yet. If I am now to hasten forward ..."

All at once she saw the coldness of his purpose. He was just a greedy peasant. The Mortimers were in trouble; he'd get them out of it if they put enough grease in his palm. There was nothing more to him than that. She was less annoyed at this discovery than at the feeling that her instinct had, for once, let her down. "I see," she sneered. "How much?"

"For myself, I want two years' schooling. For the child, I want four years' support."

These strange, and strangely modest, "demands" threw Lady Mortimer back into confusion. But momentum carried her on. She drew herself up and said, "Support for the child – yes. For *sixteen* years, if you wish. I'm prepared for that. Why stop at four? But schooling for yourself? It's out of the question. You must realize that."

"Oh must I indeed?" He was alarmed. This was one demand he could never concede.

"Of course you must. We've just spent a small fortune on your apprenticeship. And now you demand two years of schooling on top of it – pshaw!"

He thought of his years at the bench and forge, not to mention the roller, the lathe, the miller, the grinder, the polisher – long hours spent in making valuable items for the Mortimer stock; and all for a pittance. A small fortune, indeed! He drew an angry breath to speak.

But she cut across him. She had been watching his face, which had plainly showed first his hope, then his fear; it caused her to realize that her instinct had not, after all, misled her. There was something ... *different* about this young man, something extraordinary. "Two years' schooling in what?" she asked.

Without a moment's hesitation Freddy told her: "Mathematics, chemistry, and natural sciences."

The choice startled her. Somehow she had suspected he would try to become a gentleman – with Latin, Greek, fencing, and so on. "At university?"

"At the Sam Hall Methodist College in Newcastle-upon-Tyne."

His very preciseness made her smile at last. "You have been busy!"

"Newcastle should be far enough away for your comfort?"

She barely heard this afterthought, for she suddenly saw what it was that fascinated her about this young man. Something within her had seen it at once and held her in check. Perhaps the awareness had been within her, unrecognised, since the day of the flight. To call Freddy Oxley "extraordinary" did not explain one tenth of it. Anyway, she had always known he was that. If she had bothered her head about his future at all (which naturally she had not) she would have guessed he was the sort of fellow who might in time rise to become a very solid works manager. Not until today did she realize that, given the right start, there might be no limit to the heights he could reach.

The notion filled her with a novel excitement. Young Oxley was offering her a rare power – the power to control another's destiny. In a way such a power was not rare, for she exercised it every day – but only to keep people in their proper places. Indeed, had she not come to this interview determined to do precisely that to this little ex-apprentice? But something about him, his confident manner, his tough assurance that, come all the world against him, he would get what he wanted, a hardness at the core of him, now held forth this most glittering temptation to do the other thing, the rare thing – to elevate him from his present lowly station and place him, almost at her whim, wherever it might please her. It was a temptation she could not resist.

Did he know it? Did he, too, have some guiding instinct that had led him to make this strange demand of her, rather than all the other more obvious ones?

"Very well," she said evenly. "I agree."

He swallowed audibly and breathed out in relief; but he said nothing.

She understood his hesitation and smiled. "You have my word," she told him. "I'll put nothing in writing – as I'm sure you'll understand – but you have my word. Is it enough? Will you accept it?"

Images of Dixon, half-formed cautions from the Dixon vocabulary, clamoured for his mind's ear. But he shrugged them aside and answered, "Yes, of course I do."

CHAPTER ELEVEN

THEY BURNED THE GRAND SOARER. The estate workers said they had understood their orders to that effect; Sir Toby later maintained it was a mistake – all he had told them to burn was the rubble of the old barn. Perhaps it was Clive's doing, or even Lady Mortimer's. The truth would never be known.

The news reached Freddy when it was much too late. By the time he arrived at the scene of the fire, only the willow-work outline of the machine was recognisable – and the four wheels, which one of the workers had salvaged before they started pouring on the coal oil. He was surprised at how little the sight of it affected him. He stood there, half out of breath, looking down at the crackling timbers, and almost had to search himself to dredge up any sort of feeling at all. And then it was hardly sorrow – not deep and bitter sorrow. Merely a regret for something that had been inevitable. The end of childhood. There was almost a satisfaction in it. The feeling of a clean break.

He looked around at the others' faces and saw Clive among them, a little apart, on the far side of the blaze; wreathed in fumes and the shivers of the heat, he looked devilish enough.

Clive said something but the flames and smoke absorbed every syllable. Freddy tried to ignore him but they had too many years, too many crises, too much laughter in common for it to end so flatly. It called for blood. He walked around the blaze.

Clive looked away as he approached. "I could have saved half of her," he said. "But then I thought why try? It's all over, anyway."

There was a long silence while they both stared at the flames. The outlines of the Soarer were less clear every moment. "So," Clive said at last, "Fredders now has everything he wants."

"Are we talking about practical things like food and shoes?" Freddy answered in a mild, conversational tone. "Or about airy rubbish like trust and honour?"

A couple of the estate workers caught Clive's reaction and began to peer deep into the glowing charcoals, wearing intense "I'm-not-listening" stares.

"We've got to have this out," Clive said.

"Let's go for a walk."

Clive looked awkwardly toward the Old Way, beyond the empty gamekeeper's cottage.

"You're expecting Ann," Freddy accused him.

"A farewell," he confessed.

"We'll go and sit on the wall then."

"God but there's something inhuman about you," Clive told him. Yet he followed him to the verge of the Old Way. What else could he do?

It was a bright and sunny September day but away from the fire it felt suddenly chill. They sat at the foot of the wall, leaning against it, out of the breeze. There the sun soon established a new warmth for them – or at least for their bodies.

Clive began: "There is no excuse for what I did. No possible apology could ..."

"I wouldn't even look for an excuse," Freddy cut in. "Just a reason." Nervousness made him fish out his penknife and start whittling away at a piece of wood. He had no particular final shape in mind.

"Reason!" Clive gave an ironic snort. "You want a reason for *that*?" When Freddy volunteered no response, he added, "It must have happened a million times down the years."

"Causes then," Freddy persisted.

"The cause is something in the blood. Christ, surely you know! You're in love with her, too."

"It must be different. What I feel for Ann would never lead me to take her to a brothel at dead of night."

"It wasn't like that. It's not a brothel, anyway."

"Nor to my own bed."

"Then it is different," Clive said.

Freddy experienced a sudden flush of anger. He thought he detected a note of patronage in this flat assertion, implying that "different" meant "inferior."

"If she'd been 'someone's sister,' you'd never have done it. You wouldn't have taken Knox-Riddell's sister there."

Clive was silent.

"Go on. Admit it!" Freddy persisted.

"I admit it, but not in the way you imply. Look, Freddy, don't keep trying to force me to put on the gloves. Everything you feel about this whole business, the let-down, the disgust, the loathing ... loathing? Yes, I suppose you must loathe me. But there's nothing you could say to me by way of reproach ... nothing that I haven't already said to myself a hundred times, and a hundred times more severely. So don't shove me into a position of trying to justify it." He snapped the twig he was fiddling with and threw the bits away. "Now let me try and explain this 'somebody's sister' business. The reason I'd never have done it with Knox-Riddell's sister is that the very chance could never have arisen. In the last two years – I mean since women ... how can I put it? You know what I mean. Since women assumed an importance in my life and thoughts. Lord, how pompous!"

"Since your balls dropped," Freddy said impatiently.

"Exactly. Since then how many hours d'you think I've spent with girls of our age? Hours? I should think it's more like minutes. Minutes snatched here and there at dances. Not alone, of course. We never get the chance to know them properly. Just whirling around the floor, touching their alien, corseted bodies and catching that strange, herby sort of smell of them, and being frightened. What chance do we get? But it wasn't like that with Ann. When you left us alone that night, I ..."

"Did it happen then, too?" Freddy interrupted.

"Of course not. But we talked. We talked and talked and ... it was the first time in my life I've ever felt that one of them wasn't alien. We could talk about anything. There was no difficulty suddenly."

"So of course it had to be love!"

"It was love," Clive insisted stubbornly. "It still is. What else could be strong enough to make me forget – or not forget but suppress – what else could make me suppress all memory of our friendship, all my own sense of honour, even selfish things like prudence and caution. All that I just heaved overboard."

When Freddy did not answer, Clive added, "At least give me credit for not having acted lightly, wantonly ... how does it go?"

Still Freddy said nothing. The whittling wood was pared away to nothing. He looked around idly for another bit. There was one near Clive's foot. Clive saw his dilemma and reached it for him. "If you've never felt a compulsion of that strength," he said, "I hope you never may."

"Oh I have urges all right," Freddy said. "There's nothing I can do about them now. But one day – you'll see."

Clive was hardly listening. Freddy realized that the habit was ancient. Clive only listened to him on practical matters – how to build a soaring machine ... things like that.

"Here she comes," Clive said.

Without thought, without even a suspicion he was going to come out with any such words, Freddy took the greatest risk of his life. He said, "We'll let her decide."

Clive looked at him sharply. "Decide what?"

"Between us."

"But you've made an agreement with my parents. It's already decided."

Freddy shook his head. Now he was committed he could not go back. "This is more important than that." Suddenly the most important thing in all the world was for him to rub Clive's nose in Ann's rejection.

When Ann saw the two of them waiting she turned back in frightened dismay. The very fact of their standing there, side by side, implied some kind of choice on her part, whether they consciously intended it or not. But no such choice was possible; a chooser is a judge, and a judge must be in some way superior to the matter of judgement. They were two of the most wonderful people in the world – Freddy, who revered her, and Clive, who adored her; and she was not worthy to exist within a mile of either of them. How could she face them both together?

So she turned and raced back down the Old Way.

The two young men rose and ran after her. She turned then and faced them like some cornered doe. The sight of her terror rekindled all Clive's desire – and his shame, too. She turned on him. "You didn't say about Frederick." And to Freddy she said, "It wasn't to deceive you, my darling. It was to tell him why."

"Why what?" Freddy asked.

"Everything." She shrugged at the impossible vastness of a true explanation. "How did you find out?"

"I didn't. They burned the Grand Soarer." He nodded toward the Hundredacre.

She stared at him. The shock was enormous. He was sure she was going to cry. "Oh Frederick ..." she kept repeating. Her eyes searched his face endlessly, seeking a crack in his calm.

"It was an accident," Clive explained. He could not take his eyes off her. The nearness of her body, its warm-musk smell, made him shiver.

She did not notice. She was still waiting for Frederick to react. And he was wondering what he could say to make those tears start flowing; it would release all the tension between them – among all three of them. He could do nothing but shrug and say, "Everything's an accident."

She put a hand across her midriff and he understood she thought he was referring to her pregnancy. It hardened her and the potential tears were quickly subdued. A feeling of pride surged through him, taking him by surprise. He was proud of her independence. From him and from Clive.

"I'm sorry," she said. "I know how much it meant to you."

"To all of us," Clive corrected her.

"Yes!" Freddy laughed. "It brought us together, after all."

The others were too embarrassed to answer.

"And now we have to part," Freddy went on. "Me to Newcastle. You to Australia. And" – he turned to Ann – "what about you ..?"

She stared back in fright. She really was being offered the choice. She looked at Clive; the longing in his eyes, which she recognised at last, confirmed it. She turned back to Freddy. "But I thought ..."

He shook his head. Feeling trapped she turned again to Clive, to his hopeless smile. He told her, "We didn't discuss this. Freddy just came out with it the moment we saw you. He said you must decide."

"Be free to decide," Freddy corrected. Had he made a ghastly mistake?

"I don't want to be free," she said sullenly.

"You want to be ordered what to do," Freddy suggested to her. "And then you'll obey. The only freedom you want is the freedom to grumble?"

She shrugged. How little either of them truly understood her. Yet, in a way, Freddy was right. She did just want to be told what to do. No doubt they'd think it was the response of a born servant. Their love for her discounted the very possibility that she might not exactly love herself.

Freddy saw her anguish and, though he did not comprehend it, he closed his eyes against the sudden rush of love he felt for her in her isolation.

"I shan't be going to Australia," Clive announced suddenly.

They stared at him in surprise.

"What would it prove?" he asked. "I have so many relations there, I'd merely prove that families can help their own. Which all the world already knows."

"Where will you go then?" Ann asked.

"I don't know. The Cape Colony? I was looking at my old school atlas last night. We don't know a single solitary soul in Port Elizabeth. Why not go there?"

"And do what?"

"Learn to survive. Prove I can do it – prove it to myself, I mean. Also ..."

Ann saw the pain in Freddy's face and realized she could not possibly burden his life with hers. She had never loved him so much as at that moment. It cost all her will to take Clive's hand and say, "I'll go with you!" She stared at Freddy, full of defiance.

Behind her Clive closed his eyes, unable to look his old friend in the face. Freddy's expression was unreadable, his voice mild. "Your reasons?" he asked.

His calm tone dismayed her. "You sound pleased, I must say!" she replied.

He caught her by the shoulders and deliberately turned her to face Clive. "Your reasons? Don't tell me. Tell him."

She fixed her eyes on Clive's arms, spoke to them. "It's because *we* made this mess, Clive. You and me. It's our mess. It wouldn't be fair on ..." She stumbled to a halt.

"Go on," Freddy told her quietly.

"Well, I ought to be made to pay for it, too. I should suffer. The wickedness was all mine. What do I matter now?"

"Tell him the real reason," Freddy persisted, still in that infuriatingly matter-of-fact tone.

Now she was puzzled. She tried to turn and look at him but his grip was relentless. "Ow!" She struggled weakly until he relented a little. His hands never trembled when they touched her, the way Clive's did. "That *is* the real reason. I hate myself."

"Never mind hate. Talk about love. Tell him how deeply you love him."

"But I don't!" She almost shouted it. Clive saw the shock in her face and knew she spoke the truth. She appealed to him directly now: "Tell him – I never told you I loved you, did I! I always told you it was Frederick – only Frederick." She broke free and spun about, looking urgently at Freddy. "I always told him that."

There was a vast sadness in Clive's eyes, but mingled with

it a kind of grim satisfaction. To her back he said, "It isn't your decision anyway. No matter what you say, you're not coming to the Cape with me. I wouldn't take you." He watched Ann fall into Freddy's arms and cling to him as if the rest of the world had faded away. He was sure she was no longer even listening. At last his eyes met Freddy's.

He felt empty. Everything within him had abdicated. "When you said she must choose," he asked, "did you know it would turn out like this?"

Freddy nodded slowly. It was not quite the truth. In fact, he had offered Ann the choice in very much the same spirit as, long ago, he had walked down the marble steps after Clive had thrown the bomb into the fire – quite convinced of his own immortality. Ann's response had surprised him.

Clive shrugged – total defeat. "You're a clever bloody man then. One day you'll beat us all." He spoke scornfully, as if it would be a dishonourable achievement.

"Yes," Freddy said, "I will." Though he smiled, his heart was angry; this cold admiration was blunting the sting of his triumph.

"Yes!" Clive echoed. His tone was openly contemptuous now. "You know when to trust an instinct. Unlike me! I don't even know when to resist it."

He turned on his heel and strode rapidly away.

The mood changed at once. Only Ann's misery mattered now. Freddy leaned back a fraction, so as to hook his finger under her chin. Tears were streaming down her face. A great truth suddenly filled him – too important and too urgent for him to pause and wonder if it were not just wishful thinking: Ann was utterly his now – even more so than if the child within was from his own seed. He owned every particle of them both!

He had stripped the child from his former friend. Now, somehow, bit by bit, relentlessly, he would take everything else.

She smiled shyly. "I'm not crying."

He clasped her head to him, proud of possession.

She added, "It's happiness. I've got no right to feel so happy."

"Happiness for us is an accident." He touched her belly and added gently, "And accidents are also happiness."

For the first time since the disaster had overwhelmed them, she felt the stirrings of an impossible hope, too wild to articulate. But it made her laugh aloud, even a little hysterically.

Freddy, on fire with hope of a different kind, joined her.

Clive heard their laughter. He broke into a run and did not stop until he reached the Hall. If willpower were all, he would have run the full distance to the Cape of Good Hope.

PART TWO

LOVE AND GOOD HOPE

CHAPTER TWELVE

FROM CLIVE MORTIMER, IN ALGOA BAY, TO HIS PARENTS AT MORTIMER HALL
Christmas 1867:
My last night aboard! Today I went ashore and the land felt as if it heaved and bucked as did the decks of the *Pleiades* when we were caught in that storm off the Gold Coast. Captain Slingsby says the effect can last for weeks.

Well, as I said, I went ashore today and almost immediately a most extraordinary thing happened. I'd been watching the coastline through my glass all morning. Algoa Bay and the one before it, St. Francis Bay, are both fringed by white sandy beaches, stretches of rock, and, here and there, a low cliff or two. There are no startling clefts or inlets. The site for Port Elizabeth was chosen more for the big river outlets than for any especially deep water, though we got close enough inshore, I must admit. Anyway, the coastline is all a sort of scrub, which they call "bush." There are thorn trees and acacias and an enormous mixture of dry-country shrubs and succulents. It's not at all green but very drab olive and pale brown, and the thorns bleach to a kind of whitish gray, like a patriarch's beard. A little way inland, I'm told, there are sheltered valleys and escarpments with patches of forest trees. Around the town (which has 11,000 souls, though you'd wonder where they all live) people have begun plantations of softwoods, mostly pines, as there is a desperate shortage of building timber. They grow quite fast here. There is plenty of birdlife though nothing spectacularly tropical. The hoopoo, or however you spell it, is the brightest. Also animals they tell me – lions, elephant, pigs, rhino, baboons, and many sorts of antelope. I've heard a lion roar but the only animals I saw from the ship were a crowd of monkeys larking about in the tops of an acacia grove.

The town is built on a steep hillside overlooking its harbour. It's less than fifty years old and looks even younger. The place was named by Sir (something – I didn't catch it) Donkin in memory of his wife, Elizabeth, who died in Madras. I suppose they're the same Donkins whose son (or more probably grandson) was at Eton with me. There's a sort of village green at the top of the hill called the Donkin Reserve, with all the grand houses looking out across it and southward over the bay, with the town and the harbour completely out of sight beyond the edge of the hill. (Don't forget everything's the wrong way round here. The northward side is the sunny side. And Christmas, now upon us, is in their summer. *Our* summer I must start learning to say.)

The hill curves away inland to the west and the east, in both cases up river valleys. It's rolling country to the west; the east looks flatter but much of it was lost in a heat haze all day. The smell of those succulent plants and the sand is heady. I first sensed it miles out to sea, days ago. Today, the wind is blowing straight up off the Antarctic, so that you can feel quite chilly if you're exposed to it; but the minute you're beyond its reach it's like being plunged into the dry-heat room at the baths in Wych Street.

I'm sorry, I'm beginning to ramble, but there's so much to tell. The *Pleiades* is here for a week or more and as Slingsby is such dashed good company, I thought I'd be in no hurry to disembark and leap into the first house that said Rooms To Let; better see the lie of the land first. So I took nothing ashore but my card, which I left at the District Commissioner's Residence (though he's away at Cape Town at the moment). Duty done, I strolled across the said Donkin Reserve (or village green), and began to spy upon the town through my glass – seeing, of course, that side of it which had been invisible from the bay. (I took my glass ashore as well as my card, but I don't count it as it's become part of me by now.)

In the course of what must have been my third traverse my attention was riveted (and nailed, screwed, and welded, too) by *the* most extraordinary sight – a full-grown man, a white man, sitting in a rather large dog cart, being drawn along by two fine ... what d'you think? Ostriches! The ones at the zoological gardens can give you no idea of the grace and power of these creatures. Their demeanour is rather stupid when they amble about slowly, I allow; but when you see them pacing out at speed they become positively lordly. I always thought a good trotting arab horse had one of the finest movements in the animal kingdom, but a loping ostrich, striding out to some purpose, has it beat into a cocked hat.

Before this unconventional equipage quite reached the Residence its driver turned southwards and began to cross the Donkin. Two full-grown male ostriches coming straight at one is a frightening sight. I leaped aside pretty smartly and could not help cheering them as they passed.

Until that moment the driver had barely glanced at me but now, to my surprise, he stopped (not as one would stop a horse, but by turning the two birds in ever tighter circles until they had no choice but to stop). He looked back at me, or at my cravat, and said, "Are those O.E. colours?"

He leaped down and came trotting over to me, smiling and saying, "I shall have to be moving on I can see. This place is getting a d***ed sight too civilized!" I saw then that he was wearing an O.E. tie – but as a belt around his waist! His suit was of blue cotton drill and his shirt had no collar, only a bright gold stud. Yet he has the innate dignity of the true eccentric (viz., one who does not even suspect he *is* eccentric) so he carried it off easily. It made me feel wildly overdressed in my neatly laundered tropicals and topee.

His name is Kelvin Tobermory. What shall I tell you first about this most extraordinary man? He's in his forties, I'd say, though the wind and sun do screw a person's face up here. A shortie. Much shorter than me – about 5ft 8in. Chubby, but powerful. Later in the afternoon I saw him heave aside a great "pocket" of flour which a grocer called van Steen was trying to palm off on him and he made it seem as light as cotton fluff. He has a full, naval style of beard and little, beady, amused, restless eyes.

We chatted awhile and then he drove me to the Albert hotel, up near the Anglican church, where he insisted on buying me lunch. On the way I noticed he drew smiles and welcomes from the men but their womenfolk were decidedly more frosty and only gave him the merest little tight-lipped nod of the head. I must say it was charming to be abroad among women again, with their wide hats and gay parasols and their pale, airy dresses; they do decorate and enliven a town so. I was afraid this place would be utterly raw, but first impressions are agreeably contrary.

I thought Tobermory's idea in taking me to the Albert was that I should stay there until I had found my feet. But not at all. He wanted to show me how decadent the "city" as he calls it has become; in other words, the hotel is as good as any you'd find in an average provincial town in England. "You'll learn nothing about the Cape if you stay here in Gomorrah, yong," he assured me. "Yong" is a Dutch word (meaning young fellow, I think), he uses it often. He admires the Dutch greatly. Not all of them went north with that Great Trek. There's quite a good little community of them hereabouts and they mingle well with the English. Tobermory thinks I should come out and stay at Driefontein, his farm, which is about ten miles westward along the coast. I asked him what he grew there. "Thorn mostly," he said. "Whatever the baboons and pigs and elephants will permit."

I explained my purpose here – to prove I can make my own way, earn my keep, etc. "Oh have no fear," he said. "You can do that at Driefontein as well as anywhere else. Better. What sort of shot are you? A good one I hope. A wounded rhino or a bull elephant is not the sort of tenant I want on my land." He speaks with a lopsided smile and a faraway look, so I never know if he is serious or not.

His farm is huge, about twenty-thousand morgen (or more than twice that many in acres), but as it is mostly unfenced and quite indistinguishable from the bush all around, he might as well claim a million acres of the ocean for all that it brings in. He has a manager, a Dutchman called Koetzie, and between them they've been trying to scare off the big game and fence round a few hundred morgen each year. But even where they've succeeded in doing that, the battle is far from won. If they grow maize (which they call mealies), the baboons come in at night and ravage the crop. If they grow any kind of roots, the wild pigs grub up whatever the insects and termites haven't already ruined. And livestock, I suppose, is at the mercy of lions and hunting dogs, and there are several kinds of wild cat, not as big as leopards but still fierce. Tobermory and Koetzie and their Hottentot peasants have to be at it day and night, keeping all these pests at bay. On our way to the hotel he peered disgustedly at one particularly fine garden, with a lawn kept green by constant watering, and said "Love of nature, eh!"

I could not give him a definite yes, of course, but I agreed to spend Christmas and January with him and sing for my supper by potting all the rhino, elephant, and baboon I can get my sights on. Funny, I know fellows at Eton who'd give ten years off their lives for such "work." I never much cared for shooting, as you know, but perhaps it will be different here, where the quarry can give a better account of himself than your grouse or pheasant – and where the killing has a laudable purpose. We shall see.

So here I am, my last night on board and already impatient to be off. Tomorrow morning Tobermory will collect me and all my gear and drive me out to Driefontein (which means Three Springs) and the adventure will begin. No decadent city life for me! One thing – I shall be glad to see the last of young Trimble, the most junior officer on the ship. On his last voyage to India he got smitten by some oriental religion and is now besotted by it. He claims it has given his life "meaning"! Maybe so but to the uninitiated it looks a dashed sight closer to incoherence. He made my life a misery with it all – kept asking me if I really knew my inner self.

And funnily enough, now that I come to think of it, the same subject seems to fascinate Tobermory. I hope he's not another of these orientalists. At the end of our meal he told me I was a bit of a mystery. I laughed and asked him why. "Most O.E.s," he said, "especially the ones who come abroad, are empty headed fools – amiable enough, but a bullet could pass in by one ear and out by the other without doing much damage in between. How did you escape that?" When I asked him what he meant, he replied, "Oh I've met them! They come out here bursting with ready-made plans for building the empire and changing the face of the world. But you're not like that. You *look* exactly the type, but you aren't."

I laughed. But he kept on asking, "What are you like?" Most persistent fellow. Still, one can't help warming to him.

Your ever-loving son, Clive.

He read the letter several times before he waxed and sealed it. What a cheerful chap it made him sound! It was all he could ever be to his parents. If he tried to tell them how he truly felt, they'd all die of embarrassment.

Anyway, how did he truly feel?

In a word – frightened. Not of this new land, not of the adventures that must surely await him, but of the mess he had left behind – and the bits of it he still carried around inside him.

Last Easter, those weeks they had spent building the framework of the Grand Soarer had been the high point of his life. If anyone had told him then that before the summer was out he would be seized by an emotion so powerful it would force him to betray his dearest friend, his blood-brother, he would have wagered his life against the chance of it. And yet it happened.

During the two months of the voyage his feeling for Ann had changed greatly – so much so that he now, ruefully, doubted it had been love at all. He had mourned the loss of her so briefly, never with tears, but with a visceral emptiness. He suspected that if they met again, even years from now, his obsession for her would revive, but it would be an overwhelming desire for her body. Love was an emotion he had yet to discover.

Perhaps he might have found it with her? If things had gone more gradually between them. If they had given it time to grow. Instead there had been that raw, urgent ...

Give it its proper name: *lust*.

Lust had choked it. That was what he had to guard against, to subdue. That was his purpose in coming out here.

He remembered the force of it, though; and was frightened.

CHAPTER THIRTEEN

IN PIONEER COUNTRY the word "farm" conjures up the picture of a rough but sturdy homestead, a cabin of logs, say, or of sun-dried bricks, with a low-pitched roof of corrugated iron, perhaps lightly turfed over – the whole place cobbled together with the rudest of carpentry. Such at least was what Clive expected to find at Driefontein. What he actually saw as the ostrich cart came bouncing round the final bend among the thorns was so startling that for a moment he thought it must be a mirage. There, in a sheep-cropped clearing hard by the seashore, stood an English parish church, complete to its last detail. A miniature gothic cathedral, carved, it seemed, in some kind of dark-gray limestone. Around its buttresses fretted a motley collection of hens, goats, and pigs.

"Eh?" Clive blinked and shook his head.

Tobermory, who had been watching him closely, laughed. "It ain't what it seems, yong," he said. "Life isn't all singing hymns."

"But it is a church."

"Cost me a hundred and twenty. Morell and Sons of Rotherhithe make them for the tropics. Cast iron. Termites hate the stuff."

"I see. Jolly sensible then. I suppose termites must be a great problem here?"

"Not in the least," Tobermory said as he spiralled the ostriches into a dizzying halt.

The dust cleared to reveal a tall, grimly handsome woman dressed in black from head to foot.

"Mrs. Tobermory, my dear, here's the rawest, freshest thing from England. But when I saw the colour of its tie I couldn't leave it to stray in Gomorrah. He'll shoot for his supper."

She nodded stiffly and gave Clive's hand one firm shake. She had reddish hair, constrained into a tight bun whose plaits were simultaneously a concession to ornament (the only one she allowed herself to make) and a knot of discipline, binding up what would otherwise be hot and riotous. Her pale, bluish-green eyes never left his face. They seemed to peer right into him, seeking something – his discomfort, perhaps.

"We had a meal in town," Tobermory told her. "As soon as this young fellow's bags are indoors I'll show him over the place."

Clive was about to pick up his bags when Tobermory shouted something in Cape Dutch and a couple of Kaffre women came from one of the side doors of the "church" and carried them off. Tobermory followed them saying over his shoulder to Clive, "Come in and change out of those ridiculous togs."

When they met again outside, Clive was feeling much more comfortable in his tropical denim and bush shirt; Tobermory was carrying a couple of breech-loading Martini-Henrys, one of which he handed to Clive.

Cape Dutch was the language of the servants and farm workers, Tobermory explained as they set off toward the stables. It was better that way, he added. Teach them English and in no time they'd be reading the newspapers and getting thoroughly unsettled. "You'll soon pick it up," he added. "It's a bastard dialect of European Dutch. English people find it quite easy."

He turned back, facing the church. "See that tower?"

Clive turned too. Mrs. Tobermory had come out again. She was still watching him. "Yes?" he answered.

"It works here like the wind tower of an Arabian palace. Raise the trapdoor in the roof and the air just gushes up and out. Like a geyser of hot gas. Open any window or door and you've got a wonderful cooling draught, even with the fly screens."

The stables lay on the far side of the "kraal" – a maze of stone walls erected on a dusty, sunbaked stretch of mud just inland from the church. Beside the kraal was a small collection of mud rondavels with straw-thatched roofs; here lived Tobermory's Kaffres.

Apart from a few young lads, they all seemed to be women;

but of course, Clive realized, the men would be away, working somewhere about the farm. In this heat! He pitied them.

One skinny lad with tattered clothing and a crushed foot, ran lopsidedly ahead of them to the stables and began saddling the horses. As soon as the Kaffre womenfolk saw Tobermory they descended on him like a flock of crows, all shouting at the tops of their voices. It was a dispute of some kind among them and he was obviously expected to settle it.

The argument took a long time to unravel. Most of it was in Dutch though sometimes they fell back upon Xhosa for a particularly vitriolic expression. As a matter of course they included Clive in their pleading though it must have been plain he understood not a solitary word. Watching their faces he wondered if the fierceness of the sun had helped condition their languages. By forcing people to screw up their eyes it encouraged harsh and guttural sounds at the expense of smooth and rounded sibilance, the Germanic rather than the Romance.

Tobermory was as swift in his judgement as they had been long-winded. Clearly his decision was one of shattering unfairness, for all parties to the argument began to wail in unison their complaint. But he turned his back upon them and walked away. "That'll teach them," he said to Clive with a solemn, satisfied smile. "They won't hurry to elect *me* as judge again! Think I'm a bloody colonial civil servant!"

Clive looked at him in surprise. "Not exactly what we were told at Eton, what? British Justice ... position of trust, eh?"

Tobermory laughed. "Don't be such a bloody little prig!" Then he softened the rebuke. "Different if I was paid for it."

The tattered lad brought out their horses, two sturdy bush ponies, saddled with long stirrups. "Dankie, Piet," Tobermory said.

"Dankie, baas," he answered staring frankly at Clive. He had a sharp, acrid smell, quite unlike the unwashed smell of navvies and tramps in England.

They mounted. Clive felt uncomfortable with the long stirrups. "Keep an eye out for snakes," Tobermory said. "They drive the horses wild and you can be thrown before you know it. Not really horse country, this."

Clive nodded back toward the kraal. "Are they slaves?"

"Of course not. That's what the Great Trek was all about – freeing the slaves."

"How d'you pay them?"

"Mealies ... cloth ... tea, sugar, chewing tobacco – things you saw me buying yesterday in Gomorrah. Also they can work a bit of my land on their own account."

"Not money."

"Yusse yong – no! They drink enough as it is." He nodded a warning. "You'll shoot your foot off if you sling your rifle like that."

The land behind the kraal rose to a low outcrop of fragmented rock, hardly worth the dignity of the name "cliff." The horses picked their way surefootedly up the crumbling seaward face of it. When they reached the highest point Clive saw why Tobermory had brought them this way; the view northward stretched for miles and must have included most if not all of the farm. It was a featureless wilderness of bush, interrupted here and there by other rocky bluffs similar to the one on which they now stood.

"You weren't thinking of going to Kimberley?" Tobermory asked suddenly, out of the blue.

Clive looked blank. The name meant nothing to him.

"Kimberley!" Tobermory repeated. "Surely you've heard of it?"

Clive shook his head. "I don't really know the local geography. Before I came out here I just looked at the map and sort of picked somewhere vaguely middle-ish and on the coast. I didn't feel like going too far ..."

"Kimberley is hardly 'local'! Doesn't the name mean anything to you? It's been in all the papers?"

"Probably. I was rather preoccupied this summer, one way and another."

"Diamonds. They found diamonds there earlier this year. We've been expecting an absolute onslaught of every footloose ruffian and blackguard in the world." He sounded disappointed that it had not happened yet.

"It does ring a vague bell now you mention it."

"Well, we now know one thing – you certainly didn't come out here to make your fortune."

"Not really. Just to prove I could stand on my own."

"And to forget something?" Tobermory added shrewdly, making it only half a question.

Clive stared at him.

"It's no secret," the other went on. "Three-quarters of our immigrants aren't really coming *to* the Cape. In their heart of hearts they're coming *from* the old country. Or from something they left behind there."

"And you?" Clive asked, to deflect his line of inquiry.

"Oh I disgraced myself thoroughly." He laughed fulsomely. "If you've got any sense, young Mortimer, you'll see through me very quickly and move out. I'm a bad egg."

It occurred to Clive that, jocular and friendly though the fellow was, there lay no actual quality of friendship behind it all. Like many eccentrics, Tobermory was a cold fish. Perhaps it had been a mistake to accept his invitation?

They rode northward, into the noonday sun. Much of the lower part of the farm was cleared of the worst of the bush. The Kaffres did the hard work, Tobermory explained, Koetzie, his manager, did the cursing and swearing – and the worrying, too. What he himself did was not explained but Clive resisted the almost open challenge to inquire.

The field boundaries – one could not call them hedges – were composed of tree roots and cut thorn together with the larger stones that had been grubbed up from the field and manhandled, or mule-handled, to the edge. The whole place was still too primitive for luxuries like wire fences or planted hedgerows.

There was a stiff breeze off the sea, which kept them cool until they reached the uncleared areas inland. There, screened by the high scrub, yet exposed to the merciless sun, it was as if they had made a sudden leap a thousand miles closer to the equator. The aromas of baked succulents, aloes, and the hot soil was now overpowering. They combined on the dry air to bludgeon his senses.

Piping fingers of fire insinuated themselves into every crack of his clothing, up his trouser legs, in at his cuffs, down his collar. The light battered upon his eyelids making them tremble. His eyes were closed to the narrowest slits, causing his cheeks to ache from the constant strain.

"So you don't think of making your fortune in the diamond fields?" Tobermory inquired.

"It would defeat the purpose in a way. I mean, suppose I just walked across a field in England and made a lucky find, saw some ancient Saxon gold plate sticking up and then I dug around a bit and found a treasure hoard – what would that prove?"

"The folly of storing up earthly treasure? Yes, I see your point. You want to go into some sort of business here I suppose? Start in a small way, build it up, sell it when it's thriving. Prove you can do it. It would involve you in quite a bit of travel – 'going north,' as we say. You'd see a lot of the country. Meet a lot of people. I envy you. My wandering days are over."

Clive's horse did a smart sideways leap that almost unseated him. If he'd been riding with short English stirrups, it would have been a certain tumble. He glanced swiftly down as he righted himself, remembering Tobermory's warning and expecting to see a snake. But it was only a tortoise.

"They must look like moving stones to a horse," his companion said. "Most unnerving. What sort of business had you in mind?"

"Ideally one that would marry in with our business at home. Then I could hand it over to a manager and expand it when I return."

"You might stay here?"

"Oh there's no question of that, I'm afraid. I'm the only son, you see. I'd have to take over the family concerns."

"An only son!" Tobermory pounced on the revelation. "In that case, I'm surprised they let you come out here at all."

Clive laughed. "It wasn't easy. They wanted me to go to an uncle in Australia."

"I suppose you must have blotted your copybook in some way?"

"Dreadfully!" Clive laughed.

They entered a lush little valley, carpeted up the centre with tussocky green grass and fringed with heathers and a shrub that looked like berberis. Tobermory pointed it out. "Duinebessie," he said. "The berries make wonderful jam in the autumn. This valley's quite a watercourse for eight months of the year. I'm going to try to dam it this New Year. We could irrigate the whole farm. A few windmills and a couple of dozen miles of pipe. What about your business? Farm equipment and ironmongery? Anything to do with water and the management of water — you could hardly go wrong here. The city's desperately thirsty you know. It's really a ridiculous site to have chosen. No deep ocean water for the harbour, and no reliable freshwater supply for the town. They'll have to build an aqueduct soon. If not two or three. You might think of that. What's your family business?"

"Some sort of metalworking, I think."

"There you are then!"

Clive pulled a face. "I've never taken much notice of it, but I don't think pipes come into it. We do small copper tubes, but not big pipes. Pipes have seams or something. Or so I believe." At school he'd been ashamed of even that degree of knowledge; but here he began to feel an equal shame at his ignorance. To distract attention from it, and appear more businesslike than he had so far, he asked, "Anyway, can't pipes and things be made more cheaply here?"

"But of course not. All manufactures are far cheaper from England. If you have the inside rail with some English firm, you've a flying start on all the others. Think about it."

They reached the head of the little wet valley, where the water would normally spout from a cleft in the rock. Now it was a mere seepage, a hot green carpet on the stone. "That's one of the three fountains of Driefontein," Tobermory said. "We're still searching for the other two."

Clive dismounted and scooped up a handful of the water. He looked at his companion, who answered the unspoken inquiry, "A bit brackish but quite safe."

It was more than a bit brackish. Clive took only one mouthful and spat it out. It left a bitter aftertaste. The local animals must have given it a miss, too, for there was no spoor around the shallow pool. "Funny," he said. "We must have ridden miles yet the only animal we've seen is that one tortoise. And the birds, of course."

Tobermory smiled. "You don't think you'll be too busy?"

"I suppose it's more at dawn and dusk. Not midday."

"How much capital have you got?"

The bluntness of the question stung Clive into replying, "You mean how much have I got to lose!"

Tobermory roared with laughter. "I warned you – I'm a bad egg! Ask anyone."

CHAPTER FOURTEEN

THROUGHOUT JANUARY the heat grew worse, especially when the wind was northerly and blew down off hundreds of miles of parched Karroo. By way of compensation, Clive found he was acclimatizing so fast that his subjective feeling of roasting alive remained about the same. The idea that he should "sing for his supper" by hunting ferocious animals around Driefontein proved a fiction. There were no ferocious animals.

"But I'll swear I heard a lion roaring the night before we finally dropped anchor," he protested. Tobermory and his manager, Koetzie, merely laughed. Tobermory said it was more a problem in mathematics than in natural history – "how one and one makes one – or how one ox in pain plus one fertile imagination equals one extinct lion."

In fact, there wasn't a lion within a hundred miles; and very few rhino or elephant. Clive wondered why Tobermory had exaggerated so in his first account, but all the man would say was, "I thought you were a rich capitalist, yong. I was going to try and part you from your geld. Big-game hunting sounded the best attraction Driefontein had to offer."

Clive didn't believe him. "In that case why didn't you turn me out as soon as you found things were otherwise?"

He laughed. "Oh, we're a patient lot, we colonials."

Still, there were wild animals around – wild pigs for one,

and baboons, not to mention more than half a dozen kinds of antelope. And their numbers did need thinning. They could do heavy damage to standing crops. So he shot for his supper all right – and for everyone else's, too: hartebeest, eland, Cape grysbok, little duikers, steenbok, and the ubiquitous springbok. He shot far more than they could eat at once. Some of the surplus was cured in a smokehouse beside the kraal, fuelled with sneezewood chips. Clive noticed that for a day or so after his first session there the insects gave him wide berth, especially the fleas, which were otherwise the most dreadful torment. After that he took to hanging up his next pair of socks and a clean handkerchief in the smoke. The smoked socks stopped the fleas from jumping up on him, and the handkerchief, tied around his neck, kept the flying hordes away from his face and ears.

What meat they couldn't smoke was cut in strips, rolled in saltpetre, and hung in the sun to dry. When finished it was as hard as wood and, indeed, looked like thick twigs of streaky ebony. Koetzie called it biltong and claimed it was the finest delicacy in the world. You cut thin shavings of it with a pocketknife and sucked them for the strangely sweet-salty-fleshy taste and the leathery chewing.

For Clive the taste and texture held indefinable sexual overtones – like so many other things in this hot, dry, un-invigilated land. There was a violence about this sexuality that was novel to him, a pent-up force, an impatience. At home he had often watched a farmyard cock perch himself unsteadily upon a crouching hen for a brief flutter and a puzzled aftershake of the head, much as to say, "What was that?" But here the aggressive little bantam seemed more to rape the complaisant pullets that squatted for him in the dust. The brilliant sun flashed in his fierce eye as he pinned his victim's neck to the ground with his cruel little beak and asserted himself – every ten minutes. No doubts assailed that vicious, humourless little dictator. The whole harem-universe was created just for him.

And so with all the others, too. Dogs lay panting in the sun with bright pink carrots airing under their bellies. Five-legged ponies stood in the paddocks, gazing at nothing through hooded, stupefied eyes. Insects notched in pairs, and often in bizarre threesomes, struggling for release on the scorching clay. The whole spawning world trembled around him; and the heat oppressed it, bringing not liberty but obsession.

He alternated between trying not to remember Ann at all and then trying to burn her out of his memory by a surfeit of fantasy. It drove him to despair. His mind, his will, saw so clearly what had to be done. His body would not obey. His blind, unreachable flesh pined for her in stubborn purpose, never to be deflected. The enjoyment of her had become its right, as natural to it as air, as needful as drink. Her great, liquid eyes, her pale breasts, the sensitive skin over her hips – these were not *her* but an amputated part of him. Their phantom presence gave him no peace all those furnace-long days.

Yet relief of a kind came each evening, when he returned to the homestead all bloodstained and rank with the stink of buck. Then he would rush fully clothed into the broad, rocky lagoon that stood between the foreshore and the ocean, and that raging fever of the flesh was blissfully stilled.

No moment of his life could excel that evening plunge into the clear salt water. The low, slanting sun dappled an endlessly shifting net of light upon the white sandy bottom. In some curious way this light itself, playing through the shallows, gave the water special powers of rejuvenation. It teased away the dust and gore and cooled his blood. Then, revived once more, he would take off his clothes, one by one, and wash and wring each item clean, throwing it high up the beach beside his dry change of clothes. The lagoon was out of sight of the household.

From the beginning the children joined him. Tobermory's four youngsters and a horde of Kaffre infants. Their young black skin, much finer grained than his, would not wet so freely. They rose from the water and dried to rivulets almost at once. As soon as he had completed his laundry, the four or five of them who were big enough for playful roughhousing would gang up and splash him mercilessly every time his head showed above water. The game was for him to tolerate it as long as he could and then pretend to lose his temper and come at them like a lunatic paddlewheel, raising enough water to swamp a steamer. Then they would retreat in pretend terror, coughing salt and screaming moedie, which sounded like murder. But they would soon be back. The trouble with children, he decided, was they never knew when to stop. He had to retreat to the deeper part of the lagoon – and keep a watch for the little hammerhead sharks that sometimes got stranded this side of the rocks by the outgoing tide.

One day, after the children had gone home again, he lay in the limpid pool, floating on his back and treading just enough water to keep his feet buoyant. A little argument was going on inside his head; he listened to it with detached interest. Half of him said, "This is truly paradise. Why should you ever leave it?" The other half: "This is no way to prove you can stand on your own two feet in the world. What are you learning – except that you are an idle, sensual hedonist with no thought for tomorrow?"

The little octopus must have been drifting and daydreaming, too, for when the lapping water nudged them together the creature sprang to life in a sinewy, slimy flurry of all eight arms and shot away, leaving a cloud of sepia. The inkjet emerged with a kind of a whistle, which Clive, equally panicstricken, took to be an underwater scream. He threshed and battered his way ashore in a boiling of salt spray, not pausing, not looking up, until he arrived at his dry change of clothing – or the area of sand where he had left it.

The children had taken every last stitch. He gathered himself to vent a cry of rage and frustration when he noticed that their footprints led not directly back home but up into the dunes. In the corner of his eye he saw a movement on the skyline – the ducking of a head, he was sure. A flash of red, gilded by the evening sun. That made it Vera, the eldest of the little Tobermorys.

He grinned and, stooping low, ran at full pelt up the face of the dune, springing into the air at the top and leaping down the other side with a ferocious cry of "Gotcha!"

His clothes were there but no giggling band of children; only the soft whisper of the evening breeze and the distant call of a gull. And the snapping of a twig. He looked toward the source of the sound and was just in time to see the unmistakable black shape of Mrs. Tobermory, ramrod-straight, hurrying away among the dunes as fast as her coarse, heavy skirts permitted.

While he dressed, the thought of it made him grin. Ellen Tobermory, who rationed her smiles like desert raindrops, who was never lost for a prohibition backed by a biblical text, who even put frills around the legs of the piano ... Ellen Tobermory had been spying on him naked!

CHAPTER FIFTEEN

FROM CLIVE MORTIMER TO FREDDY OXLEY; MAY 1868:
I'm sitting on the side of a mountain gorge, high up on the western flank, overlooking the Great Karroo, which is a sort of vast semi-desert plain. Immediately beneath me, spread out like a toy, is the little town of Graaff Reinet, where I've been staying for the past two days. I came up here to watch the dawn and while I was waiting I fell to thinking of old times and the fun we used to have and how sober this workaday world is, and all at once I felt a great fear that if I did not write to you, if we lost touch with each other for all the time I shall be out here (three years? five? who knows?), then it would be for ever.

I could not bear that. When I think of England, I think more often of you and the times we enjoyed than I do of home or Eton or anything else. If, for the sake of all the memories we share, you can find it in yourself to overlook the deep hurt I did you, and let me know how things are with you and Mrs. O. (and the child?), then I shall be the most happy and least deserving of mortals. Perhaps not overlook, but set aside.

And how are things with me? Remember I said I chose the Cape Colony because our family knows no one here and I wished to prove myself alone? Well, who should I bump into on my first hour ashore but an Old Etonian! There is no escape from the past.

His name is Kelvin Tobermory and he's trying to clear a

large stretch of scrubland about ten miles west of Port Elizabeth. A bit of an eccentric – drives a cart drawn by two ostriches and lives in one of those reach-me-down cast-iron churches with boxlike rooms cobbled together inside.

He prides himself on being a great villain and hints that all he wants to do is to rob me – once I become rich enough. But he is certainly a most devious man (a strange accusation to make of one's host, but I shall leave him soon – and for that very reason). I stayed with him through the summer, which is our English winter, shooting buck and vermin for my keep and otherwise looking for a piece of land in P.E. where I might start a small enterprise. Tobermory gave me the idea, which is to import hydraulic equipment of all kinds, windmills, pumps, conduit pipes large and small, and corrugated sheeting for making little reservoirs or for catching the rain, which is seasonal but, when it comes, torrential. The river at the foot of this gorge, the Sunday River, is in spate now though for much of the year it is a sluggish trickle. The road (for which read dusty cart track) by which I came up to this hinterland, on a covered oxwaggon, if you please, is interlaced in many places with the smaller tributaries of this river, so that you may cross the same tributary five or six times in a day. I should have made this a new paragraph all about water so will do so now.

The land seems arid as you pass through it, full of spiky cactuses and succulents, especially aloes, which have a golden-red spike of flowers and a bitter-sweet nectar that is highly refreshing in the noonday heat. Also plantains, which look like massed bunches of tiny green bananas. There are, too, large ants, an inch long, with swollen white abdomens which you may pluck off and pop in your mouth. The taste is like chicken with vinegar. They say that between the aloe and this ant, and the prickly pear cactus in season, a man cannot starve in the Karroo.

All these plants and many more, thorns and gum trees, grow out of bare soil, dry and pinky-gray. There is no general carpet of grass or other herbs.

But I'm straying again. My point is to say that water is the key to this country. Control it and you control your destiny. Remain at its mercy and you live at the whim of Providence. Everywhere I've been, on farms and in the villages (which are pitiful huddles of corrugated-iron shacks and timber-frame bungalows set beneath Australian gum trees imported for the miserable shade they offer) the cry is the same: give us the means to get the water we lack, or to control the water we have. The litter of broken bottles and food jars is indescribable. The air is so dry they use these "towns" to treat consumptives. I should think the boredom achieves three-fourths of the cure.

In some places they will have to drill for their water and by a curious chance (is there some benevolent spirit appointed to look after me?) I met an American called Paul Eagles, who was passing through Graaff Reinet just yesterday. Three hours later and we should have missed each other. He is on his way to the new diamond field in Kimberley, where he hopes to sell rock cutting equipment for his firm in Pennsylvania. Of course, he wasn't half a day in the Karroo before he saw the potential there, too, and he was wondering how he could split himself in two, one part of him to sell drills for water down here to the farmers and the other to be in Griqualand, selling diamond drills to the miners.

The long and short of it is that I shall be his agent in P.E., through which he will import all his stock, and I shall also sell his percussion-drilling equipment to farmers and townships throughout the Cape. He says they make a toughened steel drill that will hammer its way through these clay-slate and sandstone beds "like a hot poker through butter."

He's the first American I ever met. All his conversation is exaggerated like that; picturesque, no doubt, but after a while you stop believing it, or even find yourself going to the other extreme. I am now firmly convinced that Lake Michigan is no larger than Windermere, that all Pittsburgh women are plain, and that the best thing about "'Murrikan cookin'" is the adjectives. However, if his steel drills are only one tenth as good as he claims, we shall still do amazing business here.

The sun is now quite high up over the horizon. I shall have to go soon before I bake to death. I wish you could see it all, it would take your breath away. I came up here in the dark because the twilights at dawn and dusk are so short I was afraid to miss it. The actual rising really was extraordinary. The Karroo is 3000ft above the sea, so the air is thin, and cold at nights. Despite the exertion of climbing I was glad of my long sheepskin coat I got in P.E. before I set out. (I look quite the colonial pioneer these days I may say.) Just in that short twilight before dawn I had a truly godlike feeling of looking down on the whole world. I could see the town, of course, and the wide, dusty streets. Also the farms and the clearances of the bush around them. Groves of cactus, flocks of sheep, small herds of springbok – I could see them all with a sort of gemlike clarity that made them not quite real. Or more than real, perhaps.

The profoundest silence reigned over everything, so that any sound that did arise seemed magnified hugely. I could swear I almost heard the sheep munching over five miles away. I certainly heard a dog barking well above two miles off. And the creaking of an oxwaggon and the rifle-crack of its driver's whip. The air was stretched and trembling, like an invisible skin. And it was *cold*. There is a kind of dew that forms in that dawn twilight, out of nothing. The whole land seems to break out in a cold sweat. And the sky is suddenly enormous. I admit to being homesick at times. One unexpected thing I miss is the stars, our old night sky. (Remember the observatory we built? Everything but the telescope!) The constellations are all different here.

But when I get back to England I know I'll pine for moments on the Karroo like this. Another thing I'll miss is the fruit. The melons, the oranges and grapefruit, mangoes, pawpaws, sponspek – things we never heard of. You can eat a different fruit every breakfast for a month, I'll swear. (Or you can if you're a guzzler like me.)

As for friends, I've made very few as yet. Tobermory, of course, insofar as it's possible for anyone to be friends with such an eccentric and inward person. And his wife, who is very straitlaced. But when I get back to P.E. in a month or so they say the social season will be in full swing and the D.C. throws a good ball or two. And as the only *respectable* O.E. in the district I'm promised I'll be in demand. So it will be off with the sheepskin coat and on with the lambskin gloves and the patent calfskin shoes.

Well, young 'un, if you'd rather we never met or corresponded again (which I should utterly understand), don't bother to reply to this and I'll trouble you no more. But otherwise I'll look forward to hearing from you some time before the spring (your autumn). You know there are a million questions I long to ask you, but if you intend to let this intercourse lapse, they would lie between us forever, like accusations.

My best wishes to Mrs. Oxley and good luck attend you both,

Yrs affec. – Clive

CHAPTER SIXTEEN

THE DISTRICT COMMISSIONER'S "Midsummer" Ball was the climax of the P.E. social season. The fact that it was held on the day of the local midwinter solstice was neither here nor there; the same day was the midsummer solstice back home; and "back home" was where most colonial administrators lived, in their minds. Reginald Langevin was no exception.

He was barely into his fifties but he already had one eye on his retirement to some Hampshire village, where he could lord it over creation in a grand colonial house. Not yet built, it would look four centuries old when it was. There would also be a little fishing lodge on some nearby chalkstream, and there, along its banks, he would net fat trout until he died. Meanwhile, there was a straggling empire to run.

He was a product of Rugby, the last of the old, unreformed school, before the revolution of Dr. Arnold. He did not like the new breed of colonial administrator, the next generation – earnest, dedicated young chaps from reformed Rugby and from the new schools built in its image, like Wellington and Marlborough. They had a vision of The Empire as the crowning of mankind's long, upward struggle from barbarism. One day, they believed, Pax Britannica would stretch from Greenwich round to Greenwich again and there would be universal justice, brotherhood, and harmony.

In Langevin's view this was an extraordinary belief, not least for its persistence in the face of every observable fact. To him and those of his generation the empire was an accident, a motley collection of countries England had acquired either to spite France or to frustrate Spain or to forestall Germany. All colonists were potential rebels. Most of them had had a rough time of it in England and wanted nothing more than to shake her dust off their boots and forget her as soon as possible. Imperial allegiance was something to which they drank a misty-eyed toast upon Christmas Day – and then steadily subverted during the rest of the year. It was all very well to furnish colonists with grants and every other kind of assistance; but what England really needed was a good barracks in every colonial town, good military roads or railways between them, and lots of red uniforms to fill both. Every colonist, whether he liked it or not, should have his day punctuated by the calls of the redcoat bugle or the whistle of the military train.

Time enough then for mystic dreams of universal brotherhood.

Langevin couldn't make out young Clive Mortimer. He'd seen him first at the Feathermarket Hall, whose backrooms formed a kind of unofficial gentlemen's club for the richer agents in the port. Clive was not in their league, yet, but the name of Mortimer was well known in the commercial world, so, even if he sold no more than a packet of tintacks a year, he could still hardly have been excluded; anyway, he was an O.E.

Clive found it convenient to drop in there of an evening for a mutton chop and a chinwag with the other agents. He could pick up news of what ships were due and where they were bound ... of whose business was shaky (and who ought therefore not to be given too long a credit) – and other gossip less immediately concerned with the survival and maintenance of trade.

Langevin could see at once that the young man was a cut above the ordinary agent. Several cuts above, in fact. So why was he in this backwater of a colony? He was hardly old enough for the usual black sheep, unless there was some monumental blot on the old escutcheon – and in that case news of it would certainly have reached here before now. Nor, on the other hand, was he your usual adventurer type, otherwise he'd surely be up at Kimberley making an overnight fortune.

Darker suspicions lingered. Was he a government man? The Colonial Office was constantly spying on its own officials out in the colonies. And notice how, within an hour of landing, he had met up with Tobermory, who was always rattling people's cupboards in the hope of shaking out the family skeleton. If you wanted to know the darker side of who's who and what's what out here, Tobermory was your man. What an age of bad faith ...

At that first meeting in the Feathermarket, Langevin and the enigmatic young Mortimer did no more than bow to one another. Although they had never met, they had, in the strange social custom of the day, been introduced, for Clive had called upon Mrs. Langevin "At Home," and that counted as an introduction to the husband. The second time they met, the Commissioner could hardly avoid speaking; nor, indeed, did he wish to. He wanted to get Clive to dine at the Residence, where Mrs. Langevin could interrogate him as only she knew how.

The meeting came about one morning on the Donkin, overlooking the town and the bay. Clive was at that time expecting the first shipload of pumps, water pipes, and iron sheeting from the Mortimer factories in England. Accompanying it he was also expecting to find a certain Mr. Robson who was coming out to manage the bookkeeping and warehousing, so that Clive could get on with doing what he was best at, namely selling. He had certainly "sold" the whole idea of this venture to his father, Sir Toby, who, delighted at his son's acumen and enterprise, was now arranging to invest substantial sums in this new colonial market.

The *Hyperion*, the ship carrying Mr. Robson and the first cargo, was overdue. True, it was only by a few days, but it made Clive nervous. When lunchtime came and still no vessel of her description was in sight, he climbed to the top of the town to scan the bay for himself.

Langevin was out there for his customary after-lunch stroll. There was a stone light tower at the western end of the Reserve and a fenced-off portion at the other end, where his wife and a number of other ladies were attempting to establish a formal flowerbed at the foot of a rather straggly jacaranda tree. Langevin's custom, except on court days, was to parade three times each way between these two points before retiring for his afternoon nap. On this day, when he turned and faced the light tower for the second time, he saw Clive leaning against it, steadying his spyglass against the stonework.

As he drew close he called out, "Floreat Etona, eh! A watched pot never boils you know."

Startled, Clive turned. "Oh! Good afternoon, sir."

"I see no ships, mm?"

Clive smiled. "I suppose it's ridiculous to be so impatient."

"Patience is an important virtue," Langevin said.

Close to, in bright daylight, he looked nowhere near his fifty-odd years. He had a full head of hair, still a bright coppery red. His face, in between the orange freckles, was an almost pasty white, despite years of colonial service; and his blue-green eyes were restlessly alert. Yet there was an unsmiling gravity about him that enabled him to say something like "Patience is an important virtue," as if it were a profound and mature judgement. Clive liked him at once. But then, Clive liked almost everyone at once.

"It's a shipment of windmills and pumps and water pipes and things. I could have sold it scores of times over by now."

"It's what England needs."

Clive looked at him in surprise, thinking he had perhaps said "England" absent-mindedly, meaning "this colony," or some such phrase. But not a bit of it. Langevin went on, "Get this confounded country pinned down under a burden of crops. Keep the blackguards busy. Out of mischief. The devil, you know, finds work for idle hands." Clive was still accommodating himself to this way of looking at the matter when Langevin added, "It's an amazingly fertile country, you realize, just for the want of a drop or two of rain. You'd be amazed at the lawn we've got, simply from careful reuse of our own bathwater. Waste not, want not. That's the watchword." He narrowed his eyes and nodded ferociously at the horizon, adding, "Yes, by George."

"These days, sir, it isn't the land that's crying out for

water, it's the diamond miners. The world's gone mad up in Kimberley."

Langevin raised his eyebrows politely but with little interest; Kimberley was far beyond his demesne.

Clive continued. "They need water to wash the gemstones out of the clay, you see. I'm sure if twenty ships, all laden to the gunwales with pipe and sheet, were to arrive today, I could sell every last ounce of it."

Langevin shook his head and yawned; his nap was already overdue. "All beyond me," he said. "Diamond fever. Pure avarice. Take my advice – money cannot buy happiness." He paused, as if a new thought had just struck him. His frank blue eyes pierced Clive as he said, "The love of money is the root of all evil." Then, with very little change of tone, "You're coming to the ball, of course?"

"I shall be honoured. I have already signified my gratitude to Mrs. Langevin."

The Commissioner seemed not to hear. "Seen anything of Tobermory lately?" he asked.

"Not for a day or two, sir."

"Rum fellow, what?"

Clive, unsure of his reply, merely nodded.

"Have to toddle along," the other said. And then, as if it were the merest afterthought, he added, "I hear you're moving into town?"

"I've already moved, sir. I'm more-or-less camping at my warehouse at the moment, but soon ..."

"Glad to hear it. You should never have gone out there."

"Just one portmanteau to collect."

Langevin darted him a strange look, almost as if he were trying to suggest that a portmanteau was an especially dangerous item to leave in Tobermory's care. "You just be jolly careful," he said vaguely.

Clive gave a bewildered laugh. "Of Tobermory?"

Langevin faced the sea again. After a silence he said, "It's an extraordinary world. People are extraordinary. There are those who shun power like the plague. They vanish upcountry to some sheep farm and they wouldn't even sit on a parish committee. Others guzzle it like gluttons. Can't get enough."

Clive was thinking that Tobermory fell into neither

category when the Commissioner went on: "And a few – a rare few, fortunately – hoard it as a miser hoards his gold. Such a man lives in apparent humility, seeming to be far from the centre of affairs, but he is the true baron, the hidden master of the ship of state. No one suspects his power – save those whose half-discovered secrets have rendered them his victims."

Clive was halfway down the hill before he realized he had indirectly been commanded to have as little as possible to do with Tobermory hereafter.

The same afternoon he begged a ride with a carter, out as far as Uman Gorge, from where it was but a few miles walk to Driefontein.

"I need my evening dress for the ball," he told Tobermory as he collected his portmanteau. "Are you going into town? Will you drive me back?"

"Aren't you taking one last swim? The youngsters will be disappointed." He went out to harness his ostriches. But before he'd even caught them, his wife, at the reins of a conventional pony and trap, came rumbling down from the stables. "I have to be going into P.E. myself," she said.

Clive looked at her uncertainly, and then at the gap in the thorns where Tobermory had just vanished in pursuit of his two birds.

"Get up then, I haven't all day," Mrs. Tobermory said sharply. She behaved as if she were furious at having to help him – as if she had been tricked into charity.

All the way to Uman Gorge she resisted his attempts at conversation, merely grunting in response to his overtures. But then, as they were approaching the village, she suddenly turned to him and said, quite brightly, "You'd like an orange. It's the new season. I'm gey fond o' them mysel'." And without waiting for a reply she halted the pony, threw him the reins, and went into the village store. Solemn little Chinese children, like miniature adults, came out to stare at him.

Why had she refused to speak to him until now? He had supposed it was because of her disapproval; now he had an intuition that she was simply shy. Perhaps she did not know how to while away the time in light conversation?

She emerged from the store with a whole pocket of oranges, which she handled as deftly as a feather pillow, throwing it into the bucket of the trap before he could spring down and help her. But he was in time to hand her back up. He expected her to ward off his touch but she accepted it without demur, even letting her hand linger a moment in his.

She handed him an orange and they set off again. Abstractedly, puzzled at the change in her, he peeled the fruit. The skin was paper-thin. She peeled her own orange and bit into the red-gold flesh. The tight sacs of juice burst in amber spray about her and left her lips flecked with carroty streaks. She smiled.

She was not pretty, nor was she any longer young. But there was a pure and urgent plainness about her that was suddenly appealing. A mile or so beyond the village she steered the cart off the track, over a patch of low shrubs, and into a dell of mesembryanthemum mingled with spekboom. A grove of acacias marked a former settlement, but ants and fungi were fast returning the scant remains of it to the soil. It was near the shore, too; a little way off he could hear the pounding of the surf.

"We will swim," she announced.

"No," he said, but she paid him no heed.

Leaving the pony tethered in the shade, she set off for the beach. Intrigued and curious, he followed. The path grew sandier as it wound downward, among the dunes. Marram grass and chunky green succulents straggled in clumps over the wind-winnowed gold. Not once did she turn to see if he was following.

As at Driefontein the surf was over half a mile away. But here was no broad lagoon; instead a narrow street of sand ran out between tall ramparts of smooth rock. The place was well chosen, being invisible to anyone not standing at the very rim of it.

She had shed her boots by the time he drew near. He flung himself down in the shade of an overhang and watched her, wondering if his appraisal would make her stop. But still she ignored him.

Twelve buttons released her dress, two pins her petticoats. Only her shift remained. She lifted it straight over her head and let it fall – no art, no coquetry. Her body, too, had no smalltalk.

Her skin sparkled like brilliant samite after the black of her dress. Her spare, lean flesh was laced with fine freckles. Her small breasts were the last of her youthfulness, the legacy of some impoverished Highland croft. She had probably never eaten well in her life – or never consistently. His own brand of leanness was of a different order, sleek and strong. Hers was that of the antelope, his of the carnivore.

Still without a glance at him she walked into the sea. When she was waist deep she launched herself and shrank to an auburn bullseye at the heart of an expanding target of ripples. He rose, undressed, and followed her.

Neither spoke. They stood, just within their depth in the tepid water, two breathing heads whose bodies were at liberty in a more primal element. He came almost at once, and almost without pleasure. In her disappointment she bit his shoulder hard. But then, realizing he had not gone limp, she dragged him gleefully to the shallows, to the firm, between-tides sand, and covered his nakedness with hers. He sensed that she wanted him to do nothing, as if he had bungled his turn and now it was hers. He was just to lie there and let her discover his body.

He closed his eyes and tried to remember Ann. But Ellen Tobermory would not allow those memories to return. She was too real – and, in a curious way, too experienced. She explored not the contours of his body but its sensations. She searched out its responses to each of her movements; she attuned herself to its very life. Thus, easily, she rose to some plateau of ecstasy such that every move he made caused her to moan and shiver and let out her breath like the sigh of a breeze in paradise. She helped ease him out of the shadows of his past.

They slept briefly, side by naked side. When he woke it was to find her lying half raised on one elbow, looking at him.

"Don't you feel guilty?" he asked.

She held forth an orange, as if guilt were hunger and the fruit could banish it.

He raised himself on one elbow, too, and accepted the fruit. He bit through the peel, sucked at it greedily, and then nodded skyward – "what about your God?"

"I'm damned these long years ago." It was not a joke, as one might say, "Oh – I'm a naughty girl!" She meant it.

"In that case, why are you always so prim and pious?"

"For the sake of the bairns, of course." She was surprised he needed telling.

His eyes moved restlessly over the fine, minutely wrinkled skin of her face, which seemed to be drawn inwards so that it modelled every facet of her bones. She was tense, as if she were holding her breath; and her eyes, for all their hint of amusement, flickered nervously, now holding his gaze, now flinching. How mercurial she was, he thought. Never still. The emotions darted across her face quicker than thought. The outer wings of her lips and the corners of her mouth twitched, suggesting laughter or hurt or tears or scorn, never settling. What would she have become if she had never been trapped in the black raiment of poverty and Calvinism?

Another Ann, perhaps? An hour earlier the question would have meant something, for Ann had been his only standard. Now it simply echoed in his mind, a parlour speculation. He reached out and caressed her breast, hoping to rouse her once more. But she laughed and, slipping beyond his reach, rose and began to dress herself with cool efficiency.

"How soon can we meet again?" he asked.

"Never."

"But you can't just use people like that!"

She laughed, not unkindly. "Wheesht, but you're gey young for such a fine lover!"

CHAPTER SEVENTEEN

THE MIDSUMMER BALL was a triumph. If ever the female principles of civilization put to rout the manly achievements of colonial squalor it was there in the Feathermarket on that night. It was more than a ball; it was an augury of a graceful future.

Port Elizabeth was already some half a century old – uncomfortably poised between the raw vitality of a pioneer town and the spacious garden city it might one day aspire to become. As yet there were no manufacturing trades. Of course, you could get a carpenter to shape you up some furniture, or a blacksmith to wreak you a pair of iron gates or a balcony; but there were no factories. The town was simply the entrepot to the northern, central, and eastern Colony – and for much of the trade that went up to Kimberley and the Boer republics beyond the Orange and the Vaal. It was a one-activity town, lacking all that richness of texture and character that comes from diversity.

For such a town to support any kind of a band, let alone one of the quality of the Port Elizabeth German Band, was therefore no mean triumph. Clive's opinion of it was canvassed a dozen times and his praise was greatly welcomed. Because of his background and schooling he was considered a great arbiter in these matters. And when he added that the Duchess of Devonshire herself would have been proud to hold her mid-season ball, just after Goodwood, in so fine a building as the Feathermarket, and to serve so splendid a buffet, he crowned the evening for the score of ladies who were chiefly responsible for the transformation.

True, there were some differences between this function and similar ones he might have attended at home. In England, for instance, young ladies at a subscription ball would wait demurely for their programmes to be filled; they did not, as here, hitch up their vast crinoline-gowns and go charging around from man to man, "scooping off the cream," as Tobermory put it, "before the other cats can get a lick."

"Oh I don't know," Clive said. "I rather approve of the system." He was on every list; Tobermory was on very few – but then Tobermory had come to watch and to listen, not to dance.

After yesterday's episode with Ellen Tobermory, Clive had imagined he would be unable to look his former host in the eye; but it proved not so. He supposed these last few months in the world of commerce, where you had to look interested when you were bored, or indifferent when your heart was racing with eagerness, had taught him the trick. He was surprised at his own deviousness.

It being the depth of winter, night had fallen early, making it the first midsummer ball he had ever known to begin by candlelight. It gave a gracious softness to everything and lent distance and mystery to small and familiar scenes. It also created enticing pools of darkness into which couples could waltz, kiss, and waltz out again with no apparent break in rhythm. Everyone was doing it. Such kisses meant nothing. Clive remembered one of his cousins, a Third Secretary in the British Embassy to the Hapsburg Court, telling him that in Vienna, if a young lady stayed talking with her partner between dances, the pair of them would have to announce their engagement before that evening was out or face scandal and total ostracism. Yet here the fastidiousness of genteel society mingled with the more robust ways of an earlier peasant folk – anyone could kiss anyone, practically in public. The varying rules of civilization were indeed extraordinary.

By ten that evening he had danced himself to exhaustion – or at least to that standstill between first and second wind. He begged himself out of the next set, which was a general round-robin dance and made for a lonely spot, near the door to the smoking room. He was almost there when he noticed Reginald Langevin beckoning him to join the Commissioner's party. It was a dull group, composed of senior army officers, a few foreign consuls (that is, town lawyers paid to represent France, Germany, America, and so on), and one or two leading traders. Clive was annoyed. He had already kissed two dozen girls and hoped to double the score by midnight. To stand swapping male commonplaces with people he met almost every day was not a step toward that ambition. But he saw no way out, so he joined them with all the good grace he could muster.

As he expected they were talking trade, politics, and native affairs – and, of course, Kimberley and its diamonds. "Apparently you can't walk a yard without falling over the bally things up there," one said. Another added, "They're sending out so many, the price will drop through the floor." Everyone nodded glumly. The colonel said that the miners would have to consolidate and regulate their output. The nods turned into wise-headed agreement. "Meanwhile," one of the lawyers pointed out, "a man who bought a handful of stones at market bottom would have done himself a good turn when the prices rose again."

Clive stored away the suggestion. More than half the Kimberley production came out through P.E. The few dozen people in this room had ringside seats on that market; no one in all the world would be better placed not only to judge when prices reached their floor but also to take immediate advantage of it.

Suddenly he laughed at himself. The events of this evening had stirred an earlier Clive from his slumber, the Clive of Eton and the London Season. That Clive, who expired only six months ago, would have been utterly incapable of harbouring such thoughts of market bottoms and trading advantage. He realized how greatly he had changed; yet how imperceptibly, too.

"Share the laughter," the army colonel commanded jocularly.

Clive, realizing that the truth would have been taken by half of them as a kind of rebuke, told the one about the magistrate trying a farmer for carnal knowledge of a cow. When the farmer described a particular way in which the cow had moved as he hung up his lantern, the magistrate leaned forward and eagerly corroborated him: "Yes – they always do that!"

The laughter turned half the faces in the hall toward them. But in all that sea of white Clive saw only one – the face of a girl he had not noticed before. She had not been there during the earlier dances or he surely would have seen her. That gorgeous spreading gown of white-and-lemon-striped silk alone would have ensured it.

She stared briefly at him and then returned her gaze and interest to her present partner, a woolbroker, married, with a house out in Walmer. Clive could not take his eyes away from her as she spun and glided slowly toward him. She was not strikingly beautiful, yet there was something intensely appealing about her. Long, dark, lustrous hair framed an oval face with a fine sharpness at the chin. Her cheekbones were wide, yet delicate. Turquoise bows at her neck and sleeves and ribbons of turquoise in her hair caught the colours of her eyes. Now they were large with laughter; yet when they had first transfixed him they had a seriousness that touched him far more deeply. Laughing eyes were a glutted market here tonight. Her lips were thin and finely drawn; in a different face they would have seemed pinched and even mean. Yet she was so vivacious that they borrowed life and laughter from her, and then repaid both.

As she passed, without a glance at him, he heard her say, "It was the mare I pitied. Why are they so beastly to their animals?" Her voice was richly contralto, somewhat breathless with her exertion.

Clive drifted away from the Commissioner's group. When the next round-robin began he joined in the men's circle and, by blatant deceleration before the music stopped, made sure he was opposite her. She smiled at him, the same bewitching smile she had given the woolbroker, and slipped into his arms – for a waltz so furious that all conversation was impossible. But – apart from the inconvenience of not being able to ask her name – he found he preferred it so. She danced like a dervish, laughing and shaking her long hair, and spinning like a teetotum. He had to grasp her wrists, Roman fashion, to stop her from flying among the other dancers and sending a score of them crashing to the ground. She slowed her pace, though, as they drew near to one of the recesses beyond the reach of the candlelight. Then the most extraordinary thing happened.

Until he entered that brief grotto with her, Clive fully intended to add her to his score of kisses. But it was perhaps that very thought – she would be a mere addition to his carefree tally – which held him back at the last moment. Suddenly he knew that if he was ever to kiss this young woman, he wanted it to be in quite different circumstances. To squander that moment here was suddenly unthinkable.

As soon as they were back in the light he regretted it, of course. He could sense the disappointment in her – more than disappointment. It was an affront. An outrage. He cursed his fastidiousness. He tried to steer her into another alcove but it was like pushing an iceberg. A bar or two before the waltz finished she broke from him and actually ran to rejoin the ladies' circle.

Disconsolately he dropped out and, being close to the Commissioner's party, rejoined them. Most of them had not even noticed his absence so brief had it been. Yet those few minutes had ruined the whole evening for him. He tried telling himself not to be so ridiculous. What was one misunderstanding with one woman when there were so many others waiting with his name on their cards? But it didn't work. That one nameless woman had become more important to him than all the rest.

A hand grasped his elbow and gave it a squeeze. He turned, but even before he saw who it was a voice said, with a sort of mammoth earnestness, "Faint heart never won fair lady."

The Commissioner, of course.

"I hoped no one noticed," Clive said.

The man cleared his throat. "Been meaning to say – you must come to dinner." There was a novel merriment in his eye – the one that wasn't lurking behind the oblique and trembling fold of an eyelid.

"I'd be honoured and delighted, sir," Clive said, with even less enthusiasm than he felt. At any other time he would have been appalled at his own ill manners, but now a sort of despairing recklessness filled him.

"Tomorrow night, eh? Just a quiet family supper. Leftovers, probably."

"So be it."

Langevin laughed. "It's not quite a death sentence, you know."

"I'm sorry, sir." Clive managed a little enthusiasm. The mention of food made him realize suddenly how ravenous he was. "I must get something inside me before I snap everyone's head off. Please excuse me?"

Langevin's hand wafted him toward the buffet. "Must look after the inner man. An army marches on its stomach, after all."

Among what the Commissioner would no doubt call the groaning boards, the first person Clive noticed was Tobermory, helping himself to some cold duck at one of the smaller side tables. He joined him. Tobermory looked him up and down. "From the almost vertical droop of your shoulders," he said, "from the fact that your head apparently weighs a ton, but above all from the tears streaming down your face, I'd say you've known happier moments."

Clive laughed. "You've been drinking."

"Is that what it's called?"

"And spying on me."

"On everyone. I'm not cut out for being a farmer you know. That's what I've decided tonight. If this *dorp* had a halfway decent newspaper, I'd write such an excoriating society column I'd start a new wave of emigration. You've no idea of the depravity going on here tonight." He sniffed judiciously. "It's the climate you know. By the way – what did you say to my wife? You're quite the star with her. She actually told me last night she was sorry to see you go."

Clive patted him heartily on the shoulder. "I didn't think she approved of me – or of any idle young gentleman whose ambition lies at the butt of a sporting rifle. But I was determined to make her like me before we parted."

"I wish I knew that trick." The man's eyes had a strange, cunning gleam. Did he suspect?

Clive squeezed his arm, even more heartily. "We talked about *you* of course, old boy." He laughed as if Ellen had spilled a whole budget of secrets.

Tobermory for once was at a loss. "You're a rum fellow, Mortimer," he said in ill-disguised annoyance. "What is the Commissioner's party talking about?"

"You'd never believe it!" Clive, pretending to be serious now, held forth the promise of scandal.

"What?" Tobermory was trapped into a rare eagerness.

"Native affairs ... legal matters ... trade ... and some woman called Kimberley who slides down through the market with diamonds on her bottom ... or perhaps I misheard." He could no longer hold back his laughter. Tobermory punched him.

A waiter replenished his champagne, a local vintage from Stellenbosch and very drinkable. "I'm invited to the D.C.'s for dinner tomorrow," Clive added.

"Leftovers from tonight."

"That's what the man himself promised. An army marches on its stomach, he told me."

"He has an enviable way with words," Tobermory said.

At that moment the young lady he had slighted came into the buffet room on the arm of one of the artillery subalterns, an A.D.C. to the Commissioner. Tobermory could hardly help noticing the change that came over Clive. At once his own mood altered. "Oh?" The word shot from bass to tenor; a sardonic eyebrow raised itself in mute accompaniment.

Clive swallowed. "Who is she?" he asked.

"Surely you know?"

"She's new in town."

"You're far newer! She was born in the colony, and her home has been in P.E. for the last ten years. She's just left school ..."

"But ..."

"... in Cape Town."

"Ah!"

"Haven't you danced with her yet?"

"I have, but it was too furious for conversation."

"Oh that filly would make a funeral march whizz."

Clive frowned. "Filly? Are you saying she has a reputation?"

Tobermory caught the edge of menace in the question. "Pray don't alarm yourself. Reputation, in that sense, doesn't mean the same thing out here. It's the climate, you know!" He cleared his throat. "Even the starchiest Scotch Calvinist can ..."

"Stick to the point." Clive was trying to control his anger.

"Goodness, I never saw so sudden a change in a fellow."

"Listen. Either you tell me what you meant, or you take back what you seem to be implying about her."

"Or ...?"

"Or I'll punch you in the head."

Tobermory laughed uproariously. "Good on you, young'un! You're only mortal after all. Well, to put you out of your misery, I'll let you into a secret. In fact, he says, dragging out his crystal ball and cross my palms with silver, I'd say it's beyond all doubt you'll be sitting down to dine with your lady of mysteries before another moon has risen."

The pugnacity went out of Clive. "Oh, Tobermory! Do be serious."

"I speak the simple truth. I dress it up a little but it remains the simple truth. The name you wish to know, the name of the Fair Charmer, the Captor of Your Heart and Captain of Your Soul ..."

"Tobermory!"

"I speak as her father might describe her."

Realization began to dawn on Clive. Tobermory saw it. "Yes," he said at last. "The young lady's name, the name you will whisper a million times to yourself twixt now and dawn, is Eleanor!"

"Langevin?" Clive hazarded.

"Eleanor Langevin."

Tobermory decided not to add that Eleanor Langevin was rumoured to be engaged to the young artillery subaltern who was at that moment handing her an ice and gazing deep into her eyes. The poor young fellow would find out soon enough.

CHAPTER EIGHTEEN

THE SHIP ARRIVED next day. In fact, half a dozen ships arrived next day, so competition for the port lighters was fierce. There was no deepwater anchorage inshore, and no breakwater, either. Ships could actually arrive, get caught in a storm, and have to put out to sea again until it blew over. Fortunately the day was calm and the lighters made good headway with the task of unloading and ferrying goods to the quayside. Even so, Clive could see they'd be at work all that night and all the following day beside. He really ought to stay in the port and supervise the unloading and transport of his shipment. In any other circumstances he'd have begged off his dinner at the Commissioner's, risking the social consequences, and done his duty; but his meeting with Eleanor had changed all that. Now it was unthinkable not to attend.

Anyway, what harm could come to the stock? None of it was perishable. Even if the boat sank, it was all recoverable. And Derek Robson, the storeman-bookkeeper from the home company, seemed a thoroughly competent young fellow, well able to supervise the carriage of the stock between the quay and the new warehouse, only a mile away to the west. After nearly three months afloat he was more than eager to begin. Clive showed him to his digs in town and then explained the dilemma – or, rather, glossed over the facts of it. "It's a confounded nuisance, I know," he said. "And a damnable imposition on you on your first day out here. But it's jolly important for the firm that we keep on the right side of the powers that be, especially the D.C. – so I really have no choice."

Robson was delighted to step into the breach. Clive set out for the Residence, light of heart. Despite all today's distractions he had not forgotten that Langevin had issued the invitation the very moment he had seen Clive's discomfiture with Eleanor; at the very least the father was batting on his side. The reason was not hard to guess, for, notwithstanding their enormous local power, colonial administrators are only modestly salaried; the only son of rich baronet would be a most eminent match, especially as in this case nature had already done nine-tenths of the matchmaking at first sight.

Unfortunately it was nine-tenths on one side and naught on the other. Eleanor's face fell the moment she saw him. She surely knew that a Clive Mortimer was dining with them, so this response could only mean that she had not even bothered to ask the name of the young fellow who had slighted her at the Feathermarket last night. She was polite, of course, but her manner was the coolest possible this side of outright rudeness.

She must have slept most of the day for she looked as fresh as a rose in spring. "Have you done much hunting upcountry, Mr. Mortimer?" she asked.

"Indeed, Miss Langevin," he told her. "And for the most elusive quarry of all. The cash in the farmer's pocket." Somehow his answer, which he intended to be jocular and a little self-deprecating, sounded like a reproach. He had hoped to imply, "I'm only a humble trader – I don't give myself airs." Instead it came out as if he were saying, "I'm far too serious-minded to play at hunting big game, don't you know."

"Mister Escalls is a great shot," she said with a frosty smile. Lieutenant Escalls was, of course, the young artillery subaltern, her father's A.D.C.

"It's his trade, I think," Clive said.

"Profession, actually."

"I did quite a bit of hunting at Christmas. All for the pot, of course."

"Why 'of course'? Do you not enjoy the sport of gentlemen?"

"Killing wild creatures for killing's sake? Frankly no."

"Ha, Eleanor dear!" her mother said. "I told you there are gentlemen in this world who share your opinions about the senseless slaughter of ..."

"Oh mama!" she broke in crossly. "I do wish you wouldn't remember things so. That was more than a year ago. I was just a silly little girl." Aware that she had not really recovered lost ground she added, "Anyway I was talking about grouse then. Not big game. Terence shot a hundred kudu last year. And warthogs and a rhino and all sorts of things."

"Wonderful the way he manages it," her father said quietly, "for one who's forced to live within his army pay."

She glared at him, and then at Clive, adding pointedly, "One does not have to be filthy with lucre to lead a good and useful life. And an enjoyable one."

Keeping an absolutely straight face Clive told her, "I'm sure you've heard it said, Miss Langevin, that the love of money is the root of all evil."

She was caught between annoyance and the unwilling laughter of surprise.

Langevin cleared his throat. Clive glanced at him briefly, but long enough to see him half-wink.

Clive now became aware of one of the uses of tiredness. Deep within himself he was miserable at Eleanor's hostility; yet his exhaustion overlaid it like a mild anaesthesia, reducing his tension and making him less vulnerable to her slights than he would ordinarily have been.

They dispensed with protocol to allow Clive to take Eleanor in to dinner. All through the meal Mrs. Langevin interrogated her young guest. There was nothing blatant about it, to be sure, but English ladies of the official classes have long ago perfected a technique that many a hard-bitten police investigator might envy.

To the untrained ear it would seem the lightest form of chitchat. It begins with some innocent remark like, "I do believe I may have met your parents during my last London Season. Do they by any chance go to Lady Angmering's ball?" Any ball will do, for the answer is either, "Yes," or, "No, but you would almost certainly have met them at Mrs. Wendover's."

In subsequent conversation other names will come up, giving the interrogator the required opening – as it might be: "The Latimers, you say! Are you related to them? I only ask because they are a cadet branch of my late father's family. Wouldn't it be amusing if we turned out to have them in common!" And again the answer is either, "Yes, indeed," or, "No, but we are related to the Chandos branch of the Duke of Buckingham's family. And on my paternal grandmother's side there were many generations of the squires of Pewsey."

In less than ten minutes Mrs. Langevin struck gold. It turned out that Clive's second cousin (his mother's first cousin on her father's side) was a half-brother-in-law to Langevin's paternal uncle. That is, the cousin's half-sister had married ... well, it doesn't matter – sufficient to say that the quest had reached one of its important goals: the establishment of a definite kinship (or a definite non-kinship) between the parties in play.

Thus, piece by piece, a most detailed picture is drawn out of the families, fortunes, lives, and prospects of all the players, even when they begin as utter strangers. Clive played the game with a straight bat – and face – knowing full well why he was being put through the routine. Tobermory was not the only one to suspect that he had blotted his copybook back home.

Eleanor knew the game, too, of course, and took advantage of its disguise to snipe whenever she could. "Pewsey! We visited there once, didn't we Papa. It rained all the time. You said it was the back of beyond, remember?" Or, "The iron-mongery trade must be *extremely* fascinating."

Over the dessert Mrs. Langevin turned toward Clive's experiences since his arrival in the colony. What did he think of Tobermory – was he a remittance man, and if so, in what way had he darkened the family escutcheon? Had Clive met Edgar Stanhope? Now he was definitely the family blacksheep. They paid him eight hundred a year to stay abroad. Clive finally satisfied her curiosity and explained why he had come to the Cape. It was another gloss of the actual truth: "From the moment I left Eton, Mrs. Langevin, I felt my life was about to move along preordained rails. Two or three years at Oxford, the Grand Tour or its modern equivalent, a rotten borough somewhere, perhaps, or a spell with the regiment ... and so on. A man could die without ever knowing who he truly is."

He looked straight at Eleanor as he spoke these final words; for once she had no quick reply.

"My idea in picking the Cape was that we had no relations here – or none that I knew of." He laughed. "Naturally, on my first day I ran into a fellow O.E.!"

"You're quite sure he *is* an O.E.?" Langevin asked suddenly. "You've looked him up?"

Clive shook his head.

"But I see from your face it's not the first time the question has occurred to you," Langevin pressed.

"It crossed my mind once or twice in the beginning, sir. But now? To be candid, I hardly think it matters."

"Out here you mean?" Eleanor said. "After all, what is our colony but a dull, unimportant little backwater!"

Clive shook his head vehemently. "Quite the reverse, Miss Langevin. In fact, this is the only place I know where one's family, one's inheritance – all that sort of thing – is seen in its proper perspective."

"They're still important," his hostess objected.

"But less so than what one *is* and what one does with one's life. A prince of the blood royal could come out here and make a hash of things, and no one would respect him for it. But a hedgetrimmer's son, by hard work, thrift, and flair, could become one of the pillars of society. I admire that, Miss Langevin."

Clive was not aware how similar his argument was to one she used against her mother whenever she harped on the lowly status of Lieutenant Escalls. All he saw was her annoyance – to hear it coming from him.

"Did you think like this before you left England?" her father asked.

"Not I! All I wanted was a bit of adventure. That fellow with my name who stepped ashore here six months ago would gladly have vanished upcountry and slaughtered big game for a couple of years." He pointedly avoided Eleanor's eyes. "I was actually proud of how little I knew about" – now he looked at her – "*ironmongery*. But now I'm ashamed at how much I've had to learn. I'm not ashamed, however, of the learning itself."

She understood very well that he was gently putting her in her place and telling her that her opinions about *trade* were callow and ill-informed. She glared at him. Her lips vanished; her nostrils flared. He found he was enjoying her anger. At least it was an improvement on cold indifference. He began to see her as a creature to be tamed; perhaps she was beginning to see him as a wild colt to be brought to hand. Well, either way it would be a new experience.

"Gracious, Mr. Mortimer," she said. "You're quite the revolutionary! You'll be defending the tumbrils and the guillotine before the night is out."

"It's good of you to think I'm in a condition to defend anything, Miss Langevin. For my own part I'll swear I never felt more defenceless."

"Hah!" her father said. "The quiet answer that turneth away wrath, what!"

There was a missionary glint in her eyes as she and her mother withdrew to let the men enjoy their port and a cigar.

"I won't hear a word against her," Langevin told Clive, "but since she took up with young Escalls, she's developed some peculiar notions."

"I know him only by sight, sir," Clive said.

"Capital fellow. Does his job well. Won't say a word against him, either. I don't know about you, Mortimer, but have you ever noticed that the world's greatest snobs and tufthunters are to be found not in the ranks of gentility but *just* below them."

"The ranks of genteelity."

"Very good! Must remember that. But exactly so! If you hear a man railing out against the queen, he's either an anarchist or a duke. But let him spout a panegyric of sycophantic drivel and you may place him at once. The ranks of genteelity! The port's with you, m'boy."

Clive passed the decanter. "I heard that there's some sort of unofficial engagement ...?"

Langevin shook his head.

Clive, with the anaesthetic of port added to that of his tiredness, heard himself saying, "In that case, sir, may I have your permission to call upon Miss Langevin at her convenience?" He held his breath and waited.

"*Her* convenience be damned!" the Commissioner barked. "You're one of the family, after all. Mother's half-cousin or whatever it was. Call when it suits you. And I'm delighted you ask."

From the speed and certainty of Langevin's reply Clive knew they must already have made inquiries as to his breeding and character. But in what context? It could hardly have been as a suitor to their daughter.

To show how informal their relations had become the Commissioner broke with etiquette and refilled Clive's glass. "What was Tobermory doing upcountry, d'you think?" he asked.

Clive smiled. "Your guess is probably better than mine, sir."

"The man's a scavenger. A social jackal. I'm so glad you've severed all connection with him."

It was a blunt command.

Clive softened its impact. "I often wonder, sir, how eccentrics first take up their eccentricities, don't you? I mean, when and how did old Tobermory first hitch a span of ostriches to his dogcart? And then – eccentrics are still only human. They must go on growing and developing, just like the rest of us. We grow into things and out of them. But it must be harder for an eccentric, because he's trapped by everyone else's expectations. I often wanted to ask Tobermory – what's going to happen when he's tired of living in a cast-iron church, and sick to death of riding behind a brace of ostrich?"

The Commissioner smiled. "If it's ever a choice, my boy, between a regiment and a rotten borough – pick the borough! There's an extraordinary delusion going about that politics is about policies! Well it ain't. It's about people. And you have a gift for people."

The rest of the evening passed unremarkably. Eleanor played some pianoforte pieces, most competently, though Clive suspected her slight woodenness of touch was deliberate, as if she were pointedly saying she'd parade no feelings for him. He turned the pages and gazed at her and fell more deeply in love at every moment.

"Have you got any sisters?" she asked him at one point.

"No," he said.

"Nor I brothers. Are you an only child?"

"Yes."

"And so am I."

What was she trying to establish? Or was she preparing the ground for some new argument? He had no idea; but by then he was really past caring. All he knew was that he loved her and would not rest nor give her peace until she responded to him.

He left shortly after eleven. Langevin made it clear that his invitation to drop by at any time was sincere.

A stiff breeze had sprung up and a bright moon shone among shoals of fleecy clouds. The air was rich with that succulent smell which lingers all along the Cape coast, even in the depth of winter – when, indeed, there may still be days with temperatures up in the nineties. Feeling more pleased with the world than he had any right to, he strolled across the Donkin and, leaning against the light tower, lit a cheroot. At once, as if all those pleasures were dowsed with the dying of his match, the old daily worries came flooding back. How had Robson fared with the unloading? How much was still left afloat? Would a storm blow up and send half his cargo back out to sea? How long would this consignment last? Dammit – he knew the answer to that one already: no time at all. Every bit of it was already sold.

He'd simply have to get more goods out here, as fast as the ships could bring them, or he'd miss the market. Suddenly he had an inspiration. The *Hyperion* was going on to India, wasn't she? Perhaps he could give her master a message to telegraph home from there? That would save six weeks on the time it would take a letter to get to Solihull. And if the company could work triple tides and telegraph back the main items of the next manifest in time for the master to bring it to P.E. on the homeward leg, he'd at least be able to plan and promise his sales for the whole spring.

He laughed aloud for joy. But his delight at having found the answer soon dimmed. It was so simple that only a rank amateur would have taken so long to see it. That's all he was and all he ever would be – a rank amateur. Still, did anyone else in town use this new line of communication via India? He had never heard of it. Some of his zest revived and he went home to his lodgings.

There the final surprise of the day awaited him; not the note from a now-slumbering Robson to say that all the goods were on the quayside, under guard, and half of them already in the warehouse – though that was welcome enough. One of the other ships had been carrying mail. Among several letters for him was one from Freddy Oxley. It read:

"No dout you took your time and thought hard before you put pen to paper and wrote to me. I shall now do the same. Ann is well and sends her best. The baby is dew any minute. By the time you get this it will be born. All her people say it's going to be a girl. They swing gold rings over her, tied with strands of her own hair, and claim to be able to tell the child's gendar from the circles it discribes: long and rod-like for a boy, round and hole-like for a girl. Who ever would have thought it!

    Yrs affec.
    Freddy."

Clive read the letter several times, seeking clues to all the things Freddy had *not* said. It was so opaque. Deliberately so? Or the accidental product of Freddy's uncertainty with the written word?

Perhaps Freddy wanted to keep in touch just to flaunt the child at him when it was born? Perhaps he needed an audience for that rise in the world which everyone predicted – and who better than Clive?

He disliked himself for these suspicions. If Freddy felt bitter ... well, why not? If Freddy wanted to take some small revenge before he renewed his friendship ... who would blame him?

CHAPTER NINETEEN

"BUT WHY?" her mother insisted. "Why do you reject him so ... so mindlessly – and come to that, what on earth do you see in young Escalls?"

"You'll never understand," Eleanor answered.

"Well it's not for want of trying, my darling."

"I've explained it a dozen times. What's the point of ..."

"You don't explain. You merely insist. It's like trying to ask a ..."

"It's just that you never listen," Eleanor complained. "You never let me get a word ..."

"He's penniless. He's not particularly handsome – at least, I don't think ..."

"You keep pointing out all these things that have nothing to do with it."

"He's an arrant snob."

"Just because he has fine feelings! You don't know him. If you only ..."

"Are you saying your father's no judge of character now? Hoity toity! I may remind you that your father's been judging men for the best part of ..."

"Oh mama, please please please! We've said all this a million times. I'm perfectly willing to talk about Terence, about *my* feelings, *my* judgement, *my* hopes. But all you want is to repeat ..."

"All we want, your father and I, is for you to be happy. And we don't believe ..."

"And you're a better judge of my happiness than me!"

"In this case, yes. You're blinded by ..."

"Well I'm not the only one let me tell you."

Mrs. Langevin bridled. "Meaning?"

"Let's talk about Mr. Clive Mortimer. About ..."

"Yes indeed! I would far rather talk about Mr. Clive ..."

"About being *blinded* by Mr. Clive Mortimer – which I most certainly am not."

"Oh dear."

"What do you know about him?"

"He's the son of a baronet, you can read ..."

"Now who's the snob!"

Her mother frowned crossly. "I don't mean it that way. I mean you can read up the whole family in Debrett and Burke."

"Can you read about which of them are scoundrels? Which of them beat their wives and children? Which of them are whited sepulchres and hypocrites? Oh yes – Burke and Debrett certainly tell a young girl *all* she wishes to know about ..."

"Don't be childish now. You ..."

"Conversation is impossible if you keep evading the point by calling me childish."

"Conversation is impossible if you keep deliberately provoking such a judgement."

Eleanor smiled sweetly. "Agreement at last!"

"What?"

"Conversation *is* impossible."

Her mother slumped. Speaking more to herself than to her daughter she said, "Perhaps we *are* at fault, your father and I. After all, Mr. Mortimer has never done us any harm – why should we be so eager to inflict you upon him, poor man?"

Eleanor added sharply, "I see the other half of the argument, too, mama: Terence is so odious to you that he thoroughly *deserves* me. Well, however you may arrive at your conclusion, I heartily like it. Will you break the news to papa that you have given your consent, or shall I?"

Her mother swept from the room. "You're a wicked, headstrong, thoroughly spoiled young miss."

Left alone, Eleanor lost all her ebullience. She paced the room disconsolately once or twice, almost rang for Tottie, her Indian maid, and finally sat herself down in the window seat. The house faced south, over the Donkin, so that all the bedrooms had a pleasantly shaded view of the green and of the Indian Ocean beyond. There were half a dozen vessels anchored a mile offshore and several more under full sail, farther out to sea.

A telescope lay on the ledge but she ignored it. Through it she used to be able to see Terence doing his gun drills at the battery on Baakens Kloof; but Terence was no longer there. Now that he was her father's A.D.C. she saw less of him than when he had been at the battery. She tried to picture him but could not. Only bits of him came clearly into her mind's eye – his moustache ... the gold buttons on his collar ... the bruised fingernail he was about to lose. How very romantic! she thought. She tried to rekindle in his absence those strong feelings he always aroused when he was there in person. They would not come. "Terence!" she whispered.

There was a sudden, alarming emptiness within her.

What had happened? On the night of the ball she had felt so certain about everything. Terence had been within an ace of proposing to her, she knew it. Only his nobility (the inner kind, not the kind you can buy and then parade in Burke's and Debrett, the true nobility of soul) only that had prevented him. He loved her too much to ask her to skimp and scrape on the meagre pay of an artillery subaltern. But soon he would get his captaincy, or his maiden aunt might die, and either way he'd be able to afford to ask her that sublime question. She tried to picture him asking it – his dark brown eyes, so full of devotion, begging her, miserable that she might when put to it say no. A thousand times that scene had passed through her mind; but now it sulked in the wings.

She saw that her hand had strayed to the telescope. Hastily she plucked it away. For if Terence was no longer visible on Baakens Kloof, the odious Mr. Mortimer, out at his ware-houses beyond the edge of town, was only too visible. What was it about him that made her hate him so? Certainly nothing to do with the insult he had heaped upon her at the ball.

She began to list all the things she disliked about him.

In the first place he was far too good-looking. A Greek god could hardly be more perfect. All the girls were just stupefied over him; and he affected not to notice. And that easy charm with which he treated all the world. And all the world, except her, was deceived into thinking it was his natural manner! Couldn't they see it was just a thin veneer, a mere varnish, painted onto him at Eton? All Etonians had it. They'd charm the foxes up into the trees. But it didn't mean anything. They exercised it so promiscuously that no one with their eyes open could be deceived by it.

And all this humble talk of standing on his own feet and finding out who he really was! He was only playing at it – why couldn't her parents see it? He pretended to scorn the idea of going into parliament or serving with a regiment, but when he got tired of playing the tradesman out here he'd go skulking back to England and take up that way of life with a relish. She'd risk her last penny that five years from now he'd either be trooping the colour at the Horse Guards or trooping through the division lobbies at Westminster – and no doubt he'd be telling amusing stories of his days among those quaint colonials in the Cape.

She seethed with so much anger that she didn't realize her hands had picked up the telescope and placed it to her eye, not to scan the ships on the horizon, not to raise it to Baakens Kloof, but to focus on those hideous new Mortimer warehouses and seek out the tall Adonis who owned them. She found him. He was standing a little apart from his natives, staring out to sea – no doubt thinking how wonderful he was. Old Etonians thought they had some divine right to rule the world. Her heart began to race and her breathing grew fierce. Her hand trembled. She could no longer hold her focus. Tears of fury misted her eyes.

How she loathed him!

CHAPTER TWENTY

As WINTER BRIGHTENED into spring no such warmth grew between Eleanor and Clive. She hoped he'd have to go up-country to sell his merchandise, but he claimed it was all sold long before it was landed; and true enough, the warehouse emptied again only days after that first shipment. Now, to fill in time and keep his boys, and that rather pleasant young Mr. Robson, busy, he was dabbling in a little woolbuying and feather broking. Also, through his connections with the American gentleman in Kimberley, he was handling uncut diamonds, too.

And he was so smug about it all. Whenever he came to dinner, which was far too often, the other traders and brokers teased him about how well he was doing. "You'll soon be buying up the whole town, yong," they said. And he'd pretend to be embarrassed. Yet he'd moved out of his diggings quickly enough and rented himself a smart new house at the eastern end of the Donkin, far too close to the Residence for her peace of mind.

She knew well enough what he was doing. It was quite transparent. He thought that if he appeared casually, en famille, often enough, and was kindly attentive to her, she'd grow used to him and begin to soften. Such foolish hopes!

The worst thing of all was the way he was quite obviously enjoying it. Somehow he'd discovered exactly the right things to say to infuriate her – remarks that, to anyone else, would sound most reasonable; and, as he usually made them in the presence of others, she could not show her anger for fear of seeming shrewish.

For instance, he knew how she felt about the promiscuous mingling of all classes out here. At home in England, if her father entertained tradesmen at all, they would naturally be wholesalers. (Not that one had anything against retailers; morally and in the sight of God they were as worthy as the next man. But, as Terence said, any retailer who had a smattering of finer feelings would be doocedly embarrassed at the whole business, while the rest would simply take advantage of the intimacy to pass off shoddy goods and poor service. Society would dissolve in anarchy and no one would know where they stood.) But Clive Mortimer seized every chance to praise the Colony for its "wonderful democracy" – something he intended to work for when he returned to England. It was maddening, especially coming from the son of a baronet. And, of course, he was always careful to ensure that some prominent Cape citizen was standing nearby, so she had to hold her tongue. How he loved to see her annoyance. Over those weeks he discovered a dozen similar ways to back her into this trap, where any argument would make her seem unreasonable. Just let him try it once more, she vowed, and she'd let him have both barrels.

But, almost as if he sensed that her anger was close to exploding, he suddenly ceased coming to the house, at least on informal occasions. And even on the formal ones, which as a now-prominent citizen he could hardly avoid, he would give her a distant smile, perhaps a stiff little bow, and go on talking or dancing with other guests – never with her.

When a person has suffered the racket of a hurdy-gurdy playing out in the street for what seems like hours, she prays for an end to the noise. But when at last it stops, instead of the wonderful relief she was sure she'd feel, she finds herself the victim of new doubts. "Will it soon begin again?" she wonders. "Or is the fellow merely pausing for refreshment?" Thus, playing or silent, the destroyer of her peace has taken over her life. She almost begins to wish he *would* begin again – the uncertainty being the worse half of the torment.

Thus Eleanor with Clive. To her amazement, she found herself actually wishing he would not ignore her. Even worse, she had to check herself several times in the very act of going over to him and starting a conversation on her own account.

The climax came at a private Hallowe'en ball held in the Residence. In one of the round-robin dances she ended up facing him. Even then he almost chose the lady to her left – and would have done so if it had not been Eleanor's habit to dance the circle with her arms spread wide, so that, quite accidentally, she appeared to have thrust both neighbouring ladies far from her. Equally accidentally she appeared to be holding wide her arms in welcome of Clive. Worst of all, dear Terence was only two away from them, but quite out of the running.

Clive saw he could not avoid choosing her. He did so with fair grace and danced halfway around the floor before he drew her to the edge of the throng. His movements were wooden, his voice quite flat. "I know just how distasteful this must be to you, Miss Langevin." He gave a wan little smile. "I won't inflict myself upon you any further. May I get you some cordial perhaps? I promise to make the errand last until the next round."

There is in all of us a little observer – perhaps a simplified model of ourselves – who lives an instant or two ahead of us, preparing our responses. If someone is telling an amusing tale, our little inner-self is getting us ready to laugh. And if we face an insult, that other self will prime our anger before the words are out. In short, we usually know what we're about to do because some part of our minds has already done it. Eleanor suddenly felt cut off from that essential other self. She had no idea what to say to Clive's – Mr. Mortimer's – gentlemanly offer. Or, rather, to his gentlemanly-*seeming* offer.

"Oh come," she stammered. "Come come, now." Her voice was fluttering like an ostrich plume; she hardly recognized it as hers. "We can surely be civilized?"

Again that sad smile of his. She wished he were not so good-looking; it confused the issue so. "Everything you say only increases my dislike of myself," he told her.

"But why?" She was so vehement several heads turned their way.

He saw it and suggested they should stroll out on the stoep for some fresh air. Her throat went dry. Of course, he wanted to get her out there in the dark and kiss her. What could she do? Shout out? She'd only be made a laughing stock. Her knees trembled; her heart began to pound. She let him lead her out into the dark. At the door she turned and saw Terence watching them in disquieted amazement, not to say anguish. She turned from him as in a dream and drifted out in Clive's wake.

It was a clear night with just a light zephyr of a breeze blowing down out of the north, warm and dry off the Karroo. The stars shone with a brilliance made doubly bright by the absence of any moon. The chirruping of crickets filled the air and made the night seem large. She waited for him to kiss her. She tried to prepare within herself the revulsion she knew she was going to feel; but that inner model of her soul was still asleep.

"I'm glad we have a chance to talk, Miss Langevin," he said. His voice was rock-steady, of course.

Sarcastic replies only half-occurred to her, none clear enough to utter.

"It would be futile to deny that I entertain the warmest feelings for you and have done ..." Dissatisfaction rose through his words. He faltered. "Hang it," he said. "I love you, Eleanor. I've loved you from the moment I saw you. But I know you entertain for me – I mean I know very well how much you hate me." He paused. "You do hate me, don't you?"

"Ye-es," she agreed. But somehow, though it was, of course, true, it didn't sound like it. Or not just in the way he put it. She also felt ... It was ... Well, he made it too simple.

"I knew it!" he sighed. "And by forcing my attentions upon you I've made your life a misery – and only caused you to hate me more."

She drew breath to protest but he hastened on. "Well, I brought you out here to assure you, once and for all, that I shall never importune you again. And that if you smile or make some neutrally pleasant remark to me in public, I promise I shan't take it as any kind of encouragement from you. In short, from now on we may safely observe the ordinary civilities of life in such a small community."

"Oh," she protested, "I begin to feel ..."

"No, please!" he interrupted once more. "Please don't find excuses for me – as I feel certain you are about to do. I know you – or I think I do. You are the kindest, sweetest soul who ever lived. You'd even try to pardon my behaviour, though we both know it was quite inexcusable. Please – let's agree it's all over and done with. Let's never talk about it again."

In her confusion she replied, "There is no human situation where all the fault is on one side ..."

"There you go!" he laughed. "Just as I said. I'm grateful to you for trying – but you don't know how dangerous it is, Miss Langevin."

"Dangerous?" The suggestion stirred her.

"Yes, you don't know how fragile my resolve is – how dreadfully *un*reformed I really am. Three kind words from your adorable lips ... one encouraging sparkle in your astonishing eyes ... and I might hurl myself at you and ... and ..."

"And? Yes?"

"So let's just leave things as we have now resolved them. Let's draw a veil over them and never mention them again. In any case," he went on in an altogether brisker tone, "I may not actually be here all that much longer, so even the physical temptation will be removed."

Physical temptation? She felt a certain panic. "But what can you mean?"

"No no. I oughtn't to have mentioned it."

"But you can't ... I mean ..."

"Well, if you promise to tell no one?" He gave a dry little laugh. "How extraordinary that of all the people in P.E., you should be the first to hear it! Still, it's fitting in a way, because I'm sure you'll also be the one who's most delighted by it. I fear I may shortly have to return to England."

For a long time she held her breath. She was savouring the good news. It *was* good news, she told herself. Then in a voice that sounded strangely remote she asked, "When?"

"You hide your delight beautifully. I'm grateful." He sighed. "Possibly within the next two or three months."

"But why? You've hardly been ..."

"Distressing family matters. My father is not well." He heard her draw breath to speak and added, "I didn't mean to say you'd be happy at the cause – only at the effect."

"Oh, Mr. Mortimer ..." She wished now she hadn't formerly been quite so antagonistic to him, it robbed her of proper access to ordinary sympathy.

He rescued her, though. "Please tell no one. There are reasons why I cannot yet announce it – commercial reasons, you understand." She heard the smile in his voice as he added, "My secret is in your hands. And isn't it strange – though I know just how odious you think me, I nevertheless feel utterly safe with you."

"It is strange," she agreed. A numb kind of calm now filled her. Her voice, freed from her thoughts, went on: "I feel safe with you, too."

He swallowed audibly. "In your case," he said, "as I explained, that is a delusion. Let's rejoin the dance, shall we. I'm glad we had this little chat."

"No wait," she said hastily, though she hardly knew why.

"We really must."

His hand touched her at the elbow. The silken pressure of his glove on the lace of hers was extraordinarily compelling; somehow it conferred a magical power on him. He began to guide her back to the lighted doorway. She did not want to go.

"Just one thing," she pleaded.

He paused. "What?"

"Something I must ask you. You remember the Midsummer Ball?"

"Till the day I die."

"You remember we danced together?"

"That's why I shall never ..."

"You know the alcoves down the side of the Feathermarket? You know why couples dance into them?"

"But of course I do. I must have kissed twenty girls that night."

"Well then ..." she began angrily.

He cut in quickly. "Look – we've already agreed to draw a veil over all that. It's over, past, finished, done with. Let's never mention it again. It'll only cause pain."

"Oh!" she shouted in her fury. "What do you know of pain? What do you know about forgetting?" And she turned from him and ran away along the stoep and in by the morning room and out into the hall and up the stairs to her bedroom, where she hurled herself upon the counterpane, buried her face in her pillow, and howled luxuriously.

Clive turned back toward the ballroom door. His smile vanished when he saw, framed against the candlelight beyond, the outline of Lieutenant Escalls.

"What did you say to her?" the subaltern asked furiously.

Clive, still lightheaded, was rash enough to answer, "That I love her. And always shall."

"You are a scoundrel, sir," the other replied.

Clive sighed. "Very well, Escalls. I suppose it had to come sooner or later. You say where."

The other peered out into the dark of the garden.

Clive ruled out the suggestion before it was made. "They'd stop us the moment we began. Besides, there's no light."

"All right – *you* say where."

"The moon'll be up in half an hour. Why don't we meet in an hour's time on the beach outside my warehouses. The sand's white and there'll be no one there."

Escalls bowed stiffly.

"I'll go now," Clive added. "Give it twenty minutes or so – no one must see us leaving together."

"Who'll be your second?"

"Don't be an ass! If you tell anyone, the whole crowd will turn out. This is a private matter of satisfaction between us. Do you want it to become the sport of the entire town?"

"But without a second it ceases to be an affair of honour."

"It never was 'an affair of honour.' We're just a pair of male baboons."

"You ... you scum!" Escalls was shivering with rage.

Clive was glad. The officer was the bigger and stronger by far; only the stupidity of rage could restore a little equality. Even then ...

CHAPTER TWENTY-ONE

THE SEA WAS SLICK AS PAINT; there was hardly any swell.

The forty minutes Clive waited on the beach seemed like several hours. How long did an officer need in order to change out of full dress undress? Clive himself had taken only moments to get out of his evening dress. Trust a military man to take his "one hour" literally. And sure enough, an hour to the very minute, the young subaltern came galloping up on his horse and leaped to the ground, more out of breath than his mount. "Queensberry rules?" he said.

"Modified," Clive agreed.

"In what way?"

"Well, three-minute rounds would be a bit stupid, wouldn't it – especially as we have no timekeeper. I say we fight till we drop, or one of us cries pax."

"Very well."

"Also I think it would be prudent if we avoided striking each other's faces ..."

"Frightened, eh?" Escalls began stripping himself to the waist.

Clive followed suit. Looking at the other man's bulging muscles, he was aware his suggestion must seem like cowardice. "Not a bit," he explained. "But I don't suppose either of us wants the town to know about this. The colonel is hardly likely to view it as an affair of honour, is he! To him it'll be a vulgar brawl over a woman who's worth a hundred of either of us – two white men letting the side down. It'd put your career back ten years. Then you'd never be able to marry her."

"By God, you arrant swine!" Escalls lashed out at him, a fierce blow to the ribs.

Clive, taken by surprise, fell backwards into the sand. A searing pain racked his ribs. "Supposed – to – shake – hands – first," he managed to say with winded breath.

"Buggered if I will. Come on – get up!" Escalls kicked sand at him. "You're going to wish you were never born."

The moment Clive stood he was met by another bare-knuckle jab, this time to his arm. The lack of pain surprised him; he was far more aware of his racing heart – and of a sudden, astonishing exaltation that hunted through his veins like blood on fire.

It did not cloud his judgement. That remained cool. He circled his man, watching for an opportunity, dodging several further blows – any one of which would have done the most fearful damage.

When his chance came his arm powered out like a snapping spring. His fist caught the subaltern at the base of his ribs and the recoil even knocked Clive himself back. Escalls was winded for a while; he lost the initiative. Clive got in with several more piledrivers. Escalls closed upon himself, defending his body with his arms and elbows, weaving, avoiding. He had probably expected his superior weight and strength to finish the fight in minutes.

Clive began to wonder whether, after all, he hadn't more stamina than his opponent. Perhaps his best strategy lay in trying to wear the man down. Don't try to turn the whole of the man's body black and blue, which was what Escalls was aiming for; just keep working away at one place until the fellow was in such pain he'd be forced to defend that spot. Low down one side, on the ribs, to unbalance him. And try to wear him out, too.

The realization that he was in there with a chance did wonders for Clive's spirit. He laughed aloud but it came out like the bark of a baboon. Escalls heard it and misunderstood, thinking that Clive was reviving the insult he'd made back at the dance. It reduced him to a fury that allowed Clive to begin his strategy of working away at one particular spot.

And so they sparred for twenty minutes or more, though it seemed like a lifetime. By no means did Clive have the fight his own way. He took a gruelling amount of punishment but not enough to disable him, though it was touch and go at times. Always the thought that he had the greater stamina came just in time to save him from that dreaded, involuntary cry of *pax*.

By then Escalls was clearly tiring.

The man's punching was growing wild, even a little desperate. The great shock to his pride had come in those early minutes, when Clive had sustained even his heaviest blows and come back fighting. Now, for the first time, Escalls began to realize that he just might not win; and that was when his desperation began.

The sweat was pouring down both of them. They were breathing like panting dogs and still neither could get enough air. Their lungs seemed on the point of bursting. Escalls knew he had to cool himself down, to revive his senses, which were beginning to deceive him.

But Clive was tiring, too. He no longer dodged his opponent's fists so nimbly, and, but for the other's tiredness, which robbed his punches of their proper strength, he would have fallen half a dozen times as the blows connected. They both felt roasted by the hot night air.

There was thus an unspoken agreement between them to transfer the fight to the shallow water along the edge of the sea. Steadily they circled each other, panting, occasionally lunging, rarely connecting, and always a step or two closer to the cooling water. When Clive reached it the sheer bliss of its touch was too much for him. Well, there was nothing in the rules, Queensberry or otherwise, to forbid a quick plunge between one punch and the next. He gave a roar of delight and threw himself toward the deeper water.

Escalls was a mere fraction of a second behind him. The revival it brought about was extraordinary. Moments earlier both had been at the end of their powers. The clean salt water, streaming through their hair, rippling over their exhausted muscles, restored them almost to their former vigour. In a little while they were standing back in the shallows and windmilling away with a desperation to finish it once and for all.

Of the two, Clive was the less desperate. At least he remembered his only possible winning tactic – to keep working at that one spot on Escalls' ribs. In the end it paid dividends. Escalls was in too much pain to risk staying close. He backed off and, blinking the water from his eyes – water that might just as easily be sweat as Indian Ocean – surveyed with astonishment this man who still refused to be knocked down.

In that last flurry they had both given their all. Each knew it of himself though neither could be sure of the other. In fact, there was not one good punch left between them. Clive lunged out, connected with nothing but air, and fell. Surprise caught Escalls off balance, and he fell, too. Like marionettes with their strings all cut, but with the faintest memory of movement magically lingering in their wooden limbs, they helped each other drunkenly to their feet.

Each staggered back a little, seeking to get the measure of his opponent. Escalls lashed out wildly. The punch was never going to connect. But his foot caught a stone, half embedded in the sand, and he tripped forward.

The top of his skull caught Clive on the jaw. He fell back, unconscious, and began drifting out into deeper water. Fortunately he was face up, and the cork soles to his boots kept his feet buoyant. Escalls staggered upright in a boiling of seafoam, determined to find his opponent and make one last attempt to finish him off.

At first he thought Clive must be under the water. The motionless body was not easily visible in the low, slanting moonlight. Then he saw it, no more than a couple of fathoms away. But what he saw beyond it made his guts curdle and his blood turn to ice. For a dozen yards beyond the apparently lifeless body, blue and gleaming in the silvery moon, was the unmistakable curved triangle of a shark's fin.

It was, as yet, swimming parallel to the shore, sniffing its way through the water, uncertain of its quarry, ready to turn and flee. It turned. But it did not flee. And the power of that

turn, the smooth swell of water it began to propagate, revealed
at once what folly it was for any man to remain there. Against
that ferocious creature, the strongest man on earth was helpless.
This was its element. Even in water no deeper than a man's knees
it was still invincible. As long as it had depth in which to turn on
one side, to oppose its jaws to its prey, those scimitar curves
with their myriad flesh-ripping teeth, it was the killer king.

"Mortimer!" Escalls shouted in horror.

Clive did not stir.

A remembered snippet of folklore crossed the subaltern's
mind. As long as you could see its fin, you were safe. It was
when the fin curled over sideways ...

The shark reached the other end of its sentinel leg. The
beats were getting shorter, the creature bolder.

For a shameful moment Escalls considered abandoning
Clive to his certain fate. After all, hadn't the swine deserved it?
Who would blame him? Who would even know?

He would know.

The rock that had tripped him was still at his feet, loosened
by his stumbling. It was his only possible weapon. He picked it
up and with a surge of energy that came from nowhere, waded
out until he could pluck at Clive's feet. The shark was now very
near. At any moment it would cease its parallel movements and
turn straight for the kill.

Clive slid by him, shorewards, like a waterlogged stump.
Escalls began to back toward the beach, nudging at Clive, first
with his buttocks, then, as they reached shallower water, with
the backs of his thighs. The shark, confused perhaps by the
absence of breakers into believing itself to be in deeper water
than it was, still held off its attack.

We're going to do it! Escalls allowed himself to think. But
at that moment Clive began to struggle back to consciousness –
and the shark made its lunge.

No one who has not actually seen these creatures at close
quarters can possibly imagine the sudden speeds they can
achieve, starting from nothing. Even the lieutenant, though it
was happening before his eyes, was incredulous. At one moment
the shark was several yards away, and a fraction of a second
later it was at his side. Only later did he remember that he had
actually seen its dreaded fin rolling over, away from him.

There was no time for thought. He lashed out blindly with the stone – and lost it. Something had touched his hand for there was a sharp, rasping pain there, followed by a wrench that seemed to tear out his arm at the roots. For a brief moment, until he checked, he believed that was what had happened. Then Clive gave a great shout behind him and leaped right out of the water.

He fell sidelong but Escalls had him up on his feet again in no time. "Shark!" he shouted. Clive understood at once and they raced for the shore in an explosion of water and spray. Moments later they hurled themselves on the welcome slopes of the sand.

The shark was nowhere to be seen.

Then, as they lay there panting in terminal exhaustion, there began a most extraordinary commotion, a little way out to sea, just beyond where they had been standing. The shark came bursting up through the surface like a marlin, thrashing the air with its tail as it writhed this way and that. It fell back in a boiling cauldron of white water. The reason was soon apparent. It broke the surface again and repeated its writhing. In that moment both men saw, with the clarity of a photograph, frozen in the bright moonlight, a large stone caught in the crescent of those wicked jaws.

In his desperation Escalls must have plunged the rock at the right position, and the right angle, and the right moment, for it to stick there. The miracle was even greater than that, for the stone itself must have been exactly the right size – neither too small to fall out once wedged, nor too large to enter in the first place. The monstrous driving force of the shark's body had forced it in; then those hundreds of razor-sharp teeth, curved to grip even in death, had done the rest. The beast was now in its own death throes.

Several times more it broke the surface, always writhing, seeking the counter-miracle that would shake out the obstruction, never succeeding. When the waters were still and slick once more, both men gave a valedictory sigh.

"Who won?" Clive asked.

"We did," Escalls replied. Then, after a pause, he added, "We haven't solved anything, have we."

"Did you suppose we would?" Clive let the sand trickle

through his fingers. The narrowness of his escape was just beginning to dawn upon him. "I owe you ..." he began.

But the lieutenant cut him short. "Stow it!"

"... owe you an apology at least. I didn't mean what I said, about baboons and so on. It's just that I realized my only hope was to make you lose your temper."

Escalls rubbed his ribs tenderly. "Oh yes – you kept your head all right!"

"I do love her, you know."

"If you say it ... then of course I must believe you."

"All's fair in love and war. That's what they say."

"It's what her father says."

Just at that moment they heard a horseman trotting by on the highway. The lieutenant's mare whinnied. The rider stopped and then turned seaward, making directly for them.

It was the colonel. Both men scrambled to their feet and stood shamefacedly before him.

"Escalls?" he asked as he reined in. "Good Lord yes. And you, young Mortimer! Ye gods – you haven't been swimming? Don't you know this shore is infested with sharks? You might both have been killed!"

CHAPTER TWENTY-TWO

THE YEAR 1870 was the half-centenary of the landing of some five thousand English settlers at Algoa Bay, in what had then been the sparsely populated eastern fringe of the Cape. The main celebration of the anniversary had naturally been in March, the month of the landings. But there was still plenty of celebratory steam left when winter turned to spring and the days improved. So a Saturday in late October, a month with all the connotations of "Maytime" in the northern hemisphere, was picked for a great outdoor Half-Centenary Braaivleis. The site chosen was the high open ground at the northern edge of the town, a space reserved, one day, for a gracious park.

A week or more had passed since the fight between Clive and Escalls. There was rumour aplenty, prompted by the tender way both men walked and sat; but the colonel refused to believe any of it – hadn't he met the pair of them, chatting away together on the very night they were supposed to have been brawling? His private opinion was that they had rashly gone for a dip and had a lucky escape from a shark; perhaps its rough skin had scraped them a bit. Even the "harmless" basking shark could rasp away a half-inch of flesh in a single unlucky graze. That would explain their tenderness; and the shame of such folly, behaving like newly landed rednecks, would account for their reticence.

The inconclusive end to their duel left the two men dissatisfied, though there was no longer any substantive contention between them. In fact, they were both a little ashamed of their behaviour.

It so happened that the highlight of the braaivleis day was the Governor-General's Cup – a point-to-point gallop over a different course near the town each year. As last year's winner Escalls would be automatically entered. Clive, being a passable horseman, now entered himself and, though not a word was said, it came to be understood between them that this affair would settle whatever matters of honour the shark's interruption had left up in the air.

Saturday came, bright and cloudless; it was going to be a roaster. On Friday every cook in town had spent the afternoon cutting away the tender fat from thousands of mutton chops, then dicing it in cubes and leaving it to marinade overnight in curry sauce – a trick learned from the Malays whom the Dutch had brought to the Cape. Early next day the soused cubes were speared on long acacia twigs, whose yellow sapwood added a mellow, spicy flavour to the curry. Some Africander wag had dubbed the result "societies," because they were "lumps of white fat sitting there in rows, doing nothing useful – like Meetings of the Society of Friends!" Quaker missionaries were unpopular among the colonists, English and Dutch alike, because they always seemed to take the side of the native. So the joke had stuck. And basketloads of "societies" – and, naturally, the chops from which they were cut – went up to the braaivleis grounds above the town.

Meanwhile the "boys," as tame native men were called, had dug out the braaivleis pits and loaded them with pine chips and small logs. The fires were roaring away by the time the people began to arrive. When the flames died to a glow, just before lunch, it would be time to rack the societies over them to spit and crackle and brown and go crisp. Later still, when the pits held no more than glowing ash, flavoured now with burned-off fat and traces of curry, it would be time to throw in the chops and rake the embers over them, leaving them to seal themselves and cook into that uniquely succulent dish – the braaivleis mutton chop. Meanwhile, there was a carnival to enjoy.

Port Elizabeth, the most English of colonial towns (which, considering its origins, is hardly a surprise), offered a most English sort of festival. There was hoop-la and bowling for a pig. There were skittles and darts, coconut shies and giant shove-ha'penny boards with wooden disks instead of half-pennies. The police and soldiers took turns to stick their heads through the Aunt Sally while ragamuffins and friends hurled balls of rags (and the occasional soggy orange) at them. Delicately gloved hands were plunged into tubs of bran for the Lucky Dip. The new patent ice-cream machine was a failure. In short, except for the fact that all the work was done by smiling natives and all the pleasure taken by hot and uncomfortably overdressed Europeans, all was exactly as it might have been around any village green during a heat wave back home. There the proceeds might have been for a five-hundred-year-old church steeple; here it was for an orphanage whose buildings were younger than many of its charges.

By lunchtime a merciful breeze had sprung up off the sea and everyone was congratulating everyone else on having chosen the site best suited to take advantage of it. They retired beneath parasols and awnings and prepared to wrestle the crisp-grilled societies off their twigs.

Clive arrived late, having spent hours grooming and lungeing his horse. There were points for appearance and turnout as well as for the actual racing; he didn't want Escalls to have all the advantage of his military grooms. He joined the Langevin party. It was the first time he had seen Eleanor since the night of "the duel." He could tell at once that she had heard rumours of it. She was in conversation with the colonel but several times she looked his way and smiled – not the cool sort of smile he would expect if she were merely taking up his offer of a truce, but a questioning smile that said, "don't go away – I want a word." In the end the colonel turned round to see the cause of all this signalling, saw it, and at once wafted her in Clive's general direction.

"Good morning, Miss Langevin," he got in first. "May I say I never saw you looking more lovely."

"You too," she answered with a smile that knocked him sideways.

"Oh I have to if I hope to win the cup. With me it's sheer hard work. But you can't help ..."

She interrupted the compliment. "Ah yes. I hear you and Mr. Escalls are neck-and-neck favourites."

It wasn't true. Escalls was odds-on; he was less than evens.

"He has the advantage of his uniform," Clive said. "And the grooms." He smiled. "But I have a plan."

"So have I." She laughed but would not explain.

The judges were supposed to handicap the military contestants to allow for the fact that no civilian could compete on level terms, but even so Escalls came out a clear five points ahead. That was equal to half a minute of time allowance on the point-to-point – a hefty lead on a course barely six miles long.

Clive was adjudged fourth, which gave him a quarter-minute lead. So he was there with a chance.

He knew the course quite well, having walked his horse over it several times in the past two days. As he waited for the off, he ran over it again in his mind. It followed a rough figure of eight through scrub country on the edge of the town. The first leg ran north, appropriately enough past the new orphanage in whose aid the event was staged; then it curved to the west, downhill through a recently planted pinewood. At the bottom of the slope was the crossing point of the figure eight – a tricky river leap into a wild valley. The course crossed the valley and led up for a brief run along the tree-shaded avenues of Walmer, the town's new suburb. Then, curving round to the east, it returned to the bush, downhill again to rejoin the valley higher up the watercourse. From there it was down the winding valley all the way until the last half mile. This was by far the hardest part – rough, boulder-strewn ground set among steep krantzes, or bluffs of stone. Toward the end the bush grew so thick it was impossible for one horseman to pass out another.

To make matters worse, the valley here branched into three. One wandered away to the west, eventually becoming "Happy Valley" – as he had named the site of his warehouse. The middle one emerged near the centre of the town, defining the western flank of the hill on which the Donkin stood.

The third valley, the easternmost one and much the smallest of the three, formed the last half-mile of the race course. Even then it was no straight gallop. It began with a mighty leap over a fallen tree and led via a rough uphill scramble to the site of the carnival and the finishing post. Clive knew it would need a much better horseman than himself to overtake a strong rider like Escalls on that last stretch.

"It's a four-mile race," he said to the lieutenant as they waited.

"Six, surely?"

"Not really. It's hard to overtake on that final stretch, and impossible in that thick bush down the end of the valley."

Escalls brightened even further. "I suppose you're right, egad."

"Don't smile too soon or I'll wipe it off your face," Clive promised. "I have a *plan!*"

He hadn't, of course, but he saw no harm in sowing the seeds of doubt.

At last Escalls was let go. Clive fretted while the seconds of the handicap ticked away. By the time he got the off, the lieutenant was out of sight beyond the dust of two other horses.

CHAPTER TWENTY-THREE

"GOOD LUCK!" The Commissioner's parting cry still rang in his ears. Escalls was far out of sight; he must have sped like the wind.

Yet Tickey, Clive's own mount was no carthorse. Its breeding was nothing special but it had intelligence. From the start it seemed to know this was no ordinary ride. When Clive tried to keep it under tight control, it pulled at his hands and shook its head – as if to show it, too, understood the importance of winning. An agreement thus sprang up between them that if Clive gave it its head and kept his hands only for the important moments and his spurs only for the especial encouragement, Tickey, for his part, would run as fast and direct a course as he could.

Clive was well down through the young pinewood before he caught his first glimpse of Escalls, who was just taking the water jump. He cut a tight corner after it and made straight for the uphill road to Walmer. The man could certainly ride.

Clive looked at the distance that separated them and he knew it was impossible; but when he reached the jump and felt that leaping charge of muscle beneath him, eager, excited, and yet controlled, an unreasonable hope filled him. Moments later he passed out the first of the two intervening riders.

He overtook the second one among the treeshaded avenues of Walmer. Now there was only Escalls to beat. Those leafy lanes, coupled with that commanding lead, must have lulled Escall's mare into slackening her pace. How many times must she have trotted out here on some pleasant social call? Clive, timing the difference between the moment when Escalls passed beneath the last tree and out into the blinding sun again and the moment when he himself emerged from that same shade, calculated he had regained about half the handicap. Escalls

174

realized it too when he looked behind and saw that Clive had come up from fourth to second.

"You're losing!" Clive yelled.

Escalls gave a war whoop, spurring his mare to widen the gap once more. He couldn't do that too often, Clive thought contentedly.

They plunged into the low scrub of the valley. It was here, before the thick, thorny bush began, that he had to make up those remaining seconds.

To his surprise, Tickey veered suddenly to the right, almost unseating him. This course would take them up the valleyside and, since the curve here was all to the right, make a shorter path, perhaps by several hundred yards. But it would be at the expense of a stiffish climb at the beginning and a steep descent at the end. He decided not to risk it.

But just as he was about to check the creature and force it to a more orthodox path, he realized Tickey was a better tactician than he, for only such a desperate measure would serve. Now he gave his own version of a war whoop and the horse responded; he was sure it understood.

Throughout the race he had stood in the saddle, except for the dozen or so strides when he gathered Tickey for the water jump. It was tiring, of course, to stand like a jockey for so long, but now it was paying off in the speed and freshness it allowed the horse to preserve.

Escalls, sitting in a deep military posture, more suitable for loping fifty miles over the veldt, saw what his rivals were at and began to ply the whip – much too early. Clive realized that the officer's enthusiasm was in fact his weakest point. He remembered how, just before their fight, Escalls had let himself be provoked into losing his temper – and it had cost him the easy victory he would otherwise have had.

And now exactly the same was happening here. All Escalls really needed to do, thanks to that huge lead, was to run a well-paced race, squandering a little of his advantage, perhaps, to keep his mare fresh for the final sprint. If he simply concentrated on making no mistakes, he could hardly lose. Instead, at the sight of Clive's desperate gamble – which must have looked like the threatened "plan" – he let himself be panicked into making a punishing spurt a couple of miles or more from home.

Clive crossed the Walmer road at the hillcrest, to the astonishment of one or two stragglers. The race now seemed to him distinctly winnable.

But his euphoria evaporated when they reached that part of the curve where their descent had to begin. It looked like the drop into hell. Yet it could not be avoided. They were on the right flank of the valley; the small gorge that defined the last half-mile, was on the far side, and almost a mile away. As Tickey set course gamely for that plunging descent, Clive sat deep into the saddle, lay back, and gripped for dear life with his knees and calves.

Down they went in a shower of loose rock and dust. The horse was amazing; he would swear it was loving every minute of this descending dance with death. There were times when they seemed to hang out over nothing, but they always landed, shoulder deep it often seemed, in soft sand, through which Tickey almost swam to firmer ground. Amazingly they reached the valley bottom without a tumble or a scrape.

Clive, standing in the stirrups once more, risked a glance over his shoulder. Escalls was now about five seconds behind – and his mare was showing that wild-eyed eagerness of a plucky mount near the end of her endurance.

As he plunged into the bush he knew he had won. The immediate temptation was to do what Escalls had done – pile on the pressure and confirm his lead; but he resisted it and concentrated on steering a clean path among the bush. Now he sat down again and helped Tickey to execute the almost ballet-like movements of dressage, steering its flanks and hindquarters clear of those wicked kaffre-thorns, some of which were twelve inches long.

They emerged from the bush without mishap. Now only the fallen tree lay ahead. He could not even hear Escalls behind him.

Tickey knew the country well – knew they were back near the starting place. So fierce was its eagerness to get home that Clive had to sit deep and squeeze hard to keep it gathered. Its hooves thundered on the dry ground as it pranced toward the log in that curious galloping-on-the-spot movement by which a horse stores up energy for the impossible leap.

Because of this check the length was perfect. He saw it two

strides out, rose in the stirrups, transferring the grip to his knees and getting his weight well forward. He was unbalanced for everything but the jump.

At that moment there was a flurry of colour to his immediate left. Something sprang out from behind a bush and there was a cry of "Haaaa!" – and the thwack of a stick. The horse checked, throwing Clive forward over its neck; then, seeing it was committed to the jump, it gave one almighty leap, twice as powerful as it need have been if it had come one stride earlier, and cleared the fallen tree.

If his right foot had not left its stirrup Clive might yet have cleared the jump, too. Instead he was hurtled shoulder-first into the log. The pain was frightful. The confusion of his senses was worse. The sky turned black; the ground went blinding white; he heard a roaring all round him; there was a sharp, acrid smell of ... of what? The smell of pain.

When normal sensation began to return, he was aware he was staggering around to the left of the track, some twenty paces from the tree. Tickey, he saw, was halfway up the gorge in a cloud of dust, leader if not winner.

Escalls broke free of the cover. He took in the scene at once but was professional enough not to check before the jump. He turned off immediately he had landed. "You all right?" he called as he rode up.

Clive waved at him to go on. "No bones broken. You take it. You win. Well done!"

The lieutenant saluted him and cantered off up the valley. A good winner. Clive grudged him nothing.

He was just picking his way around the end of the trunk, when he saw a movement among the dead branches. "You!" he said. It was Eleanor.

She rose, brushing herself. Her summer dress of pale green taffeta with yellow flowers was grimed with dust. "Sorry!" she said anxiously. "I didn't think *that* would happen. Are you all right?"

"All right? What d'you mean by it?"

"You're not hurt?"

"You mean you did it deliberately?"

Her lips trembled with an answer but then she turned and ran.

"Why?" he shouted after her.

When she was a good fifty yards away she turned again and called out, "I wanted you to lose."

"Come back here!"

She continued climbing.

Another horseman broke from the bush. "All right?" he called.

"Fine!" Clive waved him on. "You're now second. Good luck!"

He turned to follow Eleanor. The rider wouldn't have seen her.

In fact, the path she had taken was the most sensible way for anyone on foot to go up. If he tried following the gorge and the thick of the field came galloping through, nowhere would be safe.

Even so, the way was far from easy; he wondered how on earth Eleanor managed it in her skirts; but, just inside the entrance to a short kloof – a funnel of steeply sloping grass and almost sheer rockface – he passed the abandoned hoops of her crinoline. She was already halfway up the grassy slope.

"Stop!" he cried.

She heard his anger, looked wildly around, and then flung herself at the rock face, scrabbling for the smallest toe-hold.

He had never been so angry in his life. He suddenly saw what a terrible thing she had done. To come down there, deliberately, in order to spoil his race just when he had it in his grasp ... he seethed with fury. How could he ever have loved someone so spiteful?

He called out to her again. She heard the passion in his voice and scrabbled wildly at the steepest part of the kloof. He followed her – to what purpose, he did not know. He was too angry to work it out. Strangling would be a kindness.

Yet, behind his fury, he could also feel a streak of elation. To some primitive part of him this was even better than the race. It was real. Here was real quarry, fleeing from him, screaming, looking around with terror in her eyes. He tasted the pure joy of the hunter.

Her panic carried her farther up that sheer face than cool skill could ever have achieved; but it could not carry her to the top, which lay tantalizingly just beyond her grasp.

"I'll kill you!" he shouted. "You stupid, henbrained ... moron!"

"Go away! Go 'way!" She kicked at him, sending a shower of sharp-edged sherds straight into his face. They cut him. He began to bleed. She was appalled.

He wiped the blood from his eyes and stared at his hands. Then he looked up at her in disbelief. "By God I'll get you now!" he shouted.

"Oh Mr. Mortimer ... Clive!" she tried to appeal to him.

But he was past that now; he was almost past human speech. He leaped at her and grasped her by the ankle. She kicked out wildly but missed. It made her lose her balance. She screamed. Her fingernails tore on the rock as she sought new holds. Then she fell upon him, knocking him to the ground.

He rose at once. His teeth were bared in a snarl, as if he were about to tear at her with them. In blind panic she began to lash out at him with her fists, at his face, at his arms and chest. "I hate you! I hate you!" she yelled.

Unwittingly she had picked the three words most likely to restore him to his humanity. He saw his blood on her fists and was horrified. He grabbed at her wrists, still furious, but no longer out of control. Her left arm he caught easily enough, but her right flailed at him several more times, restoring some of his bruises to prime condition, before he trapped it.

During those last moments of her freedom she became aware that the heat of his fury had subsided. It calmed her terror, too – so much so that her shouting turned to a wild, breathless laughter, close to hysterics.

When he had both hands trapped she was too winded to voice a sound. In that wordless pause their eyes met. They were both still panting wildly. For a long moment they were locked thus; more of their calm returned.

Suddenly the indecision was over. It dawned on him that he could kiss her. He let her hands go. She clenched her fists in defence and stiffened. She watched him like a cat, but did not back away. He raised his hands to her face. All at once she relaxed and closed her eyes. When his lips touched hers they parted – and then everything was forgotten.

Those months of her dislike ... those sharp, cruel words

... her humiliation of him ... her folly here today – all melted to oblivion in the sweetness of that kiss.

When at last they broke apart she laid her head beside his and murmured, "Oh Clive – why was I such a fool?"

"I was the fool, darling. We should have done this months ago, that very first dance."

"I'm exhausted. Let's lie down." Without waiting for him she laid herself in the grass. Her hoopless skirt hid little of the form of her legs. When he hesitated, she held up her arms. "Come on!"

"They'll miss us. They'll come looking for us."

"Not here. Come on."

He lay beside her, careful inches away. But she shifted until they were touching. "Why didn't you?" she asked. "That night in the Feathermarket?"

"I already told you?"

"When?"

He shifted his weight, bringing his head above hers. Their eyes were too close for clear focus. "I said I'd already kissed two dozen girls that evening. It meant nothing. I didn't want you to ..."

She closed her eyes. Tears brimmed there. "Oh Clive!" At last she understood.

"I wanted it to be different. I thought ..."

She shook her head violently from side to side. "I don't want to hear! I don't want to hear!" He halted her with another kiss.

When she was calm again she said, "You *knew*. Even then."

He nodded. "I don't understand how. But I did. From the moment I saw you I knew I would never want anyone else."

"I suppose I was the same. Just the sight of you had such an effect on me ..."

"But you didn't even look at me."

"I didn't dare. I didn't want to. Everything was settled with Terence – in my own mind, anyway. I didn't want it upset."

"Well ... it's all behind us now. It's all forgotten."

"And you're not sorry about the race?"

"What race?"

"Kiss me again. Tell me again."

"I love you," he said, and kissed her. He said it over and over, kissing her every way he knew.

She put a finger between them. Her eyes were large as she said, "Let's marry soon? I hate the idea of a long engagement. Everyone looking at us. It's like belonging and yet not belonging." She shivered. "We do belong to each other, don't we, Clive? We already belong?"

He felt the tentative offer in the words she did not speak. He wanted her. But she was worth a thousand of Ann – and a million of Ellen Tobermory. He wanted her for always. He enfolded her even more tightly in his arms. "You are so precious," he murmured. "You're all the world to me. I want you to be my wife."

She lay happily in his arms. He ran his fingers through her hair. He shaded her eyes from the bright sky, to see them go large again.

"I suppose we'll be married in England?" she said.

"Oh, I didn't have a chance to tell you. I have a letter from home. My father has rallied. I'm to stay out here and build up the largest business possible."

Later, she put her hoops back in and they went down to the river to wash away the blood before making their way up to the carnival. She said, "There is one thing I must ask you."

"Anything!" he promised, as lovers rashly do.

"Can you tell me now why you came out here?"

"To find you, of course."

She smiled but waited patiently for the truth.

"Why shouldn't I have come out here?" he protested. "It's not for life."

"You're being evasive, Clive." She kissed him to soften the accusation.

He sighed. "I cannot answer as frankly as I would wish. The honour of another is involved. Indeed, the honour of two other people." He paused. "Actually, I mean three."

She scolded him. "Don't beat about the bush so, darling. Out with it! You mean the honour of the regiment."

They laughed.

"I can promise you this, though," he told her. "I have done foolish things – things I regret. Which of us has not? But in the end, honour was saved. Nothing dishonourable remains. Nothing that might rise and shame you, should you ever consent to be my wife."

"Consent?" She laid her head on one side and gazed at him fondly. "Doubt that the sun may rise but doubt not that!"

"I'm probably being absurdly over-sensitive," he answered solemnly, "but just once or twice these last few months I've had a fleeting ..."

"Oh!" She ran at him and stopped his words with a kiss. "You *know* that wasn't me. You know I'm not like that."

"Why then?"

She became serious. "D'you think I haven't asked myself that? I don't know. You threatened me. You're the only man who could come near ... I mean you'd just break through all ... oh dear! I know I shall regret telling you this, but if you want me as your slave, my darling, you already have your wish."

"It's the other way about," he told her.

"We're well matched then."

PART THREE:

A BROKEN WING IN TUSCANY

CHAPTER TWENTY-FOUR

MR. WATT, Provisions and General Stores, eyed the woman speculatively – not for the first time. He'd sized her up the moment she first entered his shop, some weeks ago – name of Mrs. Oxley, not long married, not a lot of money but the husband in his first salaried job, nice and steady, and good for a lifetime if they stayed. He wanted to offer her the facility of a weekly account. Women like her always had a shilling or two to spare each week – for ribbons and gloves and things. A weekly account, as his father had told him, was a grand device for diverting some of that spare cash "our way."

Yet something about this woman prompted him to caution. She always came with a list, yet she purchased on a whim, eyeing the shelves, asking for this or that as her glance happened to fall upon it. And then, when the bill was totted up, she'd gasp and tell him to take one or two things back – or, rather, to "put them aside till next time."

Today it was a packet of "unclaimed babies" – tiny sugared jellies of vaguely human outline.

"A treat for the little boy, was it?" Mr. Watt asked her.

She nodded.

"Well ... can't go disappointing the young fellow, can we. Pay me tomorrow."

"Oh, all right," she said, and pushed the packet back among her other purchases.

Mr. Watt didn't like it. Her acceptance was altogether too casual; best to put it on a formal footing. "Or tell you what," he said, "why not open a weekly account, Mrs. Oxley?"

"Would it cost more?" she asked.

"Not a penny. And we furnish you with an itemized bill each Friday – so half your housekeeping is done for you."

"All right," Ann said brightly. "I'm all in favour of that!"

It was a thrill to see the unfamiliar directions beside her name: Mrs. F. Oxley, 14 Tatton Row, Stockton. Their first proper home. You couldn't count the wretched two rooms they'd had in North Shields, between the gasworks and the railway. But Tatton Row was quite respectable; every house had an inside lavatory. True, they were a mere three streets away from some very poor quarters, but you could live there all your life and not know of their existence, unless you took the short cut to the shops. Tatton Row was also three streets away from Albert Villas, where just about everyone had their own locked pews in church.

"Will this be all for today, Mrs. Oxley?" the shopkeeper asked.

"I'll just have a look round."

He beamed. "Take your time. No hurry. We're only here to serve."

The shop was an Aladdin's cave. At the back there was stationery – everything from sealing wax to quill cutters. Out in the yard you could see drums of creosote and coal oil, and tins of paint, and rolls of bird netting. Back indoors, all along one side, was ranged a selection of servants' and workmen's clothing. From the rafters hung rubber boots and hams and coils of wire. The whole front of the shop was for grocery – flour, sugarloaves, tea, butter, rashers, ginger beer ... wherever you looked there was something to make your mouth water. The remaining side held household goods, from mops and pails to stagsheads of plaster and exquisite little doylies pressed out of paper in imitation of lace. And tucked here and there between these obvious divisions were cabinets of patent medicines, shelves of garden seed packets, jars of humbugs and boiled sweets, racks of briar pipes and snuff and tobacco ... every time you turned you saw something you had missed the time before.

Ann selected some nasturtium seeds and asked for the entire delivery to be sent round before five.

"We'll do our best," Mr. Watt promised.

She paused, toying with the idea of saying something more peremptory. Then she smiled and said, "I would be most grateful if you did manage it before five." She had noticed that among the ladies who had called on Mrs. Wilde in the old days (and how long ago they now seemed) the more ladylike they were, the more polite they had been, as well.

She had caught the right tone it seemed, for Mr. Watt now said, "You may depend upon it, madam."

Pleased with herself she walked the long way back, even though the day was raw. When she arrived at Tatton Row, she walked extra slowly to number 14, savouring its elegance and solidity every step of the way. True, it was no wider than the other houses in the terrace; it had the same moulded classical pediments as they; the same painted glass over the fanlight; yet there was something indefinably special about it to her, right down to the brass knocker on the door. ("Pressed brass, weighted up with lead," Frederick had said scornfully. "Don't polish it too hard, love!")

Indoors she told Emmy, the maid, to light a fire.

"Ooh, what'll the master say?" the girl objected.

"Just get on and light it."

Surely Frederick couldn't object on such a cold day as this? She went straight through to the kitchen to prepare their supper. She wouldn't call it "dinner" until they could afford a cook. Only then would she feel like the lady of the sort of house where people took "dinner" of an evening – when she could limit her household chores to the management of the linen and the sewing on of buttons.

Young Lawrence, who was reading a picture book by the kitchen range, came running to hug her. His head was just up to her waist now. "I'm hungry," he pleaded.

"You shouldn't read in the gloom there. You'll hurt your eyes. You should get Emmy to light the lamp."

"Daddy said not."

"I'll talk to him about it. You mustn't damage your eyes."

"Can I have some toast and dripping?"

"You'll spoil your supper. Go on with you!"

"Please, pleeeease …"

"Oh – have one of these. Now you've spoiled Saturday's treat. I was going to save them." She gave him an unclaimed baby. He managed to steal one more before he fled, screaming and giggling, from her deliberately misaimed hand.

She took one of the little jellies herself. Unclaimed babies! Who thought up such names? The soft, rubbery feel of it between her fingers reminded her of the quinine-jelly lozenges she put into herself for stopping real babies. She felt awful every time she did it, for she longed to have another, a brother or sister for Lawrence – who was so easy to spoil. But they couldn't afford one just yet; there'd be no rich grandparents to pay the rearing of a genuine Oxley child.

She wondered how often Clive thought of her and the boy. Not often to judge by his behaviour. He never wrote them a word, except for a rare P.S. in his mother's letters to Frederick: "My regards to you, Mrs. O. and the boy." He'd been back in the country over a year now, him and his new Lady Mortimer – a year and more since old Sir Toby died and he had to come hurrying home. You'd think, if he was really interested in the boy, he'd have found some excuse to visit them. His work as a member of parliament couldn't take up all his time. It hurt her that he hadn't visited. They had meant so much to each other once. Frederick was the most wonderful young man in the world and she wouldn't even *think* a thing against him. But he wasn't Clive. What men and women did in bed was only a tiny part of life; she knew that. But Clive had been ... well, there'd never be another like him. Not in her life.

And together they had made Lawrence. Surely that meant something to him? But he never came to visit. And all he ever wrote was "my regards to Mrs. O. and the boy." Men were so busy getting on with things, they didn't know how they could hurt a person by their neglect.

His mother, the dowager, was different entirely. She wrote every month. It was through her that Frederick had got this present job at the laboratory, which was really quite a feather in his cap and much better than any of the other scholars from the college had got. Mind you, Frederick had been far and away the best of them. He'd done four years' studying in just twelve months. She had never believed anyone could have such determination. How he kept so bright and healthy she still did not know. He had the stamina of ten when it came to that sort of work. But it had almost killed *her*, for the more he sacrificed of his time and energy, the more she felt she ought to contribute, too – by keeping Lawrence quiet (that was where the habit of spoiling him had started, of course), and by skimping and saving to make their allowance stretch to the books he needed and the candles he burned.

"Why not just tell Lady Newcommon we could do with a shilling or two more?" she used to ask. "She'd never miss it, and she's always saying to let her know if there's anything you truly need."

But Frederick never would. "One day," he said with relish, "we'll be rich enough for me to make a little parcel of all the money she's given us – plus all the interest – and give every last penny back to her. And who knows – fortunes can change in this world – maybe in her old age *I'll* be giving *her* a pension!"

He meant it, too. He was even going to return the money for Lawrence, to sever that side of the boy's lineage – as if paternity could be bought. Frederick had always been ambitious, of course, but now that it was coupled with this compulsion to outdo the Mortimers it had consumed him. Any man of spirit would want to repay a debt, but with Frederick it was more than that, it was almost an act of revenge. Sometimes she wondered how he'd feel about it if he ever got the power. Would it stop there?

These thoughts were interrupted by the delivery boy with her groceries. When he left, she got on with preparing the dinner. She did not notice young Lawrence sneaking back for another raid on the sweet packet until his hand came over the edge of the table and into her field of view.

Her response was automatic. She slapped him, leaving floury fingermarks on his cheek, bars of white beneath his wide, shocked eyes.

He burst into tears. But she was unrelenting. "I'll do that every time you steal!" she promised. "It's *not* funny!"

The front door opened and closed; Frederick was home. Lawrence cried even louder, preventing Ann from overhearing the conversation between her husband and Emmy. But when he came into the kitchen she knew by his face it had been about the fire in the parlour.

"Quiet!" he commanded.

Lawrence stopped in surprise. Usually Daddy was good for a hug and a ride to the moon to stop a good cry. Ann smiled. "The voice of his master! How were things at the office?"

Freddy passed his hand across his brow, as if he were sweating. "A fire?" he asked.

"I want to play bezique with you this evening, dear, and I don't want to freeze."

He smiled patiently. "There's no fear of that. If we could afford a thermometer, I could prove it to you."

"Well I feel cold. It is cold. Don't I get a kiss?"

His kiss was not so much cold as abstracted. "It isn't an office, by the way, it's a laboratory."

"When I call it that around here you should see the looks I get!"

While she finished preparing the meal, he went upstairs to the attic bedroom in which the cook would one day sleep – when they could afford her. Meanwhile he studied his chemistry there. His diploma from the college was not enough. Now he wanted an external degree of the University of London. The room was fireless, of course, even in the depths of winter. She wished she had his tolerance for discomfort and misery – but then she wished a lot of things.

The kitchen became a nursery, Emmy turned into Nanny. She fed Lawrence and herself, bathed him in the little zinc bath that hung inside the lavatory, above the door, and put him to bed. Then the kitchen became the dining room and Emmy had the evening off until eleven.

Ann and Freddy ate at eight. Tonight she had cooked him his favourite beefsteak and kidney pudding, which restored his humour; he must also have had a successful evening with the "aliphatics and aromatics," as he called it. Ann used to tell Lawrence bedtime stories about his two favourite heroes, Ali Phatick and 'Arry Mattick; she took all the names from Frederick's chemistry. They played bezique for the remaining hour of the evening. She tried to let him win because he was unbearable when he lost; but she needn't have worried because he won anyway. At last he yawned and stretched and said tomorrow soon wouldn't be another day.

She was staring into the coals. He looked at her and fell in love with her all over again, as he did every day of his life. The soft light on her skin ... those baffled but adorable eyes! If only she knew what power she could have over him – but he was careful never to show it. Ann needed a tight rein or she'd go to pieces. It wasn't that she was extravagant or wild; she'd simply go to pieces ... she'd cease to organize properly and everything would just drift along its own course.

In the race of Life they had started so far behind and with so many disadvantages they could not afford to drift one day. Nor to waste one penny. Ann had to prepare herself to manage a big household and lots of money – and lots of servants to lose it, mismanage it, embezzle it; she above all could not afford to drift.

"There's something about a fire," she murmured. "Not only the warmth. It's the life it has."

"A fire does no harm from time to time," he conceded. "One day we'll be rich enough to have fires in every room at midsummer if we want. You'll see."

"One day we'll be old."

"Old people need fires, too, dear. Even more than us. We're at the age where we can do without. There's old people in this town can't afford them at any time – but if you were to go back in their lives, ten to one you'd find they were the lads who boozed their wages or the lasses who bought fancy cottons."

She wanted to find a kindly way of telling him not to make a sermon of everything. She understood his point well enough. It was just that he never seemed to feel the rush of time – while she was the opposite. She never stopped hearing the roar of it in her ears. It was like a waterfall, spilling her life away.

Up in the bedroom she undressed in front of him, as she did every night except when his studies went on into the small hours. He didn't watch her, though – not directly. He sat with his back to her, but she noticed he took care to sit where he could see her in the mirror – just as she took equal care to stand where he could see her reflection. He never turned until she was in her nightdress and between the sheets.

She knew they would make love tonight, even before his hand snaked out for a quinine-jelly lozenge. Sometimes the beefsteak and kidney was alone enough to bring the mood on him; sometimes it was an evening of bezique; and on those rare occasions when they lit a fire, and turned down the gaslight, and she stared into the flames while he looked at her – that, too, was enough. As soon as he was in bed she opened her arms and he fell into her embrace and put the lozenge into her hand.

Tonight, she thought as she pushed it inside, tonight they would somehow break out of that cocoon of mere pleasantness. She would find the trick to unlock his caution. For he was as careful of spending himself as he was of his purse; she always felt he was doing a quick calculation as to how much he could spare this week – if anything at all. It was as if he believed you could save up pleasures, too, for your old age, like so many bags of housecoal.

In the early months of their marriage his reserve was understandable enough, what with the unfortunate circumstances and all. She had felt guilty, too, for a long time. She just closed her eyes and remembered Clive. That couldn't have helped matters. But now they were long past that – or ought to be. Perhaps it had become like one of those customs that linger on, and even strengthen, though their origins are dead and long-buried in time. She shrugged the thought from her mind, crossly; it couldn't be as permanent as that.

"Don't you feel like it?" he asked.

She took a grip on herself and gave him a low, animal gurgle of encouragement. But it was all a performance. Frederick was wonderful to her. If she behaved honestly, and only showed the passion she actually felt, he would go on and on, trying everything he knew to give her more pleasure. Sometimes, indeed, it worked; but more often it did not. And then he would grow desperate and his thing would go soft and he'd still go on trying to push it in and out. And then he'd blame himself and say he was working too hard or still thinking about some chemical formulae or something. So now she usually pretended her passion.

Funnily enough, that sometimes worked, too. Just every now and then, when she was moaning and gasping with spurious delight, the true pleasure would come rushing up out of nowhere and overwhelm her, and then she could go on and on and on until she had to beg him to stop. But it didn't happen tonight – though *he* never knew it. He let her (as he believed) enjoy three or four spells and then said, "I can't stop."

"Go on! Go on!" she encouraged.

Three quick, measured spurts and a short soak. Moments later he was asleep.

For a long time she stared at the ceiling, at the pattern of the twigs in the vase on the windowsill, where the gaslamp outside cast their shadows on the ceiling. Emmy hadn't lifted the vase to dust it; the pattern was exactly the same as last night's. Ann pretended the dark lines were the rivers of people's lives, the way they joined and parted. Real lives. Inner lives. Branches were children.

Buds were blighted hopes.

She counted the buds but gave up when she got close to a hundred.

Just before she went to sleep she remembered she ought to have told Frederick about opening the account.

Oh well – it would keep.

CHAPTER TWENTY-FIVE

THE RIGHT MOMENT to mention the weekly account with Mr. Watt never came. And then the very need to do so dwindled. She managed the budget well enough, paying weekly instead of daily, and, since Frederick gave her a weekly allowance, it balanced easily. So there was really nothing to concern him. Indeed, if ever the topic arose, she could point out that most of the money he gave her on a Friday was gone by the Saturday. It wasn't lying around all week as a temptation, either to theft, a remote possibility, or to a rash purchase – which was not so remote.

No doubt Frederick would say it was the principle of the thing – even a week's debt was still a debt. So, she decided, it was best, all in all, not to trouble him with such trifles. He worried too much about the household as it was. Almost every night he'd go into the larder to count the tins and turn them face-out again, and look at the quantities. And they all had to be marked. If she had a pound of sugar in a bag and she used four ounces, she had to cross out the "1lb" and write "12oz" beneath it – and so on for every time she used it.

At first she used to complain. Cooking took twice as long by his system; and anyway she never measured out the ingredients – she just knew how much flour and sugar and things you needed for a cake. But he persuaded her it was the only way she could keep control of things. "Suppose you ran out of sugar in the middle of baking?" he asked.

"I'd send Emmy for some more."

"And if the shop was shut?"

"I'm hardly likely to be baking at ten at night!"

"What about half-day closing?"

"I could slip next door for the loan of a cupful. But it's never happened, darling – never once in all my life."

That sort of sloppiness infuriated him. "It's the principle," he complained. "Now at the laboratory every single chemical we use is weighed out and recorded."

At least she'd managed to draw the line when he wanted her to record all weights to the nearest *half* ounce. She'd threatened to go and buy one of the new patent scales with a clockface dial instead of their simple two-pan balance.

And it was the same with the accounts. Every last farthing had to be recorded, and he wanted to see the proof of it. Her way around that was to write each item on a different scrap of paper – the back of an envelope, the torn-off spill of a newspaper, the backs of Lawrence's childish doodles, the used wrappings he brought home from work. "Well, we can't afford to waste these bits of paper, can we?" she'd reply when he complained at being given a whole sheaf of scraps. "Anyway, *I* can follow them perfectly well."

It satisfied him.

That was when she discovered Frederick wasn't really interested in following the accounts himself. It wasn't a meanness in him. True, he wanted to save everything they could – for the business he was one day going to found, the business that would outshine even the Mortimers'. But that wasn't why he was so insistent on her accounts. It was more complicated than that. Nothing about him was ever simple; he told her less than one tenth of what he was really thinking. But in this case she was fairly sure that all he wanted was to *know* she kept track of things.

But the weekly account was her undoing – or led to it. Mr. Watt, seeing how well she coped with a weekly debt, suggested transferring to a monthly account. She was terrified at the very thought of living a whole month on tick, but, because it seemed like a kind of compliment, she accepted gratefully.

That simple corner shop turned into a fairyland where she could wander around, taking this, taking that. She could even leave her purse at home – except on the last day of the month. Then the shop became a robber's den, where she was held for ransom and even if she bought only one small twist of sugar, she still had to pay out pounds. Sometimes the bill was almost five pounds. Sometimes she merely reduced it, paying off what she could and leaving the rest to carry forward.

The debt inched up until, by high summer, she was in high old trouble. It would take the best part of two weeks' allowance just to get back straight. She almost managed it. Food was cheap. The days were hot. They all ate less and she practically starved herself. But when Frederick raised an eyebrow and said, "Cold collar of mutton again?" she had to go out and buy a capon and a side of beef, and much of the good was undone.

Emmy noticed, of course. The good girl even offered a small loan. Ann thanked her but declined. Wrily she remembered that in the old days, when she herself was an upstairs maid, she'd managed to put by quite a bit – fifteen pounds – enough to wipe out this present debt four times over. Yet here she was, a respectable married lady with a family started, and she hadn't enough to spare for a curling tongs. Where had things gone wrong? Was there a badness in her that would come out in the end, despite all the good things she might do?

The day came when Mr. Watt's smile was no longer so welcoming. "I shall need a bit more than that, I'm afraid, Mrs. Oxley," he said as she paid off some of the account.

"Tomorrow," she was panicked into promising.

Fortunately he had chosen to speak to her at a moment when the shop was empty. Another time he might not be so discriminating. That was when she finally had to take up Emmy's offer of a loan. The thought of being exposed in front of another woman, a neighbour, terrified her.

"Is that all?" Mr. Watt asked when she handed it over. "I'd be grateful, Mrs. Oxley, if you could try and make it a bit more next week."

Now she was frightened out of her wits. The truth had to be faced: Frederick's allowance simply wasn't large enough. But where was it all going?

Well, there was the sherry, of course. It was supposed to last from Christmas to Christmas, but nowadays she had to keep a secret bottle to top it up from time to time. It calmed her nerves and helped her think straight. Anyway, at 1s. 3d. a bottle it hardly accounted for the shortfall. Even several bottles ...

There were also the peppermint lozenges to disguise her breath.

Even so ...

She sighed. Where was she to get more by next week? She'd simply have to pluck up her spirits and ask Frederick for it. She dreaded the very thought of that encounter. She took a little nip of sherry, to give her the courage ...

When Freddy arrived home that evening he felt at once that something was wrong. Emmy was frightened and even Lawrence was subdued.

"Where's the mistress?" he asked.

"She's took poorly," the maid answered, wafting her eyes toward the ceiling.

"Oh no! Have you sent for the doctor?"

"Tha'd best see her first, sir."

Even before he entered the bedroom he smelled the sherry. The room reeked of it, and so did her breath. At first he felt only disappointment. Then it turned to shame. Then to anger.

He shook her roughly, but she barely stirred. He slapped her face – suddenly noticing how gaunt she looked; she frowned but otherwise remained in oblivion. He began to grow worried.

He called out to Emmy to see if they'd mind Lawrence next door for an hour or so; then she herself was to go for the doctor.

First he got rid of the empty bottle. Then he ventilated the room and, sucking a cough lozenge, kissed her and tried to lick the strong taste of it into her mouth. She responded to it, lazily, in her dreams, moaning as she moaned when they made love. It disgusted him.

When the doctor came he went through the usual tests. Freddy saw the man's expression change from concern to derision. "Drunk!" he diagnosed. "This is an alcoholic stupor, man. No more."

"She's not in any danger?" Freddy asked anxiously, hot with shame.

"Only from you!"

"What d'you mean?"

"Well, I expect you'll give her a good chastizing, won't you?"

"I've never lifted a finger to her."

The doctor looked back at Ann; his gesture implied, "And just see where it's got you!" What he said was, "Six strong cuts with a light cane on the bare posteriors would stop this kind of nonsense. When she's sober, of course. Strip her and tie her down firmly. Tell her what you're going to do, then leave her for an hour to think it over." For a moment Freddy feared the man would volunteer the office himself, his eyes gleamed so brightly. "Even a dozen whacks would do no harm, you know," he concluded.

"I couldn't." Freddy cut into the reverie.

The doctor sighed as he returned to the present. He reached behind the bedside chest. "Then you'd better lay in a couple of cases of these." He held up an empty sherry bottle, one that Freddy had overlooked in his consternation.

When the man had taken his half-crown and gone, Emmy brought the boy back, fed him, and put him to bed. Then she carried two bowls of broth up to the bedroom.

Freddy thanked her, though he had little appetite. "You'd best sup the other yourself," he said.

"Wouldn't you try waking her, sir?"

"Why bother? She'd still be ..." He could not say the word. "Let her sleep it off. You get it down inside you. It can't have been an easy day."

The maid obeyed.

"Oh, sit in that chair," he told her. "You make me uncomfortable standing like that."

When she'd finished her broth she said, "You won't be too hard on her, will you, sir?"

"I can't believe it," he answered. "Did you know about it?" He saw that she did. "How long has it been going on?"

"Dunno, sir."

"Come, Emmy – can't you see this is too important to talk about punishment and being hard or soft. It's much too serious for that. We've got to *help* the mistress. I know she's done a dreadful thing, but we ..."

"You know?" Emmy was incredulous. "You knew all the time?"

He was puzzled. "Only when I came home this evening and you told me."

"Oh – that. Oh, sorry."

"What did you think I meant?"

"Nothing, sir." She squirmed.

"What's this other thing that you know and I don't?"

She shrugged.

"There's no point in not telling me. I shall keep at you until you do."

She almost yielded.

"Have no fear of the consequences," he assured her. "I know you have to work all day with the mistress, but I shall tell her I forced it out of you. I'll say I threatened you with dismissal without a character if you didn't tell me."

"Oh sir! You wouldn't do such a cruel thing."

He was tempted to say he would, but at length he shook his head. "I'll say even then I had to plead with you ... hit you ... I'll say anything. Only please tell me. I know you want to help her by keeping this secret. Well I want to help her, too – but I can only do so by getting at the truth. How can I help her if all I know is lies?"

"Say Mr. Watt told you," Emmy broke in. "Say it was him, not me."

"The shopkeeper? What is it to do with him?" he asked. But his heart was already sinking.

"It's the sort of thing he would do, anyway. And she's frit for him. She'd never face him with it."

"Frightened of him, Emmy? But why?"

And then the whole story came out.

When she reached the end of her tale the strain of telling it proved too much and she burst into tears. It made Freddy feel most awkward. He stood sheepishly and went over to her, but all he felt he could do was to ease the soup bowl from her grasp. It was an expensive Crown Derby oddment he'd got cheap at a stall in Whitley Bay. Standing in front of her he saw nowhere he could decently touch her; he went behind and put his hands comfortingly on her shoulders. "There, there," he told her. "You have nothing to reproach yourself with. You have done your mistress a great kindness."

What a little slip of a thing she was. Just sixteen – too young for such responsibility.

"Thank you, sir," she said glutinously.

He left her and went back to the bedside.

She plucked up her pinny to wipe her streaming cheeks.

"Emmy," he asked conversationally, "did you know that the human frame can tolerate a certain amount of *anything*?"

It stopped her crying. "Sir?"

"Just about anything. Take arsenic, now. Most people think that's an absolute poison. But it's not. There is a certain quantity, very small, but a measurable quantity, that you or I could take without any ill effect whatsoever. Did you know that?"

The girl looked across at the broth bowl and licked her lips nervously. "Arsenic?" she repeated.

"I'm only using that as an illustration. What I'm saying is that all the things we consider dangerous for us – they're actually safe in small amounts." He picked up the empty sherry bottle. "This stuff, for example. A glass or two at Christmas, the occasional glass during the year – quite safe." Then he pointed at Ann. "But two bottles in one afternoon ..."

"Is the missus going to die, sir?"

"Good heavens no! What gives you that idea?"

"Only when you was going on about arsenic, I thought like ..."

"No, I said that was only an example. What I want you to understand – and I'm not making a good job of it obviously – but what I hope you can see is that ..." He sighed. "To put it another way, even *good* things could kill you. Singing hymns and praying could kill you."

"I don't see that, sir."

"If you did nothing but sing and pray all day and all night. Not even eat. You'd starve to death, wouldn't you. Or die of thirst. You see – the limit of our tolerance for bad things like arsenic is very small. And with half-bad things like alcohol it's not a great deal bigger. But even with the best things, like hymn singing and praying, there *is* still a limit. Everything in moderation, you see? Nothing to excess – that's what I'm saying."

"I'm a religious girl, sir," Emmy said.

Freddy sighed again. He ought never to have started this hare; and yet it was important for the girl to understand. Otherwise she'd never be able to help poor Ann. She must stop seeing it in absolute blacks and whites; she mustn't think of helping Ann as being "too hard" or "too soft."

He tried one more time. "Look, I know the mistress thinks I fuss a lot about the house and the pantry and the way she sets about things. You know how I always want her to keep a record of everything, to know exactly where she is. It's not just record-keeping for record-keeping's sake, you know. Truly I don't give a tinker's cuss if there's eight ounces of flour there or nine ounces. That's not the point. I just want her to know where she is. If she had really kept records of her spending, do you suppose she'd have been able to run up even four shillings' worth of debt? Never mind four pounds!"

Emmy shook her head and looked pityingly at Ann. "Debt's a terrible thing and all."

"No," Freddy said, to her surprise. "It's not. A small debt, a debt you can manage, is fine. Again, you see, it's the excess of the thing. Nothing in the world, Emmy, *nothing*, is bad of itself. Only if you do too much of it, or have too much of it."

"Are you going to have to turn us off, sir?"

Freddy smiled. "No. Four pounds is a big debt, I'd be a fool to pretend otherwise. But we'll manage. You know the mistress has always wanted a cook? Well, we'll just have to put off the day. But we wouldn't say goodbye to you, Emmy. You're almost one of the family now."

The girl blinked a dozen times, quickly, and sniffed. "I'll

do all I can to help, sir. I'm ... I'm fond, like, of the missus. And ..." She nodded, not quite able to say, "and yourself."

"Bless you, love," Freddy said. "Just see to the dishes, will you? Then you get a good night's sleep. Tomorrow we must both help the mistress to start writing a nice clean page in her life, eh?"

"Don't be too hard on her, sir."

"I hope you know me better than that, Emmy." He was walking toward the door to open it for her. She caught him up. At the doorway he put his arm about her shoulder and gave it a friendly squeeze.

She froze, but when she looked up at him he saw it was uncertainty, not fear, in her eyes.

"You're an important person now, Emmy," he told her. "To the mistress and to me. I fancy we're both going to need you in this house quite a bit these next few weeks."

"I'll do anything I can, sir. Just ask us."

"Bless you." He gave her another little squeeze, followed by a gentle push in the small of her back. She leaped to the stairhead like a scholar out of school. She took the stairs three at a time, her skirts billowing up like sails.

Sweet sixteen! he thought. Her sudden youthful display of zest caused him to reflect that of the three of them, Emmy would probably gain the most from this episode in their lives – in the way of improving her maturity and knowledge of people.

He lay awake into the small hours that night, worrying about Ann and how he was going to manage to restore her old self. She was a vital part of his plan to rise in the world – quite apart from the fact that he adored her and all that sort of thing. If Clive ever heard that Ann had gone to the bad ... he shuddered at the thought of such humiliation. No – Ann must be helped back into a good way of life.

He tried to imagine what must have gone through her mind as she took first one glass of sherry, then another, then another ... but he failed. He realized it must go back further than that. To start with she had to buy the stuff. What went through her mind at that moment, when she told Mr. Watt, "And a bottle of sherry, please"? She must have known how the debt was piling up. Whenever the thought of it occurred to her, did she just shrug it off? Forget it? Think of something else?

How could a person do that? How could you have a problem in your mind and *not* worry and worry at it until it was solved? Of course, one could easily sleep on a problem, but that was different; it was just a different way of tackling it – you went to sleep knowing you'd stand a good chance of waking up with the answer. If not, you'd start worrying at it again. But this thing with Ann – she had just deliberately shut her mind to it. He couldn't imagine himself being able to do that. He couldn't even take laudanum to dull a toothache; even that degree of withdrawal from reality made him uneasy.

As he lay there, fretting over these worries, another began to nag at him: their debt to Emmy. Great heavens – what must she think of him! Why hadn't he paid her back the moment she told him? He was concerned about Ann, of course; but that was no excuse. The poor girl must be worrying herself stiff about it. A pound was a month's wages, after all. Perhaps she was lying up there in her bed, as sleepless as himself. Well, that was one worry he could take care of.

He rose, pulled the trouser press from under the bed, took his keys from the pocket, went to his dressing table, unlocked the top-right drawer, withdrew the metal cash box he'd made in his apprentice days, and extracted a sovereign. He locked everything, returned the keys, and put the press back before he picked up the candle and mounted the attic stairs.

He knocked several times before Emmy answered sleepily.

"It's me," he called.

She opened the door a crack and blinked at the light.

"I was worried," he told her.

Bewildered eyes searched his face. "Oh sir ..."

"About this." He held forth the coin. "You must have thought me very strange not to have paid you back at once."

"Oh." She took it, tried to slip it in a nonexistent pocket, and then just held it awkwardly. "There wasn't any need."

Now he saw how soundly she had been sleeping he felt an absolute fool. What had possessed him? "I'm sorry I woke you, Emmy," he said. "Just because *I* couldn't sleep. It was thoughtless."

She was shivering, though the night was warm. But something in her relaxed. She opened her door and said, "If you want to talk, sir? Or anything?"

He shook his head and turned away. "No, I'm sorry. It was foolish. You go back to sleep." He, too, was shivering now, though he couldn't understand why. When he was half-way down the stairs she called, "Sir?"

He faced her.

"I'd want to help. I've grown right fond of ... this situation."

Not trusting his voice he shook his head and continued his retreat. At the foot of the stairs he paused and looked up again. She was still there, smiling now – as if he had paid her a compliment.

CHAPTER TWENTY-SIX

IF ONLY FREDERICK would be angry with her! Really angry, instead of this solemn determination to reason her back into being "her old self." He couldn't see that by denying her the outlet of anger and recrimination, he was keeping her trapped even longer. She wanted him to hurt her, to say wounding things he'd always regret. She needed something to forgive *him* for, too. If only he'd behave like the other men around here and knock her about a bit, she'd earn that release. But his goodness burdened her with debts that were truly unpayable.

How many ways can you say sorry? How many kinds of *yes* are there? How long can a body go on trying to look and feel contrite?

Such, at least, were her immediate feelings. But they diminished as the weeks drew on. At the most superficial level, Freddy's methods worked. The arrears were paid off; the need for even an occasional glass of sherry dwindled. She did not go to pieces. That kind of emotional storm was just another of those luxuries she had to deny herself.

She wanted to go back to the weekly account, but he wouldn't hear of it. "You were right to take it," he said. "One day, when we have the money, our shortest accounts will be quarterly – you'll see. When you first started the monthly account, something in you must have felt ready to accept the responsibility. Now you've got to search in all the unswept corners of yourself, and find that element inside you, and encourage it to grow. If you take the coward's way out and go back to paying by the week, it'll be a defeat. We can only go on. Never back. We shall never go back. I'll help you."

The senior clerk in the laboratory office gave him an old ledger book that had got accidentally toasted near the fire. The damaged pages had been torn out and fair-copied into another book. Freddy brought home the remnant. For two weeks every evening he helped her to write up her day's accounts; he showed her how to subtotal them and carry down the running total. Actually, it was quite fun, she found, seeing how it all balanced at the end; but it took the uncertainty out of things. Life was drab when you always knew exactly where you were. Especially when you were at 14 Tatton Row.

For the next eight weeks he left her to do the books on her own, merely asking to see the result. After that he told her he trusted her.

The worst part was having young Emmy there on the sidelines all the time. At first Ann had wanted to get rid of her – with a good reference of course. It would even be in Emmy's best interests. Any of the fine houses in Albert Villas would take her now. If Ann herself hadn't come off a farm, that's the way she'd have had to work up. First a little clerk's house. Then perhaps a biggish shopkeeper. Then a grand house like Mr. Wilde's. The next step would have been to somewhere like Mortimer Hall. She'd been spared the first two rungs only because Mrs. Wilde had known she was of yeoman stock, and because old Lady Mortimer had given her family a good character. But lots of other girls had climbed that path to Ferndown Crescent. So it would be in Emmy's interests, as she tried pointing out to Frederick.

But he said next year would be a better time for the girl to move; if Ann couldn't face Emmy now, at their daily round, and if there was any feeling in years to come that she had shirked such an encounter, then Ann would never be able to feel she'd truly mastered her present difficulties.

"And as far as Emmy's concerned you're more than half-way there already," he told her.

"How?"

"You have her affection. She thinks the world of you."

It had been so long since Ann had felt herself to be the sort of person *anyone* would "think the world of," that it bucked up her spirits to be told so now. Yet still it was hard to labour for her own reform beneath the eyes of a little slip of a sixteen-year-old.

Often she suspected Frederick and the girl had entered into some kind of pact on that day, to wrestle together over her soul. There was certainly a strange understanding between them. If she didn't know Frederick better, she might have suspected a different sort of wrestling – and she even caught herself thinking it might be no bad thing. It was an appetite that certainly needed bringing on in him.

She began to daydream about catching them at it. When they had all retired for the night and Frederick went up to his garret to get on with studying for his chemistry degree, her imagination would often orchestrate a creaking bedspring, a cough, a sleepy sigh ... into a symphony of forbidden passion. Then she'd creep out onto the landing and listen to the soughing of the wind, the scratch of Frederick's nib, the creak of his chair, and all the other sounds of monkish study.

Back in bed she'd try to imagine the orgy of forgiveness and reconciliation they might even now be enjoying if her hopes, which were other wives' fears, had come true.

One evening, when the approach of Christmas was making her feel especially low, Frederick came home bursting with excitement. The laboratory, which belonged to the Stockton Carbonization Company, was about to expand into a new line of chemicals. "And guess who's been put in charge of it all?" he crowed.

"But why you?" she asked when he'd put her back on the ground.

"There's a loyal, wifely question!"

"I don't mean that. I mean they must have said how

brilliant you are and things like that. I want to hear what they told you."

"They didn't really need to say anything. I know more than any man there about coal-tar derivatives, especially nitrobenzol and aniline. I didn't tell you this but I discovered a new dyestuff last week. They only finished the steam-ageing tests today, but it passed. It's the first dye ever that's absolutely fast to washing and sunlight – there!"

"But Frederick, how wonderful! That must be why they gave you the job."

"It didn't hurt my chances. But also there's very few other coal-distillation companies can get their hands on the quantities of coal tar that we have. They've got to put all the top fractions into the gas they sell – for illumination, you see. But because we mainly supply coke ..."

"I thought you supply gas as well?"

"Not town gas. Only a very lean sort of industrial gas to the smelters – who don't need it for illumination. And because of that we've got tons of coal tar where others have only got pounds. So we'll be inventing and patenting dyes like nobody's business."

"How can you invent a dye. Don't they just exist anyway?"

He laughed. "Not any more. All your modern dyes are made by people like me, throwing muck into retorts and heating it – and praying it doesn't explode."

"Oh Frederick!" She bit her lip.

"Don't worry. We usually know what we're doing."

"This promotion, does it mean more money?"

From the way he paused she knew he'd been saving it for the finale. "Double!" he said. "Two hundred and ten pounds a year. Emmy may move to Albert Villas at last."

She frowned.

"With us!" he laughed – thinking she was frowning because she hadn't grasped his meaning. "The new appointment begins in January, though I start the work almost at once. So we may arrange to rent a house in Albert Villas from the next quarter day. The company is building a new, special annexe to the lab with a keystone over the door, saying dyestuffs, and Mrs. Crome is to perform the opening ceremony."

Mr. George Crome was the owner of the Stockton Carbonization Company.

A few weeks later, early in the new year, Frederick suddenly said to her, "Would you call me a greedy man, dear? In the way of money, I mean?"

"Certainly not! Who has been saying such things?"

"Old Crome. Not in so many words, but he hinted it pretty strongly. I was hurt, I must say." He grinned, looking not the least bit hurt.

"They're not going to turn you off?" she asked anxiously.

Now he laughed. "Not they! If that was ever your worry, you may put it behind you from now on. I'm far too valuable to them – and they know it. I understand more theoretical chemistry than most of the practical men they might employ, and yet I know far more practical chemistry than any university theoretician. No – the days when people will turn me off are behind us. The boot's on the other foot."

There was a determined sort of satisfaction in his tone, something she had not heard before. Frederick had always known his own worth. Now the world was waking up to it as well.

He went on, "I suggested today that the patents on the new dyestuffs, which are all filed in my name of course, should not be meekly handed over to the company, free, gratis, and for nothing."

"They should pay you?" she asked.

"A royalty – not much, but just a token recognition of my value to them."

"Oh Frederick, I hope you didn't cheek Mr. Crome."

He laughed again. "We must stop thinking like that, love. They're not our betters – Crome and his sort. They happen to have been born with money and land. They happen to have the intelligence to invest both those commodities in talents like mine. But without folk like me they'd lose it in a generation or two."

"They are paying you over two hundred pounds," she reminded him.

"Per year. And in that year my work will earn them at least ten thousand – which is more than a hundred percent return on their entire investment in bricks, mortar, raw materials, and men. You call that fair? All I asked for is a one percent royalty – a piddling hundred pounds."

"What did he say?"

"Told me not to be so greedy. Jokingly, mind. The way I might say to one of the lads, 'Don't be such a bloody fool.' But he didn't like it, I could tell. I think he's a frightened and worried man."

"Oh Frederick!"

"I hope he is, anyway."

Ann's worry was partly a pretence. Naturally, she was a *little* worried; a disagreement between her husband and his company was, after all, a threat to her lovely new home, which they'd soon be moving into. Yet deep within her she felt an elemental response to the challenge Frederick had issued; it was that touch of anarchy she always craved; uncertainty, to spice the too-sweet taste of a well-ordered life in a neat villa in a genteel neighbourhood.

That Frederick felt it, too, made her feel closer to him than at any time in the past. There was a huntsman's gleam in his eye as he told her his tale, and the shiver of pleasure in his voice. He had not won his point about the royalties, not so far; yet the triumph had been his. He had seen the fear in old Crome's eyes. He knew he was right. That night he made enormous love to her. She began to fear that the Frederick who had seemed so simple in the days of his apprenticeship might yet turn into a man more complex than she could grasp.

He was out there in the real world all day, meeting new people, new challenges, overcoming problems and opposition. The process must constantly be changing him – or at least teaching him who he was. How could she keep up? Where could she find *her* challenges?

The new building was opened in March, by which time the Oxley household had transferred to Albert Villas. They could not yet afford their own locked pew in church, but they had a living-out cook, and a living-in scullery maid who also did the coals and fires. Emmy was at last an upstairs maid. The amount of bricabrac they owned had doubled with his salary. They had sherry on Sunday after church and wine with dinner (it was "dinner" at last) on Sunday evenings.

These luxuries surprised her at first. She had feared he

would keep every extra penny to go toward his own business. But he told her that learning how to live in Society was just as important. They weren't going to be the uncouth sort of self-made people everybody laughed at behind their backs.

He also told her not to make her new friendships too deep; they were only passing through Albert Villas. She wondered how you could plan to regulate things like that – the depth of a friendship, but she knew better than to ask. He'd only say – "You just do it!"

There was a surprise guest at the opening ceremony – at least, he was a surprise until the day before. Among the Cromes' friends were the Knox-Riddells. And, by chance, Tony Knox-Riddell was actually staying at Hardiman Hall, the Cromes' place near Sedgefield. He came dashing into town and dragged the not-very-seriously-protesting Freddy from his stinks-bench and into the nearest hostelry, where they enjoyed a splendid evening raking over those good old times.

"You'll be sure to come to the ceremony tomorrow?" Freddy asked for the third or fourth time as they parted.

"Nothing would keep me away, old scout."

"Ann will be especially glad to see you again."

"Tell her I look forward to nothing more keenly than that."

Naturally Ann was delighted to hear the news from Freddy that night. "I'd almost forgotten him," she lied.

Tony Knox-Riddell had been the charming one. A bit shy but very nice.

"Try and make friends with him," Frederick told her. "He's the sort of man we want to cultivate from now on – solid bone from ear to ear, charming, and with lots of money to invest."

Tony, riding back to Sedgefield, was trying to remember Ann. There had been so many good-looking women since then. He'd probably remember her when he saw her. And he'd get on better with her, too. Married women were much easier to talk with, and much more fun generally. Apart from anything else, they were no longer "somebody's sister."

CHAPTER TWENTY-SEVEN

MRS. CROME LOOKED AS IF she could crack walnuts – and her husband – in the crook of her elbow. It gave an odd poignance to her closing remarks, as if by formally pretending to share the generally prized characteristics of her sex she might somehow acquire them for herself – or at least slip into them like some disguise, without anybody's noticing.

"Out of the lion," she said, "came forth sweetness. It has ever been so. We of that outer world which passes by this laboratory on its daily round, never venturing to peep inside its forbidding portals, we, I say, are apt to think of it as a place of horrid smells and manly danger. Yet from its tarry cauldrons there has already burgeoned forth a cornucopia of tints and hues to delight the most critical maidenly eye. Not the gaudiest tropical flower can outshine them. The butterflies hide for very shame. Here, behind these already soot-streaked walls of common brick, the genius of our age has wrested the palette from Nature's grasp and is teaching her now the colourist's trade anew. Long may that cornucopia flow! Indeed, may it now broaden to a flood, an inundation, I say – that we, the weaker and yet the fairer sex, we who I'm sure shall never comprehend the molecular mysteries of the art, may nonetheless take that art to our bosom and with it raise a new Parnassus of beauty! Oh, may we blossom and flourish as never before in the bounty of these our latest alchemists, who turn the base metal of common textiles into cloth of finest gold! In keenest anticipation of that pleasure, I gratefully declare this fine (and extremely costly) laboratory open!"

"What did you think of the speech?" Tony Knox-Riddell asked Ann.

There had been the briefest tour of inspection into the smelly bowels of the lab, followed by a hasty retreat to the public rooms of The Railway Arms, where, among prints celebrating an earlier achievement, the opening of the pioneer Stockton & Darlington Railway, the guests munched and sipped their tribute to the latest triumph of industry.

The minions were already back at their benches, where Freddy would also have been if Tony had not said, "But I insist! What – leave young Oxley behind? He's a friend of mine from schooldays."

And so Freddy came. The suggestion that Freddy might have been at Eton surprised the rest of the company – though it was true that the school had always given free education to a number of "scholars," poor boys lucky and bright enough to scrape together sufficient learning to pass the scholarship exam. Several of those present looked at him in a new light. Indeed, several of them actually noticed him for the first time.

And with Freddy, came Ann – which had been Tony's chief aim. Now that he saw her he remembered her very well, and wondered he could ever have forgotten her.

She, for her part, had forgotten those strangely pointed ears, which gave his face an expression of pixie-like intensity. At this time of day, though, he was a languid, sleepy sort of pixie. There was a permanent, hooded amusement in his eyes, suggesting that occasions like this, which others might call "time off," were hard labour to him and that when he truly came alive, late into the evening, he would squeeze more fun out of a minute than others might find in a month of holidays. It unnerved her. It acted like an obscure but powerful threat to the growing order in her life. She avoided his gaze as she answered him: "Speaking in public like that is a great gift. I envy Mrs. Crome."

Tony smiled. "Yes – she spoke it rather well. The poor dear had no notion what to say last night, you know. I wrote it for her."

"Then you're the one I envy, Mr. Knox-Riddell."

"Ah yes – count on me for fine, flowery, empty speeches."

She watched his eyes as he spoke, for he no longer looked directly at her. They were amused and restless, taking in everything very swiftly. Whenever they paused and she followed their direction she always found something of interest happening – a discussion on the verge of becoming heated, a secret glance between a woman there and a man here, or an expression or gesture that was somehow at odds with its circumstances. He missed nothing. She thought his friends must be most privileged. She would love to know him well enough to ask him his true opinion of everything. Frederick had misjudged him. Mr. Knox-Riddell was no bonehead.

She would most especially like to know his opinion of her. She was sure he saw things about her that she herself would never realize unaided.

"I don't remember that you did much talking back in the days of the Flying Six," she said.

"Ah, I often think of those times," he replied. "Weren't they extraordinary! Sometimes they seem like yesterday. At others – so long ago. Do they seem long ago to you?"

"Almost like a different lifetime."

"Oh, that sounds bad. I don't like that tone of weary regret! Surely Foxy's doing well enough, wouldn't you say?"

She nodded and looked across the room at Frederick. He caught her eye and winked back. Tony noticed, of course. His quick eyes flickered from one to the other. She almost dared to ask him what he was truly thinking; she was sure he wouldn't mind. "It sounds ungrateful, I know," she answered. "But when you get a house and family ..."

"When you settle."

She frowned, wondering why he had bothered to rephrase it for her.

"Most people call it 'settling down'," he added. "Don't you?"

"I suppose so." She shrugged.

"Don't you feel very settled, then?"

She avoided answering him. "I was going to say that, whatever you call it, it places a great wall between the present and all that happy-go-lucky past."

"So you don't feel settled!"

She laughed at his persistence. "You want to know the truth?"

"I insist upon it."

"I sometimes think I never shall – feel settled."

"I'm the same." He nodded briskly. "Well, I mustn't

commandeer your company. I'm sure there are dozens of people here you're eager to meet."

Her disappointment was acute and she showed it. He gave a satisfied smile. She realized that had been his purpose, for he added at once, "Though I must confess it's hard to snap off any true meeting of minds. Don't you feel that in some extraordinary way, without realizing quite how or why, we've managed to slip directly beneath the boom of empty social chitchat, you and I?"

Normally such talk would have embarrassed her; but he was so quiet and sincere and friendly that he made their peculiar intimacy seem natural.

"I don't know," she answered. "This is the first time I've ever been to such an occasion."

"I may assure you it won't be the last, Mrs. Oxley. Your Foxy husband is a skyrocket, believe me. Hold on to his coat-tails. He'll carry you above us all!"

Tony liked the new Foxy Freddy much less than the eager young apprentice of old; but he recognized those "skyrocket" qualities and he was astute enough to know a potentially good future investment when he met it, bought it beer, and listened all evening to its hunger.

Ann remembered that brief conversation many times during the week that followed. Mr. Knox-Riddell was right. There had been a meeting of their minds. In many ways, she thought, they were probably quite alike. He had seen that restlessness in her and recognized it at once. It was strange and refreshing. It reassured her. She was not the wayward, feckless creature Frederick so often made her feel – not that he did it deliberately, but just by being so positive in himself.

She wondered if they would ever meet again.

That Sunday, during lunch, Frederick turned to her and said, "I think we'll go to the park this afternoon."

"Sail the boat!" Lawrence piped up. "Please, daddy! Please?"

"Of course we'll sail the boat. That's our very purpose!" It was a toy steam yacht. He'd spent hours that he could ill afford making it for the boy, for his fourth birthday.

"Yes, that'll be nice," Ann agreed. It was a fine spring day, full of breeze and snatches of the sun. "If we wrap up well."

"You enjoyed meeting old Knox-Riddell again, didn't you?" Frederick continued.

She didn't hesitate. "Yes! I thought everyone was going to look down on us. But he didn't. He's such a thoroughly *nice* man."

"Then I think you'll be in for a thoroughly *nice* surprise this afternoon!"

By the time they saw Knox-Riddell himself, sauntering among the crocuses and narcissi, it was no surprise at all. But it was still very nice; she had to stop herself from breaking into a run.

The teashop was open. They took a table near the empty bandstand, sheltering from the wind behind its tarpaulin shrouds. When Frederick went off with Lawrence, to sail the yacht, she and Tony slipped back at once into their easy intimacy.

"It must be wonderful to have a son," he said. Freddy and the boy were barely out of earshot.

She wondered whether he knew Lawrence's story. "Freddy regrets having to study so hard. He'd like more time with the little lad. He's very devoted to him."

"And you, Mrs. Oxley?"

"Do call me Ann. It seems so odd for you to call him Foxy and me Mrs. Oxley."

He nodded. "Tony." He gave a slight laugh. "That's a nickname, too. I never think of Antonius." He frowned at her, comically daring her to laugh. "My father was a Roman scholar. I was almost called Suetonius. Think of being nicknamed Suet!"

"No one could call you that."

He looked down at his slim body and elegant clothes, pleased at her compliment.

The waiter came up with his trolley of cakes. "Do take some more," Tony encouraged her, leaning forward to watch her choose.

The intensity of his interest made her want to prolong it. She dithered and changed her mind and smiled at him, imitating the sort of wilting lady she'd always loathed when she'd had the waiter's office. Until that moment she never realized such a creature lay buried within her. Or was it real at all? Perhaps she was more of an actress than she realized – and here she was, reproducing the hated woman to the last flounce and simper.

It was even more strange than that. For, though she would have hated such a creature – seen as a third person – she did not dislike herself for it. And that was because of Tony. He loved to see it. His eyes shone with admiration. It was as if he were allowing her to enjoy a tiny love affair with herself. She had not loved herself much these past years; now, in this little charade of choosing a few cakes, indulging herself in the choice, he was reviving her old, carefree self-esteem.

From then on the mood between them was almost as if he loved her, too.

"Do you ever go back to visit your parents?" he asked. "Or any of the old places around Solihull?"

"I don't think you understand, Tony, how desperately poor we've been."

He nodded. Anyone else would have been embarrassed at her frankness – but not Tony. "Another person's poverty is the hardest thing of all to imagine," he said. "Pain is easy. Pain is universal. Hard labour, too. When I see a ploughboy trudging home from the fields with the rain and the darkness closing in, I remember outings in the boat at Eton when we'd rowed our guts out. I remember exhaustion like that. But poverty. It's so quiet and so ... so ..."

"So endless."

"Tell me about it, Ann. I think you could make me understand."

She told him then the one memory she had sworn to leave behind them in North Shields, never to think of again. The intensity of his eyes, the deep understanding they seemed always to radiate, compelled her not to withhold her memory.

She and Frederick had come to the end of their allowance for the week. They could have dipped into next week's but they knew that was simply robbing the future. She wanted to go out, picking rags or scrubbing floors, but Frederick would not hear of it. He said he'd go out and get some portering along the wharves. She would not hear of that. Two days they went without food or candles; only the baby ate. Freddy worked in the reference library until it closed; then he strained his eyes at his books, reading by the gaslamps shining in from the street.

"He completed a four-year course in twelve months, you know," she threw in proudly.

Tony did not doubt her; he had never seen a man more on fire than Freddy, more consumed with a passion to rise, to excel. It had taken a pint or two, but then it just blazed out of him.

And then came the worst part of her story – the part that could still wake her into a cold sweat at nights. They hadn't minded the lack of food and light so much, not for just a day or three. But to be without soap had become a torment. It was then that Ann had taken a jamjar and crept down to the shipyards at dead of night and, crawling among the rats and slithering through runnels of filthy bilgewater, had found her way to the launching ramps. And there she had scraped up the industrial soap they used for launching the keels. Thereafter, to eke out their money, she had gone back each week and gathered another jar full.

"We were clean again," she said. "But there still are times when I catch that tar and oakum smell of the ramps deep in the pores of my skin."

She turned to see his great eyes upon her, so full of tender admiration that, for the first time in her life, she found in those dreadful excursions cause for something other than shame. He could see things in her that she knew were there but could not name; he could though – he had the power of words. Vaguely she remembered a question he'd asked. Oh yes …

She changed the mood between them with a smile. "As for our ever returning to the Midlands, I expect, now that we can afford soap from the shops, we'll probably visit the old places from time to time. Frederick writes to his parents twice every month. And I with less duty to mine. Quite soon, perhaps. I suppose now that Clive Mortimer – *Sir* Clive – is master of Mortimer Hall, you must visit there quite often?"

"I do, as a matter of fact. I don't suppose you know we live near Meriden now?" He saw her start. "Does the name mean something to you?"

"My family comes from Meriden. The Howards. I have cousins there still."

"Oh then you must stay with us. You'll adore my mother. Unless Sir Clive has the prior claim? I suppose he and Foxy are still as thick as two thieves?"

For a moment she did not think she had heard him properly. Stay with the Knox-Riddells? What had Frederick been telling him? And as for the idea of staying at Mortimer Hall! They'd be lucky to be let past the gatelodge. Was Tony testing her in some obscure way?

Searching deep into his eyes she became sure that his question had been innocent. He did not know the story then. She was surprised to feel a certain disappointment. It made her realize that she wanted him to know everything, though she was not yet ready for the humiliation of having to tell him. When he knew, of course, he'd never mention it again. But the knowledge of it would always be there, hidden behind his eyes, more, not less, secure for being shared with him.

"They correspond from time to time, yes," was all she felt she had a right to say. "The dowager writes more often, though."

"Ah yes! Foxy's her discovery, in a way, isn't he. And her investment. She's an astute old bird to have seen it before anyone else."

"May I ask how you know?"

He grinned at her. "You don't mind my knowing?"

"Of course not."

"Well it was she who put us on to Foxy when he was due to leave college. She told me how brilliant he is and asked if I knew somewhere that could use him. And as we have quite a bit invested in the Stockton Carbonization Company, I thought we might as well keep it in the family. But it's all thanks to the dowager, really."

"She'll get it all back, don't worry. Frederick's going to repay her every last farthing, and with interest."

He laughed at the idea. "She'll hate that." But when he saw Ann's look of surprise he added, "Surely you understand?"

She shook her head.

"Well, Foxy's a rare bird in two ways, you know. Not just his talent. That's rare enough. But – for all his ambition and self-assurance – there's something vulnerable about him, wouldn't you say? Naive, almost? Something that's irresistible to ladies like the dowager. Don't you feel it, too? I'm sure you do."

Ann shook her head.

He tilted his eyes accusingly. "Come now. When you first met him he was a snotty little apprentice with one good suit and you were an upstairs maid. What made you look at him twice?"

Ann remembered the way Frederick had hung about outside the house, never minding the sniggering he knew he must be causing ... the way he had just walked up to her and Sally, risking every snub and insult they could have heaped on him ... and she suddenly saw what Tony meant. There *was* a quality of vulnerability in Frederick. It must show itself in different ways to different women, but it never failed to attract them. Even little Emmy was always strangely protective about him.

"I'm right, aren't I?" Tony said.

"Yes. I've been too close to him to realize it, I suppose. But how clever you are to see it – just like that! I'd love to know how he made himself appear to the dowager. I didn't think she'd even agree to see him."

"I imagine he offered her the chance to play God with his life."

"Deliberately?" She was shocked.

"No, no. This is something deep inside him. I don't think he has any idea of it. He could never sit down and work it out step by step. Instead he plans the future – all the time. From what he was telling me the other night, I don't suppose he's going to stay up here at the back of beyond for too much longer. Birmingham's where the future lies. Birmingham, Coventry, Wolverhampton ... just let him get a few more patents under his belt and the money will come looking for him." He patted her arm. "So you'll be coming back home to the Midlands again, never fear. And it's my guess you'll be staying at Mortimer Hall – at the dowager's insistence."

"We'll stay with my parents at Olton End Farm," she answered. "If we come at all."

"Oh you'll come," he said confidently.

The words ought to have comforted her; instead they stirred a great restlessness.

CHAPTER TWENTY-EIGHT

THE JOURNEY DOWN TO Birmingham was Lawrence's first long train ride. He was now five and almost made himself sick with the excitement of it all. Of course, he had been on day trips by train to Blackhall Rocks and to Whitby, but this was his first time in a "principal express." From the moment they left Stockton at eight that morning until they arrived in Birmingham, just before two, he was in and out of his seat, pressing his nose first to this side window, then to that ... down on the floor ... up on Ann's lap ... until Frederick looked up from his textbooks and threatened to truss him like a parcel and ask the guard to take him in the van. Ann played I-spy with him; Lawrence always spied things that vanished down the line long before they were guessed. They counted the gradient markers. They tried to count the dipping-rising-dipping loops of the telegraph lines. Frederick explained how you can tell in which direction London lies because the telegraph men always put the insulators on the London side of the crosspieces. For an hour after that, every time they went round a curve, Lawrence would recheck on London's whereabouts and inform the populace.

"Now you may forget London," Frederick told him when they reached New Street, their destination. "Look about you, son. This is the centre of the world."

Lawrence, confusing the description with "middle of the Earth," gazed around in wonder.

"What Birmingham makes today, the world copies tomorrow," Frederick added.

After listening to the porter and the ticket collector and several people on the bus to Snow Hill, Lawrence said, "They all talk like you and mummy, daddy."

Ann was thinking the same thing in a slightly different

form; she was thinking how nice it was to be *home* again and to hear around her, *all* around her, the speech of her childhood. Others might call it flat and ugly, but to her mind the surprised sing-song of the north-east was much worse. She remembered Tony's prediction and hoped Frederick was using this visit home as a cloak for a little discreet position hunting. He'd never tell her until it was certain, in case nothing came of it.

He had a strange idea that things you talked about became real. She could never look in a shop window and say, "What a handsome table," without his replying, "But we've already got a table." If she found a charming seaside view in a magazine – some place in Italy, say – and cut it out, he'd tell her, "Scarborough's good enough" – as if by cutting it out to keep she were hinting, "Let's go there one day."

She thought how odd it was that for him every casual remark conferred a reality upon its subject; while for her even a solemn promise was only half-real.

The local train ride from Snow Hill to Solihull was an anticlimax to Lawrence; his loyalties were still to the great express train they had left at New Street. Now all he wished to hear about was the farm. "Have they got adders?" he wanted to know. "And bees? And cows? And dogs?" She recognized his ABC book and they turned it into a game. Yes, all the farm buildings were painted with xylochrome, and one of them housed zebras – and then, thank heavens at last, it was Solihull and there was her father with the flatbed farm waggon.

She kissed him, which made him uncomfortable. She'd forgotten their family hadn't gone in for that sort of softness. He looked at Lawrence, whom he had seen only in photographs, and said he'd do. And then they hoisted their luggage and set off.

There was a plain pine coffin on the bed of the waggon. Frederick and Lawrence, having no other seat, sat upon it. They all assumed it was being taken out to one of the villages as a favour.

"Who is it for?" Ann asked.

"It's already claimed its tenant. Mary Holden. She's lying in there now. You remember her."

"Not dead!" Ann could hardly believe it. Mary was only her age. They'd been at infant school together, but Mary's father had got caught up in some queer religion and he'd taken her away.

"Died in labour," the old man sniffed. "In the union. No ring, of course. First anyone knew she was belly-up. Should have left her to be buried there on the parish." His tone was so flat and reasonable she could not tell whether the judgement was moral or practical.

Lawrence was fascinated to think he was sitting on a dead body. "Can we just have a peep?" he asked, looking at the nails.

"You'll see plenty of corpses before it's your turn," his grandfather promised. "See a dead calf when we get home. Help me bury 'un." He looked at Ann, seeking sympathy. "I was up half the night, and then lost 'un."

It was the first time he had spoken to her as he would to any other adult. Until now, she had always been, in some degree, his little girl. "You saved the cow?" she asked.

His nod was full of craftsman's pride. "She'll milk the season out."

Ann was glad he spared them the obstetric details, which wasn't his habit. His tales of ropes and tackle and of sawing off the heads of half-born stillborn calves had cast their pall over her own labour with Lawrence – though it had, in fact, been an easy birth.

"How's mother?" she asked.

"She's got a sore thumb."

Frederick told her later, "I like your dad. He comes straight to the point."

Actually, Ann thought, he comes straight to *his* point – which isn't at all the same thing. But she could see what Frederick liked in the old man – his practicality, his lack of make-believe.

Her father was now head stockman and had a substantial cottage with three bedrooms; Lawrence was in with the maid, a buxom, jolly woman in her forties. Her name, it so happened, was Agnes Lawrence. "Your first is my last," she told him at supper. To puzzle it out kept him quiet for several minutes. Then he wondered if they knew anyone whose Christian name would be Oxley, then they could find someone else whose Christian name was *his* surname ... and so on.

"If you ended up by finding someone whose surname was Agnes," Ann pointed out, "you could dance a ringaroses."

"Yes! Let's try!"

"It's getting silly," Frederick warned.

"The boy's a thinker," her father said with disgust.

The following morning they left Lawrence happily in tow with his grandfather. He leaned over the doors of the pigsties and marvelled at the size of the boar and the playfulness of the piglets and the fussy tolerance of their sleek, fat mothers. He ran at the chickens and laughed when they rose in a squawking, feathery clatter. He ran at the geese but doubled back from them in terror when they lowered their necks like snakes and waddled at him, honking and full of menace. He looked at some newborn kittens and then, ten minutes later, watched impassively when his grandfather put them in a flour bag weighted with a stone and dropped them in a bucket. At the beginning he almost cried but the old man looked at him and said he was a proper country boy not to go crying like some old woman, and when he grew up he'd be fit for work on a farm. So he shut his ears to the underwater mewing and ran across the yard to watch the milk churns being hoisted onto the cart. The coffin had gone but he did get to see the dead calf.

Ann and Frederick went to visit his parents and then to walk among all their old haunts – or those that were left. In the six years since their departure, the factory had gone, the Blythe Hundredacre had gone, the little winding lanes had gone. And in their place was a carpet of houses, fine houses, too, with one-acre gardens and stable yards. Some even had turrets, like castles in Spain.

It was a golden day in early autumn, when everything looks at its best. "I thought we might drop in on old Clive later," he said airily.

She laughed, thinking he was joking. She pointed at one of the fine houses. "Let's buy one of those first."

He grinned. She saw that he was serious. "I wrote to him," he explained. "Suggested we ought to meet again after all this time. Let the past be buried."

When she realized it was no idle joke, fear suddenly gripped her, fear of seeing Clive again. She remembered all the times she had resented his not coming to visit them. How safe that emotion had been when there wasn't the slightest chance of his doing so! But now ... it was all very well for Frederick to talk of burying the past. *His* past might be easy to lose. Hers was not.

"What did the grand Sir Clive reply?" she asked. "My regards to Mrs. O. and the boy? If we do meet him I'll put that *O* around his neck and strangle him with it."

Frederick smiled tolerantly; women have such strange likes and dislikes. "He asked us to tea."

"Not today?"

He nodded complacently.

"Oh Frederick!" She was furious. "Just look at the way I'm dressed! And you! We can't possibly go like this."

He did not flinch. "Of course we can. If we try to look like the gentry, they'll only laugh at us behind our backs. We'll go as we are. If they find it quaint, or insulting, or embarrassing ... well, it's a comment on them, not us. We're never going to pretend to be what we are not. Let's make our minds up to that now, eh?"

She could feel all sorts of objections to this apparently reasonable position but she could not find the right words. "At least you'll put on clean cuffs and a new collar. And I can change these frills for something freshly laundered," she said crossly. "What about Lawrence? They aren't expecting to see him, I hope."

"Hardly."

There were so many things she wanted to ask him. Practical questions, like was he down here looking for a job? And more difficult ones, like what were his true feelings toward Clive now? Did he even know, she wondered? Sometimes she thought he hid himself from himself as much as from her.

Anyway, there was no point in asking such questions. He wouldn't give a direct answer to the simple ones; and he'd make the difficult ones even more complicated, explaining everything with great enthusiasm and conviction, so that while the torrent of his words was actually pouring over you, you'd believe him utterly – and then the moment he'd finished, you'd be unable to remember exactly what he'd said; one or two assertions might ring on, but their context would be lost.

She'd do far better to talk to Tony about it. He understood Frederick more than she ever would.

They went back to change. Ann put on the best of her everyday finery, pleasing neither herself nor Frederick. And so to his parents for a midday dinner. Then at half past three they wandered arm in arm up the drive to Mortimer Hall. Frederick was outwardly calm but there was a contained excitement within him. She was full of foreboding.

They saw Clive from a long way off, deep in discussion with one of the gardeners.

"He's out here to head us off," Ann said. "We won't be asked indoors – you'll see. Tea on the terrace, what d'you bet?"

"My dear old friends!" Clive came running to meet them. "How wonderful to see the two of you again." He gripped Freddy's hand in both of his and shook it vigorously.

To Ann's amazement Frederick rummaged deep within his soul and came up with a self he had long discarded – the Young Apprentice. He glanced at her and for that brief instant she stared directly into the eyes of the unknown young man who had captivated her ... it seemed half a lifetime ago.

Brash little Freddy Oxley greeted Clive effusively. She could not look at him. She turned to Clive. Other memories rose and overwhelmed her. He had changed so little. For all that he was a member of parliament now, and a baronet, and the owner of a business whose size was the yardstick of Frederick's ambition, he was still the Adonis who had taken her in his arms one cool evening in the Wild Garden, who had told her she was the most beautiful girl in the world, who had been willing to throw away his career, his very life, for her.

He felt it, too. She could see it in his eyes – the way they avoided hers.

Frederick pulled his hand from between Clive's and took her arm, seized it, not in love so much as ownership. It was a gesture for Clive. But she was grateful for it, whatever his motive might be.

Clive had then to turn to her. "And Ann! You look radiant!" His voice had a politician's heartiness but as he bent to kiss her on each cheek, his breath was shivering. She had forgotten the smell of him. It transported her back at once, the way a fragrance can, to the little cottage beside the millstream. She pulled away from him swiftly and was amazed to hear a flat little voice, her own, saying, "You look well yourself, Clive. Marriage obviously suits you."

He smiled his agreement. "Tea on the terrace, I thought? It's such a gorgeous day."

"Will your wife be there?" Freddy asked.

"Of course. Why?"

"Does she know about Lawrence?"

Clive, now walking between them, linked arms on both sides and gave a squeeze. "How is the little chap?" he asked.

"The grandest in the world," Freddy answered easily.

"Good. Good. I mean to come and see him while you're here – if I may?" He did not wait for permission but went on: "Only four people in the world know that secret. The three of us and my mother – whom, incidentally, you are also about to meet."

"She's been so kind," Ann said. "All those presents, and all your news."

Frederick smiled at her and she understood she was performing well. She just wanted the day to end. An earthquake … an eclipse – anything would do.

Clive turned to her. "And we have one more guest for you to meet – an old friend."

They had no need to ask who, for at that moment they rounded the corner and the whole terrace came into view. Freddy, who had not seen it since the day of the Great Explosion, noticed that some of the flagstones had been removed at the far end to make space for a croquet lawn. And there, mallets in hand, cackling her triumph and roaring his fury, were, respectively, Gwen, the dowager Lady Mortimer and Tony Knox-Riddell. Eleanor, now *the* Lady Mortimer, heavily pregnant, was encouraging them from a bamboo and wickerwork chaise longue.

The game ended as soon as the dowager saw the new arrivals.

"I concede!" Tony laughed, doing a reverse arms with his mallet and hanging his head like a soldier on coffin vigil.

Eleanor spread her arms in a gesture of welcome, also revealing her reasons for not rising.

"What a reunion!" Lady Mortimer said when the more formal introductions were over. "Four of the Flying Six. And the fifth is not too far away – Miss Pickering is still at the Wildes', as I suppose you know, but is now assistant house-keeper there." She nodded at Ann.

"And Gray?" Freddy asked. "What news of him?"

"He's with the Life Guards," Clive told him. "As a matter of fact, he dined with me at the House last week. He's having the time of his life, of course."

Freddy caught Lady Mortimer staring at him.

She smiled. "The last time you were round this side of the house, young man, it was for a rather painful interview with Clive's father."

"One of several!" Freddy laughed ruefully, but the men-tion of her late husband disturbed him. She was into quarter mourning now; the purple suited her. He had written his condolences at the time, of course; but he wondered if it was the done thing to repeat them verbally – some passing reference, maybe – the first time one met. She divined the cause of his hesitation and saved him further embarrassment. "That was a most touching letter you sent me, Mr. Oxley. I was so grateful."

Freddy bowed slightly. "I did my share of tormenting Sir Toby. But I respected him. The more so as I grew older."

"It's kind of you to say so," she told him. "He took a great interest in you. The pity was he died before he could express it. I'm sure you'd have had quite a patron there."

"Oh Foxy won't lack for patronage!" Tony said.

"Quite!" Her agreement was frosty for she suspected Tony was teasing her.

Ann wanted to catch his eye but could not take her own off Eleanor, who was missing none of this – or, rather, was aware that she was most decidedly missing *something*. Their eyes met. Ann was first to look away. The new Lady Mortimer was certainly beautiful, though her lips were rather thin. Did she give Clive a hard time of it, she wondered? Was hers the ambition that had sent him into parliament?

Eleanor was remembering what Clive had told her – that

the honour of three people was in some way involved in the story behind his departure for the Cape. Were two of those people Tony and Ann? There was certainly something of a tingle between them – the way he kept glancing at her, the way she avoided looking at him. But how could that have made it necessary for *Clive* to go abroad? She watched and waited.

Footmen and maids came out with sandwich tiers and all the other impedimenta of the tea ritual. The three men sprang up to pass around the cups but the dowager motioned Freddy back into his seat. "You're our guests of honour today," she told him.

Ann remembered what Tony had said – that Freddy had offered the dowager the chance to play God with his life. It certainly seemed like that. She was the one, not Clive, for whom Freddy was putting on his Young Apprentice character. And the old woman was loving it.

The discovery allowed Ann to relax a little. She had dreaded this meeting – knowing it must come – ever since Tony had predicted their return to the Midlands. She feared arguments, accusations, shouting – though she saw how stupid such fears were, now. Instead it was going to be one of those terribly well-mannered "bun-fights," as Mrs. Wilde always called them, where all tensions are worked off in stiffly polite little comments and asides. She had served bread and butter and tea at a thousand such occasions. It was like a different homecoming.

And *this*, she thought, was the boring sort of society Frederick was desperate to join! A society in which none could tell what was truly meant, where it was considered terribly clever to convey one's meaning by saying the opposite: "Few ladies can wear glazed cotton like you, my dear – why it *almost* looks like silk!" That sort of thing. The gods would be kind to keep him forever at its threshold. But Frederick beamed at them all, like an orphan boy among the patrons of The Fresh Air Fund.

Freddy loved it: England – one day it would be *his* England. He loved the fine-cut white bread covered with paper-thin slices of cucumber soaked in vinegar, the weak China tea, the last of the season's strawberries with Cornish cream and a touch of crème de menthe, the madeira cake – nothing was more redolent of an English Indian summer than these. All that was missing was the distant plop of leather on willow, a sprinkling of applause, and the sound of old gentlemen waking up to wheeze a catarrhal, "Well played sir!" And he loved the game of conversation.

By the time it was over, the dowager, and thus the rest of the company, knew all that could be openly revealed of Freddy's and Ann's lives up in Stockton.

Tony, watching Ann, was more certain than ever that she was ripe for a little adventure.

Ann knew that she and Frederick were losing their roots – and would find nothing here to replace them. Obscure fears for their future began to oppress her.

And Eleanor had a new clue to the mystery of her husband's past. Yet the mystery itself had widened. Why were the Mortimers and the Knox-Riddells so concerned with the welfare of these "guests of honour" – a former apprentice and house-maid, if you please! Why did the dowager question them so closely about their tiny lives?

And why did they now sit here, taking tea like the equals they would never be?

The dowager preened herself and beamed at Freddy, whose whole new life she had made possible. He *must* return to the Midlands, she thought. She had the most stupendous plans for him.

CHAPTER TWENTY-NINE

ANN MADE NO ARRANGEMENT to meet Tony Knox-Riddell when she went to Meriden the following week; she left it to chance. It was like passing the decision to God. If they met, they met. If not ... it was willed so.

Willed or not, they did run into each other. She spent the morning with her cousins, but they were engaged that afternoon and so, after lunch, she went up to the village's main street, which is also the main Birmingham–Coventry road, to wait for a coach to Stone Bridge. From there she could walk or get a ride back to Solihull. She was early. Just as she was taking her second very slow stroll along the sunlit side, she saw Tony and a clerical gentleman standing at the gate of what was obviously the vicarage.

She nodded to him, feeling her heartbeat and thinking how silly it all was. He beckoned her over and presented the vicar to her, a Doctor Spence. They admired the glorious autumnal weather, the aspect of the village ... the abundance of autumn fruit. He had pleasant memories of a school holiday at Whitby.

And her coach went rattling by without stopping. Tony smiled at her, meaning "not to worry," Dr. Spence remembered a parish call and left them at his gate.

"I came to see him about the cricket club roof," Tony explained. But he immediately qualified it. "Actually, that was only an excuse. I felt sure you'd come today and I'd have been mortified to miss you. You are silly. Why didn't you tell me?"

He smiled at her, expecting no answer but her confusion. Instead she said, "I wasn't sure how long I'd be with my cousins."

He looked theatrically glum. "That puts *me* in place! Well, when are you expected home again?"

"No particular time."

"So the afternoon is ours. Don't worry about getting back. Our coachman will take you to your very door. So – what should you like to do? Let's walk, eh? Let me invite you home to tea. My mother would love to meet you I know."

"I'd like that, too," she said, feeling disappointed at the ordinariness of the suggestion. Yet what else might she have expected, she wondered.

"However," he went on, "tea is not until four o'clock, so ..."

"Where do you live?" she asked.

"Just beyond Four Oaks, between there and Berkswell. But as it's such a fine day, let's stroll across the fields, vaguely in that direction, wherever the stubble gives us an easy footing, and make a leisurely walk of it."

They turned their backs on the village. He did not take her arm but every now and then, to emphasize – or sometimes to soften – his words, his hands closed around her elbow and gave it a gentle squeeze. To Ann, who was reared in a different tradition, where such light intimacies were unknown, it was electrifying.

Their path ran south-east, along the afternoon-sunny side of the Blythe valley. Here, in the days of my Lord of Warwick, had stood the ancient Forest of Arden; now it had dwindled to a few stretches of oak woodland between acres of pasture and cornfield. The stubble of wheat and corn was crisp underfoot. The earth, still brown enough to show its forest heritage, was firm and lightly crazed. The westering sun fell aslant the land with a pale-gold brilliance, making every detail sharp. From the bleached autumn pastures the grazing cows watched them with an easy curiosity; the two walkers kept a sharper eye for the diamond-back outlines of bulls.

"D'you know that river?" he asked, pointing down the valley. The sun sparkled here and there on the water, which elsewhere was almost black.

"The Blythe," she replied. "It's the same one as flows through Solihull." She laughed. "The one Frederick and Clive tried to dam."

He nodded. "The same and not the same. In Solihull it's trout beck, but here it's minnow reach."

They drew near to a stile. A few paces before it they paused and took in the view. Across the valley a party of men were shooting crows and pigeons off the stubble. She stole a sideways glance at Tony and found him staring into the distance with a sort of brooding calm. She realized that she no longer felt threatened by the novelty of his nearness. Once again, as in Albert Park, it was as if they were old friends.

She looked back at the river and remembered what he had said. "Women never fish," she pointed out. "Don't you think that's strange?"

He nodded. As they resumed their stroll he tipped back the brim of his hat with the silver knob of his cane and asked, "D'you enjoy being you, Ann?"

She laughed. "Most of the time – like everyone else, I suppose."

"And in between?"

It was not something she had thought about, yet the answer came without hesitation, as if it had been waiting a long time. "In between there isn't any *me* to enjoy being."

He raised his cane, pretending it was a rifle, and potted a cow. "I know that feeling," he told her. "We make pictures of ourselves in our minds, or our parents give us pictures of ourselves – and school, of course – and everyone we meet, too. And then we try and live up to them. But the outlines fade and then we're lost. Isn't that what you mean when you say there's no *you* to enjoy being?"

The question gave her gooseflesh. His description was so exactly right she wondered she had never seen it herself. He took her silence, the intensity of her stare, as agreement and went on, "D'you have a picture of yourself at the moment, Ann?"

There was an implied promise that he would supply one if she persisted in her silence. She felt unready for that. "I'm Frederick's wife, of course," she said quickly. "And Lawrence's mum."

"And?"

She shrugged.

"Is it enough?" he asked.

She paraphrased her earlier answer. "Most of the time, yes."

He left it there and changed the subject. "I often wonder what it would be like to be someone else, just for a day. To be a woman, perhaps."

She laughed, glad to have left the uncomfortable subject of her inner self behind. "Wearing your sister's clothes?" she asked.

"No." He shook his head impatiently. "We've all done that, acting Dumb Crambos at Christmas. I mean ..." He sighed and fell silent.

All at once she understood the essential difference between him and Frederick. And Clive. It had never occurred to her before that a man could have a feminine side to his nature without being effeminate.

He pointed at the shooting party, now working its way up toward the far hillcrest. "The real pleasure of shooting, you know, is not killing. It's the wonder you feel that you, standing there, by the simple act of pressing the trigger can produce such catastrophic changes. Suppose there was a man over there, at the bottom of this field. And I ..." Again he raised his cane as if it were a rifle; this time he potted the imaginary person. "That's all it needs. One simple action, and I've irrevocably halted his life and shattered the lives of everyone close to him. It's terrifying, don't you think? And also wonderful."

She was content to let him talk.

"I don't suppose women's minds run that way, though." He explained her silence. "I'm sorry, am I boring you?"

"No, no! It's not something I've ever thought about."

"You've never imagined yourself with a gun to your shoulder and a man in the sights ... and you slowly squeeze the trigger?"

She laughed and walked on. Then she asked, "Have you?"

He slashed at the hedgerow where it had grown out over the stile. "It's a capital way of getting to sleep." He went over and stood on the far step to help her up.

At the top she paused. "You are an odd fellow," she told him.

For a moment she thought he was going to take her in his arms, as he helped her down. But he just stood there, holding her hands, looking up into her face.

In that moment she realized he had fallen in love with her. He was trying to be honest with her, in his own way – to tell her what sort of person he really was. Until then she had assumed, though perhaps not in so many words, that he would try to seduce her. She would probably have let him, too – because being Frederick's wife and Lawrence's mum was *not* enough ... because her life needed stirring ... because Tony's lightweight character (perceptive and charming though he was) could not have threatened her inner being ... because she craved again the pleasure she had felt with Clive – and knew she could find it with Tony, too.

Suddenly what was at stake between them had grown out of all proportion. It was incomprehensible to her that she could arouse such emotion in anyone; she did not feel – to herself – like that sort of woman. Yet it had happened. Tony loved her. He must have an image of her that she could not begin to comprehend. She craved to see it, to discover a different Ann through his eyes. And yet she was frightened of it, too. What if it conflicted with that increasingly shadowy outline of Ann the wife and mother? What if it were so powerful as to blot out all trace of her earlier self?

These perceptions flashed through her mind as she hesitated on the top step of the stile. Her words, "You're an odd fellow," still lingered on the air.

"Odd?" he echoed as he helped her down. "I don't think so." He let go her hand as soon as she was on firm ground.

Somehow the initiative had passed to her. He had laid out the situation; now he awaited her response. She gave a short laugh. "This is like that game where you say the first thing that comes into your head and the next person has to continue."

"Oh yes, I like that one."

"Well I don't. Not with you."

He laughed. "Why ever not?"

"Oh, you know very well. You see and understand far too much. I've watched you. I saw you at that reception in Stockton, and on the terrace at tea the other day. You notice everything that goes on. It made me wish I could become one of your closest friends because you see so many ..."

"But you already are!"

"I mean one of your closest men friends. I'm sure there are things you notice that you'd never tell a woman."

"Ask me. I'll tell you anything."

"If I were a man friend, I wouldn't have to ask. We'd be at such ease together you'd just say it. That's what I mean."

They were halfway over the field before they saw the bull. She saw it first and clutched his arm, too afraid to say anything. He turned slowly to face the animal. Then he relaxed. "It's a Hereford," he said. "And it's running with cows. It's probably safe." He looked back, past her, "All the same, it might be diplomatic if we edged our way slowly toward the top fence. We can climb through into the wood and come out in the next field."

The fact that the bull did not move but watched them stolidly every yard of their progress was all the more frightening to her, as if it were implying it could catch them any moment it wished, even within a yard of safety. By the time they reached the fence her heart was shaking her whole body.

It was wire-net fence; there was no way through it. Tony vaulted over with an acrobatic nimbleness. The realization that she was alone with the bull raised her to a new pitch of terror.

"Nothing to fear," he chided. "I never saw such a bored creature."

"But how am *I* to get out?" Her voice was shivering.

"Allow me." He leaned back over the fence and held out his arms. She hesitated. "You'll drop me."

He looked over her shoulder and, with a surprised lift of his eyebrows, said, "Oh you've woken up at last, sir!"

Her head spun swiftly round. The bull was sleepwalking toward them. She leaped at Tony and flung her arms around his neck. Deftly he swung her over the topmost wire and tilted to let her down; in the same movement his freed hand swung her skirts off the wire.

Her arm remained about his neck. The momentum carried her against him; her head sank against his chest. "I'm such a fool," she said.

Looking down, in a narrow slit of light between her arm, her bodice, and his coat, she saw his hand held stiffly beside her, fingers open, shaking. Three inches separated it from her waist. It hovered at the brink of that decision.

She lowered her own hand and pressed his to her waist, then the other. But this action lifted her head from his chest so that they now stood face to face, staring into each other's eyes. She raised a finger to touch his nose. "What's a kiss between friends?" she asked.

As Tony pressed his lips to hers the fear of what this might do to her marriage vanished. She herself dwindled to that single sweet melting point where the softness of her lips and his mingled and fused.

The kiss went on and on, as if they were afraid to break it and face each other. She tried to speak directly into Tony's mind, inches away. Seduce me now! I need to find myself again. I need to know what I'm like. I need to matter. She formed the ideas on her lips where they touched his, not in syllables but in raw, burning thoughts, powerful, naked offerings of her love, her need for love.

She saw another great difference between Clive and Tony. Clive had been magical; the spell of his beautiful body had once held hers in thrall. But, like all magic, all perfect beauty, there was a remoteness about it, too. She and Clive would always remain opposites, always call to each other across a vast divide. With Tony it would never be like that. His nature was so close to hers they were in touch without the need for words.

In the end it was the bull that separated them; it came right up to the fence and leaned its head over. She gave a strangled cry and leaped behind Tony, clinging to him. She felt the shaking of his mirth. "Don't go too close," he warned. "It'll lick you to death. It's a pet."

To prove it he went up to the beast and rubbed its ears and scratched beneath its jaws. It did everything but purr. Soon it was leaning so hard against Tony's caresses it was in danger of pushing out the fence. He gave it a great smack, to which it hardly responded, and said, "Let's move on quickly before it thinks it owns me."

She needed no second bidding; they almost ran to the next field. The bull, thinking it was a game, trotted level with them. "Lord," Tony said. "I hope he doesn't get angry when he realizes we're in earnest."

Her heart rose into her mouth; she began eyeing trees she might climb. Fortunately, the scrub at the woodland edge grew gradually thicker, so there was never a crisp moment of parting. Their glimpses of the beast, and its of them, grew shorter and shorter. By the time it reached the boundary hedge on its side, they were invisible to it. The creature let out a great bellow of disappointment, but there was no crashing of thorns and no whip in the wire.

"Whooo!" Ann fanned her face with her hand. "I must sit down." There was a fallen log at the edge of a little clearing ahead.

He went first. As he reached the log he turned to her, laughing. "There's a flock of sheep here. You're not afraid of sheep, are you?"

She drew level with him, looked at them, and decided she was not. At his appearance they had panicked to the far side of the clearing, but the grass was too tempting and they were now edging back. When the two intruders sat down, the creatures grew even bolder and fanned out all over the glade.

Ann glanced at Tony. He was leaning forward, his hands cupped over the knob of his cane, his chin resting on them, watching the sheep as if it were his profession. Those strange, pointed ears gave him a gnomic intensity.

"Well?" she asked.

"Aren't they extraordinary! They eat that stuff as if they'd never seen it before. Nibble-nibble-nibble-nibble-nibble ... as if it was too good to be true, as if they were afraid someone was even now striding down the hill to take this glade away from them."

"Tony?"

He sighed. "I wish it hadn't happened, Ann – if you want the truth."

"But it did happen. And that's also the truth."

He shrugged. "Oh, there are so many truths." He turned to her but avoided her eyes. "Here's one I won't deny. When we met again in Stockton, you took my breath away. I thought – I still think – you're one of the loveliest women I know. I wanted to ... I hoped that if we met in circumstances that would allow it, we would ..."

"Circumstances like this?" She waved at the glade.

For the first time he looked at her. She wanted him so much it ached. "That was then," he said, shaking his head. "But now ..."

When his hesitation turned to silence she prompted, "What's different now?"

"Then it was – it would have been mere dalliance. But after I left Stockton, I couldn't get you out of mind. I still can't. That's the difference. Now it would be serious." He looked away from her and intoned flatly, "It would also be lunacy." He snorted a single laugh. "But, in the currency of love, I suppose that's a minor objection."

"All this philosophy!" she said angrily. "Why can't things just happen?"

He turned to her again. "Listen, my darling – if we go any further than we already have, it will be serious. I shall want you utterly. To take you away. No Foxy. No Lawrence."

Suddenly she saw his difficulty, saw it as only someone with her background might. She laughed. It shocked him. "You're spoiled!" she told him. "You've always had exactly what you want! And exactly when you want it! Especially your pleasures. You can't imagine taking them any other way. Don't you think it's about time you tried?"

He only half grasped her point; she saw bewilderment in his eyes. Another way of putting it occurred to her. "You say you'd like to be someone else for a day? Well try being someone like me. When you can't have what you want, when you absolutely *know* you'll never get a hundredth part of it ... well, Tony my precious, it's only amazing what pleasure you'll discover in the little portion you may have. Let me tell you something." She was so agitated by her insight that she took his stick from him and stood up to pace about, prodding the ground to make her point. The sheep eyed her warily. "You hear a maidservant singing, perhaps? You think goodness what a happy little creature. Not a thought in her head ... such simple comforts ... why can't I be so contented? I'll tell you. It's because you've never had to try. Well it would do your soul good to try now. Try telling yourself that whatever may happen between us, I am *not* going to leave Frederick, nor Lawrence. Tell yourself you'll never be able to have me utterly, not for always. How often d'you suppose your happy little housemaid hates her lot? How many times a day is she ruined at the sight of all the fine things she'll never have, or eat, or wear? All the sweet flatteries she'll never be told. All the days of ease and pleasure she'll never be given. You just try watching your maidservants with those keen eyes of yours, and ask yourself – would you resent this, would you feel bitter at that? And" – she poked his waistcoat gently with the knob of his stick – "learn to be content!"

She was exultant now – to have discovered this robustness within herself. She felt that all loves and all kinds of love were simultaneously possible. She could be two people ... three ... a dozen! Her soul would enlarge itself to encompass them. They would not overwhelm her.

He took back his cane and weighed it as if he believed it might have become lighter for her touch. Then he said the one thing that could creep beneath her guard: "You amaze me,

Ann. You're one of the most astonishing people I've ever met. By heavens, I hope Foxy – and Lawrence – both have a proper appreciation of the fact."

He had laid his finger right on the nerve of her deepest discontent. She turned away, for fear that he might see it.

They walked back towards the fields and arrived at his house in perfect time for tea.

His mother, Lady Knox-Riddell, was an amiable woman, large without being fat, and quite spoiled. When she heard they'd walked for hours over the fields she raised no eyebrow, asked no question. Just to look at her, Ann knew she lay in bed until noon every day, not sleeping but actually living half her life – writing letters, seeing friends, ordering the household, sampling dress materials, being manicured.

Ann was also fairly sure that, until he had been packed off to Eton, Tony had made it a daily habit to climb into her bed and watch and wonder. She could just imagine the wide-eyed little boy beside that large, soft, pink body, younger then, in its loose and careless nightgown, her hair all let down ... perfumed, she was sure, between soft damask sheets. She could see him listening as she chatted on about all their friends, sharpening the little lad's wits, making him observant beyond his years ...

Later, when she and Tony were in the coach and on their way to her parents' home, he said, "I suppose the vote for dishonesty was cast when we came to our garden gate. That was when we had the choice."

"I don't see that. What sort of dishonesty?"

"Surely you do? If we'd walked on to Solihull, we'd have wiped today off the slate. We'd have made anything and everything and nothing possible next time we meet. Instead we've begun to live a lie."

She gave his hand an affectionate squeeze. "If I hadn't met your mother – if we'd walked on as you now suggest – we'd still have begun to live that lie at my garden gate. The only difference is that we've begun to live it in front of your mother. She's your measure of what's real and what isn't."

He grunted and changed the subject abruptly. "You know Foxy's coming to see me tomorrow?"

Now it was her turn not to answer – not to admit that Frederick had said nothing, hinted nothing.

"He wants money, of course – backing for a new dyestuffs company."

She looked into his eyes. He knew damn well that Frederick kept her in ignorance of all such plans. Tony had resented her telling him she would never be utterly his; now he wanted to remind her of Frederick's worst side. Suddenly she hated men, her need for them, their inability to keep love and jealousy and business apart, their command of the world she had to live in.

Someone told her once that lady ferrets build tunnels so narrow that gentlemen ferrets cannot follow them there. She wanted that skill now.

"Shall I give it him?" he asked. Just to make her choice quite clear he added, "It would mean your moving back to these parts. To Small Heath, to be precise."

That was three stops up the line from Solihull.

"Surely it's a commercial decision?" she answered crossly.

"Oh if only it were, it would be so easy! He'd have all the backing he wants, like a shot. But I can't just say yes – as if it would have no effect on you and me."

"What d'you want of me, Tony? D'you want me to pretend to be a wanton wife? You back Frederick and I'll grant you the Great Favour? Is that it?"

He looked away uncomfortably. "All right. I'm sorry if I seemed to put it that way. But there is a serious point to what I'm saying. The fact is I really ought to refuse Foxy's request – I may be wrong but I think the step he wants to take would be bad for *him*. It might even be a disaster."

"What are you saying?"

He squared himself to tell her: "I don't believe your man is as ready for this step as he thinks he is."

She was suddenly afraid. Frederick – a failure? She had never contemplated such a thought. She said, "Just suppose there was nothing between us – what would you tell him when he comes to see you tomorrow?"

"I'd try to persuade him to spend a little more time in learning the trade he thinks he knows so well. Not up in Stockton but down here at the Gas, Light, and Coke Company in Small Heath. Chemistry and engineering is only one tiny part of it. He should learn all the problems of moving a process out of the laboratory and into full-scale production. He should learn all the other elements of the trade – managing people, wooing customers. He should get out and meet our customers – and even *their* customers. He should travel in France and Germany – especially Germany. In other words, he should meet people – learn about people."

"When you say *our* customers ..." she began.

He nodded. "Our family is the largest stockholder in the Gas, Light, and Coke. How do I persuade him, Ann? What will make him curb his impatience for another two years?"

"Tell him exactly what you've just told me."

"And that will be enough?"

"No. But when he draws breath to object, tell him that the Mortimers didn't get where they are today just by knowing one or two clever processes and having a batch of patents in the cupboard."

Tony smiled. He understood. She was amazed that he could be so quick at some things and so slow at others.

"So that's the game, is it? Beat the Mortimers! Well why not, by God! They've ruled the roost around here long enough. Clive's getting so wrapped up in his parliamentary life he's turning into an absentee landlord. It's about time he learned that the best drug is the master's boot! And who better to teach him than little Foxy!"

CHAPTER   THIRTY

LATE THE FOLLOWING AFTERNOON Ann was alone in their room, when her mother came to her all flustered, saying that Sir Clive Mortimer was at the door and what was she to do?

"What does he want?" Ann asked. Her mother's agitation had the paradoxical effect of calming her.

"To see your man."

"Show him into the parlour, then. Surely Frederick can't be long now?"

"He's come to see Lawrence, I expect."

"It's only natural."

The calm had been an illusion; inside she was trembling. She wished there were time to change her dress; this one looked and felt jaded. It was the one she had worn on her walk with Tony, yesterday. She contented herself with a fresh collar and a quick tidying of her hair. The parlour was dark of an evening, anyway.

Clive was examining a small china dog she had once given her parents as a present from her first savings. They had scolded her at the time but they always gave it pride of place in the glass cabinet her mother's aunt had left them. He put the ornament back carefully before turning to her. "Ann!" He scooped up both her hands in his and gave them a little squeeze.

She smiled nervously and sat down. He was a bit shaky, too. But her walk with Tony had brought at least one immediate benefit: It had pushed Clive into the background as far as romantic associations went. On the terrace the other day the old feelings had challenged her; now they were history.

"Hasn't it been a pleasant day," she said.

He looked at her sideways, suspecting sarcasm.

She saw it and added, "I went out and walked for miles."

"It's the finest autumn in years," he agreed.

She remembered all the wonderful conversations they had once enjoyed, when they could talk about anything under the sun … and here they were, putting all they'd got into the weather!

"Why did you never come and see us when you visited the North?" she asked.

He gave a strange sigh, which she did not immediately recognise as a sigh of relief. "D'you think I didn't want to? I had to force myself."

"Give my regards to Mrs. O. and the boy!" she quoted with scorn.

He nodded disgustedly and looked away from her. "I must have written you a dozen letters, but where would have been the good of sending them?"

After a pause she said, "Well, it's all past now."

"Yes," he replied.

The silence returned.

"I went to see my cousins in Meriden yesterday," she remarked. "And just guess who I bumped into – Tony Knox-Riddell! We walked back to his place and took tea with his mother. What a strange woman she is, don't you think? I expected her to be much more ..." The word evaded her.

"I know what you mean," he said. "But now you've met her, don't you feel you understand Tony much better?"

"I don't really know him at all."

Clive laughed. "That's probably just as well. Tony knows that no woman in the world will ever equal his mother – for loyalty, admiration ... indulgence." He smiled, pretending to feel guilty at talking like this about a friend. "But nevertheless he has to go on proving it – if you follow me?"

"Are you warning me, Clive?" she asked.

"Well – he has a reputation, you know. And he always picks married women. If his family didn't own half the district, he'd be no stranger to the horsewhip – didn't you know?"

She shook her head and smiled, as if to say that it meant nothing to her. "Once bitten, twice shy," she told him.

He dropped his gaze to the floor. "You're absolutely right. What Tony really needs is someone very hard. An angry woman. A man-hater who just can't help falling for him but who refuses to show it – so that he'll have to court her every day of their lives."

She saw how true it was and felt a certain sadness that she could never be like that. "The very opposite of his mother," she said.

"Exactly."

She remembered that afternoon in Albert Park – how Tony had indulged her in the little business of choosing a couple of cream cakes. In such subtle ways, she realized, he could make any woman behave more like his mother. Bit by bit he would turn them into poor replicas – and then, naturally, he'd discard them, because they'd fail to match the standard.

Did it help to know these things? Some fatalistic imp within said it did not.

"Thanks for the warning," she told him. "Not that it's necessary – as I said."

"Of course not. Foxy's worth a hundred of Tony. And you don't need me to tell you that, either."

"What did you want to see him about – if I'm allowed to ask?"

"Oh, nothing of any great consequence. It was just that Eleanor was driving back from Birmingham today and saw him going into the offices of the Gas, Light, and Coke Company at Small Heath. They're looking for a new senior chemist and she wondered if he was applying?"

Ann nodded, hoping to convey that Frederick had discussed it all with her. "You can't hide anything in these parts. What exactly did you want to tell him?"

"Perhaps you can pass on the message," Clive said, rising to go. "I'm not in the least suggesting he wouldn't get the job on his own merit, but a word in the right ear can make sure his merit doesn't get overlooked. And it just so happens that we know several people on the board of the company. So, say the word, eh?"

From his smile she could tell that he was talking chiefly about the Knox-Riddells, and that he believed she did not know of their connection. Suddenly she felt very superior to him – and in the one field where he thought he excelled, too: knowing the right people ... dropping a word in the right place.

"I'm sure Frederick will be very grateful. We owe so much of our good fortune to you already that ..."

Clive laughed. "Bah! Humbug!" he said. "Foxy has a most robust sense of his own worth. Wouldn't it be dreadful if he spent all his time grovelling like Uriah Heep, telling us how ever-so-grateful and 'umble he is!"

The side window of the parlour gave a slant perspective on one corner of the yard. At that moment Lawrence came into view, staggering manfully under a great pitchfork of hay. Clive, who had intended going to the door, turned instead to the window. He watched in silence. Ann came to his side and proudly took his arm. *Tell me I've a right to be proud,* she thought. *Tell me I've done well by him.*

"Hard to believe now, isn't it," Clive said quietly.

"No."

After a pause he said, "No, you're right."

There was a further silence in which neither could take

their eyes off the young boy, who had now turned round, seeking his grandfather's approval. They heard the old man shout, "Come on! Come on, little cow's tail! We've not got all night!"

Clive spoke again. "D'you remember what I said that night we ..." He nodded toward the boy.

"You said I was your wife."

"I wonder how things would have been between us now if we had married? D'you ever think of it, Ann?"

"Aren't you happy with your wife?"

"Of course I am. But everyone plays the game of what-if from time to time. Don't tell me you don't."

"What if Frederick and I return here, to Small Heath?"

"Aren't you happy with Foxy?"

Of all the ways he might have answered her, this seemed the most extraordinary. Knowing him as she did she tried to imagine his train of thought.

"You don't answer," he prompted.

"Let me get my bonnet and I'll walk you up the lane a bit," she said. "Or did you come by carriage?"

He opened the door to let her go out ahead of him. "I did but I'll send it on ahead. You're quite right. I shouldn't ask such a question."

"We might meet Frederick coming home. You can tell him your message in person then."

When they were out in the lane Clive took her arm. His touch came like a pleasant memory. Every moment they spent together put him more firmly in her past.

"If I weren't in parliament," he said, "if I lost my seat next time round, I'd come back here and throw myself into the business with all my might. In five years no one would ever guess I'd been in the House at all."

"Really?" She could not see the point of this.

"And if the business collapsed, I suppose I'd look to our lands – become a fanatical, improving landlord. And if there was a depression in land, I'd go travelling around the country selling things. I was quite good at that once, believe it or not, out in the Cape. There's always a potential *me*, you see, waiting to take over from the present incumbent. I often think that love affairs and marriages are a bit like that, don't you?"

When she remained silent, he added, "Or do you believe in the romantic theory that we each have but one soulmate in all the world? Ordained in our stars. Destined to meet ... all that sort of thing."

"Not when you put it like that, no."

"Good!" He patted her arm contentedly.

She wanted to add that, though a man's potential careers might be packed away like so much spare linen, a woman's feelings could not. They had to be all true and all at the same time, however deeply that might offend his sense of logic. But he had made the moment too fragile and light-hearted to bear the weight of all that.

"Foxy's the same, I hope? Doesn't bear any sort of a grudge?"

"He did in the beginning. Now he's too busy with his work."

"Only natural, I suppose."

"Why d'you ask?"

"Well, when I suggested taking young Lawrence around the factory the other day – see where his father learned to be so clever – I thought his refusal was a bit brusque. That's all."

Naturally Frederick had told her none of this. She had to respond off the top of her head. "Well, it was hardly the most tactful offer, was it, Clive! He won't be proud of having been a Mortimer apprentice until he owns an industry as big as the Mortimers'. Then he'll tell the world. Surely you can understand that?"

Clive gave a rueful cough. "It seems so obvious – once you say it. Does he resent ... well, you know – Lawrence's existence?"

"Quite the reverse, Clive. He adores the boy. Ten years from now he'll have persuaded himself that you played no part in fathering him."

Clive was scandalized. "Is that possible?"

She stopped and stared at him angrily. "You mean did Frederick and I conspire to ..."

"No no no! Forgive me, Ann. Lord, what's got into me?"

She smiled and offered him a way out. "Tell me – how do you feel about all that your mother has done to help us?"

He nodded and pursed his lips. "There's something in

what you're hinting at," he allowed. "She doesn't like my going into politics at all. She'd much rather I were doing the sort of thing Foxy's doing. She says that even if I become prime minister – which, of course I shan't – my greatest achievement will still be the business I built up singlehanded when I was out in the Cape."

"And is she right?"

He shrugged. "I enjoyed it. But I couldn't do it forever."

"Does she keep on at you about it?"

"No. Give her due credit for that."

"Perhaps that's because she has Frederick to encourage instead. You ought to be grateful to him."

He closed his eyes and pinched the bridge of his nose – a gesture of his she had forgotten. The action finished in a short, explosive laugh. "I brought that on myself, didn't I!"

"You did," she agreed.

"What about you, Ann? D'you resent my mother's ... well – interference?"

"Of course not. How could I be so ungrateful? I just hope she realizes that Frederick is growing wings of his own. One day he'll fly without her."

They did not meet Frederick, and Clive's carriage was waiting for him at the head of the lane. They parted as if they were no more than the most casual acquaintances.

As soon as Clive was home, Eleanor asked, "Was it him I saw?"

Clive nodded. "According to his wife, anyway. Fredders wasn't home yet, but she confirmed it."

"She's a dark one," Eleanor said knowingly.

"Oh? Have you seen her somewhere, too?"

"No – just watching her on the terrace the other day."

Clive, feeling obscurely guilty, allowed himself to agree – in a vague sort of fashion.

But Eleanor was onto him. "What makes *you* think so, then?"

Quickly he cast around for some example. All he could think of was a suspicion that had passed fleetingly through his mind when Ann had told him about "running into" Tony. "Well, she told me she went out to Meriden yesterday. Perfectly natural, of course. After all, she has relatives out there. But then she said she ran across Tony Knox-Riddell. I didn't think anything of it until I offered our help – a word in the right quarters with the Gas, Light, and Coke, and so on. And there was a funny, superior sort of glint in her eye. As if I'd offered her a few shillings and she'd already earned a hundred guineas."

Eleanor said casually, "Well, Tony's no stranger to her, is he." She held her breath as she waited for Clive's answer.

She was astonished to see the colour rush to his ears. "I mean," she added, "from the days of the Flying Six or whatever you called yourselves. You were talking about it on the terrace the other day."

Clive swallowed and laughed. "Oh yes. He knew her then."

It was all Eleanor wished to hear. Now she was sure of it. Tony was positively the father of young Lawrence Oxley. It was all as she had suspected. The Mortimers had spared the Knox-Riddells' blushes by acting as the funnel – and the apparent source – of Tony's paternity money. It was all dressed up as a private scholarship to Freddy, who had, after all, been a Mortimer apprentice.

"It's extraordinary," Clive was saying. "She was never anything but a housemaid. I somehow can't see her scheming it all out ... going to Meriden, casually running across Tony, the biggest shareholder, in the very week her husband is applying for a position with his company. I don't like to think she'd be capable of it."

But Eleanor seemed weary of the whole business. "Let's help them by all means – especially as it's something of a family tradition. Just drop a word or two to the people who matter. But then let's wash our hands of the whole business – the pair of them."

"Oh come – Foxy's a good friend, you know, dear. I've known him since ... well, forever."

"Well, you and he can meet for the odd chinwag, of course."

"Yes. That's all I meant."

"After all, you have your parliamentary career to think of. Everyone says what a jolly fine constituency man you are, but I don't think you'd be happy to remain just that all your life. Would you?"

He saw her preparing to be hugely astonished if he answered yes. "Of course not," he told her.

"You have an advantage so few of the others possess. Most of them know the colonies only as occasional visitors or as former serving officers. In other words, their view could hardly be more blinkered. But you know the Cape better than any of them – certainly better than anyone in the present cabinet. You could become their one indispensable man where colonial and native policies are ..."

He stopped her exhortation with a kiss. "I am actually working toward it," he said. "As the saying goes in Whitehall – with all deliberate speed."

She sighed contentedly.

"How long have you been thinking these thoughts?" he asked.

"Ever since I saw you entertaining those two on the terrace. There's something about them that brings out the parish squire in you, and I didn't like it."

He let his head fall penitently on her shoulder. "Your comments are duly minuted," he said. "Henceforth the Oxleys can go to heaven or ... the other place ... as they wish. And they can do it under their own steam."

"Don't tell me," she replied. "Tell your mother."

CHAPTER THIRTY-ONE

EARLY THE FOLLOWING SPRING the Oxleys were back in the Midlands. Freddy was now assistant managing director of the Gas, Light, and Coke Company at an increase in salary of several hundred pounds a year. Despite this sudden rise in their wealth, the house in Hob's Gardens was only moderately better than the one they'd left behind in Albert Villas. Hob's Gardens was Ann's choice. Freddy had wanted a house on its own at the end of a little lane, toward Well's Green. She understood his choice. The house was classless, neither suburban villa nor country home; a good, transitional sort of dwelling for them. But from one of its attic windows she could just make out the lacemaker's cottage where Lawrence had been conceived and she flatly refused to live there. Naturally she did not give her reasons. After some exasperated argument Frederick acceded. He even put a good face on it. In Hob's Gardens, he said, they could really save.

They could also, apparently, afford a family at last. As usual with Frederick, there was no discussion about it. Their first night there he simply omitted to hand her a quinine lozenge, and when she asked, "Haven't you forgotten something?" he answered with a clipped, jocular, "No!" Ann was overjoyed, of course; but still, even though she would have said yes at once, she would have preferred the decision to be theirs rather than just his.

There had been no ill will with the Stockton company over his move. The Knox-Riddells had used their commanding position inside both companies to unite and then reorganize them. Frederick's utter dedication to his work, his visits overseas, would leave no time for his degree studies. But, as he said, he was actually writing the stuff of tomorrow's university courses; there seemed little point in swotting up yesterday's half-truths.

Ann, however, foresaw that she would have a great deal of time on her hands. Lawrence was at Dame school each day and Emmy, who had moved with the family, was by now so attuned to the running of the household, she organized it with little need to trouble her mistress. Ann had expected Tony to come calling almost as soon as they arrived. But her first visitor was a friend of much longer standing: Sally Pickering.

Hob's Gardens was only a mile or so nearer Birmingham than Olton End Farm. It lay in that indeterminate country between Solihull, Aycocks Green, and Elmdon. It was close enough to her old home for Ann to walk there, which she did during that first week. On her way back to Hob's Gardens she bumped into Sally. It being her day off, Ann brought her home to tea.

During the seven years since the time of the Grand Soarer,

Sally had changed very little, either to look at or to talk with. Two disastrous love affairs, one with a footman, the other with a butler at a house along Ferndown Crescent, had done nothing to improve her opinion of men – except to confirm that she wanted nothing more to do with them. The only man she had ever admired, she said, was Gray.

"But why?" Ann asked in astonishment. "He was awful. He was like ... what's that fellow in the Red Barn play – the one who murdered Maria Marten after you-know-what."

"That *is* why," Sally told her. "Gray knew exactly what he wanted and he'd take it as-and-when."

"But he was so crude. So unfeeling."

"You mean he wasn't sentimental. If I had his chances, that's exactly how I'd be."

"A woman couldn't be like that."

Sally smiled but said nothing.

"What did you think of the other one, Tony Knox-Riddell?" Ann asked.

"Mother's darling?"

Ann laughed. "Yes but what are the *bad* things about him, dear? Surely you can think of some."

Sally shrugged and said reluctantly, "He wasn't too awful, I suppose – with his elf's ears and his great cow eyes. But there's not a man born who won't let you down in the end. That Knox-Riddell would do it gently – flowers ... a little neck-lace ..."

"You make me shiver," Ann told her. "Where's the point in trying if you just ..."

"I'm *not* trying. *That's* the point. The whole point."

Ann understood the choice Sally had made; she risked no further argument. She had mentioned Tony as a preamble to adding she had met him again last year. She would have said no more than that, of course; it would take time for them to reestablish their former intimacy – if they ever did. But, in the face of such vehemence, even to mention Tony again would seem too persistent.

She offered to walk Sally back to the Wildes'. They had barely started down Hob's Moat Lane when Sally looked across the road and said, "Talk of the devil!"

It was, indeed, Tony. He was standing in the gateway to

Olton Grange, angrily shaking his boots and brushing mud from his trousers. It had been raining earlier and a passing delivery van had just splashed him. Why was he not in his carriage? Ann wondered.

"Dare we?" Sally asked.

"I don't think so," Ann replied quickly. "He won't know us. It's been far too long."

But at that moment the decision was made for them. Tony looked up, saw them, and called out, "Hello!" Heedless now of his mired legs and boots he darted across the road and joined them. "Serve me right!" he said, turning first to Sally. "Miss Pickering, if I remember correctly? How pleasant to meet you again. I hope you remember me after all this time? Tony Knox-Riddell of the Flying Six?"

Sally, hot with the pleasure of being recognized and remembered by name, misunderstood his glance at Ann. "Indeed I do, sir. And surely you remember Miss Howard, too – Ann Howard? Now Mrs. Oxley."

He was looking at Ann all the while Sally spoke. He took her gloved hand and brushed it lightly with his lips. "In fact, I was just on my way to see you," he told her. "Been playing whist all afternoon. I thought a little stroll would do me good."

Ann now had to explain to Sally. "I was going to tell you, dear. Mr. Knox-Riddell and I met last summer at the Mortimers. In fact, he is the proprietor of the company Frederick works for. It is through his good offices that we've returned to these parts."

Sally laughed. "I believe you – thousands wouldn't!"

Tony grinned. "Don't say you two have been talking about me! But what a most extraordinary coincidence, for I have just been talking about you." He nodded at Ann and gestured vaguely over his shoulder at the trees which hid the Grange.

"Me?" Ann echoed.

"Yes, I was telling Mrs. Homfray about you, as a new neighbour, you see. D'you know her, by any chance? Or know of her?"

Ann had been told about Mrs. Homfray even before they rented their house. The woman smoked cigarettes and had a hot reputation. Mr. Homfray was a great racing man, they said. *Whist?* she thought. Baccarat was far more likely!

"I don't believe I do," she replied.

He beamed. "Then come at once and let me present you to her. I know she'd love to meet you. Or" – he looked dubiously from one to the other – "are you both on some errand?"

"I'm seeing Miss Pickering home. And then I …"

"But my carriage can take her." He looked up at the gray skies. "It's going to rain again, anyway. And then it can come back and pick me up. That'll just give us time. Do please say yes. I know she'll fascinate you."

Ann turned to Sally with a helpless shrug.

"My gooseberry days are over," Sally said bluntly.

"Don't be absurd," Ann told her. "Come again on your next day off. We'll go into town and stroll round all the shops."

Sally looked Tony up and down, and laughed, and shook her head, and laughed again.

CHAPTER THIRTY-TWO

ANN'S INVOLVEMENT with the Homfray set was as much Frederick's choice as hers. He said that any friends of the Knox-Riddells must be sound. As for the alleged goings-on at Olton Grange – well, people were just petty minded. Show them a big house surrounded by a dense belt of trees and they'd believe anyone who said it was a gambling hell, an opium den, a cockfighting pit, or even a house of accommodation.

"It'll do you good," he told her, "to mix in a different set. You needn't adopt all their values. Look at the people I have to rub along with – some very queer customers."

He did not mention his other fear – that if she stayed at home and brooded too much she might return to her solitary drinking. He heard dreadful stories at work and in the club.

Most people thought drunkenness was a scourge of the working classes; but a liking for ardent spirits had become a regular epidemic among genteel ladies sitting around all day in suburban homes with nothing to do.

Mrs. Homfray, Mrs. Calendula Homfray, as she loathed to be called – or Calley, as she preferred – was not at all as Ann had expected. Before Tony had introduced them that afternoon, she had pictured an ample sort of woman with a gravelly voice and a braying laugh. But Calley was a small spring of energy – swift, nimble, delicate-looking, and never at rest. Her laugh was an engaging little peal of music, which often ended in a drawn-out, rising then falling, "Aaaaaaaah dear!" and a dab at her eyes. She somehow conveyed she had cornered the market in sheer *fun* and if you wanted a share, you had better stay close.

Yet there was something decadent about her. She reached out and touched people with the tips of her fingers when she talked to them – men and women. When she sat down she would squirm this way and that, to settle herself. Her lips were never still, even when she was listening rather than talking. Men watched her in fascination. Ann did not believe that much actual naughtiness went on under her roof; rather, Calley collected around her the sort of people who, while living solid, four-square, respectable lives, nonetheless enjoyed the possibility, the idea, of naughtiness.

They talked about it endlessly, some wittily, some with a worried earnestness, others with a lofty wisdom which suggested that – though they knew absolutely everything about it – nothing of that sort could ever actually intrude upon their own lives.

"Notice how they all sit well apart," Tony pointed out. "Real contact would horrify most of them."

"Except Calley," Ann replied.

"Yes, she's the cement. Without her they'd all vanish in different directions."

But Calley was not the only thing that held them together. They were all nonconformists of one kind or another.

The Hawtaynes, Guinevere and Leofric (he was Squire of Berkswell and a neighbour of Tony's), were staunch medievalists, hated industry, spun and wove their own wool, and wore the resulting cloth upon their backs. They practised wan and courtly expressions. He collected troubadour songs. She pored endlessly over pictures of dragons.

Mabel and Arthur Sturridge were freethinkers. They owned a large house in Selly Oak but they had let it and gone to live in a woodland cottage in Hampton-in-Arden. It was surrounded by a high and impenetrable privet hedge behind which, the locals said, they took off their clothes and walked around the garden naked. Like most of the angrier sort of atheist they hardly ever stopped thinking about God and His nonexistence.

John Gulston-Stevens was a campaigner for divorce and women's rights. He was happily married and had eight children. His wife organized the whole parish but never came to Olton Grange; she considered herself to be above such frivolity.

Frank Durand wrote strong, sensuous poems to an unnamed angel; only their anatomical vagueness permitted their publication or reading aloud. Everyone knew that the object of all this passion was Millicent Hardy, though she and Frank always sat well apart. Whenever he read his latest outpouring she folded her hands across her lap, like a coy academy nude, and smiled enigmatically at the carpet.

Millicent herself believed that vegetables have souls. She had written a book called *The Morality and Sagacity of Flowers*, which was full of imaginative but not very practical ideas about love.

And so forth. There were a dozen or more of them.

From the beginning Ann could not see where either she or Tony fitted in. But then it struck her: They were the audience! Without them the group would be forever at rehearsals, never actually performing. Hers was the passive role. Wide-eyed interest was all they demanded of her. Tony was the claque; he was there to murmur *bravo*, to throw in the witty aside that helped ease the show along.

Calley had the strange habit of putting her guests' cloaks together on one of the spare beds, so that, during their visits, their clothing enjoyed all the intimacy their wearers so fastidiously shunned. At the end of her third or fourth afternoon among the charmed circle, Ann went up to adjust her hair and retrieve her cloak. Hers and Tony's were the last. She picked up his coat and laid her cheek on its soft collar of sealskin; then she turned to see him at the door, smiling at her.

"Well now," he said, coming over to her. "Here's the real thing."

She slipped into his arms and lifted her face to his. He ran his lips up and down the taut skin of her neck, making her shiver. "Calley won't mind," he told her.

It cost all her will to shake her head. "Soon," she promised. She wanted to be sure of Freddy's baby first. "D'you mind? D'you think I'm being silly?"

"Of course not. I want you to be free, make your decision freely. It's not a favour you owe me."

She chuckled. "You sound like Arthur Sturridge on The Beauty of Free Love."

"You're not overwhelmed, then?"

"I wanted to tell him it's never free. There's always a price."

"You should."

"Oh yes – and reveal myself as a woman of experience. No thank you!"

He hugged her. She felt an unease in him and asked what it was.

"Don't grow up too fast, my darling," he answered. "Keep something of the Ann I met last year."

"I don't know how to do that." Though she was flattered at his request she also realized he wanted her to remain the sort of woman who could be moulded by precisely such flattery.

"It's easy," he told her. "Just don't be too honest."

From that evening on he made no further advances. The game of waiting, it seemed, had a thrill of its own.

After a few weeks Ann grew bored with their endless earnest talk. The novelty had gone. One afternoon, when Tony was not there, Calley asked her to stay behind. When they were alone the woman lit fresh incense sticks and sat down beside Ann, making her usual wriggles and sighs. "And what d'you think of us, Ann, dear?" she asked. "Aren't we the strangest people?"

"You're all very kind," Ann answered guardedly.

Calley was surprised. "Kind?" she repeated, as if it were a

very rare word. "I've thought of us in many ways but never that."

"I don't understand why you keep inviting me – except as Tony's friend, of course."

"Ah yes! Tony's friend. He has brought so many here!"

Ann knew well enough what she was driving at but was not going to give her the satisfaction of curiosity. "He's so good natured," she explained.

Calley laughed, once again cornering the market in fun. "Is it true you were ladies' maid to Mrs. Wilde of Solihull?" she asked.

"No. Just an upstairs maid. I'm sure it's no secret."

Calley raised her eyebrows, as if this show of frankness were especially praiseworthy. "We have that in common, then," she replied. "I began as a lady's maid." She laughed at Ann's surprise. "You didn't know that, did you." She glanced away and shook her head. "Origins ..." she murmured. "Talking of origins, did you know that Tony was sired by a royal duke? That's how his supposed father earned his barony. I forget which duke, though. It's the one with the pointed ears – as if we couldn't guess! Don't ever tell him I told you, though. In fact, don't even mention it. But the inheritance is there – that roving eye ... the incurable itch."

"Did his father *know*?" Ann asked.

Calley stared at her intensely and touched her arm. "Men are so strange," she said. "They can know something with one half of their minds while the other half remains in complete ignorance of it. I'm sure you've noticed that."

Ann smiled ruefully.

"They're not to be trusted," Calley added. "They are deceivers all, including our own dear Tony." Her smile became even sweeter. "But I hardly need tell you that!"

Ann was torn between dishonesty and disloyalty.

Calley went on. "Ah – how many times have we seen the dear boy's head turned by a dark eye, a heaving bosom, a pretty tress of hair? So exactly like his royal sire!"

"It's a side of him I'd hardly know," Ann pointed out.

"That's what's so extraordinary about you," Calley assured her. "It's usually over so quickly with him. When Tony brought you here, I thought aha! Here's yet another of his little married women from Aycocks Green. I thought you'd last about two weeks. I kept the bed aired. But ..." She raised a hand in a gesture of bafflement and brought it gently to rest on Ann's arm. "I'm sure I shock you," she added – with such an absurd air of pride that Ann saw, for the first time, that there was a vulnerable, naive side to her nature.

"Not really," she replied.

Calley wriggled with approval and clasped Ann's hand to her. "Now you're being honest, Ann. I do love all my friends to be honest. We must not let these awful, drab people who live, who exist, who drag out their existence all around us" – she waved vaguely at the nearby suburbs – "we must not let them do our thinking for us."

She's like a whirlpool, Ann thought. *She sucks people in and drowns them.* The smell of the incense was by now over-powering. Calley suddenly sprang to her feet and went to open the window. "Such a dreary time of year," she said. "What else is there to do but sit around and talk? No wonder you're beginning to tire of us."

"Oh but I'm not," Ann had to say.

Calley's smile was radiant. She came back and sat beside Ann. "Really? You're not just saying it?"

To convince her Ann had to take her hands and squeeze them warmly. "I love coming here. I love the friends you've made."

"And me?"

Ann laughed. "Yes of course."

Calley was almost crying. She leaned forward and gave Ann a sisterly kiss. "Bless you my dear," she murmured. "We already have so much in common – as I said. I'm sure that as time goes by we'll discover more and more." She sat back and laughed and wriggled. "Won't that be fun!"

Ann nodded and wondered if she could decently rise to leave.

"I tell you what!" Calley said, as if the thought had just struck her. "About this time of year, when everything is at its saddest and dullest here, we usually fold our tents and steal away to Italy. Do you know Tuscany in the spring?"

Ann shook her head.

"Ah! Firenze! Carrara ... Pisa ... the Toscano Emiliano!

All the magic of which the world's greatest art is but a pale shadow! Why not come with us?"

"I'd love to," Ann said, with more certainty than she felt. How many was "we"? Would Tony be included? She added, "But of course I must ask my husband."

"If you say you must, you must," Calley answered with an air of brisk superiority. "I'm sure I shan't ask mine."

Freddy was delighted at the idea. In his climb up the social ladder he had been afraid of leaving her behind.

Ann was happy, as well. It was too early to be absolutely positive but she felt reasonably sure she was carrying Frederick's baby. It would be safe to go to Italy in the same party as Tony.

CHAPTER   THIRTY-THREE

THE SETTING WAS straight out of a Florentine painting. Beside the farmhouse an open, sunlit grove of oranges and figs stretched in a narrow band along the hillside, between the dusty road and a perilously low stone wall. Beyond the wall was a sheer drop, a hundred feet or so, to a narrow valley filled with more commercially spaced olive trees and an invasion of stunted lombardy poplars. The far side of the valley rose through terraced vineyards to a pinnacled wilderness of goat maquis.

Beside the orchard wall, in the pleasant shade of its trees, Ann and Tony sat at a plain wooden table of some antiquity; they could look directly down at the tops of the olives and poplars.

But Tony's eyes were upon Ann. The sun, stealing among the orchard leaves, gave her a halo of gold and spilled with Italianate generosity upon the white linen cloth between them. Its warm fingers reached on down into the valley and struck long shadows across the early-summer slopes. Reflected light

off the cloth gave her face an angelic pallor and tinted all her
features with exquisite delicacy.

"You look like the Piero della Francesca madonna," he
told her.

He looked like a nervous pixie. She didn't often see him
with his hat off in public. She wanted to tell him so but his
solemnity overwhelmed her.

"It's not what I feel like," she replied. It made her wonder
if she wasn't good enough for him; he often told her she looked
like something else, usually something far more poetic than she
felt.

"Tell me?" He reached across the table and touched her
hand.

"I don't feel English out here," she answered. "I don't feel
un-English, either. Nor Italian. I can't explain it properly. It's
not like a day at the seaside back home. Something has been left
behind. I'm free of something."

There was an unease in his eye. These were not the things
he wanted to hear.

The farmwife cleared away the remains of the duckling.
She scraped them straight into the valley below, where a gang
of quarrelling jackdaws had already assembled. Moments
later she brought out brimming bowls of green figs and fresh
cream.

Tony tried again. "This setting ... this light – it's perfect
for you. I've never seen you look more beautiful, Ann."

She could quite happily sit there in easeful silence, soaking
in the dappled sunlight, eating the figs, drinking the strong
Tuscan wine, meeting his eyes, smiling at him ... until it was
time to rise and drift hand-in-hand into the farmhouse, where,
no doubt, a big feather bed already lay opened, and water and
towels were at hand. But for some reason he could not do that.
And she did not know the words to make it easy. In some
indefinable way they had delayed too long.

She reached across and squeezed his hand. "That's because
I'm happy, darling." She gave a radiant smile. "I think I'll
remember today as one of the happiest ever."

He pulled a figstalk from between his teeth and flicked it
far out over the olive grove below. He sighed.

She followed the trajectory of the falling stalk until its

green was lost in the ochre, olive, and viridian background. She remained looking in that direction, at the far side of the valley.

"Toilers in the vineyards," he murmured, making it sound like the title of an old painting. Then he turned to her. "I love watching people at work, don't you? I love meeting them coming home from the fields and vineyards in the evening, all dusty and streaked with sweat. I know just how they feel – the ache, the exhaustion, the trembling-with-hunger, the utter hollowness, the longing-for-a-wash. It makes me so glad I'll never have to work like that."

His words brought back one of her childhood memories. "Yes! When I was about six I remember pressing my nose to one of the cottage windows when it was raining and watching the field girls out there, soaked to the skin. I could almost feel the wind through the pane of glass. I could see it chasing the droplets furiously round and round in the corners. And I could just imagine how frozen they must feel and I was so glad to be all snug and warm inside."

The memory pleased him. "That little child could have had no inkling of what lay ahead," he began.

"She certainly knew she was going into service. That was made clear very ..."

"Yes, but since then. All that's happened since. The train of events that has brought us both here to Fiesole today – you couldn't possibly have imagined that. Doesn't it make you fearful of the future? If the past can be so ... wayward, where will you be ten years from now?"

"There's no point in thinking about it."

"Oh, I believe you ought to. I always knew young Foxy was bright, but he's really without an equal. With most people, you know, you can get a sort of feeling about their ultimate level, the heights they're going to achieve. As they go up the ladder, it's as if they get shorter and shorter of breath. It becomes harder for them to learn the next set of skills or the next batch of knowledge. But not Foxy. You put a plate in front of him and by the time he's devoured it, his appetite's doubled. He takes everything in. Forgets nothing. And some-how he manages to keep it all in the front of his mind." He broke off and looked away. "Funny thing is – I find I don't care

for him all that much." He looked at her and smiled. "Nothing
to do with you. But I sense there's a coldness in him."

"He's not without emotions." Ann felt she had to defend
him.

"If you say so."

"What's the point of telling me all this, Tony?"

He frowned. For a moment he had lost the thread. Then
he remembered. "He's going to be running the whole business
before long. A year at the most. Then he'll be in for a big slice
of the profits – the lion's share, in fact. In actual income, if not
in capital, you'll be about as rich as the Mortimers, you realize?
You ought to think about the future, Ann. You'll have your
marbled halls and flunkeys before you can draw breath."

She popped the last fig into her mouth and pushed her
tongue through a crack in its skin, into the gritty, sweet heart
of it. The seeds crushed between her teeth. "I don't think I
want them now," she said glutinously. The sound of her voice
made her laugh and she had to cup one hand beneath her chin.

"That's new." He was annoyed that she was not taking
him seriously. "What would you prefer?"

She gulped down the fig and made a vague gesture at the
farm and olive grove.

"Simplicity?" He looked dubiously at her. "Like the
Sturridges?"

"No, not like them. I could never make a sort of religion
out of it."

"Is this just today's whim? Because of all this?"

"No. I mean, *all this* is a good example. But really my
feeling grows out of something Sally Pickering said to me. She
said, 'If you could choose anything you wanted, would you
honestly want a damp English country house full of damp
English history. And a wet English husband to give you wet
English children. And then ponies. And going to endless hunt
balls and county balls and charity balls. And would you want
to live amid tons of personal rubbish, and keep a few dozen
servants whose only purpose in life is to smash it little by little?
Because honestly – that's all that upper-class life seems to
consist of!' And it made me wonder, Tony."

"What would Miss Pickering herself do?" he asked.

Ann looked at him accusingly. "Why this interest in her?"

"Because it obviously impressed you."

"Sal hasn't enough imagination to work out an alternative. She's one of those people who very easily sees what's wrong, but it never occurs to her to dream up improvements."

"What would you want, then? If it isn't marble halls?"

"Just to be free to be myself." She leaned toward him and became animated. "It's strange, the power of a phrase, isn't it. When Sal said 'a couple of tons of personal rubbish,' it made me look around our home with new eyes. All those little knicknacks I've collected these past years, the things we keep under glass and shift and dust every week ... I looked at them and thought suddenly what ever could have possessed me! *They* possess me, of course. I'd gladly smash them and ..." The idea petered out.

"And what?"

"I don't know. There must be something else. I just wonder if Frederick will ever understand."

His face saddened. "You're changing so quickly these days."

She smiled. "Look on the bright side. Suppose I'd failed to realize any of this until I was forty – when I was really trapped inside it all! Two *hundred* tons of it, perhaps!"

"What will Foxy do with his money then?" he asked. "If you won't let him build you a golden cage?"

"He'll find some other way to rub the Mortimers' noses in it."

"Oh is that still the game?"

She had spoken half in jest. His seriousness forced her to reconsider. "I don't know," she said. "He has an amazing ability to hide himself from himself. He's a labyrinth, and he imagines he's as simple as an open book."

Tony wanted no more talk of Freddy. "Let's get back to you," he said. "This something else you want must be something very simple?"

"Yes but simple in every way. The *choices* must be simple. Look at the knot we're in now, you and me. Why can't I simply put my hands over the table ... like this ... lay them in yours, and say, let's be lovers!"

For a moment the question took him aback; then he grinned. "Yes – why can't you?" His smile narrowed slightly as he added, "Did you know about this place – that it offers that kind of accommodation?"

"Only when I saw that woman's eyes. I wondered, of course."

"You don't feel it makes me seem too calculating?"

She laughed. "I can't believe you still worry about what you *seem*!"

He was wholly serious again. "I worry far more at what we are about to awaken."

She stood and moved clear of the table. He rose into her arms and pressed his lips to hers. His tongue eased into her mouth and she melted to him. From the door the farmwife scolded them in Tuscan.

Her windmill arms dusted them into a long whitewashed passage that ran the full length of the house. The light was green and dim and cool; plants in profusion shaded every little window. The only open door lay at the far end of the passage.

In all essentials it was exactly like the room in the cottage Clive had taken her to, except that here were dried flowers in the fireplace and orange blossom hung on branches so close to the open window that their fragrance heaped the air.

"You are so ..." he began before she stopped him with a kiss.

"You're ..." he said more gently, but again she halted him.

Then he understood.

He loosened her buttons and ribbons and began to explore her. He kissed her throat and eased away all the words that were stuck there. He undressed her completely before she touched a single button of his. She crushed herself to him, naked against the fine cotton of his suit, relishing her freedom. Her desires grew until she thought they would drive her senseless.

Then she pushed him back on the bed and removed his clothing, too. His fingers and his lips found every fold and cranny of her.

His chest and limbs were hairless and strangely childlike, as slim and sweet and desirable as a young boy's. She could hold herself back no longer. She threw herself over him and almost at once began to thrill.

He felt what was happening and, by some means, held her

back. She squirmed and wriggled but his response kept her maddeningly short of release.

She begged. She moaned. She bit him. She dug her nails into his back, feeling in each of these actions a pleasure she had never before experienced. And that, she suddenly realized, was the point of it all: not to walk again down the old ways of pleasure but to find new ones, to create them if need be.

She surrendered then to his skill. They lay entangled, moving very slowly, until each little wriggle became a torture; it concentrated every atom and nerve and every particle of their thoughts upon each other – or, rather, upon the single, sensual being they had now become.

His climax took him unawares. But she had felt it growing. She felt, too, his getting ready to withdraw, and she flung her legs up and around him and clung so tight she felt a cracking in her joints. The sudden, powerful throb of him, deep within, released her at last. For a moment she lost all control of herself.

But no sooner was it over than she felt the stab of a renewed desire – and of annoyance, too, at the sight of him, soft and foolish at her side.

Then she knew what he had been afraid to awaken.

CHAPTER   THIRTY-FOUR

THE GIRL CHILD who was born the following February had a curiously sharp little fold of flesh at the apex of each pointed ear. In others ways, too – allowing that she was as wizened in the face and as crushed about the skull as any other newborn babe – she might as well have had the name *Knox-Riddell* tattooed in scarlet letters clear across her brow.

Freddy, who had so desperately wanted this baby, would not be kept out of the room, despite the protests of the midwife,

Mrs. Harvey. So he saw Angelica, as they had decided to call it if it were a girl, before Ann. Her first glimpse was indirect – through the shame and anger in his eyes. She wished she were dead. She had felt so certain – so absolutely certain.

As Mrs. Harvey handed the baby to her, he put a finger on the swaddling, a gesture curiously like a boatman fending off a piece of flotsam with a hook. "Another one," he said flatly.

Mrs. Harvey snorted. "If you can't be more encouraging than that, Mr. Oxley, you were best off out of this room."

"For once," he told her, "I quite agree with you."

"Frederick!" Ann called after his departing back; but he did not even hesitate.

"Men!" Mrs. Harvey said happily. "Their stomach's not as strong as what they think."

Ann looked down at little Angelica, saw Tony's ears and Tony's cheekbones and Tony's mouth, and she burst into tears.

It was nine in the evening. Freddy went straight down the road to Olton Grange. The footman said Mrs. Homfray was not at home, but he had seen her outline at an upstairs window as he stormed up the drive. The flunkey closed the door. Freddy took one leap at the wistaria and Russian vine and shinned his way up to the balcony over the porch. He was about to break the window when the figure of Mrs. Homfray loomed out of the darkened room. Silvered in the moonlight, with the stark shadows of the glazing bars falling across her, she looked like some imprisoned ghost. She opened one side of the casement three inches but held it on the stay.

"Is Knox-Riddell here?" Freddy asked.

"No. Go away." It was not convincing.

"He'll have to face me sooner or later."

She hesitated.

"If he truly isn't here, I'm going directly to his parents' home," he threatened.

"What's it about?"

"You know very well what it's about. Those fine freedoms you encourage beneath your roof."

It brought all his simmering fury to the boil just to see her there, in all her elegance, in that dignified old house. Her foul ideas and odious way of life were subscribed to, paid for, by industrious and upright people like himself. He grasped at the window frame and wrenched it off its stay. She fell back before him as he stepped into the room.

"Tony!" he roared.

"I shall send for the police," she told him. She must have heard how empty the threat sounded for she added, "It will ruin your wife's name."

"My wife!" He gave a hollow laugh. "She stopped being my wife nine months ago. And as for her name – what name is that? Homfray's horizontale? Knox-Riddell's remount? How could I do more than the pair of you have already done?" He lifted his chin and yelled once more: "Tony!"

The door opened but it was the butler, armed with a shotgun; behind him was the footman, holding a pitchfork. "Shall I send for the constable, madam?" he asked.

"Yes!" Freddy said.

"No." It was Tony. Five minutes earlier he must have cut a most elegant figure in his padded silk dressing gown and tasselled fez; now those same garments made him look ridiculous. "Thank you, Summers. We can deal with this," he added.

The two servants withdrew. Mrs. Homfray lit a pair of gaslamps and pushed the window to; she had to wedge the back of a chair beneath its handle to hold it closed.

"Let's sit down?" Tony suggested.

Freddy remained standing. "All I came to say is – your whore is now yours. I don't suppose she'll be fit enough to move for a week or so – which will give you time to make arrangements for her lodging and collection. I shall not be in the house. You may take the little bastard, too. I'll not own her."

Tony looked at him, sizing up his anger, but said nothing.

Freddy felt compelled to fill the silence. "The boy will stay with me. I shall be leaving the company, of course."

"Who'll look after him?" Mrs. Homfray asked.

Freddy thought of telling her it was none of her business but saw, instead, the chance to score. "A true and loyal servant. Who do you think has been looking after him all these months, while your peacock friend here and his harlot have been learning the Meaning of Life and all those Values of the Spirit you're so keen on?"

Tony spoke up at last. "Say what you will about me, Foxy old scout. I deserve it all. But not Ann. I know how it must seem to you, but it hasn't been like that. I don't deny I love her, and nothing would delight me more than to take her as you suggest. I've wanted that ever since we met again in Stockton. But she won't come. D'you think I haven't already tried? If you weren't so blind about her, you'd see it for yourself."

"Ah yes!" Freddy sneered. "She loves me, eh? Never stopped telling you? Lay swooning in your arms, bleating on about her undying devotion to me!"

"It's the truth! She worships you, man. You're all the world to her. But you're impossible to live with. She's a skylark and you tie her down. She's as fathomless as the deep, and you measure her to the nearest half-ounce. She loves you and she can't live with you – or the only way she *can* live with you is to find some convenient, sympathetic ..."

"Stop!" Freddy shouted. He could feel all his certainties dissolving in this honeyed casuistry. His anger was his only toehold on the future. "You can talk till the moon turns to cheese," he said. "No doubt you could twist me around so I'd end up paying you to live under our roof. But nothing can ever alter the fact that great wrongs have been done. You and she are *wrong*."

Tony shrugged. "How can I deny it? We have mortally wronged you. But to *be* wronged doesn't make you right. You are not right, either. You, too, have done wrong. You've tried to stifle one of the finest spirits ..."

Freddy leaped to his feet and strode from the room, pressing his hands ostentatiously to his ears. Mrs. Homfray caught up with him halfway down the staircase. Her touch on his arm slowed his pace. He lowered his hands and, turning to her, said, "You and your beliefs have ruined the happiest of marriages. When you think how the courts punish little children who steal pocket handkerchiefs, what do you suppose you and he deserve?"

"I am so sorry, Mr. Oxley," she said. The tears sprang from her eyes and ran copiously down her cheeks.

As he went back out into the dark he knew it had been a mistake to come here in the immediate fury of his discovery. He had forgotten how easily the polished and urbane upper classes could confuse the simplest issues; it was as if simplicity were a condemnation in itself.

Three strides down the driveway he heard Tony's voice calling from the balcony above. "Foxy! I'll be there next Friday, as you suggest. But I hope you'll have thought over what I said – and talked it over with her."

Freddy did not pause.

"For the love of God, man – don't leave her alone now. Especially now."

Freddy ran.

But that will to run was the only animus left within him. His direction was heedless. The full enormity of what those two had done was just beginning to reach him. Now that he had seen the interior of the house he began to picture them at it. Ann, his beautiful, adoring, adorable, darling wife – and that snake of a friend, in his absurd silk gown and hat; he could just *see* them lying there, entwined together, saying now, my darling, now, and yes, oh yes, and all those wonderful, urgent, savage things he thought belonged only to the dark and magical warmth of their marriage bed.

Several times he shook his head angrily, as if that might dislodge the waspish images. Then other memories returned. Since Stockton, Tony had said; he had wanted Ann ever since they met again in Stockton. Is that where it had begun? Was his own promotion and move to Small Heath owed to some foul compact between them?

No. Of that at least he was sure. He knew his own worth by now.

His heedless flight, vaguely in the direction of his parents' house, had brought him to the gates of Mortimer Hall. Where all the trouble had begun. God, they were as incontinent as dogs, these upper-class men!

He should go up there and beat Clive's brains out. He was suddenly far more angry with Clive than with Tony. He counted to ten. He walked a hundred measured paces. He let the cold of the night seep into his very bones.

A quarter of a mile he walked, beyond the gates. But something kept calling him back. He had to see Clive tonight. For what purpose he could not say, but the urge was overwhelming. He turned and retraced his steps toward the Hall.

This obedience to instinct was a habit he had learned more and more to trust of late. The demands of his business had faced him with more decisions each hour than he could solve in a day of careful reasoning, step by step. He had developed a faculty that somehow leaped over all those stages.

Ann used to joke about it. "One half of your brain has no notion of what the other half's doing," she would tell him. In his mind's eye he saw her smiling face now. *Oh Ann! Oh Ann ...*

He swallowed the lump in his throat; he shut his eyes tight against the tears. He crossed the road, turned in at the gate to the Hall, strode up the long drive, and rang the front doorbell. It was a while before Old Soakum answered. Freddy had forgotten the cocky little apprentice who had come to this same door to bargain with an earlier Lady Mortimer – until he saw the old servant's look of disdain.

Freddy stared coolly back at him. "I trust Sir Clive's at home? It's most urgent that I see him tonight."

Old Soakum, who was not a forgetting man, said, "Wait." He intended shutting the door on Freddy but the young man radiated too much power and authority to permit that now. Awkwardly he beckoned him inside. Within the minute Clive came running from the drawing room. "My dear friend! You must be frozen without a coat. Come in where it's warm. We haven't yet retired."

"Have you somewhere we could talk?"

Old Soakum coughed. "There's a fire in the morning room, sir."

Clive nodded. "Take Mr. Oxley there and bring some brandy. I'll go and warn the others not to wait up for me."

"I hope I don't intrude," Freddy said mechanically.

"Not at all. You've brightened one of the year's most tedious evenings." Then, feeling his words were too conventionally hollow, he gave Freddy a light punch on the shoulder and added, "Old Fredders always came first."

Though a part of him still felt angry at Clive – knowing such anger to be unreasonable – Freddy wondered that he could ever have thought of coming here to fight him. They were bound by ties far deeper than those of marriage, deeper even than straight kinship. At the very height of his anger,

when he had felt most murderous – just a few short minutes ago
– he would still have given his life to save Clive's.

That was what had called him here tonight – that bond of
blood which knew no love, no hate, nor hot nor cold, neither
change nor degree of any kind. It was his lodestar, the one fixed
point of his firmament.

"Well now," Clive said when they were alone in the
morning room. "What's afoot? Nothing ghastly, I hope? The
baby is due, isn't it?"

"The baby is born. A girl."

When Freddy added no more, Clive swirled his brandy
and prompted, "Well?"

"It has – she has little knots of gristle in her ears here.
Pointed knots. They are quite unmistakable."

Clive needed no name. He sank his head in his free hand
and shook it slowly, rubbing his eyes. His voice sounded lost.
"No, Fredders. Don't even think it."

"I've just spoken to Tony Knox-Riddell. There's no doubt
about it."

Clive put aside his glass and stood. He paced the room,
banging his fist against his open palm. "How do we escape
killing?" he asked, putting himself and Tony on the one footing.

Freddy felt cheated, as if Clive were stealing a drama that
was rightly his.

"What can I do?" Clive begged. "Ask anything of me."

"I wondered if you knew where Gray was. I wouldn't like
him to feel left out."

Clive stared at him in horror. "You can joke about it?"

"Or go mad. I've considered that, too."

"Ann's all right, is she?"

"She had an exhausting labour. Otherwise there were no
complications. Don't start pitying her. She made the bed she's
lying in."

"My God – I can see you're bitter. I wish you were angry,
you know."

"Then you should have been at Madame Homfray's half
an hour ago."

"You came straight here? Why here? I mean I'm glad you
did, but still – why?"

Freddy shrugged. "I just ran and ran – and then I found

myself outside your gates." He shook his head at the inadequacy of his explanation. "I don't know why I came. It's nothing to do with you, after all. I suppose I can't think of anybody else in the world who knows me well enough to be absolutely honest with me at such a time."

"You make me feel ashamed, Foxy," Clive told him. "I've had the most unworthy suspicions of you at times."

Freddy smiled. "Of course you have, old boy. It's what makes you such a valued committee man."

Clive chuckled, despite himself.

Freddy asked suddenly, "Tell me – what d'you think of Ann?"

Clive was lost for a reply. He knew that bland assurances about her charm and beauty were out of the question; yet he could think of nothing else to say. To fill the silence he seated himself once more.

Freddy added: "Come on – let's say you are her soul's advocate before God on Judgement Day – what do you plead in extenuation?"

"Oh – that's rather a different question." Clive took up his brandy. For a while he stared into the depths of it, then he looked up. "I don't believe you really want to hear what I think, Fredders. What would it signify? It's what *you* would say that's important. Forget God and the Judgement Seat. Just tell me what you ... or just talk to me about Ann. I'll listen."

Freddy, too, was silent quite a while, collecting his thoughts. At last he said, "There's a hunger in her that I can't describe. It's as if" – the words dragged their way out of him with leaden emphasis – "as if she's always waiting for something to happen. She doesn't know what it is, but when it comes along, she'll recognise it."

"But isn't that true of most people?"

Freddy shook his head. "This ... *thing* she's waiting for – it's something that'll *never* happen. She'll still be waiting for it on the day of her death." He clenched his fists in frustration. "I'm not saying it properly. It isn't one single thing – that's the point. It keeps changing. It's a will o' the wisp. I remember ..."

He relaxed and subsided into silence.

"Yes?" Clive encouraged.

"There was a time when we mismanaged your father's

allowance to us, in North Shields. We couldn't even afford to buy soap and she went down to the shipyards and scraped up the stuff they put on the launching ramps. It's a kind of soap. She hated doing it, but at the same time there was a sort of pride in her at being able to. I was proud of her, too. We shared the same ... we shared ... everything. But now she's gone somewhere far beyond that. I can't describe it. She has no learning to speak of. Not book learning. But she listens to all those strange people who swarm around Olton Grange and it's like ... what were those maidens whose singing charmed Ulysses?"

"The sirens."

"Yes. It's like siren songs to her. You could tell her – even the wisest man who ever lived could tell her – that God gives most people *nothing*. Even to the richest and most powerful family on earth He gives only a farthing's worth of all the world's possibilities – but to you and me and her: nothing! You could tell her that, and she'd agree. But it wouldn't make any difference. She still wants that extra ... something."

Clive sat silent, waiting.

Freddy continued, "She wants everything to be true, everything to be possible at the same time. When I saw Tony just now he swore she still loves me, and d'you know – I think I believe him. But I also believe she loves Tony. In some strange way, it's all possible simultaneously in her mind. She once told me she cut one of her dolls to shreds, not to see what it was made of, but to discover her own feelings about it. Then she howled on and off for days because she couldn't cuddle it any more." Freddy was almost in tears at the intimacy of the memory. His voice shook as he spoke, but he went on, "Can't you see a frightening parallel with ... what she did with you? And now with Tony? She has cut me and herself to pieces."

Clive shook his head sadly. "I'd like to believe that what she and I did was dignified by anything so ... so profound. In truth I think it was nothing more than the Old Adam."

Freddy sighed. "The Old Eve, actually. I can't live with it any longer."

Clive looked at him through narrowed eyes, not certain whether the statement was to be taken literally.

"I've told Knox-Riddell to come and fetch her when he wants – when she's able. Her and the girl."

"Oh dear," Clive sighed. "One can't blame you, of course. What about the boy?"

Freddy seemed not to hear him. "I still love her, too," he added. "She can be so wonderful."

Clive nodded. "I wish I could remember her exact words that night when we saved the Grand Soarer from the gales, when the old barn collapsed. She made me realize how different time is for a woman. You and I can set our sights at fifty. We can say, when I'm fifty I want to be such-and-such. What could Ann say? When I'm fifty, I'll be worn out with child-bearing? I'll have skin like an autumn beachleaf? I'll have emptied a million coal scuttles and the dust will be in my soul? She said something like it then, that night. There was a terrible urgency in her to live, to understand things. She spoke as if time was a runaway horse and cart bearing down on her."

Freddy finished his brandy and declined a refill. He passed his hand over his brow and said, "You're a good fellow, Clive. A good advocate. She should be grateful."

"Successful defence – client hanged," Clive commented dourly. "Are you going home now?"

"I hadn't thought. I was going to my parents, I suppose."

"You're welcome here, you know. I don't need to say it."

Freddy thought of the dark, damp world outside and realized he could not face it again ... could not face a further set of explanations ... more half-truths. "I'd be most grateful," he said.

"The only thing is I have to leave for Westminster quite early tomorrow. Your staying the night is bound to make the tongues wag and at breakfast you'll face two of the most experienced interrogators in the country – without me to protect you."

"Oh, I'll be gone before breakfast," Freddy promised. "I think I'm going abroad for a while."

It was another of those conclusions – the ones he leaped to without the need for thought.

CHAPTER THIRTY-FIVE

GWEN, LADY MORTIMER rode into the stable yard from her early-morning outing. Freddy was just sneaking out by the back way, expressly to avoid such an encounter. He had no idea she was an early bird.

"Our young man of mystery," she cried, slipping from her horse and handing it to a groom, all in one smooth action. Man and beast vanished in a cloud of heady-smelling steam. The day was crisp and frosty.

"Good morning, Lady Mortimer. I'm on my way to work. Already a little late, I'm afraid."

"Nonsense. You can't possibly go like that. You look ghastly. I shall send word."

Freddy resigned himself and accompanied her in to breakfast.

"I met your mother-in-law while I was out," she said. "You're a father again, I hear. How are they both?"

"Well, thank you."

She refrained from commenting that it was a strange time for a man to sleep away from home – except that her silence was, in itself, a thunderous comment.

Eleanor was already at table. She merely toyed with some toast. He knew she did not like him. She was impatient, as keen for him to go as her mother-in-law was for him to stay.

He expected the interrogation to begin at once, but the meal passed in terse pleasantries and then the household vanished on private errands. Eleanor ordered a carriage; the dowager went upstairs to change from her riding habit. He drifted into the library and wrote his letters of resignation, checking every word against the dictionary, for he knew he was an atrocious speller.

The more he thought about this decision to go abroad, the

274

more he realized it was right. His instinct again. He needed the break – not in the usual sense, but a break from the Mortimers and the Knox-Riddells. From now on, whatever he might do in life, he'd do it on his own. He'd go abroad somewhere and start from the very bottom – not as a chemist (for even that he owed to the Mortimers) but in his original trade, as a mechanical fitter. He'd watch for his chances, and he'd come back with enough to start his own business, which he'd then build up until the Mortimers and the Knox-Riddells of this world would come cap-in-hand to his front door. Emmy would look after Lawrence. He was already impatient to begin.

Eleanor drove straight to Hob's Gardens, where she found Ann sitting up in bed, much calmer than she had expected. She congratulated her on the baby, who was at that moment being bathed in the kitchen – and leaving the household in no doubt as to her dislike of warm water. Ann behaved as if she was being complimented on third prize in a cake competition. Eleanor tried to share one or two intimate memories connected with the birth of Rosamund, her own eldest; Ann merely nodded.

"Mr. Oxley probably found it all a bit much," Eleanor ventured. "I expect you know he spent last night at the Hall?"

"He's better off there," Ann said.

The utter self-absorption of this remark angered Eleanor, but she controlled herself. "Of course, Sir Clive is immensely fond of your husband and would do anything for him. I only hope he won't feel let down."

"Frederick would never let anyone down, Lady Mortimer."

"No, no – I mean the other way about. I hope Sir Clive won't let him down. My husband is so very busy, you see. These are crucial years in his parliamentary career – years when he will rise above the ordinary ruck of M.P.s and establish ..."

"It's not Frederick," Ann began. Then she quailed at the impossibility of the explanation.

Eleanor pressed on. These two self-absorbed, demanding young people had to realize how unimportant they were. "Already he's becoming an authority on affairs in Southern Africa. Only last week the prime minister himself ..."

"It's not Frederick," Ann repeated. "Don't you understand? It's me!"

"You?" Eleanor hesitated. "No, I don't understand."

The baby had stopped crying.

"I'm the one who spoils things for everyone," Ann said flatly.

Eleanor was aghast. All her stored-up words, everything she had thought of saying, shrivelled within her. How could she have misread the situation so? There were tears in Ann's eyes but she was trying to behave as if they were not there.

"Come!" Eleanor was mortified now at her own insensitivity, and desperate to comfort Ann. "We don't all feel as joyful and loving as the journals like to pretend. When poor little Rosamund was born I positively disliked her for weeks. And I hardly need say how guilty I felt – oh, the self-accusation! But it passed, you know. Even the blackest mood passes in the end."

"Time for a feed!" Emmy brought the now-quiet Angelica to her mother.

"You don't mind?" Ann asked.

"Of course not. I'm the one who should ask."

With a strangely mechanical gesture Ann bared a breast and lifted the baby to it.

"Oh the little darling! May I?" Eleanor knelt near her to see the child closely.

Smiling, never taking her eyes off her visitor's face, Ann deliberately rearranged the swaddling to reveal the ears. She saw the recognition dawn in Eleanor's eyes – and saw it quickly smothered. "Such dear little faces they have," Eleanor said, avoiding her gaze.

It was the moment when Ann first realized she and Angelica would have to go away. She'd take the girl and find work somewhere.

The thought of seeking Tony's help flashed through her mind but she rejected it, almost with abhorrence. There'd been enough of that already. She'd borrow a few pounds from Sally and see it through on her own. She'd make something of her life on her own.

In the depth of her misery that thought – "I can achieve something *on my own*" – came to her as an immense comfort.

On her return journey to the Hall, Eleanor told her coachman not to hurry. She needed time to think. Having misread the situation so drastically, she wanted no further mistakes.

She realized that Freddy's instinct to run away last night had been quite right. The difficulty now would be to prevent his return – or, rather, his immediate return. (Clive had told her nothing of Freddy's decision to go abroad; he thought it was just one of those things people say at times of stress.)

If Freddy could be found six months' urgent work away from here, Eleanor thought, away from Ann and that living little accusation, time might do its mending.

It might not, of course; nothing was certain – except that if he stayed, the daily salt in the wound could only make it worse.

She'd have to see Tony. The very least he could do now was to devise some way to get Freddy out of Solihull for a while, preferably abroad.

She settled back among the upholstery, pleased to have reached so sensible a conclusion. She began to think about Tony and Ann. What folly! Fancy behaving as though the bargain over Lawrence had extended to a second child!

She still wondered what had made it necessary for Clive to go out to the Cape. Perhaps there was a similar skeleton in his cupboard, still unknown to her? But it was ridiculous for anyone to go for such a trivial cause. If the sons of gentlemen were exiled for getting maidservants into trouble, the entire court and parliament would have been exiled to the colonies generations ago.

Perhaps Clive took exception to the arrangement – which was really an abuse of Freddy's honour – and had gone abroad for a year or two to register his protest. She remembered that day when he told her "the honour of another" was involved – and then had corrected it to the honour of two people – and then of three. It implied that the second and third persons were not the sort one usually associates with the notion of "honour" – such as an apprentice and a housemaid.

Perhaps, then, Clive had felt the humiliation of Freddy so keenly that, in a fit of anger he had gone out to the Cape. He had been rather impetuous in those days. But from the moment he arrived there, time and distance had begun to heal the insult, so that in the end only his marriage to her and the need to consolidate a thriving new branch of the family industry had kept him there.

She was not completely satisfied with this explanation, but for the moment it would do.

A footman came into the library just after eleven; he announced to Freddy that biscuits and sherry were being served in the morning room. It seemed to be some kind of code for "the dowager commands your presence." She was there, anyway, dressed for walking, in a grand Inverness cape and a hat such as alpine climbers wear. "It's turned into a fine morning," she said. "Eleanor's out somewhere. Thought we might take a turn around the terrace and disturb the gardeners. One of Sir Toby's old coats wouldn't look too ridiculous on you. What d'you say?"

"I shan't need a coat, thanks."

It was a fine sherry. Its vapours opened every channel in his nose and head; all his weariness seemed to fall away. Outside, a bright, wintry sun had left just a hint of frost in the crannies of the stones.

"February filldyke," she mused. "He's not filling many dykes this year."

"It rained last night around three," he told her.

"And what was keeping you awake at three? Are we going to hear?"

Freddy hesitated. He had prepared for everything but a direct question.

"Surely you know there's a great concern for you in this household?" she said, watching him closely; then she added, "Why that disbelieving smile?"

"There was a time, Lady Mortimer, when you wouldn't much have mourned my death."

Her shock seemed genuine. "How can you say it?"

"I'll tell you the very day and hour. When we flew that machine we made, the Grand Soarer. After the first little flight the others said let's stop, but I said no, I wanted to make a proper flight of it. And you said, if ..."

She cut in, "If this young man wishes to do the thing properly, I don't think we should stand in his way."

"That's right!" It surprised him that she had remembered.

"And you supposed it was because I wished to see you ... die? Good ..."

"Well, I surely wasn't your son's favourite friend?"

"I thought what you did that day was the most exciting thing I'd ever seen. When you soared aloft, you carried me with you, every inch of the way."

Freddy stared at her intently. Her memory must have completely reversed the events of that day.

She went on, "I often wondered why you never built another soaring machine. When you came to earth that day you had the look of a man who'd conquered the impossible. Have you forgotten how you felt?"

"Certainly not."

Their aimless stroll had brought them to the top of the great marble staircase. He took the first step down. "It was the same feeling as I had on the day of the Great Explosion. Did Clive ever describe it to you? Exactly what happened, I mean?"

She followed him down, catching hold of his arm to steady herself. "It was one of those sal-volatile episodes," she said with a stage shudder.

"I walked down these steps" – he began to relive it for her – "no faster than this. The fire was burning under there. I had induced Clive to throw the bomb into it by pretending I was going to run. But then, when it was too late for him to fish it out again, I just sauntered down. I knew the bomb could go off and the stairs would shatter around me. But somehow I knew I wouldn't be touched by any of it. I felt truly immortal. No – I felt ... oh, it's so hard to describe. I felt as if the world was paper thin, like a scene played out in shadows on frosted glass. And the glass was just about to shatter and I'd see the real world beyond it. That's the most exciting feeling I ever get."

She looked at him admiringly. "I don't think there's anything you'd set your mind to that you couldn't do."

"I hope you're right, Lady Mortimer," he said. "I've just decided to go abroad."

"For the company?"

"No. I mean to give it all up. Start afresh."

She gripped his arm like a bird of prey. "But you can't. It's quite impossible."

"My mind's made up."

"But we've ... I mean ... you've put so much into it!"

"And so have you. And for that reason I wish I could be more frank with you. All I can say is that I've had an almighty ... well, Tony Knox-Riddell and I have fallen out. Rather sharply. I have no choice."

She relaxed again. She even laughed. "Oh is that all!"

"No, it's something quite fundamental, I promise you. There's no question of ..."

"Is it money?" she asked, cutting straight through his hesitation.

He looked sharply at her to see if she were serious.

She smiled. "I thought so. How much?"

He shook his head. "It isn't that. I wish I could explain."

Her nostrils flared angrily. "So do I young man. Indeed, I think you *owe* me an explanation."

He turned on her then, pulling his arm away and jabbing a finger that stopped just short of touching her. "That's it! I *owe* you an explanation. I *owe* Knox-Riddell my present position. I *owe* my membership of the club to Clive. Dear God, it's a wonder there's any scrap of me that's not pledged in some way to one of you. Don't you see?"

His earnestness frightened her. She tried to soothe him. "Well, my dear – when I said *owe*, I'm sure I didn't mean it in that mercenary sense. But it does you great credit to be so sensitive upon the point; it shows a fine, discriminating nature. What I meant was that surely, over these years, we have built up a friendship, you and I, that has long ago effaced all question of mere financial obligations between us – in either direction. Surely you feel it?"

The hair bristled on his neck. She was *good!* Of course she had meant to remind him of his debt to her when she first spoke of "owing." But how swiftly and adroitly she had recovered the situation! If there were more women like her, then thank heavens they weren't in business.

She left him no choice but to accept her new line of attack and meet it as best he could. He smiled ruefully. "You're right to rebuke me," he conceded. "I am absurdly sensitive upon the point. But I must go abroad for a while. Trust me that far. It has nothing to do with you, or Clive, or any of those obligations of friendship and support we have created between us over the years. It is something quite, quite different."

She could see him outmanoeuvring her again. She said what must have been the first thing that came into her head.

"If you feel the Knox-Riddells are keeping you back, then what about all the Mortimer businesses?"

He was nonplussed. "I'm sorry? What about them?"

"Well, you know yourself what a fragmented lot they are. Little workshops all over the place. Just because they've always been like that everyone thinks it's splendid. Wilde won't hear of a change. I've long maintained we need a new broom."

"D'you mean me?"

"Who better? You practically grew up in the business. And no one could accuse you of sticking in the mud."

He was fascinated at this quite unexpected turn of events. "Have you the power to …"

"I have enough shares – don't you worry. And don't think, either, that this is some spur-of-the-moment decision. I've discussed it many times with Clive – ever since Tony Knox-Riddell began singing your praises."

"Clive would be against it, of course."

"How d'you know?"

"He had a dozen chances to mention it last night."

She looked away in disgust. "That boy has no real interest in the company, except as a milch-cow for his political ambitions. He'd give it away for votes." She smiled again. "Fortunately, thanks to the vagaries of the marriage settlement acts, while I live I can outvote him in the one place where it matters. I can offer you the management of the companies."

He whistled but his lips were dry. Even his tongue was barely moist enough to wet them. "I tell you what," he said at last. "I'm completely bowled over by this offer. I'm going to kick myself tomorrow, I know. But I still have to turn it down."

She almost exploded in her wrath, but he gripped her arm and managed to make her listen.

"I simply couldn't accept it without Clive's wholehearted approval. It would cause such a rift between us. But you saw how I hesitated!" He laughed in self-mockery. "You know what a temptation it is, even now, to accept."

"Well then …" she began, happy again.

"So let's say this. I'll go abroad – as I planned – and for all those good reasons that I cannot divulge at the moment, but which I ask you as a friend to accept in trust. Meanwhile, you go to work on Clive. If it's as sensible as it sounds, you'll make him see it. I know you will. And I promise that, win or lose, I'll come back a year or so from now – and then, if you still want me, and Clive agrees, you have me."

He saw, by the glint in her eye, that to give her the objective of winning Clive around had been an astute move. She would grumble a little longer, cajole him some more, but she'd accept his offer in the end.

And so it proved. "But let me also say this," he continued. "If I come back as rich as I hope to be, that money goes into the business, too."

"Of course," she agreed lightly.

"Even if it's enough to outvote you all?"

She wasn't so happy about that.

"When I come back, I shall never again work *for* anybody," he said. He saw the hurt look in her eye and added, cajolingly, "Don't be like that, Lady Mortimer. You're the one who made me what I am."

"No," she said quietly. "I merely *allowed* you to be what you are – and that's quite a different thing."

Before lunch Eleanor found an opportunity to corner him. "It's so nice to see you here at the Hall, Mr. Oxley," she said. "The pleasure has been all too rare. I hope it means that the pressures of your work are beginning to ease at last?"

"They will," Freddy told her. "Very soon now."

Her momentary uncertainty at this reply told him she knew something. Had she driven over to see Tony this morning?

She smiled. "I'm so glad. I wish I could say the same for Clive. His parliamentary obligations seem only to multiply."

"But he thrives on it."

"Yes." She looked at him sharply. "Of course, he has the right background."

Freddy looked around them, at the oak panelling, the ancestral portraits, the suits of armour. "All this," he said.

But she shook her head. "No, I wasn't referring to that. After all, think of the thousands of idle young men who grow up in even grander surroundings and yet who do nothing with their lives. They're becoming a scourge. I'm sure, without mentioning any names, we can both think of several instances."

He laughed. "Are you trying to convert me to socialism, Lady Mortimer?"

She laughed with him. "May I offer you a sherry, Mr. Oxley?"

He declined. They went into the morning room, where she seated herself; he stood by the mantelpiece, staring into the fire.

She tried again. "The background I referred to has nothing to do with breeding. It's available to any man."

When he did not immediately respond she thought over what she had said and wished she had put it differently. "Available to any man" was hardly a happy choice of words! "What I mean," she went on, "is this. I don't think the prime minister picked Clive to chair this committee on African policy simply because of ancestral portraits and half a ton of ancient chain mail."

"That's certainly true," Freddy agreed. "Those years he spent out in the Cape will prove the best investment he could possibly have made in his political career."

Eleanor was quick to press her point. "Not just that, Mr. Oxley. You see, if he hadn't gone into politics, what he learned out there would have stood him in equally good stead if he had taken up the reins of our family business. These divisions – politics ... business ... and so on – they're so artificial. It's experience that counts, especially experience overseas."

He kept a straight face. "Yes, I have found my visits to Europe of immense value. They've opened up my eyes to so many different ways of doing the same thing. We British can all too easily forget that the rest of the world exists. We think our way of doing things is the only possible way. Oh no – I firmly believe in the value of travel and overseas experience."

She could not believe her luck. "You yourself now – you never considered a protracted period abroad? Six months, say?"

"No." He tried to look as if the idea had never occurred to him – but as if he realized it ought to have. "It's certainly something to mull over."

She smiled happily. "You and Clive are so alike in many ways, you know – despite all the more obvious differences."

"Oh? In what ways?"

She looked down and blushed. She did it very well – not too much. "It's probably impertinent of me to say this. Please don't think I mean it to be. But it's occurred to me more than once lately that the single element which may be lacking in your astonishing progress is precisely what we have been discussing. Oh, how awful of me to be talking to you like this!"

"Please! I'm delighted you do. The quality I most admire in anyone is candour."

"That's another way in which you and he are alike. I'm sure that – with the experience you've already gained – you could turn a six-month visit abroad into as good an investment in your future as he made of his four years."

The luncheon gong summoned them.

"I can't tell you, Lady Mortimer," he said as he took her into the dining room, "how happy I am that we had this conversation."

CHAPTER THIRTY-SIX

ANN PRESSED HER CHEEKS to the railings of the Foundlings Hospital at Coram's Fields. The cold iron hurt but she welcomed the pain. Without it everything seemed unreal. The money Sally had brought to the hospital was all gone. There could be no more. Anyway, Sal had been followed that time; it would be too risky to try again.

Ann was watching the little foundlings at their play, trying to persuade herself how happy they were. But in her heart she knew the only happy child in sight was barely a month old and presently lay snuggled against her, warmly wrapped and fast asleep. Little Angelica had a full belly, too, though how much longer the milk would last Ann was beginning to wonder; she herself was reduced to hide and bone. Soon there would be no kinder home for the baby than the steps of the Foundlings Hospital.

"Which one's yours?" asked a voice at her side.

Ann pulled her face from its lodging and looked at the stranger, a middle-aged woman with the comfortable appearance of a cook or housekeeper. "None," she said, glancing down at Angelica. "Not yet."

"How long since you ate?"

Ann avoided a lie. "She's just been fed."

The woman smiled. "And you? You look like you could just about do with a nice cup o' tea."

Ann shrugged. "Well, I won't say no."

"A morsel of meat pie wouldn't go astray either, I dare say."

They introduced themselves; Ann gave her maiden name. The stranger was a Mrs. Curtis, cook to a gentleman's household in Gray's Inn Road. They walked down Lamb's Conduit Street and found a modest little eating house, where they settled themselves near the window. Angelica woke briefly, blinked at the light, and fell asleep again. "She's ever so good, really," Ann said.

Mrs. Curtis sighed. "I give mine up to the Coram's seven years ago, next apple-christening day. That's why I took the job in Gray's Inn Road – so as I could come down in my time off and keep an eye on him, little Peter."

Her lip trembled so violently at the name, Ann was afraid to inquire if the lad had died.

"That's why I asked you which was yours," Mrs. Curtis went on. "See if you had my trouble."

The meat pie came. Hot food had never smelled so scrumptious; for days Ann had crossed the street rather than walk past the open door of any eating house. "What trouble was that?" she asked when she had the first few mouthfuls inside her.

"I thought I should always know my own little Peter. Never forget him, not with his great big nose and all. But they keep them in for three years, see? I didn't know that. There's a little court out the back where the infants play, but you can't see it. They're four years old before they come out to church of a Sunday. You should have seen me that day! No better than a bride, I was. The old ticker was all over the place, like a cake of soap in a washtub." She fell into a reverie. A sadness filled her.

"Did he recognise you?" Ann asked.

The woman shot her a bitter look. "Him! Recognize me? I didn't even recognize *him*. By the time they're four, they all look the same. They've all got that same pinched face, the same flat eyes, the same pointy look. He could have died. I don't know. He could walk past me – I come here every week, see, like today, on me day off – he could walk right past me. How would I know? I should ought to of had the little mite tattooed."

Ann wondered why she still bothered to come in that case.

Mrs. Curtis answered the unspoken question. "I watch them at their play, see? And when one of them does something special, catches a ball that the others'd drop or wins at hoop-and-hook – I say to myself, 'That's my Peter!' You've got to keep the memory alive, haven't you."

Ann finished the pie and tried hard not to glance toward the counter. "Want another?" Mrs. Curtis asked.

Hot with shame, not daring to look up and meet her eye, Ann nodded. She explained, "The old lady who boils sheeps' heads in Little Ormond Street, she usually gives me a cup of broth, but she wasn't there today."

Mrs. Curtis gave the order. "Little boy? Or a gel?" she asked while she poured out more tea.

"Angelica," Ann said.

"Still, boy or gel – what's the difference at that age? She's got a dozen good years ahead of her, I say, no matter what. A dozen years before any man can ruin her life. Is that wedding ring real, love?" She laughed at herself. "Don't mind me, I'm as nosey as the cat."

"It's real."

"Old man popped off?"

Ann frowned.

"Kicked it?" Mrs. Curtis explained, looking heavenwards. "Gone to join the choir invisible?"

"Oh ... no. Nothing like that."

"Better off without them. Some of them."

"He's better off without me. That's the truth."

Mrs. Curtis put her head on one side and considered her shrewdly. Ann was torn between gratitude for the food, which implied some small obligation to satisfy the woman's curiosity, and her own desire not to think about it all – especially about the inevitable separation from her baby, which could not be postponed much longer.

"You been through a bad time," the woman said. "Anyone can see that. Got any family? Anyone who'll help?"

"I've shamed them all."

"Washed their hands of you, eh? Are they out looking for you?"

"I expect so. They'll give up in the end, though. A month or two, a year, maybe, and they'll accept I've gone. They'll be better off."

"And you? How are you going to live?"

"I was in service six years. I'll find a place."

"Without a character?" She made a doubting, upside-down grin. "You'll have to watch it, my dear. You don't need me to tell you where starving women, pretty, young women, can end up."

Ann sighed and shrugged. "I'm not much above that even now."

Mrs. Curtis shook her head. "Don't you believe it, my love! You're a mile above it." She walked her fingers to the edge of the table. "You can be an inch from it, see, but a mile above it. But you take that step – you may think it's only an inch" – she walked her fingers off the edge of the table and let her hand fall dramatically – "only an inch … but it's a mile to climb back up again. A million miles for some. You want to be very careful."

"Surely someone'll help? There must be places …" Her voice tailed off. What did it matter, anyway?

She gazed out of the window. On the far side of the street she saw a tall, respectable gentleman walking slowly by in the direction of Coram's Fields. "Who is that?" she asked. "I've seen him in this area several times lately."

Mrs. Curtis screwed up her eyes to clear her focus. Then she grinned and struck herself on the forehead. "The very man! I'd forgotten him. Now *he* could help you. He's helped a lot of girls like you."

"You know him?"

"For years. To talk to, you know. He's often round the Coram. Mr. Netherbere. Charles Makepiece Netherbere – a most charitable gentleman. A one-man charity, you might say."

"Does he live nearby?"

"Not as I know ..."

"Only I thought ..."

"Oh – because he's often round the Coram? No – stands to reason, my dear. Everyone's got their place in London. Where are you going to find fallen women, eh?" She dug a thumb vaguely southwestward. "Down the Garden. And where would be best to catch 'em afore they fall?" The thumb swivelled around northward. "The Coram. You lay little girlie there on the foundling steps, ten to one you'll turn round to find Mr. Netherbere waiting behind you with a slip of paper in his hand. And on that slip of paper – the directions to a good Christian house where you may find a place before you fall. The very least you'll have a bed for the night until he can get you set on."

A wild hope sprang up in Ann's mind. "D'you know him well enough to ask him – for me? Perhaps he could find me a place where I could keep my baby?"

Mrs. Curtis smiled sadly and shook her head. "Now where in all the world will you find a place like that?"

"She's born in wedlock."

"You'd be willing to prove it?"

Ann's enthusiasm subsided. "Still, he might know of one. I'd work for nothing – no wages. Just our keep. Ask him, please? Oh please, please, dear Mrs. Curtis!"

Miming hopelessness, but infinitely obliging, the older woman rose to her feet. "God knows," she said, "I'm the last to want to see a mother separated from her own little mite." With a brave smile she went to the door. The proprietor merely nodded; she was obviously a regular here. Through the window Ann saw her cross the street and diffidently engage the charitable Mr. Netherbere in conversation.

Soft into the ear of the still-sleeping Angelica she whispered, "It's all going to be all right, my darling. Mama's going to find us a home. No more sleeping out in the shelters. It's going to be all right."

She went on saying it even as she saw Mr. Netherbere shaking his head. But then he stopped. He tugged thoughtfully at his beard. He nodded gravely. He shrugged. He put his hands together as if about to pray. He rubbed them slowly, in deepest thought. He shrugged again and nodded, as if to say that in this infinitely variable world all things were possible, however remotely so.

Mrs. Curtis returned. "He'll try. There's not much hope, but he'll try."

Ann's heart vaulted the moon. "Oh, thank you, thank you, thank you, Mrs. Curtis. You're a dear, kind soul and I can't even ..."

"I can't even stay," the woman picked up the words and laughed. "But you can. Stay in here where it's nice and warm till Mr. Netherbere comes back. Have another pie? Or a slice of apple tart?" She took a silver threepenny bit from her purse.

"Oh I couldn't," Ann began.

But the woman pressed it into her hand. "And don't think of paying me back, dearie. One day, when you're on your feet again, you can do some other poor unfortunate, or *near-* unfortunate, a good turn. Just say a little prayer for me then. That's all the thanks I want."

"For you *and* Peter," Ann said.

Mrs. Curtis frowned. Ann feared she had trespassed, but it was the frown of habitual grief, soon gone.

Then Ann had time to reflect upon the goodness of people – and her own deep unworthiness. It was more like two hours before Mr. Netherbere returned. Angelica had just finished another little feed. Ann's long-empty stomach was twisting and rumbling in its fight to remember what to do with food.

Mr. Netherbere had the kindest eyes imaginable – though in her present mood Ann found everything about him kind and good – his deep, reassuring voice, his quiet, unhurried air, his obvious sympathy as he listened to her answers. He began by asking several questions about her background and years in service. Then, saying he could only help her if she was entirely candid with him, he asked her to explain how she came to find herself in such circumstances. She confided to him everything except the true names of those involved, including her own surname. He seemed to accept the need for her reticence, and he heard her out in earnest silence. When he spoke at all, he called her Miss Ann. Even at the most shaming moments of her narrative his eyes held not the slightest cast of judgement. Jesus himself, she thought, when he heard the tale of the woman taken in adultery, must have listened in just such a manner. All he seemed concerned to establish was that she had severed herself from her past and that no one was going to come looking for her.

"It would be most embarrassing for me, and for those kindly people who offered you sanctuary, if some irate husband began to harry us all with writs for crim-con and damages for the loss of your services."

She assured him he need have no worries on that score. Frederick would be heartbroken for a while, but time would teach him how much better off he was without her.

With every word that Mr. Netherbere spoke, of course, she longed to break in and ask him if he knew of a place where they would accept Angelica, too. At last he put her out of her suspense. "Well, the best I have been able to find, Miss Ann, is a position with a wealthy family in British Guiana. D'you know where that is?"

She shook her head, hardly daring to speak.

"In South America. It sounds a long way away, doesn't it. But the steamship has changed all that. The voyage takes weeks, now. Not months. And it needn't be expensive, either." He waited for her to ask a question but none came. He went on. "They're a family called de Santos. Mr. de Santos is one of the country's leading traders. A protestant – which is less common there than here – but that is how I know of him, through our church. He wants … well, I suppose one would call it a governess, but not to teach his children. Merely to hold English conversations with them for a part of each day. But, like a governess, you would live with the family. And the emolument – are you interested in the, ah, financial …"

"If I may keep my baby, as I said to Mrs. Curtis, I'd work for nothing." She saw his face and stopped. "No?" she asked bleakly.

He flinched. "Mr. de Santos is the very soul of charity. If he were here now, if he could see you and the dear little angel – how well you named her! – I entertain not the slightest doubt but that he would consent at once to accommodate the pair of you. But" – he shrugged helplessly – "Mr. de Santos is not here. The only thing I may suggest, dear Miss Ann, is that you lodge the child with some relative, perhaps, and go to Mr. de Santos for a year. You will earn sixty pounds in that time, for fifteen of which you could voyage back to England, collect your child, and return to Mr. de Santos. As I say, I have no doubt but by then he will be so pleased with you, he'll consent at once." He patted her arm encouragingly. "Think it over, anyway."

"There's nothing to think over," Ann said quickly. "Or nothing new. I've had four weeks already. I'll ... see to the lodging of the baby and then ... well, what then?"

He took a card from his case. "I live not too far from here, as you see. Do you know your way?"

Coldbath Square. It was near Mount Pleasant. She could even see the house in her memory. "I know every cobblestone for miles," she replied.

"Well," he smiled happily, "those days are already behind you now. And as for this separation from your loved one – a year may seem a long time, but it will go quickly enough, what with the excitement of your journey and the novelty of a foreign country. It will pass in a twinkling, you'll see. Er ... how long will you require to settle the child? I only ask because there is a ship sailing from Tilbury on tomorrow's tide, bound for Demerara."

Get it over with, Ann thought. She looked outside. It was dark. "An hour," she said. "I'll be with you in an hour."

They parted at the door of the eating house. He took all his good cheer with him. Left alone in the cold street, Ann hugged the tiny bundle of her baby to her. "Only a year, my little love," she whispered. "Mama's going to make a new home and a new life for us. Only a year."

She took a discarded newspaper from a litter bin and found some shelter between two brick buttresses outside a pub at the corner of the street. There she gave Angelica her last change, using the newspaper as a napkin. She also tried to give her one more feed, but the previous one had been too recent. Angelica took a couple of sucks and lay back contentedly, with pearly drops of milk at the corners of her tiny, cupid lips. Ann took out Mr. Netherbere's card and a stub of a pencil. Crossing out his name and address, she wrote on the back,

"Angelica – protestant – not yet baptized." She read it and added, "Please love her."

Then, walking as slowly as she could, promising herself she'd remember every dreadful step of the way, she wandered back to "the Coram," as Mrs. Curtis had called it.

"I love you," she whispered again and again into the swaddling of the hot, contented little bundle in her arms. "Mama loves you."

She pressed her cheeks to the railings. Once more, the cold, familiar iron brought its welcome pain, without which everything seemed unreal. At last the time had come to lay the baby down upon the steps.

But she found she could not do it. One more hug, she thought. How long had she said? An hour. Surely only half an hour had gone by? And Mr. Netherbere lived only twenty minutes away. So she had another ten minutes. Tomorrow, when her heart would be aching for just one sight of her little baby, she'd curse herself for not using these last free ten minutes. She walked off into the dark again, rocking the tiny bundle and humming a formless tune to show herself how happy she was.

In just such ways must condemned men snatch crumbs of comfort until the abyss opens beneath them. I'm alive. I breathe: the air tastes good. No headache. Hello legs – still there, eh? Scratch – it still feels good. How rewarding each moment can be made!

She squandered ten minutes, rich in such moments. She was back at the railings. Now the tears were streaming down her face. She pressed one hot kiss after another on baby Angelica's tiny eyelids, her milky lips, her fine, tight skin.

At the last she remembered Mrs. Curtis's words: "I should ought to have had the little mite tattooed." Panic seized her. How would she recognise Angelica again?

In a year, surely she couldn't change so much?

In a year she'd be unrecognisable.

How do you tattoo a baby, anyway? Would she have time? When was the next ship to South America? Would Mr. Netherbere wait? Perhaps the position would be filled by then.

But how *was* she going to recognise her baby again?

Those ranks of pinched, starved, miserable faces paraded before her mind's eye. Terror-stricken, she imagined herself here, a year from now, two years – how long might it take? – searching among them for a sign that unequivocally said, "Angelica!"

"I should ought to have had the little mite tattooed."

Suddenly she knew what she had to do. A great calm descended on her.

She walked directly up to the front steps. For the last time she hugged Angelica to her. She let her lips nuzzle softly over that fine, fine skin, back along the chubby cheeks to the tiny ear. "I love you," she whispered one last time. "It's all for love. It's all for love!"

And then she bit clean through the top of the ear.

The baby's piercing shrieks harried her all down that odious street.

And round the corner.

And into the dreams of the waking nightmare of her life.

CHAPTER THIRTY-SEVEN

"I DON'T SEE WHY I should tell you anything!" Sally said defiantly.

"Because you did her no good by going down to London and taking her that money," Tony answered patiently.

"And what good did you do her!"

He nodded, conceding the point. "But what should I do *now*?" he asked. "That's the question you're so unwilling to face. What now? Should I simply abandon her? Walk away? Say hard luck and get on with my own life – which, as you know, is one long round of selfish pleasure and idle amusement? Or should I ..."

"It wouldn't be the first time."

He looked at her steadily until she was forced to drop her gaze. "How little you truly know me," he said.

"I know men!"

"Which conveniently saves you the chore of getting to know any individual of the species? You can judge us all, sight unseen?"

"All I know is that the man who *should* be out looking for her is buying tickets to South America or Canada or somewhere, and the man who ruined her life can't wait to find her and finish it off."

"And yet you, the one person in all the world who might actually help her, are sitting here in Solihull, a hundred miles away, moaning about the rottenness of things but actually doing sweet ... nothing." He sniffed. "I could put it stronger."

The first stirrings of uncertainty crept past the ramparts of Sally's righteous anger. "If you find her ..." she began reluctantly.

"If Freddy hasn't already gone – he's going to Venezuela, by the way, at the end of the week. If I can find her before that, I shall do my utmost to repair things and restore the marriage. Otherwise I shall cherish her and look after her and ... let things take their course. I do love her, you know. She's not like ... other women in my life you may have heard of."

"Me and half Birmingham."

"Oh come – it's not as bad as that."

"Well anyway, what d'you expect me to do? I'm not a lady of leisure, you know. I've got a job to do in this house."

"All I want is to know where she is in London. Considering the condition she was in when she left here, it must be a hospital." He risked a smile. "Not St. Thomas's. I know that much."

She frowned. "Were those two men yours?"

He shook his head. "No, they were regular police, out of uniform. We know the chief constable of Staffordshire. He arranged it."

Sally shook her head. "Ann was right then. She said I'd be dodged. It was her idea to go to St. Thomas's first. In the front door, out the back. They were a pair of bunglers, those two! They turned about the moment they saw me go into St. Thomas's. Couldn't wait to get into the pub."

She rose and left the room, saying, "I'll bring you her letter." A short while later she returned. Tony read it in silence. "The Paddington Hospital," he said at length. "I'll telegraph London. I can easily make the midday express. Perhaps there'll be some answer by the time I arrive."

"She won't still be there," Sally said bitterly. "She was fit again by the time *I* arrived. They were going to put her out the next day."

"It's somewhere to start," he replied.

He arrived at Euston just before four o'clock that afternoon. He had barely reached the end of the platform when he was aware of a woman walking rather closely at his side. It was Sally. He stopped and stared. Her smile was savage. "Like a leech!" she told him.

"But ... how?"

"I told Mr. Wilde there was something very important I forgot this morning. He brought me to the train."

Tony frowned in bewilderment, still not understanding the situation. "But if we were on the same train ...?"

"Yes, I omitted to tell him that."

"Well, Miss Pickering, it had better be jolly important."

"It's ever-so-jolly important."

He waited. All she did was smile. "Yes? Yes?" he asked tetchily.

"Simply this: I'm not going to let you find her and then twist her round your little finger. When you find her – I'll be there! As I said – like a leech."

He looked around in acute embarrassment. "But it might take days. The matter is delicate enough as it is. I haven't even brought my manservant."

She revelled in his discomfiture. "You can't be afraid for your reputation, surely?"

"But it's out of the question."

"Try and stop me! I'll dodge you a sight better than those two oafs you set on to me."

"What about your work at the Wildes'? You're not a lady of leisure, you know."

"You'll think of something to tell them, I'm sure."

He realized they could not stand there arguing much longer; already they were attracting attention. "I can't prevent your coming to the hospital, I suppose," he allowed wearily. "But that's as far as you'll go. You'll take the next train home."

She mock-curtseyed; in her eyes he could see the defiance already building. There were very few women he actively loathed. In fact, now he came to consider the matter, there was but one. Strange, really, because objectively speaking she was quite handsome.

No message awaited him, so his telegraphic inquiries had yielded nothing. He went out, intending to hail a cab, but Sally said, "Why don't you try to follow her path as closely as possible? She wouldn't have wasted money on a cab."

"Walk?" he asked.

She nodded at the entrance to the underground railway.

He looked at it and then back at her. "One thing puzzles me. Here she is, alone and friendless in a strange city. Standing just here, feeling ghastly and wondering where to go. Why pick Paddington Hospital?"

"The ticket collector told her. His brother's a porter there."

"Then we'd better start with him." They wasted ten minutes seeking a ticket collector with a brother at the Paddington Hospital. One of the others placed him – Ted McGregor – but this was his day off.

Tony bought first-class underground tickets but Sally insisted they travel the two miles on the slatted wooden seats of a third-class carriage, directly behind the engine. And infernal miles they were, with the acrid tang of sulphur on the air, and the sparks swirling back through banks of smoke and steam, almost outshining the dim oil lighting of the carriage.

She turned to him and, putting her mouth near his ear, said, "Try and imagine her – exhausted ... running blood ... sitting here. A long way from your boudoir at Olton Grange, wouldn't you say!"

He closed his eyes and nodded. Then he gripped her forearm and said, "Don't stop, Miss Pickering. I deserve it all. Indeed, I deserve far worse."

His submissiveness confused her; she realized there was nothing she could say that would go too far. She had licence to revile him in any way and to any degree she might wish. It was a glimpse of power that suddenly frightened her. Her heart began to pound. Why did she not snatch her arm from his gentle grip? Because it would humiliate him before all these artisans, their fellow-passengers – and he would relish such humiliation. Oh – an Honourable Snake indeed! Love him – hate him – no matter; he would encompass it all and put your emotion to his service!

At the hospital they had a record of Ann's admission, and of her discharge eight days later. But that had been three weeks ago. She had called herself Ann Howard. One of the attendants told them the baby had been baptized Angelica, but the mother had been unconscious at the time; indeed, they had despaired for her life. But she was strong. She'd made an amazing recovery. The birth had not been registered there so far as he knew.

At that the trail ended.

"Now I'll see you to your train," he told Sally.

"And I'll see you in hell."

Fury seized him. Shaking with anger he walked blindly away up the corridor. But she, having visited the place before, knew it led nowhere so she stood her ground. All the way back he fixed his eyes upon her. "We must come to some modus vivendi," he said as he drew near again.

She frowned. "What's that? Some kind of lodging house?"

"Yes," he replied grimly. "A lodging house for our mutual dislike. You may taunt me all you wish, Miss Pickering, but you'll never provoke me into answering you in kind. However, don't let my forbearance deceive you. I dislike you as heartily as you dislike me."

His sudden show of spirit, despite his quietness of tone, startled her. She could think of nothing to say.

Satisfied he went on, "But we neither of us came to London to give scope to these mutual feelings. We could waste a lot of time snapping at each other like spoiled dogs. We could also miss valuable evidence. So may I suggest we concoct some reasonable story, something that will not require us to be on more than formal terms with each other, and then, swallowing our differences as best we may, set about the one task, the only conceivable task, that can unite our action?"

She nodded her tight-lipped agreement. Buried somewhere in his suggestion she felt there lurked an obscure rebuke, but she could not isolate it. His desire to find Ann and help her was genuine. She had to allow it. Perhaps a man could be nine-tenths bad and one-tenth good; but for Sally to admit as much was a huge concession. To admit it of the Honourable Snake was little short of a miracle.

The story they concocted was that Ann had vanished in a delirium following the birth of her baby. They had traced her to the hospital but now feared she was wandering, perhaps suffering from loss of memory. Tony was her brother-in-law; Sally her half-sister – a degree of relationship that could be entirely formal but which would explain their sharing the same lodging house. Tony naturally wanted them to use different houses but Sally said, "Oh yes – wake up and find you absconded!"

For two days they visited other hospitals, showed Ann's likeness to the keepers of every conceivable charitable house where she might have sought lodging or a crust ... all with-out the slightest flicker of recognition. A woman who sold sheep's-head broth in Little Ormond Street half-recognised her but couldn't be sure; the woman she knew was much thinner.

That third evening in London found them in despair. "Where would you turn next?" Tony asked Sally. "If you had avoided charity and had run out of money."

Her embarrassment answered him. He was horrified. "She'd never do that, surely?"

Sally, who had behaved impeccably for two days, could contain herself no longer. "No! She'd never do that. Not Ann. Not left to herself, she wouldn't. But what if she'd already been made to feel like she was dirt? What if she'd already told herself a million times that death was too good for her? And what if she got no milk left for the baby? *Men!*"

"Let me have her likeness," Tony said. "I'll go and make some inquiries."

"I'm coming, too."

"Absolutely not! I will not hear of it – most unsuitable."

She stared him out. "Covent Garden's the place the young lads all snigger about," she told him.

They had taken lodgings at the King's Cross end of the Gray's Inn Road. From the moment they stepped outside the door it seemed they fell into a sea of prostitutes, and they were still two miles from Covent Garden. London was seething with fallen women. It had been raining that afternoon and the streets were wet and gusty. The cold damp air struck a chill through any sort of outer garment.

"They call it 'turning gay'!" Tony said, looking at the drab, sorry creatures all around them. She didn't answer. He stared at her stony profile, wondering what on earth was going on inside that sharp, vulpine mind.

For a while neither had the courage to approach any of the women; then Sally took the picture from him and went straight up to one of them, a dignified matron of forty, who looked more like a moral crusader than what she really was. She listened attentively, looked at the picture, and shook her head. "Sorry, lovely. She's not trod this patch."

"Are we doing the right thing?" Sally asked her. "Going the right way about it?"

The woman smiled bleakly. "Why not? There's only twenty miles of streets filled with gay women like us. You could see them all in a week."

"She's rambling," Tony said.

"Have it your own way, sir. That's the watchword." She turned back to Sally. "You'd stand a better chance with the soft eggs."

"What's that?"

"Charities."

"Oh we've tried them."

The woman looked surprised. "What, all of 'em? Soup and Hymns? Soap and Service? The Pillars of Salt? ..."

"Wait a mo, wait a mo," Tony said. "What charities are these?"

"For gay women of course."

"We haven't tried those."

Ten minutes later, armed with a list of addresses, they were on their way to the first, the Dr. Addison's Memorial Home for Unfortunates, in Mecklenburg Street, which was just around the corner.

The guardian of the home, a Mrs. Mullens, listened impassively to their tale. She was a large woman, of formidable appearance, with a mouth that opened and shut like a trap.

"The child would be a better guide," she advised. "Seek the child. She'll lead you to the mother."

"Where might a child be lodged?" Tony asked. "Newborn. Only a month old."

"There must be a thousand places," she answered. "A thousand women with dead infants and milk to sell ..."

"To sell?" Sally echoed. "But where might a baby be taken in free?"

"In precious few places. Babies aren't too hard got, if you take my meaning."

"But such places do exist?"

Mrs. Mullens shrugged. "The most famous of them is just across the street. The Foundling Hospital. Coram's, they call it. But they only take in babies after interview. Saturday mornings. The committee has to be satisfied of the mother's previous good character – and her future. So if you suppose your unhappy sister was turning gay ..."

"We didn't say that," Tony cut in. "It's just that we can't ignore any possibility, however remote."

"You could try there."

"What if someone just leaves a baby on their doorstep?" Sally asked.

"They send it on to the union workhouse in Clerkenwell – and may God have mercy on its soul!"

Outside they looked at the imposing, classical dignity of the Foundlings Hospital; it contrasted so strongly with what they imagined of Ann's condition that both of them could smell disappointment even at that distance.

"Let's follow our original plan tonight," Tony suggested. "At least while the women are about on the streets. And then, if we draw blank, we can return here tomorrow."

But as they turned away Sally stopped. "We're so close. It's only just over there. They can't bite us. I'm sure she'd have seen little Angelica settled first, no matter what. She'd have settled the baby and then sought a place in service. And that fits everything Mrs. Mullens said about previous and future character. Ann would have done anything rather than what we're thinking."

Tony looked at her sourly. "A somewhat different tune from the one we were hearing an hour ago?"

"I was angry then. I only wanted to rub your snout in it."

"And now?"

"Christ, what d'you think!" she flared. "I'm frightened – that's what. Twenty *miles* of streets like these! You go over there and pour the old Eton on them. I'll bet your dad knows half the committee."

Silently he led the way over the street to the small side door. There, as she had sneered, his Etonian charm gained them entry and an instant conduct to the study of the governor-in-residence, a Mr. Tanqueray Bulstrode, of Harrow and Brasenose College. He welcomed them cordially, offered them port, which they declined, listened to their request, decided that the events to which it referred had occurred far below his sphere of responsibility – if, indeed, they had occurred at all, and passed them on to the matron, Miss Mundy.

Miss Mundy was small, bony, and sharp as a little bird. She inventoried the pair of them as she listened to their tale. "Ye've told it so often, ye can hardly credit it yourselves now, eh?" she said with a smile that made them feel acutely uncomfortable. "Well, I think I may have good news for ye, so ye'll need tell it no more."

She led a jubilant couple through tall stone corridors, down bleak stone staircases, worn deeply by the passing of countless clogged feet, through lower-ceilinged and then positively cramped stone passageways until they supposed they must be in the antechambers of the underworld itself. The age-old smell of boiled greens lurked in every crack and pore, overlaid with the more modern aroma of carbolic.

At last they stood before a door that had been painted chocolate brown as a small concession to cheerfulness. There was no doubting what lay beyond; the bellowing of a dozen lusty lungs, penetrating the stout oak, painted the picture before the door was opened and thirty little cribs were revealed. A single nurse curtseyed at them and continued her rounds, popping comforters back into squalling mouths and bringing temporary peace.

Tony had not seen Angelica at all. It was Sally who said, "It's her!" when they were still only half way up the ward.

"With the injured ear?" Mrs. Mundy said.

They drew close and halted in a half-circle around the crib. "Her ear was all right when last I saw her," Sally said.

"Well, it wasn't when we found her."

"*Found* her?" Tony asked. "Didn't the lady bring her here?"

"You're sure this is the child?" Mrs. Mundy insisted.

"No doubt of it," Sally answered.

Tony looked at the accusing features, saw himself there all too plainly, and said nothing.

"She was left on our doorstep the night before last," the matron told them.

"But I thought you didn't take in ... well, foundlings – despite your name."

"Normally we don't, but in this case the mother had left a note." She looked across at a tall cupboard. "Just a moment." She went to it, opened one of the doors, and took out a large tin cash box, from the depths of which she drew forth the card Ann had left inside the baby's swaddling.

Tony read it. The simple phrase, "Please love her," brought him to tears. It made Sally cry, too. They each felt angry to be sharing the emotion. Tony recovered first. He turned the card over and spotted the crossed-out name and address on the other side.

"Who is Mr. Netherbere?" he asked. "Of Number Six, Coldbath Square, Mount Pleasant?"

"He is the gentleman who vouched for her. We sent one of our beadles to see him the following day – yesterday – and it seems he is connected with some Christian charity that places errant young women of good character into sympathetic homes. He was not aware of our procedures here – nor of the fact that 'Miss Ann,' as he called her, had simply abandoned the baby. He has promised to bring her here on Saturday, from Tooting, I think. But he said nothing about her having lost her memory. I think you ought to be prepared to find that she has made a free choice, you know. I know nothing of the circumstances, of course."

"Tooting?" Tony looked again at the card.

"Ah yes. Mr. Netherbere lives by Mount Pleasant, but he has found her a place with a family in Tooting. Anyway, Saturday is the day on which the governors convene to consider applications for places. So the baby may stay until then – after all, what's one more among five hundred!"

Tony looked uncertainly at his daughter. Sally laid her hand gently on his arm. "No, brother-in-law, dear," she said. "Look at the poor little thing's ear – she's best off in here for the moment."

He turned to the matron. "The doctor has seen her?"

She nodded. "He's quite happy it'll heal over in a week or two."

"Because if it's a question of money or anything ..."

"It would make no difference." She cut short their final look at the sleeping baby and ushered them out of the noisy room. The silent corridors were cold and dank.

"May we return tomorrow?" Tony asked. "We shall, of course, be taking the baby with us when she has recovered."

"See Mr. Netherbere first, eh?"

When they were out in the street again, he turned to Sally and said, awkwardly, "Thank you."

She steered herself away from his closeness. "For nothing!" she snapped.

At eight the following morning they called at Number Six, Coldbath Square, Mount Pleasant. Their repeated hammering brought no response, until the basement door of Number Seven was opened and a manservant put out his head.

"Gawn away!" he called.

"D'you mean Mr. Netherbere?" Tony asked with sinking heart.

"Gawn away," he repeated more slowly, as if to foreigners. "And one of the two women. Good riddance."

"In what way d'you mean – gone?" Sally asked. "Please – it's very important to us."

The man's attitude softened. He took a step out into the area and, shielding his eyes against the sky, looked up at them. He was in rolled shirtsleeves and wearing a green baize apron; he must have been polishing the silver. "It's my opinion he's done a bunk," he said. "Filled a big pantechnicon yesterday. All his furniture. Then he hung about a bit, him and one of the women. Keeps looking at his watch. Then finally he says they can't wait no more. So he whistles up a cab, down Rosebery Avenue, and off they goes."

"What women were these?" Tony asked. "Was this one of them?" He leaped down the area steps and showed him Ann's picture.

He sucked his teeth and shook his head. "No – old, they was. Or older'n this. Forty if they was a day."

Sally was still upon the front steps. "Is that one of them now?" she asked. "Look quickly. She's just turned away from us – crossing the street, now. See her there – by the milkman?"

The fellow sprang up the steps. "Yeah – that's her," he said. "The fat one."

The other two were already running.

The woman had made the mistake of popping into a little eel-pie shop across the Farringdon Road. They had her cornered. Her fear gave her away, otherwise they would have approached her more diffidently. "Where is Mr. Netherbere?" Tony asked in his most authoritative tones.

"I've never heard of him," she said.

Tony turned to Sally. "Go and fetch the constable."

Before Sally reached the door, the woman said, "Wait."

They turned to her. "Why d'you come following me?" she asked. "Wasn't that you on his front steps just now?"

"The house is empty," Tony told her. "Mr. Netherbere vamoosed yesterday."

Her mouth and eyes went wide in shock. "He never did. He never would!"

Tony went to the door and beckoned her. "Come and see."

They stayed close by her side as they marched back across the street to Coldbath Square. As they ascended the steps she pulled a key from her bag and opened the front door. She stood back like a servant, to let them in; but Tony, suspecting a ruse to slam the door on them and leave them locked inside, took the key from its housing and turned to her, unsmiling. "Ladies first," he said. "It looks as if you're going to be stuck with the rent – if not worse."

Her position did not sink in until she had seen the third empty room. "The villain!" she shouted suddenly. "That evil-hearted, double-dyed villain!"

"Your only hope now, Mrs. ...?"

"Curtis."

"Your only hope, Mrs. Curtis, is to turn Queen's evidence. It's quite clear your partners in crime have left you in the lurch. I'm sure I don't need to tell you what the penalties are for the vile business in which you've been engaged. And you will suffer them unless you lead us to the real villain."

"Inspector!" Sally cut in sharply. "Shall I get the sergeant to come up here and take down her statement?"

He was quick. She knew what a gamble she had taken but, heaven be praised, he was quick. "Thank you, Miss Jameson," he said gruffly. "I think we'll let Sergeant Evans and the constable go on sorting out all those documents." He pulled a notebook from his pocket. "I haven't quite forgotten how to write." He smiled grimly at the woman.

"Documents?" she asked anxiously.

He gave her a wink of fiendish triumph. "Ho, yes indeed! Quite a nice little business, wasn't it – while it lasted. Now, suppose you tell me everything you know about Mr. Netherbere."

She quickly reached a decision. "Netherbere!" she sneered. "He took that off of some coach in Devon, when he scarpered once before. Netherbere! McKenna's his name. George McKenna."

Tony wrote it down. He was warming to the deception despite a heart full of foreboding. "Perhaps you'll start by telling us your name, too. Your real one," he said.

"Brill," Mrs. Curtis sighed. "Miss Erica Brill." She nodded toward Sally. "Who's she?"

"Complainant-in-person."

"You must be the first what come back to tell the tale," Miss Brill replied. "Not one of mine, was you."

Her story was more bleak than their darkest fears had painted it. McKenna and his two accomplices, posing as sympathetic and charitable folk, lived by enticing desperate young women to places like Turkey, Morocco, and South America on every kind of pretext. Dancers would be prima ballerinas, chorus singers would become divas, ladies' maids would be transformed into governesses. Their only true qualification was that no one would be too worried about their disappearance. "Slipped up with you," she added ruefully. "Which one was it?"

"My sister." Sally showed her Ann's likeness.

Miss Brill sucked in her breath sharply. "Damn! I had a feeling about that one. I should ought to of trusted it."

Sally saw Tony's hand begin to shake, his knuckles whiten. In an unthinking moment of true sympathy she crossed to him and gripped his shoulders.

Miss Brill was instantly alert. "'Ere!" she said, rising to her feet. "What's all this, then?" She looked at the pair of them. "You ain't the traps."

Tony leaped to her side and squeezed her arm until she cried out at the pain. "No, we ain't the traps. And what that means, Miss Brill, is that you're going to be very lucky to leave this house alive."

She went deathly pale and sat again. Tony stood behind her and thrust Ann's picture in front of her once more. "Where is she?"

"I was mistook. I never seen her in my life."

Tony suddenly took hold of her bodice and ripped it from her. She screamed. Quick as a cat he crushed it to a ball and stuffed it into her still-open mouth. He held her to the chair with a wrestler's grip. "String in the next room," he said to Sally. "Get it."

She ran to obey.

Miss Brill, shaking now with terror, kept nodding her head and making muffled cries.

Sally returned with a discarded ball of strong twine. He bound the woman's wrists together behind her. Sally, holding the gag for a moment, gazed into the woman's contorted face. "I think she'll talk," she said.

"Just wait a mo," Tony told her grimly. One-handed, the other holding the gag again, he took out a cheroot and motioned Sally to light it for him. He puffed it up to a bright red glow and then held it near the woman's naked forearm. "You understand?" he asked.

She nodded wildly. Tony removed the gag.

She sat very still and stared at the glowing cheroot. "By God, you would!" she said.

He put his face close to hers and breathed out the fumes as he spoke. "By God I would! For what you've done? I'd love every minute of it."

Sally watched all this open-mouthed. His triumph over the odious woman was hers, too. It gave her a visceral thrill just to see it. In that moment all her hatred of him was forgotten.

"Now tell me everything you know about my brother's wife. That's who we're talking about."

The woman had guts. "The first thing I'll tell you is that baby's yours!" she sneered. "I saw it."

Tony was relentless. "Tell us where she is now. *Exactly* where she is. And *exactly* where she's going. And when? Everything." He puffed up the cheroot again.

She told them: Ann was now aboard the *SS Hecate*, bound for Demerara, where she believed the charitable Mr. de Santos was waiting to meet her. She would go ashore and never be heard of again. They could easily check it. The *Hecate* sailed from Tilbury yesterday morning.

Sally hurled herself against the wall and began to thrash her arms at it, heedless of pain. "While we were here!" she shouted. "Here in London!"

Tony tossed the cheroot into the empty fireplace and went over to try to comfort her.

"We're forgetting something," he said. "There's Freddy. He's sailing for Venezuela, which is just next door to British Guiana. Surely when he hears what's happened, he'll ..." He paused.

"What?" Sally asked.

"Tell me today isn't Friday."

"It is."

He slumped. "Freddy's already sailed" – he looked at his watch – "six hours!" Then for her sake he deliberately cheered up. "I'll write to him. There may even be a cable service. I can certainly cable America – charter a boat to be waiting at Demerara ... oh there are so many things we can still do."

But she was no longer listening. She had turned her face back to the wall and was weeping silently. He went over and put his arms around her. She did not resist.

PART FOUR

THE GOLD OF EL AVILA

CHAPTER THIRTY-EIGHT

FREDDY OXLEY TO LAWRENCE AND EMMY:
(From the Engine Depot at Caracas)
My Dears:– Here at last! We had a smooth and un-eventful voyage out. All were sick at first, of course, the passage from Southampton through Biscay is notorius, but soon found our sea legs. I borrowed a pedometer from a Swedish miner called A. Gulberg and by it walked 10 miles though I doubted its truthfullness; took it apart later and improved it though he didn't think so nor thank me for it. He is with us here in Caracas for the moment buying guns and pans and mules to go inland where he is to prospeckt for gold for his company at 20 pounds a month and if he finds it he is to get 500 on the report and 300 at the opening of the mines and 200 paid-up shares so he will do very well (or not at all). He urges me to join him but I must stay near the cities and places of industry.

At sea we saw flying fishes and porpoises and whales. I always pictured the ocean as empty and was amazed at the amount of life going on all the time. Some flying fishes are as big as pike others small as butterflies. When they came on deck we early birds gathered them up and had them done nicely for breakfast. Life aplenty on board, too. The first class passengers had dancing up on deck and we were permitted to watch and it was high-jinks, I can tell you! On our last day on the *Nile* before we changed to the *Essequibo* at Barbadoes I went to the stoke hole for a good look round, there are six boilers and three fires to each boiler, eighteen in all. A stoker gave me a shovel and I fired up for a bit and had to pay my footing for so doing. Not nice work at 100deg. She had six miles of pipes for the water, which must not get above 1.9 of saltiness, and enough dials to make one giddy. But with all sail bent on and both engines going we fairly dashed it, doing nearly 400 nots on the best days so we covered the 3500 nt. miles from Southampton to Barbadoes in fine style. Eleven days to Barbadoes and four on to La Guayra.

The *Essequibo* was a different kettle of fish. In fact, a kettle of fish would have been preferable. Our luggage was kept under tarpoalings and was soaked in the squalls but no great harm done. Barbadoes was too hot for comfort and Gulberg and I went shoping and walking all day and saw maze and sugar cane and a cactus at least 30ft which makes the one in the Bottanic Gardens look like a toy. The people were bothersome especially the young boys and we had to give two in charge of the police who pestered us so. We saw HM Gunboat *Garnet* in the harbour and you would have been proud to see it so trim and neat. The land very flat, but St. Vincents is much prettier with a mountain and a fort and not so dusty and very green. We got our shoes mended there and rested in a grove of nutmegs and clove trees and then sailed for Grenada where we had no time to go ashore or so they said but we would have had plenty in fact.

We saw Trinidad and Venezuela in the distance by moonlight, very clear and silvery, and were escourted from the Dragon's Mouth all the way into Port of Spain by a large porpoise. Thence all along the coast to La Guayra which is said to be the loveliest port in the hemisphere and even the whole world, it certainly is very beautiful. It felt very hot to me but the people of Caracas go there to cool down, so I'm told, and now I'm up here in Caracas I can believe it! Mr. Fraser, our General Manager, says we'll soon get used to it and it's healthy enough if you keep of the drink except a little wine in the water to poison the insects.

The journey from La Guayra to Caracas is only 24 mls but takes three hours as it climbs over 3,000 ft, a single-track line, all curves. At one place the line runs along the side of a gorge with 2,000 ft of a drop, nearly shear. We were also stoped by langousters, a sort of grasshoppers, so thick on the line that the wheels just slipped. The fireman had to throw sand upon them to make them stick. Also a landslide of which there are many, this one a small one. Mr. B.R. Nicholls (also called Firey

Knuckles), the driver of Number 1, says there are sometimes 4 or 5 ton rocks on the line and they have to send for blasting powder. He says the powder is of poor quality, though, so if I can lay in a little store of carbolic and some nitric acid, I could start a nice litle chemical business here in reliable explosives. And I should begin here where I left off in Small Heath! We shall see.

We, the four engine drivers and relief, and the three English machine engineers, mess at a lodging house near the depot but it is too costly and Mr. Fraser has agreed to set up temporary quarters in the goods shed until our houses are ready. We were promised houses and cabbins when we signed up with the company in England but Mr. Fraser says he was not told of it and has not been given money for such a purpose. Also the clothing provided is very poor and I must use my own moleskin trews and flannel shirts, despite the heat, which is bad enough outside, but inside a firebox is intollerable when I have to go in to cure the leaky copper pipes.

That is only one of my jobs. I am also in charge of casting the iron and all lathework. The lathes came out with us and are still in their crates as it is more urgent to cast up some spare wheels because of the constant derailments. They blame the mule drivers who are losing their trade to our new railway.

I've had little chance so far to walk about, except into the town for stamps etc. The country is steeply hilly and covered in thick, green jungle full of strange ferns and huge butterflies, in places so thick you must cut your way forward with a machete and you must always carry a pistol against snakes. I have not seen a snake yet.

This evening I may walk out a bit. Firey Knuckles says he'll shew me some of the local sites. He gets his name from his frequently having "a drop taken" as Charley Clancey, driver of Number Three, puts it, and often thereby getting into fights with the citizenry and police, and sleeping in jail and getting docked some of his pay. But at all other times is as good-humored and mild-mannered a gentleman as you could wish to incounter. I'll tell you what we see in my next.

Goodbye for the moment then my dear son, be good and obedient to your darling Emmy who is so good to look after you. I think of you both v. often and wonder what you're doing so far away. Try to think well of your mama and forgive her wherever she is.

Yr loving father.

CHAPTER THIRTY-NINE

FIREY KNUCKLES had gone aside to relieve himself, not to pollute the stream. Freddy remained at the heart of the glade. It was early evening and the whole forest was coming to life. Here, where men had once cut and burned and moved on, there were no giant trees reaching for the light and shutting it off from the forest floor; this glade, created by a great shelf of rock only sparsely covered with soil, was the first clearing they had seen on their wandering up the steeply sloping hillside. To reach it they had followed a wildly meandering game trail amid a tropical profusion of ferns, shrubs, tall grasses, and sapling trees. It was like standing in a flower shop, blind and half-drunk; the perfume of wild ginger, deadly nightshade, hibiscus, and other plants was overpowering.

Their trail had run across the stream, and the stream had brought them up to the shelf, across whose face it had, over the long millennia, scoured a channel – a series of hollowed-out pools linked by miniature chutes and waterfalls. Freddy knelt and drank directly from its surface. It was cold and fresh; the spring could not be far away.

As he sat and waited for Firey to return he realized how close this scene was to the European idea of a tropic paradise: the balmy mountain air, poised between the heat of the day and the cool of the night – the virgin green all around – the endless background of frogs and cicadas, the shrieking of the parrots and other exotic birds, flashes of astonishing colour in the brilliant dark-dappled light of the setting sun; and there below him, through the thinning of the trees on the downhill side of the glade, he could see the kindling lights of Caracas, deep in a bowl of a valley between huge knuckles of mountains.

It reminded him of another paradise – as Ann had described it: the marbled terrace of Mrs. Homfray's villa in Florence, where the whole party had sat of an evening, amid the white-splashing fountains and the tall, black-green cypresses, all gilded in the lowering sun. The images were the same – stone, splashing water, trees, the birds, the evening light. He thought of Ann herself – that wonderful, childlike spontaneity of hers ... all her soft, ample beauty. He pictured her asleep, as relaxed and vulnerable as a baby.

He rose and stumbled to a nearby tree, placing its stout bole between him and the point where Firey had vanished. And there he burst into tears. He tried telling himself how stupid it was, how dangerous. He pressed his brow hard against the finely indented bark, hard enough to hurt. He rapped his knuckles against the bone above his ears. And he said her name many times, as in the first evenings of his love.

But the rage of it passed, and then he told himself these were no more than the phantom pains that soldiers feel when the surgeons take off a limb. There was no real Ann there any more. Tony had amputated her. It would pass. He would hobble on without her.

Fearing his companion's return, which was, indeed, over-due, he ran back to the water and, lying full stretch at its margin, buried his face in the cool, leaf-dark depths.

Firey, who had watched most of the episode from the edge of the clearing, now felt it safe to emerge. "If it's not the runs, it's t'other thing," he said by way of explaining the length of his absence. "We'd best get back. Dark falls quickly here."

"I was thinking how like paradise it is," Freddy said. "Down there at noon in the engine yard, what with no shelter from the sun, and the heat off the boilers and all, it may be close to hell. But up here ... now, when it's cool ..." He spread his hands around them.

"It's a strange paradise as lacks good ale, see tha," Firey answered.

"I've never been a great one for the beer."

"Aye? Well it doesn't lack women, I can tell thee. There's some reet little fireworks in't Plaza."

Freddy laughed. "Nor women, either. Not in that way."

Firey was at a loss. If paradise was not defined in terms of ale or women, what was left?

They chose to follow the stream, whose banks were generally clearer than the surrounding forest.

Firey continued his gentle fishing: "We've all got us reasons, no doubt. If you took all dozen on us, Englishmen out here, I 'speck you'd not find one reason in common. I came for t'money. I'd be hard put to earn in a month back home what I get in a week here, see tha."

"The money's very good," Freddy agreed.

"Art saying tha didn't come just for't money then?"

"I'd not have come without it," Freddy agreed carefully. "But also there's the adventure. I thought what other chance might I get? I couldn't leave a *big* family, not so easily."

"Th'art married then?"

"Aye."

"And a bairn or two, I dare say?"

Freddy hesitated between saying "one" and "two," and finally just said, "Aye," again.

They came to a point where the stream had undercut a large boulder and they had to leap to the far side, where the way was now easier.

"I'm not ower fond o' women, either," Firey confided. "I'm partial to the odd frig, of course, but I'd abhor seeing t'same face each breakfast time. I couldn't abide that."

"Matter of taste," Freddy allowed.

"I don't think we were intended to live together, to have and to hold, from this time forth, and all that carry-on. It's impossible. Stands to reason. That's what breeds the mischief."

Freddy steered the conversation away. "Stands to what reason?"

"Plain matter of observation, see tha. Shut thee eyes and picture a man – any man. What's he doing? Playing cricket, isn't he! Or football. What do us lads do round here in us spare time? Cricket. Football. Go out shooting parrots. Go to't Plaza and sup ale, or what passes for it. Now when did you last see a lass at any o' them things? Or fighting wars? I think that's why we used to have wars every which while. The men couldn't stand t'women no longer. They felt riddled wi'em. They had to get away. But now, d'you notice, we've had very few wars this century? That's 'cause we can travel more easy, see? We can escape the bloody women. Stands to reason." He looked back at Freddy, sure of his agreement, and added. "I don't miss 'em, anyroad."

Freddy, sure now that Firey had seen him break down, was embarrassed. He sought a distraction. The undercut boulder that had forced them to change sides loomed menacingly above them, half of it etched against the rapidly deepening twilight. "That won't be long in coming down," he said. "Are there rocks like that overhanging the line?"

Firey spat affirmatively into the stream. "It makes life interesting," he said. "There's one place they call Zic-Zac – I've never seen the line completely clear there. Always summat falling. They say it's muleteers what lost their business to us, but I don't believe it."

"Why don't they blast the hillsides free of all such hazards?"

"Aye, they should ought to have done, and that's a fact. But Mr. Fraser said that when Mr. Brassey was building't line he swore he'd go mad if he saw one more penny spent on blasting powder. Cost him a tidy fortune as it was. So I don't reckon as they did a proper job. Either that or they was all skimming off a bit on't side."

"Interesting," Freddy said.

The stream vanished into a culvert. They had reached the road, a dusty track that wound at a gentle downward slope along the hillside, past the depot and into Caracas.

"Anyway," he added, "why were they still using blasting powder?"

"All they could get, I suppose. They probably had to make it on't site, see tha."

"Even so, there's easier explosives to make than powder. And cheaper."

"Tha knows all about it then!" Firey said with a hint of sarcasm.

Freddy ignored it. "And a lot easier to use. A three-foot bore is about all you could put in this sort of rock for powder.

But with picric acid or nitroglycerine you could go to two or three times that."

"Oh aye. I thought tha were a wheelwright and copper fitter?"

"My last work was with dyestuffs – some of which you have a job to stop them turning into explosives, so I picked up a bit about it. I wonder if Mr. Fraser would be interested in buying some good quality explosives? We might get a canny little second business going out here."

Firey laughed. "Art serious?"

Freddy waved a hand at the forest all around – a gesture that was almost lost in the deep twilight. "We're not short of starch, after all. Just import a few carboys of nitric acid and phenol – there's a ship to or from New York or Galveston almost every week – and we could be turning out xyloidene and nitro-mannite by the gallon."

"Or blowing us all into kingdom come!"

"You might. I wouldn't. We've got plenty of cool, running water to keep the reaction temperature down. And it's only dangerous while it's liquid. Once you've got it safely absorbed in dried clay powder, or diatomaceous earth if we can find any, you can play cricket with it."

"Well, I'll go around th'ouses! Tha'rt serious an' all."

"If there'd be money in it, I'm serious, Firey. I'm not interested in a tinpot little railway. I'm looking for business."

"Doing what?" There was respect in his tone.

"Who knows?" Freddy laughed. "It could even be making explosives." He risked adding, "And guns. Why not? I was trained as a metalworker – casting, dropforging, boring, tempering ... there's not many know all that *and* the chemistry of explosives. Aye – why not!"

Firey shook his head in wonderment. "And I thought as I was showing *thee* around!"

A short while later they saw the lights of the depot among the trees. "Anyway," Freddy added, "it'll help take my mind of cricket and football and boozing and hunting and going to war."

"And women," Firey added.

Freddy punched his arm playfully. "I knew I was forgetting something."

Next day a mail boat came. There was only one letter for him. He opened it and looked first at the signature.

Tony Knox-Riddell.

He had opened it to see if it contained money, or made any reference to their business. The name Ann, Ann, Ann leaped up from a dozen lines. He threw it, unread, into the fire of his forge.

CHAPTER FORTY

IT WAS THREE WEEKS before the first carboys of nitric acid and phenol arrived from Galveston; by then Freddy and Mr. Fraser, the manager, had fallen out. It happened by a most tenuous thread of coincidence.

The Englishmen were all dissatisfied at their lodgings, which were airless, cramped, none too clean, and expensive. But Manuela, the owner's wife, was a good cook; had it not been for that, their resentment would have boiled over into open revolt.

Freddy, being such an outstanding craftsman, was greatly appreciated by Mr. Fraser. So when the men wanted to get up a deputation to learn what progress was being made, not only with permission to convert the goods shed to temporary lodgings, but also in the building of more permanent quarters for drivers and craftsmen, Freddy was their natural choice as leader.

At first all went well. Freddy was firm but respectful and Mr. Fraser was a model of all that a manager should be – making it clear that he agreed with his men in principle but he could not commit the company without something in writing from head office. The situation was accepted on both sides, and whenever Mr. Fraser had occasion to go into the workshops he would make some good-humoured comment upon the delay and on the torments the artisans must be suffering at their lodging house.

But then, quite suddenly, his attitude changed. He became coldness itself. All his good-humoured joking was replaced by a heavy line in sarcasm until Freddy was at last driven to ask in what way he might have given offence.

"Think you can play the Dixon with me?" Fraser snapped. "Well think on!"

The explanation of this enigmatic comment came from the deputy manager, Mr. Albright, a born oiler of troubled waters. It turned out that Fraser had once had dealings with "old" Dixon when he had been "young" Dixon. In fact, the young socialist had come within an ace of transportation to Australia, and Mr. Fraser, who had then been his foreman, had been the chief prosecution witness at his trial. The charge had failed upon a technicality, a rebuff that Fraser had never forgotten.

How Fraser had come to hear of the connection between Freddy and Dixon in the first place was no mystery. Freddy had said to Firey: "Old Dixon would have gone at this business like a bull at a gate. But see how much easier it is to get your own way by being reasonable ..." This sentiment had somehow found its way back to Mr. Fraser, who chose to see it as an arrogant boast – as if Freddy thought he was twisting Fraser round his little finger.

That, at least, was Firey's explanation. Freddy believed that Fraser had also come to realize that he was no ordinary wage-earning mechanic; he was out here to feather his own nest.

Whatever the truth of it, Freddy was now marked down as a troublemaker. Even his resignation as leader of the deputation made no difference; he simply became, in Fraser's mind, the gray eminence behind it all, manipulating the men's discontent while keeping his own head below the parapet.

Freddy began to prepare for his dismissal. Fraser was right in a way. He himself would do the same if he found some mechanic working for him under borrowed plumage. He remembered the Swede, Gulberg, who had gone upcountry somewhere, looking for gold. They had a loose arrangement to communicate poste restante via Bolivar on the Orinoco;

Gulberg was some hundred miles away in Yuruary, where the richest gold fields were, but Bolivar was his base. The letter would take three weeks to get there – and then it might sit in its pigeonhole for six months. So that was a long shot. His "canny little second business" in explosives was now of more immediate relevance.

A mile or so into the forest, beyond the clearing he had reached during that evening walk with Firey Knuckles, he discovered, on a later solo ramble, a former coffee plantation. It had no doubt been abandoned for something more productive and more easily worked lower down the slope. The forest had reclaimed most of it, but two stout, stone-built sheds remained, the haunt of lizards and small monkeys, which he soon chased out. A nearby stream provided the vital water for cooling the reaction and dowsing it if some emergency arose. His only hard labour was to reglaze the windows, one in each shed, and hack down the growth in the yard of the former plantation. On his way back from these visits he was always careful to pick an armful of ferns of as many different kinds as he could manage. He would spend the rest of the evening pressing and cataloguing them in an amateur way, to disguise his true purpose up in the forest.

When all was ready he hired Amalfia, the least criminal-looking of the local muleteers, to carry his carboys and other materials up to his forest laboratory. The man left the desolate spot almost at once, warning him not to forget how swiftly darkness descends. Freddy was itching to make just one small batch of xyloidene, a process he knew well. In the longer term he wanted to experiment with extracting starch from the bagasse left over from sugar refining, as a prelude to making the even more powerful nitro-mannitol; he could get bagasse for nothing, so the process could be ten times as profitable. But Amalfia was right to warn him. Reluctantly, he stayed only long enough to fit a new brass padlock to the door. People would steal anything here, whether or not they knew what it was – and whether or not it was of the slightest use to them. They might not smash a window, but they would take an unbarred door as an invitation.

Freddy's first month's wages had come to thirty-one pounds. He'd had to pretend to be a mere mechanic, so the company had paid five pounds directly to Emmy, for the household expenses; a further three had been deducted to part-pay for the voyage out. Of the remaining twenty-three only one remained. But his board and keep were settled to the end of the month, so he should get by, if he lived frugally until next payday. He had sent several hundred pounds of his savings out ahead of him, to a bank in Caracas; but that was only for dire emergencies.

The evenings were long but the daylight hours were unfortunately scanty. The swiftness of the sunset gave him an hour at best, long enough each day to make only a fluid ounce or so in safety – and then only if all went well. This left Sunday as the only day on which he could carry out any serious manufacture.

One evening the flow of cooling water fell to a trickle and he had to dash outside to investigate just as the reaction reached its critical moment.

At any second he expected an explosion to tear the shed apart, killing him and flattening everything for several dozen yards. He began to curse his own stupidity and impatience. Why had he not at least had the sense to move the earlier product to some place of safety? The one ounce in the reaction vessel would do little more than lift off the roof; the stone walls would certainly contain it. But there was the best part of a gallon in the room, stored in jars and phials. It would take out half the hillside.

The fault with the water was soon located and rectified. A stone had become displaced in the small dam he had built to divert some of the water down an ancient channel to the shed. A passing anteater or some other small animal must have dislodged it. He replaced it and ran back to the shed.

Though he knew he was in mortal danger anywhere within a half-furlong of the place, and certainly no safer one side of it than the other, it still required all his pluck to open that door and step back inside. Then the familiar narcotic of imminent and violent death claimed him once again. His heart raced and a new sort of blood surged through him. He was no longer afraid.

His own personal time stretched while that of the world shrank. The door took an age to open. A leaf, dislodged from a spider's web, fell as if through glue.

His vision grew sharp as never before. He could see the veins on the falling leaf, the minute hairs on the spider's legs, the black holes at the ends of the straws protruding from the carboy – he could even see how far each deviated from a perfect circle. It was a power of vision such as only gods are granted.

Godlike he sauntered to the retort, lifted it from its cradle, and lowered it gently into the rapidly refilling water sump. Moments later he dared to feel the temperature of the glass and was glad he had resisted the temptation to swirl it round so as to hasten the cooling. It must have been within half a degree of spontaneous detonation – possibly even less. Indeed, perhaps even now at the heart of the vessel there were a hundred million or so molecules, enough to fill a pinhead, just teetering at that threshold. If the reaction had been a little more advanced when the overheating occurred ... if the product had been a little more concentrated ...

Intellectually it did not bear thinking about, but emotionally it was a possibility in another world, not in his own personal charmed universe.

When the danger had passed, the first thing he did was to move the jars and phials of finished product outdoors. A little way upstream was a small waterfall with a rocky ledge behind it. There he left his explosives, where it was always cool.

The second thing he did was curse out loud. Night was falling swiftly; in ten minutes it would be dark. It was already as cold as only a tropic night can seem, and here he was, stuck up a mountain, soaked to the skin, without candles or firewood.

In what little light was left he picked all the ferns he could and added them to the straw from the carboys. It made a tolerable bed and he might have slept at least part of the night if it had not been for the menacing racket from the forest all around. He was just dozing off when some large snuffling creature pushed in at his door. He sprang up and with much shouting and kicking drove it out again. Wondering which of them had been in greater terror, he locked the padlock, climbed back in through the window, and tried again to sleep.

There was now a bright moon, larger and redder than it had ever seemed at home. It was almost bright enough to work by. Freddy was toying with that idea when he heard the crack of a twig and a rustle from across the clearing. He rose and peered out of the window, and then immediately drew back into the shadow; for there, emerging from among the trees, was not the deer or other animal he had half-expected to see, but a man.

The mere fact that the man was carrying a gun was not as menacing out here as it would have been at home; but there was certainly menace in the way he carried it. He had the lithe, alert movements of a hunted animal. The crackle of the twig had brought him to the very peak of that alertness. Now he walked in ghostlike silence, placing one foot carefully before the other, swinging his whole body from the hips so that his eyes and his gun traversed the entire field before him with each step.

He was making directly for the two sheds. Freddy shrank against the innermost wall and did his best to control his breathing. The whole forest had fallen to silence, as if it, too, were watching in that same terrified fascination.

The man examined the empty shed first. To Freddy it seemed to take an hour though it was probably only a few minutes. Then he heard the intruder lift the padlock and try it. The man made a low birdlike noise. Freddy saw several other men break the cover of darkness at the edge of the clearing. They, too, were dressed like peasants, with nondescript soft hats of the small sombrero type. They, too, carried guns.

But they were all now relaxed, talking and laughing softly, like men who lived half their lives in shadows and silence. They were obviously preparing to sleep in the empty shed; the locked padlock must have led them to believe the place was deserted.

Freddy saw the dilemma he was in. In an hour or so it would be dawn and he would have to make his way down to the lodgings for breakfast. To remain silent now and emerge only then would needlessly arouse the suspicions of what was plainly some kind of clandestine band. Better to face them at once. Anyway, what right had they to invade his demesne like this?

He went to the window, threw it wide open, and said, in English, "What d'you think you're doing here?"

Half a dozen guns swung instantly upon him. The silence was total.

"Go away," Freddy added. "This place is mine."

The man who had come first into the clearing – the leader to judge by the way the others looked to him – said something in Spanish.

"Go away," Freddy repeated, shooing at them as one would at stray cattle. "Vamoose."

They all broke into spontaneous laughter. The leader nodded at the man nearest the window, who advanced and put the barrel of his shotgun against Freddy's chest. He clearly did not expect Freddy to seize it and thrust it angrily away, for the movement almost knocked him off balance.

"Mine!" Freddy shouted at them.

The man with the shotgun now took deliberate aim at Freddy but the leader swiftly put himself between them and stared the fellow down. Then he turned to Freddy and said, "Inglesi?"

"Yes. Si. English."

"How do you do?" the man said slowly and with difficulty.

Freddy gulped with surprise, thrust his hand through the window, and answered, "How do you do. My name is Oxley. Freddy Oxley."

Now it was the man's turn to be surprised. He took Freddy's outstretched hand and shook it, somewhat bemused.

"Oxley," Freddy repeated, pointing to himself with his free hand.

Understanding dawned. The man's name was long and proud and Spanish and quite unpronounceable; all Freddy caught was Miguel. Introductions over, Miguel somewhat surprisingly repeated himself, more carefully but more confidently. "How do you do?" He pointed vaguely into the dark interior of the room.

"Ah!" Freddy laughed. "*What* do I do? What am I doing?"

"Si! How what do you doing?"

"Railway," he said, ashamed that he had been here almost two months and still had not learned the Spanish for "railway." He added: "Chooof chooooof chooooooof!" and tried to imitate an engine whistle.

It was not what Miguel meant; he said something cross and pointed to the ground.

"Ah – here?"

"Si."

It came down to sign-talk. "Me." (Point to chest.) "Walk." (Walk fingers along windowsill.) "Sun." (Point to sky – shield eyes.) "Go down ... me ... sleep ... here."

Miguel was not fooled. He pointed to the padlock, which was hardly something a benighted stroller might carry; he also pinged an inquiring fingernail against the newly glazed windowpane. And he waited with a confident smile for Freddy's explanation.

Freddy laid a finger against his nose in what he hoped was an international gesture of secrecy and then, having nothing to lose by it, handed out the key. When Miguel came in he showed him the little apparatus he had and then, on a sudden inspiration, said, "Sugar!" A spanish-sounding word, *a-zoo-car*, popped into his mind. Was that right? He said it, anyway.

"Ah! Azucar!" Miguel understood something by it, anyway.

Freddy shaped a large volume of some vague raw material in the air before him. He pointed to a retort and gestured a repeated reduction in that volume until he could grasp it between finger and thumb. He hoped that by this he had managed to convey the idea of refining. Finally he popped the imaginary ball of refined product into his mouth and gestured a sublime ecstasy.

Miguel understood. They all understood, and looked at him with interest. Indeed they understood so well that they wanted to taste this ultimately refined sugar at once.

Freddy had to laugh and say *manyana* five times (he knew *that* word, all right!), and gesture five passages of the sun across the sky, before they understood that his first production run still had some time to go. Again Freddy laid a finger to his nose and said, "Sssssh!"

They waited while he locked up and then escorted him down to the road. Dawn was breaking.

He had just left them, waving a cheery farewell, when a shot rang out from the bush that flanked the way. He heard the whirr of a bullet overhead.

Then all was confusion. He flung himself flat on the ground and began to worm his way to the grass at the verge. There was continuous wild firing from guns of every make and calibre, mingled with the shouts of men, some excited, others in pain, as well as the neighing of frightened horses.

Gradually the shouting began to predominate over the shooting, until, Freddy realized, it was all over. He sat up and saw the band of men, his erstwhile comrades, being herded together in the middle of the trail by a chattering and excited troop of regular soldiers. He knew their uniforms well for they were the best customers of the railway; almost every day there was a special military train to or from La Guayra. Despite all the shooting no one seemed to have been killed, though one or two were wounded and needed support.

He stood there at the roadside, uncertain what to do next – go over to the officer in command and introduce himself, or set off at once for the depot, making it clear that the incident had nothing to do with him?

Suddenly one of the soldiers saw him and shouted to the officer, who shouted something back. The soldier and a comrade detached themselves from the party and ran over to Freddy. Being English and therefore above all these incomprehensible local squabbles, he felt no sense of danger. "Buenas dias," he said with a smile.

One of them kicked him. The other did something painful with the butt of his rifle.

"English!" Freddy shouted angrily, pointing to himself. "I'm English, damn you. I've got nothing to do with that rabble." He pointed at the bandits, as he now assumed them to be.

A rain of kicks and blows persuaded him it was futile to offer any further explanation. "You'll be sorry for this," he shouted at them as he reluctantly joined the other prisoners.

They paid him no attention.

Fifteen minutes later, as they shuffled past the boarding house, he shouted out for help, calling on Firey and several of the others by name until he was silenced by another flurry of rifle butts and boots.

Half an hour after that, he lay bruised and naked on a filthy earthen floor in a makeshift cell of teak and corrugated iron in the backyard of the military prison in Caracas.

Every now and then he called out for someone to come – someone who spoke English – but there was never a response.

CHAPTER FORTY-ONE

DURING FOUR DAYS, though it seemed like forty, he languished in that wretched cell, refusing the uneatable food but being forced by the heat to drink the foul water they served him. It quickly gave him dysentry. Then they were forced to move him to hospital.

Some days later he came round from his fever to find Firey sitting at his bedside. "Tha'st set cat among't pigeons," he said cheerfully.

Freddy closed his eyes, afraid this was just another figment of his delirium.

"There's damn near a strike among all't lads," Firey went on. "On account of t'way Fraser won't stick up for thee."

Firey was no figment then; he was too coherent. "Tell it me," Freddy murmured in a voice that had to struggle up through sheets of phlegm.

"They said they'd caught thee wi' a band o' rebels. And Fraser said that's right, tha wert a rebel in England and tha'rt naught but a rebel here. He as good as told them to chuck away't key. There were a right carry-on at't depot, I can tell thee. We all took us guns and set out to free thee. Singing *Rule Britannia*. It were right grand. But for Albright it'd've been battle royal."

Freddy managed to clear his throat. "What's happening now, then?"

"We only cried it off when Albright promised to tell't British consul. Has he been to see thee?"

"I don't know. Perhaps. You're the first as far as I know."

"Ye look terrible."

"Ta! Call again – I've been in danger of laughing to death."

Firey chuckled happily. "Thall't live! I'd've come before but I was in jail me'sen. Is there aught tha wants?"

"Pure water." He had an image of a running stream, the one by the abandoned plantation. How remote it all seemed now. A different life.

The consul, Mr. J.P. Manning, came that evening, just after a visit from several of the other lads. By then, Freddy's basic good health and rugged constitution were beginning to reassert themselves. Manning explained that there was little he could do while Fraser refused to vouch for Freddy.

"But it's all a misunderstanding, sir," Freddy burst out. He could say nothing about his having been virtual manager of the G.L.&C., of course, but he explained the misunderstanding about Dixon as best he could. He saw the consul more than half-believed his version of it; but the fact remained that Fraser's judgement was an insuperable barrier to Freddy's freedom.

"The best I can do," Manning said, "is to engage you a good local lawyer. Have you much put by?"

"Not a penny, sir." This was certainly no time to reveal his bank account.

The other pulled a face.

"But the lads would probably have a whip-round," Freddy offered. He'd repay them later, of course.

It became more hopeful. "And I can certainly see to it that the authorities don't return you to that dreadful oven of a cell. That was a disgrace. I may tell you I put in the strongest possible protest over that."

Freddy's heart sank. "You mean I have to go back to prison, sir? Can't I give my parole?"

Manning shook his head. "Too many Europeans have done that and then simply vanished up country."

"But I'm not a European. I'm an Englishman."

"They don't make such fine distinctions, I'm afraid, Mr. Oxley."

Freddy saw that the man had gone soft out here. *Fine* distinctions, indeed! But all he said was, "I'll be grateful for any assistance you may be able to give me, sir."

Four days later he was back in prison, but this time it was the civil jail – Firey's second home; and Freddy had the cell that was normally kept for ex-presidents and other distinguished prisoners. It had a soft feather bed and its big windows, though stoutly barred, were able to open wide. And the lads held a whip-round to send him in good food. At a purely physical level he was living as well as at any time in his life.

But, such is the relativity of the human condition, these blessings only served to make him the more restless. In the daylong, nightlong hell of those first four days he would have given his right arm to be so comfortably housed; now he could think of nothing but ways to get out – legal ways, of course, for he had no stomach to be hunted through even such scrappy jungle as he had seen close to the city. He sent for paper and pen and wrote daily letters to the prison authorities, the chief of police ... even to Guzman Blanco himself. All were met with total silence.

After a week of this, the consul returned, this time to act as interpreter (and referee) for an interrogation by an army colonel. Among his interpretations Manning also conveyed that the military were unsure of their ground with him. Despite extreme torture, all the rebels who had been captured that same morning were unanimous as to Freddy's innocence.

Outwardly Freddy remained calm. If Eton had been his school, she would have been proud of him. But inwardly he was all a-shiver. True, his entire stock of explosive was safely hidden behind the waterfall, but it would only need some half-competent chemist, even a local pharmacist, to take one look at the remaining phenol and nitric acid, and they would know exactly what he had been making. So – should he tell the truth at last, or should he stick to the lies he had told the rebels?

The colonel began with a question that nearly threw him: "Is it true that you are a revolutionary in England, too? Did you not once try to blow up the home of your employer?"

That was another of the stories he had told Firey Knuckles. It took some time to convince the colonel of the true nature of the prank.

After that the man's questions were somewhat perfunctory, as if he had become convinced of Freddy's innocence and were merely looking to close the file. But when it came to his final question, "What were you doing up there in that shed?" the honest answer, "making explosives," simply stuck in Freddy's throat and refused to be uttered.

Taking his courage in both hands he explained that before he left England he had been working at a chemicals factory; and here in Venezuela, prompted by the large amounts of bagasse he had seen being thrown out of the sugar refineries, he was working in secret on an idea for chemically extracting more sugar from the waste.

"Was it successful?"

Freddy shrugged. "I had hardly begun."

And there the matter rested ... and rested ... and rested. Freddy's incarceration was now more a result of bureaucratic delay than of anything more sinister. But still he chafed to be free – and earning again.

His fifth week of incarceration was coming to a close when Firey visited him in a state of high excitement. It was mid-afternoon, so Freddy naturally asked him why he wasn't working.

"Eah!" he chuckled. "Tha'd think as t'world had come to an end. Down at Zic-Zac, half't mountain has fallen down on't track. They say as it'll take two or three weeks to clear. And Guzman Blanco's playing all merry hell. He's in't middle of a big push against't rebels and he's shifting his men around like spinning tops. And now, wi't line blocked, they can't move hand nor foot." He laughed. "He says he's going to cancel't English concession and get some German outfit in to run't railway. Poor old Fraser's like a bear on hot coals."

Freddy's chance had come at last. He wasted no time in relishing the situation, but took up pen and paper and wrote to Fraser:

Whatever your opinion of me, you must believe me when I say I have the means to clear the line inside two days. If I have not heard from you by tonight, I shall send a copy of this letter to General Blanco.

Firey carried the note away with him.

Within two hours Freddy was summoned to the office of the prison governor, where he met not just Mr. Fraser but Guzman Blanco himself. Freddy knew the man at once. He had, in fact, seen him during his first week out here; the whole depot had been thrown into a turmoil because the dictator had wanted to take a train that day.

To say that he was tall and distinguished, though true,

fails to convey the sense of utterly ruthless power that hung around the man like a special sort of atmosphere. He resembled a death's-head with a thin veneer of cold flesh. To be near him was like being close to an uncaged tiger – a tiger who presently happened to be well fed and contented, but one who might at any moment turn and rend you to pieces. Freddy was not in the room three seconds before he knew how useless it would be to persist with the lie about sugar refining; he had had some notion of saying that the same chemicals could, just by chance, be used for making explosives.

So he told the truth, embroidering nothing and leaving nothing out. The general had his own interpreter. Freddy hated to hear his simple narrative being repeated in the man's fawning, deferential whine. But the General kept his eyes on Freddy, those cold, reptilian eyes that plumbed the very depths of him. The interpreter could have squeaked like a mouse for all that it mattered; Guzman Blanco could see the truth as it emerged, whether or not he understood the words (and Freddy felt sure the man understood a great deal more English than he admitted to).

The worry of it all must have driven Fraser insane, for his first words were, "D'you seriously expect us to believe you weren't making explosives for the rebels?"

Freddy ignored him; he went on looking steadily at the General. "Pay no attention to this man," he said.

"Convince me," the General told him.

"If I were working for the rebels, why should I now offer to clear the line for you, sir?"

"People are funny about wanting to live."

"Then I can only assure you I was not working for them."

"But why make explosives at all?"

"As I said, sir – for the railway. To bring down all the loose material that keeps falling on the line."

The General was still uncertain. His lips chewed nothing; his ice-cool eyes dwelled in Freddy's, forcing him to add a further explanation: "As soon as I heard the whole line had originally been cleared with blasting powder, I knew why they had done the least amount of blasting necessary to open the line. I'm sure I don't need to tell the general the difference between the power of gunpowder and that of modern explosives!"

The General turned those withering eyes on Fraser. "True?" he asked.

Fraser glared at Freddy and muttered something about the original specification (which, of course, had been drawn up in the days of Falcón, when Guzman Blanco himself had been a rebel leader). The General waved him to silence and turned back to Freddy. "And you, young man, can clear the line in two days, eh?"

Freddy asked Fraser, "What's the bed at that point? Describe it to me."

"Rock. It's a rock ledge, about twenty-five feet wide, with several thousand tons of loose soil and scree spilled down upon it. As fast as we move it, more comes down."

Freddy smiled his satisfaction. "And blasting powder, of course, can't throw it far enough."

"We've sent for some better explosive. A Royal Navy gunboat gave us five shells, which we took apart, but it wasn't enough."

"But there's firm rock beneath?"

Fraser nodded.

Freddy turned to the general. "Two days," he promised.

The general stood. They all stood. "What are you waiting for?" he asked.

"Quite a lot," Freddy said deliberately.

They both turned and stared at him in astonishment.

"From you, sir, I respectfully request free passage from this place and your assurance as an officer and a gentleman that whatever charges may be pending will be dropped." He had thought this part out most carefully. He turned to Fraser. "And from you," he added, "or from your company – I don't care which – one hundred pounds for the job."

Fraser turned purple. "I'll see you in hell!" he stormed.

"Then it's two hundred pounds," Freddy said calmly. "And it will double every time you ..."

Guzman Blanco interrupted. He sounded angry but Freddy could sense an amusement behind it. "I'll have you tortured," he threatened. "All I need to know is where the explosive is hidden. We can do the rest."

That was something Freddy had not thought of. He swallowed and, though he had no clear idea of what he was going to say, shook his head and gave a slow, confident smile.

"No?" the General asked. "Why not?"

A sudden wild thought occurred to Freddy. "Because," he said, "when this is over, I am the man who will give Venezuela the best ordinance in the whole of South America."

Guzman Blanco roared with laughter. Like a lot of bullies the General appreciated someone who stood up to him. He clapped Freddy on the shoulder, making his head reel, and, turning to Fraser, said in English, "Two hundred." It was a command.

"Four!" Freddy risked saying, but the General just wagged a finger at him.

The interpreter was still speaking the final words after the General had left the room: "And for you, Mr. Oxley, you have my word, the word of Guzman Blanco, that, when you have cleared the line in two days, you are a free man."

CHAPTER FORTY-TWO

"SHOULD OUGHT TO OF looked at it first, see tha," Firey said complacently.

Freddy remained morosely silent. Half the mountain seemed to have spilled across the track. An ant army of men were shovelling the looser stuff off the edge, where it fell in smoky downward plumes that seemed to dissolve into the air. Now and then a rising draught would catch one of them and bend it up in a graceful U. Marooned among the dwindling debris were larger rocks that only machines or explosives could shift.

Taking any one hour with any other, there might seem to be progress; but day-by-day comparisons showed that no sooner was a foot of bare track gained here than it was lost at some other point. The mountain relentlessly refilled the shelf as fast – or rather as slow – as the men cleared it. In places where the men had not yet even reached, the depth to be cleared was close to twenty feet.

"Try and shift that in one blast and tha'llt crack all't rockbed," Firey continued.

"I'm thinking," Freddy answered.

"How much blasting 'ast tha done?"

"I told you – I began when I was nine."

That silenced Firey for a while. Freddy calculated there was the best part of five thousand cubic yards of rock and shale to be cleared, not counting the thin layers at the edges of the fall, which would in any case be more effectively cleared by hand.

"Six hours gone," Firey reminded him. "Forty-two left."

"And naught done! Can't you say anything useful?"

"Aye."

"What?"

"If they could shift half that muck by hand, you could blast the other half wi'out risking cracks in the bed."

Freddy raised his eyes heavenwards. "Very useful. And it wouldn't take above a week."

"It's the only way."

"Then we've got to find the *other* only way." He turned his back on the scene of the disaster. "I'm going for a walk."

He went up into the forest that skirted the rockslide on the Caracas side. There was a fairly well-marked trail; somewhere ahead must be a coffee plantation or fruit orchard. After a few hundred yards he came to a clearing where some freak wind had flattened half a dozen trees, leaving the rest of the forest standing. He sat on the trunk of one and peeled away a few remaining strips of bark. There was a scurry of crawling things. What a prolific country this was! Turn over any stone or leaf and there it was – seething, burgeoning life. Despite their peeling bark, the trees could only have fallen during the last few weeks; some of their foliage was still green. Yet new growth, quickened by the unexpected kiss of the sun, was already springing up all around. Scars healed quickly here.

That was certainly true of the scars of his imprisonment.

After six hours of freedom it already seemed a distant night-mare. Perhaps that was because deep inside himself he had been impatient rather than angry. He had known it was all a mistake. He knew he did not belong there. He knew they would sort it all out before long and he would be free again. In spirit he had never been in jail; he had remained out here all along.

This wasn't getting any muck shifted off the line.

Thank heavens Guzman Blanco wasn't out here, storming around and frightening everyone. Was it a good sign? Either he had absolute confidence in Freddy or he smelled disaster and wanted no taint of it on himself.

How to shift that vast overburden of rock and ... mess?

Something Firey had said flashed before his mind's eye – a tantalizing glimpse of a hint of a suggestion of a possibility ...

Why had he come away from the scene of the fall? Shouldn't he be there?

No – it was the wrong way to look at it – too much useless information crowding in. The sun was too bright.

What was it Firey had said?

He took out a pencil and began drawing on the bleached wood of the fallen tree – a section through the hillside: a slope of scree and rock, a vertical cut, a horizontal rockbed, and then a steep fall into the valley. Loosely he shaded in the fallen debris. He drew a cross – the explosive charge – at the bottom of the shading, in the angle where the vertical cutting met the horizontal rock shelf. He brought the pencil point down on the charge, to detonate it.

In his mind's eye the tiny chemical demon that lurked unseen in the pale liquid suddenly grew to a monstrous giant, flinging off his covering of shale and hurling away the great boulders with a mighty ease.

Then he pencilled in the new cracks and fissures, deep into the rockbed – half of which he could now imagine sliding away into the valley below.

He moved along the treetrunk and quickly sketched out a second cross-section. What about raising the location of the charge a bit? Leave a cushion of loose shale between it and the bed to absorb the impact? How much, though? A foot? Two feet? He tried to imagine himself, a man carved in stone, imprisoned in the rockbed, with the explosion going off in the dirt above him. What distance would be kindly to such a creature?

He gave up the effort. The forces involved were far beyond his imagination. Yet his return from that blind alley revealed to him one important fact: Strictly speaking it was not a simple question of how thick a cushion to leave between the charge and the bed. The calculation involved a complex balance between the size of the charge, the nature of the overburden (how much loose dirt ... how many big boulders?) and the innate strength of the bedrock – was it already slightly fractured, for instance?

Could he answer any of these questions?

No.

So there was really no point in going on thinking about it all.

No. Not really!

He could place the charge anywhere he liked – one position was as good as another?

Exactly.

He shrugged and drew three crosses in the overburden, not quite at random. One was on the rockbed itself; one a third of the way up; and the last about three feet below the surface.

Which should he choose?

Tip! Tip! Tip! He touched each in turn, idly, with the pencil point.

Suddenly the hair rose on his neck. He stopped breathing. His whole body was racked with an unbearable tension.

"Wheeeee!" He flung the pencil in the air, followed by his hat.

He had solved it!

Not one explosion but *three* – bang-bang-bang – a tenth of a second apart. In a way, Firey had given him the answer, except that he'd been too dazzled by the problem to see it. Take half of it off by hand, Firey had said, and you could use a smaller charge that wouldn't crack the rock. Well, you could just as easily take half of it off by explosives – or a third, to keep the size of the charge down. Then, while that bit of muck was lifted off, poised in the air, so to speak, you could get in another bang – lift off another third ... and so on.

The beauty of it was you didn't need to have all those

unknowable answers about the depth and consistency of the overburden and the exact fragility of the rockbed; doing the job piecemeal gave you a huge margin for error.

He picked up his hat, did not even try to find the pencil, and set off briskly to return to the site.

Firey saw the jauntiness in his stride long before he could make out his expression. "Eeee!" he called out. "Th'art like a pasha wi' two pricks. Didst meet Moses up there or what?"

"It's three pricks, Firey, me lad! Not two! We'll poke that muck off the hillside with three little pinpricks." He explained the method he had devised.

"Well," Firey answered, "I know naught about blasting but it sounds just't ticket."

"It was your suggestion. You said get half of it off and the rest'd be simple."

Firey beat his chest and made a prizefighter's winning gesture.

"Well, seriously girls ..." Freddy deliberately calmed down their euphoria. "That was the easy part. Now for the hard work. I was going to absorb the liquid xyloidene into dry clay powder and detonate it with a burning fuse, but this calls for accurate timing – about a tenth of a second, I'd say. And it would be disastrous if the two upper charges didn't go off and the bottom one did – that really would fracture the bedrock."

"You've lost me, lad."

"Simply this." He scored a depression in the ground with his toe. "Imagine I had a cup – an eggcup even – of the liquid down there." He picked up a small pebble. "I can drop this anywhere into that liquid and" – he let the pebble go; it fell into the dent – "bang! It explodes. Hit the liquid anywhere, see, and it will explode. But" – he put a short, stout twig beside the dent and an English threepenny bit upon it – "There's a solid charge, with a detonator on it, and" – he dropped another pebble; it missed by inches – "Nothing! You've got to be so accurate with solid explosive and detonators, see? We daren't risk it."

"So – we drill holes and pour the stuff down?"

Freddy laughed.

"What's so funny?"

"You'll see! Let's go back to the depot. My head's busting

with all the things still to be done – bring the explosive down the hillside, rig up some kind of detonation apparatus, cut umpteen lengths of copper tube ... you did your Mechanics, didn't you? What's the acceleration due to gravity? Or, to be exact, how far does a falling body move in a tenth of a second? The *first* tenth?"

"Eighteen inches," Firey guessed.

"We'll give it two feet."

"Ho!" Firey parodied him grandly. "We'll give it thirty inches!" He laughed. "Power's a grand thing, eh?"

"What d'you mean?"

"Doesn't tha realize it? Th'art king o' Caracas for't next thirty-eight hours, lad. Say aught tha will, they'll obey thee. Say tha needs every gold candlestick in't city – they'd ransack th'ole place, cathedral and all, and bring thee every last one. No questions asked!"

Freddy laughed at the fantasy though he knew that what Firey said was true.

As they climbed aboard his engine and opened the steam valve, Firey looked back and said, "I can't wait to see that lot shift. Half a mountain pushed up into't sky!"

"I'm afraid not," Freddy told him. "We'll do it one short section at a time. Less risk of bringing down a fresh rockfall."

For the next twenty hours he worked without rest. The plan was to put the xyloidene in test tubes at the bottom of copper pipes of appropriate depth. At the top of each pipe would be a weight, held by a pin. When the pin was jerked out, the weight would fall and detonate the charge. He handed the problem of making that part of the apparatus to Tommy Walsh, the best of the artificers. He himself took a dozen men and all the test tubes in Caracas up to the abandoned farm, to bring down the explosive.

There the first thing he did was to range them in a semicircle and stage a brief but sobering demonstration. He took a single phial of xyloidene from its hiding place behind the waterfall and from it withdrew, using a suction pipette, a few drops of the liquid. All his movements were careful to a degree that seemed ridiculous to the onlookers. With the pipette well stoppered, he replaced the phial and tiptoed back to the centre of the semicircle.

"We get your point, Oxley," Casey, one of the drivers, said impatiently.

"I wonder about that," Freddy replied.

Dramatically he held up the pipette, its tip almost six feet above a piece of bare stone. He took off his finger and let fall a single drop. There was a loud report that startled even him. There were whistles and cries of amazement and fear.

He looked along that row of faces, blanched white beneath their newly acquired tans, and said, quietly, "Each of you will be carrying one fluid ounce, sealed in a test tube and wrapped in damp rags. The vibration of ordinary walking won't set it off. But if you drop it, you'll vanish in such tiny bits not even the rats would think you worth the scavenging."

They hardly breathed.

"You'll leave at half-minute intervals – that's how long it will take me to fill each tube. You'll wait a hundred yards away up there and come forward one at a time, when you hear my whistle. On your journey down, you'll sing – one line out loud, one in your head. If you hear the man below you, stop. Go on singing, on and off, to warn the man behind. But stop where you are. Don't start again until there's only silence before you."

"What song do we sing?" one of the fitters asked.

The others turned on him in derision but Freddy raised his free hand as if it were obvious: "Nearer my God to Thee, of course."

For the three remaining hours of daylight Freddy filled and stoppered the test tubes. They brought him lanterns and sandwiches and he worked through the night to use up his stock of phenol and nitric acid. It took half the following morning to ferry that lot down. By then the supply of test tubes had run out and they were using everything from perfume bottles to spice holders. These took longer because he first had to fill each container with fine, dry sand, and then pour off exactly one fluid ounce of it – so that precisely that volume would be left to fill with explosive. It was vital to have the same quantity in every charge.

Then, with a last weary, bleary look around the "factory," he left to see how the other work was progressing. On his way down there was a sudden tropical thunderstorm. The rain fell in curtain rods and the path became a torrential stream. He walked on through it, feeling more refreshed when it was over than if he had had several hours' sleep. But it did not last. By the time he reached the depot, the invigorating wetness of the rain had turned to the deathly soaking of his own sweat. The sun beat down and the humidity climbed toward a hundred.

Only twenty hours were left, and not a single shothole was yet drilled.

Tom Walsh had made a first-rate job of the copper pipes. The idea was that the diggers should pioneer a hole down to bedrock. Then the pipe could be lowered to the right depth. He had made nicks at twelve-inch intervals down the length of each. Next the test tube full of explosive would be lowered on strong linen thread, inside the pipe; Walsh had blocked the bottom of each pipe with a lump of soft putty as a cushion for the unstable xyloidene.

The detonator was a small cylinder of lead, brought to a point like a sailor's marlin spike. It fitted inside a short copper tube that, in turn, fitted into a sleeve at the top of the explosion tube, like an extension of it. The detonation tubes were of three lengths, to give the three slightly different timings: a foot, three feet, and six feet. The lead detonator was held by a small bolt that passed through holes in the tube wall. Each bolt had a hundred-yard-long tail of fine stranded ripwire that could be led back to one central firing point.

That, as far as Freddy could see, was the only weakness. "There could be a difference of two or three feet in the slack between any given ripwire and another," he objected. "You couldn't pull them all evenly taut, because you'd risk pulling out one or other of the pins."

But Walsh had thought of that. He led Freddy to the back of the shop, where Mr. Albright himself had devised a machine like a small version of the ballista with which Roman armies once hurled stone and fireballs into beleaguered cities. The Romans had used whippy woods like yew and willow; this one had the best spring steel from Sheffield. When it was cranked up and the pin removed, its arm would swing through fifteen feet of arc in less than half a second; at that rate it would hardly matter if one of the ripwires was as much as two yards longer than another.

Freddy patted Walsh on the back and nodded appreciatively at Albright. "What can go wrong?" he asked.

They loaded all their apparatus, and enough pipes and explosive for two dozen shotholes, onto an inspection van behind Firey's engine. Then they set off gingerly for Zic-Zac.

When they reached the rockspill, Freddy picked the first point where the depth of overburden reached at least ten feet. Through an interpreter he explained to the officer in charge what he wanted in the way of shotholes, showing him a little sketch he had drawn.

The officer smiled and translated it into military terms: three ranks of men, eight in each rank, in open order, three inches of daylight between shoulders, each man with a pointed crowbar, and a single command: "Dig! Hup-down, hup-down, hup-down, hup ...!"

Freddy had thought he might snatch a little nap while the holes were dug; he was hardly back at the inspection waggon when the officer cried halt.

They laid planks beside each rank of holes, to avoid treading loose shale down into them before the copper pipes were placed at the appropriate depth (or at what Freddy prayed was the appropriate depth). As soon as each pipe was placed, they trod the loose dirt tight to hold it there. Nothing could get in at the bottom thanks to the plug of putty.

The men who had handled the test tubes down the mountainside were veterans now in the business of moving liquid xyloidene. They carried it from the van to the firing site.

The soldiers watched with incredulity the precautions that were being taken: only one man to move one test tube at a time; each one to be placed by Freddy, beginning at the farther end; not a single detonator to be placed until the last charge was loaded; and then no movement in any direction that might accidentally yank out one of the pins.

But every man of them absorbed the message.

Sixteen hours were now left; eight of them would be in darkness. Freddy realized it was going to be impossible to do it all this way, one short section at a time.

They cleared the hillside of everyone except the scouts on lookout near the summit. Each wire had been led back without mishap to the ballista, which was now in a sandbagged redoubt, eighty yards from the shotholes.

"Anyone done any pigeon shooting?" Freddy asked.

Casey raised a thumb. "The king o' King's County," he said.

"Then you poke your head over the parapet and watch through these glasses." He handed him the binoculars, part of the equipment of the inspection van. "Tell me if you can see the overburden actually being lifted in three separate bits. It'll be very quick so keep your wits about you."

"And you?" Casey's tone suggested he felt he had "been volunteered."

"I'm going to watch the stuff above." It occurred to him that they could have pegged down white tapes on the slope above, as a later check on any movement. Too late now. One couldn't think of everything.

What else had he forgotten?

Before the question could bite he nodded at the officer, who drew out his pistol and fired three spaced shots. Everyone ducked except Freddy, Casey – and the officer.

Albright snapped out the ballista pin. The arm whistled as it sliced the air. A spaghetti of wire filled the redoubt. There was a two-part roar, muffled then sharp. Then a splattering of firing pins against the sandbags. A part of the sky ahead was suddenly dark.

Freddy had to force himself to watch the slope; as far as he could tell, nothing moved. But the dark patch of exploded earth at the edge of his field of view seemed disappointingly small. About all that could be said for it was that it went in the right direction – out into the valley rather than straight up and down.

"It seemed to come out in one," Casey said in a neutral tone. "Twas fierce quick so it was."

The others must have felt the same sense of deflation for a distinct mood of anticlimax, tempered by the false heartiness of disappointed men, settled upon them as they scrambled back to survey the scene.

When they reached it, however, they could only stand and gape. You'd think a giant witch's broomstick had dealt the mountainside one mighty swipe and swept it bare. The line emerged from the nearer pile of debris and, three or four yards later, vanished into the farther pile; but in between it gleamed. A few small heaps of shale on the up-blast side of the metal were all that marred an otherwise perfect job.

"Good!" a voice boomed in English. "Ver' good!"

They all turned. It was Guzman Blanco; he must have been watching in secret from somewhere close by – one of the army tents at the edge of the landslide, perhaps. Through his interpreter he asked, "What now?"

"There's no time to do it all like that, sir," Freddy said. "Not length by length. We'll have to do the rest in one single blast and take a chance on fetching down more rock. In terms of stress per unit of length, it won't be greater than this."

He could tell that the interpreter made a hash of that; but the General got the point nonetheless.

"Can the soldiers drill the shotholes through the night?"

"How many?"

"Half a dozen men, taking it in relays, working eight hours."

Guzman Blanco conferred with his officers and said it could be done. The problem lay in mounting enough night patrols to keep away snipers. "You will have dinner with me," he added to Freddy, pointing back up the line toward Caracas.

All Freddy had wanted to do was sleep, but suddenly he was wide awake again.

CHAPTER FORTY-THREE

DESPITE THE GRANDEUR of the presidential palace, Guzman Blanco lived rather simply. That evening they – the General, two or three ministers, and their wives – dined in a small suite somewhere near the back of the building, overlooking a flower-filled courtyard decked with lanterns. The meal was spartan in its simplicity, for which Freddy was grateful; a stomachful of rich food would have finished him in his present tired state. As it was, only the scratchiness of his borrowed evening dress kept him awake.

The drone of the General's interpreter did little to help. The man sat near his elbow, not quite at the table, and summarized the conversation. Sometimes he was deliberately vague – "They are discussing penal matters ..." – which could mean anything from the cost of prison skilly to improved methods of torture. At other times the conversation became more international, with talk of the Russian threat to Turkey, the likelihood of war in Europe, and the possible interference with trade in the hemisphere. At one point the General turned to Freddy and asked, "What d'you think of Disraeli? What will England do?" – as if Freddy were some kind of indiscreet ambassador.

"Disraeli will do for England what the General would do for Venezuela," Freddy replied.

Guzman Blanco laughed approvingly. "You should also add that in matters of mutual interest your prime minister would strive zealously to safeguard the legitimate aspirations of my country."

"There's enough English railway proprietors, bankers, and merchants out here to remind him of that," Freddy answered.

The General laughed even more heartily. "Yes, the best hostages are always self-appointed."

It was the only direct exchange between the two men during the entire meal. Freddy kept himself awake in awkward smalltalk (via the interpreter, of course) with the General's wife on his right and the wife of a minister to his left; they clearly had no idea who he was or why he was there. Even Freddy himself began to wonder.

There was a great deal of laughter and seeming good humour but Freddy noticed that the men watched each other warily. The spirit was more one of truce than of comradeship – the sort of truce that prevails among creatures at a waterhole. So, he thought, the war against the rebels was more serious than was generally admitted.

When the ladies had withdrawn, the men kicked off their boots, cigars were passed around, and the footmen served a drink that seemed to be made chiefly of grenadillas and rum. Freddy drank only the smallest sips.

At last Guzman Blanco turned to him and, through the interpreter, gave a brief history of the revolution – *his* revolution, of course, not the one now being waged against him. He spoke of the bad days of Falcón, the misery of the people, the legitimacy of the struggle, its triumph, the freedom of the elections ever since ... the new prosperity ...

It suddenly dawned on Freddy that he was being recruited to the General's cause. The man obviously distrusted the ordinary springs of human action – fear and self-interest. He knew Freddy was afraid of going back to prison and that he stood to gain two hundred pounds when he cleared the line (a feat that now seemed assured). But these were not enough; the man had to bind him with the positive ties of loyalty and fervour. Freddy was too tired even to pretend.

When the general saw the lukewarmth of Freddy's response, he merely smiled and said, "At least, young man, you have learned the two most important lessons in the business of war."

Freddy pricked up his ears.

"First, you must make your price when the other man is weak – as you did with Fraser yesterday." He chuckled. "The poor fellow thought you were a wicked socialist, and hey presto! – you're a more dangerous capitalist than he will ever be!"

"And the second lesson?" Freddy had to ask.

"Oh that! Yes, you must only deal with the winning side, of course. In Europe it's different. Europe has an older civilization, more devious. They quite expect you to deal with both sides. But here it's an iron rule. Follow it and you won't go wrong."

It struck Freddy that the winning side was not necessarily the government; in his tiredness he almost said as much.

Uncannily, as if he had read Freddy's thoughts, Guzman Blanco added, "That's why a civil war is the supreme test of any general."

As Freddy was crossing the plaza on his way home there

was another downpour. He should have taken shelter but
tiredness drove him on. Mr. Albright's white tie and tails were
soaked but what did it matter? What did anything matter? He
had reached a pitch of fatigue where he began to doubt his own
reality.

The cooling of the rain should have made sleep even
easier, yet it would not come. Within five minutes of laying his
head upon the pillow Freddy knew he was not going to be able
to sleep; in a curious way he was almost *too* tired for it. His
mind floated in a nightmare list of things not done – or were
they? – things he had not personally supervised – things that
could so easily go wrong still.

Half an hour later, when he had run through the events of
the coming morning for the fifth time, he realized he might as
well be up and about, doing all these things instead of lying
there, uselessly awake and worrying about them. He rose and
dressed in his workaday drill shirt and trousers and, leaving a
hasty note for Firey, slipped out into the warm predawn night.
At the depot he switched the points and took out the hand
trolley, which was easy enough for one man to pump downhill
to Zic-Zac.

He arrived just as dawn was pushing a spectacularly green
and icy light up into the eastern sky. A great hawk, or an eagle
perhaps, was already quartering the bare slope of the mountain,
borne aloft on thermals rising from the still-warm rock. He no
longer felt tired, just a little apart from the world around him –
an observer, even of himself.

The troops had finished the holes and were now laying
continuous lines of planks beside them. There was no officer in
charge, only a corporal; they were surprised to see him about
so early and he obviously fell several notches in their scale of
importance. The corporal offered him a cheroot. It was small,
cheap, and strong but to Freddy it had no taste at all.

He probed several holes but found none that needed
further work. That in itself was a tribute to the General's
leadership.

He counted the holes and the remaining explosion tubes.
They had plenty. The test tubes of xyloidene had been placed
in a sandbagged hole overnight, invulnerable to anything but a
direct mortar bomb. He counted them – more than enough.

He counted the detonation tubes ... the ripwires ... he even counted the sandbags. There was nothing else to do. Why had he been so worried?

It was daylight now; the others would be here soon. In any case, there was plenty of time. As he and Guzman Blanco had parted last night, the General had waived aside the promise of forty-eight hours and had set the explosion for noon; he wanted to make a spectacle of it for the ladies of his "court."

Freddy strolled away up the line and then followed the track he had taken yesterday – or was it the day before? Time had fused into one swimming continuum. Whether one day or two, the forest had put on as much growth as he would expect in a month in his own little vegetable patch in Albert Villas.

A pang of memory stabbed him at the name. Why had he thought of Albert Villas rather than Hob's Gardens?

They had been happy in Stockton, that's why. A happy, contented little family. Ann had always had her guinea ideas but in Stockton they had no scope. Only when she came down and mixed with the Homfray set ...

Forget it. Why keep thinking about Ann? The idea was to start afresh.

Consciously he sought images of Lawrence and Emmy – strolling in fields of poppies and cornflowers ... down by the boating pool ... walking solemnly to church of a Sunday. Soon, surely, there would be a letter from them?

At the edge of the clearing he paused. There was a man sitting on one of the fallen trees – the one he himself had sat on to make his sketches; indeed, it seemed that the man was studying them.

"Buenas dias, senor," Freddy called out, slipping his hand into his pocket and lightly cradling his revolver there.

The man looked up. He could have been Miguel's brother – but then so could half the male population of the country. "English?" he asked.

"Yes." Freddy walked over to him.

The man tapped the drawings on the treetrunk, already half-obliterated by the rain. "You?" he asked.

Freddy nodded.

"Then you are Mr. Oxley, the saviour of Guzman Blanco." There was a harsh edge to the question. "I'm an employee of the railway company," Freddy replied. "I'm clearing our line."

"And saving the hide of Guzman Blanco."

Freddy shrugged. "Who are you?"

"Iago." The man stared hard at him as if the name should mean something. When he saw it didn't, he gave a bitter laugh. "You're just a dumb slave," he said. "A brilliant, genius, dumb slave." He regarded him speculatively. "What shall we do with you?"

"I'm glad you approve of my little sketches," Freddy said, to hide the noise as he cocked the hammer of his revolver.

The ruse failed. "Don't," Iago told him evenly. "At least half a dozen of my men have you in their sights."

Freddy grinned. None of it was real. "What about the army, they're only half a mile away, you know."

"You can risk that, of course."

"And killing me wouldn't stop them clearing the line. I'm no longer necessary."

"Oh we wouldn't kill you. A man who can make such powerful explosives in such a crude little factory ... no we certainly wouldn't kill you."

"What then? What d'you want?"

Iago gave a coldly amused little laugh. He had black hair and pale blue eyes – very striking in that part of the world. "What do we want? We want to deny any further services from you to Guzman Blanco. We want to divert those services to us. But above all at this moment what we want is to avoid hurting you so badly we'd have to carry you away from here. We want you to walk with us."

"You talk as if you were waiting for me? You couldn't possibly have known I was going to come here."

"There's an ambush party down at the line now. We thought you'd come down soon after dawn. The Grand Event has been put off until noon, no?"

"What makes you think I'll agree to work for you?"

"Are you immune from hunger?" Iago asked. He read the contempt in Freddy's eyes and added, "You don't seem to be much of an idealist. I don't suppose the plight of the Venezuelan poor would move you very far."

"Talking of moving far," Freddy began; but then his mind

lost its grasp of the rest of the sentence. He heard the words still on the air but they suddenly had no meaning. "Moving far ..." he repeated mechanically.

"Two hours' walk," Iago said. "Surely you can do that?"

"I know what I was going to say – you could still ambush the supplies ... the explosives. I could point out the truck to you."

"Well tried!" Iago smiled. "We know they moved the explosive into a ..." lacking the word, he pointed at the ground and gestured a hollow space. "Last night."

Far up the line there was a whistle. Engine Number One. Firey's own.

"The ambush will create a ... a divertition?" Iago said. "We'll slip away then. Perhaps you'll make that pistol safe and hand it to me?"

"Ambush?" Freddy took out the gun.

"To show the General how weak he is on every flank." Iago held out his hand to receive the weapon.

"But that train – its driver is a friend of mine. They're all friends of mine."

"I have friends there, too. Anyway, no Englishman will be harmed." The man was growing impatient.

"But if they're shot at, they'll shoot back."

"That would be different, of course. Come on. We have no more time."

They could hear the slow thunder of the train now.

Freddy raised his arm, pointing the revolver toward the sky. "I could create a diversion, too."

Again those cold, merciless eyes. "You would exchange the certainty of your death for the probability of your friends' survival. I didn't think you such a fool."

Freddy wished his head were clearer; thoughts kept grinding to a halt in a kind of limbo where meaningful words echoed themselves into nonsense ... certainty ... probability. They became interchangeable and alien.

And suddenly it was too late. A volley of shots rang out from somewhere down the slope. Then, after a brief, shocked silence, it was answered by a regular fusillade. There was a lot of shouting and blowing of whistles.

"Come on!" Somehow Iago already had his gun and they

were slipping away among the trees. He was at the centre, half captive, half honoured guest. What about his knife? Had they forgotten it, or did they think their guns made its possession pretty useless? He looked about him. There were more than half a dozen – indeed, more than a dozen. He could not count them all, flitting among the trees.

On a sudden inspiration he said, "The men down at the ambush – they're expecting you to back them up with this small army here. This was going to be your big counterpush – before the line was cleared."

"We have a bigger prize now," Iago said.

"They'll all be killed."

"They expect to die for our country, for the revolution."

In his tiredness, Freddy suddenly saw everything with a brilliant lucidity; it would never have happened if his mind had been clogged with everyday trivia. "There are no people left in your life," he told Iago.

"What do you mean? I care only for the people."

"You talk of the poor. *The* poor. But they don't exist. This man is poor because he has bad land. Another because he had bad parents. Another – bad luck. Another – bad habits. There are a thousand reasons for being poor. How can you talk about *the* poor? I'll tell you how – in the same way you can abandon your comrades to certain death down there. They, too, aren't people any more. Just a group. Proud to die for the revolution – that's all that matters."

For a while Iago appeared not to have heard. Then he said, "If you take away faith and noble things, what is left? Only selfish things – money, fear, starvation, lust ... the humans need more than this. We need sacrifice."

The clarity of Freddy's insight grew clouded; it was all ceasing to matter. There was gunfire down the valley; any one of those shots might mark the death of a friend, but it had no meaning. His ability to comprehend had been stretched to its limits. Now it burst like a party balloon. All he could take in was this decaying branch, that fern, Iago's heels rising and falling ... the path ahead.

The men around had faded into the forest thickness. He looked about him and saw them from time to time, quiet ghosts among the mighty tree trunks. It was some seconds before he realized that apart from the expected rebels, somewhat farther off, he had also glimpsed the greeny grey of the regular army uniform.

Or had it been an illusion? He longed to look again but feared that his doing so might alert the others. It would be better to turn his mind, or what remnants were left of it, to the implications of what he thought he had seen.

But it was hard. His exhausted faculties could no longer assemble a logical train of thoughts and consequences; instead came a seething of questions and conclusions.

How many were following? He should try to make a break for it. Had the General expected some attempt at kidnapping – was he a mere decoy? They'd do nothing while he was still there among them. Or was he expendable? Someone had said he was no longer needed – quite recently. So he was expendable. If the army was following in force ... what then? Perhaps not completely expendable. Guzman Blanco was another of those idealists who had forgotten people. Perhaps they'd wait until the last moment, hoping for a chance to pick the others off and rescue him. Only *the* people. He ought to create that chance.

It was the only conclusion he came to. He must create a chance for the army to fire safely, killing the others but not him.

Now who was forgetting that rebels were also people!

No – they'd already done it for him, surely?

Oh, what did it matter? The only thing to think about was getting away. Look for a shallow gully beside the path – something to drop into. Or a river. Even an old abandoned building. He looked, and looked ... and flogged his mind when it strayed, and looked again ... and yet again.

For half an hour he staggered among them, always gently uphill, winding this way and that, seeking some avenue of swift escape. It was so long in coming that he almost missed it – a slit in the rockface, seven foot tall and wide enough for him to throw himself inside it without breaking any bones against the sides; yet it was not wide enough for them to come in after him more than two abreast. A less exhausted Freddy would have wondered, too, whether the followers (if they existed at all) would be quick enough to see what he had done and take advantage of it – in short, would they open fire before the rebels could follow him into the cave?

But such thoughts were beyond him. Merely to see the cave mouth, to work out what it was, and what he must do, took all his concentration. They were level with the opening and past it before his muscles leaped to a decision – and he was halfway into the dark before he properly grasped the fact at all.

There was a loud confusion of rifle shots, but who was firing he could not tell. Someone shouted, "Not there, you fool! Not there for God's sake!"

It had to be Iago but it sounded like any excited man – more frightened than angry, strangely enough.

He hurled himself deeper into the darkness. The shooting continued. The darkness became a living, friendly creature, engulfing him.

But it was a creature with the most appalling breath. The air was filled with a nauseating stink of rotting flesh. Perhaps some animal had crept in here to die?

Like smelling salts the stench brought every nerve suddenly alive. A terrible foreboding overcame him.

Then there was a hiss.

An oily touch. A weight.

A pair of glinting eyes weaving close with machinelike grace.

All at once he was as awake as if he had slept the clock around. This was no mere cave; it was the den of some great snake. Even as the fact dawned on him the creature threw one coil around his ankles – and he knew what snake it was.

It spun him like a toy as it threw on more coils, binding his shins and calves, his knees and thighs, with such relentless and unimaginable power that once it reached his chest he knew it would crack him to a pulp. He barely had time to whip his dagger from its sheath before it threw another coil around him, pinning his left hand to his hip.

He lashed out at it blindly, furiously, hitting rock, piles of leaves, old bones, and, just occasionally, that cold, smooth, and curiously oily flesh.

The creature had run out of length. It had used its body up in coiling around him as far as his waist. As long as that one arm was free to wield the knife, it did not dare bring its head and the first three feet of itself any too close. For the moment there was a stalemate. Freddy's eyes were now growing dark-accustomed. Fingers of the rising sun, pushing in through the forest mists, struck fire in the rock around them; so bright it hurt to look. Even the borrowed flash of it on his knifeblade was slightly painful. And the glint of it in those beady eyes was terrifying.

In this approach to death he felt none of that earlier godlike aloofness; here he was not the one in control.

The constrictor began a tactical shift of its grip. It remained tight as a hangman's noose about his waist but it uncoiled itself from around his ankles. He watched in helpless fascination as its liberated tail quivered and flickered around the cave. Whatever it touched it instantly coiled around; but if the thing it gripped then moved, it would uncoil and resume its search. Its movements proclaimed it had all the time in the world.

Suddenly he realized what it was doing. If it could find a firm grip, it could then straighten itself out and break every bone in the lower half of his body. Then he'd be in no condition to resist. But without that purchase, on rock or on tree, its strength, though still awesome, was not quite great enough for that lethal embrace.

He had to get near the opening, where the men outside could see what was happening. How intelligent were snakes? His lower legs were now free. If he tried to get to the cave-mouth, would it realize his purpose and work to prevent him? So should he fool it by seeming to want to get further inside? Or was it so unthinking that it would press on with its own purposes regardless of what he tried to do?

The best course was ...

The least worst course was ...

The least worst course ... he couldn't think any further. In fact, the only thought that came into his head was something Firey had once said to him when they were discussing snakes in general: "If you see a big one, try to bag him whole. Pop him in a sack and suffocate him. The skin's worth a lot more then."

More of Firey's useful advice!

The snake got a small purchase around a pinnacle of rock. Seconds later it broke off, but in that brief interval Freddy had experienced the mighty power that had caused the rock to break. A little more or a little harder and his hip girdle would now be in fragments of most monstrous pain inside him. That must never happen again. Already the questing tail with a life and brain of its own was seeking a new purchase.

"Help!" he shouted.

Snakes are deaf, aren't they?

This one must have felt the vibrations through his body for it tightened what was obviously until now a mere holding grip. The walls of the cave burst in golden stars and swirled around him. Blindly he slashed out at the creature. He must have hit something; it relaxed and hissed furiously.

He saw its tail reaching for a flute of rock, not free like a pillar, but enough of a column, and with enough of a crack behind it, to allow its tail some purchase. Desperately he scrabbled with his heels in the dirt of the floor, inching them toward the cavemouth; relentlessly the tail stretched back, back ... toward the cleft.

"Help!" he shouted again and slashed out at the creature's head.

By chance he caught it – perhaps it was just at the start of a strike against him with its jaws. At all events the knife went straight through it, piercing the skin at its throat and emerging again behind its skull.

He gave a cry of triumph. Now surely it must die, or at least relinquish its hold?

With a hand shaking from the exertion he held the head pinned to the rocky wall, waiting for its muscles to tire, waiting for the relaxation that never came. The thing thrashed and wriggled, seemingly oblivious to any pain the blade might be causing. He could not keep it up much longer; his own muscles were already shrieking their agony.

He relaxed for the merest fraction of a second, but only to stab again, and then again. It still had no effect.

And then he saw his mistake. The snake suddenly abandoned all caution. Its instinct to go for a slow kill, safe to itself, had been overturned when Freddy made it a matter of the creature's own life or death. The coils rippled swiftly up and around his chest, within cutting distance of the knife – if only the knife were not fully engaged in a seemingly hopeless attempt to cut off the head.

He could no longer breathe. A brilliant black snow was

crowding out the world. Not even a gurgle could escape his throat. At last he was dying. He was truly dying.

Ann came rising up out of the black snow, her arms outstretched. She was dead already. Dead and smiling, welcoming him. They would be together again. At last and forever. It was all he really wanted.

The darkness was complete. He no longer even felt the need to breathe. All the struggle had gone out of him. There was a peace such as he had never experienced before. The peace that passeth all ...

Then a roar that shattered the universe. Sparks of gold fell all about him. Winds rushed into his chest and rose like wine into every cranny of his brain. They boomed and howled in glee.

The black snow dissolved. Or filled with hands. He floated in a sea of hands. Sweet angels bear thee ...

His own hands floated. The knife had gone. He saw the head of the boa constrictor, all blasted open. It fell upon his chest – ruined. He looked up into the eyes of Guzman Blanco and burst into tears.

"It's all right. You're all right. Safe!" The General said.

"I was trying to keep it whole," he sobbed. "I wanted to preserve the entire skin."

CHAPTER FORTY-FOUR

HE WENT UP THE MOUNTAIN, a decoy; he returned, a legend. He was back in Caracas when he next awoke, in the Hospital of the Little Sisters of Mercy. As he stirred back into life he had a vague memory of being prodded into consciousness some time earlier – hours? days? he could not say. Someone had wanted him to witness the second Great Explosion of his life – the one that cleared the line at Zic-Zac. He had a brief image of several thousand tons of rock and dirt hanging over the void and then falling with a dreamlike grace. Perhaps it was all a dream.

He looked about him. The first person he saw was Firey Knuckles, in the bed next to his.

"Tha did it!" he said the moment he saw Freddy's eyes open. "Line's clear. Army's shifted. Revolution's a wet firework." He laughed. "And every engine-driver, platelayer, and engineer in't company wants a job as shotfirer and blasting supervisor!"

Freddy smiled at the thought. "And why are you in here?"

"Ambush. Got shot in't foot."

"Oh Lord! Is it bad?"

Firey sniffed philosophically. "They had to take it off at th'ankle, see tha."

"Oh Firey!" Freddy groaned, sinking back on his pillow. In his spinning head, memories stirred ... himself and Iago in the clearing above the ambush. Wasn't there something he could have done to prevent it?

"Could be worse," Firey told him. "What's an engine-driver want a left foot for, anyroad? They say Casey may not live. He was hit very bad."

"Was anyone killed?"

"Not among the English. Casey was worst. He's in't military hospital."

"Does it hurt? Your foot."

"Bit early to say. I've not done that much jumping on it yet."

Freddy grinned. "Am I wounded? Why am I here? What's wrong with me?" Gingerly he began to feel himself for sore places; they seemed to be everywhere.

"Nowt broken. Just bruises. Tha'st been asleep two days, tha knows – like a babby. Eeay, but that must have been a grand scrap wi' yon snake! Twelve foot, they measured him at. He flung thee around that cave like a wasp in a bottle. Do'st tha remember it?"

Freddy nodded. "Not very well. I remember the stink of it. And the touch – very silky. And its eyes."

"It were Guzman Blanco his'sen who shot it. Tha wrestled

it out into't daylight and he shot it." He laughed. "Do'st recollect what tha said?"

Freddy shook his head. "Almost. Something about ..." The memory was there but would not come.

"The whole of Caracas is on about it. Th'art a bloody legend, see tha. When Guzman Blanco shot th'head to bits, tha stood up, grasped him by't throat, and shouted to his face: 'Tha damn great fool! I were trying to preserve't skin!' That's what they say. Bloody hell!" He shook his head in admiration. "Fighting a twelve foot boa constrictor with kid gloves on! Trying to preserve't skin! Tha could stand for president and win tomorrow, I tell thee."

Freddy sat up again. "It isn't true," he told Firey. Odd scraps of memory were coming together now. "I vaguely recall, some time in the middle of the fight, the sunlight must have struck it or something – anyway, it looked very beautiful – and I remembered something you'd said about trying to preserve the skin of any especially large snake. But I'm sure I didn't say anything like that to the General. Did I?"

"It's what they're all saying, anyroad."

Freddy lay back again. His head swam. Sitting up was all right, but lying down too quickly made him dizzy. When the world stopped spinning he asked, "Have I really been here two days?"

"Aye. Old Fraser's been in and out like a double-acting piston. He's down at La Guayra now but he asked us to tell thee – he knows he did thee wrong."

Those earlier memories were much clearer. "Maybe not. If he'd not taken agin me, I'd not have felt such an urgent need for a second line of business ... no jail ... no xyloidene ... none of this would have happened."

"There's more – he says Guzman Blanco'll give thee anything tha asks for, within reason. Fraser told us to tell thee tha might ask for one percent of't company stock held by't Venezuelan Government. Be worth a tidy pile one day."

"Oh yes!" Freddy said sarcastically. "It would suit the company to get as much stock as possible back into English hands!"

"Eee, I never thought o' that! Fraser's right about't General, though," Firey went on. "He'd give thee't moon if it were cheap enough. So when he asks thee, what do'st tha want – tha'd best have aught in mind. He's not ower fond o' shilly-shallying, isn't our General."

Freddy closed his eyes and tried to think of something to ask for. What did he really want?

Contracts ... concessions ...

"Tell thee what I'd ask for." Firey interrupted his train of thought.

"What?" He sat up again.

"I'd ask for land. Out on't south side o't city. It's plain as the nose on your face – this railway's going to extend that way as soon as't present line's paid back a bit o't capital. And there's only one valley as makes any sense to build it in." He winked. "I'd ask for a goodly slice o' yon particular plum pudding."

"You may be right."

"Course I'm right. No maybe about it." A faraway look crept into his eyes. "There were two fields at th'end of our street when I were a lad. Belonged to our grandad. We sold them off in a hard time. Got forty pound for 'em, which looked like a fortune. Sold 'em to a bright young lawyer called Stafford. Ten years later, Stafford sold't same land to't Lancs and Yorks Railway for five hundred! I could've been squire of Hunslett if we'd kept them fields."

"If you had all the money you wanted, Firey, what would you do?"

"Buy land ... big house out in't Dales ... a hundred servants ..."

The ease with which he rattled it off made Freddy interrupt: "Would you really? Have you ever actually thought about it?"

Firey halted in midflow. "Happen not," he admitted. "I know what tha's thinking – tha's thinking I'd buy a pub and kill me'sen inside a year."

"Why not buy the brewery and do the job wholesale?"

Firey laughed. "Happen I'd do none o' them things. Happen I'd buy me'sen a steam engine." Like a cat on velvet, he spread himself over this dream and added contentedly, "Aye – a steam engine and a gang o' good men. That's what I'd do."

Freddy was puzzled. "But Firey – if you kept your slate clean out here for only four years, you could put by enough to buy your engine anyway."

The man was not so easily pried out of his heaven. "We'd never settle. Travel from John o'Groats to Land's End leaving copies of us'sens in every willing lass!"

"There's nothing to stop you doing it now," Freddy repeated.

"Four bloody years!" Firey said harshly. "I know just what'd happen. I'd scrimp and I'd save, four years – not a sup. I'd crucify me'sen. I'd live on cat collop and chimpings. And happen I'd put by five ... six-hundred pound. And on't voyage back ower Atlantic, ship'd go down. And me inside her. I'd drown in th'undrinkable. And with every gulp I'd think this could've been good Yorkshire ale! I'd die in rage for every tankard I never supped. So I reckon I'm as better off supping it while I may."

"It's a matter of time, then? If you could make the five hundred pounds in just one year ...?"

"Aye, I'd be tempted then," he admitted.

That afternoon they allowed Freddy to get up and sit in the garden beneath the dappled shade of a large acacia tree. The rainforest came right up to the southern wall of the hospital and the gardeners fought a ceaseless battle with volunteer seedlings of its shrubs and giant trees.

He wrote letters home, playing down the drama of these recent days but talking of the country's commercial openings. His heart was Midland once again.

After supper there was a great commotion and Guzman Blanco himself was ushered in by several excited nuns. His attitude could not have been warmer if Freddy were his only son. This emboldened Freddy to ask how the General had known about his abduction by Iago and the forced march up into the mountain.

Guzman Blanco smiled contentedly. "I know you, Oxley. And I know Iago, God rest him. You are the honey in my pot. Iago was the wasp who cannot keep away. Iago must try to stop you. Failing that – try to make you work for him. Failing that – keep you prisoner. Last of all – kill you."

Freddy remembered his conversation with the rebel leader

and thought he could not have summarized the choices more precisely. He nodded.

"And you," Guzman Blanco said, tapping Freddy's forehead. "What do you do? You are the man who walks alone! Where do you make your explosives? Deep in the forest, alone. I watched you the other day, the first day you saw the blockage on the line. What do you do? You go off, alone. Whenever you have problems, you go somewhere alone. I know you – see."

Freddy realized how true it was, and wondered he had not seen it himself before – or not in so many words. Even his being here in Venezuela was due to that instinct to strike out alone. "Did you follow me?" he asked.

The General put imaginary binoculars to his eyes and smiled. "But the second time, when you ran into Iago, *then* I followed you. I wanted Iago to lead us to his camp. When a man thinks he has made his biggest triumph, he is then at his most careless."

Freddy had cause to remember this warning when, at the end of their conversation, the General made him the offer Firey had predicted. With a smile Freddy repeated the words and added, "May I give you an answer tomorrow, General?"

He had no doubt he would do as Firey had suggested – ask for land along the probable line of the next railway – but some caution held him back from saying so at once.

The following morning he found among his effects the knife with which he had held the boa constrictor at bay. The tip of it was curled over where he had blindly struck the rock wall of the cave. He showed it to Firey. "See – I told you it was but poor metal, this. Look how it's bent."

Firey laughed at the memory and turned to share it with the doctor, who was prodding at the bandages on his stump. "Ye've never seen the like o' this man when it comes to buying a knife. Just an ordinary knife for sharpening pencils and cutting ferns and things like that. I was with him in the shop. The shopkeeper shows him one. He doesn't like it. 'Got any more?' he asks. Shopkeeper shows him another, identical pattern. Our Frederick doesn't think much to that one, either. 'Got any more?' Same thing. Still doesn't like it. 'Got any more?' Shopkeeper pulls out the whole bloody drawer – *twenty* knives! Friend Oxley here considers all twenty. Takes him five minutes – and even then he's only narrowed it down to six. 'Can I take these over to the door?' he asks. 'To see them in the sunlight!' By now the shopkeeper's just standing there, gawping like a fish. 'I hope you don't want any screws, young man,' he says. "'Cos I've got several *thousand* o' them!'" Firey threw back his head and roared with laughter. "All that – just for *one* knife. And a bad'un at that!"

The doctor, who had good English, gave Freddy an apologetic glance and laughed. Half of Freddy saw the humour of it and joined in; but the other half protested, "It may have been a bad'un, but it was the best one there. I had the satisfaction of knowing I'd got the best there was."

The laughter redoubled.

Freddy added, "No one could go into that shop after me and come out with a better bargain."

They still couldn't see it, so he gave up.

The doctor pointed to the knife. "I could go to that same shop and get nineteen better bargains now!"

Freddy nodded his sad agreement. "Still, I couldn't throw it away. It saved my life. I'll see if I can straighten out the tip."

After lunch he borrowed a screwdriver from a visiting carpenter and pried apart the furled-over tip. As it opened it yielded from its grip a sliver of pale yellow metal.

Freddy stared at it. His heart stopped. His mouth went dry with the fear of what he might have found – or, rather, with the fear that it might be mere fool's gold. He went to the hospital dispensary and begged a small test tube with a few dribbles of concentrated sulphuric and nitric acids, mixed. Into it he dropped the sliver of metal.

There was no reaction. Still not daring to hope, he corked it tightly and placed it on the windowsill. If it was still there by evening, there would be no doubt.

"Tha'rt not going to blow us all to kingdom come?" Firey asked jocularly.

"I wonder," Freddy replied.

At supper the little slip of metal was as pristine as when it first fell from the tip of his knife.

It was gold. Beyond all possible doubt it was gold.

Now he knew precisely what stretch of land he would be asking Guzman Blanco to grant him.

CHAPTER FORTY-FIVE

A GOLD CLAIM was more assured in that part of the world if it had as a sleeping partner some senior member of the government. Freddy's claim to the El Avila mine, as it came to be known, was as certain as the result of next year's election, for his sleeping partner (at fifteen percent) was none other than Guzman Blanco.

The letter to Gulberg at Bolivar had produced no response by the time Freddy left the hospital; but these were still early days. His first call was at the depot office, where he collected his promised two hundred pounds from a now most-friendly Mr. Fraser. He paid off the ten-odd pounds remaining on his fare and sacrificed twenty-six of his due wage in lieu of notice.

When he stood on that dusty track above the depot and realized he was free – free to turn left for Caracas, or right for El Avila, or go straight ahead into the forest, to the abandoned plantation where he had made the explosives ... or, indeed, free to stretch himself in the grass at the verge of the road – he was as contented with his lot as he had ever been.

But it did not last. The one thing he was not free to do was to take his wealth and go back to England. His wealth was still imprisoned in the living rock around the constrictor's den.

There was so much groundwork to put in before he could even begin to mine in earnest that within weeks he began to lose heart. They ran a drift into the lode as far as his amateur skill allowed, to prove its yield and to gain at least a little experience – and, indeed, the yield was high. But even the few cubic yards of muck that came out with it were bothersome to deal with by hand. Clearly he was going to have to raze a lot of jungle, lay miles of road – and rail – and plan the siting of the spoil heaps carefully. The last thing he wanted was to find himself, a year from now, having to relocate thousands of tons of spoil that could, with a little forethought, as easily have been dumped elsewhere in the first place.

A year from now? Already it sounded like a sentence.

Firey came out of hospital after five weeks' convalescence. He was forced to trade an engine-driver's well-paid job for an engine-driver's miserly pension. Freddy appointed him overseer in the day-to-day running of the mine. But within a week he could tell that Firey would never take to it. He didn't even approach the business with common sense. Once, when a great overhang of rock fell and only by the grace of God failed to kill anyone, all Firey said was, "If I'd known that was going to happen, I'd have fetched it down deliberate, see tha."

Freddy set him to overseeing the clearing of the jungle. What Firey really wanted was to lay railroad from the main line up to the mine compound. He'd be good at it, too, Freddy believed; it was closer to his natural trade. Perhaps when Gulberg came, *if* Gulberg came, he'd give Firey the contract. Everything depended on Gulberg.

When Freddy wasn't at the mine he was making explosives; this time it was all safely absorbed in kieselguhr for detonation with proper mercaptan fuses. He made enough to satisfy the needs of the railway and the army, but, though the money was rolling in nicely, it didn't satisfy him. Out here he was still a one-man band. He ought to be at home in England, where he could find dozens of men with the necessary skills. With the money he'd saved and the income from the goldmine, he could be making thousands of pounds there rather than mere tens here. He could produce enough to satisfy Venezuela any old wet Saturday evening. More than that – if he could take up the dowager's offer, if he could bring all the Mortimers' capacity and expertise in iron and steel under his control, then he could start manufacturing guns, too. His head was already bristling with designs.

He toyed with the idea of going to Guzman Blanco and explaining it all. Surely the man was shrewd enough to see the sense of it? He, Freddy, wouldn't dare wriggle out of the bargain because the General could always appropriate the mine and stop the flow of gold. But his instinct for people told him it wouldn't work. Guzman Blanco liked to touch flesh.

As a precaution, to show he was committed to Venezuela, Freddy commissioned the General's own architect, a man called Mendez, to design and build a new explosives factory, down near the line. To make sure that word of it got back to Guzman Blanco, he put the man through hell. What was really just a large, simple, four-square warehouse with plain partitions was discussed and designed with all the ache and pain of a national monument. Freddy almost selected each individual pebble to be used in the concrete foundations. There was a port-warehouse foreman down at La Guayra who terrorized his porters by taking out his glass eye and leaving it "to watch over them" while he went off and got drunk. Freddy had something better: his reputation as a fanatical perfectionist. He could safely leave Mendez and the builder to spread the word, for neither doubted that if, when the job was done, Freddy found anything amiss, he'd blow the entire building up and make them start again.

At last Fate was kind. The two missing elements in Freddy's scheme to leave Venezuela – with the General's blessing – came to him on the same day, in the form of a telegram and a letter.

The telegram was from Gulberg, saying he would arrive at La Guayra in two days' time "with good news."

The letter was from Clive, written on House of Commons notepaper:

Dear Foxy, When you made no response to Knox-Riddell's letter we all assumed you'd washed your hands of Ann. Perhaps you had at that time. Certainly no one could blame you. But from odd asides in your more recent letters to me, I think I detect a softer tone? And on that slender inference I beg to let you know how matters now stand. Forgive me for being repetitious – most of these details were in Knox-Riddell's letter, but I have to assume you discarded it. Indeed, I shall assume you chose not to read it at all.

Ann sailed from Tilbury with four other young women on 4th April, 1877, on a ship called *Hecate*. She was bound for Demerara in British Guiana, calling at Barbadoes, St. Vincent, and Port of Spain on the way.

As Freddy read the details, the hair bristled on his neck. She had sailed just a few days ahead of him; and Demerara was

only a few hundred miles down the coast from here! But why?
Who did she know in Demerara? He read on:

We have tried to trace the *Hecate*, but she is a tramp,
owned by her master, a Captain Moran, who sails with his wife
and family and has only an agent here, at Bristol. The agent
tells us that Moran must have picked up a catch cargo at
Demerara, most probably for Europe (or America or South
America or the Orient – in order of likelihood). If Europe, we
shall know soon enough, otherwise not at all.

The next bit, Foxy, old friend, is hard to write and will be
even harder to read and bear, but it cannot be shirked. Ann was
told she was to be governess to the children of a Mr. de Santos.
No such person existed. The vile creatures who lured poor
Ann aboard the *Hecate* (all now facing lengthy imprisonment,
thank God) were in the business of selling unsuspecting young
women into slavery (not to mince words) overseas, of what
kind you may imagine.

Yet I cannot believe Ann was so easily duped. I am
sure that on the voyage out she had time to reflect on the
amazing promises that were made to her and to realize how
false they must be. I am equally sure she must then have found
some way to escape at one or other of those earlier ports of
call.

This we must all most earnestly hope!

In all conscience, Foxy, someone must try to find her and,
if it is not already too late, rescue her. For whether she escaped
or not, we cannot imagine her condition to be anything but
parlous. What have we been doing, you may justly ask? Knox-
Riddell hired a mercantile-fraud investigator from New Orleans
who scoured the harbours and likely parts of the mainland,
sent highly impressive reports, demanded a small fortune, and
said the trail was "colder than a dead turkey."

I have made such strenuous and insistent inquiries through
our consular offices that I am almost *persona non grata* at both
the colonial and foreign offices. All to no avail.

Short of chucking up our careers and coming out there
ourselves, there is nothing further to be attempted from this
distance.

I don't know whether your obligations to the railway

company will prevent you from making your own investigations at Barbadoes etc. It will certainly not be a matter of money for, as you see, I enclose a Letter of Credit for you at the Imperial Bank in Caracas. (By the by, in case it should ever arise in the future, you should know I was forced to tell a little white fib to Eleanor about it. I said it was for fifty pounds but as you see it's really for a thousand. Not a penny spent in the search for Ann will be grudged by yrs. truly.)

As to little Angelica, she was rescued from the Foundlings Hospital (though one should not say *rescued* from so admirable an institution) by Knox-Riddell, who has made arrangements for her care in Solihull.

If you are able to commence a search for Ann, here is a list of the other young women who also sailed on the *Hecate* on that same date. It was provided by one George McKenna, alias "Mr. Netherbere," the wretch chiefly responsible for ensnaring them; but we trust its accuracy:

1). Maria Dawson (chanteuse; told she'd be prima donna at the Opera in Caracas; tall, dark, well-built, fluent in Spanish)

2). Betty Jameson (ladies' maid; told she'd be governess to a rich coffee planter in Brazil; average height, fair, with freckles, slim, missing left eye tooth, speaks with a slight London accent)

3). Letty Lockyer (orphaned daughter of an itinerant preacher; told she'd be a teacher in British Guiana; short, plump, auburn, with markedly sloping-down eyelids and longish nose, speaks with West Country accent)

4). Rosina Williams (piano teacher; offered position at a military musical academy near Port of Spain; quite similar to Betty Jameson but taller and more frail-looking, has no marked speaking accent, fluent in German)

You know I would gladly come searching for her myself, let tongues wag where they will, but my parliamentary duties preclude it. The Russians crossed the Danube in June and we are on the brink of war. If they invade Turkey, I do not know how I shall vote. The country is very bellicose, of course, but they little know how ill-prepared we are! And in the Cape (which, as you know, is a special interest of mine) we shall soon be at war with the Kaffres. Something, or some*one* more likely, is stirring them up. There is a bad smell about it at the Colonial Office.

There was so much about wars and rumours of wars that the explosives manufacturer in Freddy began to fear he was missing the boat.

At the end of the letter was a P.S.:

Please share my conviction that Ann is too alert to have remained deceived for the three long weeks the *Hecate* required in order to reach Barbadoes. She is not undergoing the abominable fate that was prepared for her. I know it. Do not ask how, but I feel so sure of it.

He folded the letter with a sigh. Until this moment he had not realized how accustomed he had grown to life without Ann. She really played no part in his plans now. In shutting out the pain of her betrayal and loss he had somehow shut *her* out, too. And suppose he found her? What then? What part could she play in his future?

No – Clive was surely right. Ann wouldn't have been deceived. She must have made a new life for herself by now. Why upset everything? Too much time had gone by.

It was so easy for Clive and Knox-Riddell to parade their good intentions and pay their conscience money. And anyway, how could he succeed where a professional investigator had failed? Come to that, why *couldn't* Tony Knox-Riddell travel out here and finish what he'd started? He lived in utter idleness.

Nevertheless, Freddy saw that the letter – on that impressive notepaper, too – made exactly the sort of appeal to which Guzman Blanco would respond. Freddy's long-desired departure from Venezuela could now be dressed up as a matter of honour and chivalry.

The dictator was, indeed, most sympathetic. When he heard that one of the young women had been promised a position at the (as yet nonexistent) opera house in Caracas he grew angry, as if the deceit had somehow touched him, too. He promised to set in train his own investigation, both in Caracas and at the seaports, seeking out the receivers of this wretched trade. If any of the women had been abducted in Venezuela, he would find them. Looking deep into those stern, cold eyes, Freddy had no doubt of it.

Next day he was down at La Guayra, waiting for the arrival of Gulberg. A sailor on the *Nile* had told him that a good naval wife would always look out for her husband's ship from the quayside, never from the top of a hill. "Hope's the worst deceiver," he said. "Did you ever see a young woman more than twenty paces off who wasn't a rare beauty? It's the same with ships. Every one of them on a fifteen-mile horizon is rigged the way you want her to be. But down on the quayside the horizon's never more than three miles off."

Freddy eyed the hillsides all around the port but resisted the temptation to climb them and use his spyglass. Instead – and to lend colour to his request to Guzman Blanco – he passed the time inquiring along the wharves for any news of the *Hecate*. He drew a blank, of course, for he wasted no money on it. No one had even heard of her.

When Gulberg came his news was good indeed – or good for him. He had discovered gold fairly swiftly. "You'd have to be a blind fool (which the most of them are) to miss the signs of it in Yuruary," he said. He had thus fulfilled the terms of his contract with his employers. Then he had gambled his profits on a private expedition to a remote corner of the region, where, again, he had found gold beyond his most optimistic dreams. At this point in the narrative, however, his face fell.

"The trouble is it should cost a fortune to bring men and equipment into the region. I can impossibly get such money myself, so I must give greatly much more share than she's worth to some moneylender, some greedy banker, to acquire the capital from him."

Freddy saw his chance. "You've made the claim?" he asked. "The mineral rights, they're yours?"

Gulberg's gesture said, *d'you take me for a child?*

"And no one can go in and steal it while you're away? Just take it?"

"If it can be done with pickaxes and mules, should I be here?"

Freddy grinned, "Then how would you like to *earn* your capital, here, in Caracas?"

"Where?" Gulberg asked suspiciously.

"In *my* goldmine." And he went on to tell the story of the finding of El Avila and how well the lode had proved out.

The Swede threw up his hands in disgust. "It's a land for children to find gold in! I'm wasting my time."

"But you'll manage El Avila for me while I'm away? One third of my share? I have to go away for a month or maybe two."

"Of course," he answered glumly, but Freddy could see he was delighted not to have to share his windfall with a bank. "You want a written contract?" he asked.

The Swede shook his head.

"Good."

In a year or so's time, Freddy thought, when his business in England was established and he returned to Venezuela with his first big guns and ammunition, he would propose a merger of the two mines, leaving Gulberg to manage them both. But why confuse the man with such an offer yet?

Gulberg brightened. "Come," he said, downing his whisky in one gulp. "Let's find a couple of women and glad us of this town. We've both deserved it."

Freddy declined the offer. All he wanted now was to get away.

"Ah come on!" the Swede urged.

"No. I have to look for somebody."

"I help you – here in La Guayra?"

"No. The Guianas, Brazil, the islands … all over. It's a relative of mine who's disappeared."

"Then we have time. A woman won't delay you more than an hour."

"I don't want to."

"Are you for serious? Don't *want* to? What's that?"

Freddy gave a baffled laugh. "How can I say it more plainly? I simply don't want a woman like that."

"Never in the life?"

"Never. Of course not."

"What means it – *of course not?* If I ask you have you ever bought a meal, have you ever bought a shave … hired a hotel room? … should you answer me, *of course not?*"

"It isn't the same thing at all."

"You're that judger of herring who never tasted fish!"

"I'm the judger of *me* my friend."

Gulberg shook his head. "Cold fish."

Freddy rose, smiling, and patted him on the shoulder. "Cold sea," he answered as he left.

CHAPTER FORTY-SIX

FREDDY'S ROUTE HOME retraced that of his outward voyage, that is, by local vessel from La Guayra to Georgetown, Barbadoes, where, after a few days' delay, he was to transfer to a larger, transoceanic ship. Georgetown had also been the *Hecate's* first port of call. Having a few days to kill, he decided to make at least some inquiry after Ann and the other women. Not that he was weakening, he quickly assured himself, but when he next met Clive it would look bad if he had made no effort at all. The women's abductors must have allowed them ashore at Georgetown, if only to lull any suspicions they may have formed; someone might just remember seeing them; five young European women travelling together would not be too common a sight.

Curiously enough, his voyage to Georgetown was on the *Essequibo*, the same vessel as had brought him *from* Georgetown almost six months earlier. But the moment she rounded the new light at Needham's Point and slipped into the calm of Carlisle Bay, he realized that if they had jumped ship anywhere, they had certainly not done so here. It would have been like trying to escape a hot pursuer by leaping down a well.

The *Essequibo*, her engine barely turning, drifted into the Careenage at the mouth of the Constitution River. From his earlier visit he remembered passing a hotel with a pleasant-sounding name, down near the wharf; now, with the help of his spyglass, he found it again – the Ice House. It looked cheaper than the Marine, which he could also see, some way up the hill. By chance they berthed at the wharf immediately opposite the Ice House.

In the character of a tourist he engaged one of the deck-hands to carry his bags across the quay. As he paid him off he asked the fellow which were the busiest ports among the islands and along the north coast of the continent.

"Naval too?" the man asked.

"No, just passenger and cargo."

The man listed them: "Havana, Georgetown, La Guayra ... Port of Spain maybe, Porto Bello maybe, Kingston yes. Some season yes, some season no."

"But around this time of year?"

"Yes."

"Any others?"

"Plenty maybe. I not sail others."

"If you wanted to jump ship," Freddy began ...

The man looked at him in fright. "I not jump ship. I not jump ship ..." He repeated the assertion angrily several times as he made a hasty retreat, leaving behind an odour of panic, a compound of sweat and some cloying, garlic-like spice.

Freddy's room was up on the first floor, overlooking the Careenage – another advantage of the Ice House. He threw wide the windows and, sitting well back in the room, out of sight from the street, took out his spyglass and began a minute survey of the dockside and each of its buildings. Exactly what he was looking for he could not say, but he observed carefully and noted everything.

He had only an hour or so in which to watch the comings and goings of the little port. The sun went down around five thirty; before six, darkness had descended. The tide was just short of high and work continued on one ship, hoping to sail with it; but the other warehouses shut their doors and all the deckhands went ashore. The long, sweeping line of the quay-side, so dominant a feature by day, was now broken into a dozen little islands of light, mostly taverns, set against the darkness and making it even more impenetrable.

He had taken full pension at 5s. a day so, though not yet hungry, he went down and claimed his supper. Then he returned to his room and resumed his vigil, now daring to sit closer to the window. But he soon grew bored. People at leisure were so predictable; he would far rather watch them at work.

He began looking at a crane down on the wharf below him. Its oiled surfaces gleamed in the light from the Ice House bar. The pawl that held the ratchet wheel had been forged with a satisfyingly beautiful curve where two straight sides would have served just as well; old Dixon would have approved. He was just thinking he could draw its mechanism from memory when a young girl came from out of the darkness and leaned against it. She was sucking a guava or some small fruit, and looking about her, sharp eyed. She was at work.

There was an encouraging whistle from the *Essequibo*, still tied up immediately opposite his window. The girl swung her hips against the crane, launching herself toward the sound. The whistler was in the dark – a mere shape, imperfectly glimpsed against the shimmer of lights on the water beyond. How could any man do that – go with a girl he'd never seen before, a girl who was only a dim-lit silhouette in the dark?

And what about her? Freddy watched the girl, strolling so casually, still sucking the fruit, going to do that most intimate thing with an invisible stranger. Was he tall or short? Skinny ... fat? Black, white, yellow, clean, dirty, shaven, or bearded ..? Was he the deckhand who had brought up the baggage – all that sweat and garlic? It mattered not to her – or she dared not let it matter.

He shivered, not merely at the foul mystery of human depravity, but also because this hackneyed little scene was too close to everybody's fears for Ann.

The girl vanished into the dark that engulfed the man, but with his spyglass Freddy could just make them out as dimly resonant shapes against the blue-black tropic night all round. They moved up toward the bows where there was a coil of rope and some tarpaulin to lie upon. The girl settled herself and presumably drew up her skirts. The man was upon her at once. A little way up the wharf someone lit a lamp. By the minimal increase in the general illumination he saw the girl popping the last of the fruit into her mouth. She put her arm around her partner, not in affection but to wipe her fingers on his shirt. A minute or so later the man stopped moving. Shortly after that the girl was back on the quayside, leaning against the crane. She

fished in her bag and took out another small fruit. She bit a hole
in its skin and, sucking gently at its heart, looked around again
with those alert blue eyes.

The quay was deserted. There was laughter in the hotel
bar. With that same deft, sexy movement of her hips she
launched herself in its direction. After one or two paces she
looked up and caught Freddy staring down at her. She paused
and pointed at herself and then at him, lifting her eyebrows in
obvious inquiry.

His heart stopped. There was something about her movement – not her features, not her colouring, not her figure, but
simply her movement – that reminded him of Ann. It provoked
one of those moments of total recall when the brain slips into
some supernatural state and experiences everything at one and
the same moment instead of in the usual sequences. In later
years, when people tried to describe to him the feeling of
religious conversion or some other powerful emotion, his mind
always leaped back to that overwhelming moment when he
glanced down at a quayside slut and exploded with all his
memories of Ann, memories he thought he had long suppressed
– from the goddess of Ferndown Crescent to the anguished
woman who had brought Angelica into the world.

In that instant he knew he could not go back to England
until he had found her. Whether or not she would come back
with him ... whether or not she had sunk beyond the reach of
earthly salvation ... he had to find her.

Down on the wharf the girl was no longer looking at him.
She was already striding toward the Ice House. He did not
notice her departure for his mind was still heaped with memories
of Ann. How *could* he have supposed he might return to
England with an easy conscience if he had not done all in his
power to find her out here?

Yet even as he bathed in this new glow of righteousness,
that stolid, practical streak in his character rose once more to
the surface. If his time in this hemisphere had taught him
anything it had taught him about the many ways to power, the
varieties of success; above all it had revealed to him the envy
and malice of lesser men. If he returned to England and achieved
everything he now hoped for himself, the whispers would soon
go about: He had not *wished* to find Ann; he had been glad of

her disappearance, for what could she have been to him but a hindrance? A wink, a knowing tilt of the head, would even make him party to her abduction. So, if only for the sake of his own career, he'd have to do more than simply go through the motions of searching for her.

Thus the new Freddy, hard, determined, thrusting, excused the remnants of the old, whom he now saw as too soft, too forgiving.

The girl down on the quay must have taken his hesitation as conditional assent, for she came straight upstairs, knocked at his door, opened it, and stood there smiling hopefully. "Made your mind up, honey?" she asked in what sounded like West Country English – or it might have been Irish.

She was pretty even at close quarters, with her blonde, curly hair and those enormous blue eyes that looked so innocent.

"I don't want what I saw just now ..." He nodded toward the quay.

"Were you watching?" She looked at his spyglass and laughed. "I can do a lot better than that."

"No. I want information." He jingled some coin in his pocket.

Her eyes narrowed. "You the police?" she asked.

He shook his head.

"Not that you'd admit it, anyway. Just in case you are, let me warn you – I've got friends here, too."

This sounded promising. "Come in awhile, anyway. You're not missing much down there." He jerked a thumb toward the wharf.

She brushed past him and flung herself at once on the bed. Without lifting her skirts she parted her legs and brought them together, wrapping the cloth around them and revealing their form.

"D'you know a ship called the *Hecate*?" he asked "She calls here quite often, I think."

The girl nodded toward the spyglass on its tripod and giggled. "You're one of *them* – you want to watch it. Tell you what – give us a dollar or two and I'll go back and give that sailor a free turn ... if I can remember him. What was he like? Did you get a good look?"

"No. I ..."

"He'll take a good long time now the cream's skimmed off. You'll get your money's worth."

"Listen ..."

"I'll bring him up here if you want I should. You can sit close behind the curtain. He wouldn't ..."

"Listen! It's nothing like that. Truly! I'm trying to trace a young woman. My sister, in fact. She came out here on a ship called the *Hecate*, from London."

The girl frowned and looked at him askance.

He added, "She thought she was coming out to a respectable post as governess. But I fear it was a trap. I fear she's ... she's been forced into ..." Unwilling to offend her, he simply waved in her general direction.

The girl looked down at herself, saw the sculpting of her limbs beneath the thin skirts that covered them, and blushed. At first it struck him as a strange response but then it dawned on him that immodesty, like passion, could also be faked; in her private life this girl might easily be as reserved as any of her more respectable sisters. It was an unexpected bridge across a divide he had assumed to be absolutely unbridgeable. He looked at her with a new interest.

She sat up and plumped out her clothing. Earlier she had lain in such a way that her bosom stood out provocatively; now she somehow collapsed it to half its former size. In these new circumstances she seemed so ill-at-ease he was forced to add, "I don't mean to insult you, Miss ...?"

"I'm known as Kate," she answered.

"I am Frederick Oxley."

"What was that ship, Mr. Oxley? *Hex* ..?"

"*Hecate*. She must call here two or three times a year. When my sister was aboard she must have called in April."

"Ah. I was working Port Royal then. Keep moving, see. Business drops off when they get to know you too well."

"How many ports have you worked in, then?" he asked. If she knew her sort of trade at them all, she might be quite useful, even though the people who had gone to such pains to lure the women out here were certainly not going to put them to work at the two-shilling level along the wharves.

She shrugged.

"Good heavens! How old are you?"

She grinned. "Eighteen."

He shook his head at the pity of it.

"How old's your sister?" she asked. "Does she look like me?"

Again he shook his head. "I know nothing about ... this sort of thing. I hardly know where to start."

"A cherry!" She laughed delightedly and looked at him in a kind of wonder; then a crafty glint stole into her eyes. He could see he represented some sort of challenge. "I don't meet many of your sort," she said.

He went on impatiently: "Whoever abducted her went to a great deal of trouble and expense. The rewards must be great, too."

"Rewards to them, you mean. Not to your li'l sister."

"Exactly. But where is that likely to be? What sort of establishment?"

The girl pursed her lips in thought.

Freddy tried to prompt her: "It would have to be some kind of high-class house, wouldn't it? But how would I find such places? Are there any here in Georgetown?"

The girl frowned at him. "Now listen, honey – if that's all you wanna know, you don't need to go through all this!" She licked her lips. "What's it worth?"

"Even suppose I knew the place – how would I discover if my sister was there?"

"Just go in through the front door like any other swell. 'Course, she might be upstairs doing business. But give it an hour – that's about the longest. There's only one possible place in Georgetown, though."

"Where?"

She smiled knowingly and rubbed her thumb upon one lean forefinger. He took out a handful of coins and counted two shillings into her open palm. She shook her head. Two more ... and then two more ...

At ten she closed her fist and gave him the address. "It's a little side alley off Tudor Street," she explained. "Not far from the Bridgetown Club. The cabman will know, anyway." She smiled and added, "Jack down in the bar would have told you for the price of one rum."

He shrugged.

"But this was more fun, wasn't it," she challenged. "Already it's more exciting, no?"

He shook his head. "I don't like this having to pretend to be a customer of the place. I don't suppose you'd consider going there instead of me? How much would you want for that?"

"There's some very fancy high-yaller dames in there."

He shook his head.

"I don't believe it! I didn't think there was a man born!" She drew up her knees and hugged them to her chest. "Would it be worth as much again?" she asked.

Silently he handed over a half-sovereign.

She pocketed it. "I'll tell you right now. I don't need to go up there. Your sister isn't there."

"But they might use some other name for her. She might be too ashamed to ..."

She was shaking her head. "That isn't the point, dear Mr. Frederick. The point is wherever she may be, she's being held against her will."

"Therefore?"

"Well, it just ain't the sort of place where they could do that."

He felt a great surge of relief. "You're sure?"

"Tell the truth, I don't think there's anyplace in the whole British administration where they could do it. She'd have to be in some place like Martinique ... Hayti ... some French place." She shuddered theatrically.

"Go on talking," he said. "You may think you've taken that money off me pretty easily, but I'll tell you – you're earning it. Tell me everything you can that might help me."

By nine o'clock that evening he had paid her five pounds and he considered every last farthing of it worthwhile – especially as it was Clive's money he had just decided to spend on his search.

She was American. He had never heard an American accent before; to him she still sounded Irish. She had grown up on a farm in Kentucky, of strict parents – a strict and tyrannical mother and a strict but weak father. When she was thirteen he had whipped her hard and then raped her, so she'd run away.

She found she was pregnant so she had gone to a woman who could fix it. But the police had been there, waiting, and she was given over to the Sisters of Love and Charity.

"They told me it wasn't really my daddy who got me belly-up. They said it was God who really done it. Something about cree-ation and pro-creeation. I didn't catch it exactly but I remember it was God who did the important fixing. So they told me I just had to carry that baby all the way."

"The Sisters of *what*?" he asked.

"Love and Charity." She grinned. "Bet I know something about God you don't know."

"What?"

"Well, if his kid's anything to go on, he's got hair all over and his fingers are missing and all glued together, and funny eyes and no lip. And he died that same night. And there'll never be another." She stared blankly at him. "I can't have no more. And I just used to love kids. How 'bout that!"

For a while she'd been put in a waifs and strays in New Orleans but that had been even more stifling than the farm.

Then one of the boys off a neighbour's farm had come down to the city and seen her across the street. He won some money gambling and had taken her out of the home. For a while they'd lived very high, and she had learned all about sex and men. Then he got killed in a gunfight and she had to start out on The Life – at fifteen, though she had looked as old then as she did now. She was never going to look any older.

She'd worked in two or three houses in New Orleans and then a sea captain had taken her away. She got bored with him and jumped ship in Port Royal. After that she'd worked all around the Caribbean. "First I was only in the five-dollar houses, but then I got wise."

Freddy nodded his head toward the wharf and asked in disbelief, "That's wise?"

She nodded. "Sure thing. In a five-dollar house a girl can make thirty a night. But she won't *keep* thirty – no sir! She'll be let have twelve. But after deductions for the doctor and the laundry and the maid and the liquor and the perfume and like that ... well, she's lucky if she don't end up working off some debt!"

In the time Miss Kate had been freelancing she'd put by

over four thousand dollars. Another year and she'd have enough to go back to Kentucky and open up the best house in town – her home town, of course. She was going to rub their noses in it.

The thought of it pleased her so highly she laughed aloud, as if she already owned the place. "I'll need one honest, incorruptible man," she said, looking at him carefully. "You wouldn't be interested I suppose?"

"It's tempting," he said, to keep her talking.

"That won't do. This man must be beyond temptation. Are you married?"

He nodded.

She looked deep into his eyes and said, "It's not your sister, it's your wife."

He nodded again.

"I like you, Mr. Frederick," she said simply. "I like you so much I'm set to do something foolish."

"Oh, not on my account, please," he said, not too convincingly.

"Don't worry. In this game anything that helps someone else without any benefit to you is foolish. I'm going up to that high-tone house I told you about and see if your wife isn't maybe there after all."

"But ..."

"Listen, if this was April, she'd be there against her will – which, like I said, is impossible. But this is what – November?"

"Soon."

"That's six, seven months. She might have no will left. I've seen it. Have you got any picture?"

He shook his head; she was shocked.

"We parted on bad terms," he explained. "When I left England I never meant to see her again. But since then ..." He was on the verge of cracking up.

"That's all right." She touched his arm gently.

He took a grip on himself and showed her the descriptions Clive had sent him. He also told her what Ann looked like; he knew her so well she proved quite hard to describe.

Miss Kate was gone the best part of an hour. "I guess it's good news," she said on her return. "She's not there. Descriptions are so hard. One or two kind of fit. But none of those ladies was so beat in spirit, like they'd have to be."

He laughed with admiration at the ease with which she had discovered these things. "Did you just walk in?"

She grinned as if the question were the height of simplicity. "I know my way about there. I've helped out, gala nights. On my terms, not theirs."

He cleared his throat. "And ... tonight. I mean ... did you ..?"

She punched him playfully. "Why Mr. Frederick! You care!"

"No!" He blushed.

"You do! You do, too!" She threw her arms around his neck, laughing, and kissed him on the ear. "I know you want to go to bed with me," she whispered.

He unpeeled her arms and held her gently at a little distance. "No," he told her. "I like you too well. I honestly do."

She frowned, not understanding him at all.

"It would be like ..." he tried to explain. He knew exactly what it would be like but could not find the words. Suddenly they came to him. "It would be like going to bed with someone's sister!"

She still had not the faintest notion of his meaning but she saw his sincerity and decided to take it as some kind of obscure compliment. "You're the darndest man," she said. "Did you eat yet?"

"I had supper here at six but it was my first real meal today. I could eat again."

"Supper *here*!" She was aghast. "You must have a gut of steel. Yeuch! Tell you what – I'll go home, slip into something respectable and be back in a shake. You put on fresh whites and I'll show you the best food in Georgetown. Ackee rice, salt fish, papaya juice, banana pie ... you haven't eaten!"

"The best food in Georgetown" was, apparently, served in a down-at-heel little cabin out past Government House. It certainly was very good. The time was near midnight when, like any swain and his lass, he saw her back to her lodgings, which turned out to be just around the corner from the Ice House. He almost thought he might snatch a kiss, just for friendship's sake. But at the door she turned to him and said, "Listen, Mr. Frederick, I've just had the damndest idea. I can turn an easy twenty dollars a day around these ports – in not very pleasant circumstances, I'll allow. But I think I'm worth five of your pounds a day to you. I know every port you're going to need to visit. I know all the houses ... the fancy men ... you *need* me. Your ears need me!"

"My *ears?*"

"And your nose. And your fingers. They'll cut them out of you as soon as look at you, I tell you. You ask one wrong question at one wrong time or place, and you're dead! Ain't your life worth five pounds a day to you, Mr. Frederick?"

"But five pounds is thirty-five dollars!" he objected.

She let out a silvery peal of laughter.

Then he remembered the folly of his innocent-seeming question to the deckhand this morning, about jumping ship. "Very well," he said.

To judge from her response, his acceptance of the suggestion meant a great deal to her, far more than her casual attitude in making it had implied. A thought suddenly struck him. "If what you say is true, then you yourself ran quite a risk when you went to that house this evening. You must have asked some fairly pointed questions."

She shrugged, unable to deny it.

"Yet you didn't ask me for any more money."

"You already paid me a lot. Oh hell – let's just say you brought out the honest woman in me."

"But you were possibly risking your life. And you'll certainly be risking it in the weeks to come."

She smiled fondly and said, "You sure you don't want me tonight? You already paid."

He shook his head. "Goodnight, Miss Kate." Then, feeling the gesture should be grander than that, he lifted her hand and brushed it lightly with his lips.

She let it linger there. "Well I declare, Mr. Frederick. If this ain't going to be the damndest adventure!"

CHAPTER FORTY-SEVEN

IN THE LONG HISTORY of the West Indies and its motley of explorers and travellers there can have been few couples more oddly matched than Mr. Frederick and Miss Kate. For more than three months they roamed the Caribbean, from Montego Bay to San Fernando, from Anegada to Tortuga, following the smallest hint, the vaguest suggestion, the merest whim.

"We must go about this business as scientifically as possible," Freddy told her at the beginning.

"How's that?" she asked.

"Well, first search vigilantly for clues. We must miss nothing. Next – put the evidence into some sort of order. Then construct a hypothesis – a provisional guess, if you like – about where she is. Then test it."

"Sure," Miss Kate said. "That sounds fine. Let's start in Hayti."

"Why Hayti?"

"I don't know. I've just got a feeling about it."

"Have you been there?"

"No. That's one place I never was. Those Frenchies, they're flooey about you've got to have bits of paper. You got the right bits, they're easy as old shoes. Seems a cold idea to me, I mean, if I was a revolutionary, first thing I'd do is I'd buy me some good papers. They buy easy in those French places, anyway. Then it's cartay-blanchay. You English are soft plush about papers, but you can't be bought so easy."

On the voyage to Hayti, however, they discovered it was an island without roads, without hotels, and, as far as anyone knew, not a single white man or woman.

"Not even the French officials?" Freddy asked their informant.

"The French? What would the French be doing there?"

"I know – let's go to Martinique," Miss Kate cut in quickly. "That's *definitely* French. The Empress Josephine was born there. A man told me that once."

"The same one who told you Hayti is French?"

"Well, it surely sounds French. You can't blame me for that."

The incident was typical. Freddy, in his ignorance of the region, did his best to be methodical and thorough; Miss Kate, knowing almost too much and guessing what she didn't know, worked by inspiration and whim. Curiously their successes and failures were about equal – with many more of the latter. Freddy wondered if they wouldn't do as well by staying put in one bar and letting the gossip of the region pour over them – or by simply spinning a coin.

On arriving at a new place he usually spoke with the officials – the harbour master, the superintendent of the docks police, and so on – while she exercised her talent for finding people he would never have run down in a year of inquiring – the macquereaux, McGimpers, shills, fancy men, and pimples, as she variously called them.

Their discoveries were as varied as their sources, but gradually, among all the conflicting "certainties" they were offered, there began to emerge a consensus that the women on the *Hecate* could not be on any of the islands. It had to be the mainland.

One macquereau said the islands were too small; someone would talk. Maybe one lone crazed planter might hold a single unfortunate European woman against her will, but not five – and then to sustain a regular trade … no, no, it could only be on the mainland.

The prefect at St. Pierre maintained that, in the islands administered by the European powers, the bribes necessary to conceal the trade would be far greater than the trade itself could afford. "And I am a specialist in this field," he added unsmilingly.

A sea captain told them that if the women were transhipped from the *Hecate* to some other vessel, then it would have to be a small one and the job would have to be done as close to the final destination as possible. Any vessel caught in such a trade would be impounded at least until the trial. The captain of a large vessel would therefore be taking an expensive risk – for which he would demand a fat fee. Again, the trade could not afford it. For the same reason he thought the duped women would remain duped all the while they were on the *Hecate*. Even her master wouldn't necessarily know of the conspiracy.

But there was conflicting advice, too. At one extreme the maydam of a swell intimaterie in Port of Spain poured scorn on the whole idea; willing freeborn women of every size, shape, colour, race, and age were too freely available for anyone to run the risk of kidnapping. At the other extreme a fortune teller at Port Royal saw the entire voyage of the *Hecate* in lurid detail; four of the women, she told them lugubriously, were dead; only Ann had survived. She was on her way back home to England.

During those months of inquiry their own relationship underwent many subtle changes, so slowly that most of them passed unnoticed at the time. Many seemed more like arguments than adjustments.

They had one serious misunderstanding right at the beginning; it almost ended their association. When they paid their fare to Hayti but disembarked at St. Pierre in Martinique, the Dutch captain refused to refund the unused portion; so Miss Kate stole one of the ship's compasses and some navigational instruments. Freddy was furious. At first his reaction puzzled her; she thought she'd done a wonderful thing. Then she grew so frightened – like a child – that he relented and forced himself to be calm again.

He realized it must be hard for her to see it as theft. In her view, other people's right to property was slim at the best of times; it vanished altogether when the other person tried to cheat you. To call her action "theft" meant going back to the pious values of her childhood. And in her recent "adult" life those values were like suicide.

Indeed, she was still at heart a child. And that was the danger. She had an aged and cynical knowledge of the world (or, rather, of the ways of men and of the world men have built) and she believed it promoted her up among the greybeards of civilization. To her there was no difference between knowledge and understanding.

Her beauty, too, was childlike. The rich sexuality that

hung about her, in her movements and her laughter, was more in the minds of the men who saw it (himself included) than in her. He had noticed the same disturbing quality in certain young girls around the age of ten; they seemed to possess a grown woman's beauty and charm, and to walk with the knowing swing of their older, nubile sisters; yet they were, in fact, as innocent as any other child of that age. Miss Kate knew how to smile coquettishly and "sashay around," as she called that style of walking, and she "knew" the effect it had on men – but only in the way a zoologist might "know" the effect of a scorpion's mating dance on the two partners. Inwardly it meant absolutely nothing to her. It was just a splendid, funny trick.

At first she thought their not sharing a bed was a quaint game, like seeing who could hold their breath the longest. She teased him about it. She had heart palpitations – couldn't he feel them? She had pains there and there – would he be an angel and massage them? She flirted with waiters and ship's crew to make him jealous. She slipped into his cabin and left her flimsy underwear between his sheets.

One night it all came to a head. It was on their second visit to Martinique. They had been told of a certain famous courtesan who might be able to help them. She was a devotee of the opera and the arrangement was for them to attend a performance at the St. Pierre Opera House and, if she liked the look of them, she'd talk to them afterward.

The performance that evening was *Orpheus and Eurydice*. It affected Freddy deeply, especially in that heart-rending scene where Eurydice decides Orpheus does not love her – because he dare not look at her. Orpheus has, of course, promised not to look at her until they are out of Hades; if he breaks his word, he will lose her forever.

But it was only the power of the music, the impossible, nightly triumph of the lone human voice over sixty orchestral instruments. The mood vanished with the final curtain.

Miss Kate was oblivious to all that. She just enjoyed the whole evening – the grand music, the spectacle, the tragedy, the richly dressed crowd – they were all one great swirl to her.

"Such times, Mr. Frederick!" she said, her eyes dancing. "I could come back here."

The suggestion that she could tolerate anything twice was a high compliment. He watched her as she looked around the auditorium and he realized she would like to meet them all. Everyone was different, a new challenge. Even if one or two were dull or full of their own importance, she would enjoy them – not because she lacked taste but because they might make one good joke or tell her one interesting story, and that would be reward enough. Time was still infinite for her. There would always be more people to meet and they couldn't all be dull or pompous. He wished he could borrow that kind of youth. It had somehow passed him by.

The great courtesan must have approved of them because they were ushered into her box as soon as the final curtain fell. She was a large woman, well past her youth and given to gestures that were grand enough to compete with the opera they had just seen. She fascinated Miss Kate, who was always looking for people to copy; she tried on personalities the way other women try on hats. But as her story progressed they both felt a dreadful let-down.

"The man you seek, monsieur," she said at last, "the Bluebeard of Martinique, the closet-Casanova of St. Pierre, is none other than ..." and she named the prefect of police.

By this time they both knew the man well, had even dined at his home. The allegation was absurd. It was plain to them that the prefect had slighted her once, cast her off as a lover, perhaps, and she was now seeking her revenge in whatever way it might offer itself.

Freddy was fascinated. The depth and intensity of her hatred mesmerized him; he had never before encountered an emotion that was so nearly tangible. The air about her sizzled with her ancient rage. Her eyes compelled belief; he had to look away before he could hear the voice of his own reason.

But Miss Kate soon grew bored – and that was a mood she could not conceal. Before disaster could strike he hastily thanked the old woman, made their excuses, and withdrew.

In the cab on the way back to their hotel Miss Kate sat as far apart from him as possible. The disappointment of the old woman had ruined her evening. She blamed him for it.

"Aren't you sometimes afraid of all the emotions you don't understand?" he asked her.

"Jealousy!" she sneered. "Jealousy's not an emotion."

"Oh?"

"Course it isn't. Look how it's destroyed her. If it was an eee-motion, how could it do that!"

He laughed.

It was a mistake – with her in that mood, it was a mistake.

"Jeeee-hoshophat!" she shouted angrily. "You, Mr. Frederick, are a pain in the dumbelle!"

She imagined he was laughing at her for her youth, for the narrowness and predictability of her feelings. She, on the other hand, considered herself mature and complex.

He went chastened, she grumpily, to their separate rooms.

In hotels in the English parts of the West Indies, they were usually given rooms on different floors. In French hotels, however, they were invariably put in adjacent rooms with a connecting door. That night she had not been in bed fifteen minutes before she rose and flung open the door between them. She was nude.

"You asleep?" she asked – superfluously, for he was sitting up between his sheets, writing his diary.

He did not answer but watched her in silence as she walked directly to the unused half of his bed. Lifting the covers, she flung herself beneath them. It was a large bed, though, and she was nowhere near touching him. "Now!" she said, looking up at him with a smile that was more malicious than seductive.

She had to prove she understood – that she really was grown up. He suddenly found that he wanted her. Partly it was simple lust, but even more than that it was a tenderness toward her, an understanding of her discontent, a desire to give her the one triumph she now craved.

He was on the point of yielding to her when he felt an even stronger curiosity that tugged him in the opposite direction. This was her ultimate gamble. Short of tying him down she could go no further than this. How, then, would she respond if he *still* refused?

He leaned over and kissed her lightly on the forehead. "You're wonderful, Miss Kate. A dear and wonderful sister, and I love you most tenderly."

She turned her back to him and hunched the sheets around

her. She was trapped in emotions – her own and his – for which the past years had done nothing to prepare her. A man's sex is like a machine, isn't it? Every girl knows that. You press a lever and it works. It doesn't argue back, or talk about its sister.

Later, in the dark, he heard her weeping. He reached over and began to stroke her hair, surprised to feel how fine and soft it was. She relaxed and fell asleep almost at once.

In the small hours he awoke, shivering with the urge to take her in her sleep. But he mastered himself and it soon passed.

In the morning she was still there, smiling fondly down at him, waiting for him to awaken. When he did, she stretched herself like a cat and said, "That was heavenly, Mr. Frederick."

It was so convincing he wondered if he had forgotten it. She saw his bewilderment and laughed.

Over breakfast she said, "You really don't want me that way, do you? I didn't believe it until now."

He gave her as much of her triumph as he dared. He pretended he could not look her in the eye. "I'm afraid of what might happen if we did," he confessed. "We're good friends, don't you think? I mean, apart from the occasional angry moments, we get on very well together. I love your company and I could never – I mean, I see it now – I could never have continued this fruitless search on my own. It's only because you're there to cheer me up. You're like … a butterfly. You sparkle." He reached across the table and stroked her hand. "That's what I really, really need you for, dearest Miss Kate."

She stared at him, mouth open, vainly grappling with these alien ideas. She had all the skills in the world for dealing with that other thing, but none for this. Or did she? Strange, new, uncertain feelings were stirring inside her, pushing her in contrary directions. She was no longer in command of herself.

A week or so later, early in February, 1878, they were on a Danish ship, the *Garman*, heading, as it happened, for Georgetown, Barbadoes.

"We're beginning to go over the old ground yet again," he said. "I think our search had better end here, where it started. It's as good a place as any."

"You're not giving up!" She was aghast.

"No – I'll turn my attention to the mainland. They can't be on any of the islands. We've surely proved that."

"But you'll need me there, too."

"You've got your own life to lead, Miss Kate. I can't commandeer you forever."

"But I don't mind," she said. There was a hint of desperation in it.

"Well, you think it over. Surely you've got enough now to go back home and rub their noses in it? The best house in Kentucky – remember?"

"That!" she said scornfully, as if he were talking about the dolls of her childhood.

"You didn't mean it?" he asked. "Was it a lie?"

She shrugged. "People need lies," she said evasively. "Maybe even your need to find your precious Ann is a lie."

The remark drew blood. Was she just striking out at him, any stick to beat a dog? Or was she actually gaining mature insights at last?

They were both again at the rail as they steamed into Carlisle Bay and headed for the Careenage. By long habit Freddy put the glass to his eye and scanned the ships at anchor or berthed at the wharves.

Suddenly he stiffened. He lowered the glass ... blinked ... raised it again.

"What now?" she asked.

Silently he handed the glass to her. "Tell me if I'm seeing things. It's at the wharf just upstream from the Ice House."

She found it quickly. "Heavens!" she said. "Is *that* how you spell Heccarty? Why didn't you say? I thought it was like the Irish name only with a *c*."

Before they were even tied up Freddy leaped ashore and raced back along the quay and up the gangplank onto the *Hecate*. There he accosted the first man he saw. "The women," he shouted breathlessly. "Where are the women?"

The man looked warily at him as at an escaped lunatic.

"You know damn well who I mean," Freddy challenged. "The women you took on board at Tilbury on the fourth of April last year."

The man raised his hands as if to say, "You expect me to have been with this ship so long ago!"

At that moment the master appeared on the deck above. He looked sternly down the companionway and barked, "Bates! Who is that man?"

"My name is Oxley, sir," Freddy snapped back. "You are Captain Moran, I presume? I'm inquiring into the disappearance of five women from London in April last. I have reason to believe they sailed in this ship."

The master folded his arms and looked calmly down. "You may be about your business, Bates. And as for you, sir, I don't know why you talk in that way. Your information is quite correct. There is no doubt the women sailed with us. I have never concealed the fact – why should I? It was a regular passage as far as we were concerned. All above-board and ..."

"Above-board!" Freddy exploded. "The women were abducted. You abducted them. You ..."

"Have a care, sir!" the master thundered. "Who are you, may I ask? The name Oxley means nothing to me."

"Then it damn well should! It is the name of one of those women – my wife. Ann Oxley."

The other became conciliatory at once. "Please, my dear sir, come to my quarters. Your anger is quite understandable – especially as you plainly know only half the story." He held out a hand, ushering Freddy aft.

Seated in the master's quarters, a glass of the master's whisky in his hand, a bewildered Freddy heard the other half:

The women had, indeed, been passengers from Tilbury. The *Hecate* was to carry them as far as Port of Spain, where they were to board different vessels to their various destinations in the hemisphere. But when they had arrived at Port of Spain, half those vessels were not there and the masters of the rest protested that the onward voyages had been cancelled or had never been properly arranged in the first place. The women were simply stranded there. Several of them had attempted to get in touch with their prospective employers but without success. All this had happened while the *Hecate* had been tramping between other ports. When she returned to Port of Spain, Captain Moran had offered the women free passage back to London, but, after thinking it over, all of them had declined.

"They had some harebrained scheme for making a living out here," the master said.

"Have you any idea what it might be?"

The man stared at his whisky, shaking his head. "That opera singer, she was at the bottom of it. You'll find the answer in Port of Spain – you mark my words."

"But I've searched there already. Three times! Not a trace of them."

"Depends where you looked rather."

Freddy blushed. "I didn't think they'd be free agents."

"Yes. Well, I'm sure it was nothing like that. You go back to Port of Spain and raise your sights a bit."

They stayed at the Marine Hotel this time. That evening Miss Kate did not come to his room to take dinner. He waited awhile and then went up to her room on the floor above. She was not in. At first he supposed she might have left for good, but too many of her things were still lying around.

He picked up one of her négligées and ran it fondly through his fingers. He was going to miss her. She had been such good company. He folded the garment and was turning to put it in the drawer when he caught sight of her, standing in the doorway and watching him with the strangest smile.

Had she seen?

He blushed and guiltily dropped the négligée.

But there was a sadness in her smile.

"I came up to see if you wanted dinner," he explained.

"I've been making my own inquiries," she said. "And I know where Ann is – all of them. I know where all of them are."

"Where? For the love of God ..."

"Why didn't we think of it? A piano teacher ... an opera singer ... we should have thought of it."

"Music? But Ann isn't the least bit musical."

"Oh fie and shame on her," she said sarcastically. "And after all those lessons you paid for! Well, Mr Frederick, you're in for a surprise." She pointed at the floor. "Just go downstairs. Take your dinner in the dining room with all the others, for a change. Somehow, I'm not hungry tonight."

He walked awkwardly past her. Shyly she put out an arm to stop him. She leaned toward him and gave him a gentle hug, following it with a light kiss. A sisterly kiss. Before he could speak, she thrust him into the corridor. Then the lock clicked home and he heard her begin to cry.

CHAPTER FORTY-EIGHT

THE MARINE WAS A ramshackle sort of hotel, cobbled together out of three or four adjacent private houses, with "annexes" in the garden for the staff. The dining room was built lean-to the middle house and had a covered pathway to the kitchens, which were placed in the former stables. To one side of the pathway – a blister in the wall of the dining room, an after-thought to an afterthought – was an alcove with a stage. It was large enough to seat a quartet in comfort – a condition that eluded the five young women who occupied it when Freddy entered the dining room that evening.

They were singing *Only a fading dream*, or, rather, the woman at the centre – Maria Dawson from her description and voice – was singing; three others were la-laing and humming a close-harmony background. The fifth, who could only be Rosina Williams, was at the piano.

He searched their faces but Ann was not there. He was looking for a plump, bonny young woman with long, fine, fair hair. Then one of them turned and slipped quickly away through a side door to the alcove-stage. By some remembered trick of her movement he realized it was Ann – but she had turned into a slender young lady with dark-red hair piled high on her head. He ran after her, almost knocking down a waiter as he sprang out into the courtyard. He was just in time to see the flash of her dress at the coach house door.

In her panic she had trapped herself, for the back entrance had been bricked over when the stables had been converted into kitchens. The old coach, unused these many years, was still swaying slightly when Freddy entered.

"Ann?" he called softly. "Darling? Do come out."

There was only silence.

"What d'you expect?" he said, raising his voice to its normal pitch. "D'you think I've driven myself mad these last months, searching for you here there and everywhere, just to abuse you or hurt you when I find you at last?"

There was a creak, followed by a further silence.

"Darling?" he prompted.

Above the distant strains of *Only a fading dream*, above the nearer clatter of the kitchen, he heard the sound of gentle sobbing. He smiled to himself; forgiveness welled up within him. Whatever sins she might now confess, he was already telling her in his heart that it did not matter.

He went to the coach and pulled open the unlatched door; his sight was growing used to the gloom. Through her fingers, her large, wet eyes were staring at him. Some sort of stage colouring was running in streaks down the backs of her hands. "I knew it was too good to last," she said.

The despair in her tone was so contrary to everything he had imagined for this moment (when he had dared to imagine anything at all) that he could only stand there, one foot upon the step, and stare at her.

She heaved a great sigh, as if to vent away her present mood. "You'd better come in," she said. "We must talk, I suppose."

He climbed in and sat beside her. He wanted to take her in his arms, to kiss her without stopping, to hold her, to crush her ... but this sudden, deflated coolness left him marooned at the heart of his own expectations. Even if she were angry with him it would be more acceptable, more understandable than this.

"How can you have been looking for me everywhere?" she asked. "We haven't been hiding."

"I wasn't looking in ... I mean I didn't think of music. I didn't know you could sing a note."

She laughed. It was the first hint of any joy in her. "Nor did I until we were stranded in Trinidad. I mean, not for a living. We're not bad though, are we!"

"The two bars I heard before I realized who you all were sounded ..."

"Where have you been looking, then?"

When he didn't answer she said, "Frederick!" But then she qualified her shock. "I suppose I was close enough to it in London."

"And closer still on the *Hecate*!"

"What d'you mean?"

"Well surely you know why you were being brought out here?"

"To be governess to a family in British ..."

"You mean you really don't know! You still don't know. Mr. de Santos didn't exist. I thought you knew that much."

She shook her head. "I never actually reached Georgetown. I mean the other Georgetown. We left the *Hecate* at Port of Spain and ... well, all the arrangements seemed to break down."

"Exactly. Someone in England must have been busy on the Brazil cable, letting people know the game was up. That man in London ..?"

"Mr. Netherbere?"

"Well that wasn't his real name. Anyway, he's in prison. And his accomplices. They're all in prison now."

The news plainly shook her.

Freddy continued: "I'm talking about all five of you, not just you, Ann. You were all to be ... well, I can see you understand it now."

"Oh, Frederick! Don't tell them. Don't tell anyone. It's too horrid even to think about."

After a pause he asked, "Why did you refuse Captain Moran's offer of a free return to London?"

"London!" she snorted. "I never want to see London again."

"That isn't what I'm really asking, Ann."

She turned to him and gripped his arm. "I'm no good, Frederick. I've only ever brought you unhappiness. And Clive. And poor Tony. I'm ... I have some fatal ... I'm just not a good person."

"Ann – that's simply not true! You're the most wonderful ..."

"Except here, with The Angels. With them – with *us* – I ..."

"Angels?"

"The Angels of Harmony – that's our name. It was Maria's idea. She's wonderful. D'you know, she ..."

"Oh never mind all that, darling. The only thing that matters is I've found you again. We can go back home now. As soon as you've packed we can leave."

"Oh but that's quite impossible. I mean we have a contract to fulfil."

He smiled, like a new stage manager. "I'll buy you out of it. I can take care of you at last, darling. I mean properly. We're rich now." He laughed as if to imply that he could still hardly believe it himself. "In fact, we own a gold mine in Venezuela. Honestly. I've made more money in less than a year out here than I could have made in ten in England."

"Oh, you'd make money anywhere, Frederick. It's always been there in you." Her tone was flat; she showed no interest at all in his news.

"Well don't sound so pleased," he said.

She sighed. "As for my coming back ... it's hard to explain this, my dear, but please try to understand. These last few months I've come to realize that my whole life – I mean *all* of it – was one long, terrible mistake. I was told, from when I was a tiny girl, they told me I was to go into service, and marry in service – and for all I knew die in service. That was the only ... the only" – she hit her forehead angrily – "the only picture I had of myself. I never questioned it. No one ever told me I could *be* something else. Then I met you ... and Clive ... and I was uprooted from all that. I didn't know what I was. All I knew was that I *could* be something else."

"But you were! You were my wife. You *are* my wife. You're the mother of our children. Oh Ann! Do say you're coming back to us. I love you. People say – oh it's so easy to talk – they say love is perfect forgiveness. Yet it's true! I love you so much I've not only forgiven you all that, but all the future, too. Anything! Everything!"

"Oh Christ!" she almost screamed. She rose and flung herself from the coach, leaving him in a cloud of dust. At the threshold into the yard she paused and added more calmly,

"You're just talking out of sentimental old sermons. All these words mean nothing!"

He caught up with her halfway across the yard. The swiftly fading light seemed bright as noonday now. "Let's go for a walk," he said. "Sitting still in the dark, close together, it's ..."

"How can I make you understand?" she asked tonelessly.

Hesitantly he took her arm. As they went out past the front of the hotel he looked up at the window of his room. Miss Kate was there, staring out to sea. Attracted by the movement she looked down, saw them, and angrily drew the curtain. He remembered he had left a hundred dollars in his wallet in his daytime suit. Still, he hadn't paid Miss Kate for a week or two. He must owe her fifty pounds by now.

"Shall I fetch your cape?" he asked Ann.

She shook her head. "I'll never feel cold again – not after London."

"You haven't asked about Angelica."

"She's better off without a mother like me. Anyway, don't worry – I'd always be able to find *her*!"

Freddy, who knew nothing of the business with the baby's ear, was mystified. In any case, her first remark seemed more important to pursue. "You do yourself such wrong, Ann," he began.

But she grew agitated. "I've got to make you understand. You don't know me, Frederick. You've never known me. No one ever has – only Maria and the others, the five of us. I've never been myself until we were stranded in Trinidad. That's when the very last shred of that old picture in my mind, the picture of me was stripped away. Did that ever happen to you? Can you imagine ..."

"Calm yourself, love. I believe you. I can understand." He clasped her arm more tightly in his. She gave an answering squeeze – the first intimacy between them since she had fled from the stage.

"And it wasn't just me. It happened to all of us. When we were offered free passage back, d'you know – we all nearly accepted it. We were actually packing up our belongings when I just happened to say I had nothing really to go back to ... and Letty said nor had she ... and then we all agreed. Except Maria.

She could get a job singing anywhere, of course. She was the only one who had anything of herself left. And she said let's try and get work as a singing quartet, with Rosie to play the piano. Maria had taught us all a lot of harmonies to while away the voyage, so even then we were quite good. Anyway, the manager at the Union Club said we were pretty fair, and he gave us a try, and we were a grand success. I mean, we're the only all-female musical company around. And we're a lot better since then. I'll tell you how good we are. We ..."

"All right, Ann. I believe all that. I understand all that. But when you say you had nothing, you must have imagined I was still as angry as that night ..." He paused.

She could feel he was holding his breath. "What?" she asked.

"My God! It was this night one year ago! And I forgot ... I forgot!" He stopped and tried to hold her with his stare. "Our little Angelica is one year old tonight!"

She walked on without pausing. "It won't work, Frederick," she told him flatly.

Her lack of emotion annoyed him. "But surely now you know I haven't turned against you, and ... and our marriage is still there – and our children – when you know we need you so much – and we're not short of money now – I mean surely that changes everything?"

She didn't answer.

"Surely?" he repeated more gently.

"What d'you want me for?" she asked at length.

"What d'you mean?"

"Exactly what I say."

"Well, I've already told you – to be my wife. To come back and manage ..."

"Where? Solihull? Birmingham?"

"Oh no doubt about that. I've a mind to go into explosives and armaments. The Midlands are the obvious place."

The silence that greeted this prompted him to add, in a more hesitant tone, "... or ... you say where. You decide."

She burst into laughter. "Frederick! D'you ever listen to yourself?" The question, which she had intended as a piece of jocular scorn, made her pause. She saw a serious point at its heart. "In fact," she added, all laughter gone now, "*do* you know yourself at all, I wonder? Tell me about Clive, for instance. You and Clive."

"Clive?" Her apparent change of tack bewildered him.

"Yes. Why did you go to him on the night that" – she smiled – "a year ago tonight? I suppose you left England soon after that? What happened between you? How did you feel about him then? And have you changed since? I want to know what sort of thinking has been going on in your head this last year."

He felt a small panic beginning to grow. Whether or not he had changed, Ann certainly had. "There hasn't been much time for that sort of thing," he said lamely. "Not for thinking."

They had arrived at the waterfront. The evening was now dark. He caught only occasional glimpses of her by the light of quayside lamps and windows as they passed. It added to his panic, to the feeling that they were drifting in and out of contact with each other.

"More or less what I expected you to say," she told him. "I don't believe you. I'm sure you think about yourself and the past and the future all the time. Perhaps not in words, though."

There was a hint of flattery in her tone. He wanted more of it. He racked his mind desperately for any sort of answers to her questions. "The funny thing is that when I saw Angelica, when I realized what had happened, it wasn't Tony I hated. It was Clive. I wanted to kill him. If he'd been in the room, I think I would have done."

"So why did you go to him?"

"Because ... because ... I don't know!"

She gave a little cry of exasperation and sprang in front of him, beating his chest with her fists, but more in token than in true fury. "You *do* know!" she cried. "You just won't face it. You keep it all locked away inside ... festering!"

Two seamen were passing. One sniggered and made a crude gesture. Freddy waited until they were beyond earshot.

"It wasn't really Clive I hated," he explained. "Only a part of him. It was the same that first time, back in the Grand Soarer days. Old Dixon got me all fired and steaming against Clive. But Dixon's Clive was a Boss, an Oppressor. That wasn't my Clive. Only a part of him. And when I met him ... it all evaporated. Well, not completely. But ... you know. Oh how can I explain it!"

"Go on! Go on!"

Again that flattery, stronger now. She knew what she was doing all right. He took her arm. "I should start courting you all over again, Ann. You're a different person. When I said I want you to come back and be my wife again, I was wrong. You could do *that* job inside an hour each day. What I really want is for you to come back and be yourself – during the other twenty-three hours, anyway."

She shivered and pulled her arm away as if he had some contagion. "My God – I had forgotten you! It's completely instinctive, isn't it! You have no idea you're doing it."

"What?"

"You can twist anyone. Any woman, at least. I can see just how you managed the dowager. But I don't suppose you could do it if you planned it – consciously, I mean. You couldn't face yourself."

He turned from her toward the dark waters of the Careenage. He saw a bollard immediately before him and settled on it gratefully. How could he explain to her about Clive? That he hated him *and* loved him. That he would never forget or forgive the betrayal and yet he would never let the memory of it cloud his actual dealings with his old friend and blood brother?

But that, as he suddenly realized, was no longer his real problem. His feelings about Clive, and even hers, were now beside the point. His problem was Ann, the real Ann, behind him, here on this darkening waterfront; the Ann he no longer dared to face.

That other Ann, the one he and Miss Kate had sought all over the Caribbean, had been infinitely pliable to his will and imagination. She had had her taste of freedom and found it bitter; she would have been so grateful to him for finding her like this – for being willing to take her back without conditions, without even a word of reproach. She had been an easy Ann to love and yearn to find.

In a sense he was looking for her still ... seeking her vainly in this tough, bright, self-reliant, and utterly unrepentant woman who had somehow usurped Ann's mind and body.

An irony made him shiver: Miss Kate, for all her outward toughness and would-be sophistication, was actually closer in spirit to the woman he had been looking for.

From behind Ann put her arms around him and rested her chin on his shoulder. The nearness of her, the soft touch of her hair upon his cheek, filled him with a primitive longing. But there was also fear – for that new Ann, the stranger she had become.

"Stay out here, my dear," she said. "Don't go back to England. Don't see Clive again. Sever all those old, poisoned roots. Will you?"

The suggestion was unthinkable. What was the point of being cock-of-the-walk in some tinpot little foreign country! He nuzzled her ear with his lips. "Come to my room tonight," he whispered.

It had no effect on her. She straightened herself and turned to face the way they had come. "You're driven to it, I suppose," she said. "But who am I to talk?"

"If I stay out here" – he grasped her arm to stop her walking away – "will you leave the others and be with me?"

She unpeeled his fingers. "Ten seconds earlier," she said coldly, "that question would have deserved an answer. I pity poor Clive. Those few, mad, young, impulsive hours are going to cost him dearly, I can see."

"You're wrong, Ann. I honestly have no thought of ... well, from time to time, of course, I remember his betrayal and I still resent it. I won't deny that. But you seem to think ... well, that I'm unhinged about it or something."

She turned to him. "That's not at all what I think. I think you're a whole boxful of people all crammed into one body. There's Frederick the Vengeful who hates Clive and would like to kill him. And Frederick the Stalwart who's Clive's blood brother and would lay down his life for him. And Father Frederick, who wants me to come back and be wife and mother. But Frederick the Lover sees how little that prospect attracts me and so *he* says, 'No no – come back and be *yourself!*' Tell me, my dear – how long did it take you to get over my desertion?"

He thought back to that night, exactly twelve months ago – the rage with Tony, the deep discussion with Clive ... and then next day, the fencing match with the dowager, followed by the bit of amusement at Eleanor's expense. And all within twenty-four hours of the most terrible discovery of his life. He realized there was a certain truth – no, a certain caricature of the truth – in Ann's judgement.

She took his silence for chagrin and, turning to walk back to the hotel, said in a gentler voice, "It's actually the most wonderful thing about you, too, of course. It's why you'll never be defeated. They could demolish you utterly – and ten seconds later there'd be another Frederick standing there, unscathed, smiling ... ready to step over the corpse and carry on. But I can't keep up with you."

He drew level. She slipped her arm through his. An easeful silence settled between them.

"Perhaps I could change," he offered tentatively.

She replied with exaggerated reasonableness. "Prove it to me. Stay in the West Indies. Use your new money to start some kind of business here. And then a year from today – since anniversaries seem to mean so much to you – I'll come to visit you, and if you've done all that, if you're settled to it, then I'll leave the girls and start a new life with you."

"Back in England?" he tried.

She dug him sharply with her elbow.

"What you're asking is unreasonable," he complained.

"If it was reasonable, there'd be no point in asking it."

"You're asking me to give up all my ambitions, but you'd be giving up nothing."

She gave a single, ironic laugh, a shout almost.

It stung him. "All right – what *would* you be giving up?"

She stared solemnly at him. "Oh Frederick – I don't think you want to know that."

The reply made him angry but he contained himself. He wanted to force her to a proper answer. "Just tell me about your life nowadays then," he suggested pleasantly.

She took it as an excuse to change the subject. "Well, since you've been scouring the fleshpots of the West Indies looking for me, I'll tell you this – The Angels of Harmony are so good we can make it a condition in our contract that if we are approached or molested by any customer, that customer will be ejected from the premises."

"That's not the sort of thing I mean," he complained.

"Perhaps not. But it's what I want you to remember when you've gone your way and I've gone mine. With most performing groups, you realize, it's usually a condition that any female in the troupe must spend part of her offstage time 'entertaining' the customers. Well, we're the very opposite of that, and it's something we've insisted on from the start. The Union Club manager, he advised us. Of course, his place didn't need such a condition. But the first hotel where we tried to insist, the owner laughed in our faces, so we went to his rival. Fortunately he'd seen us at the Union, and he agreed – and we took away all the other fellow's trade. He went down on his knees! That's how good we are. So rest easy, my love."

They had taken a more direct route back and were now at the foot of the short hill leading up to the hotel.

"Don't come to any quick decision," he said. "Think about it tonight, and let's talk about it again at breakfast?"

She sighed, gave him a quick kiss, and ran ahead of him, indoors. To have answered in words she would have had to tell him that by breakfast time tomorrow The Angels of Harmony would already be at sea, bound for Rio and their next engagement. She was not brave enough for that.

The first thing he did on entering his room was to check on his hundred dollars. It was all there. Somehow the pleasure it gave him coloured everything else. Though he could give no reasons for his confidence, he nonetheless felt certain Ann would change her mind. Whistling happily, *Only a fading dream*, he took his towel and sponge and loofah and went for a bath at the end of the passage.

The moment he was in the water, Miss Kate came hastening down the corridor and slipped into his room. Safely inside she undressed down to her most "sexalted lingery."

A few minutes later, Ann put down her suitcase and tapped gently at that same door. She could not leave him on the false promise of that last kiss.

But suddenly Miss Kate stood before her, clutching a large silk scarf about her slender figure.

"Oh, I'm sorry," Ann stammered in confusion. "I thought ..."

Miss Kate recovered herself quickly. She saw a chance for some light amusement. "Are you for Mr. Frederick, too?" she asked. "Same here, honey. Come in – he didn't tell me but who cares! This is going to be some intimaterie!"

Ann picked up her suitcase and went storming back up the corridor.

When her laughter died, Miss Kate took fright at what she had done and returned swiftly to her own room, where she began at once to pack.

When Freddy awoke next morning, there were no longer any women in his life.

PART FIVE

ONLY A BIRD IN A ROYAL HAREM

CHAPTER FORTY-NINE

THIS SECOND AND SEEMINGLY FINAL loss of Ann was a great shock to Freddy. In the end what helped him accept it was the realization that she could go, just like that, no note, no word of goodbye. For those first few days he thought about her a great deal; there was little else to do while he leant upon the ship's rail and watched the ocean slipping by. It was not what she had said but the image of her that chiefly haunted him; indeed a protective veil seemed to have fallen over his memory of their conversation. He recalled how striking her new, red hair had been, the way it framed her face, so thin now, so vibrant, her eyes so alive. She was the only one he had ever loved or wanted; all the womanly qualities he most admired were now focused on that image. It tugged at his heart every time he thought of her.

But toward the end of his voyage home, these nostalgic indulgences gave way to the returning memories of what she had said. She seemed to think that buried inside him was another Freddy who nursed a bitter resentment against Clive and who sought nothing but revenge – a hidden Freddy, concealed even from himself. It was absurd, of course. How could there be two people inside one person? And how could anybody think thoughts without being aware of them? It was like saying you could travel abroad while all the time your body stayed at home.

But there was more sense in another of the things she had told him, when she said there was an almost infinite number of Freddies inside him and that if one was defeated another would spring up and take his place. If you didn't interpret it too literally, he had to agree there was a certain truth in that. He had never seen any point in letting adversity get you down. However despairing life might appear, there was only one thing to do – look for its positive elements and seize them. Miss Kate had been like that, too. She'd touched the blackest pitch without being defiled; she'd lived though hell-on-earth and she'd come out of it singing like a linnet. By the time he reached Liverpool he realised he was actually more sad at losing Miss Kate's company than at having failed to win back Ann.

And then, when he looked down at the quayside and saw young Emmy standing there with Lawrence beside her, both leaping up and down like the children they were, all thought of his emotional losses vanished. Day was just breaking; their enthusiasm put a new seal upon it. The future was all that mattered now.

"Well, this *is* nice. I certainly didn't expect to see you here," he told them when they were on the train. "When did my cable arrive?"

"Day before yesterday, sir," she replied. "You aren't angry, I hope?"

"Do I look it?"

"It's just we couldn't wait."

"Well I'm glad. I've been starved for a friendly face."

Lawrence asked, "Why couldn't mummy have come with you, daddy?"

"Because, as I said, she and the other ladies in the choir had signed a contract – a solemn agreement – to complete their tour. Breaking your contract is like breaking your word."

"And when it's over, will she come back then?"

"We all hope so. We must pray for it – and keep a place in our hearts always prepared for her." Before the boy could ask anything further he turned to Emmy. "And what of baby Angelica? No longer quite such a baby now, I'm sure."

The girl's eyes flagged a massive scandal but all she said was, "Mr. Knox-Riddell's looking after her."

"Oh? Well we can soon put a stop to that."

"Him and that Sally Pickering." Again her eyes spoke volumes, closing off the subject until Lawrence was safely back in the nursery at Hob's Gardens.

Only then did she add what had been the scandal of the district for the best part of the year: Tony Knox-Riddell had married Sally Pickering. Half of local Society, including Mrs. Homfray's set, had dropped the Knox-Riddells entirely; the other half would dearly like to follow suit but as they owed their livelihoods, either directly or indirectly, to that family, they could not afford to show their feelings.

"No one would have minded so much if that Sally Pickering had been a bit humble about it," Emmy told him, passing on the received local wisdom. "But she stepped into the lady-of-the-manor's shoes as if she was born to them. She's smart, see. She's kept her eyes and ears open all these years. She knows just how everything's done. So she never put a foot wrong."

Freddy laughed. "So they can't forgive her, of course. Thank you, Emmy – you may have saved me a little heartache on my own account – considering the way I hope our lives and fortunes may change in the not-too-distant future."

Later that evening, when he had retired to bed and was going through recent issues of the local trade newspapers, Emmy brought him a cup of hot cocoa. There was one for herself, too.

"I hope you don't mind, sir," she said. "I thought that what with your having such a long, tiring day it might just set you at your ease."

He was decidedly *ill* at ease to see she was in her night attire, though a heavy woollen dressing gown made it perfectly respectable. However, the steaming cocoa smelled very good. She picked up the tray, with her own cup upon it, and was about to leave when, on an impulse, he pointed to the empty chair at his bedside and said, "Stay and sup it with me. Tell me what else has been going on."

She pulled the chair away to a respectful distance and seated herself with a contented smile. "D'you remember the last occasion, sir, when I supped in your bedroom? Though then it was soup, not cocoa."

He had to think back. "Oh yes! *That* day is best forgotten."

"And you so eager to pay me back that pound!"

He nodded. He was remembering that he still owed Miss Kate at least forty pounds. He wondered if they would ever meet again.

From then on the cup of cocoa and the little chat became a nightly ritual, a winding-down of the day's frenzy – and such frenzied days Freddy had never before known. He had always been a demonic worker but now, with land to buy, a factory to design and build, raw materials to secure, markets to cultivate ... he worked with the stamina of ten. It helped that there were no distractions in his life, no Ann to worry about, and a household that, thanks to Emmy, ran like a machine.

She was a miracle. She seemed to know his slightest wants even before he felt them himself. She never consulted him about the meals, because it would have taken up his time, but they were always what he would have asked for if she had; and the vegetables were cooked just the way he liked them; and the quantities were perfect. Whatever suit he chose, it was ready pressed and aired; the stains of today were always gone by tomorrow. When he came down at six, the carpets were already swept and beaten and the fires laid, though they would not be lit until evening. And every Saturday she would set before him the week's accounts, perfect to the last farthing. They were done on the double-entry system, which she had studied out of a book in the *Paternoster Penny Library*.

But her greatest service of all was simply to sit and listen to him over a cup of cocoa, last thing at night, and occasionally (more frequently as time went on) throw in a little comment or opinion of her own. What she had said of Sally – that she was smart and kept her eyes and ears open – was no less true of herself.

It was Emmy who conducted the negotiations that resulted in the return of Angelica to the Oxley household. Both Tony and Sally were distressed, but Freddy was the child's legal father and there was nothing they could do about it. No one ever commented on the missing tip of her right ear. She fretted for a week or two and then settled happily enough to her new home.

"When Mrs. Oxley returns, she must find all her family waiting for her," Freddy said.

Emmy replied that they were her feelings exactly, and added with a sigh, "However many years that might be."

The dowager was furious when Freddy declined her renewed offer of the post of general manager of all the Mortimer companies.

"She seems to think I made some kind of solemn promise to her before I went away," Freddy complained to Emmy. "She doesn't understand how things work in business – how one takes certain decisions from purely precautionary motives. To outsiders they may sound like promises but insiders understand them for what they are."

"What does Sir Clive think?" Emmy asked.

"She practically called me a traitor today. Sir Clive? Well, he's against it, of course. He doesn't want *any* new broom sweeping through his ramshackle kingdom, and especially not one called Oxley. Understandable, of course. The man has his pride."

"So does her ladyship."

Freddy half-frowned, half-smiled at her. "Go on."

"Did you ever look at it from her point of view?" Emmy no longer called him "sir" when they were alone.

"It's hard to know what her point of view is, Emmy. She hasn't much time for her son – I mean as a man of business. Proud of him as a junior minister, of course, but ..."

"No. I mean her attitude to you."

He sighed. "Well I don't think she's ever *liked* me, for all her kindness and gener..."

"You think it's kindness?"

Freddy was at a loss how to answer. Naturally he could not tell the girl the truth.

"That's what I mean," Emmy went on. "The Mortimers don't exactly have a reputation around here as give-it-all-away philanthropists."

"They're not skinflints, either, Emmy."

"No. Just very careful. So why did the dowager make this exception in your case? Did you ever ask yourself that?"

He stared at her levelly. "Did you?"

She nodded confidently. "If the mistress told me once, she told me a dozen times how, that year before I came to you, how you did a four-year course in just twelve months. And I wasn't in the house a week before I felt it, too."

"Felt what?"

"That nothing was ever going to hold you down. I used to lie awake up there, listening to you in the next room, your pen nib going scratch-scratch-scratch till all hours. And I knew it, too. You're a star – and that's what the dowager must have seen, too. I mean if I could see it, surely to goodness she could?"

It was a convenient gloss upon the truth. "You mean I'm her investment," he replied. "And I've stopped paying a dividend."

Emmy nodded. "That's the size of it. Men invest money, but women always invest a bit of themselves, too. She's got a bit of herself invested in you, Mr. Oxley, and you've cut her off from it."

He shook his head ruefully. "If you're right, Emmy – and I'm sure you are – I don't see there's much I can do about it. I'm certainly never again going to work *for* anyone else."

She grinned at him. "You'll find a way, sir. That's another canny thing about you – once you understand a difficulty, you always find a way around it."

A month later Freddy presented himself at Mortimer Hall, where, Eleanor being away (as he had earlier made sure), he was received by a distinctly frosty dowager.

"I am not At Home," she told him.

He looked out over the empty terrace and said, "So much the better." Then, turning his warmest smile upon her, he added, "You have such an amazing knack of knowing exactly what it is that troubles me at any particular moment, Lady Mortimer. It's almost frightening. I think there's no one else in the world with so sure an instinct."

She, having no idea at all what might be on his mind, tried to look wise while she waited for him to drop a hint.

"At Home," he prompted. "All those social customs. Visiting ... leaving one's card ... when to leave only one, when to leave two ... when to fold down the corner ..."

The dowager frowned. "A gentleman couldn't possibly leave two. His wife would, of course, if she called alone. The second card would represent her husband. And one must *never* fold down the corner."

"You see!" He threw up his hands and sighed at the arcane complexity of this one small corner of the vast field of etiquette. "And that's only the beginning. What about entertainment on a grander scale? Giving a ball – invitations, the order of precedence ..."

She smiled and took his arm, walking him away from the window and back toward the sofa. He half-relaxed. "My dear boy," she said. "What has brought on all this?"

Reluctantly, as if she were squeezing an admission out of him, he said, "I suppose you know Lord Monckton?"

She shook her head. "Not even by sight. I know *of* him, naturally. Do you?"

"Yes. I met him last week."

Monckton was financially interested in a company that made special steels, some of which Freddy would be using in a field gun he had designed. Freddy had seen a short paragraph in the *Military Gazette*, saying that the recent manoeuvres of the Imperial Austrian Army had revealed particular deficiencies in its light artillery. Censorship in the Habsburg Empire was strict, so the release of this interesting snippet was like an advertisement saying, "Arms manufacturers please apply."

At his meeting with Lord Monckton, Freddy had wondered aloud whether any of his lordship's acquaintances had an entrée to the Imperial War Ministry. Monckton had seen the point at once. If the new Oxley gun proved as good as it looked on paper, and if it therefore attracted orders from the greatest army on the European mainland, the market for special steels would be not only secured but greatly enlarged.

"Your friend Sir Clive Mortimer's the man to see," he told Freddy.

"It would be better coming from you, sir," he had replied. He wanted no favours from Clive.

"Then you must arrange a meeting. Nothing too direct, don't you know. Politically we don't see eye-to-eye. A dinner party, perhaps? A small affair – no more than thirty – which will give us a chance to talk casually but in confidence."

Freddy briefly summarized all this for the dowager. Then he laughed. "Can you imagine a dinner party for thirty at Hob's Gardens! We'd have difficulty seating eight. Obviously no one's told him where I live."

"Yes, I see your difficulty." He could almost hear the cogs of her brain whirring.

"There's the banqueting room at the club," he continued. "But I think he's expecting some social occasion. Wives and so on. It'll have to be at one of the big hotels in Birmingham, but what I came to ask you is which is the best book for me to learn up all those rules about precedence and sending out invitations, and so on?"

She laughed and patted his arm soothingly. He relaxed still further; she had taken the bait. "My dear boy, it's quite absurd. We must put on our thinking caps."

She rose and toyed with a flower arrangement for a while. "Of course," she said at length, "you could always rent my house."

"*Your* house? I don't understand."

"The one I ought to be living in – the dower house. That gloomy Queen Anne place down in Ravenscroft Way. It's not in the best of repair, but it has a good ballroom and dining room – ample kitchens and cellar and that sort of thing."

"Me? Live there?"

"No no no. You'd die of the damp and decay inside a month. It's utterly uninhabitable. But you could keep a couple there on board wages and hire chefs and footmen and things whenever you needed."

"What a splendid idea – no capital outlay!" He pulled a face. "But I'd still need that book on etiquette."

"Nonsense! All you need is a hostess."

"Ah! But she's away, touring around the world."

The dowager laughed. "Actually, she's standing before you at this very minute – thinking that for a clever young fellow you're sometimes remarkably obtuse."

"Emmy, my girl!" Freddy told her that night. "You're a marvel. How I should ever manage without you, I just dread to think."

She laughed as she replied, "Well, bonny lad, that's one thing you'll never need bother your head about."

CHAPTER FIFTY

"WE SHALL HAVE TO make up our own rules," the dowager said. "For new arrivals in a district the form is well established. Local Society calls on them and, if they pass muster, they get invited out to dine here and there."

"I'm a new arrival," Freddy pointed out.

"Quite. But you're a new arrival in the district where you were born and where you've lived most of your life. You're a new *vertical* arrival and all the rules are for *horizontal* ones. So, as I say, we must make it up as we go along." She considered the wording of the invitation. "*Mr. Frederick Oxley and Gwen, Lady Mortimer request* ... You see, even the precedence is wrong yet somehow the other way about it sounds worse: *Gwen, Lady Mortimer and Mr. Frederick Oxley request* ... It makes you sound like my butler. Oh and talking of upper servants, that little housekeeper thing of yours, d'you think she's quite up to this sort of occasion? She looks so young."

"Oh, Emmy will astonish you. Have no fear there."

"I must say, the suggested menu she brought me was excellent. I suppose she copied it directly out of some ladies' magazine."

"If I know Emmy, she has a penny notebook somewhere with a hundred dinner menus all ready and waiting."

The dowager looked at him sharply. "So she's out of the same mould as you then!" She shivered theatrically. "How many more of you are there – down there in the Lower Depths?"

He laughed. "Enough to keep your dividends rolling in nice and smoothly, Lady Mortimer."

She brightened. "Yes – there is that."

She was in her element, of course, arranging this grand dinner party to launch Freddy into local Society; for too long she had had to yield to Eleanor in such affairs. True, there had been one or two moments of doubt. After her initial enthusiasm she'd had a dreadful attack of cold feet – until Lady Cottesmore had pointed out that Daisy de Vere hadn't been too proud to act as London hostess for "Cap'n" Churley, the railway magnate, and the Prince and Princess of Wales – and even the Duchess of Devonshire – had gone to those balls and dinners.

Provincial Society was naturally much slower to take to it, but such innovations had to come. It was Freddy Oxley and people like him who were making what new wealth there was – and they were smart enough to know it, too. If established Society didn't let them in, they'd form a new one of their own. And a vulgar, uncultivated affair it would be, too. They would drive out all delicacy and refinement. And that would be the end of everything worthwhile.

So she threw herself into the arrangements, heart and soul.

"Thank heavens for your little Foxy," Eleanor said to Clive. "If I'd been obliged to give one more dinner with your mother's *help*, I should have bolted."

"I wonder whose idea it was for him to rent the old dower house?" Clive mused.

"Perhaps, while she's so totally preoccupied, perhaps I could arrange a Friday-to-Monday? What d'you think? Between Ascot and the Twelfth, say. A big one for the party. D'you suppose the Grand Old Man himself would come?"

"Mother says it was her idea, but I've a suspicion it was young Foxy's."

"Clive! You're not listening to me. This is important."

He took her hands in his. "I am listening, darling girl – and trying, in the most tactful possible way, not to answer."

She withdrew her hands sharply and tossed her hair. "I'd like to know why."

He sighed. "Because I think you're being premature. I imagine Gladstone has just about heard of my name – and knows me well enough by sight to waggle a vague paw in my direction when I step out of his way in the House. We've dined with precisely two members of the cabinet – and on one of those illustrious occasions we were a last-minute makeweight because they'd otherwise have been thirteen. It's quite impossible to invite the party down here for a Friday-to-..."

"Oh!" Eleanor clenched her fists and shook them at the empty air.

Clive laughed. "And you know it perfectly well yourself, my dear."

"Do I? All I know is that little Freddy Oxley, who hasn't dined at a single table in the entire county, who has barely completed the purchase of the *fields* in which to build his factories, and who doesn't ..."

"The factories are actually half finished."

"Which is the same as saying only half begun. My point is that he doesn't let any of these scruples prevent him from throwing out invitations to the cream of the district. Lord Monckton! Good heavens – think how delighted we'd be if he came to dine with us."

"But he's a Tory."

"So is my father, in case you've forgotten. And if we're only ever to dine the Whigs or Liberals, what a very dull time we'll have of it."

"Anyway, the whole thing was Monckton's idea from the start. To meet me. He has his own Foreign Office connections but for some reason he doesn't wish to deal through them – prefers to go at arm's length through me. Probably suspects failure is inevitable but doesn't want to appear to be dragging his feet. I wish I knew whose idea it was to rent the dower house."

"Your mother's, of course. It's a perfect excuse not to go and live there herself. She's run through all the other excuses – it's damp ... it's haunted ... it gets a malarial miasma off the Blythe ... it's too far away – when all the time it's a perfectly habitable house, or could be for the want of a few hundred pounds. But this one is perfect. She can't go there now because young Fredders will be giving a dinner there or a ball two or three times a year!"

Clive nodded. "You're probably right, dearest. It probably wasn't Foxy."

She caught something in his tone, hinting that what he really meant was, "It wasn't Foxy *this time*." The nuance intrigued her and she abandoned her former line of conversation. "What is it between you and him?" she asked.

He shrugged and tried to resume his newspaper. "I told you. We practically grew up together."

"But why are you always on your guard for some possible

insult from him – or more than that. You often seem to suspect him of trying to serve you a bad turn."

He looked up with an amused smile. "Do I? I'm not aware of it, I assure you." He returned to the paper with an air that said, *Now I simply must read this article.*

She let him settle, let his guard begin to drop, and then she said quietly, "It has something to do with Lawrence, hasn't it."

He stiffened at once. She saw the blood drain from his fingernails where his hands gripped the paper. But he pretended to go on reading. "Lawrence?" he asked abstractedly.

"I'm sure of it."

It forced him to look up at her. "I don't follow." But his eyes said otherwise.

She nodded confidently. "Lawrence and Tony Knox-Riddell. I know it's none of my business – and before the girl was born it was very loyal of you to keep quiet about it all – but now the secret's out, among us anyway, don't you think you're carrying it too far?"

"Carrying what too …"

"Whatever oath of secrecy you swore to Tony – when your mother agreed to pay Tony's paternity money to the Oxleys as if it were some kind of private scholarship from her. You see – I've worked it all out."

He gave her a rueful smile, suggesting he was a fool ever to have thought he could deceive her for long. "An oath is an oath, nonetheless," he said. "Anyway – what more could I add to what you've already guessed?"

"You could explain why you so often suspect Foxy of plotting something or other against *you*. If he's sharpening a knife for anyone's back, surely it's Tony's?"

He frowned and pinched the furrowed skin across the bridge of his nose – always a sign that he was about to concede some point gracefully. "Tony, Gray, and I were so close at that time, you see. And Foxy, too. He took the betrayal (I name no names, mind you) – he took it very hard. I don't think he discriminated much between the three of us."

She was horrified. "You mean all *three* of you played wanton with …"

"No no! Of course not. But …"

"But he *suspected* all three of you?"

"No. He knew that the three of us, our combined presence if you like, he knew that's what had bowled Ann over. And ..." He licked his lips, uncertain how to continue.

She rescued him. "And Tony took advantage of it." She nodded sagely. "Yes, I can understand his point of view. Still, surely he can see how well he's done out of it! Does he suppose he'd now have your mother working double tides to arrange a dinner for Monckton and half the county if it weren't for all that?"

"Well, I hope he sees it that way. I must say I was surprised when he turned down mother's repeated offer of the general managership."

"Are you? I'm not."

"How d'you explain it then?" he asked, laying down his paper at last.

"Obviously he thinks he can do much better on his own. Anyway, what would it be? One more grace-and-favour gift from the Mortimers! Enough to make him wonder if he'd ever be free of us. No – he's much happier as things are. He's rid himself of a wife who'd only be a social liability where he's going. And ..."

"But he begged her to return with him!"

Eleanor smiled pityingly. "And whose word do we have for that? No! Ann was his ladder from the basement up to the ground floor. Now he's got your mother twisted round his little finger – as I suppose he always had. But she's just another ladder to him. One day he'll have no use for her either."

"Oh, I think you're much too hard, darling."

"You'll see," she said confidently.

Clive laughed. "What sort of power d'you think he has over mother then?"

Her surprise was genuine. "Don't you see it? Oh surely! It's the power to do precisely what she's doing now – to make a silk purse out of a sow's ear. Somehow, back in the days when he was just an apprentice – probably the day he flew that soaring machine – she often talks about that – but somehow he allowed her to have a glimpse of himself at the very pinnacle of Society. Lord knows how because his view of such things must have been pretty hazy while hers was sharp as crystal, but somehow he managed it. And from that moment on it's been a sort of addiction with her. She's going down in history as the great patroness of the legendary Frederick Oxley."

She waited for Clive to agree but saw instead a lingering doubt. She went on: "Remember how she was when they were living in Stockton – a job which she secured for him, incidentally – remember that time when they came here and we all had tea on the terrace? He was *her* protégé. And then again look at how dreadful she was when he came back and wanted to branch out on his own! She hadn't a good word to say about him – until he asked her to be his hostess."

"But that was *her* idea, not his. She told us."

Again that pitying smile. "If you plant an acorn in the garden, my dear, isn't the oak tree yours? Or do you say it belongs to the garden!"

Clive shook his head in amazement. "I had no idea!"

"Of what?"

"All this. I didn't realize you dislike him so much."

"But I don't! I'm not saying I'd pine away for want of his friendship, but I certainly admire him. He's a terrier. And he's quite fearless. He knows exactly what he wants and he goes for it until he gets it." She rose and added, as an idle afterthought, "We could do with more like him."

Left alone, Clive reflected that here was yet another way in which Freddy might yet drive a wedge between the Mortimers – mother and son, son and wife. The only thing he was unable to decide – as always – was whether it was deliberate, or whether it arose simply because Foxy was ... Foxy: a figure who unwittingly held all three of them, in their different ways, quite mesmerized.

CHAPTER FIFTY-ONE

IN EVERY RESPECT but one the dinner that launched Freddy into Society was an outstanding success. Profiting from Emmy's judgement concerning Sally Pickering's disastrous entrée, he made no attempt to disguise his origins. He was genial but not familiar, expansive but never florid, attentive without being fawning. Grand ladies had accepted his invitation, hoping for some amusement at the sight of a boorish little arriviste aping his betters – not to mention the pleasure of commiserating with Gwen Mortimer at the depths to which she had descended. They were agreeably surprised by the shy, quiet young man they met; and they were all the more impressed to note the respect in which Lord Monckton obviously held him.

But there was more to his conquest than that – there was something *directly* appealing about the young fellow. Such a realization sat uncomfortably in bosoms where maternal feelings had never truly flourished, yet it could not be denied. He carried about him – despite all those dynamic qualities which had brought him to his present position – he carried a hint of the little-boy-lost. There was never a moment when he actually floundered, but there were several when he seemed on the point of doing so. And the extraordinary thing was that women who had come precisely to enjoy such a spectacle found themselves holding their breath and willing him not to fail. The relief when he came through each petty crisis without stumbling was almost tangible.

Eleanor, who watched him closely and coolly all evening, delivered her verdict to Clive: "He's incredible. I don't think he's fully aware of what he's doing or how he does it. But he's a master."

"I wish you liked him more," Clive told her.

She laughed. "Oh no you don't!"

The men were impressed, too, but in a different way. They had expected lavish hospitality, of course, and, since Gwen Mortimer was involved, they knew it would be refined. But they had also expected Freddy to seek a return for this investment – hints about joining the Masons, or about being put up for this club or the other ... or just that certain look in the eye which says, "And when am I to dine at *your* table?" Yet there was none of it. Quite the contrary, in fact. Somehow he managed to suggest that *he* held the secrets *they* should be trying to worm out of him. Many a hardened capitalist there was surprised to hear himself passing on, "just between ourselves," some useful tidbit – and felt absurdly rewarded by the shrewd nod and smile which greeted it. Such confidences are in themselves a sort of invisible investment; Freddy ended the evening with half a dozen new supporters of that kind, none of them quite understanding how it had come about.

As to the main purpose of the affair – the meeting between Lord Monckton and Sir Clive Mortimer, which took place over billiards – that, too, was successful in the immediate sense. While Monckton put up a break of forty-seven, Clive was provided with all the facts he needed for a strong approach to the Foreign Office, not simply on behalf of the yet-to-be-built Oxley field gun, but for the welfare of the still-infant steel industry as a whole.

In the long term, though, the occasion proved abortive. Eight months later, by which time the Oxley gun was built and undergoing its trials, the Austrians gave the contract to Creusot in France.

"A political decision, naturally," Clive said. "They'll regret it. But I'm sorry for you, young'un."

He thought Freddy hid his disappointment well. Actually, all Freddy was hiding was his delight. He had been beside himself with the worry that he might just possibly win the Austrian contract, for he was beginning to realize how much capital was involved in the iron and steel industry. The chemical side of his business was a very modest bidder by comparison. If he had been given the contract, he would have been forced to go into the market looking for capital; and that was the one thing he was determined never to do. While he lived, The Oxley Co. would have but a single owner; he would be answerable to none but himself.

In fact, during those first years, Freddy underestimated just about everything, except his own stamina and determination. He grievously underestimated the capital his business might consume, the time it would take to develop each gun or each new explosive compound, the loyalty of yesterday's satisfied customers ...

There were occasions when he needed to be three people – and he could wish that Ann's eccentric judgement on him was indeed true. He ought to be in Europe to conclude negotiations with some foreign supplier ... but just then Guzman Blanco would want him to advise on certain aspects of Venezuela's industrial progress ... or the laboratories were finding it impossible to stabilize Oxlite, the newest and most powerful explosive in the world. There was always an actual or incipient crisis of that kind in the air.

Several times over those years the strain of it proved too much, even for him, and he went down with colds and thrush and sore joints and aching gums – a hotch-potch of debilitating symptoms that added up to nothing the doctors could put their fingers on. So they bled him for safety's sake and left him in a state of exhaustion that usually worked the cure. The convalescence was the worst part. He fretted constantly to be up, and Emmy had to be quite severe with him, scolding him for being such a child and for having no consideration for others. He compromised with her to the extent of having a specially adapted draughtsman's table fixed to his bed and indulging in an orgy of new designs. As in that forest clearing near Zic-Zac, all his best ideas came to him when he withdrew a little from the hurly-burly of the business.

Curiously enough whenever he returned to the office, he found that all the usual problems had come and gone, solved without his aid. "Why didn't you tell me about this?" he would demand angrily, holding up some two-week-old memorandum warning of an impending calamity in the works. "Read on!" they would reply with a smile. "We had it well in hand, as you will see." And it was true. He grasped the obvious conclusion to be drawn from such incidents yet he lacked the final dash of courage to apply it. He still felt he needed to be in daily touch with every branch of his creation; it had become an extension of his own nervous system. He had eyes in Europe, the Americas ... ears in Turkey, India; when he flexed his muscles, things moved in the Cape, in China ... in places he could hardly locate on the globe. He could not bear to be isolated from a single thread of that sprawling, ever-growing empire.

But those episodes revealed one thing to him at least. He had somehow managed to gather around him a team of associates who were competent, dedicated, and almost as hardworking as himself. They had to be in order to survive. Like many an autocrat – and he was certainly that – he quite admired people who stood up to him. Many had been too frightened and they had fallen away. Those who had the courage were the ones who, after half a decade of this unconscious winnowing process, remained. It made for a rough ride at times, especially when his brightest ideas were taken mercilessly to pieces and none of his past successes were allowed into the balance. But the company thrived on it, and so did Freddy. It became his world. Nothing mattered unless it could be related to the business. Ann was just a name; Miss Kate a distant memory. Lawrence and Angelica went through all the usual dramas of childhood, but the events surrounding their births were by now mere echoes of long-forgotten disquiet.

From time to time people asked after Mrs. Oxley. It became convenient to explain her travels abroad in terms of her health. In the local mind Ann became a permanent invalid, hastening in darkened carriages or cabins from spa to watering hole, and specialist to specialist. Even Lawrence, who had grieved bitterly at the loss of her, gave up asking in time.

Before the business was two years old they moved – only a hundred yards or so up the road, it is true, but the house, Hob's Hall, was much the biggest in the street. It had stood there long before the suburb was laid out. Emmy seemed to expand with it. She had been badgering him for months about the need for larger premises, telling him how absurd it was for someone in his position to go on living in a little suburban villa. Objectively she was right, but his reasons for the delay were the same as those that had made him so modest at that first dinner he gave. In social matters he would always lag behind people's expectations, just as in those of business (or so he hoped) he would always leap ahead of them.

Emmy, too, discovered the secret of survival close to Freddy. The house was *hers*. He trespassed in the running of it only at her whim. Though never impertinent she bossed him about the place without compunction, complaining about candle-grease and soup stains and mud brought in on his shoes; she called him "bonny lad," which amused him, though it scandalized Clive and the dowager; but she ran the house so that everything lay exactly where he would put his hand to it, and never a whisper of the servants' discords or jealousies was allowed to reach him.

And every night, whether he retired at ten or in the small hours, she was there with the cup of cocoa and the day's small-talk to fill his mind and to blanket the eternal problems of the business. Sometimes there was nothing to say. Then they would sit, three-quarters facing each other, he in bed, she in her chair, and stare into space or at the flame of the oil lamp. Then he would glance surreptitiously at her and tell himself how little difference it would make to their lives if he and she were man and wife. He often wondered if she felt the same.

He remembered how Miss Kate had come into his room that time, with just one notion in her mind – and how hard it had been to convince her he was not the sort of machine that other men had taught her to expect. How different it would be with Emmy! She would need no such explanation – indeed, he doubted if a thought of that nature had ever crossed her mind. She was the most relaxing woman and the best company he had ever known. When she drained the dregs of her cocoa and said goodnight, the loneliness that followed was often acute. He longed to ask her to stay but dared not risk the misunderstanding it might cause; if she took it amiss, all the good things in their relationship would be swept away for ever.

Even so, there were moments when she would look back over her shoulder as she stood at the door, when he would almost swear she was willing him to ask her to stay. Perhaps she felt lonely, too? Perhaps she wondered if there wasn't some way of suggesting that she stay – but without raising unworthy thoughts or suspicions. How could one ever tell?

Early in 1881 both Ann's parents died within weeks of each other. With the first real money he had made, Freddy had settled a pension on them, as, indeed, he had on his own father (his mother by then being also dead). He had also bought them a life tenancy of their cottage and four acres, all of which now reverted to Olton End Farm.

He wished there were some way of letting Ann know, but she had severed all links with her former life. He wrote to the owner of the Marine Hotel, explaining the situation and enclosing a letter for her in case The Angels ever returned there. Her parents' effects were put into boxes and stored in his attic.

His tenure of Hob's Hall was no more than two years old when Emmy once again began pressing him to move to an even larger place. And not just *any* larger place, either, but to the magnificent Valiant House, set amid two hundred landscaped acres in Elmdon Park. It had been untenanted for a year and she had heard the lease could be got cheap. In a way Emmy was right. Hob's Hall was still too small – large enough for a vicar, perhaps, or for a rising young doctor with half a fashionable practice still to build, but absurdly small for a man who was by now one of the most thriving private industrialists in the Midlands – indeed, in the entire country. Had it not been for the facility afforded by the Mortimer dower house, he would have been forced to move a year earlier.

But that facility – and, even more, the lady who provided it – could not simply be ignored. If he took Valiant House, it would look distinctly odd for him to go on using the dower house for his entertaining; people would resent it. But if he then transferred his entertaining, the dowager would be furious. One of the very purposes of her existence would be removed.

So, for once in his life, he decided to allow a problem to grow until the weight of it became insupportable. He dithered so much over the decision that Emmy had to hold her tongue for fear of becoming shrewish on the subject. But, after two further years the matter could no longer be postponed. Even Freddy admitted it. The modesty of Hob's Hall was damaging his reputation. Some were calling him a miser; others were saying that The Oxley Co. was by no means as prosperous as appearances might suggest.

In a sense it was true, though not in the way that gossiping tongues might intend. They were now selling the Oxley Mark III Light Field Piece. The Heavy Rear Battery Gun, which had a range of several miles, had finished its development and was now entering production to a five-year order book. The new explosive, Oxlite, had impressed both civilian and military customers; the Navy was keen to use it because one of its forms was impervious to water. And mining contractors couldn't get enough of the fast-burning Oxlite fuse, which they liked for the same reason. On the surface, then, the business looked good. Yet, apart from a few trial pieces sent to the Imperial German Army, they had made not a single sale of large ordinance to any of the great European powers.

If Freddy had not known Clive better he would have

suspected the government of thwarting sales to what were, after all, potential enemies. But Clive assured him it was not so. He even arranged a meeting between Freddy and the chancellor of Her Britannic Majesty's Embassy in Vienna, who gloomily told him that trade in most of Europe, especially in arms and ammunition, was riddled with bribery and corruption; the farther east one went, the worse it grew. The Ottoman ministers were so deep in corruption that you could sell them waggon-loads of rust if only the "oil of angels" were copious enough. The chancellor's purpose was to warn Freddy to stay out – not to defile the fair name of a British firm with such dealings – so Freddy held back the one question that almost burned his tongue, namely, "Where can I get lessons?"

He was obviously going to have to scout the territory for himself. This decision coincided with pressures to move to the still untenanted Valiant House – and also, as it happened, with Lawrence's Easter vacation from Eton. Freddy decided that a brief "holiday" – the first of his life – was in order. They would begin in Vienna, then move on to Constantinople, and thence ... who knew where?

CHAPTER FIFTY-TWO

THE VIENNA OF 1883 was the heart of the world. By comparison London was a comfortable provincial town, as solid and un-exciting as her menus. Paris was an exhausted jade picking herself up from the last binge of revolution and waiting nervously for the next. Berlin was no city at all, just a pompous stage setting hastily thrown together over the past two decades to express the imperial ambitions of the Kaiser – a sprawl of stucco and plaster façades behind which her proud, impoverished burghers led lives of desperate meanness. Rome was still the medieval city of a medievally divided nation, her ancient ruins haunted by hope and malaria in equal proportions.

But Vienna ...

Even Freddy, whose judgement of any city, home or foreign, tended to be strictly utilitarian, sensed it every time he visited; nothing else could explain the affection he still felt for the place despite the many rebuffs and disappointments it had served him. Yet, as he now realized, he hardly knew the city at all. Indeed, the first few times, his business had kept him entirely in the suburbs. The army agency for the purchase of small arms had then been housed in the Artillery Arsenal, two miles south of the centre. For convenience's sake he had stayed at the Victoria hotel in Wieden, halfway between the Arsenal and the West Station; the name "Victoria" had a reassuring ring to an Englishman – and it was only half the price of the city-centre hotels. Thus all he had seen of Vienna was the largely industrial quarter between Neubau and Margarethen. His later attempts to build on his successful small-arms sales by seeking orders for field pieces had taken him to the Rudolf Barracks at the northern tip of the old city, but even then he had continued to stay at the Victoria, where he felt at home; so he still knew no more of the place than could be seen from the windows of a hackney carriage.

One of the purposes of this visit with Lawrence was to remedy that deficiency.

"Just look at those ramparts!" Lawrence said the moment they stepped outside the West Station. The hundred-and-eighty-year-old defences stretched away in the early-morning light, north and south, curving around the western suburbs.

Freddy smiled and shook his head. "They may look impressive enough but a direct hit with just one of our latest shells would knock it flat. So take a good look, my boy – never again will anyone in his right mind ring a city with stone like that."

"We're spoiling everything," Lawrence commented.

"That's a demonstration I'd love to mount for them!"

Freddy had decided not to stay at the Victoria this time. Industrial suburbs are pretty much the same the world over. Instead he had consulted friends at his club, particularly Clegg-Pearsen, a most experienced traveller.

"Remember," the man had told him, "for all their

cosmopolitan charm, the Austrians are not and never will be a truly civilized people. When one of their emperors dies, d'you know what the blighters do? They pull out his guts and bury them in the cathedral. Then they cut the heart out of him and put it in the Augustine church. And the rest – for what it's worth by then – they inter in the Capuchin church. See what I mean? They're nothing but orientals, for all their pride. Scratch off the veneer and the old barbarian shines through. Speaking for myself, I never feel happy staying actually *in* Vienna. Keep them at arm's length – that's what I say." He had then offered a number of suggestions.

Freddy had settled on the hotel at Kahlenberg, up in the Vienna Woods, some five miles north of the city – a good enough "arm's length," he supposed.

The cog railway up from Nussdorf was planned but not yet capitalized so they had to take a cab all the way to Grinzing, thence along the valley to Himmel, where an extra horse was spanned in for the steep climb up by way of Vogelsangbirge. What with the detours they had made in the city, stopping off for lunch and a walk in the Prater, they did not reach Kahlenberg until late that afternoon. There, after tea, they saw what made the long journey across the city and up into the mountains worth every extra kreuzer it had cost. First they strolled among the trees to the Leopoldsberg, the last spur of the Vienna Woods; there the steep fall to the Danube, nine-hundred feet below, was spectacular enough. But on their return, the view of the evening sun from the terrace of the Josephsdorf castle made all the rest forgettable.

Vienna herself lay at their feet, her old stone buildings glowing with a pale rose colour that grew stronger with the sinking sun. Beyond lay the vast plain of the March, suffused with a dark, verdant green, testament enough to its amazing fertility. Snaking across it and turning away eastwards, the blue of the Danube fell into blackness, as if its flood plain, the far, wide Puzta, had devoured all the light from the vaulted sky above. Farther eastward still the Carpathians were slowly turning from gray to violet. Their great buttresses of stone seemed liberated from the earth; they hovered tremulously just above it, fearful to wander. And to the southwest, toward the fading day, the far-off Styrian Alps began to glow with a supernal red, an oriflamme that no degree of familiarity could make seem real.

Freddy stood there, wishing he had the words to express a hundredth part of the wonder such a panorama stirred within him. He remembered a sunset in Caracas, that first evening there, in the forest with Firey Knuckles. Memories of Ann at Calley Homfray's villa in Tuscany hovered at the edge of his mind.

He looked at Lawrence and saw that he, too, was stricken mute by it all. A little pang caught at his stomach; for the first time in years he saw a trace of Clive in the boy – that calm Etonian confidence and the unmistakable tilt of the·head that went with it.

It was Eton, of course, he told himself. Not Clive. Just coincidence.

He was about to return his gaze to the view below when a movement farther up the terrace distracted him. A woman stepped out from behind a piece of topiary and stood at the balustrade. She, too, was transfixed by the view.

He saw at once that it was Miss Kate but could not believe his eyes; he thought it was some trick of the light, coupled with the slightly unreal state induced by the splendour of the scene. Then she turned toward him, giving the kind of casual glance strangers give one another on such occasions; but this casual glance turned into a riveted stare.

He felt sure then, though her face was in the shade and all he could see at this distance was the line of gold laid upon her by the lowering sun. "Lend me those binoculars a moment," he said to Lawrence.

"What is it?" Lawrence was astonished to see his father turn them upon the woman, who was openly staring at them. He was even more astonished when his father raised his hat and shouted, "Hello!"

"May I ask who?" he asked as they began to walk toward her.

"When I knew her she was a Miss Kate Kendall. I met her in the West Indies when I was seeking your mother. In fact, she was quite a help to me. She could ask questions I couldn't."

"What sort of questions?"

"She's American but she's all right. In fact, it was she, not

I, who finally discovered your mother's whereabouts." They were very close by now. Freddy raised his voice and called to her: "I've been looking everywhere for you, Miss Kate! I still owe you forty pounds."

With laughing eyes she ran to him and impetuously threw her arms around his neck, giving his ear a light kiss. "Oh Mr. Frederick! Don't ever change!" Then she looked beyond him and saw Lawrence, watching them with his mouth agape. She winked at him and pushed Freddy to arm's length. "And nor you have – you've not changed one bit. But don't tell me this is young Lawrence!"

Freddy stepped aside, still holding her arm. "Lawrence – come and meet ..." He hesitated, turning to her. "Is it still Miss Kate Kendall?"

She grinned as if that were the cleverest thing. "It surely is."

"Miss Kate Kendall. And this is young Lawrence Oxley – who gets less young every day."

"Don't we all."

They shook hands gravely. Then Kate laughed. "Well, Mr. Frederick, he didn't get his good looks from you!" She misread the fleeting pain in Freddy's eyes and laughed again, chiding him. "I mean *your* good looks are quite a different kind! Oh my mouth! My mouth! How long have you been in Vienna?"

"We've just arrived. This is our first stroll."

"But that's astonishing – we've been here three weeks. Next week and you'd have missed us. Where are you staying? We're at the hotel in Kahlenberg."

Freddy's incredulous laugh told her they were staying there, too. But his question was, "Who, if I may ask, is *we*?"

She looked uncertainly into his eyes, checking first the right then the left, as if each might convey a different message. "Oh – the things I have to tell you! But where to begin?"

Lawrence, taking a hint, said, "Well I'll just toddle back and start dressing for dinner, pater."

Freddy nodded but Kate said quickly, "No – don't do that. I'll explain why. Let's just walk up and down, huh? Whooo! All this is just starting to reach into me. Are you *real*?" She touched him and laughed again.

He took her arm and they began walking back the way he and Lawrence had come, toward the Leopoldsberg. Lawrence hung behind until she half-turned and beckoned him to join them. She took his arm and let each man feel he was her chief support. When they reached the end of the terrace she wheeled them around; in this way they strolled back and forth several times while she told him her story.

She began by reminding him of the night their search for Ann had ended in Georgetown, Barbadoes. She said nothing of the thoughtless trick she had played when Ann had come to bid him goodbye. She merely explained that, their search being over, she had taken the next boat out – bound, as it happened, for Rio. Imagine her surprise, the followng morning, when, while taking a turn on deck, she saw Ann standing at the rail with the tears running down her cheeks.

There was some further editing at this point, gliding over the explanations that passed between her and Ann (which had, in any case been fictions), and coming at once to the heart of the matter. "The Angels had done pretty well since they started, so much so, they figured they needed some kind of a manager, someone to fix the bookings up ahead, write the contracts, gouge the geld, count the baggage in and out ... that sort of thing."

"Surely they could count their own bags," Freddy objected. Then he caught her eye. "Oh, you're joking."

She laughed. "Only very slightly, I do assure you. Musicians! Anyway, the only reason they hadn't already hired a manager was they didn't want a man busting in on the sorority. So ... by the time we reached Rio, guess who was their new manager! And guess who still is – no longer so new, mind you. Oh, have I aged in this job!"

Freddy swallowed hard. "So ... when you say *we* ..."

She nodded and watched him carefully. No one looked at Lawrence, who was aghast.

"And you're at the Kahlenberg?"

"All six of us. This is the end of our first European tour, here in Vienna. Why did you pick just that hotel, Mr. Frederick – out of all the city has to offer?"

He waved his hand across the view. "Because I suspected there might be this ... godlike prospect. Why did you?"

"I didn't. Not me personally. It was Rosie. She found out Mozart wrote *The Magic Flute* here." She laughed. "I guess our reason's not really so different from yours – just a different approach. Also Beethoven, you know."

He frowned. The name was famous. He'd noticed it on a plaster bust someone had donated to the club.

"The composer," she added.

"Ah – that Beethoven!"

She chuckled, thinking he was joking, and waved a hand at the treetops below them. "His house is somewhere in there."

Freddy, unsure as to whether or not Beethoven was still alive, nodded knowingly.

Kate cleared her throat delicately and said, "I think, Mr. Frederick, you ought to prepare yourself for the possibility that you've already received the warmest welcome you're going to get today."

Freddy leaned forward and, glancing nervously at Lawrence, gave him a brief, cool smile.

The boy stopped dead, forcing them to stop, too. His look of incredulity shaded rapidly into anger. "For heaven's sake!" he said sharply. "*She's* the deserter!"

Freddy counted down his fury.

Kate stepped nimbly between them. "Do I stay here," she asked Freddy, "and try to help Lawrence understand? Or do you do that while I go back and warn Ann?"

"Understand?" Freddy asked warily.

"Well yes. In a way Lawrence is absolutely right. I can certainly see his point, can't you? Ann *is* the deserter. Except that we both know" – here, though still ostensibly talking to Freddy, she turned her eyes on Lawrence – "that in the real world of grown-up men and women nothing is ever quite so cut-and-dried as all that. I'm sure if it was explained to Lawrence, he'd see it." Now she turned back to Freddy and, nodding her head toward the boy, said, "He's no child anymore."

All Freddy's anger had evaporated. In some obscure way he felt she had rebuked them both. "I'll try," he promised. "You go ahead and tell her."

Lawrence just stood there and watched Kate go; he could not take his eyes off her.

CHAPTER FIFTY-THREE

"FREDERICK, MY DEAR! How simply marvellous to see you again!" Ann came down the last flight of stairs like a prima donna, her arms open wide to welcome him and everyone else in view. Behind her were the rest of The Angels, smiling politely, looking abstractedly about them, eager to be off.

She kissed him continental fashion, left and right, merely grazing their cheeks together. Her hair was black now and she wore a heavy perfume, musky rather than sweet. There seemed to be nothing left of the Ann he had known except for the enigmatic look in her eyes, which could seem both innocent and all-knowing, baffled and wise, at once.

"And Lawrence," he said, standing aside.

She saw the boy stiffen. She shook his hand, then took it between both of hers, saying, "You've forgiven me by now, I hope."

"Of course," he answered awkwardly and withdrew his hand.

She looked happily at the pair of them. "Are you coming to see us tonight?"

Lawrence was amazed that of all the questions she might have asked she chose that.

"Is it your grand finale?" Freddy wanted to know.

"No, that's tomorrow."

"Oh we'll come to that then. We'll feel fresher."

"Lovely! Wonderful! If you should change your mind, we're at the Hirschberger in the Prater."

"But I'll stay and have dinner with you two boys," Kate said. "I'm strictly a daytime Angel now."

"Let's meet over breakfast tomorrow," Freddy suggested to Ann.

"I'd adore that. Ten o'clock. I'll get up early. Must bolt now."

She was halfway to the door when Freddy caught up with her. "I was sorry about your parents," he said awkwardly. "This is my first chance of ..."

Ann was awkward, too. "These things happen. You were very good to them, I know. I was so grateful even if I didn't actually write and say so. That was a sweet letter you sent me after ..."

"Oh good, you received it. What am I to do with your parents' things?"

She looked surprised, then trapped. "I don't know. I don't know."

"It's all right, dear, we'll talk about it another time."

Inspiration struck her. "Sell them and put the money toward Angelica's dowry. Oh Lord, I feel so guilty about everything."

"No don't distress yourself. I shouldn't have asked."

They exchanged shy smiles. "I simply must fly," she repeated.

"I know." He returned to Miss Kate and Lawrence.

When they were in the carriage Maria Dawson, referring to the earlier, more public conversation, said, "You handled that rather well."

Ann nodded glumly. "It's only the beginning, though."

Lawrence's coolness had shaken her. She knew he was fifteen by now but she had not expected him to be so tall and self-possessed. Nothing remained of the ebullient, assertive, outgoing little lad she had known. But then how much remained of the Mrs. Oxley of Hob's Gardens, either!

The sight of him had disturbed her at deeper levels, too. Though he bore little physical resemblance to Clive, she saw at once those qualities which Freddy had glimpsed and suppressed on the Josephsdorf terrace. It cut through all her defences. Clive had just turned nineteen when she had met him; the sight of Lawrence revived not memories but emotions.

At dinner, after Kate had caught up with all of Freddy's news, she turned her charm on Lawrence. Watching them, Freddy began to realize what the boy's life had lacked since Ann had left – that feminine engagement and interest in his thoughts and achievements. Emmy had always been there for the big emergencies, of course, but that wasn't the same thing as the minute and dedicated interest Kate was now showing.

She sounded as if she were making no more than light conversation, yet she drew from him ideas and admissions that amazed Freddy. He'd always known that Lawrence was interested in history, but now it seemed he knew the story of Vienna almost stone by stone. He had "swotted it up" before they came away; yet not a word of it had he spoken while they were driving through the city. He also seemed to know quite a bit about music. And geology. And almost anything Kate cared to draw him out on.

She, as always, proceeded by inspired guesses. "Watching you walk today," she told him at one point, "you looked to me like a man who's good at gymnastics – or fencing, maybe?"

Lawrence gave an embarrassed little laugh. "As a matter of fact I got my house colours in foil and epée this last half."

"You never told me!" Freddy said.

He shrugged. "I didn't want to seem boastful, pater."

"Well what else has happened? Are you perhaps a Windsor page? Or Head of Boats? Have you been elected into Pop?"

Poor Lawrence was red as a radish by now. "Of course not!" he muttered.

"Well when these things happen, I do hope you'll let me know. I'd be sorry to hear about it first from the butler."

"Your son is a man to watch, Mr. Frederick," Kate warned. "Just when you think he's lost behind you, suddenly he's a half-mile out in front."

Freddy shook his head. "Yes – I had no idea I'd raised such a dark horse."

A short while later Lawrence, feigning exhaustion, made his excuses and retired to his room. There he stuffed a bolster in his bed, to look as if he were asleep in it, and left the hotel by a side door. The paschal moon was nearing its fullness, casting enough light for him to run down the path to Nussdorf, where he caught a train into the city. From the Franz Josef station he walked along the bank of the Danube, a mile or so, skirting the old city until he reached the Aspern Bridge. He crossed the river and walked the remaining half mile to the Prater-Stern, the meeting point of all the major thoroughfares. There, for the first time, he had to ask directions. Another of the things he had "swotted up" before leaving England was a map of Vienna. The directions he now sought were for the Hirschberger café.

"What a splendid son you have, Mr. Frederick," Kate said as soon as Lawrence had retired. "At the risk of sounding disloyal, I'll tell you I think Ann is loco. I truly do."

"Call me Freddy," he suggested.

"Oh no, I'm much too fond of Mr. Frederick. You'll just have to put up with that."

"It was all right when you were that worldly-wise little waif in Georgetown, but now ..."

She gave a little wriggle of delight and grasped his hand. "Oh yes – do tell me about me now." When he hesitated she added slyly, "Am I still your kid sister?"

The laughter eased his awkwardness. "Certainly not. I suppose you always were remarkable, except that you hadn't had much of a life ... I mean, not the right opportunities to show it. But watching you with Lawrence just now, and at Josephsdorf this afternoon ... well, you can certainly manage people. I'll wager you're the best thing that ever happened to The Angels. You said I haven't changed – and unfortunately I think that's true. I don't suppose I ever ..."

"Oh listen!" she protested.

"But *you!* You've really thrived on it, Kate."

She pouted at the name.

"All right – *Miss* Kate if you insist. All the charm and ... and – yes, beauty ... that were hidden in you – oh, I'm no good at this sort of talk. D'you mind if I have a cigar? Is there a smokers' lounge here?"

She put on her wrap and they went out on the terrace. The whole of Vienna, a diadem of twinkling jewels, was spread out before them. In the relative dark it was easier for her to say, "I may talk a little skittish, Mr. Frederick, but don't think I'm not grateful."

He remembered the money he still owed her. In fact, he almost mentioned it.

"You were the first person in my life who treated me like a human being. To my mommy and daddy I was just a ... a *thing* they had to beat the catechism into. And the sisters. Then everyone else either saw me as a gold mine or ... some place to get an itch scratched. But to you I was a person. A *real* woman. You gave me back that feeling I was real. Right from that very first evening. Remember that dinner I took you to?"

He chuckled.

"You know what I wanted to do right after that? Kiss you! I was horrified – well ... horrified and then kind of sad. Because I hadn't any of *those* kind of kisses left, you see. And then that other night, in Saint Pierre, when you said I was your sister – well! That was like as if I'd had my hair over my eyes all my life and you just ... pulled it away."

Freddy puffed at his cigar, wondering whether he ought to say anything. At length he asked, "Why did you run away, when we found Ann at the Marine that night?"

Kate hesitated. She was close to confessing the truth but could not quite bring herself to it. She told him a different truth, the one that would have ruled if only she had not played that idiotic joke. "I saw you and Ann go out arm in arm and I knew I had to get out of your life and then I realized I couldn't possibly go back to the old life. Ann says we've all got pictures of ourselves inside us. You gave me a new picture to live up to, and then when I had to think what will I do now, I saw the old picture for the first time in months and I just ran from it. I just ran."

"Leaving me owing you forty pounds," he said.

Kate laughed until the tears ran, until people looked at them askance. "Ever since we met again this afternoon," she said as she calmed down again, "I've been looking for something you and that son of yours have in common. And now I see it. You both *hold* things inside you. Different kinds of things, I know. But you both do it."

Freddy puffed contentedly. "You were marvellous with him. Watching you I began to realize all the things he's missing, not having a mother."

She paused before she responded. "I don't think you should let your hopes grow any, Mr. Frederick. Not in that direction."

She watched him mastering his annoyance and realized it was something he did quite often. She had imagined he would collect a bunch of yessirs around him; now she saw he had not. He was an even rarer man than she had always known him to be

– one with strong ideas and a burning will to succeed, who nevertheless *listened*.

"It can't be much of a life ..." he began.

"Have you heard The Angels?" Kate interrupted.

He shook his head.

"Well they are good. They're the best. I tell you – after this European tour my job's a shoo-in. I'll be fighting off the bookings from this on."

"Even so – always on the move. Hotels, hotels, hotels – a different one every few weeks. I travel on business, too. So I know."

Kate chuckled and shook her head. "No sir! You don't know. I've seen some bad acts these last five years. I mean people who ... you'd wonder how they can even bear to look at themselves in the mirror. But it's all worth it for that one short moment when the limelight is on them and they're standing centre-stage. Now if that's how it is when you're *bad*, can't you imagine how it is when you're good? I've seen Ann go on with a raging toothache. And come off with it. But in between – while she was up there – nothing! So you could be as rich as J.P. Morgan, I don't think she'd come back to you."

He gave her a curt little smile and nodded. She liked that – the way he wasted no time on dead ends. Her eyes were accustomed to the dark by now; she could see every change in his expression.

"So what's next?" he asked. "You say Vienna's the end of your tour."

"Uh huh. We're all taking a six-week vacation and meeting up in Alexandria."

"Why Alexandria?"

"Oh, some of the girls are going to Italy and Egypt. And two are going to Greece. And Ann and I are going to the Holy Land and then down to Petra and back across the Sinai by camel. Won't that be something! All my life, ever since I saw those bible pictures, I wanted to travel in an eastern caravan." She watched the ideas forming just behind his eyes. "What are you scheming now?" she asked.

He was surprised. "Was it so obvious?"

"To me."

"I must be more careful. I was just thinking – on these

travels of yours, you wouldn't want to be bothered with Lawrence, I suppose?" He saw the doubt in her eye and added, "Just him. Not me."

"But this is supposed to be your vacation with him. Don't you want to get to know him? You haven't made much of a fist of it so far."

He pulled a face. "Until this evening I'd have disputed that. But I think it's more important for him to be reconciled to his mother – and this is the only chance. If he still thinks of her as a deserter ..."

"You're not hoping to bring her back that way, are you? Because that wouldn't work either, you know."

"Oh Miss Kate! You're a very direct young woman."

She bowed her head in mock repentance. "Sorry. It's just that I don't want you to be hurt."

He threw away his cigar, half-smoked. "Let's go back indoors. Would you like a nightcap?"

She asked for a Benedictine.

"What d'you say?" he pressed. "About taking Lawrence? Perhaps you and Ann could wander around Vienna with him tomorrow? Make your minds up then. And meanwhile I could go and do a spot of business with the army."

She laughed. "That's your limelight, I guess. That's your centre-stage – a piece of paper saying party-of-the-first-part agrees to supply ten-thousand guns etcetera."

When she put it like that she forced him to understand – at a level far deeper than her earlier words had reached – exactly why he had lost Ann forever, why her true marriage was now, and always would be, with that centre-stage.

Lawrence found the Hirschberger easily enough. It stood immediately before the hall that had housed the Great Exposition of '73. The place was packed. The Zahlmarquer summed up his age and meagre purse at a glance and put him near the back, which pleased him well, for he did not wish his mother to see him. He ordered a Capuzin and Sachertorte and, because the run and the walk had made him hungry again, a Dirndl ice to help it down.

A comedian was reading a string of jokes off little cards, not pausing for laughter, which was, in any case, sparse. Lawrence did not understand a word but he realized that the crowd tolerated the fellow only because he was racing through his act like an express train. He bowed right, left, and centre while he was still telling the final joke. The little string band struck up the closing bars before he reached the punchline, and he vanished to a sporadic clatter of applause and ironic whistles.

Lawrence already burned with shame for his mother. If this was the level of the acts that booked into the Hirschberger, he could just imagine how awful The Angels of Harmony were going to be. Yet something within him was not too distressed at the thought. Her failure would make her human again, accessible to his comfort and sympathy. It would give her a reason for returning home. They could even laugh about it in years to come – mother's idiotic idea that she could thrive and prosper on her own!

He had not long to wait before her humiliation began. The master of ceremonies sprang upon the stage and announced their names, one by one. There was a moment's expectant silence and then, as the first of The Angels, introduced as Miss Maria Dawson, parted the curtains, the applause broke over him. It was deafening. Men and women all around him stood and shouted and whistled and stamped their feet. He wondered the fabric of the building could tolerate such an onslaught.

When his mother was introduced as Miss Ann Howard, he barely managed to stop himself from standing and shouting, "No!"

The first chord of the piano, quickly taken up by the little house band to one side of the stage, brought a silence that was equally stunning. Miss Maria Dawson stood at the centre; his mother was to her left. They began to sing: "Oh sad was my heart when from mountain and glen ..."

A collective sigh went up – and Lawrence sat there, stunned at the revelation. It was not going to be a humiliation but a triumph. The hair rose on his scalp, on the nape of his neck. The voices blended so beautifully, the words carried so crisply, as if to him alone; their tone caught the inner meaning of every phrase and turned it into effortless melody. He sat there, his head bowed, enraptured.

But when he looked up, when he saw that it was indeed his mother standing there, smiling with all the confidence of an artiste who knows she is supreme, he felt a new emotion growing within him.

Anger!

It was so strange, so unexpected, that for a moment he did not recognize it.

That was *his* mother standing there, enchanting all these hundreds of strangers, holding them spellbound with the beauty of her voice. Between them and her he felt a kind of pact, which excluded him as surely as any shutter of steel.

He rose to his feet and, grateful again that he had been placed so far back, stumbled out into the Prater. For ten minutes he simply walked, counting his footsteps, banging his heels down until it hurt. The reverberations shivered up his spine and broke the dwindling melody that still poured from every open window of the café. Passers-by paused to listen, transfixed at the purity and grace of the sound. He wove his way among them until the swish of the evening breeze in the trees above him drowned it.

His mother had no right to be so good, he kept thinking. He had heard his friend's mothers and sisters singing at parties and family entertainments. Their pleasant but uncertain voices had struggled through, *Pale hands* or *Say not that baleful word*, while their eyes had craved indulgence and love and forgiveness and all the other emotions such ordeals are designed to confirm. And whether they managed it well or ill they had all been grateful to step out of the role of chanteuse and become again themselves – dear sister, dearest mama.

But what he had just seen in his mother's eyes – that was the very opposite. Up there on the stage, with that noble, golden sound pouring from her lips, she had become more truly alive than he had ever seen her. He would never be able to forgive her for the fact that she was ten times – a hundred times – more real outside their family, outside their home, outside his life, than she ever had been in it.

He realized he was walking deeper into the Prater. His only way back was the way he had come. The fear that, if he left his return too late, he might meet her in the street or on their way back to Kahlenberg, forced him to retrace his steps at once, forced him to pass the café again. For their finale, and by way of a special tribute to Franz von Suppé, who was actually in the audience that evening, they were singing a selection of songs from his operettas. Lawrence did not recognize the melodies, of course, but he caught their unmistakable Viennese lilt and heard the audience, still beside itself in rapture.

Then, feeling more alone and more truly lonely than at any time in his life, he walked disconsolately home along the banks of the Danube. The black black Danube.

CHAPTER FIFTY-FOUR

AT BREAKFAST Ann's warmth and affection were no more personal than they had been the previous evening. She continued to treat Freddy like some good friend she had known years ago and was delighted to have met again. All her talk was of the success of their present tour; at last, she said, no theatre in the world would be able to close its doors to them.

"The funny thing is I don't remember you ever singing a note," Freddy told her.

"And what about you?" she countered. "You didn't discover all the things you're good at until you actually got into that world. Why isn't that funny, too? When you first went to college you were going to become a leader of the toiling masses."

Lawrence giggled, delighted at the revelation.

Freddy shifted uncomfortably. "I was only his age then. Anyway, it's different for men."

Ann let it go with a little shrug. "I don't know about men and women. I only know about me and you. Let's decide what we're going to do today. Nothing *too* exhausting because you simply have to come and see us tonight."

It was decided that she and Kate would take Lawrence around the city; in fact, *he* took them, rattling off whole pages of Baedeker wherever they stopped. He followed his mother's

example and treated her like a jolly aunt he hadn't seen for
some time. It enabled him to hide his disappointment from her
– or so he imagined.

Frederick had decided to spend the day looking up friends
in the chemistry department of the university. On the way he
happened to pass the War Ministry. He went into the vestibule,
intending merely to leave his card and try to arrange a meeting
for some day next month, when he would be passing through
on his way back from Constantinople. To his surprise he was
asked to wait.

In fact he waited quite a while but the tedium was
punctuated by a series of visits from secretaries of increasingly
exalted grade. Each seemed unable to believe his junior's
assertion that he was, indeed, *the* Mr. Frederick Oxley,
inventor and manufacturer of the Oxley field guns and of
Oxlite. Each apologized that he should have been kept waiting
in such a lowly corridor and then conducted him to an anteroom
still more grand than the one they found him in. He had been to
Vienna many times but he had never before received such
treatment as this.

In what he felt sure must be the ultimate anteroom he
became aware that he was being watched. He gazed uncomfortably about him. In one corner sat another man, also waiting;
he was staring at his boots, deep in thought. In another corner a
clerk was scratching away with a squeaky pen, dipping it
mechanically in the ornate inkwell at the start of every line.
Then, in the corner of his eye, Freddy saw that the door by
which he had entered was slightly ajar. He knew the secretary
had closed it. He clearly remembered the click of the latch. But
now, as he turned his full gaze in that direction, the gap
vanished and he heard that click again. A few moments later he
was ushered in to meet a general who was also a duke. Most
important of all, though, the man knew his gunnery.

General Szep, Duke of Salgo-Torjan, spoke through an
interpreter but he understood Freddy's replies without such
aid. His mind was sharp. He asked all the questions Freddy
himself would have asked in his position. He knew to the last
dot and comma the performances of every weapon in Europe,
from Krupp, Schneider, Armstrong ... He wanted to place
Freddy's guns precisely in that array.

They spoke of products outside the present scope of The Oxley Co., but Freddy had the strong impression he was being prompted to turn his thoughts in those directions – armour plating, fuses with a time delay, new shrapnel projectiles with more accurate altitude fuses. The General closed their discussion by requesting a demonstration of the latest Oxley field guns some time during the summer. They parted with mutual protestations of goodwill and interest. Freddy's mind was now so bristling with ideas that all he wanted was to return at once to Birmingham and develop them. He regretted the necessity to go on to Constantinople – and even the fact that his life and Ann's had crossed yet again.

In the entrance foyer he paused to adjust his cravat in one of the tall mirrors. On the facing walls each glass was staggered so that they would not create infinite perspectives. Glancing obliquely, out of curiosity to see whether or not such a perspective was possible at the very edge of the mirror, he noticed another visitor, also adjusting his dress – or at least that is what he pretended to be doing the moment he saw Freddy's eye upon him. Freddy felt sure that this was the person who had been spying on him through the slip of the door in the general's anteroom. He bent to brush some nonexistent lint from his trousers. Then he retied his shoelace, taking long enough about it to force the other to leave ahead of him.

The man was tall, well built, and elegantly dressed – in a way, too elegantly. The pale gray cravat was well chosen, but the pearl pin that held it was much too large. The silver knob on his cane had a showy diamond stud at its centre. His gloves were left carelessly unbuttoned as if he sought to create a fashionably raffish appearance for which he was at least ten years too old. The one thing all this would-be elegance could not disguise was the man's walk. It was springy, ready to pounce to either side – the walk of a carnivore. He knew Freddy was following him and he did not like it.

He walked down the Burgring, past the museums and the Hofburg, on past the new Opera. There, at Kaerntnerstrasse, he crossed the road and seated himself at one of the tables on the terrace of the Hochleitner Café. Freddy walked up to him as if he intended to speak. The man became tense, staring at the passers-by like one who seeks some familiar face. The fine leather of his gloves almost burst, so tight did he clutch the head of his cane. Without pausing, Freddy swept on by and sat at a table several yards beyond. The man was facing away from him now. His great bull neck added to the aura of ruthless strength that somehow hung about him.

When the Ober came for his order, Freddy put two kreuzer on the tablecloth and pinned them with his finger. "The gentleman in gray, sitting alone, between here and the central opening – does he come here regularly?"

The waiter shrugged uncomfortably.

"At least you may know his name?" Freddy persisted.

The waiter licked his lips. "A man once called him Patriarca," he said reluctantly.

"Is that a name or a title?"

The waiter shrugged again. Freddy let go of the coins and ordered a Nussschwarzer and Linzertorte. Before it arrived, Patriarca was joined by a delicate, pretty young lady who was also slightly overdressed. Patriarca rose to greet her, but the ironic smile on his face suggested that the action was a joke rather than a courtesy. The touch that guided her into her chair was one of ownership; the chair was the one from which he had just risen. When he seated himself again, he could watch Freddy out of the corner of his eye. He was the sort of man, Freddy thought, who did most of his watching that way.

Freddy gave him little chance. He finished his cake and coffee, and, leaving the money on the table, quitted the terrace by the side entrance. The British commercial attaché's office was just around the corner in Kantgasse. He went directly to the house and summarized his interview with the General for the attaché, who naturally offered him cypher facilities. Freddy composed his messages to his deputies and was on the point of leaving when he asked casually whether anyone in the office had ever heard of a person called Patriarca.

"It surprises me that *you* haven't heard of him," the attaché answered. "Is he in Vienna?"

"I believe I've just seen him. He followed me out of the ministry."

The man nodded, as if that fitted well with what he knew of Patriarca.

"May I ask why I should have heard of him?" Freddy continued.

"Perhaps the news hasn't reached you yet. He's a Greek, though some say he's actually Russian. He's lived most of his life in Constantinople. He's tried his hand at nearly everything, most of it illegal."

"Is he rich?"

"Just lately he appears to have become very rich. He claims to represent the Muraviev Cartel."

"Ah! I see why you expected me to have heard of him." The Muraviev Cartel was a group of Russian arms manufacturers. Freddy shook his head. "I doubt this story. The Muraviev would have to be fairly desperate to employ such a man."

"Perhaps they are. Whatever business he's in, he'll pursue it ruthlessly." He smiled. "Now, whether you believe the tale or not, I imagine you'll want to send home a further message?"

Freddy agreed.

Before he left the building he went to a window and looked up and down the street. No one seemed to be lurking about. He returned to the café but Patriarca's table was now occupied by others; he was nowhere to be seen.

By the time Freddy returned to the Kahlenberg to dress for the evening's festivities, he had put the whole incident from his mind. It was a laughing, carefree party that set off for The Angels' final night in Vienna.

This time Lawrence was prepared for the experience. He sat back in his seat, where the shadow of a potted palm fell over the upper half of his face, put the tips of his index fingers together and placed them against his lips in an attitude of a judicious connoisseur, and – sidelong – watched his father.

There was no comedian. Tonight, a pair of jugglers preceded The Angels. The circuslike atmosphere led Freddy to expect the women to sing a few knockabout choruses and a sentimental ballad or two. Nothing prepared him for the musical feast that followed. Lawrence watched familiar emotions pass across his father's face: the slightly patronizing expectation, the happy bewilderment at the rapturous reception The Angels received, even before they had sung a note, the shock at the beauty of the first few bars ... and then the stunned realization that here was singing of an international standard – and that little Ann Howard, farm girl, housemaid, wife and mother, was part of it.

In his bewilderment Freddy looked first at Kate, who winked confidently at him and mouthed silently the words, "I told you!" Then he looked at Lawrence but, unable to see the boy's eyes, and supposing he was watching his mother, looked away again. In that moment Lawrence had seen the grief of a man bereft; swiftly it had shaded into a kind of bleak understanding. If he had not been here himself last night, he would not have comprehended it. He felt closer to his father at that moment than at any time in his life – and, in consequence, so remote from his mother that she might as well have been a stranger.

The finale was the same selection of songs by Suppé, though tonight the great man himself was back at his post at Theater an der Wien. The reception accorded by the crowd was, if anything, even more rapturous. The Angels were almost swamped by bouquets of flowers. By then, Lawrence saw, his father had adjusted to the experience; he was standing and shouting himself hoarse with the best of them. How he envied his father that facility – to see what was sterile and avoid it, to nurse no grudge, to adapt to reality in the twinkling of an eye.

He stood and joined in, wondering if mere practice could teach him the art. His mother saw him and blew him a kiss. He laughed. Perhaps it was possible.

They all went on to a riotous dinner in private rooms at the Roget-Clément in the Casino of the Nobles, where Lawrence entered into the spirit of the thing more than any of them. He understood it better than his father, or even Miss Kate. It was like an end-of-term rag.

The following evening the four of them left for Constantinople. Lawrence had wished for at least another week in Vienna but his father promised him they would make it up on their return, or come back in the summer.

No one could guarantee their safety in the trains that ran beyond the Carpathians, which were often stopped and looted by brigands. But Freddy went back to see General Szep and through him arranged to hire a private sleeping coach, complete with kitchen, dining room, and sitting room, from Count

Szigismondo, one of the perennially hard-up aristocrats of the Old Nobility. He refused the Count's own retainers and chose instead servants recommended by a friend at the British Embassy. This luxurious equipage was to be attached to a series of trains travelling through Hungary and Romania to Constanza near the mouth of the Danube on the Black Sea. From there it was an overnight journey by steamer, down the coast and through the Bosphorus to the imperial city.

The count's carriage was the last word in luxury. Cut glass, polished rosewood with delicate inlays, rococo ceilings, richly patterned moquette upholstery, deep carpets, crisp damask table linen ... nothing was skimped that might help the impoverished nobleman feel at home.

Freddy handled the heavy silk curtains. "Perhaps there's something to this bankruptcy business – something they leave out of all the books," he joked.

"D'you suppose The Angels will ever be rich enough to afford anything like this?" Kate asked Ann slyly.

"As if we'd want it!" she answered.

"Go on!" Kate jabbed her in the ribs. "This beats *our* kind of travel."

Ann sat back and let the deep upholstery embrace her. She made no reply.

After what seemed an interminable wait the train began to move out of the Staadtsbahnhof. Almost immediately it crossed the Donau canal and then the mighty Danube itself. From the high steel viaduct the city was once again a fairy carpet of kindling lights; here and there the darkling outline of a barely lighted palace or an unlit church rose against the dusk, a deeper hue than the humps of the Vienna Woods beyond. Lawrence tried to locate the Kahlenberg but it could have been any one of half a dozen lights. *How temporary everything is,* he thought.

Kate knelt on the sofa and put her head next to his; she pulled one of the silk curtains around them, shading out the carriage lights and leaving them in a little world of their own.

"She's one beautiful city," she murmured to him.

"Mmmm!" In two short days he had grown to like Miss Kate enormously. He wished that she rather than "Miss Ann Howard" were his mother. She was the one grown-up he could talk to.

"She's just beginning to stir herself," Kate went on. "Try and imagine all the life those lights are witnessing!"

The train snaked out over the flats of Marchfeld. Distance lent the dwindling brilliance all the charm of a toy.

"There's the Hofburg," he said. "I wonder what the Emperor's doing at this moment?"

"Working," Kate replied. "They say he never stops."

"And that must be the Opera," he went on. "Everyone must be in their seats by now. I've never been to an opera. I'd love to go. I bet you've been to millions. Can you remember the first one you ever went to?"

"Indeed I can. Your father took me. It was in Saint Pierre in Martinique. *Orpheus and Eurydice*. Oh that was an evening!"

"I know the story." He remembered tedious hours of Virgil and Ovid and Horatio, bitterly grudged at the time but not now. "Orpheus can't talk to her or he'll lose her. But she doesn't understand."

"That's right. They knew things, those old Greeks. More people lose each other through talk than by silence."

He could think of nothing to add.

After a while she said, "Wouldn't you love to be a little bird, Lawrence? A little night bird, so that you could fly in and out of all the lighted windows and see whatever's going on?"

He laughed. It was the fantasy of the perfect life. "You'd be able to understand them," he said. "But they'd never ask you to join in. They wouldn't even notice you."

On through Marchegg steamed the express, now in a dusk that, from the well-lit coach, seemed darkness itself. Only a thin band of paler darkness sat upon the distant Alps, behind the train; but it was enough to reflect upon the marshes and tussocky islands that nudged aside the sluggish waters of the river March. They traversed this dreary waste on a long stone viaduct, with one ringing span of iron.

On the other side was Hungary. As if it had been waiting to greet them, a wild boar dashed along at the foot of the embankment, frantic, ferocious. At last it grew exhausted and stopped. In that instant it must have looked up at their carriage, for the lamps reflected back in its eyes, twin points of an astonishing blood red.

CHAPTER FIFTY-FIVE

LAWRENCE HAD MANAGED TO pick up a German edition of Baedeker's guide to Constantinople before they left the Staadtsbahnhof. With the help of the servants they had hired to go with their carriage he battled his way through it so that by the time they arrived at Constanza, three days later, he knew as much about the Ottoman capital as he had previously learned about Vienna. He had also acquired a smattering of Austrian German. Kate was impressed, and said as much – which encouraged him to go further than he would have done for his own needs. Ann was reminded of Clive, another of those who go through life easily picking up things as they pass. Freddy, who had never considered the boy in a practical light before, began to see that he might one day make a most useful contribution to the business.

At Constanza they paid off the servants and sent them back with the empty carriage. Freddy wanted to keep the maid to serve the two ladies. Kate hesitated but Ann would not hear of it. "One more mouth to feed," she said. "One more body to accommodate. There's nothing she can do that I can't do myself in half the time."

The boat, a steamer called *Colomba*, was waiting at the quayside. They appeared to be the only train passengers for the boat, though there were plenty of Romanians, or perhaps passengers off earlier trains, already aboard. It took an army of porters a good quarter of an hour to argue their ten cases from the quayside onto the ship.

Then, though the sailing time had passed, they waited. The deck hands stood around, ready to cast off; their officer kept consulting his watch.

"What's the delay?" Freddy asked him.

He shrugged and pointed vaguely ashore.

Some five minutes later a carriage drawn by a pair of horses came at full gallop down onto the quay, only just managing to stop in time; two yards more and one of the horses would have piled breast-high into the gangway.

A tall, powerful man sprang from the interior even before it had stopped. He was quickly followed by a young lady of some beauty. The man's walk was unmistakable as they strode up the gangway.

"Patriarca!" Freddy said as the officer briefly joined him at the rail.

The man nodded. "Now we sail."

"Who is he? Why did they delay our departure for him?"

"A director of the company, I suppose." He turned to his deck hands and began the business of casting off.

Kate, who had come out on deck at that moment, observed Freddy's interest and was just in time to see Patriarca and his companion step swiftly across the deck and into the purser's office.

"D'you know him?" she asked.

While they strolled down toward the purser Freddy told her what had happened in Vienna.

"Is it the same woman?" she asked.

"I couldn't be sure."

Kate laughed. "Well *I* know her anyway."

He stared in surprise.

"Sure. I've met her in every port and city in the world."

There was no Patriarca on the passenger list. When Freddy described the man and asked for his cabin number the purser's bewilderment seemed quite genuine. "I assure you, Mr. Oxley, there is no one of that name or description on board."

"I'm talking about the man who delayed the boat's departure. He went in by that door not two minutes ago."

"Ah! A mere courier. He brought a diplomatic bag, that is all."

"And his cabin?"

The purser looked him straight in the eye and said, "He has immediately returned ashore, sir."

Kate pulled at his arm. "Quite like old times!" she said.

They dined early because they all wanted to awaken at five

and watch the sunrise over the Bosphorus. Neither Patriarca
nor his companion appeared for dinner.

The first to arrive on deck next day were Lawrence and
Ann, in time to see the false dawn set the eastern horizon
aglow. It was a bleary pink light that made the hour seem
especially chill. Ann shivered and pulled her furs around her,
clasping them at the neck from inside.

"It'll be another twenty minutes yet," Lawrence said.
"Shall I go below and see if there's anyone about? I might stir
up a cup of coffee."

"You're an utter angel," she told him.

As she watched him go she wondered which of his two
fathers he resembled more – Clive to whom life came easily,
who never planned anything until the situation was actually
upon him and he could see its possibilities – or Frederick, for
whom the objective was far more clear than any of his immediate
circumstances, and who could either brush those circumstances
aside or bend them to his purpose. The lad had acquired the
best of both, she decided, which was why he could afford to
remain so quiet about his gifts and achievements.

Five minutes later he was back with two steaming mugs of
chocolate. By the light of the one feeble oil lamp that guttered
above them she could just make out his hand, offering one of
them to her. "I have a bag of Marie biscuits in my cabin," he
suggested.

"No no. This is divine."

They sipped noisily, to fill the silence and share their
pleasure. They cupped their hands around the porcelain, grateful for the warmth. They stared at the now-darkening horizon,
eager for a sign of the true first light.

"I'm so glad we've met again," Ann said.

"Mmm. Me too."

"Oh go on with you! I know very well you don't approve."

He said nothing.

"I hope you'll understand one day, though. Does your
father ever talk about me?"

"He used to tell people you were travelling to various
places, implying it had something to do with your health."

She chuckled. "In a way it was no lie."

"Lately the subject hasn't come up much."

"He should divorce me. He has sufficient grounds, after all."

Lawrence looked away, acutely embarrassed.

"D'you remember Stockton?" she asked.

"Yes!" The change of subject relieved him. "That steam yacht the pater made. In Albert Park."

"You never knew I took to drink while we were living there, did you."

It stemmed the flood of his enthusiasm. "It's really none of my business," he said awkwardly.

"But it is, Lawrence. Your silent disapproval of me makes it your business. Also the fact that, whatever else you may believe, I do love you and it distresses me to see you repeating the mistakes your father once made. Or some of them."

He held his breath for a moment, then let it out in a rush.

"So, at the risk of boring you or embarrassing you or shocking you – or simply making you angry – there are one or two things I have to tell you." She drained the last of her chocolate and stooped to place the mug in the scuppers, between her feet. The exertion of her rising spilled over into her voice, making it more peremptory than she intended. "You needn't say anything. Just listen."

He stiffened, squaring his shoulders and staring fixedly at the horizon. Pure Frederick.

"Your father saw in me an ideal that I could not possibly live up to. I don't believe any woman could, but that's by the way. The point is *I* certainly couldn't. And when I failed to match that ideal – by coping badly with the household accounts, by taking to ardent spirits, as the doctor called it ... oh, and just generally mismanaging myself and life and things – when I failed, as I say, he was so utterly good and forgiving that I was left feeling doubly awful. Can you understand me so far?"

He did not stir.

"I'm not asking whether you approve – just whether you understand. Well, never mind. Of course in those days it was as if my eyes were still closed. I knew something was wrong with my life but I couldn't say what. There was nothing I could put my finger on. Quite the opposite, in fact. There was I, born the daughter of a farm labourer, sent into service at fourteen, and now the mistress of a fine little household, with an

ambitious and successful husband like your father and a grand
young son like yourself ... what *could* be wrong!"

Lawrence nodded emphatically.

"I couldn't answer that question until I joined up with the
other girls and we formed The Angels. And between leaving
home and meeting them I went through a form of purgatory ...
such depths as I hope you'll never know, Lawrence."

The appeal behind her words frightened him.

"Not that I want your pity, or even sympathy, but I want
you to understand our lives from my point of view."

"*Your* life," he said, like an accusation. "*We* don't seem to
come into it."

She smiled. "Oh darling – can't you imagine what sort of
wife I'd have made these last five years? Can you honestly see
me as your father's hostess – a former housemaid! How many
of the people who sit at his table because of the name Gwen,
Lady Mortimer would come if it were just your father and me!
And if they did, it would just be to laugh at one more example
of Sir Georgius Midas and his social pretensions. My absence
has opened doors to your father that would never have opened
with me at his side."

"But none of this is why you left us," Lawrence said.

She nodded. "I'm just trying to show you that – whatever
my reasons, and whatever you may think of them – my
departure has been an unmixed blessing for your father."

The lad nodded reluctantly and looked away, unwilling to
concede but unable to disagree.

"But you're right, dear. My reasons for deserting you are
strong and selfish, not meek and holy like that." She paused
before she said, "Tell me – you saw us at the Hirschberger.
What did you think?"

He tilted his head and breathed out through his nostrils.
She remembered how Clive had often done that when cornered.

"You heard the crowd that night you came. But you
should have been there the night before! Von Suppé himself
was there and you should just have heard them cheering then!
Can you imagine what it would be like to be as good as that and
yet to be forced instead to do for your father what Emmy does
and what the dowager does?"

"But that's a wife's *job*!" Lawrence insisted.

She withdrew all those tiny, fragile feelers she had reached out toward him. "Yes," she sighed. "You're quite right. It's a wife's *job!*"

"Don't you want to come back at all?" he now felt bold enough to ask. "Not even in the slightest ..?"

"Of course I do. You may find this hard to understand but I still love your father. There'll certainly never be any other ..."

"How can you talk of divorce then!"

"*Because* I love him, you goose. Because I want what's best for him. He should marry again."

"You're right – I *do* find it hard to understand. Very." He stooped and picked up her mug, which he carried indoors.

Dawn was just breaking. She watched it for a while and then, having seen many dawns in many strange lands, walked aimlessly around the deck. Dawns reminded her of aching tiredness and eyes red from cigar smoke. Why she had agreed to get up and watch it she couldn't understand – no more than she could now say why she had agreed to this "family" journey as far as Constantinople?

She found Lawrence leaning against the rail on the *Colomba's* starboard side. The dim outlines of Turkey-in-Europe were just beginning to emerge out of the fading night. She stood beside him saying nothing. He felt her need for his company but could not respond.

"Of course I'm tempted," she said, as if their conversation had not been interrupted. "I hate the endless succession of hotels, and having no home. Tours like the one we've just finished leave one utterly drained. So when your father tells me he's thinking of moving into Valiant House and how successful the business is and how much *more* successful it will be if he secures a good contract here in Constantinople ... well of course I'm tempted. But I know that within three months I'd be screaming to get away again."

The words finally released that element of stubbornness in Lawrence. He found he was able to put his arm around her.

To his surprise – and to hers – she stiffened. She had craved only his understanding. She wanted to see him smile as she continued her life in her own way. But this gesture of his went beyond all that. It was not so much Lawrence's arm that encircled her as a newly budded family tentacle, drawing her back.

"You're saying you have no self-control at all!" Lawrence cried as he snatched his arm away. His voice was filled with anger at her rejection.

She throttled a scream and walked away. After a few paces she turned and said, "You're such a wise *idiot!*"

Kate, who had been hovering in the doorway, now judged it time to emerge. "Darlings! Thank you so much for calling me! Has anyone woken the lord and master?"

A few minutes later Freddy joined them and they lapsed easily into their roles as jolly-family-plus-friend.

It was a glorious sunrise but it was a mere curtain raiser to their first view of Turkey, at the entrance to the Bosphorus. It looked like a country whose people live in endless, idyllic holiday – a series of bright villages, mosques, kiosks, and palaces. The European side seemed the richer, with many country villas; the eastern shore was full of mystery – quiet old Ottoman houses with their grated windows, minarets, and wind towers, and oriental fountains playing in the shade of dark cypresses and ancient plane trees.

The nearer they drew to the city, the more densely packed were the buildings, so there was no precise point at which one could say that Constantinople began. But when the *Colomba* rounded the point at Beylerbey, there it all was, suddenly before them – indeed almost on top of them. An early morning mist shrouded the basin where the waters of the Bosphorus, the Sea of Marmara, and the Golden Horn all mingle. Rising out of it, the three cities of Constantinople appeared to be staring into each other. On the Asiatic shore rose the great amphitheatre of Scutari. Directly opposite, on the European shore, reared Pera, the Christian quarter – tier upon tier of houses and palaces, all so tightly packed together that from this angle the trees and vines seemed to be squeezed upward by the pressure of the crowded stones. And between the two, on a tongue of land beyond the Golden Horn, rose the grand domes and stately minarets of St. Sophia, the Old Seraglio, the Suleimanieh Palace ... in a word, all the mystery and glory of Old Stamboul, ancient Byzantium itself. Though Stamboul is the last city in Europe, it is nonetheless more Oriental than either Pera or Scutari, the two Asiatic cities of Constantinople. Between the three of them, riding at anchor or flitting through the mists, were steamers, sailing vessels, and a myriad kaiks – the gondolas of the Golden City.

The *Colomba*, her engines barely turning over now, slipped quietly past the modern palaces of Cheragan and Dolmah Baghcheh, white as snow right down to their marble quays, before which the three imperial yachts rode at anchor. On she drifted, past the yachts harbour and the Saly Bazaar, where at last the Sea of Marmara itself came into view, smoky, atmospheric, scintillating. Suddenly they were among it all, the bustle, the bright colours, the babble of strange tongues ... the exotic smells that wafted by and were gone. They disembarked at Galata, the boisterous, disreputable district that crowds the foot of the hill of Pera, from where it thumbs its dirty nose at silent, shrouded Stamboul, just across the waters of the Golden Horn.

Freddy wanted to send the other three on to their hotel while he waited to see Patriarca disembark; he had some idea of trying to follow the man. But someone back in England – Clive probably – had been pulling strings. An envoy came from the British Embassy inviting them all to breakfast, so they had no choice but to leave at once. Customs formalities were waived.

There were some dozen English visitors for breakfast that day. Ann said to the ambassador's wife, "I hope we're not discommoding you."

"Four tourists more or less is neither here nor there to me," she answered resignedly.

"You must long for a posting to Tibet," Ann responded with a laugh.

The woman's remark had been carelessly dismissive rather than deliberate. The fact that Ann had turned it so easily aside made the wife look at her visitor with respect. There was, too, a sadness that her official position made it difficult to cultivate such little seeds of human contact.

One very aristocratic party from Surrey – name of King-Penefather – divined Ann's and Freddy's humble origins within seconds and were very nose-in-the-air throughout the rest of the meal. Ann caught Lawrence's eye and smiled triumphantly at him. He took her meaning and conceded the point with a nod. When they took their leave the King-Penefathers pointedly refused to shake hands.

Lawrence took his chance. "By the by," he said over his shoulder. "Have you a young relative in Chavasse's?"

Chavasse's was a junior house at Eton.

"Yes. He's my son," the older woman of the party answered frostily – also with a touch of surprise at the revelation that the son of these two rather common people should be at the same school.

Lawrence now drove the coffin nail home. He broke into a slow smile and said with relish: "Aaaaah!"

He hoped he managed to convey that the young King-Penefather's life would become sheer hell next half. After a few paces he turned back to give her another smile. Judging by the anguished frown on her face, he had succeeded.

"Serve her right," he said with satisfaction.

Kate gave his elbow a squeeze. "There's a hard, determined streak in you," she told him.

Later, after they had settled everything into their rooms, they met on the hotel verandah for a cup of rich, coffee-flavoured mud while they planned the day. Before any of them could speak Lawrence said, "Four is such an unwieldy number. Someone's always fretting to be ahead and someone else is always hanging back for one last look. So I propose to take Miss Kate and show her the *real* Stamboul. Why don't you two do whatever you like and then we'll meet up at dinner and compare notes?"

Ann knew Lawrence's purpose well enough – to throw her and Frederick together in hope of a reconciliation. She shrugged and then, so as not to seem curmudgeonly about it, gave Freddy a warm smile and said it would be delightful.

"You little schemer!" Kate said to Lawrence as they set off for the day. "Ann says your father's nickname was Foxy, but you're ten times worse."

"I don't suppose you're complaining," he said, boldly taking her arm.

Unseen by him she gave a most satisfied smile. "Sure ain't!" she said. "Couldn't have wished it better."

CHAPTER FIFTY-SIX

ONLY MOMENTS AFTER Lawrence and Kate left the hotel, an envoy arrived from the Grand Vizier inviting Freddy to an audience with the Sultan, Abdul Hamid. The description, "an envoy of the Grand Vizier," led Freddy to expect something out of the Arabian Nights, but Mr. Nubar Lotis wore a suit from Savile Row and spoke impeccable French and English. He was an Armenian Christian, in his fifties, florid rather than fat, and blessed with an impressive head of shiny black wavy hair. He was delighted to hear that Mrs. Oxley was of the party; of course His Majesty would consider his house ten times honoured if she would consent to visit his harem while he himself enjoyed the inestimable blessing of Mr. Oxley's company.

Unfortunately, this being Ramadan, the Sultan could not receive him until after sunset, but meanwhile the royal carriage and the imperial kaik were at their disposal, and if they would care to visit the Old Seraglio, he, Mr. Lotis, would do his humble best to act as their guide; they would see many parts of the former palace that were closed to ordinary visitors.

Of course, they accepted with delight.

From the beginning Freddy had his doubts about this Mr. Lotis. He pretended to be a mere guide – little more than an office boy. Yet he radiated power and self-assurance. The whole point of today's jaunt was not to fill the hours until sunset, it was to allow Lotis, and thus the Ottoman government, to size up this potential supplier of arms and ammunition.

They took the royal carriage down to the Top Haneh landing stage, where they boarded the imperial kaik, a magnificent gilded skiff with no fewer than eight oarsmen, and set off

460

toward the private jetty at Seraglio Point. Freddy decided to play no games. "Do you know a man called Patriarca?" he asked Lotis.

He saw a thousand answers flit quickly behind the man's uncertain eyes. Then Lotis laughed. "Of all the nations in the world," he said, "do you know whom we Orientals dread dealing with the most?"

"The Arabs?" Freddy guessed.

The laughter redoubled. "Not at all. No – it is you English. You always come directly to the point and you always mean *exactly* what you say. You've no idea how disconcerting that is to us. Because you always tell the truth, we simply don't know where we stand with you."

Freddy grinned. "But it does help you to avoid answering questions."

"Questions?" Lotis asked innocently.

"Patriarca."

Lotis sighed. "Ah – Patriarca. Well, did you notice a kaik that pulled away from Top Haneh just after we left? Don't look now, but it's the one with the scarlet prow. The man in it is a Russian called Vedyev. He works for Patriarca. I think you must assume, Mr. Oxley, that every action of yours since leaving Vienna has either been observed by or reported to Patriarca."

"That would be expensive," Freddy said. "His commission on sales must be impressive."

"Sales?"

"I understand he's a representative of the Muraviev Cartel."

"You *are* well informed, Mr. Oxley. But in my view the Muraviev offers him only the most temporary of homes. Patriarca will look for" – his eyes lingered in Freddy's – "something bigger."

Freddy nodded. "We must be ready for him then."

Lotis turned to Ann with a gracious smile. "Do forgive us, Mrs. Oxley. How tedious this must be for you."

"On the contrary," Ann told him. "I had no idea my husband's world involved such ..."

He supplied the word she could not find: "Undercurrents?"

"Yes. I thought only my world, the world of the theatre and concert hall, where everybody smiles all the time and calls everyone else darling – I thought only we lived with those undercurrents."

Lotis laughed with delight. Before he met the Oxleys he had expected his day would be dull.

Their landfall was at Kaik Haneh, from where, the day being fine and brisk, they walked around the foot of the ancient fortifications to an enceinte on its western flank, reminiscent of a medieval fortress. There, Lotis rapped on a small, iron-studded door and they were immediately admitted. Beyond lay a scene of incomparable splendour and luxury – the ancient palace of the caliphs of Turkey. Stamboul itself is a city of whispers, but the high walls excluded what little noise there was; a profound silence reigned over all. Cypresses as tall as minarets, and of a green so dark as to seem almost black, towered over ancient plane trees, grotesquely withered and distorted by the years. At their feet tall grasses grew between the disused flagstones. And beyond – a mighty backdrop to dying and resurgent nature – were the galleries of the Seraglio itself, long colonnades in the ancient Turkish style whose verandahs were still covered in their medieval frescoes. Here the ambassadors of old had trembled before the might of the sultan; no one then had dared call Turkey "the sick man of Europe."

Lotis led them back almost to the point where they had landed – except that they were now inside the wall. Crossing the first courtyards they noticed, to their right, a number of impenetrably closed gardens, over whose hedges and walls they could see, amid groves of cypresses, ancient kiosks; though the windows were shuttered, these pavilions had an occupied air.

"Does someone live there?" Ann asked.

Lotis nodded. "Imperial widows ... aged princesses. They live out their days here, a kind of foretaste of paradise, don't you think?"

Toward Seraglio Point they climbed up by marble stair-cases to a lofty, white promenade. "Asia," Lotis declared impressively, waving his hand across the blue expanse of the sea toward the rest of the city. "This is the very limit of Europe."

It amazed them to stand in such quiet solitude at the heart of the mighty city – to watch the kaiks and larger vessels bustling to and fro, and to hear the muted roar of commercial life along the waterfronts. Before they began their tour of the old palace, Lotis pointed silently across the water where a kaik with a scarlet prow rode at anchor; its occupant was pretending to fish.

The first kiosk they came to was closed "even to the Faithful," Lotis explained; it housed the mantle of the Prophet in a case studded with precious stones, all polished but uncut, as is the Oriental way. Then there was the Kiosk of Baghdad, lined with Persian porcelains whose value was now beyond price.

"You see these red flowers?" Lotis pointed to a detail of their painting. "The colour is from real coral. The art of liquefying such corals has been lost."

Freddy thought, *Give me a good modern laboratory and I'd soon find it again!* Ann caught his eye and smiled; she knew well enough what sort of challenge such a statement would pose to him.

The next building, the imperial treasury, had iron-grated windows, like a prison-of-no-recourse. The etiquette for entry was strict and unvarying. The guardian summoned his twenty subordinates, who lined the path, ten to the right, ten to the left. The door required three keys to open it, one held by the guardian and one by each of his flank men. Inside, the grated windows made the rooms rather dark; ten of the guards accompanied them through the chambers.

But here at last they were in the land of the Arabian Nights. No cave of Aladdin or Ali-Baba could match the riches now displayed before them – the hoarding of eight centuries of rulers who, for most of that time, had been masters of the ancient world. As the visitors' eyes grew accustomed to the dark the first things to shine out were the diamonds; their scintillations flashed from every case and rack and tier until they became quite dazzling. By then the objects themselves could be glimpsed – a profusion of them, of every age and all beyond price. Caskets for spices, jewel boxes, gem-studded robes, ceremonial swords ... here were weapons from the time of Yenghis Khan, and even from the days of Mohammed: daggers and scimitars of silver and gold, laden with precious stones. There were golden chests of every size; one was crusted with rubies, another with sapphires. On one table, quite casually, stood a casket carved from a single giant emerald, which must have been as large as an ostrich egg. Another room was filled with coffee services and flagons and pitchers of exquisite form and beauty. Yet another was given over to precious cloths – from tissues of fairylike daintiness to great caparisons of gold thread for camels and horses; also saddle cloths of silver and gold, bordered with flowers of precious stones. At one end stood ancient thrones of state, made for sitting cross-legged in the former royal manner. One was a blaze of rubies and pearls; another was studded with emeralds and sapphires, making it seem to ripple like the sea as they filed past it in wonder.

But the climax was in the last chamber of all, for there, motionless and terrible behind sheets of glass stood the twenty-eight life-sized puppets of the sultans who had ruled between the fall of Constantinople and the end of the last century; as each of them died he was brought here in effigy, wearing his court costume and ceremonial arms. And there they now stood, shoulder to shoulder, grotesquely lifelike, dressed in wonderful brocades embroidered with mysterious designs of occult significance, turbanned in silk with magnificent aigrettes of jewels ... all that wealth forever possessed by, yet forever denied to, the ruler of the day. Entombed in that one huge case of glass, the mannikins were beyond the reach of feather duster or polishing rag. So time had quite literally dulled their brilliance; even the diamonds shone with a yellow, exhausted kind of light.

"Murad the Conqueror," Lotis translated the little etiquette that stood before each figure. "Suleiman the Magnificent ... Mohammed ... Mahmud ... Once men shuddered with dread at the very syllables."

Surveying it all, Ann remembered Sally's jibe about the bourgeois lust for possessions – "a couple of tons of personal rubbish ... you have to clothe, feed, and pay a small army to clean it. And little by little they smash it to pieces." Here, in such palaces as this, was where such fancy bred.

"Well?" Lotis asked as they came out into the sun again.

Freddy shook his head sadly. "They just didn't understand wealth, did they," he said.

"Oh?" Their guide's surprise was genuine.

"Yes – any one of those baubles – I mean, they're very pretty, and don't think I'm ungrateful or anything – but any one of them could have paid for a better harbour, a new bridge, a hundred miles of good military road, schools, hospitals ... This love of gold and jewels and earthly show, it's what killed the Roman Empire in its day – and I'm afraid ..." He looked around him and shook his head. Then he brightened and smiled at Lotis. "But perhaps it's not too late, even yet."

Lotis chuckled. "Perhaps, if we shake our treasury coffers well, we'll find a leftover beshlik or two for guns."

"Pray you do," Freddy advised.

Lotis took them next to an inhabited palace – that is, one kept ready for the sultan, though not once in the past twenty years had he actually set foot in it. The universal white marble steps led up to airy, open apartments with a magnificent view over the entire city and its waters. The rooms had been decorated in the last century, in the French style of Louis Quinze, but with an indefinable Oriental quaintness added to it. There were white and gold wainscots to show off the cerise and lilac brocades, studded with pale white flowers. Every room was lofty, pale, wide – filled with an enormous sense of tranquillity, as if no one had ever raised his voice there.

The etiquette was again strict, but quite passive as far as the visitors were concerned. They simply followed Lotis's lead as the slaves brought handbasins and cool water and towels and Turkish slippers and coffee and sweetmeats. At last they were able to sit. Away to the north, beyond Pera, Lotis pointed out the new imperial palaces of Dolmah Baghcheh and Tcheragan, set amid a whole series of stately older buildings and mosques. Their gleaming images shimmered in reflection over the Bosphorus. Opposite lay Scutari, with its domes and minarets, its vast cemetery and gloomy cypress groves. The rest of the view was filled by the wide blue reaches of the Sea of Marmara across which little grey smudges of steamboats trailed plumes of black smoke.

In a while they were served luncheon. Lotis, not being a Mussulman, ignored the customs of Ramadan and joined them in a mouth-watering succession of small dishes – kabobs, pilaffs, salads of raw vegetables, very crisp and succulent, and yaurt to finish with. He asked Ann if she would like to retire to rest for an hour or so, saying that there was no telling how long this evening's festivities in the harem would go on. She accepted the offer. He and Freddy went out to promenade up and down the verandah.

To the north Freddy could just make out the kaik with the scarlet prow, still at anchor. He pointed it out and said, "Tell me what you know of Patriarca's history."

Lotis began at once, as if he had only been waiting to be asked. "He was born Vasil Petrov, a Russian Jew, though he prefers now to be thought of as Greek Christian – Basil Patriarca. Somehow he has persuaded a Greek priest in a small village north of Athens to furnish him with a genuine baptismal certificate. When he was two his father came here to Constantinople, where he set up as a tailor. But both parents died in an epidemic shortly after and he was left to fend for himself. He was then seven, I believe. Like all this city's jetsam he gravitated pretty quickly to Tatavla." He raised his eyebrows. "You've heard of this place? Tatavla?"

"I think I saw it on the map," Freddy admitted. "It's north of Pera, inland from the modern palaces."

Lotis stared at the city's northern skyline. "Yes, it's just out of sight from here. Never be tempted to go there, my friend. By day or by night. The guides will tell you that *all* of Constantinople is dangerous after dark, but that's just to make you hire them. However, of Tatavla it is true. The entire scum of the Orient and the Mediterranean mingles there. No vice or depravity is so monstrous it cannot be gratified there. And the worst of all, the very dregs of the very dregs, are the *tulumbadschi* – the firefighters."

Freddy turned to him in surprise.

"Oh yes!" Lotis laughed. "In Constantinople the firefighters run to the fires chiefly in order to loot the premises. If they like what they get, they may – as a passing favour, you understand – condescend also to extinguish the flames for you. The *tulumbadschi* taught young Petrov his morals. But he is also clever – oh yes, a most astute man. Quick to learn. He never needs telling twice. He's fought his way to the top of every illicit trade in the Orient – drugs, pearls, guns, women – he controls them all. With these eyes I have seen him kill a man, and that man's only crime was to walk too hastily around a street corner and bump into our hero. He slit the fellow's throat on the spot."

"And the police can do nothing?"

Lotis merely smiled.

"So now," Freddy went on, "he is beginning to yearn for a little respectability?"

"As Basil Patriarca, yes."

"And as agent for the Muraviev Cartel."

"He will be your biggest problem."

It was a moment or two before Freddy realized that this warning was also a confirmation that he had passed whatever scrutiny Lotis was there to administer.

"In what way?" he asked.

"Patriarca has powerful connections here, inside the government. I'm sure you know that politically we are all at sixes and sevens. It's like a silent civil war – after our brief flirtation with democracy. His Majesty is doing his best to take back the reins of power. The parliamentarians try to frustrate him at every turn."

"I feel sorry for those who find themselves caught in the middle," Freddy ventured. "They are in a most delicate position."

Lotis hesitated and then said, "Quite. We Armenians are always caught in the middle, of course. We are, you might say, the middlemen of the world – limping along at ... er ... two percent?"

"Two percent sounds extremely modest."

Lotis struggled to appear extremely modest. Then he chuckled. "Do you know the guns-and-butter scale of political values?"

Freddy smiled. "It sounds as if I ought to."

"In the early stages of a war, guns are more important than butter. But when we say that the war reaches a turning point, that's precisely what we mean – butter is suddenly more important than guns. That is the true moment of defeat. After defeat, butter becomes more important even than loyalty or moral scruples. That is total defeat." Then, in case Freddy had not fully grasped the point, he added, "The same is true of a civil war, of course. Even a silent one."

"What precise form would Patriarca's interference take?"

Lotis shrugged, as if to hint that the forms were too numerous to mention. But he listed a few. "Certain vital parts of your consignments would be mysteriously lost. Your vessels might be intercepted by the Greeks (he has influence there, too, as I said) who would delay them on spurious charges that would take weeks to elucidate. Manifests would be lost. Demurrages would be extortionate. Sailors would jump ship at the last minute …"

Freddy put up his hands. "I understand. And I'm grateful – truly. I shall have to find a way of dealing with this gentleman."

"It will be expensive."

Freddy raised his eyebrows.

Lotis smiled. "The contract would have a little extra percentage to allow for it."

"Mmmm." Freddy was pleased to hear it but remained unconvinced. "What does the man want out of life? For what would he sell his own grandmother, as we say?"

Lotis was approving. "I see I may leave it to you," he replied. "You understand that the game of selling has only one rule."

"I'm sure I'd like to hear the way you express it, though."

Lotis marshalled his thoughts and then, chewing on his smile, said, "In Germany sell boot polish. In England, soap."

"And in France?"

"France is more interesting. In France you should wait for offers. Spurn nothing."

Freddy laughed. "And America then?"

"The same rule applies. What would America sell its grandmother to possess? History! Sell them Germany, England, and France – stone by numbered stone."

Freddy was enchanted at Lotis's inexhaustible fund of Oriental cynicism; and Lotis, for his part, was pleased to have such an appreciative audience. Ann, when she rejoined them, was woman-of-the-world enough to enjoy it, too. For what remained of the afternoon, while he showed them over the rest of the Seraglio and the mausoleum of Selim II, he delivered himself of several further gems.

In *his* map of the world, he told them at one point, Liechtenstein was a continent, Canada … a mere parish.

When they talked of gratitude in public affairs he asked if the Archbishop of Canterbury ever mentioned Martin Luther.

From the shelter of the mausoleum, during a torrential shower of rain, they noticed a pack of stray dogs fighting over the carcase of an ass. "Ah look!" he said. "Victorious Arabs!" But later in the same conversation, when they were talking about the threat to the Ottoman government from its disaffected Arab subjects, he said, "You can take a hammer to microbes, but they'll kill you just as surely."

His final advice to Freddy, when he left them back at their hotel, with promises to collect them at dusk for their audience with the sultan, was: "In the Orient you cannot find a needle *without* a haystack – the two are inseparable."

"What an astonishing man," Freddy said to Ann as they watched him go. "Isn't the world full of extraordinary people."

She took his arm affectionately and walked with him across the foyer. "Oh Frederick," she sighed. "I do sometimes wish you weren't so damned *nice*!"

CHAPTER FIFTY-SEVEN

FROM HIS STUDY OF the book and maps Lawrence had no difficulty in guiding Miss Kate back to the waterfront. In one way there were no surprises; his eyes were prepared to find the streets and squares – and such larger buildings as the Galata Tower or the Yeni Mosque – exactly where they were. But what the books and maps left out were the fine details of the scene.

It was a marvel, the way the sunlight came delicately tumbling through the leaves of the plane trees and dissipated itself among the fronds of the vines, which grew in profusion in all the quiet squares. Too, there were the haunting smells of the city ... the universal tang of coffee ... the sweet, sharp reek of Turkish tobacco ... spices from Persia ... perfumes from Cyprus – the two wanderers saw all the strange scripts of the Orient on the crates and bundles the porters were carrying up the hill from the wharves below. Draught horses seemed unknown in the city; instead there was this human army, all dressed alike in brown frieze dashed with black and red, struggling up and trotting down the steep streets of Galata. Their vests, opened low at the neck, showed muscles straining at their burdens and skin tanned almost black by the sun.

The carriage from the embassy had taken them up via the Yeni Tsarchi, the widest and steepest of the streets leading to Pera. Now, showing off, Lawrence led Kate down through a rat run of little alleys. Like the sleazy quarter of any other city in the world at such an early hour, Galata had a worn, dejected, hung-over air. The brawling taverns, the alcazars, the divans – all were closed and shuttered. Kate, watching Lawrence slyly, affectionately, saw that he considered himself a great man of the world to be running the gauntlet of this dangerous maze.

Down at the waterfront they hired a kaik. "To Ayub," he told the somewhat surprised boatman.

"Where d'you sit?" Kate asked as she climbed aboard.

Lawrence pointed toward the great curled prow. "You just sprawl on those cushions."

"Oh sprawling – that's one thing I am good at!"

"Shall I see if I can get you a parasol?"

"No, I don't breakfast often enough with the King-Penefathers to worry about my freckles."

They joked light-heartedly all the way up the Golden Horn, with the hushed Mussulman town to their left and the brash modern city to their right. Even after they passed beyond the wall of ancient Byzantium, the contrast continued, with the holy suburbs and the dervish monastery on their left and the naval arsenal, the artillery barracks, and the powder batteries on the opposing bank.

"What's this Ayub place we're headed for?" Miss Kate asked.

"The heart of European Islam," he quoted.

"Yes but what is it really?"

"The book says tourists don't go there. So I thought it would be a good place to start."

They soon discovered why tourists shunned the area. At its centre was a vast series of graveyards and mosques.

"Still – you can learn a lot about people just by looking at their cemeteries," Lawrence said uncertainly.

Miss Kate remembered the simple graves around the homesteads in Kentucky, the fussy bourgeois tombs of Père Lachaise, the military-classical mausoleums of Berlin ... and allowed he had a point. "Depends if you *want* to learn it," she said.

Tall ranks of dark-green cypresses enclosed a great desert of pavilions for the dead, everything from lofty catafalques crowned by turbans of stone to airy kiosks of richly sculptured forms right down to the simplest slabs of marble. Here and there a pierced arcade gave visions of inner courtyards, vistas of strange tombs, patched with fading gold leaf, half-submerged in tangles of wild roses, grass, and brambles. An ancient stillness brooded over all, broken only by occasional chanting from a nearby mosque or the scurrying shape of a dervish priest.

"D'you believe in God, Miss Kate?" Lawrence asked.

"Of course," she replied.

"*This* much?" He waved his hand all around.

She shrugged. "Maybe not." She looked at him. "How about you?"

"I wish I could." His eyes endlessly quartered the cemetery, seeking a glimpse of something that was not visible.

On their way out they passed three pretty little Turkish maidens, the eldest about ten, gambolling among the graves and creating an odd splash of colour in their grown-up dresses of bright red and green.

They took a kaik back as far as the old city wall, where they disembarked on the Stamboul side. "Where can we find something to eat?" Lawrence asked the boatman. He had to mime the question.

The fellow shook his head vehemently. "Ramadan," he said. The explanation meant nothing to either of them.

But the man was right. Through one narrow, black, mysterious street after another they wandered. Curled-up bundles of yellow-skinned dogs snarled at them; curious children followed them; and the few men who were about eyed them askance; but there was not the sniff of a single cooking pot, and every little café was shuttered. The traffic in those streets could never have been great at the best of times, for grass and herbs sprouted from every crack between the stones.

"Which is more dead?" Kate asked gloomily. "Here or back there? It's quite a contest."

They were both ravenous by the time they arrived in the "improved" streets beyond the Sublime Porte. There at last they found the cafés open – for the tourists, of course. The waiter explained the meaning of Ramadan, celebrating the month when Allah sent the Koran down to earth, a month during which no Mussulman eats or drinks between sunrise and sunset. But the feasting *after* sunset, he told them, was a sight not to miss.

They ate kabobs with rice and saffron, following it with little cakes of a cloying sweetness that cried out for the bitter Turkish coffee to wash them down.

"Don't you feel we're desecrating something holy?" Lawrence asked her. "Eating before sunset."

"Nope!" she answered.

He laughed and agreed ruefully. "You can't just take over customs and feelings like that, can you."

They spent the afternoon like any other tourists, wandering around those parts of St. Sophia and the Old Seraglio that were accessible to the Infidel – unaware how close they were to Ann and Freddy. The sky above grew increasingly disturbed as the afternoon wore on. A sulphurous hue filled it from the east, flecked with dark gray that shaded off to purple and finally to black. Toward five o'clock the tension broke in a torrential downpour. They avoided it in the nick of time by following the crowd into the bazaar.

Even on the brightest day the lighting in there would have been dim enough; today it was little more than a mist of twilight, which turned the everyday confusion into total chaos. Here was no rank and column of ordered kiosks and market stalls. Instead each trader created a sprawling island of his wares, leaving the narrowest channel between himself and his neighbours.

"It's an ant colony," Lawrence said.

The "ants" were men, mostly in capes of red, and women, all veiled in white, swaying to and fro as they struggled to get through, while the merchants entreated them to buy, buy.

As their eyes grew accustomed to the gloom they saw that beyond the higgledy-piggledy of the entrance there were, indeed, regular streets and avenues, all teeming with people. There it was easier to move and they wandered around in fascination for half an hour. Lawrence bargained with a couple of stallholders, looking for little presents of silver. Kate watched him in fascination but was too seasoned a traveller to want any more "souvenirs" to cart around the globe. They found a little café, even darker than the bazaar itself, where they sat amid the gleam of rich Turkey carpets and old Persian tiles, and drank yet another tiny cup of coffee and watched the honeyed tobacco smoke drift out and turn everything gray.

Kate chose that moment to spring the question on him. "Do you want your mother to come back, Lawrence?"

He stared at her in astonishment, as if she had violated some unspoken rule of the day.

She gave him a knowing smile. "That's why you took me off on this jaunt, isn't it – to some place like that cemetery, where we'd be certain-sure not to meet up with them?"

He slumped. "You make me sound such a scheming rotter."

She reached forward and squeezed his arm. "You know that's not true, now. You're a wonderful companion. I'll never forget today – never. But I'm not fooling myself you did it for my benefit."

He cheered up at that. "You think I'm wrong?" he asked. "To want her to come back to us I mean? You sound as if you do."

"I asked first."

He sighed. "Well of course I want her back. Isn't that natural?"

She said nothing, forcing him to ask, "What do you think?"

She paused, as if she had not expected her own opinion to be canvassed. At length she said, "I can't understand why any loving husband would want a miserable wife waiting for him each evening – or why any loving son would want to be greeted by an unhappy mother at the end of every term."

Now he was silent.

"Don't you understand?" she pressed.

"No! A mother loves her children. That's what I understand. A wife loves her husband. A woman loves her home. I can understand all that. But when my mother says she loves my father but won't come back home ... when she says she wants him to" – he lowered his voice still further and whispered the word – "*divorce* her, precisely because she still loves him ... well then, no, I don't understand."

"Did she say that? Is that what you were talking about this morning?"

He nodded. "What about you, Miss Kate? I mean, I can see what fun it must be trotting about the globe and being so successful – and getting paid well into the bargain. But in the end – isn't it all just empty? Don't *you* want to settle down? Don't you miss not having a home of your own ... your own children?"

She smiled fondly. "But I'm not your mother," she said.

He misunderstood her and blushed. "Yes, I'm sorry ... I had no right to ask ..."

Now she laughed. "I don't mean *that*! You have every right to ask. After all, I'm the one who started in on these personal questions. What I meant was – perhaps you don't know – I ran away from home when I was fourteen. I've been globetrotting a lot longer than any of The Angels. So if I say I hanker after a home and all ... well – that's just nine years of rootless wandering talking. And here's another thing – your mother has the added reward of being on stage. Surely you feel it." She paused and then added casually, "After all, you went and saw her two nights running when we were in Vienna."

He gasped. "How did you know that!"

"Well now, a girl on her own in this world has to spend a lot of time looking into men's eyes, young and old, trying to work out what they're thinking, what they're planning – and trying to stay just one step ahead of them."

He slumped in his seat. After a while he said, "They don't teach us *any*thing at school, do they!"

"Oh I don't think you need worry, Lawrence. You're

already streets ahead of any other fifteen-year-old man I ever met."

He bucked up quickly. "Actually I'm in my sixteenth year."

"Already!"

The storm passed. Even in the depths of the café the air grew brighter. They left the bazaar, blinking at the strength of the evening light. The lowering sun was striking inwards, almost horizontally, against the whitewashed stone walls of Pera, which towered above them across the water to the east. They strolled down past the Custom House to the New Bridge, where all the steamer ferries berth; that short walk was a leap through the centuries, from the smells of the bazaar – a blend of coffee and sandalwood and spices – to the reek of coal and steam and hot oil.

In Galata the working day was ending. The shutters were off the alcazars, where the singers and acrobats were already arriving. The taverns were filling; the demimondaines sat in doorways, showing their calves and ankles, or they leaned provocatively from upper windows, showing even more. Lawrence pointedly failed to notice them. The porters were leaving their work and settling in the divans, calling for nargilehs and coffee.

"Let's rest awhile," Kate said. "My feet just hate me."

"But it's only another couple of hundred yards."

"Just ten minutes, huh?"

"It's a dreadful area."

"It could teach you as much as any old cemetery."

They sat on the nearest divan and bought yet another cup of coffee. "But they're so miniature, these little cups," Kate pointed out, "I still probably didn't reach my daily ration yet."

Neither touched the plate of raki sweetmeats.

The porters lay on their divans, smoking their nargilehs; the endless gurgling of the bubbles was in itself a kind of narcotic. The men stared dreamily at fragments of the dark-blue Sea of Marmara, merely glimpsed between the tall apartment houses. The wreaths of their smoke hung on the drifting air. Sometimes a more powerful but momentary breeze carried with it the scent of absinthe and aniseed.

Pedlars passed, ringing bells and shouting their wares,

usually sherbets or cakes or fruit. On a main road, two streets away, a heavy tramcar went by, preceded by couriers blowing trumpets to clear the way. A young Turkish blade, out for a bit of excitement, cantered his horse along the lane, crying "Bestour! Bestour!" The ladies called down interesting-sounding suggestions and laughed; the porters stared after him in unruffled stupefaction. The alcazars began to hang out their flags so that now one could tell what tonight's performances would be. Here there was an Italian pantomime; there it was a group of Hungarian ladies, singing Strauss. Cymbals, tambourines, bells, and drums were already beginning to sound. A party of sailors came through, all in white with red fezzes and collars. They knew everyone, shook hands all round, introduced their sisters and mothers, whose large, dark eyes danced merrily above their long veils of pink or blue. They, too, filled the divans, spilling out into the roadway. Their officers sat among them, smoking cigarettes in golden tubes.

At sunset there was a great display of fireworks a mile or so away, near the royal palaces. They saw occasional starbursts and rockets above the roofline – and over in Stamboul there was a persistent glow, as if the whole of that quarter were on fire.

Kate and Lawrence sat there until night fell, until time had no meaning; they watched it all in silence. She could not remember the last time she had sat and gazed dispassionately at the passing scene in just this way – never probably, or not since that first day in New Orleans. She watched Lawrence, too – drinking it all in. At last she said, "You are *just* like your father, you know."

"In what way?"

"That time when we were looking for your mother, every ship we sailed he had to go down to the engine room and talk with the engineer. He wanted to know how many miles of steam pipe ... what was the pressure and temperature ... the degree of saltiness. He kept a special little book where he wrote it all down. He couldn't feel happy on any ship until he knew things like that. And you're the same about cities. You've got to know how they work – first Vienna, now here."

He nodded, delighted at her insight. "When you said that – on the train when we left Vienna – about being a little bird that could fly in and out of all the windows without anyone really noticing ... well that was so exact. You understand people so well, Miss Kate. I wish I did."

"Oh you're well on the way," she assured him.

When they left, he took her arm to guide her among the crowds; the nightly Babel of Galata was by then in full swing. As they drew near to their hotel he gave out a great sigh.

"What's the cause of that?" she asked.

"If my father did ... divorce ... my mother ..."

"Yes?"

"I'm only saying *if*."

"Of course."

"Well ... d'you think he might marry again?"

Lightly she pinched his arm and answered: "Stranger things have happened."

CHAPTER FIFTY-EIGHT

ANN LEFT A NOTE for Kate and Lawrence. Lotis arrived in the royal carriage punctually at sunset. He took them a roundabout way, across the Azab Kapu bridge to the Stamboul waterfront, so that they could see at close quarters the garlands of fire that ringed the minarets of every mosque.

"These are exciting nights for the ladies in all the ordinary harems," he explained. "They go out visiting from house to house. The eunuchs walk before them carrying lanterns. The happiness of the women is childlike and very moving."

Ann drew breath to speak but then held her tongue.

"There is a saying," Lotis told her. "The destiny of the cage is to seek out the bird."

"Not strictly true," Freddy pointed out. "The destiny of most metals is to rust away."

"... which is why the best cages are made of gold," Lotis laughed. "Tonight, Mrs. Oxley, you will be visiting the most stupendous golden cage on earth." For the first time they noticed a harsh edge to his laughter.

When they returned to Galata via the new bridge they could see that a large part of the Phanar district, beyond the Selim Mosque, was on fire. "Vaugun-vâr! Vaugun-vâr!" the cry went up. Even the royal coach had to pull aside as a great mass of people poured over the bridge – beggars, children, sailors, half-naked men on horses ... Among them were gangs of wild-looking thugs who, though roped to great pumping engines, were running as fast as their legs could carry them. Other carriages were being rocked from side to side until their occupants paid a ransom to be left in peace. Some even tried it on the royal coach – until they noticed the cypher of the palace.

Freddy looked at Lotis. "*Tulumbadschi?*" he asked.

"*Tulumbadschi.*"

The drive to Top Haneh and on through Fundukli was a complete contrast. The streets were deserted. The sky ahead was one gentle blaze of green and white, not this time from an impromptu fire of houses, but from the lanterns and Bengal lamps that ringed the palaces. The carriage rattled across the grated barriers into the royal district and they galloped on among brilliant illuminations. White globes were set out in all the gardens, and the sky was spattered with the falling red and blue stars of rockets.

The way led uphill to a second grating, beyond which whole battalions of cavalry and infantry formed a close-packed human hedge, barring their way. Every man carried a torch or a lantern. There were almost as many officers as men, all wearing the oriental dolman with its long flowing sleeves. There was no martial ferocity about them, though. They seemed withdrawn, lost in some religious meditation, hypnotized by the light and the fireworks.

The coachman gave the password and the ranks parted in silence to let them through. They stopped before a pavilion close to the Yildiz Kiosk, the present rather modest royal palace. Though the pavilion was completely deserted, every room was brightly lit, both from within and by the outdoor illuminations. They entered and went upstairs, where they stood at the windows and gazed out over a vast sea of men, all standing there in that same absorbed and mystic silence.

And then, so quiet that at first it might have been no more than the massed breathing of that great army, came the strains of sacred music from the mosque – male voices, high-pitched but limpid, trembling through the quarter-tones of eastern chants. The building itself, radiant from within, seemed to have walls as thin as alabaster. Every path and alley in the surrounding gardens fanned outward from its portals; the lanterns and Bengal lights strung out along their sides continued the symbolism of that radiance. And hanging above the garden, by some invisible means, was a giant transparency upon which gleaming Arabic characters were picked out against the night: *Allah is great. Allah is merciful.* In the far distance, riding quietly at anchor on the Bosphorus, the vessels of the fleet were dressed overall and lit from stem to stern.

The music touched Ann. The long, high notes were sustained without fatigue while other voices, an octave lower, endlessly renewed the chant. It captured an aspect of religion that had always eluded the sacred music of the west; it was a direct expression not just of the eternal *littleness* of human existence but of God's sadness at the gulf between that littleness and humanity's vision of the infinite.

Mankind will always *want*, it seemed to say.

In western religions, by contrast, mankind is always found wanting.

An open landau drawn by richly caparisoned horses galloped up one of the avenues and halted before the marble steps of the mosque.

"Now you'll see the Sultan," Lotis promised.

From nowhere, it seemed, some thirty attendants gathered, each carrying a huge lantern draped in white silk. They lined up behind the landau. Other carriages drew up to one side of the mosque.

"For the royal princesses," Lotis explained. "The women worship behind the men – up in the gallery."

The chanting beneath the cupola of the mosque rose to an impassioned, exultant crescendo. A great sigh went up from the soldiers: "Allah! Allah! Here is our Sultan!"

Yet when the ruler himself appeared they fell back into

that old, profound silence which was so much more impressive than cheers.

The royal progress along the short drive between the mosque and the Yildiz Kiosk was extraordinary, for the horses went immediately from a standing position into a full gallop – a manoeuvre for which they were especially trained. The other carriages did the same. And sandwiched between them the men with the lanterns ran wildly to keep up. Seconds later the kiosk gates clanged together and the troops closed up behind the vehicles with a clashing of their drawn swords. And the public ceremony was all over!

A eunuch was waiting to conduct Ann by a maze of small pathways fringed with berberis and other thorns to the harem. Meanwhile an aide-de-camp brought the two men to the royal apartments. All around the Yildiz and down the hill to the Bosphorus were fairylike palaces of incomparably greater beauty; but Abdul Hamid II had built this simple, sober pavilion to his own taste, and here he lived and worked. The only luxury lay in the magnificent Turkey rugs, which deadened every footfall.

Tonight the antechambers were full of generals and admirals, and, of course, their aides-de-camp. There were glittering dress uniforms of every kind, some western but most oriental; red fezzes, black astrakhans, and white dolman capes predominated. They spoke in whispers; the presence of the sovereign hung over all. It sobered Freddy to realize that, though Turkey might be an increasingly spent force among the nations, she was by no means finished yet. There was enough power gathered in this room to tear apart the fabric of the civilized world.

Lotis, acting as interpreter, introduced Freddy to several generals, including Osman Pasha, the heroic defender of Plevna in the war against the Russians, six years ago.

"We could have done with a hundred of your guns then," he told Freddy.

"Or even ten," Freddy answered.

The Pasha chuckled. "Yes – we've all been told how good they are."

The Grand Master of Ceremonies came to conduct them to a little side room, where the Sultan was holding his audiences.

Freddy looked at Lotis, seeking a cue for his own demeanour. The Armenian was calm and casual. "You get on well with generals," he said approvingly. "You know how to cheek them without attacking their dignity. They enjoy that when they're off-duty."

Freddy remembered Guzman Blanco. "I had an excellent teacher," he said.

At the arched entranceway they bowed in the court salutation. The Sultan, lying at ease upon a divan, watched Freddy with interest. Out of the corner of his eye Freddy saw Lotis give a small, confidential nod; that slight inclination of the head was the man's entire "report" on Freddy's suitability for the proposed contract. Thus in all despotic governments the fate of men may hang on a nod, on the droop of an eyelid.

Had it not been for the ceremony Freddy would not have been able to distinguish the ruler from any of his generals. He wore the same uniform, and his brown military cloak was identical to theirs. He beckoned them to approach.

They talked, through Lotis, for some five minutes but not a word was said of guns or indeed of any military matters. The Sultan first asked Freddy's opinion of Constantinople.

"I hope all westerners who come here, when the new railway is fully opened, will learn as much as I have, sir," he said.

"And what in particular is that?"

"How to preserve the best of the old traditions without allowing them to choke us. It is something we seem utterly incapable of doing, yet your majesty's people achieve it without effort."

Their entire conversation was of that kind – dealing in generalities without falling back upon the most obvious platitudes.

"You have impressed him," Lotis said after they withdrew. "Now come and continue the good work among our customers." Without any change of pace he added, in the same quiet tones: "The order, by the way, will be for four-thousand light field guns; twelve-hundred medium ones, and six-hundred heavy, rear-echelon pieces. And we want you to design us a new gun – a very heavy one – for the navy and for the batteries along the Dardanelles."

Freddy felt the blood draining from his face. The order would make him the largest arms manufacturer in the world. It was also far beyond his present or any likely capacity.

Ann had met surprises, too. Her notions of a *harem* derived from pictures by French romanticists and their imitators – paintings displayed in the less salubrious locations on her various tours. She was prepared for vistas of naked or lightly draped maidens, all lying around, ready for their master's inspection and choice.

Only the apartments accorded to her expectations.

Despite the day's surfeit of magnificence, she could not help marvelling anew at the matchless luxury of the Yildiz harem. Yet apart from the splendour and age of the building she might as well have been visiting any first class hotel. The women were dressed like women indoors anywhere else in Turkey; some, indeed, were in western dress and would not have looked out of place at any small dinner party in London or Paris. Only the eunuchs were as she had envisaged them, with their shirtlike tunics open to the waist, showing off their sleek, black skin, their gorgeous turbans, and their lethal-looking scimitars.

She was met, not at the main door but at a kind of inner entrance that seemed to mark off the private quarters; the young lady who greeted her was in western dress. "Good evening, Mrs. Oxley," she said. "I am the Princess Yasmé, His Majesty's fourth wife."

Her English was perfect; she had been tutored in England, she said, and had attended schools in Milan and Rome. When the formalities were over, she cast aside her dignified manner like a coat and became almost girlish. "Everyone's dying to meet you," she said. "Is it true you are an opera diva?"

"Not quite," Ann laughed and described The Angels.

"Oh but that's even more exciting! Five women travelling around the world together. Doesn't it make your head spin sometimes?"

"Sometimes."

The corridor led directly to a kind of large drawing room, overlooking the Bosphorus. Most of the lights had been extinguished to allow the ladies to watch the fireworks; but as soon as the princess clapped her hands the lamps were turned up and the introductions began. There were only fourteen wives – another surprise for Ann, who had expected dozens. As with Yasmé, the first greetings were extremely formal, beginning with the Sultana herself; but as soon as they were over, it was all smiles and laughter again. Tea and little rice cakes were served and they all sat around Ann like schoolchildren at story-time; they plied her with questions at a merciless pace.

There was no pattern to their inquiry. They could go directly from what the ladies of New York would be wearing this summer to the character of Lady Beresford, or some other member of Queen Victoria's court ... to the merits of silk or cotton next to the skin. Their hunger for news and gossip was, Ann thought, a kind of gluttony. Starving men presented with a laden buffet would satisfy their hunger in just such a manner – cramming in a little of this, a bit of that ... as their eyes fell upon it.

But they were practical, too. They touched her evening gown and wanted to know who made it ... how many yards of this or that material ... what quality she had requested ... and above all what price she had paid. And they wanted to know all about travel – the routes and the prices. They were especially interested in the new luxury trains that were appearing in many countries. This very summer, they told her, a new "Orient Express" was going into service between Paris and Constantinople by way of Vienna; people said it would be the last word in luxury.

At length, when the tide of questions began to ebb, Yasmé shyly asked Ann if she would favour them with a song. As she spoke she sidled over to one corner of the room, where stood a magnificent Scheiner grand piano.

"I've brought no music," Ann said, following her. "I'll just have to do the simple chords."

She sang some of the von Suppé pieces they had performed at the Hirschberger, then *Die Lotosblume* and *Ich grolle nicht* by Schumann. All were rapturously received. Halfway through the first of the Schumann songs, Yasmé put her hands over Ann's and took over the playing. Ann was astonished; she was the best accompanist she had ever heard.

"You play superbly," she told the girl. "D'you perhaps sing as well?"

The princess looked as if she were about to say no but the others all cried out, "Yes yes! She does!"

After a further show of reluctance, she sat at the piano and played the introduction to the Habañera from Bizet's Carmen. From the first note of the song itself Ann sat there in thunderstruck amazement. Yasmé could have walked onto any opera stage in the world and have won standing encores. She was not just a good singer; she was a great one. Her voice had undoubtedly been trained. Milan and Rome, she had said. Of course – that was it.

All through her song Yasmé avoided Ann's eyes. Ann supposed it was because the princess knew she was making *her* singing sound like that of some tipsy barmaid. But at the end, when she was about to leap up and hug Yasmé and tell her how superlative she was, their eyes met and a mute, desperate appeal flashed between them. *For the love of pity, do not tell me how good I am,* it said.

A most dreadful sense of desolation filled Ann. She clapped and laughed with the rest of the wives, but her heart could have wept the spirit from her.

Then they played cards – not bridge or any of the sedate games but a raucous form of beggar-my-neighbour. Yasmé went on strumming at the piano, waltzes and polkas, mostly. Two of the wives danced, not as male-female partners but side-by-side, with their arms about each other's waists, allowing both to do the female steps in unison.

"What d'you think of us?" Yasmé asked Ann quietly, taking advantage of the distraction of the others.

"This is the most luxurious place I've ever been in," Ann answered carefully.

"Yes, I believe it!" Yasmé laughed. "Now say you'd adore to live here."

Later, when she saw Ann looking at one of the eunuchs, she asked, "Are you wondering about them?"

"A bit." Ann smiled shyly.

"Well they don't. The white eunuchs, the Georgians and Circassians, are only castrati; they could but they're never allowed near the harem, of course. The black ones have everything removed. It's horrible. I've only seen it once. The man wept when he showed me." She gave a bitter little laugh.

"It's true, you see – there *is* always someone worse off than oneself."

Ann now felt bold enough to ask, "Will the Sultan send for one of you tonight? How does that work?"

Yasmé shook her head. "In Ramadan he sends only for his concubines. There's usually about forty of them, all virgins. They live in dormitories over in the other wing. They dance and sing for him – not lasciviously, like in the taverns, but not modestly either. Then, when he's seen enough, the Mother of the Maidens arranges them in a circle around him and he throws his handkerchief to the chosen one. Then she's supposed to almost faint with joy while the others have to crowd around her and kiss her and tell her how lucky she is." A compulsion had seized Yasmé. She was no longer telling the story – she was reliving it. "Then he goes to his chamber while they bathe her and perfume her and deck her with the family jewels. Then they sing and chant her all the way to the Sultan's door, where the Eunuch of the Door takes her to the Chief Eunuch, who gets permission for her to enter. Then she has to crawl across the floor and crawl in at the foot of his bed and crawl up until she's at his side."

"And then?" Ann asked; the ritual had so absorbed her that she had, for the moment, forgotten its purpose. She blushed as Yasmé laughed. "I mean after," she corrected herself.

"Oh after. Well, now that she's been deflowered by His Majesty, she's a Royal Concubine and she gets apartments and slaves of her own. They're in the central part of the harem, between the wings for the ordinary concubines and the wives. I'll show you on the way out. If she has a boy child, she'll be promoted to the status of wife. That's how it happened with half of us here. The others were political alliances, of course."

"Were you always a princess, Yasmé?"

"Not I! My father was a quite small, quite ordinary merchant. Nubar Lotis and Son, General Importers, Tunnel Square, Pera. I think you can guess what I was going to be."

"Oh ... Yasmé!"

The princess forced herself to smile. "Not at all! As I say, there's always somebody worse off. And my father is *now* a very important man in the office of the Grand Vizier. And my brother is *now* a colonel in the best cavalry regiment. And my mother is *now* one of the queens of Pera." Here the sarcasm went out of her tone as she added, "And my son is, now and always, the most beautiful young man you ever saw – though he is only three."

At the end of Ann's visit Yasmé asked if she would kindly send the music of the new operas as each was published. "You can send it to my father," she said. "I'll give you his address."

"I know your father," Ann told her.

Yasmé showed no surprise. "He was the only one," she said, more to herself than Ann.

"What only one?"

"He hated what happened to me. He was so proud. The government must be mad to employ him – but of course it would never enter their heads that he wasn't the happiest man in Pera."

They kissed warmly and parted. When Ann turned back at the end of the corridor for one last look, all she saw was that one forlorn figure marooned there at the heart of all that splendour.

It was a different eunuch who brought Ann back to the royal carriage. Neither Frederick nor Lotis had arrived yet. The fellow made sure she was comfortably seated and then pulled down all the blinds.

When he had gone Ann sat there in the dark, waiting for Frederick, thinking of poor Yasmé, and trying not to cry.

CHAPTER FIFTY-NINE

"SOMETHING WILL TURN UP," Freddy said, not too convincingly. "At the moment I feel like a starving mongrel who's found a freshly dead whale on the beach."

"But isn't that good?" Lawrence asked.

"It would be except for this one catch. Beside the whale stands a guardian who says, 'If you take so much as one single mouthful, you must eat the lot. If you leave anything, I'll shoot you.'" He laughed. "Still, that's only one of the difficulties. The other is Mr. Patriarca."

By mid-morning a third had been added – in the form of a cable from the dowager: YOUR PRESENCE URGENTLY NEEDED HERE. LIFE OR DEATH SITUATION. PLEASE CABLE RESPONSE.

He replied: SITUATION AWKWARD HERE TOO. CAN YOU INDICATE THE NATURE OF YOUR PROBLEM?

The rejoinder was: NO. JUST COME PLEASE. TRULY DESPERATE.

By then it was evening. He replied: LEAVING SOONEST. WILL CABLE YOU AGAIN EN VOYAGE.

Those were not the only cable exchanges involving Freddy that day. In fact, he spent most of it at the embassy's chancery section, communicating in cypher with The Oxley Company's offices, warning them about what he now called "the whale difficulty" and the thousands of gallons of midnight oil they were going to need in the months ahead.

Nubar Lotis called by arrangement at noon, back at the hotel. They worked together over sandwiches and pilsner in Freddy's room. By then Lawrence and the two women were off for a day trip around the Prince Islands. Freddy showed Lotis the cables from the dowager.

"What d'you suppose it means?" Lotis asked.

"It means I have little time for the usual Oriental niceties. How soon can you get the contract drafted?"

Lotis patted his bag and smiled.

Freddy did not smile. "Why so quick all of a sudden?" he asked. "I've had men battering at your door for years. And to no effect. Even at the height of the war with Russia, you ..."

"When we were at war with Russia, The Oxley Company was only two years old."

Freddy conceded the point with a curt nod. "Nevertheless, I've been seeking to do business ever since."

Lotis's face creased in a cynical smile. "I'll tell you what's different now – *even the generals are afraid*. Didn't you smell it in the palace last night? For years (even centuries perhaps) we've bought our weapons on the basis of who could afford to return to us the largest proportion of the bill by way of gifts. It made for poor weapons but happy generals. One should not overlook the advantages of having happy generals. But now the wolves are gathering." His pale, well-manicured finger pointed to all corners of the earth as he listed the names. "Russia. Oh what Russia would give for a warm-water seaport! Austria-Hungary, falling apart herself. Our dismemberment would feed her and keep her together for a century. And anyway, she dare not let Russia build herself a new back door. Germany – the rising star – wants hegemony over the whole of this region and an outlet into the Persian Gulf. The Baghdad Railway is only the beginning. France, too. Now that the corpse of Africa has been divided – in the sense that future squabbles will be dog-versus-dog rather than dog-versus-trussed-goat – now the eyes of Europe are looking eastward. Yet we Turks must turn our backs on Europe in order to deal with the Arabs. Therefore we must have a good shield behind us." He patted the bag containing the draft contracts. "Even the most avaricious general can understand that."

"But still ... there are many other companies in Europe, most of them bigger than mine."

Lotis shrugged expansively. "It had to be an English company. Of all the European powers England leans most favourably toward us. She has more interest in seeing Turkey strong than in helping to carve her up. Anyway, she already has indigestion – or sunburn, more likely – from her other acquisitions. Or are you saying there is a better *English* company than yours?"

"Of course not! But it's a large order. A lot of eggs to put in one basket. You could have asked several of us to form a cartel and so spread your ..."

"Never!" Lotis suddenly shed his schoolmasterly air of detached cynicism. "We wish to deal with just one person. If you have any ideas of leaving here with this large order and then farming it out among your fellow manufacturers, you should forget them this instant, Mr. Oxley. We are not interested in any such arrangement. It is you and you alone. Or it will be one of the others and them alone. But" – he relaxed and gave a winning smile – "I know it will be you. I've made the closest possible study of you for the past three years, you and your company."

"Then you must know I have nothing like sufficient capacity to fulfil the order."

"Aieee!" Lotis pretended to tear out his own hair. He looked around the room like a trapped animal. "This dreadful disease of honesty! I do so hope it's not contagious."

"But if you've made as close a study of me as you claim, you must already know that."

"Of course I do. But I also know you. You'll overcome the difficulty."

"How do I arrange to see Patriarca? I must deal with him before I go."

"It will be expensive."

"I believe not."

Lotis's eyebrows shot up. "Don't deceive yourself that you can bluff him, my friend. Nor frighten him."

Freddy smiled. "Just tell me how I may get in touch with him."

With a resigned tilt of his head Lotis said, "For an Oriental there would be so many ways. But you – you alone of all the men I know – you can use the most surprising one of all. Go straight up to his front door and knock!"

Freddy laughed. "Where does he live?"

"At the top of Pera, off the street called Serkis. You can't miss the house, it's built in the style first made popular by Atilla the Hun. If you're quite determined to deal with him, remember this. Whenever the play *Othello* is performed out here, the Moor himself is seen as a gullible clown. The hero is Iago. And that, mark you, is among the more civilized of our citizenry. Not even in a hundred generations would the off-spring of Patriarca climb upward to such a level of civilization. Now you have the first glimmering of an idea about the sort of man you'll be dealing with."

Then Lotis produced the draft contracts. They haggled for the best part of an hour and knocked them into a shape that was highly pleasing to Freddy. They initialled the papers and left them for redrafting and detailed discussion between both sides' legal experts. Of many concessions that he won, the prize was a down-payment of a quarter-million pounds sterling on signature of the final documents. Lotis promised that letters of intent and heads of agreement would be ready for collection at the Grand Vizier's office by noon tomorrow.

Around teatime Freddy walked up to the street called Serkis; he had no difficulty identifying the style of Atilla the Hun. A high wall surrounded the entire property. Surprisingly, it was painted pink but its top was guarded by rotating iron spikes, wickedly sharp. Inside was something the size of a small palace, but only the pantiles were visible from the road, a sea of terracotta beyond a palisade of cypresses. The entrance gate was of solid oak, cross-banded with straps of iron; even the little wicket gate within it – at which Freddy now hammered with the knob of his cane – was studded with rows of iron spikes.

The tyler spoke only French. He slammed the gate in Freddy's face while he went to fetch the major domo. Even that august official had very limited English. "Password," was about all he could say intelligibly.

"*My* password is Oxley. I'm sure it will get me in." He handed over his card.

The man was gone the best part of five minutes; Freddy was still kept out upon the street.

When the major domo returned he handed back the card, saying, "You write. Your business."

On the back of the card Freddy wrote, "I have something to sell which all your money could not otherwise buy. The price is most reasonable."

This time the man brought back a note: "Mr. Basil Patriarca requests the pleasure of the company of Mr. and Mrs. Frederick Oxley to dinner this evening at eight o'clock." It was signed illegibly over the title: Secretary.

"You can go alone," Ann said when he showed her the invitation that evening. "What d'you want me for?"

He eyed her warily. Ever since the visit to the harem she had been a little strange.

Later Kate came to him and said, "Ann's told me about this invitation. Why don't I come with you?"

"Oh I don't want to involve you, Miss Kate."

"But I'd like to see the fellow. Anyway, there are things I want to tell you."

"About Patriarca?"

"Yes. One or two. But mostly about Ann – things she's said to me today."

And so it was arranged. Lawrence dined with his mother and they each went early to bed. Freddy and Kate left the hotel with plenty of time in hand. They told the cabby to circle about until eight, when he was to leave them at Patriarca's door.

"Tell me about Patriarca first," Freddy said. "How d'you come to know anything about him?"

Kate chuckled. "Oh Mr. Frederick – there's nothing sentimental about you, is there! The one thing I know about Patriarca is that he hires beautiful women to ..."

"Yes I wondered about that," Freddy said sarcastically. "He had one with him the first day I saw him and then again on the *Colomba*. I wondered if it was just coincidence."

After a pause she said, "Will you let me finish? I had a talk with the woman on the boat, after dinner that evening, after you'd all turned in. She was Austrian but she had quite good English. The interesting thing she told me is that he hires her quite often yet he's never once touched her. And the girl who introduced her to him in the first place – she said the same. He has this whole string of beautiful women – pays them a small fortune to be seen on his arm – but he never touches them."

"What's the point of all that?" Freddy asked.

"Well what did you think when you saw him – always in the company of those gorgeous creatures?"

"I don't know. I didn't pay them much attention."

"Oh golly I'll scream in a minute! Well for your information, Mr. Frederick, anyone *else* would think he's playing the blue-assed baboon – to put it crudely – saying to all the other male baboons, 'Look what I can afford that you can't!' In short, stoking up the envy of the crowd and then basking in it."

Freddy laughed in semi-belief. "Well, I've heard of some pretty rum people in my time! But what does this tell us about him?"

"To me it says only one thing – he's mightily concerned for the world's opinion of him."

Freddy was silent a long while. Then he said, "Yes. By George, Miss Kate, I think you may have saved me a small fortune – if not my life. I believe this evening must now follow quite a different plan."

"What had you intended then?"

"I was going to offer him the Oxley agency for the entire Austro-Hungarian Empire."

"What?"

"Yes. It's not worth a bean, but he's not to know that. And if by his efforts he turned it into something of value – well, he'd be worth every penny I'd allow him to steal."

"And now?"

He patted her arm. "I shall still make the same offer, because it's all I have. But wrapped up with it I shall also offer him something quite priceless – something I don't own and never *could* own, something I have no right whatever to promise!" He laughed at the neatness of it but would not be drawn further. "Now," he went on, "you also said something about Ann?"

Reluctantly now, Kate let go of their previous conversation. "What happened last night?" she asked.

"We told you at breakfast – I met the Sultan, Ann visited the harem."

"Did she say anything about it?"

"She said it was very luxurious, which is hardly surprising – but the wives seemed like fairly ordinary upper-class Turkish women. Apparently there were other categories of women there but she didn't meet them."

"Didn't she tell you about Mr. Lotis's daughter, Yasmé?"

From the shock on Freddy's face she could see that Ann hadn't mentioned the encounter. So Kate herself told him – all that Ann had told her.

"And this Yasmé, she was going to be an operatic singer?" he asked.

"One of the greats."

Freddy whistled. "No wonder Lotis seems bitter at times. He may be a man to cultivate rather more deeply than I had intended."

Kate made a strangled sound.

"What now?" he asked.

"Holy Mo, Mr. Frederick! Can't you see what it meant to Ann? It was like Fate talking right into her ear. Here she is, having met up with you again and finding you a whole lot more mellow and mature, and more attractive than ever, and life is obviously going well, and the hot blood of youth has cooled or whatever it was between you – I mean, I don't know what went wrong ... anyway, there she is thinking maybe it wouldn't be too bad, settling back in the bosom of the family ... when – *whammo!* The proverbial voice trills out a warning: 'Love's the most rebellious bird that ne'er a man can tame ...' Only the irony of it is *this* bird's in the famous gilded cage, and Ann recognises a sister! Like I said – that's the warble of Fate in her ear. And I'll tell you – right now all she wants is to catch the next boat to Tyre or Haifa. Such as tomorrow."

Freddy was less affected by this news than she had expected. He considered it a moment and then said, "I had more or less written off any chance of her returning, you know. I suppose I saw it in her eyes in that café in Vienna when the crowd were going wild with their applause and she just stood there letting it wash over her. There's nothing I can offer to replace that, is there." Something in the notion seemed to please him, for he added: "You see! It's what we were saying about Patriarca – it's the *intangible* things that people really want. If you can offer them that, you have a hold on them for life. But if you're reduced to offering mere gold, you've already lost them. In the long run you've lost them." He squeezed her arm. "I'm so glad you came with me tonight, Miss Kate."

Baffled, she made a noncommittal noise and stared out of the window.

"Will you also be going on to the Holy Land?" he inquired.

"Are you asking me to stay?" She held her breath for his reply.

"No no. I have to go back to England at once. Tomorrow morning if possible. I've asked the embassy to see if they can arrange a berth on a Royal Navy vessel going that way. Lotis thinks that's the quickest."

"Yes, I'm going on with Ann," Kate said flatly.

"You must let me know everywhere The Angels visit," he went on. "Cable me as soon as you confirm the bookings. I travel quite extensively these days. I'd love to see you from time to time. You especially." He raised a hand and touched her cheek. "You'll find this hard to credit, I know, but when you slipped away from me like that, in Georgetown, although it had been Ann we were searching for, it was *you* I missed most on the voyage back home."

At precisely that moment they pulled up before Patriarca's door; Kate had no chance to respond.

Lotis was right. Patriarca *was* a barbarian. The interior of his palace was magnificent but cold. Its use of marble was grandiose, showing none of those softening influences that were so apparent in all the Turkish royal dwellings. The objets d'art scattered so liberally and prominently about the rooms were from every continent and period; they were the indiscriminate loot of an army, not one man's considered collection.

The major domo led them through a series of showy anterooms to an open courtyard at the heart of the building. It was planted with a rich profusion of semitropical shrubs, and fairy lanterns bordered every path. The illumination they shed was needed, for otherwise the visitors would have been blinded by the light that shone from the far end of the court. And there, at the threshold of a magnificent banqueting hall, stood Patriarca, a dark, powerful shadow. Behind him were the silhouettes of three women. As soon as he saw Freddy and Kate he turned around and sent two of them away.

"They'll be heartbroken, I'm sure," Kate murmured.

"My dear Mr. Oxley! And Mrs. Oxley, too?" Patriarca advanced to the top of the short flight of steps that led up from the courtyard.

As Freddy shook his hand, feeling very much like David before Goliath, he replied, "No. Miss Kate Kendall is a very good friend of the family. Mrs. Oxley is exhausted and begs to be excused."

Introductions followed. Patriarca's companion was a Miss Dirmikis, "a very good friend of *my* family," he added with a knowing smile. His English was fairly good but guttural; his voice was deep and resonant. That carnivorous aura was ten times stronger at close quarters – above all in his eyes, which were pale and cold as sapphires.

They went immediately to the table. Patriarca wanted to know how Freddy had enjoyed the Old Seraglio. He spoke about yesterday's itinerary in detail, right down to the shower of rain. He wanted Freddy to understand he had been observed every step of the way. It was the same with Kate. "So it was you, Miss Kendall, who went out with young Master Oxley – such a handsome, self-assured young fellow!" But why had they gone to Ayub? What a melancholy place! And at least they could have gone to see the dervishes dancing while they were in that quarter ... and so on.

It was heavily done. Freddy showed not the slightest surprise; he behaved as if he were royalty and it was only natural that a sycophantic commoner like Patriarca would show such minute interest in his doings. Kate, taking her cue from Freddy, did likewise. So when, after ten minutes or so had gone by, with the man proudly showing off his knowledge of their movements, and the pair of them responding as if it were the most natural thing in the world that they should become the immediate centre of any milieu in which they chose to move, the message penetrated even Patriarca's thick hide and he changed the subject angrily.

He began to speak of Lotis. His first few comments were cautiously critical, but when Freddy showed no inclination to defend the man, Patriarca dropped his guard and poured out a tirade of unbridled abuse. Lotis had been a nobody, a small merchant who could have been destroyed with one little warehouse fire. It would have been so easy to arrange. The idiot had spent a fortune on his daughter, hoping she'd become an opera singer. Instead it turned out she had a voice like a foghorn and would never have made it, not even into the chorus of a cheap provincial opera. So Lotis had been forced to pander her to the Sultan. She was never destined to be more than a royal concubine but she'd had the luck to produce a son who was now the ruler's favourite. So all of a sudden the little shopkeeper thinks he can lord it over Pera ...

When he ran out of steam Freddy drawled in his best Etonian imitation, "He's a pompous little bureaucrat but he has an amusing turn of phrase."

Kate saw his purpose then. He was out to suggest that this whole visit to Constantinople was a kind of slumming trip. They had stepped down off the Great British Olympus for the regrettable necessity of transacting a little business; but nothing impressed them. She was glad of this insight for, remembering her conversation with the young lady on the *Colomba*, she had intended suggesting to Patriarca that Freddy was the most sizzling and masterful lover any woman could desire; she was quite confident she could manage that without in the least arousing Freddy's suspicions.

So when Patriarca asked Freddy what he thought of the royal court, Kate said – as if it were an amusing observation they had already shared – "So very different from life at Windsor!"

Freddy smiled appreciatively at her. "Quite."

Patriarca's eyes grew larger. "You attend the court of Queen Victoria? But since the death of her poor husband ... has she not retired?"

"There are no public functions, of course," Kate explained. "The court has been reduced only to those nearest and dearest to her. Those who remember ... *him* ... in the days of his greatness."

Freddy nodded sagely. "Those who won't overdo their sympathy – in fact, who won't overdo *anything*."

Kate took his point.

Patriarca was well on the hook by now. "But your visit here," he said with a knowing smile, "it was worth it, no? You've done good business?"

"Pretty much what one expected," Freddy said evenly. "Three or four thousand light field guns. A thousand or so of the medium size." Patriarca's jaw dropped. He had not expected his little fishing question to provoke an answer for which he would have paid richly. "Five hundred-odd heavies (or is it six? I hate carrying figures in my head, don't you?). Oh yes – and they want me to design a very heavy battery gun. All these are military secrets, you understand."

Patriarca gulped. "But why d'you tell *me*, Mr. Oxley?"

"Oh I have a reason." He looked at the two women, as if to say that it would keep until they withdrew.

The servants came and went, immaculate, unobtrusive. The dishes appeared and were whisked away with smooth efficiency. Freddy approved. Though Patriarca may have grown up among the ratruns of Tatavla, five hundred yards (and yet a million miles) from this house, he had learned quickly the way things ought to be. From his own experience he knew that servants often try to pull the wool over the eyes of a master who is not "top drawer"; he couldn't imagine them trying it on this fellow.

"D'you visit London much, Mr. Patriarca?" he asked.

"For Tattersall's auctions, yes. Otherwise my business keeps me here ... you understand."

"Yes, I'm beginning to wonder about doing business out here in the east. Is it wise or foolish?"

Patriarca beamed. "Oh very wise, Mr. Oxley – especially now that you've come to me. Many have not done so. Many have failed. Some have even died."

"Uh huh. I was thinking in more general terms."

Patriarca frowned. "Explain, please."

"Well, I don't know what it is but the farther east I travel, the less secure I feel. Not in my person, but in the way of business."

"Ah yes! The risks! Shall we perhaps talk of ..."

Freddy interrupted. "They're not small! The dogs of Russia, Austria-Hungary, Germany, France. And there are enemies within, too ... the Arabs ... and the government in a state of civil war. Perhaps you're so used to it you've learned to discount it. But if I had substantial assets here, I'd want to move some of them to safety. That's why I wondered how often you came to London."

Patriarca nodded brusquely at Miss Dirmikis. She smiled at Kate and said, "Shall we leave the gentlemen to their cigars?"

The meal had reached nowhere near that stage, but Kate complied without surprise – just like the well-brought-up young English lady she was pretending to be.

Patriarca chewed obsessively on his lip until they were gone. As he seated himself again he said, "One big trouble with England is if you don't know a duke or an earl ..." He completed the sentence by slitting his throat with his finger.

Freddy spread his hands in a gesture he had learned from Lotis. "That is why, when we visit each other's countries, we should always place ourselves in the hands of someone who understands the local ways."

"Austria I understand," Patriarca went on. "The emperor talks only to his army officers and to the old nobility. Oh – the money I threw away on the new nobles! If you haven't sixteen quarterings in your coat of arms ... pffft! You know the new nobility must even stand apart at the palace balls! Yes! They stretch a silken rope across the ballroom and the new nobility must stand below it and only watch. They're not permitted to dance even."

"Whereas our Prince of Wales seats more commoners than aristocracy at his table."

"Jews also."

"Yet even in Austria the English milord is more respected than most of their own nobility."

"And you?" Patriarca asked. "Have you dined there, Mr. Oxley?"

Freddy stared into those sapphire eyes and wondered how many violent deaths they had witnessed. "Not yet," he replied. "But with an order this size ..."

Patriarca licked his lips and smiled. "Yes indeed. Yes, I see. You begin to interest me greatly Mr. Oxley."

"I understand you're acting as agent for the Muraviev people. I presume you could buy yourself out of that?"

Patriarca sniffed. "They could be bought off, yes," he answered carefully.

"You see – with this order, which I have mentioned, plus one from the Austrian government, which perhaps I should not mention – but which I have reason to believe you are aware of" – not a flicker of an eyelid from the man – "I shall need an agent out here of vastly greater calibre than any I have employed heretofore. Indeed, I would not think of this new agent as an employee. More as a partner."

Patriarca gave a cynical laugh. "I understand! Partners share risks!"

"But that's why it would be so ideal for you. I ask myself: In the whole of the two eastern empires – what man is better placed to reduce those risks to nothing? And anyway – you're rich enough not to worry about *immediate* profit. You have reached that stage in your career when, like me, you can afford to take the long-term view, surely? If not I've come to the wrong man."

Patriarca frowned.

Freddy looked surprised. "But I thought we understood each other. The British government is not like other European powers. Look at the common men who have been raised to the aristocracy in the last twenty years – the railway contractors, the iron barons, the bankers ... many of them were born in little two-room cottages. I myself was born in such a home."

"It will be very nice for you," Patriarca said off-handedly. "Lord Oxley – yes, very nice."

"Oh Mr. Patriarca!" Freddy looked pained. "I am not talking about *me!*"

The man stopped breathing. His fingers, which had been drumming on the table, twitched feebly and were still. His eyes bulged.

"Yes!" Freddy cried. "*Now* you understand!"

"But ... is it possible?"

"For the man who made such a handsome contract with the Ottoman army? And the one we're now cooking with the Austrians? Provided he becomes a naturalized British subject, of course."

"You would tell them *I* did that?"

"*We.*"

Patriarca closed his eyes and smiled.

In a dreamy voice Freddy said, "Sir Basil Patriarca! I think – when you become naturalized – you must shorten it to Patriarc. Sir Basil Patriarc. Yes! Much more robust."

Patriarca laughed. "I must think. I must think."

"Of course you must. Give the idea time to sink in, eh? Come and see me in London in a month or two." He chuckled as he added, "Bring your contribution."

He had never seen a man change more violently from laughter to fury. "Contribution!"

"Yes, of course. A performance bond we may call it. We'll place it on joint deposit with the interest going to you. I'm not a bloodsucker – just a careful man. And a modest one – I should think a hundred-thousand pounds will do."

Patriarca spluttered incoherently – but there was a hint of fear in his eyes, too.

"We'll reduce it by twenty-thousand for each satisfactory year so that in five years – five good years – all need for a bond would have vanished."

Anger ... fear ... and now bewilderment. The man was remembering what Freddy had said about moving some of his assets to London. The Tatavla animal still raged within him, but the astute man of affairs was just beginning to glimpse the new terrain now opening up before him.

Freddy risked leaning forward and giving his arm a squeeze. "As you say – you need time to think. Take three months if you wish. Make all the inquiries and calculations you like ... Sir Basil!"

CHAPTER SIXTY

"SCUM!" FREDDY SAID as soon as they were in the cab and on their way back to the hotel.

"Oh dear – did it not go as you expected?" Kate asked.

"It went exactly as I expected. In a way that's the worst thing of all – not a single redeeming feature. No, that's not the worst. The worst of it is, the very very worst, is that every word I spoke is most probably true. Patriarca will be the best representative I could possibly have – in these parts, anyway. He'll increase the business tenfold. We'll both make a fortune. He'll become a naturalized Briton ... and they'll give him a baronetcy."

"Is that what you told him?"

He leaned his head gently on her shoulder and nodded. "Oh Miss Kate – dear Miss Kate – I'm weary of this business already, and I haven't even begun! Shall I throw in the sponge? Why don't we all go and live in Venezuela and vegetate until we rot? Doesn't that sound like paradise?"

She did not answer.

"Mmmm?" he prompted.

"You'd change your mind before we even reached the Atlantic."

He sighed at the truth of it. Now she leaned her head against his. The perfume of her body carried him sharply back to that night in St. Pierre, when she walked naked into his room and lay down beside him. He was filled with a sudden, almost overwhelming desire for her.

He sat rigid, hoping it would pass.

It did not.

"Why d'you suppose he withholds himself from those women he hires?" Kate asked.

"Perhaps he's afraid of them?" Freddy ventured.

"A man like that? Yet you could be right. Miss Dirmikis told me she's very fond of him and would dearly love to sleep with him. But she says he's like a horse that shies. Why are men sometimes afraid of women?"

Freddy racked his brains for a suitable answer. At length he said, "Perhaps that's not the reason. A man like that, as you say. Perhaps he thinks that to yield to them would be like revealing a weakness. I'll bet he goes back to Tatavla and picks up some really filthy slut and beats her senseless – gets his revenge for the weakness those beautiful women reveal in him."

When she did not respond he asked what she was thinking.

"Poor world!" she said.

They arrived at the hotel. "Shall we just drive around for a bit?" he asked. "I need to wind down. Get rid of this bad taste Patriarca's left in my blood. Or are you exhausted?"

"No, I'd like that."

He told the driver to go over to Stamboul. "You can see the garlands of lights on all the minarets," he told her. He was sitting straight again now, a little apart from her. "How did you stay so pure, Miss Kate? So good in spirit?"

She laughed. "How d'you know all that about Patriarca? Going to Tatavla and beating up some ugly slut – how d'you know about things like that?"

"Just a guess. Good heavens – you don't suppose *I* ..." He fell into silence, wishing he hadn't added that outburst.

"What *do* you do, Mr. Frederick?"

"Nothing."

"Really? You never want a woman to share ..."

"Well of course I do. I'm not a eunuch."

"So?"

"So ... what?"

"You never go out and just pick one up?"

He shrugged uncomfortably. "I'm often tempted, of course. But it passes."

"And you let it pass? Why? If you're thirsty, I'm sure you go out and buy a bottle of wine. Think nothing of it."

"But ... people are people. It's wrong. I mean ... people aren't *things*. Not like things you can buy."

She sighed.

"I'm right, Miss Kate," he insisted.

"I know, I know. It's just so unfair. Men are either so awful it makes you shrivel to be near them, or they're just *too* damn nice! You know? A little awfulness can sometimes be very good for the soul."

After a pause she put one finger on the crease of his trousers, at the knee, and moved it an inch or two toward him.

He trapped her hand and then lifted it to his lips.

She jerked it away angrily.

"We'd be risking so much," he explained.

"I can take care."

"No ... I mean – our friendship. All the good things we have between us. There's no one else in the world I can feel so close to, so comfortable with, as you, Miss Kate. Look how five years of absence simply melted away within minutes of our meeting each other again in Vienna. That's too rare to risk."

She swallowed noisily; he heard it above the rumble of the wheels.

She snuffled.

"Oh there now!" he said.

She turned to him, leaning into his shoulder, and howled, letting the astrakhan of his collar absorb the noise and the tears. He held her tight and stroked her shoulder and ran his fingers into her hair; and in a while she grew calm again. "I'm sorry about that," she said.

He squeezed her again. "I'm the one who's sorry."

When they reached Stamboul he paid off the cab and they walked along the waterfront to let the cool night air drive the redness from her eyes. About halfway between the two bridges they were approached by a small, laughing crowd: two huge men strode out ahead, carrying lanterns; two others similarly brought up the rear; and in between trotted a couple of dozen veiled women, pushing and giggling. Freddy remembered Lotis's description, last night. "It's the harem of some rich merchant or pasha," he told Kate. "Apparently in Ramadan they all go out and visit as many other harems as possible. Those are eunuchs guarding them."

Kate watched them vanish up one of the pitch-black side alleys. "No one has the answer, do they!" she said ruefully. "Not marriage. Not the harem. Not ... what I got into. There isn't an answer!"

He took her arm. "If I hadn't married Ann ..." he began.

"Yes?" She squeezed his hand to encourage him.

"Oh, I know so much more now. I feel so much wiser."

"You mean you'd make a wise mistake now instead of a foolish one."

He sighed. "No. I made the wise mistake when I was seventeen. Do you know that Lawrence wasn't originally my son?"

"What d'you mean!" she began. "Of course he's ..."

The tension in his arm, the pressure of his hand around hers dried the words in her throat. "Oh Mr. Frederick," she said, almost in a whisper. "Do you really want to tell me this?"

"Ann and I were already courting but ... well, I was sent away for a few weeks and Ann had her head turned by the son of the local squire. Oh, it sounds ridiculous – put like that. He was actually my best friend. He's Lawrence's ... what can one call him? Begetter."

"Why d'you want me to ... share this knowledge?"

He thought about it and said, "I don't know. I suppose I want to offer you something that's important to me. There's more."

She remained silent.

"This friend's parents paid something for Lawrence's upbringing. They also helped me through school. That's how I got started. Then a few years later Ann had another child."

"Oh my God!"

"I haven't told you yet."

"You said *Ann*, not *we*."

"Ah. Well this time the father was another boyhood friend. So I didn't beget either of my two children."

Miss Kate stopped.

"What now?" he asked.

"Was that just before she ran away to the West Indies?"

"Yes."

"And yet you still tried to find her? You still wanted her back?"

"She was more important to me than any of that."

"Was?"

He made her walk again. "Yes, I think it's over now – for all the reasons I mentioned earlier. Goodness – it seems days ago. Was it only this evening?"

"Will you divorce her?"

He was silent a long while before he answered. "I don't know. We'll see."

"That's extraordinary about Lawrence. I'd never have guessed. Even now I can't see it. I mean he's so like you in so many ways."

"That's not strange. I'm the only father he's ever known. We're not animals. Instinct is only a tiny fraction of our make-up. Almost everything else is what we choose to make of it – or are deluded into making of it."

"D'you ever see this friend ... Lawrence's father?"

Freddy chuckled dryly. "You know those cables I received this morning?"

"Ann told me. Something about a dowager?"

"She's his mother. She, or they, seem to be in quite serious trouble. She's not one to exaggerate or send out hysterical messages over nothing."

Kate gave a little laugh. "So now you're going back to save them from whatever it is!"

"Ironical."

She turned aside and leaned against the river wall. The garish lights of Galata twinkled in a never-ending pattern all across the Golden Horn. The raucous voice of its nightlife carried clearly to them.

Her beauty moved him. He wanted to ask her if she might one day think of settling down. But why should she? She was even younger than Ann. There she was, travelling around the world, making good money, enjoying life, meeting people – she'd always loved that. Why should *any* woman who enjoyed that sort of life want to exchange it for the petty routines and cares and squabbles of domesticity? He absolutely understood Ann's point of view.

But he envied the young man who would one day sweep Miss Kate off her feet and appear so *wonderful* to her that she'd sacrifice it all for him.

"Penny for your thoughts," he said.

"I was thinking about the lives of the saints."

He laughed. "Of course! Stupid question, really."

Her laughter joined his. "No, that's a book I was reading back in Vienna. The previous occupant of my room left it behind. You know most of them led terrible lives. People were just awful to them. I kept thinking how could they *do* this to Saint Soandso when he was so obviously a saint. But that's the point, I guess. It *wasn't* obvious. You could live next door to a saint for years and not know it."

He realized she was getting very tired. They walked briskly back across the bridge and up through Galata, looking neither right nor left, not stopping at any of the myriad distractions, barely talking.

Five minutes after he had retired for the night, there was a timid knock at his door. It was Kate, holding a note in her hand. He recognised Ann's writing at once.

"Dear Kate: Call me weak if you will," it ran, "but I feel great dangers for me every hour I remain. I discovered a cargo boat sailing tonight for Haifa and I have arranged to travel by it. I shall go straight to Jerusalem and there wait for you seven days. After that, if you do not come, we shall meet as arranged at Alexandria. If you want to know what prompted this it was when the midshipman came up with a message for Frederick saying that passage had been arranged aboard *HMS Ulysses* for Mr. Oxley and his wife and son. The navy must have misunderstood our intentions, but *you are free to make what you wish of it, Kate!*"

Freddy looked around his room. "No note for me, of course. No – she never does when she runs away." He smiled at her to show he was joking. "What does she mean – you're free to make what you wish of it?"

Miss Kate did not answer directly but just stared at him with a strange, compelling, unreadable expression. A mad idea crossed his mind: She could pretend to be Mrs. Oxley ... return to England with him ... wait while he secured a divorce ....

I must be going insane, he thought.

Why was she staring like that?

"Well?" she asked with a smile. She hardly dared breathe; she could almost hear his mind working.

What can I say? he wondered. He had to say something. He blurted out the first thing that came into his head. He picked up the note and remarked, "Blue paper. She used to like green."

Miss Kate turned away and shuffled toward the door.

"You're not going to vanish overnight again, are you?" he asked, again meaning it as a joke.

She faced him. He had never seen her so weary.

"No," she said.

PART SIX

HOME TO ROOST

CHAPTER SIXTY-ONE

"WELL?" THE DOWAGER ASKED peremptorily. She had brought Freddy straight up to her own drawing room the minute he returned from Barcham and Browne, solicitors to the firm of Mortimer.

"In a nutshell, Lady Mortimer, the company's situation is serious – but not, I think, hopeless. Unless there are horrors yet to be discovered."

"Oh there are bound to be." She wrung her hands as she paced restlessly about.

"I can understand why people have been afraid to turn over too many stones. What we've discovered these past two days is bad enough. Wilde was obviously as mad as a hatter; they carried him off just in time. But he must also have been some kind of genius to keep such a ramshackle collection in any sort of running order. D'you mind if I sit down?"

"Please! Oh look how I'm forgetting myself." She watched him lower his frame into the chair, as carefully as an eighty-year-old. He sank his head into his hands and massaged his eyes.

"Oh you poor dear," she said.

He looked up at her and smiled. "I mustn't take credit for being utterly selfless. I have an interest to declare."

Curiosity made her frown.

"I'll come to it later, if I may. At the moment I would sell my soul for just one glass of your sherry."

"Of course, of course!" She went toward the bell cord and then, thinking better of it, changed direction and filled his glass herself.

He took the merest sip and leaned back, closing his eyes. He could not remember the last time he had felt so utterly exhausted. "Be with you in a moment," he promised.

"You'll dine with us tonight? We can eat up here if you're too tired to dress."

"I think Clive and Eleanor should hear what I have to say, too."

"Very well, very well." She did not like it. She wanted to digest his news and recommendations before the others were told anything; but Freddy was determined not to play the game that way.

"Can't you give me at least some idea?" she asked.

"I'll give you one trivial example of the horrors we're finding," he told her. "Wilde used to keep the record – the *only* record – of an entire month's stock transactions on a single sheet of foolscap paper. What's more he kept it *in pencil*, so that he could bring it up to date every few days. I had to use a magnifying glass to read it. You'd think he trained little beetles to do his writing. One of the office clerks told me they had to sharpen the indiarubber before they erased anything, otherwise they could accidentally wipe out two or three items at a single stroke, any one of which might be a record of stock transfers worth hundreds of pounds! It actually happened, more than once."

"And nobody questioned such an idiotic system?" the dowager asked.

Freddy almost answered her but held his tongue.

She snorted. "I know what you're thinking! The man who should have questioned it was braying his head off in parliament."

"That's hardly a fair description of a son who's hailed on all sides as the rising star of the Liberal Party."

His defence of Clive was so lacklustre that the dowager grew anxious once more. "Why don't you try to sleep for just an hour, you poor dear? There's a daybed next door. I'll go and arrange a buffet dinner so that we can send the servants off. I'll get them to bring you one of Clive's dressing gowns."

He warned her, "You may need some Oxlite to wake me."

Yet when they woke him, only ninety minutes later, he felt as if he'd slept the clock round. His evening clothes had been fetched over from Hob's Hall; the freshly starched and laundered linen was like a tonic. He was a new man.

It did not, however, make his message any the easier to deliver.

Clive was as direct as his mother had been. "Well – are we solvent still?" he asked as soon as the four of them were alone.

Freddy looked around at them: Clive, out of his depth, angry with himself, wishing the problem involved people or political affairs; the dowager, having seen her circle of friends depleted from time to time by bankruptcy ... having visited those "fallen gems" in their thrifty lodging houses in Normandy ... now imagining herself among them; and Eleanor – strangely calm ... holding herself aloof from it all. Each of them was looking to him as to a conjuror; he'd surely know some trick for saving the day.

"Solvent?" he repeated. "It'll be a week or so yet before anyone can answer that, I'm afraid."

"But surely it's just a matter of adding up two columns," Clive objected. "Assets one side, debts the other." He gave a hollow laugh. "There's no difficulty in listing the debts."

When Freddy did not immediately answer, Eleanor asked, "Isn't it as simple as that?"

"First track down your assets," Freddy said. "I don't know if you're aware of it but Mortimer's owns no fewer than ... well, have a guess. How many separate bits of property d'you suppose you own? I'm not talking about individual houses, now. Take the whole of the Blythe estate as a single property – and the same for the Eastcote estate. How many separate parcels of land and sundry buildings do you imagine you own?"

Clive shrugged. "Forty?"

"Two hundred and twenty seven!"

They all turned and stared at him in disbelief.

"It's true. In fact, we're still counting. And almost all of them are just ... things like a small blacksmith's forge at Great Barr, an old tithe barn near King's Norton, four or five strips of land beside the Warwick and Birmingham Canal, the abandoned brickfield at Claydon, an oakwood at Brierley Hill ... it just goes on and on and on. We shall have to send out a lad with a pushcart and a camera. His first task will be to find the wretched places and then photograph them. Then perhaps we can begin to form some estimate of their worth. *Your* worth."

"Two hundred and twenty seven!" Clive was still reeling.

"We know what they cost, but whether Wilde got them cheap or paid through the nose, no one can say."

"And Mr. Wilde bought them all?" Eleanor asked.

"All during the last five years. Lord knows what was in his mind. It may turn out he was being very astute. Each one of these properties may be so situated as to block any potential development, thus giving it premium value to the developer."

"Or?" the dowager said.

Freddy sighed. "The possibility has to be faced. Wilde may have fallen off his rocking horse, as they say round here. We may never know. He confided in no one. He was a law unto himself."

"When he should have been a law unto *you!*" the dowager spat at Clive.

Freddy interposed quickly, "There's nothing to be gained by ..."

But Clive interrupted. "No. Let her get it out. She won't be happy until then."

For the first time in his life Freddy asserted himself over all of them. As the dowager drew breath to flare back at her son, he said, "Quarrel as much as you like when I'm gone. But I still have a long furrow to plough – and an early start tomorrow is essential. May I tell you what I propose?"

"Can we afford to wait while we discover whether these properties are assets or liabilities?" Clive asked.

"That's what I'm coming to. There's no doubt about the main assets, of course: the three large factories and their associated foundries, warehouses, roads, reservoirs, and so on. And also the two housing estates, Blythe and Eastcote, where most of the workers live. There's little argument about their value."

"Except that the capital which should have gone into maintaining and improving them has been frittered away in these other ..."

Freddy cleared his throat. "Before you talk their value down too far, Clive old sport, you should know that The Oxley Company is your most likely purchaser."

"You!"

Only Eleanor was unsurprised. Her self-contained smile suggested she had known it all along.

"In fact, I'm far and away your most likely purchaser. I doubt if you'd get another, things being as they are. Trade, as you know, is in the doldrums. Very little is ..."

"You needn't tell me!" Clive interrupted. "That's why all this has come to a head so suddenly."

"But it just so happens that I managed ... I mean I arrived in Constantinople on *exactly* the right day – pure stroke of luck ... I managed to secure an order that exceeds the present capacity of The Oxley Company. All during the voyage back I was trying to work out schemes whereby I could lease your factories from you, so that ..."

"Or subcontract the work to us!" Clive suggested.

Freddy fished in his brief case and pulled out a document, which he passed to Clive. "Heads of agreement with the Ottoman Government. Clause thirteen, para two. You'll see it expressly forbids any subcontracting."

Clive pushed it back with one finger, unread; he was more than a little surprised. "I'll take your word for it, Foxy. You needn't ... I mean, I'd believe you without your producing documents."

"It's important to me that you know I'm being completely open and straight. What I'm proposing is that my company should buy the factories and the estates, as they stand, for a hundred and sixty thousand pounds. Cash in the hand – tomorrow, if you wish."

"But where would you lay your hands on that amount?" Clive asked.

Freddy was tempted to say he'd take it out of Petty Cash. "It's just a fortunate moment," he said. "Last week I couldn't have raised half of it."

Eleanor was watching him guardedly. The dowager seemed favourable to the idea. Clive asked, "And the other two-hundred-odd properties?"

"It gives you time, you see. You can investigate their true value – which frankly is something I have neither the time nor the patience to undertake. And you can sell them or keep them as you think fit."

"I follow! You get the good parts, but I may keep the rubbish. Is that it?"

Freddy explained patiently. "You need immediate cash.

The good parts are the only ones that have any immediate value. Of course, if you're already convinced that the rest *is* rubbish and you'd care to throw them in at a rubbish-price – five thousand pounds, say – I'd be forced to take them. As I freely confess, I'm in a desperate hole, too. I must either buy a factory or build one."

"In fact, a hundred and sixty thousand pounds seems a fair price," the dowager said.

"It's about thirty thousand more than the factories and housing estates are worth," Freddy pointed out.

"We're not looking for charity ..." Clive began.

"And nor am I offering it. There's one thing I haven't mentioned yet. I've been dreading the moment when I have to tell you this but I have to make it a condition of the sale that Mortimer Hall and Park are included in the transfer."

For a moment they were too stunned to reply. Then they all shouted at once – it was impossible ... never ... he must be mad ... he must suppose they were mad ...

He waited for the storm to die sufficiently to allow him to interrupt: "It's understandable you should take it like this. After all, Mortimer Hall is your ..."

"I'm glad you don't suppose we're freaks!" Clive said.

"Just hear me out. You'll have life tenancy, of course, and at a peppercorn rent. My company will maintain the fabric of the property and not seek dilapidations. I hope it goes without saying that the necessary legal agreements governing the tenancy will always be interpreted generously in your favour ..."

"By God, you've planned this!" Clive said. He was no longer listening. "This is something you've worked for all your life. You want the lot! Nothing less will do."

Eleanor was watching Freddy with a catlike contempt.

He appealed to the dowager. "I planned this, eh? Do *you* believe that? When did I ever beg you or Clive to let Wilde have a free hand? How often have I warned you about the direction things were taking? And how could I possibly have planned this depression in trade?"

"Stop it, Mr. Oxley!" Eleanor said at last.

Everyone turned to her in surprise.

"Stop what?" Freddy asked.

"Driving wedges between us. You already know we'll have to sell out to you. Be content with that."

It was Clive who objected first. "See here now – it's by no means certain we'll have to sell out – not to *him*, anyway!"

Eleanor faced him calmly. "We have no choice, dear."

"I'm afraid she's right," Freddy began.

Clive rounded on him. "You just shut up!"

But Freddy continued, trying to show them how reasonable his plan was: "I'm not seeking the property for myself, you understand. Not to move into, I mean. If I moved anywhere, it would be into the old dower house. But anyone looking at a map of your company properties can see at a glance that the existence of the Hall and estate, slap bang in the middle of it all ... well it does knock thousands of pounds off its value."

Clive hammered the table with his fist. "Never!" he shouted.

Freddy shrugged. "It's your privilege, of course. May I ask what you propose instead?"

"Perhaps we'll sell off these other properties."

"I should think five thousand pounds would be your maximum return in the present market. Some of them won't even pay back the legal costs of the conveyance. Still ... five thousand is better than nothing."

"We let you in," Clive said bitterly. "We show you the books in the hope that – as a friend – you'll be able to suggest a way out, and instead ..."

His mother interrupted. "We *made* you," she reminded Freddy. "You were a nothing, a nobody, a little worm of an apprentice. Everything you have you owe to us – and well you know it. I ask you now, if there's a shred of decent feeling inside you – if you happen to have one hundred and sixty-five thousand pounds to spare – when fifty thousand would probably save us ... don't you see what the decent thing would be?"

Freddy closed his eyes and shook his head against the impossibility of bridging the gulf he now saw opening up between their perception and his. "Fifty thousand pounds would save you, eh?"

"Yes!"

"Save you for *what*, Lady Mortimer? For more of the same?"

She shrugged angrily and looked away.

"Exactly," Freddy said. He turned to Clive. "I'll give you the fifty thousand," he promised. "But on one condition. You give up your political career tomorrow. Indeed, tonight! And you apply yourself to the running of your business for the thirty-hour day and the eight-day week it's going to require. That's what I'll have to put into it – and I've probably forgotten more about running a business than you'll ever know."

Clive looked at him, trapped, haunted. "Oh it's all just tricks. Tricks! Tricks! You'd have talked Jesus into jumping off the temple. But I know full well that this is the culmination of a deeply laid plot. You know what it goes back to – and so do I."

Freddy asked Eleanor, "What d'you say?"

She turned her back on him.

"If you had a spark of decency," the dowager said, "you'd give Clive the money without conditions. When I think of what we've done for you!"

Freddy lost his temper at that. "You're drowning!" he yelled at her. "Don't you understand? You're drowning. You're a hundred yards from the shore. And you're begging me to throw you a rope that's only fifty yards long. What possible good d'you imagine can come of it?"

She went to the door. "If you're simply going to hurl abuse at me, then all communication between us is at an end. I intend to cut you in future. Do not embarrass me or yourself by approaching me in public." Her parting words to Clive were: "None of this need have happened if you had heeded *me!*"

Freddy went to the door and called after her: "You didn't say it! When you've thought it over and realized I'm right, I shan't remember you said it."

She swept upstairs as if he had not spoken.

He turned back to the others. "It must be especially hard for her ..." he began.

"Viper!" Clive shouted at him. "I ought to have you thrashed. I ought to have you put out on the dung heap where you belong."

Eleanor touched his arm gently. He flung himself from

the room. She turned to Freddy and said quietly, "So now you have it all."

"And all you'll have is a hundred-odd thousand once your debts are settled – plus a life tenancy here! Good heavens, my offer is worth double what anyone else is going to give you. The trouble with you people is that you were born with money, you grew up with money, you've never known life without money – and so you imagine it's as natural as air."

"We certainly don't put it before friendship."

He shook away her words angrily. "Listen! Your opinion of me is neither here nor there. Just put it on one side for a minute and *listen*! Mortimer's probably is insolvent. In three or four days, we'll know for certain. If you are and you continue to trade, you will be breaking the law. Clive could go to jail for it."

She turned white. Freddy continued, "The only legal course open to you then is to go into liquidation. And I can assure you, with trade as it is you'd be absolutely hammered. You'd come out of it with next to nothing. Perhaps I should have explained all this. I thought you all knew. I just didn't want to rub it in. Frankly Clive has been an absolute B.F."

She flared up at that. "Oh – so not content with turning Clive and his mother against each other, you now seek to do the same between me and him!"

Freddy threw up his hands in despair and started toward the door. "I give up!" he told the oak panelling.

But she ran ahead of him. Her eyes flashed, her nostrils quivered. "Oh no you don't! You're not going away from here without someone telling you a few home truths. What harm have the Mortimers ever done you? Answer me that!"

He stared at her, uncertain as to how much she knew.

"See!" she crowed. "You can't answer. You may think I know nothing of what happened long ago – nothing of Lawrence's true parentage. But I've worked it out."

"I see." He was very calm now. "If you think that has played any part in these affairs, then ..."

She ignored him. "I know that Lawrence's true father is Tony Knox-Riddell."

It stopped Freddy in mid-sentence.

But there was no stopping Eleanor now. "I know that

money from Tony was somehow funnelled through the Mortimers to you – to pay for your start in life. And I can just imagine how you blackmailed it out of poor Tony. I've seen some examples of ruthlessness in my time but never anything like tonight's display. How you can live with yourself, I can't imagine – but it's patently obvious that no one else can live with you. Just think of that now! Every friend you ever had has deserted you now. You've alienated them all. God help the two thousand men who were once proud and happy to work for Mortimer's!"

"Have you finished?" he asked.

"Yes – except to repeat what the dowager said. We shall all cut you from now on. You are dead to us."

Calmly he stared back at her. There was no point in trying to argue. "Then these are my last words to you," he said. "Some time before you die, before Clive dies, I want you to tell him what you've said to me tonight. And then tell him I replied that I would not come between you and him."

She flared up again. "You'd never get the chance!"

"That isn't what I mean. Just tell him I said it."

When he had gone she stared at the space he had left, remembering his strange parting words. The curious thing was she had intended running straight to Clive, to tell him how she had put the Oxley bug in its place ... how utterly she had squashed him. But now, because of what he had said, because of that supreme confidence which never seemed to desert him, she could not face it. All her elation had gone. In its place was a gnawing fear, formless as yet.

Freddy returned home, too tired to understand what a dreadful thing had just happened; he barely got undressed before he fell into bed. He was fast asleep when Emmy arrived with the cocoa. She shook him gently but he did not stir.

She sat on the edge of his bed a long while, looking fondly down at him, sipping her own cup. She left his there to get cold, so that he would know of her visit in the morning. She bent over and kissed him tenderly.

"My dear master," she said, relishing the words. "My dear, dear master."

Then she turned down the wick of the lamp and went off to her own little room.

CHAPTER SIXTY-TWO

CLIVE AND HIS MOTHER held out for the best part of two months. They tried to find a buyer – any buyer – other than Freddy. He, meanwhile, went ahead with alternative plans to build a new factory in fields out beyond Knowle. At first each potential buyer was enthusiastic; the name Mortimer was still one to conjure with. But when they looked closely and saw what chaos the works were in, they backed off pretty quickly. One of them told Clive that the various components of the Mortimer windmill pump travelled twenty miles around the workshops during their manufacture and assembly. If the job were properly organized, that figure could be cut down to half a mile. But, as the man pointed out, no one was going to buy such headaches in times like these.

In the end the Mortimers realized that Freddy had actually offered them what would be the market price in a good year, and they accepted. But his insistence on taking the Hall as well still stuck in their throats. They refused to meet him, and on the rare occasions when their paths accidentally crossed, they cut him dead.

One change often precipitates another. The Mortimers had no intention of accepting a life tenancy from Freddy. They made arrangements to rent Valiant House instead. But then Tony Knox-Riddell offered them his place out near Meriden. His mother had died the year before; it was now clear that, because of Sally's origins and her high-handed behaviour, they would never be accepted socially in the Midlands, so they had decided to buy a villa in northern Italy, where they would probably see more of their true friends in a month than they would in a year back home. So Clive and Eleanor bought the old Knox-Riddell estate.

This created difficulties for the dowager. She had few

friends out Meriden way and her increasing age would make a misery of her frequent journeys back to her old stamping grounds. At the last moment, therefore, she decided after all to accept the life tenancy of the Hall. "I'll live till I'm a hundred, just to torment the urchin," she laughed. They never referred to Freddy now – always "the urchin."

Freddy himself moved into the old Queen Anne dower house down on Ravenscroft Road. Most of the county, who heard only the Mortimer side of the argument, turned against him. His social life ceased to exist. Not that he had time to notice it; he was so frantically busy reorganizing the old Mortimer factories, retraining the mechanics and labourers as artificers, foundrymen, lathe-turners, and drop-forgers, and designing the heavy battery guns for the Dardanelles fortresses – not to mention trying to stay one step ahead of Patriarca, and keeping all his former clients happy – plus the thousand other cares of a large and growing business. The Ottoman contract had made The Oxley Company the largest arms manufacturer in the British Empire; other provisional orders were coming in, together with requests for demonstrations from powers as far flung as Argentina, America, Persia, and Japan. The British Government had to be kept closely informed of all these developments.

For months, and ultimately for years, Freddy lived on sandwiches and light ale. He ate standing up at his drawing board, or "on the hoof" – walking around the factories – or at whatever time he could manage, between his various appointments. Many a night he slept in a light truckle bed at the office.

By the end of that first year his half-dozen most senior managers were each carrying more daily responsibility than he himself had borne twelve months ago. In recognition of the fact, he cut each of them in for a share of the profits. Remembering Eleanor's parting jibe, he devised a similar profit-sharing scheme in the form of twice-yearly bonuses for all weekly paid hands – the first of its kind in the industrial midlands. The company was one of the few to escape the great engineering strike of '85. That, too, did not endear him to his fellow industrialists; but by now he was becoming too important to be simply cut or ignored.

The last guns for the Ottoman contract were delivered at the end of '86. Patriarca, true to Freddy's prediction, had meanwhile secured two more orders of similar size from the Austrian and German imperial armies. The British Government could no longer overlook the importance of Freddy's achievement. He had by now endowed libraries and schools, parks and hygienic footbaths, wings of hospitals, university chairs in organic chemistry and the new science of metallurgy, not to mention scholarships in science and mathematics for gifted poor children – "Oxley scholars," as they came to be called.

In '86 Gladstone's government (and Clive with it) gave way to the first administration of the Marquis of Salisbury. In the '87 honours list Freddy was created a viscount. Clive lobbied strenuously against the appointment, but he was now relatively powerless. In any case, sentiment in London, which knew little and cared less about parochial Midlands squabbles, was against him; most people felt that Freddy was long overdue his ennoblement.

Friends advised him to assume a territorial title – Lord Solihull and Lord Knowle were two suggestions. But he felt that smacked of dishonesty; he was not of the landed, territorial classes. It was a man called "Oxley" who had won the honour, and that was the name which should be ennobled. Thus he became the First Viscount Oxley of Ravenscroft. The day he put on the ermine robes and took his seat in the House of Lords was the most nerve-wracking in his life; but Lord Frampton, one of the two who flanked and introduced him on that day, said he'd seen an eighth duke who, on *his* introduction, had been "in an absolute blue funk and shivered a jolly sight worse."

All through those years Miss Kate faithfully sent him the details of The Angels' advance bookings. Mostly they were to places he never visited or no longer had time to visit. He did only the major capitals now – and then only when negotiations were already well advanced. But even there his luck was out. When The Angels played London he was in Venezuela; when they were back in Vienna, it was impossible for him to leave St. Petersburg; when they were in St. Petersburg, he had to stay in London. It became a standing joke that the fates which had brought them back together in '83 had regretted the folly of it ever since. The letters from Kate dwindled in frequency and finally, in '89, petered out altogether.

Then, to his surprise, in 1890 he saw a notice in *The Times* announcing a concert at Sadler's Wells to be given by The Angels of Harmony. He was in Paris at the time but his business there was less well advanced than his agent had hoped so he decided to leave it to simmer for a week while he returned to London and surprised Miss Kate. And Ann, of course. He wondered if she knew she was now Lady Oxley.

It was a raw November night when his train drew into Victoria Station. A thick fog had settled on the city, delaying his carriage. He stood on the pavement outside, tasting the sulphur in the air and marvelling at how deeply the fog muted the incessant roar of the iron-wheeled traffic. To fill in the time he telephoned the theatre to confirm that The Angels were, indeed, appearing that night. They were. By the time his carriage drew up in the station forecourt he was as excited as he had been when waiting for Ann to appear from the Wildes' house in Ferndown Crescent ... how long since? Lawrence was twenty-two now, so it was twenty-three years ago. It seemed so much longer than that.

For the first time in years he thought of those days again. He remembered the evening Clive and Tony and Gray had first seen the Grand Soarer. Such exuberance! The shadows that hung over their lives were then still far in the future. And where were they now? Gray was in prison after that awful rape on the 11.20 to Aldershot. Tony was in self-imposed exile in Italy. And Clive, out of office, was said to be turning into "a teeny-weeny bit of a bore," as Emmy reported the local gossip over the teacups.

He mourned the loss of Clive's friendship; but he never doubted that one day they'd make it up again. Clive would realize how wrong he'd been.

In places the fog was so thick the footman had to leap down and, straddling the kerb and gutter, wave the horses on with a carbide torch. When they finally arrived at the theatre he found it in a state of pandemonium. The fog was as dense inside the building as out. There was more coughing than singing coming from the stage and the performers were saying they could not continue; in any case, half the house could see nothing of the performance beyond vague movements, as if through several layers of gauze. Freddy went round to the stage door.

The doorman was a real Cerberus. "There's a lot of dirty old men calls theirselves Lord This and Lord That, my lord," he said.

Freddy gave him his card.

"There's a lot who consider a shillin' for a hundred cards werry well worth the inwestment, my lord."

Freddy, more amused than annoyed, said, "I wonder do many of them claim that their *wife* is to be found among the artistes?"

The fellow's eyes twinkled. "Now that is a new one, my lord. What might her name be? There's no Oxley among ..."

"No her professional name is Howard. Ann Howard."

The man checked the list and shook his head. "Nor no Howard neither."

"Ann anything?"

"No – no Ann."

Freddy was at a loss. "Is Miss Kate Kendall in the house then?"

"And who might she be?"

"She's their manager, surely? Kate Kendall."

At that moment a young artiste happened to come out of one of the dressing rooms. She heard the name and turned at once toward Freddy. "Excuse me, did you say Kate Kendall?"

"Yes. Is she here?" Freddy looked carefully at the girl. She was not one of The Angels, he was fairly sure of that.

"She's left The Angels – didn't you know?"

He felt the blood draining from his face. "How? Is she all right?"

The young woman smiled encouragingly. "Right as rain. They retired – that's all. Last year it was."

Ten minutes and a tot of brandy later Freddy had the full story. Letty Lockyer and Betty Jameson had both died of yellow fever in the summer of '89, in Freetown. The remaining Angels had taken on two new girls but somehow the spirit had gone out of it for them and they had decided to sell out the name and goodwill and retire on the proceeds. Maria Dawson, the main singer, had returned to England where she was now pursuing a solo career.

"And the other three?" Freddy asked.

The woman couldn't be positive but she was pretty sure they had settled in Rio de Janeiro, where they had started an academy of music and dance.

Wondering why Miss Kate had not written to tell him all this, Freddy went not to his own home in Belgrave Square but to Lawrence's set of chambers in The Albany. Lawrence was then at Gould's, the merchant bankers, on the understanding that when he was familiar with the workings of the City and the money market he'd return to The Oxley Company. The people at Gould's said he was "a real chip off the old block" – quick on the uptake, a phenomenal worker with a memory like an elephant. The only criticism they had was that he kept things too much to himself. He never volunteered his opinion; one had to drag it out of him – yet it always proved more apt and incisive than any of the waffle that others had been spouting for hours.

"It's a grand night to be indoors," Freddy said as Lawrence let him in. "I have some most extraordinary news for you."

"I'm afraid I have some news for you, pater." His tone was grave.

"Am I going to need a brandy? I mean another brandy?"

"Oh I shouldn't think so. It's the dowager Lady Mortimer. I'm afraid she's dying. She's asking to see you. In fact, she's been asking for days but – for one reason or another – word has only just reached us."

"Yes, I can imagine."

There were no more trains that night but the two men were both on the first one out of Euston the following morning, arriving at New Street before seven. They had sent a telegram ahead so their arrival was expected. It was Rosamund, Clive and Eleanor's eldest daughter, who welcomed them to Mortimer Hall.

"Young Toby has been taken ill," she told them. "Daddy had to take Mummy back home."

Of course! Freddy thought. "I hope it's nothing serious. How is the dowager?"

A tear trembled in Rosamund's eye. "I can't imagine

what's keeping her alive. She asks for you, over and over. Could you ... I mean, I know you've been up travelling half the night, but ..."

"But of course I'll go to her at once." He smiled. "I don't know this house at all well, I'm afraid. Which room is it?"

She led the way upstairs. "I'll wait for you in the morning room, pater," Lawrence called after them.

"No no – you come, too. She is a great and noble lady and was always very kind to you. You should see her one last time."

But when Freddy stood beside the bed and looked down at the appalling remnant that lay there, he regretted having asked his son to share the moment. A skull covered in fine gray silk, wetted and plastered to the bone, would have been a less distressing sight. Her head was so light and fragile it hardly dented the pillow. The sheets and blankets, tucked firmly in on either side, gave no indication whatever that a body lay beneath them.

At first Freddy was sure she had already died. There was no sign of breathing.

"Dowager?" he bent low and murmured near her ear. "Lady Mortimer?"

Her eyelids trembled. A small noise escaped her throat.

"I'm here. Freddy Oxley – the little urchin, eh! You said you wanted me."

Rosamund watched with bated breath, her eyes wide. Lawrence stole a glance at her. It was four years since he had seen her last. She was eighteen now, lovely to look at.

"Ox ... ley?" the old woman managed to say. Her voice was thick and gravelly.

"Freddy Oxley. I'm here. I've come to see you."

They became aware that she was struggling to get one hand above the counterpane. Freddy didn't like to touch her bedclothes. Rosamund came forward and lifted the sheet. "What d'you want, grandma?" she asked. The odour from beneath the sheets was of camphor.

The old lady's eyes were open now. They peered vaguely about her until they found Freddy; then they fastened on him and never let go. "Him," she said. "Him." Her hand wobbled in his direction.

He reached forward and grasped it as tenderly as he could. Lawrence put a chair behind his knees; he felt it and sat down gratefully. The young man touched Rosamund gently on the sleeve and beckoned her to come a little way off.

The dowager was trying to say something. The phlegm gurgled in her throat. Freddy leaned nearer to her, turning his ear to her lips. "God be good to you," he said.

She gurgled again. There was anger in it now.

"I have never ceased to be grateful to you," he went on. "That breach between us was a terrible pain to me. I'm glad it's over at last."

A fury seemed to possess her at this.

"When spring comes," he added, "I'll wheel you about the terrace and we'll look at the daffodils and laugh over all the good old times."

"Mortimer!" Her voice broke at last through the congestion in her throat.

"Mortimer? Yes?" he encouraged.

"Mortimer ... inherit."

"Go on!"

Her grip on his hand intensified. Where did she manage to find such strength in an arm that was wasted to nothing?

"A Mortimer will inherit!" She managed it at last. The triumph filled her with laughter; her dreadful, dying, eldritch cackles filled the room.

"Of course!" Freddy told her. "Of course!"

She must have thought he did not understand for she repeated the cry: "A Mortimer will inherit!"

"Of course!" Freddy repeated. "We always knew it!"

She looked up into his eyes and realized that he had cheated her of her final triumph. Her body had died days ago; only her will had kept it alive until this moment, to crow her triumph over him. And still he had cheated her. She gave one final, terrible cry of despair and died. The three of them watched in anguish as her flesh sank into that utter stillness of death.

Freddy reached his free hand forward and closed her eyelids. "The Lord be merciful unto her and bless her," he said.

Their echo of his *amen* seemed to remind him of their

presence. He looked up at them, almost in surprise. "Ten minutes?" he asked. "Her soul is still lingering. We have many memories to share."

"Of course." Rosamund led Lawrence down to the morning room. "Oh why have our parents fallen out!" she said angrily. "Your father's such a good man."

He smiled ruefully. "It's years since we played together, Ros. Remember?"

She nodded and smiled back at him. There was a new light in her eye, a sort of devilment. She was sizing him up.

"I've missed you," he said. "What have you been doing with yourself?"

"I climbed the Matterhorn."

"Did you!" He was agog. "I hadn't heard that."

"Oh yes, that was before the expedition to the North Pole but after I went big-game hunting in Africa."

He laughed. "Oh, I see."

"In short, Lawrence, I've done all the wonderful, fascinating things every young girl does by the time she's eighteen. Actually I sing like a corncrake. I play the piano as well as Humpty Dumpty can straddle a wall. I adore dancing almost as much as I do standing out in the rain at midnight. Oh what is to become of me!" Her effervescent good humour overcame her. Then she was ashamed. "No no, this will not do! How dreadful of me. Do forgive me. I'm a bit light-headed, what with ..." She raised her eyes toward the ceiling. "Have you had breakfast?"

"Hours ago."

"Luncheon then. Your father looks as if he'll say no, so we'll take his refusal for granted. But you look hungry."

He nodded. The realization was just dawning on him that in many ways she was like Miss Kate. She was commanding and self-assured without ever being bossy or mannish.

She looked at him, still sizing him up. "They say you're a silent one. Strong and silent. Do your thoughts run deep? What are you thinking now?"

He was forced to laugh. "I'm thinking it's a good thing you say you're not always like this. You'll frighten your suitors off in droves."

To his surprise she became quite serious. She was on her

way to the bell sash but she turned aside to grip his arm while she said, "You've seen through me. I don't think I want you to stay."

"Seen through you?"

She let go and went on toward the bell sash. "It is my firm intention never to marry. I can't imagine anything more drab than marriage, can you?"

"Let me see. I would say *The Theory of Unfunded Government Debt* ran it a close second. Or how about *Dobbin's Evidence on Small Notes in Ireland*?"

She laughed with delight. She obviously found very few people who attuned themselves so swiftly to her idiosyncratic humour. "Oh damn our parents!" she said.

"Yours, actually," he told her. "The pater has always been ready to bury the hatchet."

"But he did steal this house from them."

Lawrence shook his head. "Now if I answer that, you'll defend them ... and that's how family feuds begin. I vote we leave it with their generation."

"Montagues and Capulets," she said, looking at him critically. "But you don't look Mediterranean enough for Romeo and I'm too old for Juliet."

"And anyway, you're not going to marry."

"That too." She nodded. "What d'you suppose Grandma meant – a Mortimer will inherit?"

"She was just rambling."

"You don't think there was a secret pact between them, long ago, to leave it all to my young brother, Toby? You wouldn't remember him. He's not ill actually. That was just an excuse. My parents are hiding here – in the west wing. Your father could embarrass them beautifully if he decided to walk around his property. Shall I suggest it or will you?"

"Rambling seems to run in your family."

She gurgled with laughter. "Oh Lorry – I miss you, too. I'm coming up to London after Christmas. Will you take me out somewhere? Will the fair and proud possessor of your heart object?"

He pretended he had to work that one out. "Ah, you mean will *I* object. D'you know, Ros, I don't think I shall."

CHAPTER SIXTY-THREE

CLIVE AND ELEANOR came out of the west wing as soon as they saw the Oxley carriage departing.

"Grandma's dead," Rosamund told them.

They had expected the news for so long it came as no shock. "A merciful release," Clive said.

When all the immediate arrangements had been put in hand they turned again to their daughter, asking her what it was that the dowager had so earnestly desired to tell Lord Oxley.

"She just rambled," Rosamund answered. "It made no sense at all. But Uncle Freddy was so ..."

"We've told you never to call him that," her mother said sharply.

"He was so kind and gentle. I wish you could have seen him. He made her death so peaceful."

"Hmm. When you say rambling – you mean literally just muttering nonsense sounds."

"No, she just went on and on about inheritance. Rambling."

"Inheritance?" Eleanor's ears pricked up. "What exactly did she say?"

"And the Mortimers. She went on and on about inheritance and the Mortimers."

"Rosamund!" Eleanor flared up. "You are the most aggravating ..."

But Clive cut in. "Listen, dear girl." He took up both her hands and squeezed them earnestly. "Just tell us her exact words, eh?"

"She said 'A Mortimer will inherit.' Those were her exact words: 'A Mortimer will inherit.' I told you – she was rambling. But Lord Oxley was sweet. He just kept saying to her, 'Of course he will ... Of course he will' – to soothe her. And as soon as he said that, she passed away and he closed her eyes. And she looked so peaceful. I do wish you had seen it."

Eleanor was pacified – until she noticed that Clive was rather more thoughtful than his mother's words seemed to warrant. When Rosamund had gone, she asked if he supposed they actually meant anything.

He shook his head but she could see it still absorbed him. At length he turned to her. "One thing I never asked you. That final night with the urchin – if I remember it rightly, mother lost her temper and went upstairs. Then I followed her. And you stayed behind to see him off the premises and count the spoons. Did he say anything to you then?"

He saw the colour rise to her cheeks; she became agitated. "Nothing of any weight," she replied.

"You can't remember?"

She sighed. "Oh very well. I wanted to tell you at the time but the fact that he *expected* me to made me dig in my heels. So I never said anything. As far as I can remember, I told him I knew all about Lawrence's true parentage and how kind the dowager ..."

"You said *what?*" Clive was suddenly as pale as the wind.

"Don't worry. I told him I'd worked it out for myself. He knows *you* didn't tell me. Anyway, I also said ..."

"How did you work it out for yourself, may I ask?"

"Well I'd had my suspicions for a long time, ever since that day he and Ann took tea with us on the terrace and Tony Knox-Riddell was there. And I saw the way they kept looking at each other. And then the moment I clapped eyes on her second baby – Angelica, was it? – as soon as I saw it, there was no doubting he was the father of that one, too. Plus the urchin's behaviour at the time – not to mention Tony's." She reached forward and pressed his arm. "I didn't have to be the brightest girl in the class to work it out that Tony was the father of both Ann's children, dear. Give me some credit. Anyway – I seem to remember I said all this to you once before. You just smiled then and said clever girl or something."

Clive swallowed. "And you said all that to Foxy? What did he reply?"

Eleanor, surprised to hear him revert to the affectionate

name of their boyhood, answered, "After I'd told him I knew Tony was Lawrence's father, I asked him what harm the Mortimers had ever done him. That made him blush! I've never seen him so tongue-tied."

"He didn't say a word? Not a single word?"

"Well that was the extraordinary part. He told me to tell you all this 'one day before you die'! Such drama! And I was also to say that he replied he would not come between us, you and me." She laughed. "He would not come between us! I ask you!"

Clive smiled wanly and said, "I think I'll go up and sit by mother for a while."

When they buried the old lady, Freddy sat watching from his carriage, a little way off. Clive almost went over to him but the vehicle moved off while he was still debating how he might explain his action to Eleanor. Some months later they happened to run into each other in the corridors of the Foreign Office. Freddy smiled and nodded, as he always did at such encounters. To his surprise, Clive did not sweep on by in the usual stiff-necked manner. Indeed, he stopped.

"I've been talking to Sir Henry Holland," he said.

"Ah yes."

"They want to set up a commission to look into native affairs in southern Africa."

"It's long overdue."

"Indeed. Indeed." Clive scratched the bridge of his nose and added awkwardly, "Look – I heard what my mother said to you. It was unforgivable to throw that in your face at such a time. You behaved every inch like a gentleman."

Freddy nodded gravely and turned to go. But Clive added, "And shortly afterwards, Eleanor told me what passed between you and her on the night when ... well ..."

"I remember the occasion," Freddy helped him.

"I don't think I could have shown such restraint as you did then. Your behaviour was impeccable."

Freddy waited, as if he expected more.

Clive cleared his throat. "Well, I just wanted to tell you."

To Clive's surprise, Freddy pulled a punch on his arm. He was grinning broadly. "One down. Two to go!" he said brightly and walked on.

Clive watched him out of sight; an undeniable drabness hung about the space old Foxy had once filled in his life.

Freddy had meanwhile received the long-awaited letter from Miss Kate, telling him in much greater detail the news he had heard in outline at Sadler's Wells. The only substantive addition to fact, however, was that they had settled not in Rio but in the Cape – at the Villa Rosalia in First Avenue, Walmer, just outside Port Elizabeth.

The news set Freddy to wondering whether the G.O.C. Artillery, in that selfsame city, would welcome a demonstration of the Oxley Mark VI Medium Howitzer? He replied to Miss Kate at once, saying that now they were no longer whizzing about the globe in all directions the chances of their meeting again were vastly more favourable.

During those early months of 1890, Lawrence and Rosamund met with increasing frequency. She had come up to prepare for the season at the town house of her second cousin, Sir Peter Warley, the son of Mrs. Langevin's sister. Like his uncle, Sir Reginald, this Peter had been a colonial administrator, too. But five years in the Gold Coast had broken his health and he had retired to live the sort of semi-invalid existence that usually guaranteed three extra decades of life. His wife Marjorie spent so much time fussing over him that she was only too glad when Rosamund decided to take her maid as chaperone and spend the afternoon strolling earnestly around the Royal Academy or the Victoria & Albert or sitting in the Ladies Gallery at the House of Commons.

"You gels are so serious-minded these days!" Lady Warley would say.

And so Rosamund was liberated for glorious walks in the park, laughing among the daffodils, and talking with Lorry about whatever came into her head. He was the most wonderful companion she could wish for because she never had to explain anything or excuse anything, and however wayward the thought, he could follow it.

One warm June day at the height of the Season they were sitting beneath a parasol in Hyde Park – well away from the fashionable areas around Rotten Row – discreetly sharing an ice and talking about marriage.

"It's all my mother thinks of," Rosamund complained.

"She thinks that if I'm not auctioned off by the end of this Season – or at the very latest the end of *next* Season – her whole life will be one abject failure. Honestly! D'you think I'm ready for it?"

"No," he answered firmly.

She hit him playfully. "You needn't be quite so definite."

"But you're not," he repeated. "I think it would be hateful to see you knotted up with ... well, not to name any names – to be knotted up with any of the fellows I've seen you dancing with."

"Hah – dancing! Don't!"

"Off to Italy for a six-month honeymoon. Can you imagine?"

She shuddered. "I'm going to a desert island to get married. Where no one can look at me. I'd hate them looking at me and thinking she's *his*. Belonging! I couldn't bear it. What's it like for a man, Lorry? How would you feel about a gaggle of women staring at you and thinking he's *hers!* Doesn't it make you shiver? What d'you think I ought to do?"

"About marriage?"

"No – life in general. I want to *be* things before I marry. Where does one learn to be a femme fatale?"

"I'm sure you wouldn't enjoy it," he told her. "A femme fatale is as much the prisoner of her reputation as the most respectable lady is of hers."

"I'd like to do what your mother did. Except that I can't sing a note. But I think she's had the most fulfilling life. Don't you?"

This conversation reminded him of something Miss Kate had told him, but he couldn't remember what. He fell into a brief reverie, thinking of Miss Kate and their unforgettable day together, wandering through Constantinople.

"Did I say a Bad Thing?" Rosamund asked.

"Not at all. But my mother isn't the only such woman, you know. I was remembering Miss Kate. She was the business manager – manager*ess*, I suppose one ought to say – of the choral group to which my mother belonged. She did all the advance bookings and arranged the hotels and transport and kept the accounts for them."

"Oh, the lucky thing! That's what I'd like to do."

He laughed. "You wouldn't think such a woman would have her unfulfilled dreams, would you. But she did. D'you know what hers was?"

Rosamund shook her head with a sharp, birdlike movement that made all her ringlets sparkle. Her eyes were wide with fascination. She had no idea, he realized, what effect her youth and beauty could have on a man. "Well tell me!" she commanded.

"Miss Kate's dream was to travel in an Arab caravan across the desert."

"To Samarkand!"

"To Aleppo, actually. And then on to Petra in Nabatea."

"Rose-red city, half as old as time. Oh she's right! I want to do that too. I want to do everything. Don't you? Absolutely everything."

"Not on my own," he told her. "But I'd love to accompany *you*. I think you'd make it all twice as alive, twice as sparkling."

Impetuously she grabbed his hand, "Oh yes, Lorry! Let's just go! Tomorrow?"

"You just say the word, little grasshopper."

Something in his tone made her look into his eyes. There she saw the seriousness behind his jocular offer. She withdrew her hands at once. "Oh no, Lorry – not you, too."

He smiled. "Not in that way, Ros. Not with burning ardour. Not with impatience. But with deep affection. With endless tolerance. With ... fond bewilderment. With warmth as wide as an ocean."

"I think of you and me more like brother and sister, you see."

He nodded. "The rest will follow, Ros."

"And you can wait?"

"Of course."

She shook her head. "No – I'd feel you waiting, watching me."

His smile was slow. "Why should you? You haven't noticed it for the *past* six months."

She raised a hand to his cheek. "Oh you poor darling!"

He could see she didn't mean it – not deeply. She was just trying out a new emotion. He knew he must give her time. "Nothing's changed," he said.

"But it has. Now I'll know."

"You'll forget. That's your nature."

But she couldn't forget. They met once or twice more that summer but she was watching him all the time, nervously waiting for some renewed declaration of his love. Then she said they ought to give each other up for a while, to see how it affected them. Reluctantly he agreed; he knew it was part of that time she needed, time to mature, time to explore her own emotions, to accept the pain of growing up and *not* being able to do everything.

They did not see each other for six months and when they did, the circumstances were so bizarre that not even Rosamund, in her wildest flights of fancy, could have imagined them.

CHAPTER SIXTY-FOUR

THAT NOVEMBER, when "not seeing each other" had endured almost six months, Lawrence got word to Rosamund suggesting they should meet again. She panicked. She knew that if they resumed where they had left off last summer, she would be trapped by her own emotions into doing something rash. She still felt unready for that. The alternatives in her mind were vague but powerful. There were things she wanted to do, to be, before she became someone's wife, even Lawrence's wife. What things? Just *things*. Her inability to name them, to set them up against his simple request for a meeting, alarmed her.

So when she heard that her father had been appointed to chair a commission on native affairs in the Cape, she decided to work night and day on her mother to make it a family visit – not to include her younger brothers and sisters, of course, just her father, her mother, and herself. "You could look up your old friends … you could show me all the places you knew when you were growing up …" She found a dozen arguments.

Eleanor was half-inclined to the suggestion – to see again the playgrounds of her youth – even before Rosamund spoke about it; the girl found herself pushing at an open door and so their visit to the Cape was speedily arranged.

In the meantime Freddy had gone ahead with his arrangements to demonstrate his light field pieces to the military in Port Elizabeth – in particular to one Colonel Escalls, Officer in Command, Artillery Training. He suggested to Lawrence that he should take leave from Gould's and accompany him. Together they could look at the possibilities for expansion in the Cape, whose great mineral wealth, especially in coal and iron, was just becoming apparent. They could also take Angelica, who, rising fifteen, was now old enough to profit from a voyage overseas.

"It'll be a nice surprise for your mother to see us all again," he added.

Though Lawrence had his doubts on that score, he said nothing about them. In any case, he was daily expecting a reply from Rosamund, so he found many reasons, all strictly professional, as to why foreign travel was utterly out of the question. Freddy had a quiet word with the elder Gould. Then Lawrence got wind of Rosamund's intended trip with her parents and wished he had not burned his boats so thoroughly. He was racking his brains for good professional grounds for a visit to the Cape after all when, greatly to his surprise, Gould handed him several. Freddy, Angelica, and Lawrence sailed for Cape Town one week behind Clive, Eleanor, and Rosamund. Of the six of them, Lawrence alone knew the precise state of affairs; Freddy had known vaguely that Clive was due to go out there some time this winter but had no idea he had already left, much less that he had taken Eleanor and Rosamund with him.

Cape Town is a magical landfall. The almost geometrical flatness of the summit of Table Mountain, which dominates the town and looks as improbable after the hundredth inspection as it did on the first, proclaims and goes on proclaiming that here indeed is a foreign land, quite unlike anything at home. Though the Mortimers had taken sea tickets all the way to Port Elizabeth, the promise of that magic lured them ashore. Once their feet touched land, the land that would always be so

special to them, nothing could induce Clive and Eleanor to
return to the ship. Instead, though it was the height of summer,
they went on by train.

The beeline to P.E. is about four-hundred miles, almost
due east; but a succession of mountain ranges prevents the
railway from taking such a route. Instead it runs northeast, up
over the Great Karroo to a one-barber village called De Aar
Junction, about four-hundred miles inland; from there a branch
line winds its way two-hundred-and-fifty miles down to the
coast, through Middelburg and Cradock, down the valley of
the Great Fish River, between the majestic peaks of the
Tandjiesberg and Winterberg mountains, levelling out in the
coastal plains at Addo, just north of the city. It was a two-day
journey.

Though the month was December, some freak rainclouds
had lately swept inland. Their haphazard passage had painted
broad swathes of green across the arid veldt – not the lush green
of England, but the vibrant olive-green of numerous little
shrubs and succulents, the strident silver-green of dry savannah
grass, and the hot chrome-green of thorns and cactuses. There
was, too, a desperate frenzy of desert flowers, quickened by
the rain, soon to wither in the summer heat. Rosamund gazed
upon it all in wonder; even hours at the carriage window could
not dim her sense of awe. The endlessness of it all – the
wildness that would never be tamed! How puny by contrast
were the marks of man. The down-at-heel little villages they
passed, pathetic huddles of gum trees, windmill pumps, and
corrugated iron ... the homestead-farms, minute patchworks
of order in a vast, indifferent desert – these were never going to
dominate that sere, God-proclaiming landscape; they would
always be mere accidents – blemishes, almost – upon the face
of it.

She wished they need not hasten among it so; she would
love to take a trusty pony, a good hunting dog, a light rifle, and
wander through it for a year or more.

Eleanor and Clive, by contrast, were disappointed. They
remembered all those elements no train journey can reveal: the
thin, dew-cool air of early morning on the veldt ... the silence
of it all ... the overpowering aroma of sunbaked cactuses ... the
heat underfoot from the thin, red soil ... the stark clarity of

nature's myriad life-and-death struggles, in webs, in pits, behind leaves, under stones, beyond the next little koppie ... through all of this the train carried them in an anaesthetic sort of isolation.

On their final dawn they steamed into Somerset East, where there was a two-hour pause for breakfast at the station hotel. Eleanor and Clive left the mutton chops and eggs to the other passengers and, taking nothing more than a small basket of fruit, walked out into that remembered Eden. Only then did they feel they had truly returned.

A little way to the east of the town they found a koppie from whose top they could watch the sunrise. A weathered stone outcrop gave them comfortable lodging. As they sat and waited, and looked all about them, long-forgotten details returned: the astonishing red of a squashed cochineal bug in its soft web of white on the glossy green of a prickly pear ... the warning grunt and clatter of a retreating porcupine ... the terrified, dusty, pitterpat of a little klip-dassie ... the tethered buzz of unseen insects, warming to the advancing day. Clive wished the aloes were still in flower, that he might taste again their bittersweet nectar.

He glanced sideways at Eleanor, and thought what a noble woman she was; how dreadful his life might have been if he had never met her. "What are you thinking?" he asked. "Not still worrying about the girl?"

"No, I was thinking it was a pity we have to go on to Durban next month. Why can't you hold all your hearings in P.E.?"

"I'll see what I can do. We shall have to hold *some* sessions up there."

"Perhaps by then we'll have discovered that none of our old friends are left. Everyone moves on so much these days. The upper classes are turning into gypsies."

Clive hit his head in a gesture of annoyance. "I knew there was something I meant to tell you. I saw it in the *Argus* the day before yesterday under Forthcoming Social Events. The Staff of the Headquarters Barracks in P.E. are entertaining at a Ladies' Night on New Year's Eve ... and I'll give you one guess as to who is President of the Mess Committee."

"Not Terence!"

"Colonel Escalls himself."

"But I thought he'd been posted to India – years ago."

"Indeed he was. Twelve years ago – and served there with distinction. But he's back again now and in charge of gunnery training. So there's something to look forward to, eh? Sometimes the gypsies return."

"I wonder if he ever got married? It didn't say Colonel and Mrs?"

"Well it wouldn't anyway. Not an officers' mess function. Talking of old friends, I ran into old Foxy Freddy recently."

Eleanor looked at him in amazement. "Old friend?"

Clive shifted uneasily. "I think we may have done him an injustice, you know, my dear."

"I should like to know in what way." Her nostrils flared. He knew the discussion was going to be futile.

"Well, he did give us a price well above the market value of the business – even including the Hall and estate."

"But it was your ancestral home. No money could have bought it! Only the beastly necessity to stay out of Carey Street."

"Nevertheless, it turned out to be the best thing that ever happened to us. One has to admit it. We're *natural* landowners, you and I, not industrialists. The business just went to pieces in my hands. But look at what I've been able to do in the way of improving the Knox-Riddell estates. If old Foxy hadn't given me the push, I'd never have made the leap on my own account, quite apart from the fact that we simply wouldn't have been able to afford it. I don't think you realize – if he hadn't bailed us out, we'd have been living in squalor in some wretched little twenty-room suburban villa, wondering how to find wages for a mere half-dozen servants."

She snorted impatiently. "You may put what gloss you like on it, my dear. The fact remains that the urchin was not thinking of *our* good when he bought us out. He's only ever been out for one thing: Number One. He's used and discarded everybody he's met along his path. He's ruthless, single-minded, and utterly without finer feelings."

"I happen to know better, at least with regard to the finer feelings."

She raised her hand to his cheek and touched him fondly.

"You'd see good in Jack the Ripper. I know you. Well, if you want to resume your acquaintance with him, nothing I can say will stop you. But please don't expect me to meet or entertain him. If I ever meet him again, I shall walk up to him and kick his shins. I shouldn't be able to stop myself."

The boat carrying the Oxleys made better time of it. The day after the Mortimers settled in at the government guest house in P.E., Freddy was standing in front of the Villa Rosalia, three miles away in First Avenue, Walmer. Beside the gate a discreetly green notice board whispered: THE WALMER ACADEMY OF MUSIC AND DANCE – proprietors:– Miss Rosina Williams, Dip. Kl. (Vienna), Miss Ann Howard, C&G (Lond), and Miss Kate Kendall. Lessons in all Branches of the Musical Arts for Private or Professional Exponents. Coaching for the Examinations of all Leading Bodies. Greek Dancing. Phonographic Cylinders Cut. Practice Rooms. Musical Soirées ... The words sprawled impressively on down the board, finally reaching: Next Meeting of the Port Elizabeth Choral Society: ... the space where the date might be chalked was blank.

It was a whole biography, set forth in gold letters with black-relief shading. He turned to look at the house.

The ground floor was of stone or brick, plastered over and whitewashed. The weathered surface made a perfect background for the magnolias, wistarias, and other climbing shrubs whose bark and foliage softened its starkness. The upstairs was boarded in white-painted wood, in the common colonial style. On the western side a wide, shady, ground-floor stoep, or verandah, supported broad, open balconies above. The double-slope of the mansard roof reminded him vaguely of Paris. Pale chiffon or chintz curtains were gathered in bows at all the projecting gable windows. Not a masculine touch was to be seen.

The garden must have been one of the first to be planted in the suburb. The trees – pines, jacarandas, figs, loquats, and one magnificent judas tree – were large and sturdy. Bougainvillaea and other shrubs, also in their maturity, were out in full bloom. Hidden somewhere in their depths a hoopoe vied with a Chopin sonata drifting out through one of the ground-floor windows. Butterflies shivered their way from flower to flower. Close to the gate he saw a tortoise slithering over the pine-needles; in the sunshine beyond, a pair of lizards soaked up the sun and watched him with wary aloofness.

It all looked so foreign – almost designed to exclude him.

With his heart in his mouth he pushed open the gate and walked up the winding stone pathway to the door. A houseboy was watering a small patch of lawn, greening it to English standards; he set down his can and walked ahead of Freddy to the stoep, where he gave the bell-pull a tug. Freddy smiled his thanks. As he waited for the ring to be answered he turned for another survey of the garden. From here he could see that it was much larger than appeared from the road, for it ran in a series of terraces down into the valley – the same valley (though Freddy did not know it) through which Clive and Escalls had raced in that point-to-point so long ago. The second terrace was a broad lawn. Upon it a lithe young woman in flowing drapery was conducting a Grecian-dance class – a group of children, alternately gambolling like lambs and then pausing to wave their arms like fronds of seaweed. The music presumably came from a phonograph, but their laughter and the folds of the terrain prevented the sound of it from carrying up to the house.

It was some seconds before he realized that the young woman was, in fact, Miss Kate. Her short hair, the Grecian robes, and the dark green sweat band had combined to deceive him. A maid answered the door.

He pointed to the lower lawn and said, "I've just noticed the young lady I wish to see."

He took a step out onto the upper lawn. Chopin and the hoopoe were still fighting it out. When he reached the sunlight she saw him. For a moment they froze; then she threw wide her arms and ran toward him. The enthusiasm of her embrace almost sent him flying. She was already breathless from the dancing, but the excitement and the laughter made it worse. She patted her breast and mimed a heart attack. "Why didn't you say?" she asked over and over. And "Where are you staying?" And "How long are you going to be here?"

Then she remembered her class, who were watching all this in bewildered amusement. "We've only a few minutes left," she told Freddy. She got him to rewind the phonograph while she organized them to give a brief display of the morning's lesson, which he found charming.

When the children ran back to their dressing rooms, the gardener came to carry up the phonograph, but she told him to leave it there as she had another class after lunch. "Oh I *wish* I could cancel it," she complained to Freddy. "We could all go swimming then."

They strolled back toward the house. He shook his head. "I'm afraid not, Miss Kate. This afternoon I'm seeing Colonel Escalls about ..."

"The Colonel?" She put her hand to her brow. "D'you know him? Good heavens it's *you* he was mentioning! He said someone was coming out here to test some guns. It was on the tip of my tongue to say I knew *you* – but you know how discreet we all are nowadays. No one here knows Ann is Lady Oxley – you've seen her?"

"How d'you know Colonel Escalls?" he asked.

She smiled archly. "Ah, it's a small world – or hadn't you noticed? Do I take it you haven't seen Ann? You mean you came to see me first? Goodness, how flattering!"

"I'd just rung the doorbell when I spotted you down there. You look absolutely lovely, Miss Kate."

The compliment stemmed the tide of her enthusiasm. She almost said something and then blushed. They had reached the foot of the steps leading up to the stoep, which he now saw continued around the shady south side of the house as well. The sound of the piano was coming from one of the rooms just above them. "That's Ann playing," Kate said. "She's studying for the silver. She'll get it of course. I'll go and tell her you're here. Then I'll change. You'll stay for lunch, naturally."

She led him into the drawing room. It was spartan in its simplicity – plain wallpaper, plain carpets, plain curtains, plain furnishings. He had never seen anything quite like it. The colours were all in the range from white through pale gray to lavender and mauve, which emphasized the warmth of the unstained wood in the chairs and bookcases. The pictures were simple, too, in a dreamy sort of fashion – young ladies, clad only in the smoke of autumn leaves, staring out at you with large, dark eyes, filled with intimations of death. There was a drawing, too – of a modern English parish church, probably one of those cast-iron copies, set way out in some arid patch of local scrub.

There could be no doubting that this was Ann's home – her home for life. Nothing here was rented, not even the furniture. The Chopin stopped. She probably even owned the freehold. He wandered around, touching the fabrics, the plain wood, the smoothness of the plaster. He did not notice Ann's entry until, in the calmest voice, she said, "Hello Frederick."

He turned to face her. She came toward him holding forth both hands. He took them. She offered her cheek for his kiss.

"You've achieved it at last," he said, looking around.

She nodded and smiled with satisfaction.

"It's monastic."

"Yes," she said.

"No regrets?"

She put her head on one side and looked at him fondly. "Of course there are – more than I want to think about."

"But they're all past."

She nodded.

"Good."

"Why didn't you say you were coming?" she asked.

"Because when it came to it I didn't know whether I'd actually have the courage to come and see you."

"Frederick!" She did not believe him.

"I know, I know. I just wanted to leave the choice open."

She laughed. "Now you're the one who wants everything to be possible and all at the same time." She drew his attention to the paintings and asked what he thought of them.

He said they were very pretty.

She laughed. "Kate painted them."

He looked at them more closely. "Actually, they're beautiful."

"And so is she."

"I thought she'd be married by now."

Ann shook her head pityingly but all she said was, "Dear Frederick!"

"How does she know Colonel Escalls?" he asked.

Ann's expression prepared him for some dismissive or scornful reply but then, thinking better of it, she gave a sly smile and answered, "None of your business sir she said."

Then, to change the subject she went on, "Will you come to us for Christmas Day? It's quite ridiculous. We have goose and plum pudding and mince pies just as if we were home in England – though the weather is scorching hot."

"All three of us?" Freddy asked.

Her eyes went wide. Lawrence she had more than half-expected, once she saw Frederick; but it was a shock to hear that Angelica had come out, too. With some misgiving she agreed.

Angelica always kept her hair well combed down over her mutilated ear, but shortly after they arrived for the Christmas Day party – while Ann was showing her over the house, she swept it back and, with a nervous little smile, said, "See? It's not at all bad, is it."

She was right. Over the years Ann's guilty imagination had magnified the wound out of all proportion. Ann raised her hand and touched the lobe. "Oh, I'm so sorry, my darling," she said.

"But you needn't be. I'm so proud of it."

"Proud!"

"Yes, of course. Whenever I was miserable I used to put my thumb in my mouth, like this, and with the other hand I'd stroke my ear" – she showed Ann how – "and I'd think of you and how desperate you must have been …"

"You've heard the story then?"

"I know you ran away and you were desperate and you had to leave me on the steps of the Foundlings Hospital. And how else could you tell a month-old baby how much you loved her?"

"Oh my dear!" Ann threw her arms around her and hugged her tight, partly to conceal the tears that had sprung into her eyes.

When she felt calmer she held her daughter at arm's length and asked, "And you've forgiven me?"

"For what?"

"For running away. For making such a mess of all your lives? I know Lawrence hasn't."

"I think he has now, mama. I mustn't call you that, must I."

Ann smiled ruefully. "It would be best if you didn't get in the habit while you're out here. I'm very firmly *Miss* Howard in these parts. It might cause one or two raised eyebrows, to say the least, if the Hon. Lawrence and the Hon. Angelica Oxley started calling me mama all of a sudden. Anyway, what about Lawrence – you were saying?"

"Oh yes. We were talking about you on the boat and he was explaining how you went straight from service into marriage and only later found out that art was your true master. And ..."

"Art?"

"Music. The art of music. And artists have to follow their inspiration no matter whom it may hurt – and it probably hurts them more than anyone."

Ann looked at her askance, as if she suspected a leg-pull.

"Honestly," Angelica insisted. "Isn't it true?"

"Is Lawrence keen on some young lady who fancies she's a bit of an artist?" Ann asked.

The girl shrugged.

"Well it sounds like it. The sober truth is that I made a mess of my life, and your father's, and ... everyone's. And if I'd stayed, things would only have got worse and worse. So I went. That's all. I wasn't following some great artistic ... whatever you call it. I just ran away. It's as simple as that."

But later, when Angelica heard her mother play the piano and sing, she knew better.

Kate was delighted to renew her friendship with Lawrence, whom, of course, she hardly recognised. After dinner, as the day began to cool, and before the swift sunset fell, the pair of them walked out beneath the jacarandas and relived that memorable day in Constantinople.

"Did you ever go back?" he asked.

"No. Did you?"

"I don't think I could. Or if I did, I'd stay away from Ayub and the old bazaar and the Mussulman part of the city."

"Does your father go back?"

"Sometimes. Quite often, actually. Mostly to keep an eye on Sir Basil."

"Patriarca?"

"Patriarc, he calls himself now. He's the biggest thorn in our flesh as well as being our greatest asset in the whole of eastern Europe – at one and the same time. I don't think he's really trying to cheat us any longer. It's just a sort of game he and the pater like to play."

"I can't get over your being so tall, Lawrence. And so handsome! Now there must be some young lady?"

"You're the only one I'll ever love, Miss Kate," he said easily.

"Hmm!" she replied. "Well I know better."

He was silent.

"Golly, you haven't changed any," she told him.

On Boxing Day they all went out for a braaivleis at a deserted, rocky cape called Skoenmaakerskop, halfway to Uman Gorge. Though the bush around the city was fairly tame, Lawrence could feel how wild the country was. In the middle of the road, on their way to the spot, they had to stop to let a frightened puff adder slither away into the grass; one could easily imagine baboons and wild pigs behind every bush, around every bend. It was a raw sort of country, he felt, a place for simple, clear decisions – a physical country that purified the soul and washed away the casuistry of the old civilization. As they rode home in the evening, he relaxed in the happy exhaustion of his muscles, felt and tasted the seasalt on his skin, gazed around at the high, wide sky, and knew that if Rosamund said *no* to him out here, it would be final, absolute. There could be no ambiguities about it, as there would have been back home.

"By the way," Freddy said, "we three have been invited to the Headquarters Mess for their New Year's ball. Colonel Escalls sent a runner down with the invitation before we left the hotel this morning."

Ann turned pale. "But we've been invited, too. We always go."

They decided on a common story. Ann and Freddy had known each other since childhood, having grown up in the same village. They had met again by chance some years ago in Vienna ... and so forth. The rest followed without any need for emendation.

At around that same moment Rosamund and her parents were returning to their guest house, having spent the afternoon at a small private party in the Residence. As she was about to step over the threshold she noticed an envelope lying on the mat. She picked it up. It bore the crest of the HQ Mess.

"Read it," her father told her.

"The President of the Mess Committee," she said, carrying the card to the last of the daylight at the window, "requests the pleasure of the company of Sir Clive and Lady Mortimer and their daughter Rosamund at a New Year's Eve Ball, beginning at eight-thirty p.m. ... evening dress ... buffet supper ... RSVP." She looked up happily. "The answer's *yes* of course!"

CHAPTER SIXTY-FIVE

"YOU TWO PROBABLY know each other?" Colonel Escalls said.

Clive had, in fact, just noticed Freddy – about three seconds earlier. In any case, as the veteran of half a dozen elections, he was well used to showing no surprise at the most surprising introductions. Freddy, for his part, had known in general of Clive's visit, though not of its precise coincidence with his. Both men behaved perfectly; they greeted each other as fervently as any two Englishmen who had not met for a decade or so.

"Hello Foxy," Clive muttered as he held forth his hand.

Freddy shook it warmly as he murmured, "Old sport."

"Well isn't that extraordinary," Escalls said, beaming at the pair of them.

"This fellow and I practically grew up together," Clive told him.

Freddy's mind was racing. "I do hope Lady Mortimer's here," he said.

Clive took his courage in both hands, "Yes indeed. She'll be delighted to see you again. Young Rosamund is with us, too."

"Oh good. But you'll never guess who else I met. I don't know if you remember Ann *Howard*?" He made the pause significant "*Miss* Howard? Used to live in Ferndown Crescent?"

Clive did not let him down. After a moment's reflection he replied, "Why yes, of course! You don't mean to say she's here?"

Freddy turned to Escalls. "I know you know her, Colonel. She also grew up not half a mile from Mortimer and me."

"But she's lived out here several years now," the Colonel replied, as if it somehow cast doubt on Freddy's remark.

"Did you know she was out here?" Clive asked Freddy.

"As a matter of fact I did. I ran across her some years ago on a visit to Vienna and we've kept in touch on and off ever since."

His tone was so airy and offhand that Escalls grew suddenly jocose. "Aha – I see! Cherchez la femme! I thought it wasn't just the lure of a second summer that brought you out here!" He winked at Clive, who laughed and pointed at Freddy. "Oh this man is a very dark horse, Colonel." Then he turned to Freddy. "Do come and meet Eleanor."

"I'm most anxious to," Freddy said with emphasis. "And I hope we're not too late," he added under his breath as they went in search of her.

"That was hairy," Clive said. "Look, young'un, time's short. I've behaved badly toward you – unforgivably. So if you can take as read all the apologies I ought to have made long ago … well, may we let our handshake back there mark the end of it all?"

Freddy clapped him on the back. "Three down, none to go!" he said.

"You made a splendid job of Mortimer's. Thank you for not changing the name."

"As a shrewd man once told me – it was werry well worth the inwestment."

Clive laughed. "You're in good spirits tonight. I take it no one out here knows about … Lady Oxley?"

Freddy was serious again. "No, and we very much wish to keep it that way."

Clive pulled a face. "I hope Eleanor will agree. I'm afraid she still harbours a grudge … If I could've told her the truth without compromising Ann's honour – and Lawrence's – and yours, of course – I'd have done it long ago."

"She's seen me," Freddy said, nudging Clive and inclining

his head in Eleanor's direction. She was staring at him with an expression that would heat up mustard.

"My dearest!" Clive called, a little too loudly and much too soon; people all around were startled by his exuberance. "Just look who's here! We've come seven thousand miles only to bump into our oldest friend."

"Lady Mortimer." Freddy stood a yard off and bowed stiffly.

In that fraction of a second she realized she could not possibly show her husband up after such a public announcement. A political hostess to her fingernails, she gave Freddy a dazzling smile and held out her hand. "Lord Oxley! But this is simply splendid!"

They chatted as such friends might be expected to chat – until, that is, any local interest in them had died away. Slowly they drifted to a less public corner of the anteroom and there Clive explained as briefly as possible the dilemma over Ann.

Freddy watched her closely. Though the mask of her face was so well trained, he nonetheless saw a little glint of malicious amusement there, swiftly concealed.

"Of course," he butted in with an affable laugh, "if it were up to me, I would infinitely prefer the whole thing to come out ... for the truth to be made public, you understand."

"But why?" she asked.

He shrugged diffidently. "One ... grows lonely, you know."

"Shrewd! Shrewd!" Clive said to him a little while later. "You should have been in politics, Foxy – you'd have run circles around us there, too."

"Yes, I think we may safely say the secret is well and truly bottled. Now I must find Ann and warn her about your being here. Oh my God – too late!"

Ann was staring at them like a gargoyle. But Clive put her at her ease at once. "Miss Howard!" he cried. "How delightful after all these years! I claim no superhuman powers of memory, though – Lord Oxley told me you were here. Isn't this quite extraordinary?"

Between them he and Freddy kept up the conversation until the sprinting of her heart slackened enough for her to introduce Miss Kate.

While they were talking Clive spotted Lawrence. He turned at once to Freddy. "You didn't mention you'd brought the boy! But how splendid. Since Rosamund insists on breaking all her partners' toes, it's slightly less embarrassing if one knows the wounded party. She put half of London's eligible squad into wheelchairs last summer."

Lawrence pretended surprise at seeing his "Uncle Clive" – and delight, of course.

"Go and find Rosamund," Clive advised. "Book her for the waltzes. She's less lethal at them."

Lawrence had the presence of mind to stare in surprise at this advice.

"It's all right again," Freddy told him with a nod of his head toward Clive. "The feud is over."

"Oh dear!" Lawrence replied, with a lugubrious grin at Kate. "A whole new set of rules to live by!"

He found Rosamund standing among a group of other "young gels" under the sharp eye of three military-matronly wallflowers. She had her back to him, her hair was cut differently, she was wearing a gown he'd never seen before, yet he knew her at once.

His stomach was a whole butterfly farm but he managed to keep his voice casual enough. "Hello Ros! Your pater has warned me to claim a waltz. He says I might stand less chance of permanent injury that way."

For a moment he felt sure she was going to faint. She just stood there and stared at him, unbelief in every movement of her eyes. The band struck up a polka. "This'll do," he told her, moving close and holding up his arms in the dance position.

Automatically she took the cue and moved off with him onto the floor. She was actually a moderately good dancer; it was just her habit to denigrate any of her feminine achievements.

"Oh thank you," she said, breathing out a huge sigh of relief. "One second more and I'd have dropped. What on earth are you doing here? I still can't believe it!" She pinched him until he said, "Ow!"

Before she could ask any more questions he told her that their fathers seemed to have buried the hatchet; he also warned her about "the Lady Oxley difficulty."

She understood. "I just hope my mother will cooperate.

She detests your father. I doubt if she'll ever relent. I can't understand them."

"I'd better not be seen too much with you this evening, then," he said. "It shouldn't be difficult – not after the practice I've had."

"Was it hard?" she asked.

"What d'you think!"

Now that she was over the shock of seeing him again, she was surprised at her own calm. She remembered the turmoil he had aroused when he had confessed in that odd, sidelong way of his, that he loved her. She had expected some of it to return when they met again. But it had not. Instead there was this strange calm within her, as if no real decisions would be called for.

"Was it hard for you?" he asked.

"It was necessary."

"That's not the same thing."

She shrugged.

"But did it work?" he added. "Did it have any effect?"

She looked up at him and smiled. "Has nothing changed with you?"

"It's stronger, that's all."

"You're absolutely sure?"

"I've never felt more sure of anything in my life."

She digested this in silence.

"Well?" He held his breath.

"It doesn't frighten me any more," she admitted. "I thought it would."

"You've been going to not-answering-questions classes. *And* you got the gold diploma."

She laughed and laid her head briefly beside his. "I'll give you an answer before this ball's over," she promised.

Then a thought struck her. "If 'Miss Howard' is here ... does that mean Miss Kate is here, too?"

Lawrence pointed her out.

Later Rosamund wished she had not made her promise so specific. The evening no longer seemed quite as infinite as it had then. She found herself standing not far from Miss Kate. She edged her way toward her and introduced herself. She did not mention Lawrence but spoke of the friendship between her father and Lord Oxley. Kate was delighted to meet her. After a few pleasantries, Rosamund came straight to the point. "I once heard Lord Oxley telling his son Lawrence – you know him I suppose?"

"Oh very well. He's a darling man."

"Yes. Well, the conversation was about remarkable women – women who'd achieved something in life instead of just turning themselves into bloodstock. And naturally the subject of Miss Howard came up. And ..."

"Ah, you know about that – *Miss* Howard? You know she's here tonight?"

"Yes, I know about that."

"Good."

"Anyway Lawrence was saying what a rich and satisfying life Miss Howard must have led and Lord Oxley told him there was one woman even more remarkable than Miss Howard, and that was Miss Kate Kendall."

Kate's eyes grew large; the black of her pupils was like an upwelling of ink. The transformation took Rosamund aback. Then it made her thoughtful.

"He said that about me?" Kate asked.

Rosamund nodded, watching her intently now. The flush in Miss Kendall's cheeks was extraordinary, as though a red spotlight had accidentally caught her.

"Well, I can't think why, I'm sure."

"Oh yes ... he said you hadn't any obvious talent like Miss Howard but by sheer force of will and strength of character you'd achieved even more." She was so fascinated at Miss Kate's response that she left too long a pause before adding, "It was because you hadn't made any false starts in life. Whereas Miss Howard – I don't know her at all well – but apparently she'd tried her hand at several things with very little success. But you just went straight for the main chance and seized it!"

Rosamund's personal commitment to this false but flattering biography was too obvious for Kate to miss. "It's warm in here," she said. "Shall we go out for a stroll? You won't need a wrap or a boa, I promise."

"I'd love that," Rosamund said gratefully.

The HQ Mess was not within barracks. It stood on a long sliver of manicured land beside the Baakens River, about a quarter of a mile from its junction with the sea. It being summer, the flow of water was sluggish, moving each way with the tide; but because of the fall of the land, very little salt water reached even this far up. Just above the mess two low weirs kept the rest of the river penned back. The face of it glistened black and silver beneath the moon. The gentle gurgle of falling water was restful; the smell of it, green-weedy fresh.

"Now," Miss Kate said, taking Rosamund's arm, "Lord Oxley told you no such thing, did he! Not that *last* bit, anyway."

It amused Rosamund that Kate couldn't let go of the earlier compliment. "No," she confessed. "I added that myself. But I'm sure it's true."

"So what was the point? What did you really want to tell me? Or" – she lingered a little – "ask me?"

Rosamund was delighted. "I didn't know it was going to be so easy to talk to you!" she exclaimed in surprise. "You see, the thing is this. There's a man who's asked me to marry him, and in one way I want to say yes. I very *much* want to say yes, because I love him. But in another way I feel there's the whole world out there and I don't want to shut myself away from it."

"Is this man a Mussulman or what?"

"No! Just an ordinary – or actually extraordinary, but you know what I mean. An English gentleman."

"Rich?"

"I'd still love him if he had nothing."

"Fine. So he's rich. I haven't heard your problem yet."

"Well I want to ... I want ... oh, you see – that's the thing. I don't really know what I want – and yet I know I want it! I have no particular talent. That's why I pricked up my ears when Lord Oxley mentioned you. All right, perhaps I did exaggerate a bit, but only a bit. Lord Oxley thinks the world of you – honestly."

"We're talking about you."

They had reached the upper end of the garden. For a moment they looked out into the thorn scrub, ghostly in the moonlight; then they turned and began to retrace their steps.

"How did you begin, Miss Kate? Where did you learn all the things you needed to know to become the business manageress of The Angels?"

Kate skirted around the question. "Listen, have you an income of your own?"

"Yes. Or I will have when I'm of age – in just over a year from now."

"Could you live on it – I mean, without starving?"

"It's about a thousand a year."

Kate whistled. "Then there *isn't* a problem. You can do whatever you wish. Know what I'd do?"

"Oh do tell me!"

"Go to Trebizond. Join one of the regular caravans up to Aleppo – you can hire bearers and a dragoman. You needn't worry, because the Arabs are scrupulous about high-born women travelling alone. Princesses get sent to distant sheikhs with just one servant to guard them, and they pass through the hands of the most awful ruffians yet they come to no harm. Anyway, from Aleppo you could go down the old trade route from Babylon, down through Philadelphia and on to Petra."

"And there?"

Miss Kate was silent a while. "Well now you've really come to it," she said. "You see, I've actually done all that – all I've just told you. But when I was there I realized I was only just skirting the *fringe* of it. Beyond all that country there lies a vast, forbidden continent."

"Forbidden?"

"Oh yes. Only Mussulmen are allowed there. It's sacred; they kill all infidels who try to enter it. What I'd like to do – if I had my time over – is learn Arabic well enough to pass for one of them, learn their religion too, and then travel all that country. That's where Alexander the Great went, you know – and it defeated him! How about that? And the frankincense that one of the Three Wise Men brought to the manger? That came from down there somewhere. I'll bet there's whole ancient cities – like Petra – just waiting for someone to discover them."

Suddenly Rosamund's heart was beating fast; she had never heard any idea so exciting as this. *And it was all quite possible!* Here was this amazing woman, telling her that all she had to do was want it enough and it could be hers.

Kate watched her, saw the idea taking root, envied her. Then conscience prompted a warning: "But there is a price, you know."

They had reached the door to the anteroom. The light fell across Miss Kate, giving her eyes a new intensity.

"Yes?" Rosamund prompted.

"The price is loneliness. You'll have all the fulfilment you want until you're ... what? Thirty-five? Forty? But from then on in it starts looking ... pretty bleak."

"Oh, I'll risk that," Rosamund said confidently.

But just as they parted she witnessed a silent little tableau that made her pause and think again. Their stroll back among the crowd had brought them close to her father and Lord Oxley, deep in conversation. Lord Oxley noticed them and smiled, especially at Miss Kate. Then he turned back to his conversation. To look at Miss Kate you would have thought the sun just went out. For a moment Rosamund found herself staring into the very soul of desolation. The nakedness of Miss Kate's pain was swiftly covered, of course; she had had much practice. But that, too, was just as heartrending.

Kate saw Rosamund's eyes upon her. She smiled at once. "Don't all the men look marvellous in their uniforms!" she said.

Rosamund nodded and forced a smile in return. As she went away in search of Lawrence she realized she had perhaps just been given a most privileged glimpse of ... twenty years from now. She had seen not Miss Kate but herself, staring at Lawrence across a crowded room, Lawrence comfortably married and settled. Her expression would be just like that.

She felt lost – until she noticed Lawrence standing alone near a potted palm. She knew she could not take the risk. With no pause for thought she went straight up to him and said, in a voice that barely rose above a whisper, "I'll marry you on one condition, my darling."

He froze, not daring to look at her. "Name it."

"Make it irrevocable. Make it so that I'll never be able to back out. Announce it here, tonight, suddenly."

Now he looked at her, bewildered. "But this is hardly the occasion."

"You'll find a way. Your father would. If you're his son, you'll *make* the occasion – I know you will."

His eyes raked the ceiling. "Oh for the days of dragons!"

But he found the chance, just as she predicted.

At midnight they all joined hands and sang *Auld lang syne*; then they raised their glasses to toast in the year 1892. Into that sea of vague, generalized goodwill, into the dying fall of the old year, he projected his voice. "If I may have your attention for a moment?"

A hush fell; they all turned to him in surprise.

"I'm sure I'm going to embarrass everyone dreadfully, but I simply cannot let this evening pass without sharing with you all something of its very special nature to me. Colonel Escalls! Gentlemen!" His roving eye picked out officers' uniforms at random. An officer placed a chair behind him and patted his arm. He thanked the man and stood upon it. "I'm sure I pre-empt someone far more qualified than me to make a speech of thanks. I'm sure, too, that everyone here has his or her special reasons for gratitude. Yet none, I venture now to swear, none can exceed mine in heartfelt fervour."

Their eyes were guarded, neutral. He had yet to win them.

"Gentlemen, when your president extended your invitation to Sir Clive and Lady Mortimer (whom many of you, I'm sure, will remember from years ago) and to my father, Lord Oxley, he was not to know – he had no way of knowing – that they had not been on social terms for almost ten years."

A gasp went up. This was not Good Form.

But Lawrence held up his hand and continued. He had to sweep his eyes around carefully, so as to avoid the patches of tiger country containing the Mortimers and Lord Oxley. "Naturally I should not be standing here now, saying all this, if such were still the case. But tonight, as you must by now have guessed, a small miracle has happened among us – the schism is over! It is a very *large* miracle for those of my generation who grew up together and have keenly felt the deprivation of one another's company."

The smiles were back; women were even checking on the readiness of their handkerchiefs.

"The origins of the schism are history now – and the sooner the dust buries them the better. We have ten lost years to reclaim. So to you, Mr. President, and to you, Gentlemen, we raise our glasses for the most heartfelt toast you have ever received. May I ask you all to drink to our hosts tonight, and to couple with it the toast of" – he lifted his glass high – *"Friendship – life's jewel!"*

"Friendship – life's jewel!" the cry rang out. There was applause. There was a great dabbing of handkerchiefs.

Only Rosamund was looking at him in anguish. He had forgotten the most important thing of all.

He winked at her and raised his hand once more.

"However!"

His cry brought renewed silence.

"I have not yet told you the half of it. Not one hundredth part. The wise heads that rule our nation's destiny know it. The princes who order our commerce know it. Any man or woman who gives the matter a moment's thought knows it! Such arrangements cannot be left to the airy sentiment of a moment, however fine, however deeply felt. They may vanish as swiftly as ... why, as swiftly as the quarrel that occasioned them."

There was laughter and applause. Freddy turned to smile at Kate; but she was staring at Lawrence in consternation, her hand to her mouth – and that mouth wide open.

"No," Lawrence continued. "Such arrangements demand a more formal cement. And *that* is why tonight is a thousand times more special to me than any of you may so far have guessed. For tonight, when the Montagues and Capulets may at last walk arm in arm at peace, tonight Romeo escapes the blade, tonight Juliet spurns the poison cup, and together they set their seal upon the torn parchment of their family trees. In short – Miss Rosamund Mortimer has done me the honour of consenting to become Mrs. Lawrence Oxley!"

Kate's cry of "No!" was lost in the deafening roar of applause that now filled the ballroom. But Ann heard it. She herself had been on the point of screaming out the same word, and but for the astonishment of hearing Kate say it, a fraction of a second before her, she would have let it slip – and thereby have furnished material for gossip to last out the century, and to spill all the way back to England, too.

Another chair was fetched. Rosalind, blushing like a rose and smiling like a sandboy, stood beside Lawrence. He put his arm around her and hugged her. More toasts followed. There was a cry of, "The parents! Where are the parents!"

Freddy and Clive, pale as cinders, stared at each other.

"We must seem to concur," Clive said under his breath. "We can sort it out later."

"Indeed," Eleanor agreed.

Freddy nodded.

Smiling, they went forth together to mark with their approval a union that two of them knew to be forbidden by all the laws of God and man.

CHAPTER SIXTY-SIX

ELEANOR WAS DUMBFOUNDED. It particularly annoyed her that she was forced to whisper, for fear that Rosamund, who should still be blissfully asleep in her bedroom next door, might wake up and overhear. "But of course I shall be there," she insisted. "If the little maidservant Ann Oxley is permitted to attend, then ..."

"I haven't said she will be," Clive interrupted. "We just happen to be using the garden of the Villa Rosalia – because it's so private."

"But if you're using her garden, of course she'll be there! A mere housemaid – what does she know? I'm astonished to hear that you propose to exclude me."

"That's not what I propose at all. It's just that someone has to stay and keep an eye on Rosamund. If she gets the slightest wind of ..."

"You mean to say Rosamund won't be there either!"

"Of course not."

"Nor Lawrence?"

"No. A far as I'm concerned it'll just be Foxy and me."

Eleanor sounded as if she were choking.

"Why – what did *you* suppose?" Clive asked.

She forced herself to be calm. "I supposed what any reasonable parent would suppose. In fact, *I* see no need for a meeting of any kind. Rosamund is not yet of age. You would simply inform her that you forbid the marriage. And I would take her back to England. And then, of course, in our own good time, we should find her someone suitable."

"And tongues out here wouldn't wag?" Clive asked pointedly. "Especially after Lawrence's efforts last night! My God – he nailed every flag in the locker to every mast in the fleet! You know very well – the wagging of the tongues out here would soon be heard in every drawing room in London. You'd step off the boat into a thicket of American reporters."

Reluctantly Eleanor conceded the possibility. "Very well then. We *all* gather out there in the villa garden, and we simply lay down the law."

"And what reason do we give?"

"Reason? She's only nineteen! One doesn't give reasons to children."

Clive put his arms around his wife and smiled. "She is only a few months younger than you were when you agreed to marry me. Now just think back to how you felt at that time. What would you have done if your father had simply 'laid down the law.' Eh?"

She shrugged uncomfortably.

"You know precisely what we'd both have done," he went on. "And so you see our greatest danger now – that she will get wind of our opposition and elope. Someone must stick by her like a leech, from now until you both leave – and it can't be me."

After a pause Eleanor said, "I don't like it. What am I supposed to do with her? How do I occupy her time?"

"Why don't the pair of you go shopping – look for things for her trousseau. Arrange ..."

Eleanor almost exploded again.

"Yes!" Clive insisted. "Even chaperone her with Lawrence. Until Foxy and I have worked out some way of presenting them with a fait-accompli, she must not get the slightest inkling of our opposition. You were magnificent last night, and I'm sure you can maintain the masquerade for just a little while longer."

Still with the greatest reluctance Eleanor agreed – for this one day at least.

Rosamund awoke knowing there was something new and

glorious in her life. When the memory hit her she almost cried for the joy of it.

"This is much the most sensible way," she told her mother at breakfast. "We can have our family early, you see. Stop at three – that's quite possible these days, or so Megs Davison says – dump them in the nursery, and then vanish into the forbidden continent. It's the best of both worlds, you see."

"Of course it is, dear." Eleanor had no idea what the girl was babbling on about.

"Where's father?"

"He went to see the urchin – I mean ... Ffff ... Lord Oxley."

Rosamund bubbled over with laughter and squeezed her mother's hand. "I know you don't approve, mumsie. I can always tell when you're putting a political face on things. But he's just sweet. You'll see."

Out at the Villa Rosalia, on the seventh and last terrace down from the house, on a lawn that was barely reclaimed from the dense thorn scrub that encroached from all around, Freddy, Clive, and Ann paced slowly, aimlessly, up and down. Lunchtime was approaching; they were all growing hungry, tense, edgy. The meeting had not gone smoothly.

"It's obvious," Ann said. "You simply must tell Eleanor."

"There's no *simply* about it," Clive retorted.

"But if she imagines that our objections amount to no more than the fact – which isn't even *true* – that our two families are still really quarrelling ... well, it'll just never work."

There was a pause before Freddy said, "I'm afraid she's right, old scout."

Clive nodded unhappily. "If only it didn't involve your honour though, Ann. And Lawrence's. And yours also, of course, Foxy. D'you believe Lawrence should be told, too?"

"I do," Ann said flatly.

"No!" Freddy was so insistent they halted and turned to him in surprise. He stared back defiantly. "I'd rather the marriage went ahead than that."

"But ..." Ann began.

"There's the danger of an elopement," Clive explained. "It's the biggest of all our dangers in my view. It's out of the question to tell Rosamund, but if Lawrence knew the true ..."

"No!" Freddy insisted. He took a step back and looked from one to the other. "You shall not take away my son! I've invested twenty-three years in him – twenty-three years of *me*! And now you suppose that in five minutes you can take it all away!"

"But what if they elope?" Ann persisted.

"Tell Rosamund then," Freddy replied.

"But she's had the most correct, the most sheltered up-bringing," Clive objected.

"So had Ann," Freddy told him.

"Balls, Freddy!" Ann shouted at him – astonishing them both. "Forgive my bluntness but you are making me very angry." She stared at him, breathing furiously.

He grew angry too. "Any minute now you'll be telling me I had nothing to do with it," he challenged. "Well let me tell you – I've played the only decent part in this whole sorry business. Are you going to tell me that all the paternity I've lavished on that son of mine counts for *nothing*? D'you mean to say that one small squalid accident, which happened nearly a quarter of a century ago, can still wipe it out?"

Ann and Clive exchanged worried glances.

"Nothing can change the biological facts, dear," Ann said soothingly.

"What did you imagine we were going to discuss, Foxy?" Clive asked, in the same conciliatory tones. "When you came out here this morning, you must have had some plan in your mind."

Freddy merely chewed his lip, distrusting the politician in Clive.

"I mean let's begin at the very beginning. We are all agreed, I assume, that this marriage is to be prevented at all costs?"

"Naturally," Ann said.

They looked at Freddy. "Not at *all* costs," he told them.

"But you know what sort of marriage it would be!" Ann said, trying not to flare up again.

He gave her a withering look. "I may be trained in chemistry and mathematics but I've probably picked up more biology in passing than you could learn in the rest of your life. So don't start trying to teach me about ontogeny and genesis."

"You mean there are no biological objections?" Clive asked, astounded at the suggestion.

Freddy turned on him. "I am not going to let myself get shunted off onto irrelevant lines of argument. Someone must keep this discussion in order."

Clive raised his hands in disbelief. "And I suppose you'll be saying next that there are no legal objections either."

Freddy looked at him as if he were a simpleton. "What on earth are we talking about things like this for?" he asked. "They simply have no relevance."

"You mean you see no legal objections?"

Freddy gave an impatient snort. "Of course there are no legal objections! How could there be? But in any case it's beside the point."

"I give up!" Clive said.

"Hear hear!" Ann agreed. "We don't seem to be talking about the same thing at all." She touched Freddy's arm. "Suppose we let *you* start, dear? Clive asked you what you had in mind when you came to this meeting. Propose it now."

He looked from one to the other. "I don't know. You're beginning to force me to change my mind. I mean, I agree that my immediate reaction was the same as yours. But now you're making me consider it more carefully, more rationally – all the little side-issues that weren't immediately apparent – I'm beginning to think it's not the end of the world."

"Dammit!" Clive exploded.

But Ann put her hand up. "No – hear him out."

Freddy continued: "If it means telling my son that he's not my son, then I say a thousand times no. On that I shall not budge."

"All right," Ann said. "Let's take that as granted. Lawrence is not to be told. You still agree that in principle this marriage is one to be avoided?"

Freddy sighed. "I'm no longer prepared even to say that much. I want to know exactly what is being proposed in its place."

"But one of them *must* be told," Ann went on. "We cannot run the risk – the near-certain risk – of an elopement. Therefore it will have to be Rosamund. Is that what you want?"

"Of course I don't *want* it! But don't go on at me as if I'm the one who created this mess."

"Now we have it!" Clive broke in bitterly. Ann tried to stop him but he insisted. "All this talk of burying the hatchet … it doesn't mean a damn thing. You've always wanted to punish me for what happened that time, and now it's clear you always will. You'll take pound after pound after pound of my flesh – any time you can get it!"

Freddy looked at Ann, almost as if he expected her to defend him from this charge. At least, that is how she interpreted his gaze. Sadly she shook her head. "It's the same thing I told you, darling, that evening in Georgetown, all those years ago. You cannot face the truth of it. Somewhere inside you, so deep you can't even feel it, that worm of bitterness is still gnawing away. Until you can spit it up – and that means facing yourself honestly – you'll always be blind to the truth. *We* see it." She looked at Clive. He nodded. She turned back to Freddy. "But you're blind."

He spun angrily on his heel and walked away from them. He almost blundered into a kaffre thorn. He reached out a finger and pressed it firmly against the tip of the longest spike within reach, a wicked monster, almost a foot long. He increased the pressure – and the pain – until the tip of it pierced his skin. The poison burned.

He was right! All this talk of Ann's was just airy fairy nonsense – the words of a song, rearranged to bamboozle him. He was right. Lawrence *was* his son – by investment. By law. By common consent. By love. They had no right to take him away. He walked slowly back to rejoin them. He'd have to use cunning now.

"Well?" Ann asked with an encouraging smile.

He smiled back. "Let's see if some luncheon can't improve our tempers."

They both sighed with relief. "Good idea!"

They set up a table and parasol on the next lawn, so that they could continue their discussion without disrupting the rest of the household. Halfway through the meal, a distraught Eleanor came hurrying down the path. "Is Rosamund here?" she asked.

The shock in their faces answered her.

"Oh that little devil!" She sat down at the table and burst into tears. "She told me she was coming directly here!"

Five minutes later they had the story out of her. Rosamund had eventually sensed her mother's unease. She had, of course, been bubbling over all morning with her delight and Eleanor had not been able to keep up the pretence. In the end she'd been goaded into saying too much. The girl had stormed off and leaped into the first passing cab, shouting that she was coming out to the Villa Rosalia to confront them all. It had taken Eleanor some minutes to find a vacant cab and follow her. Now it was clear that she had gone straight to Lawrence, presumably at the hotel.

Clive looked daggers at his wife. "None of this need have happened," he said.

"Indeed it need not!" she replied pointedly.

"The main thing now is to find them," Ann cut in quickly. She looked pleadingly at Freddy. "If it's you who runs across them, tell them anything – anything you like – it needn't be the truth – but this marriage *must* be stopped!"

The sight of this former housemaid laying down the law and speaking as if it were *she* and *her* family that would be slighted by such a match was suddenly more than Eleanor could bear, especially on top of her present distress. She stood up. "I hardly think it's your place to say such things!" she said in her most peremptory tone.

Ann reacted angrily. "I should think it's my place above all others to say it!"

"Ann!" Clive warned sharply.

Eleanor caught his tone and swung round on him. The guilt she saw there left her completely shattered. He looked away.

Quickly she turned to Ann. Ann looked away, too.

Then to Freddy – where she saw not guilt but anguish.

She sat down. "Oh ... my ... God!" she whispered.

No one spoke.

"But how blind I've been! 'A Mortimer will inherit!' "

"Clive begged me to be allowed to tell you," Ann said.

Eleanor buried her face in her hands and began to cry again, softly this time, almost soundlessly.

"I told him no," Ann went on. "I couldn't hurt Frederick."

"If only we'd known," Eleanor sobbed.

"Would it have helped?" Clive asked. "Were *you* aware of anything going on between Rosamund and Lawrence?"

She went on sobbing.

Suddenly it struck her. She looked up at Freddy. "All those things I said to you!"

He smiled. "But I knew you didn't know the truth."

"You 'wouldn't come between Clive and me'! I see it now!"

He shrugged. "How could I have told you?"

She shook her head in amazement. "And you just stood there and took it! You let me call you every filthy name I could think of ... and not by a flicker of an eyelid ..."

Clive had meanwhile risen and come to stand behind her. She turned in her seat and, half rising, buried herself in his arms.

"I never held a word of it against you," Freddy told her. "I was glad to spare you – for your sake. And for Clive's, of course."

Ann looked at him sharply. It was just too unctuous for words. Yet the mild sincerity of his voice almost swayed her against that judgement – even her. Clive and Eleanor, in their overwrought state, were completely won over.

"Let's go and find them," Freddy said. "We'll need good horses. Is there a livery nearby?"

CHAPTER SIXTY-SEVEN

LAWRENCE AND ROSAMUND rode in silence, as fast as the terrain permitted. They took any path that led more westerly than the one they were on, and in that way came by degrees upon the coastal road to Uman Gorge. He recognised it only as far as

Skoenmaakerskop; after that it was wild country to them both. For a mile or so they galloped, but then, realizing they had passed only a few farm waggons and one empty stanhope, they relaxed their pace and pulled their horses aside for a breather.

"I still can't believe it," Lawrence said as he helped her dismount. "It was all a sham."

"Every word of it. Every smile. Oh Lorry, darling, don't let us *ever* be like that."

"I wouldn't know how to begin."

They held each other tight, still shocked by their parents' duplicity.

"What do we do now?" she asked.

"Find the first preacher who'll marry us. I don't care what denomination – Hindoo, Jew, Confucian ..."

"Oh yes!" She laughed. "Won't that teach them!"

They were in a grove of gum trees, though the settlement for which it had been planted had long since gone. A little way away they could hear the pounding of the surf. The rich smell of coastal bush was all around.

"What a beaut of a country!" he said. "We could settle out here."

"We don't need to settle anywhere," she murmured happily.

"Shall we stroll about a bit? I think we're safe enough here. We can't be seen from the road."

They tethered their horses on a long rein, allowing them the chance to graze, while they walked off hand in hand toward the sea.

"The *best* thing that can be said in their favour," she told him, "is that it's all snobbery."

"Snobbery?"

"Well, what else? Suppose they are genuine about burying the hatchet. It must mean they don't mind your father as a friend. But nothing closer than that. They couldn't possibly have a former apprentice actually in the family."

Lawrence digested this in silence. It was plausible and yet it rang false. He gave up with a sigh. "I wish I could talk it over with the pater. But perhaps he's in it with them – whatever *it* may be. We can't risk that." A sudden thought struck him. "Perhaps they've got both our futures planned for us already!"

"How?" she asked.

The path grew sandier as it wound down toward the shore. Only marram grass and chunky green succulents dotted its golden whiteness. They were beyond the thorn shade now; with nothing but the onshore breeze to cool their half-acclimatized bodies.

"What if they have some political match lined up for you – one of the Hoare boys, or the Hickses. And some industrial pairing-off for me. Amanda Whitworth or one of the Vosper girls. Something like that."

He felt her shiver at the thought, and pulled her close to him. She hugged herself into his embrace and shut her eyes. "Let's do what you suggested," she said. "Just ride until we find a minister. I don't give a fig what denomination either, just as long as he's licensed. And we'll pay him whatever he wants to marry us on the spot."

He took her hand and led her the last winding hundred yards among the dunes. The surf was pounding a quarter of a mile away, at the farther edge of the rocks that fringed the shore. Immediately before them those same rocks rose to embrace a sandy lane of shimmering water.

"Swim?" he suggested.

She heard the shiver in his voice – and an answering tremor in hers when she said, "Yes."

They undressed with their backs to each other and ran swiftly down into the water. At first they laughed and splashed each other as they had when they were children, but when they drew close together a great seriousness came over them. She drifted into his arms, raised her feet from the sand, and wrapped herself about him.

"Mmmm?" he faltered.

Her grip intensified. She hardly felt what he did. She lay against his heaving chest, feeling the hammer of their hearts, looking dreamily at the water and seeing her small issue of blood turn it pink, feeling no alarm, feeling nothing except the goodness of his pleasure. Some inner wisdom promised her that next time would be different, better. It hadn't exactly been what Eve had risked all Paradise to know.

He almost collapsed. Then he could not stop shivering. "Did it hurt?" he asked shyly.

She kissed him softly. "Now we *must* find that minister."

"Oh Ros, I do love you so. You're all the world to me."

They dressed and rode on westwards. After the blood she had expected a tenderness but there was none. On they went, through Uman Gorge and into the wild coastal bush. In a few miles they came to a small ridge from whose crest there stretched before them vast tracts of pasture, green and obviously irrigated. But the object that caught and held their eye, far down the shallow valley and so close to the sea that from here it seemed to spring from among its waves, was a perfect replica of an English parish church.

"Our vicar!" Lawrence said. "It's an omen, I'm sure. Let's go and see if he'll marry us!"

She was trying to remember something. "I think father told me about this once. It's not a real church. It's one of the local curios, but there was something else, too. I've forgotten."

"Well, church or not, perhaps they take in travellers, anyway. Let's see." He urged his horse forward.

The drive wound around in a lazy semicircle so that they approached the place from the west. A tall, fair-haired woman in her middle age stood at the door, shielding her eyes against the lowering sun. "You're gey welcome," she said in a strong Scots accent. "I'm Mrs. Tobermory. Himself will be home soon."

CHAPTER SIXTY-EIGHT

THREE DAYS LATER, when news of Lawrence and Rosamund reached their families, there was a second meeting of the clans on that most private and secure of grass terraces at the Villa Rosalia. Ann, Eleanor, and Clive were subdued, shocked. Freddy, by contrast, was impatient.

"Why should this man Tobermory go out of his way to

help them like that?" Eleanor asked. "*And* throw us off the scent."

"He didn't exactly lie to me," Clive pointed out.

"And he didn't exactly tell the truth, either! Why should he want to hurt us?"

Freddy gave a clipped laugh. "What harm have the Mortimers ever done him, eh, Eleanor? It's becoming your standard question. Let's hope it hasn't got the standard answer!"

Clive leaped to his feet. "Now chuck it, you!" he shouted.

For a moment it looked as if they would come to blows, but Ann moved between them. "This will lead nowhere," she said, and then, turning to Eleanor, "It really doesn't matter why Tobermory did it. Probably sheer cussedness. He's well known as a troublemaker here. He loves nothing better than to egg people on in whatever folly they wish to engage in, and then later he'll find some way of making them pay for it."

"Blackmail?" Freddy asked.

"Not for money. Perhaps in the early days but not now. He's one of the richest people around here now. No he does it for favours ... information ... or just the sense of power it gives him. So forget Tobermory. The question is, what do *we* do now? I suppose we're quite sure the marriage is legal?"

They all looked at Clive, who nodded unhappily. "It's a sect of lunatics, The Brothers and Sisters of The Last Day, but some equally deranged idiot in Cape Town saw fit to license them and so ... yes, the marriage ceremony was valid."

"Then," Ann said, "we have only two choices, surely? We must tell the youngsters the truth and either seek an annulment, or" – she mimed hopelessness at the very idea – "they must live apart."

Freddy saw at once the impossibility of either course. *Wait a bit*, he thought. *Let them talk it out.*

No one felt inclined to say anything.

"Are there any other suggestions?" Ann asked.

"An annulment would be so public," Eleanor objected. "Absolutely everything would come out. We'd be finished in England. We'd have to sell up everything and live abroad. Who would marry our other daughters?" She looked at Freddy, whom she now saw as the only decent person in the whole business. "I don't suppose it would affect your business, Foxy, but socially it would be the absolute end of you. Angelica would be in exactly the same position as our girls."

"I quite agree, Eleanor." His smile was warm, sympathetic; it said, *We both know what fools these others are.*

Clive was still fuming. "All right, let's hear your brilliant suggestion," he taunted.

Freddy answered mildly, "I want Ann to tell us about this other choice – living in continence. Or *you* tell us, Clive! I didn't realize either of you knew much about the subject."

"By God you swine!" This time it would have been blows if Ann had not leaped at Freddy first.

"If all you can do is throw that *one* mistake endlessly in our faces then you can just get out. We don't need you here. We're perfectly capable of telling Lawrence the truth whether you're present or not." She saw him go pale and knew she had found the right curb.

Clive saw it, too, and seated himself again with a smile.

"Now," Ann went on, still commanding but more reasonable. "Have you anything positive to contribute?"

He licked his lips and looked at them, trying to size up their mood. It did not satisfy him. "I will put forward my suggestions when the rest of you are quite agreed that the other two choices – what you mistakenly call the *only* choices – are out of the question."

They looked at each other.

"The remaining choice is to say nothing, do nothing, and let the marriage go forward," Clive objected. "That's equally out of the question."

"Never mind that," Freddy persisted. "All I want is to hear you agree that the open scandal of an annulment is unthinkable, and that telling them the truth and asking them to remain married but live apart – as if they had quarrelled, or as if there were something unspeakably odious about one or other of them – is also ... too ridiculous to put forward seriously."

Again there was an uncomfortable pause.

"I suppose he's right," Eleanor said at length.

Ann sighed. "I didn't mean that I *liked* either course. But ..."

Clive looked up at Freddy, the only one still standing.

"All right, Oxley. You might say we're agreed." He rubbed the bridge of his nose.

"That's exactly what Lawrence does!" Eleanor cried. "Every day I see more and more resemblances. Why was I so blind!"

"Please Foxy?" Clive said, ignoring her.

"Well first let's look at the legal situation," Freddy said. "I imagine at the back of all our minds is the fear that one day all this might come out into the open and if we'd allowed the marriage to stand, knowing what we do, we'd all be accessories to a criminal offence."

"I wouldn't say it's at the *back* of our minds," Clive replied. The others murmured their agreement.

"I'm talking about *legal* incest now," Freddy emphasized. "I'll come to the biological aspects in a minute. Let's just focus our attention on the legal question."

He sat down, a little way apart from them. They leaned forward eagerly; his confidence, the suggestion that he had worked it all out to the last little detail, gave them an absurd feeling of hope.

"Legally," he went on, "there is no question but that Lawrence is Lawrence Oxley."

They nodded, but he underlined the point nonetheless. "Under *Father's Name* on his birth certificate it says Frederick Oxley – not written in pencil – no little question mark set against it."

They nodded again, even smiled a little.

"So *legally* there's no doubt Lawrence is an Oxley. And *legally* there's no doubt Rosamund is a Mortimer. So *legally* there can be no question of incest. No possible prosecution on those grounds." He let that sink in before he added, "Our only fear would be if Ann went into a commissioner for oaths and swore out an affidavit that the information on the original birth certificate was a lie."

Ann laughed at the absurdity of it. They all laughed.

Suddenly they found themselves looking at each other in amazement, as if to ask, *Can this be true?*

"Let's turn to the biological question," Freddy went on. "I suppose you've all heard of the name Ptolemy?"

"The Egyptian pharaoh?" Clive asked.

"The most famous of them. He was also a mathematician and astronomer – one of the most brilliant the world has ever known. He was, in fact, Ptolemy IX – the ninth of his dynasty in a direct line. He was the result of the union between his father, Ptolemy VIII, and his father's full sister."

He allowed that to sink in.

"One swallow doesn't make a summer," Clive said.

Freddy held up a finger, the conjuror in command. "Ptolemy VIII was the result of the union between *his* father, Ptolemy VII, and *that* father's full sister."

Again he paused.

"But why?" Eleanor asked, horrified at the very thought of it.

"Because the Egyptians believed their pharaohs were gods. It was unthinkable to them that gods should marry mortals – for the next pharaoh would then be only half a god ... and so on."

"You mean they *all* married their sisters?"

He nodded. His smile said, *Now you see it!* "Every single Ptolemy, from the first to the eighth, was the result of the union between a brother and his full sister. And the last of the line, after eight generations of brother-sister marriages, was one of the most brilliant men in the entire history of science." After a pause, he added, "Lawrence and Rosamund are only *half*-brother-and-sister, of course. I think that settles what must be our principal anxiety on the biological side."

"What happened to the ninth Ptolemy?" Clive asked.

Freddy looked at him pityingly. "How much insurance do you want, man?"

They chuckled and again there was that wonder among them that perhaps the unthinkable was not quite so unthinkable after all.

"Anyway Clive," Freddy added, "when you want to strengthen the bloodline of your prize Hereford or your champion Yorkshire White, how do you set about it?"

Clive nodded as he grasped the point.

"How?" Ann asked.

"He sires them onto their siblings or their own progeny, of course."

"Does that mean their sisters and daughters?"

"And their mothers," Clive added.

Ann shivered. "I always thought animals had nobler natures than people."

"The point is the stock improves and thrives."

"I no longer understand any of it." She looked intently at Freddy. "But by heavens, you'd better be right!"

"Is there any marked defect in your family?" he asked her. "Any lunacy or congenital deformity?"

She shook her head. He looked at the other two; they shook their heads as well.

"Then the odds in our favour must be many thousands to one."

A profound silence reigned.

"I can't believe this is happening," Clive said. He looked from one to the other of them. "We *know* the truth. We all know the honourable answer to this dilemma. Yet here we are ..." His hands finished the sentence for him.

Freddy said nothing. The two women looked briefly at each other but not at the men.

"Surely we're not agreeing?" Clive insisted.

"But think of the alternatives!" Eleanor said. "The ruin and disgrace of at least two families – and Lord alone knows how wide the ripples might spread. Four unmarriageable girls ... sons with blighted careers ... all our work, all our lives – just thrown away ... it's, it's, it's ... unthinkable. Utterly out of the question."

"What of conscience, then?" Clive asked.

"Conscience!" she sneered. "Where was conscience a quarter of a century ago? This isn't conscience, it's the remorse of the murderer who wants his victim alive again."

"But the *law*." Clive tried another tack.

She cut him short again. "The law is in the Bible. The sins of the fathers shall be visited on the children even unto the seventh generation. That's your law."

It was as if Clive were seeing Eleanor for the first time. "You *want* some kind of retribution! My God, you want it to go wrong!"

Freddy interrupted: "The only laws we need worry about are the laws of nature, old scout. And they don't get repealed and re-enacted with every new administration." He meant the remark to be jocular, for the argument between Clive and Eleanor was unnerving him. But his earlier taunts were not yet dead enough; his tone accidentally revived something of their spirit.

It forced Clive to square up to the decision. "Very well. If no one else can bring himself to do it, I can see I must."

"What d'you mean?"

There was a commotion at the gates, laughter, shouts of *coo-eee!* It was Lawrence and Rosamund, the Hon. Mr. and Mrs. Oxley. Ann stood up and ran to the top of the steps, from where she would be visible. "We're down here!" she cried.

"I shall tell them," Clive said. "Immediately. Get it over with."

Eleanor stood up, her eyes blazing. "If you do any such thing, I shall leave you." She saw the anguish flood into his eyes but she did not flinch. "I mean it," she insisted. "I was never more serious about anything in my life."

Ann rejoined them. "Clive's right," she said flatly. "We could not live with our consciences."

The youngsters were coming down the path.

"But didn't you listen?" Freddy asked Ann. "Didn't you hear a word I said?"

He looked at the pair of them but neither could meet his eye. "Of course we did," Ann told him. "I'm sure it's all true. I'm sure we believe every word of it. But there is still the matter of conscience. If Clive doesn't tell them, I will." Her voice broke on her tears. Clive went to her and put an arm around her. Unwittingly, an animal in pain, she hugged herself to him.

Eleanor watched them, speechless.

"Hello!" Lawrence called. "What on earth are you all doing down there!"

Now that they were in sight of their parents their boisterous cheer deserted them a little; ancient habits of deference began to reassert themselves.

"Come on down here a moment," Clive said solemnly, letting Ann go.

Freddy stood there aghast. His blood had turned to a gel. He had felt so sure of his arguments – so sure he had won them over. He sought for more words but none came.

The youngsters walked slowly down the last flight of

steps. "What is it?" Rosamund asked. "You look as if some-one's died."

"There's something we have to tell you," Clive replied.

"Someone *has* died!" Rosamund's jaw dropped.

"It's ... it's more serious than that," her father told her.

Wordless, they almost tiptoed forward, scared by the terrible fragility they now felt in the very air around them.

"Clive!" Freddy's agonized cry rang out.

Clive looked at him and saw a soul stripped naked. Lord Oxley had vanished ... all his confidence, all his clever arguments, layer after layer of Freddy had fallen away. All that was left was the little boy who had shared his youth – the one, true, original Foxy. He stood there now, mute and pleading, *My blood brother! Do not do this to me!*

The two youngsters held their breath, staring first at one, then at the other. They saw Clive's eyelids waver and fall; they saw him slump where he stood.

"Ann," he said, passing responsibility to her.

But Ann had seen it, too – that defenceless mite who stood revealed yet again at the heart of her old love, her only love. She thought of all the hurt she had done him over the years, not because she had wished to but because he was what he was, and she what she was, and neither of them could help it. And like Clive she realized that, honour and conscience notwithstanding, she simply could not do this to him.

In a way, the decision was made not seconds but years ago. She and Clive had had to live with their soiled consciences all their lives. No new act of purification could cleanse them after all that time. The decision to say nothing now, to live with that *knowledge* of wrong inside them for the rest of their lives, was already ancient.

She saw that Eleanor was right in saying that the sins of the fathers – the parents – were laid upon the generations. But she was wrong if she believed it was because a vengeful God stored them up and carried them forward; the truth was even more bleak than that. The truth was that the parents survived their sins and could change neither themselves nor their history – they remained forever prisoners of their time and blood.

Thus Ann, too, lowered her eyes.

"Well?" Lawrence risked asking.

Eleanor seized the initiative. "We hope you'll both be very happy."

They were ecstatic. "Oh is it true?" Rosamund asked.

"*Is* it, Clive?" Eleanor repeated.

He nodded. Then, unable to face them, he walked away.

"Ann?" Eleanor asked next.

Ann did the same as Clive, but walked off in a different direction.

"What's the matter?" Lawrence asked.

"They need time," Freddy told him. "All this has been a bit of a shock, but they'll get over it. Just give them a little time." He smiled as at a sudden thought. "You can well afford it now."

CHAPTER SIXTY-NINE

THEY NEEDED MORE THAN TIME. They needed air, space. Above all they needed to get away from the atmosphere of the Villa Rosalia – even Ann. They needed to ventilate the sadness, the anger, the cowardice – even the sombre, resigned joy of their acceptance. They gathered up the makings of an impromptu banquet and fled to the coast. Kate and Angelica came as well.

To Nordhoek ... but there were other people there, two shy ladies and an elderly gentleman.

To Skoenmaakerskop, or Skoenies, as Eleanor called it ... but a party of African women were doing their washing there – a whole year's production, it seemed.

On they went, out along the road to Uman Gorge.

"We don't want to end up at Tobermory's!" Ann joked.

"Oh here's a place," Kate called out. "We've not been here for donkey's years."

They had arrived at a grove of gum trees, though the settlement for which it had been planted had long since gone. In the distance they could hear the pounding of the surf. The rich smell of coastal bush was all around.

"There's a lovely, long, sheltered pool down here," Kate explained to the others.

Lawrence looked at Rosamund and smiled.

Clive recognised it, too, the moment they were out of the thorn shade and onto the sandy path that wound down to the sea. The marram grass and chunky green succulents that littered the pale-golden earth seemed hardly to have changed since he and Ellen Tobermory were here. They babbled to one another all the way, heaping a litter of words – any words – over the thoughts they would never again speak out loud. The last hundred yards of the path lay among the dunes – and suddenly there they were, standing on the harder, tide-washed sand, with the pale lane of water nestling between its flanks of rock. The surf was thundering a quarter of a mile away.

"Paradise!" Lawrence said.

"Then where's the tree of knowledge?" Angelica joked.

"We ate it all," Ann told her.

Everyone laughed. They were all hungry.

The younger ones took Angelica and scavenged for driftwood. Clive and Freddy argued about the scientific way to build a fire, but the fire took hold and burned brightly just the same. Their wives portioned out the bread and cheese and fruit; the braaivleis would have to wait until there was a good hot bed of ashes.

Later Rosamund found herself swilling the plates and cutlery alongside Ann. "I owe you an apology," she said. "What do I call you – Lady Oxley ... Aunt Ann?"

"Just call me Ann. What sort of an apology?"

"Oh, for all the things I thought about you. I mean I could understand the others being surprised and getting upset and so on. But not you. You chose a free life for yourself. I thought that of all the women I know, you'd be the one most likely to understand. So I thought the most dreadful things against you."

"Well as long as you only thought them."

"All our laughter and smiles when we came back to the

villa – that was just to keep our courage up, you know. If you'd still been all sour, I was ready to let fly."

Ann chuckled. "I'm glad we saw sense then."

"What would you have done if I had?" Rosamund asked.

"There are some things in life you just have to learn to take," she replied vaguely.

"I don't suppose we'll ever know now – what you all had against us."

"Not from me, you won't."

"It wasn't just the family quarrel, I'm sure of that. Lorry and I think you already had quite different partners arranged for us."

"Aren't parents beastly!"

Rosamund laughed. "Yes – such scheming things!"

"And now you'll soon be one of us," Ann pointed out. She felt she ought to add, "Or so we're all hoping." But she could not bring herself to it.

Rosamund's laughter again. "I know!"

They had built the braaivleis pits a little way off, not to be bothered by the smoke. Ann saw Clive bent over them, tending the fire, turning the stubs of pine branches in toward the heart of the flames. Idly she rose and sauntered over to join him.

"Well well!" he said flatly, not looking up. "Weren't we the brave ones!"

"I couldn't possibly blame you," she answered in the same matter-of-fact tone. After a brief silence she added, "I know this is an awful thing to say about anyone – and God forgive me for even thinking it – but you don't suppose Frederick actually planned this whole awful business, do you? Years ago, perhaps?"

Clive was silent – but not, she noticed, surprised. "So the same thought has already crossed your mind," she said.

He nodded bitterly. "I took it more as a comment on myself than on old Fredders, though. I still can't believe we've all connived to accept this ghastly situation."

She agreed so wholeheartedly she could think of nothing to add.

He went on, "I don't suppose I shall ever know a moment's true peace again – not ever." He almost looked up at her. "Did you ever get whacked at school?"

"Of course."

"You remember the fear – no, it was worse than fear – the *dread* that hung over the whole day? How your mind would keep stubbing its toes on that one recurring thought: *Soon I'll be getting it!* And your guts would just curdle up inside you? Now it's going to be like that every day until we die."

"We've deserved it."

He was startled into looking at her. "Oh no! Surely not, Ann? It was such a *little* sin. The smallest shift in our circumstances would have made it no sin at all. Oh no – God is not so malevolent."

"Then you have to fall back on believing that Frederick planned it."

Clive nodded morosely. "And yet in a way that would be to elevate him above even God."

She saw how perfectly he had adopted the political mode of thinking, which works by preparing good reasons for and against everything, and then drawing on either set of arguments, or both, as expediency dictates. He was waiting for a clearer view into her mind.

"You were right the first time," she told him. "If we think such things of Frederick, we actually reveal our own murky souls, not his."

"I was right the second time, too," he added. "This *is* a ghastly mess. We *are* condoning something quite monstrous. And we shall never stop paying for it."

She was about to argue, to say that he was being altogether too pessimistic, that there were many currencies for such payment and that misery and rue were only two of them; but then she saw that his train of thought was a great comfort to him; it allowed him to swallow the nausea, to stifle that scream of judgement.

"The one person who's surprised me in all this," he said in a more conversational tone, "is Eleanor."

"In what way?" Ann remembered the ferocity of Eleanor's insistence.

"I've always lived with this fear that one day she'd stumble upon the truth. I thought it would break her up completely."

Ann gave a dry little laugh. "Well that's one fear less."

"To me she's always been the very soul of propriety. A

pillar of morality. It's her vehemence that is so surprising. She seems to have none of our qualms about it." He looked up at Ann and caught her shaking her head in a knowing kind of pity. "What?" he asked.

"You don't really know much about women, Clive. Morality's a fine and noble thing as long as it works in support of the family. But just let it try threatening ...!"

A long silence followed while Clive digested the news; there seemed to be nothing more to say.

"We must keep in touch," she suggested emptily.

"Yes," he lied.

Later, he and Freddy went for a walk over the rocks. After a quarter of a mile or so they came upon a sandy stretch of beach. They walked along the tideline, where hundreds of Portuguese men-of-war lay stranded. Their glassy bladders had dried tight in the sun, begging passers-by to burst them underfoot like miniature party balloons.

"I'll tell you one thing, Foxy," Clive said solemnly, ignoring the fun his feet were having. "After this you'll make bloody sure young Angelica doesn't go near the Knox-Riddells!"

Freddy breathed out sharply. "A hit," he acknowledged. "I felt that."

"Well, I have to get my little dig in where I can."

They came to a whole school of balloons and enjoyed a frenzy of popping. "Seriously though," Clive said as they resumed their stroll, "don't you think we can agree to draw the double line across the page now? Ann and I have paid enough, surely?"

Freddy stopped and grasped his arm. "My dear friend," he said earnestly. "Not once, from the days of the Grand Soarer until now, not once have I said or done a single act against you. You've picked up this ridiculous notion from Ann – you needn't deny it – I saw you talking to her just now. But you just try going back and asking her to explain it in detail. She can't! She's utterly loony on the subject – thinks I'm not one person but half a dozen. How she supposes that six people can cohabit in one body without bumping into each other and making life impossible all round, I just can't imagine. And it's the one thing she can't explain, of course."

Looking into his eyes Clive saw nothing there but honest bewilderment. They continued their stroll.

"I came close to it once," Freddy admitted. "That night Angelica was born I wanted to kill you."

"Me!"

"Well, Tony was such a sop about it. Anyway, you were the one who ..."

After a healthy pause Clive prompted: "I was the one who what?"

"No I can't explain it. But you were the one I would willingly have killed. Yet you know very well what response that brought out in me."

"Do I?"

"Of course you do – I came to see you."

"Oh well, naturally I remember that." Then he added, "You didn't *seem* very murderous."

"But don't you see? That's my point. I was frightened. The desire to kill you ... frightened me. I had to see you – to overcome that bloodlust. That's what I'm saying – I've never done or said a single thing to hurt you. I may have *felt* the impulse, but my first reaction was to see you and ... and quell that feeling." He punched Clive lightly on the arm. "So just take anything Ann says on the subject with a grain of salt, eh?"

Clive, who knew exactly what Ann meant when she said that Freddy was like half a dozen people cohabiting inside one common body, realized that Freddy would never be able to grasp it. He let an easeful silence bury the echoes of the topic and then asked, "What about Ann, anyway?"

"What about her?"

"Are you just going back to England once your field-gun trials are complete? And is she to stay out here?"

"Oh I expect so."

"You don't want to marry again?"

Freddy paused too long before he said, "I wouldn't want to put her through the scandal of a divorce."

"Ah. Is that all?"

"I don't know about *all*. It's quite a strong objection, surely?"

Clive considered the matter and then said, "You might not have to."

"In what way?"

"Ann's people are dead, aren't they?"

Freddy nodded. "Some years ago."

"So all the people in the world who know that Ann Howard of Walmer is actually Lady Oxley are here at this beach today. Am I right?"

Freddy thought about it and agreed.

"How did *you* find out she was here?"

"Miss Kate wrote to tell me. She always kept me informed of The Angels' whereabouts."

"But presumably you'd also made inquiries on your own account?"

Freddy was about to say no when he remembered the evening at Sadler's Wells. "In a way, yes. But it was a dead end. One of the new Angels, the second lot, told me they'd gone to Rio de Janeiro. But Kate later told me that was only for a few weeks. Just to cover their traces."

"Oh really?" Clive pricked up his ears. "Why did they need to cover their traces?"

"Well, can't you imagine what the local matrons in P.E. would say if they knew that the respectable Misses Howard and Williams and Kendall had all been on the stage! What – touring the world and singing in clubs and bars! They'd lose every pupil inside a week."

"In other words, it's going to be pretty hard for anyone to trace Ann."

"Almost impossible, I'd say."

Clive laughed. "Then the problem's solved. When did you last see her – as far as the world is concerned? That time in Turkey wasn't it?"

"Yes. Eight years ago."

"Seven years is all the law requires. You're already home and dry. Lady Oxley is now missing-presumed-dead. Sandy Lauderdale got free of his wife last year that way. There's half a dozen cases every year – they never make more than a line or two in the rags. No scandal, you see."

"I'll have a word about it with Ann some time before I leave for England. I say – it's the day for shredding our consciences all right!" They turned about and began to retrace their steps. "Talking of conscience – and scandal,"

Freddy went on. "Isn't Eleanor *the* most surprising woman?"

"In what way?"

"Well I've often wondered if you had ever told her the truth about you and Ann. I assumed you hadn't because I felt sure it'd break her heart. Yet look at her! I've met first-class generals with less power of command and decision."

He looked up at Clive and caught him suppressing a little smile, patronizing, knowing. Freddy raised his eyebrows.

"Ah, Foxy," Clive explained. "You're a great man in many ways, but I'm afraid you know little about women. Eleanor's a tigress fighting for her litter. She'll use morality if it's on her side, but she'll turn on it and rend it to bits if it's against her."

"All's fair in love and war, eh?" Freddy suggested brightly.

"It boils down to that."

"And do you approve or disapprove?"

Clive shrugged. "It's like approving or disapproving of the tides. Or the Niagara Falls."

Freddy laughed. "Oh then we're not so different from the women after all!"

Clive couldn't quite see the connection but he let it pass.

They all went for a swim, except Ann, who volunteered to look after the braaivleis, and Clive, who now wanted a further word with her. The men undressed on the beach, the women went to the far end of the creek. Their bobbing heads met halfway amid a lot of splashing and laughter.

"What did you talk about with Frederick?" Ann asked as she raked the hot ash in over the chops. "Oh that heavenly smell! I don't think I could ever leave this country."

"I asked him if we couldn't say the bill is paid at last."

"And?"

"He can't see it, Ann. There's no malice in him. He just can't see it."

"I could have spared you the effort. Frederick always has good logical reasons for anything he does. He'll never understand they're really only masking the true ones. I used to be able to talk to him. There was an evening once, in Barbadoes, the night they tracked me down ..."

"They?"

"Him and Miss Kate."

"Oh really? Tell me more!"

She smiled. "In a mo. But that evening in Georgetown we walked and talked together for a long time and I got him within a fraction of an inch of understanding it all. But he slipped away from me and I've never been able to get him close to it since. Our ways of thinking have drifted too far apart. Or perhaps I just don't feel it's urgent any more."

Clive lobbed a pebble into the water and watched its ripples widen. They dwindled to nothing before they crossed any of the ripples from the rest of the party. "Tell me about Foxy and Miss Kate."

"Oh yes. He met her shortly after you wrote to him in Venezuela, and he persuaded her to join in the search for me. I don't know what she was doing before he found her. I suspect she was the daughter of an hotel owner – or a ship's master, perhaps. Anyway, she had some local knowledge of the Caribbean that was useful to him. Also she quite obviously fell head over heels in love with him, and I'd imagine ..."

"You think so?"

She poked at the meat. "Oh yes – no doubt about it. In fact, she still is. Not that he'd ever realize it, of course."

"When you say they searched for you 'together,' you don't mean they ... you know?"

She laughed. "Frederick?"

Clive saw her point. "What an extraordinary fellow he is!" He joined her laughter but then became serious again. "Miss Kate, eh? Well now – what about that? Don't you think she'd make him a perfect wife?"

Ann shrugged an eloquent gesture of hopelessness. "But how?" She turned the chops. "I'd give anything to find a way, but neither Frederick nor I could take the scandal of a divorce."

"What about you, Ann? You wouldn't be lonely?"

She smiled. "I've met the dearest man."

"Aaaaah!"

"Nothing like that, Clive! He's much older ... well, not much, actually. But he's one of life's bachelors, so he *seems* a lot older. His only passion is music. He's the local church organist – oh and so much more. He arranges all the musical life of P.E. And we've become such friends, you know. I've never met anyone I feel so safe with. If Freddy ever divorced me, I could quite easily imagine myself marrying Desmond, but it wouldn't be that kind of marriage. We'd just be two hackney horses, two musical hackneys, out to pasture."

Her smile said it was all just a pipe dream.

"I have an idea," Clive said.

They talked earnestly together until the others left the water.

On the way home, just after they reached Skoenies, Ann said she knew a short cut to Walmer through the bush. Angelica begged to be allowed to go back into P.E. with the others. To Ann's great relief, Freddy consented.

He, Ann, and Kate took the three outriding horses and set off through the bush. They had not gone far before Ann said, "Now that we're alone, there's a question I must ask the pair of you."

"Fire away!" Freddy said jocularly. Nothing could spoil today now.

"When Lawrence stood up at that New Year's Eve Ball and announced his engagement to Rosamund, you, Kate, blurted out *no!* Ever since then I've been wondering why?"

Kate swallowed audibly. "Did I?"

"You know you did."

"I didn't hear her," Freddy lied.

But Kate laughed suddenly. "I remember now. Yes. Rosamund and I had just had a talk outside, all about not marrying too young, not settling down too early. I thought she'd taken my advice. I was just so disappointed."

Damn! Ann thought. "Listen Kate," she said. "This is much too important for any half-truths now. Be honest. Trust me. I think the reason you've just given is only part of the truth. Now tell me – am I right?"

Kate looked across at Freddy, her eyes full of troubles.

"I told her," Freddy admitted curtly.

"About Lawrence? About his true parentage?"

"Yes."

Ann had manoeuvred her horse between them. "I thought as much," she said. "Oh dear."

"I'm sorry," Kate told her.

"So am I, my dear. Truly sorry."

"What d'you mean?"

The words seemed to drag out of Ann with the greatest reluctance: "I mean ... it'll no longer be possible for us to go on living under the same roof. I couldn't bear the thought of you knowing ... that." She winked, but Kate did not notice. The judgement seemed to have shattered her. She stared at the ground, fighting back her tears.

For pity's sake look at me! Ann tried desperately to project the thought, but Kate's eyes remained lowered.

"Ann!" Freddy chided. "That's not like you!"

"How d'you know what's like me?" she flared up, hoping that a sudden display of anger might startle Kate out of her reverie. "When have you ever known what I'm like?"

"What about me?" Kate said distantly. "If only you knew about me!" She looked up at last – and found herself facing an orgy of winking from Ann.

"I realize you've probably known it for years," Ann said, babbling now to mask her relief. "But it wouldn't be the same. Now *I'd* know you know."

With her eyes she desperately signalled that Kate should drop back. "You'll have to find somewhere else to live," she concluded harshly.

Kate reined in and buried her face in her hands. Ann rode on.

"Now look what you've done!" Freddy said. "Just because you're angry with me today, there's no need to take it out on poor Kate."

He dropped back, too. Ann did not hesitate. "Oh you do whatever you like," she shouted angrily and spurred her mount to a canter. She only just managed to stop herself from singing as she sped among the trees with the wind streaming through her hair.

"There now," Freddy said consolingly. "There, there! Take my handkerchief."

Kate blew a deal of salt into the white linen. "Ann's right, though," she sighed. "I'll have to leave the villa."

"The devil you will!" he said stoutly. "We'll soon talk her out of that. Don't know what's got into her."

"No!" Kate shook her head firmly. "*I* wouldn't feel right now. Even if she changed her mind. It would never be the same again. There'd always be the feeling that ... oh well, I don't suppose you'd understand."

"I'm sure I do," he answered uncertainly.

"You must think we all developed hides like an elephant's – knocking around the world the way we did. Me especially. You must think I long ago lost all my finer feelings."

"Kate!" He was shocked she could hold such an opinion of him. "You're the finest woman I've ever met."

She looked at him, full of disbelief. "What about Ann?"

"Much finer than her. In the end all she could do was run away. But you're different. When you run, you always go ... well – *towards!* You're so positive."

She nodded, as if she half-believed him now. "I'm sure that'll be a great comfort to me."

"You won't have to leave," he said.

"I will."

"What'll you do?"

Scream, she thought. *Any minute now.*

His horse fretted. In calming it he was brought right to her side, so that their thighs were touching. "Kate?" he said hesitantly.

"Yes?"

"You wouldn't consider ... no, I have no right to ask it."

Kate screamed – and laughed – all at the same time.

"What?" he asked in astonishment. "Why did you do that?"

"Because you're like a twelve-year-old. Just *say* what's on your mind."

"You're so fine and beautiful and young – and I'm sure there are dozens of men ... just waiting."

"Waiting for what?"

"To marry you, of course."

Her eyes raked the heavens. "Jeehoshophat, Mr. Frederick! I can see I'm just going to have to do this myself." She dropped her reins, and his handkerchief, and took his hands in hers. "Are you asking me to marry you?"

"Yes." He said it like an admission of guilt, of defeat.

She laughed for sheer joy and leaned forward and her adorable soft lips came up to his ... and his whole world turned over.

Back at the Villa Rosalia, while Kate was dressing for dinner, Ann slipped into her room. "Well?" she asked, taking the hairbrush from the maid and gesturing for the woman to leave them.

"I don't know what to say, Ann. Why did you do it?"

"Tell me what happened. What he said."

"I thought I'd kept my feelings about him secret. You must have known them all along."

Ann gave her a playful pat with the brush. "About as long as you've known the secret of Lawrence's parentage, I'd say. So that makes us even. Now tell me before I beat it out of you." She laughed at a memory. "Oh, I could have killed you this afternoon when I was winking at you like a mad lighthouse and you just sat there refusing to see me."

Kate giggled for shame and buried her face in her hands before she looked up and said, "He asked me to marry him, of course."

"Just like that?"

Kate looked at her pityingly. "I had to work for it."

Ann nodded. "I can imagine. Did he also tell you this idea that Clive put into his head – that there need be no divorce? Ann, Lady Oxley, will be presumed dead. No one else will come looking for me. So the way will be open for Kate, Lady Oxley."

Ann was so busy with Kate's beautiful hair she did not see the tears in her eyes until the silence caused her to look up. Then she smiled and, putting her arms around Kate from behind, gave her a mighty hug. "And what's more, my love, you'll give him all the joy I was never able to provide, and you'll find all the happiness you yourself deserve. I'm more certain of that than of anything else in the world, Kate dear."

But as she straightened and prepared to lay down the hairbrush a further thought struck her. "There is just one thing..."

"Yes?"

"We had a maid. Emmy Hunter. She can't have been more than fifteen or sixteen when she came to us. We were struggling to keep up appearances on a hundred pounds a year then – even less, perhaps. So you can imagine how it was. Well that same Emmy Hunter is now Frederick's housekeeper – has been ever since he returned from Venezuela. She more or less brought up Lawrence and Angelica."

"You think I won't get on with her?"

Ann shook her head. "The other way round. You know Frederick, so you won't misunderstand me when I say she's far more than just a housekeeper to him. I remember one or two things he told me that time in Vienna. She gets him safely tucked up in bed every night, brings him a nightcap of cocoa, sits there on a chair beside him in her nightgown, and they talk over all the business of the day. You don't need me to tell you that, Frederick being Frederick, it's all extremely proper. But you may be equally sure that our Emmy thinks she owns him. So just be prepared for her, eh?"

Kate shook her head in rueful fondness. "Oh the tangles that just weave themselves around that man!"

ENVOI

FROM KATE (LADY OXLEY) IN SOLIHULL TO ANN (LADY OXLEY) IN THE CAPE:

The Dower House
15th January, 1893

Dearest Ann,
Twenty adorable fingers! Twenty darling toes! Of course our cable will have told you the fact of it, but nothing can convey our relief. You can imagine! Never were two babies so pawed over and pored over as those. Mr. Frederick (of course) was so sure of it that he claims to be disappointed they weren't born talking French and riding bicycles, but he's as happy and proud as the rest of us. (I only call him Mr. Frederick when he's being pompous now.)

They still have no names. Lawrence and Ros will dither until the legal date for registration has passed, I'm sure. I scoured all the books for names that go together, from Castor and Pollux to Pelion and Ossa, but they don't like any of them. Clive said that Pelion and Ossa was in very poor taste, and I confess that, having gone back and checked on it, I'm bound to agree. So I've resigned as a provider of names.

Eleanor goes around saying how wise and right Foxy was and everyone should listen to him always and forever. Oh, he has a new champion there. Still, she's been sweet to me, helping me master all these dreadful things about etiquette and precedence. How did we manage all those years without knowing whether a bishop sits above or below a second secretary? Or caring.

You were absolutely right about little Emmy Hunter! Such a pity, but the minute I walked into this house I knew we couldn't share it. I'm sorry for all her years of devotion – and she really did bring up Lawrence and Angelica wonderfully, but she just couldn't yield. She was very unhappy over at Mortimer Hall at first but Lawrence says she's settled in fine now. But why didn't she get her hooks into Freddy all those years when she had the chance? You or I would have. There is a very docile streak in all the English working classes I've decided. You and Freddy were so lucky to have escaped it.

Talking of Mortimer Hall and the things that happen the minute you walk into a house, I was there when Rosamund and Lawrence moved in. He said to her, this is your kingdom or this is your empire – something like that. And she turned white as death and said, *a Mortimer will inherit!* Apparently those were her grandmother's dying words to Frederick. You and I know what the old bitch meant, of course, but Rosamund is convinced her g'ma was a clairvoyante! History hasn't a chance, has it?

Congratulations on getting the gold, by the way. Now you have it, what'll you do? Either give up the piano altogether or just play it for fun – that's a tough choice. Seriously, you could take up the organ. Desmond would love that. Accidental brushings-together of hands *and* feet! No I mustn't tease. You really ought to marry him, you know. You're made for each other, just as Freddy and I are.

The Prince of Wales came to dine with us just before Christmas. I know I told you all about it last time but I still can't believe it. I keep checking the diary. What I forgot to tell you was that Sir Basil Patriarc was there and behaved very well. Frederick says it's a new cure for the criminal classes – give them all peerages or knighthoods, something to live up to. However, when I look at the way some of the existing peers behave, I'm forced to conclude it's already been tried.

Frederick himself continues in sparkling health. He truly isn't working so hard now. We take quite a lot of time off and get about and meet people and see things. And why not? He has good deputies and isn't this what he's worked for all those years? I know *I* haven't deserved it but I've never learned that art of questioning my luck.

Remember all those earnest conversations we had about him, you and I, before I left the Cape? I've sometimes tried to get him to open up a little about his feelings for Clive. They're great friends now and see a lot of each other, but I'd like to hear him talk about the past. He won't, though. The nearest he ever got to saying something near the mark was once when he closed off my "idle" questioning by saying, "All's fair in love and war." I told him love *is* war – and you know ... he's beginning to believe it!

Well Ann dear, enough of this. I'll write a more balanced, sober, LADY-like letter (to include Rosina, too) when we've all recovered from our relief and joy. From time to time the enormity of the situation still strikes us (except Freddy), but we catch each other's eyes and shrug uncomfortably and smile what encouragement we can. And bit by bit it dwindles.

Well, what else *can* we do?

All our love for now,

Kate.